CLOAK

TIMOTHY ZAHN

For David —

2/9/18

SILENCE
IN THE
LIBRARY

ISBN 978-1-941650-35-6

First Printing December 2014
Edited by Hollie Johnson and Corwin Zahn
Cover and interior design by Kelli Neier

Set in Tinos
Printed in the United States of America

Silence in the Library, LLC
Havelock, NC, United States of America
www.silenceinthelibrarypublishing.com

To those of you, friends and family,
who never gave up faith in this book.
Thank you.

CONTENTS

PROLOGUE

THE ROOM WAS small and dark, the only light coming from the soft glow of a simple reading lamp resting on a corner of the equally simple desk. Set in the wall across from the desk was a tiny but serviceable window, and it had been a gloriously clear day when the general entered the building an hour earlier. But the window was heavily curtained, and not even a glimmer of the sunshine outside was getting through.

The room seemed dusty, too, as if it hadn't been used in months. Perhaps it hadn't. Certainly the starkness of the place was in sharp contrast to the pomp and ritual that was so much an integral part of the present occupant's public life. Perhaps he only used this place for special occasions, when secrecy was required.

This was certainly a special occasion, the general thought grimly. And secrecy was absolutely required.

There was a movement at the desk, and the general turned from his unseeing contemplation of the curtained window as the middle-aged man in his oddly rumpled outfit turned over the final page of the proposal. The rumpled clothing, again out of place with his public life, also seemed to fit the room.

For a minute the other man continued to gaze down at the open folder, as if by sheer force of will he could change it or perhaps make it go away entirely. But the folder stayed as it was, and with visible reluctance he lifted his eyes to his visitor. "There's no other way?"

The general suppressed a sigh. They'd been over this so many times in the past few months. But he supposed it wouldn't hurt to go over it again. "You've read the reports," he said, pitching his voice to the same low level. There was something about the room that discouraged loud speech. "We've tried every quiet method we can think of. His protectors are simply too good."

"Good enough to stop a sniper's bullet?"

"Do you want him to become a martyr?" the general countered. "Because that's what an assassin's bullet would do. A bullet or any other obvious and overt action. It has to be done subtly, or the threat he stands for will gain momentum we may never be able to stop."

"Subtle? *Subtle*?" The other slapped a hand down on the folder, the sharp crack painfully loud in the enclosed space. "This is your idea of *subtle*?"

"When you kill one man, motives are easily traced to their source," the general said stiffly. "When you kill a thousand, the sheer number of possibilities makes any certainty impossible."

"A thousand," the rumpled man murmured, looking down at the folder again. "Will it be only a thousand? Or will it be tens of thousands? Perhaps even hundreds of thousands?"

"Not hundreds," the general assured him. "Almost certainly not even tens. Remember, the building is surrounded by a great deal of open space, and the yield of the weapon is extremely small. This is very much a surgical strike."

"Or what passes for a surgical strike in the nuclear age," the other said, still gazing at the folder. "There's no other way?"

"If there was, we wouldn't even be discussing this," the general said, sternly throttling back a wave of impatience. "Our only other choice is to sit back, do nothing, and watch one man bring down the nation. To sit back and do nothing as the work of decades collapses into ruin. To let the lives of our founders be just so much wasted sacrifice and blood. If he succeeds—if we let him succeed—there will be nothing left but chaos."

He stopped, his ears ringing, suddenly aware that he'd raised his voice past the room's natural tolerance for noise. "And that chaos wouldn't stop at our borders," he continued more quietly. "Never forget that. Within the year it would spread across the continent. Within two years, perhaps, the entire world would be in the same state of ruin."

The rumpled man gave him a cynical smile. "A nice speech, General," he said. "Carefully designed to stir the emotions, strengthen the resolve, and quiet the fears."

"I assure you, I didn't mean it that way," the general said stiffly. Sometimes he forgot how astute this man was at reading people.

"Of course not," the other said, almost as if he believed it. "So now it's a matter of our small handful of patriots saving the world from chaos, is it?"

"I wasn't exaggerating, sir," the general said. "You know the situation even better than I do. It has to be done. For the good of the nation."

"Yes," the other said with a sigh. "I was simply wondering how well that line of argument will play at our trial."

"There won't be any trial," the general said firmly. "Any publicity would automatically mean failure. We can't afford failure."

"No." Standing up, the rumpled man walked around his desk to the window. Leaning against the wall, he lifted the edge of the curtain and gazed out. The light sweeping in past his face, the general noted, was diffuse and subdued. It must have clouded up. "No one saw you come here?"

"No one," the general said. "My car has tinted windows, and I put on a false license. No one will be able to trace any of this back to you. Certainly not with any proof."

"For use at the trial that won't be happening, no doubt."

"Sir—"

"Never mind," the other said, waving a hand resignedly. "Will there be any difficulty getting hold of the weapon and moving it?"

"The equipment and personnel are already standing by," the general said. "The common wisdom, of course, is that such a theft is impossible. It shouldn't be a problem."

"Does it have to be a nuclear weapon?" the other asked, dropping the edge of the curtain and turning back to face the general. Trying one last time. "Why not use a conventional bomb, or even a surface-to-surface missile?"

"Two reasons," the general said. The rumpled man knew all this, too. "First, the delivery would be problematic at best. Remember, he'll be well guarded and moving among other well-guarded people, all inside a large building. The package must by necessity be relatively small, and that small a conventional explosive simply would not be enough to guarantee success."

"Not even with this magic invisibility device you plan to obtain?"

"Not even then," the general said. "But there's a second and even more important reason. Conventional bombs, no matter how powerful, don't really destroy anything, but merely break it into very small pieces. Those who would study the aftermath would be able to piece together enough of the explosive or missile to determine its origin. At that point, those responsible might possibly be tracked down."

He lifted his eyebrows. "At which point, the trial you mentioned most certainly would take place."

The rumpled man snorted gently. "And a nuclear weapon is, of course, so *much* less traceable."

"Their relative rarity will actually work to our advantage," the general said, ignoring the sarcasm. "Trust me on that."

"Of course." The other shook his head. "Trust you. On that, and on so much more." He sent one last look out the window, and then smoothed the curtain back into place, cutting off the last invasion of even subdued sunlight into the darkened room. "What about the money you'll need?"

"It's already been appropriated from various funds."

The dark eyes frowned. "Already?"

"Yes," the general said. "Invisibly, I assure you. One of my people is quite good at such things."

"And if I now say no?" the other demanded. "What then?"

"Then we simply put it back," the general said, striving to keep his voice calm. It wasn't nearly that easy, of course. A great deal of the money had already been spent over the past months, a detail he hadn't felt it necessary to trouble the other with. "We cancel the operation, send everyone away, and sit back to watch the disintegration—"

"I know, I know," the other said, the brief spark of resistance fading away. He was fighting it to the end, the general knew, fighting against the need for this action.

But the moral twisting was all for show, or for conscience. The end result was no longer in doubt. The general was good at reading people too.

"And this—what did you call it? It will be ready in time?"

"The Cloak," the general said. "And yes, our man assures me the preparations are nearly complete. The inventors have scheduled a demonstration, in fact, for three days from now."

"And your own zero hour?"

"Our opportunity comes in ten days," the general said. "We should have no problem meeting that schedule."

The other grunted. "I hope your man knows what he's doing," he said, crossing back to the desk and sitting down.

"He does," the general promised. "He's an experienced professional, and we're paying him a great deal of money to deliver the Cloak. And I'll be there to supervise the entire operation, his part included. I can leave as soon as you make the decision."

The rumpled man opened the folder again, leafing uncertainly through the pages. "It's so complicated. So very complicated."

"But necessarily so," the general reminded him. "And all of the most crucial aspects are ultimately under our control."

"Things can still go wrong," the other countered, looking up at his visitor. "Don't forget, they'll be barely a step behind you the entire way."

The general smiled tightly. "The operative word being *behind*," he pointed out. "I assure you, one step is all we'll need."

The other dropped his gaze to the folder again. "My son's going to school near there, you know," he said obliquely.

"The blast won't affect him at all," the general said, a wave of relief washing through him. So that was the real reason for this sudden reticence. Not politics, not even conscience. Just family. "It's a tactical weapon, with a yield less than a quarter of a kiloton. He may feel the ground shake a little if he's paying attention. Other than that, he'll learn about it from CNN like the rest of the world."

The other took a deep breath and closed the folder. "Then I suppose there's nothing more to say," he said, handing it back to the general. His eyes, the general noted, didn't quite meet his. "You said you'll be leaving immediately?"

"I can be on a plane for San Francisco in twelve hours," the general said, studying the dark eyes carefully as he accepted the folder. "There are a few details I need to take care of here first."

"Yes." Turning away, the rumpled man pulled another piece of paper from a small stack on the far corner of his desk. "You'll keep me informed, of course."

"Of course," the general said, sliding the folder back into his briefcase and backing toward the door. Yes, he was going along with the plan. But he wasn't convinced. Not really. "Good day, sir."

The other nodded but didn't speak. Quietly, the general left, closing the door on the small, dark, dusty room and the small, rumpled man. He would feel better, the general decided, when this was all over. Which it soon would be.

In exactly ten days.

THE
FIRST
DAY

01

FBI DIRECTOR FRANK McPherson hurried down the White House corridor, moving as quickly as he could without his haste looking obvious, cursing the early-morning D.C. traffic, the lack of proper workmen's pride on the part of Virginia's snowplow crews, and President Andrew Whitcomb's minute-miser quirks. Technically speaking, these informal Wednesday security meetings weren't supposed to start until seven, and he still had five minutes before the conference room wall clock chimed them to order.

But Whitcomb's philosophy was that meetings started as soon as everyone was assembled. Since no one wanted to keep the President waiting, everyone made it a point to be there a few minutes early, with the result that the seven o'clock starting gun had gradually but steadily drifted backwards until the typical opening report had actually been kicking off around six forty.

So four minutes early, McPherson was as a practical matter sixteen minutes late. Maybe this would set the time clock back to where it was supposed to be, which in itself wouldn't be a bad thing.

He only wished it had been someone else who had done it instead of him.

The others were indeed gathered around the polished oak table as he strode in through the door. At the head of the table sat Whitcomb, skimming through a file with the State Department logo on it. To his left, National Security Adviser Cynthia Duvall and Homeland Security's Deputy Secretary Spence Logan were engaged in quiet conversation over an open folder lying midway between them, munching their respective croissants between comments. Logan was a relative newcomer to the group, having taken over from Secretary of Homeland Security Dobbs while the latter recovered from kidney surgery, and

McPherson knew that Logan and Duvall had clashed on a number of occasions, usually over accessibility issues. But for the moment, at least, they seemed to be getting along well enough.

At the end of the table opposite the President was General Eldridge Vaughn, coordinator of Military Intelligence for the Joint Chiefs. He was sipping coffee as he wrote precise notes on a pad of paper, a barely-touched donut on the plate beside him. To the general's left, CIA Director Lawrence Cohn was just polishing off what looked to be his second danish as he leafed through a thick folder of his own. The sixth chair, sitting between Cohn and the President, was empty.

There were quite a few intelligence and analysis groups that weren't represented at these informal get-togethers, not to mention the various Cabinet heads who figured prominently at the monthly Security Council meetings. McPherson knew of at least two directors and one Cabinet undersecretary who had permanently bent noses over what they considered to be a massive snub.

But Whitcomb was President, and he got to make the rules. These were the people and agencies he felt most comfortable with, and if this was how he wanted to get his midweek situation overview, that was the way it was.

Personally, McPherson would be just as happy to let someone else have the FBI's slot for a while. His days started too early as it was.

"Mr. President," McPherson said as he closed the door behind him. "Sorry I'm late."

"Good morning, Frank," Whitcomb said, giving him a nod. "I make it still three-minutes-to. Coffee?"

"Thank you," McPherson said, dropping his briefcase at the empty place and stepping over to the coffee urn. He drew an aromatic cup of the President's private blend, giving the pastry tray a longing look but leaving it untouched. Last weekend's back-to-back dinner parties had added three pounds to his frame all by themselves, and he'd already put off the necessary caloric penance for two days.

"Let's get started," Whitcomb said as McPherson sat down with his cup. "What's new at the CIA, Larry?"

"Not much, actually," Cohn said, opening his folder. "We'll start with the Middle East."

Keeping his movements small and unobtrusive, McPherson pulled out his own summary, listening with half an ear to Cohn's rundown of the current state of woes outside U.S. borders. Aside from a handful of new additions, most of the hotspots were the same ones that had been outlined at last week's meeting, and the week before, and the week before that. The world was clinging to an ice-covered slope, McPherson had long since concluded, with some areas losing ground while the rest hung on for dear life.

"—and finally, we have some preliminary reports of odd activity yesterday at the Indian nuclear weapons research lab near Raipur," Cohn said, turning to the last page in his folder. "Probably not an accident, at least not a major one. A fair number of military personnel were involved, but there were no indications of major clean-up crew mobilizations. We also saw no sign of emergency medical personnel or vehicles. Our current educated guess is that it was a training exercise."

"But you don't agree?" Whitcomb prompted.

Cohn's lips compressed briefly. "I have no information indicating otherwise," he said. "But something about it doesn't feel right."

"Could there have been an attack on the facility?" General Vaughn asked. "Plenty of countries out there who'd be more than happy to find a shortcut into the nuclear club."

"There was no indication of actual combat activity," Cohn said. "As I say, our information is still sketchy, most of it gleaned from satellite data and intercepted communications. We're currently stirring our various humint sources in the area; hopefully, we'll have something more solid in a day or two."

"Maybe they're gearing up for more tests," Duvall suggested, making a note on her pad. "Both India and Pakistan issued new statements last weekend blasting the U.S. position on further nuclear testing in south Asia. Pakistan in particular made it quite clear that any U.S. economic pressure would be met with serious consequences."

"Keep digging into it," Whitcomb said to Cohn, making a note of his own. "If they've had an accident we'll have Secretary Jameson offer our assistance in cleaning it up. Give us a chance to be helpful and get a closer look at the Raipur facility while we're at it. Any other comments on Larry's report? No? General Vaughn; you have the floor."

There wasn't, as it turned out, much new on the Military Intelligence front either. Logan, when it was DHS's turn, had a few new wrinkles on cyber-attack tactics that McPherson hadn't heard, and he took nearly two pages of notes with an eye toward how they might affect the Bureau. It was his turn next, with not much more to add than Vaughn had.

"It looks like civilization is at least holding its own for the moment," Whitcomb said when McPherson was finished. "Questions about Frank's report?"

"I'm still not happy about these merger talks between the Klan and those neo-Nazi groups," Duvall said, tapping the end of her pen against her list of notes. "What makes you so sure they *aren't* going to get together?"

"The size of the egos involved," McPherson told her. "They recognize that holding these talks buys them some free publicity—"

"All of it bad, of course," Logan murmured.

"There's no such thing as bad publicity for people like that," McPherson pointed out. "Seriously, Cynthia, I wouldn't worry about it. They all have their little duck ponds, and none of them is going to give up any real power to the others. It's all for show."

Duvall didn't look convinced, but she nodded and laid down her pen, a probably unconscious signal that she had no further questions. Whitcomb glanced inquiringly around the table, and then leaned back in his chair. "All right, then," he said. "Let's hear this week's Goose List."

As always, McPherson threw a surreptitious look at the far end of the table. As always, Vaughn's lip gave just the faintest twitch of disapproval. At sixty-three years old, the general had grown up in a time and subculture where the term "to goose" carried a very definite and decidedly undignified physical context. Whitcomb, fourteen years his junior and from a different part of the country, either wasn't aware of the other meaning or simply didn't care. For him, the name "Goose List" referred merely to those people and nations he'd honked off that week.

Three months after its introduction, Vaughn was still not happy with the term. But then, McPherson had always considered Vaughn too stiff for his own good. The man had been born forty years old and probably already in uniform.

"I mentioned earlier the Indian and Pakistani statements," Duvall said, shuffling one of her papers to the top of the stack. Unlike Vaughn, she'd taken to the Goose List concept like a duck to bread crumbs. "Apparently, Iran's also decided to be mad at you on their behalf. The Iranian foreign minister delivered a speech a couple hours after the Pakistani statement in full support of their non-interference demand."

"Not surprising, given their aspirations," Whitcomb said. "Anyone else?"

"Mexico's rather peeved about your comments at last Friday's press conference," Logan said. "The one where you denounced their continued ineffectiveness on the cross-border drug issue. One of their people, I forget which one, blasted you on one of the talking-head shows Sunday."

"They should be happy Operation Calling Birds wasn't directed at them," Vaughn rumbled. "We could just as easily have hit Mexican sites instead of Colombian ones."

"I'm sure that thought has occurred to them," Whitcomb said. "As a matter of fact, if the DEA's final report gives the raid high enough marks I may consider making Calling Birds an annual event. With a different target each time, of course.

"Our Christmas Eve present to the world's drug lords," Vaughn said.

Whitcomb nodded. "Exactly."

"I'd suggest we not make any sweeping plans in that direction quite yet, sir," Duvall cautioned. "The Colombian government is still nearly as mad at us as the drug lords are—General Lopez had some scathing things to say about you yesterday. A few more of these unilateral raids and you risk wiping out years of bridge building with our southern neighbors."

"I wouldn't worry about it," Whitcomb said. "Most of Lopez's anger is for public consumption. Besides, I don't mind taking heat if a problem gets fixed in the process. Anyone else?"

"Speaking of crime lords, Russia's mad at Thursday's statement that further investment would be tied to a crackdown on their organized crime networks," Cohn said. "North Korea says you're a puppet of South Korean financial interests, the Chinese are concerned about our debt structure, and Argentina's blasting you on both Calling Birds and your Mexican statements."

"You can forget the Argentinean stuff," Whitcomb said, waving it away. "It's a new government, and they're trying to show how independent they are of Big Brother to the north. Anything new with the various terrorist groups?"

"Oddly enough, they've all been pretty quiet," Cohn said. "The bombings in Iraq and Israel are about all they've got to show for the week."

"There hasn't been any increase in chatter, either," Duvall added. "Either everyone's on vacation or they're all in think-tank mode trying to come up with what to try next."

"Well, stay on it," Whitcomb said grimly. "They may be waiting for the UN conference in hopes of grabbing extra publicity." He turned to McPherson. "Frank, you're being rather quiet. Am I so loved and adored by all our nation's citizens? Or are my enemies' press-release writers sunning in Rio with all the terrorists?"

"Enough of them are still at their desks," McPherson assured him. "Particularly those on Reverend Kirkwood Lane's staff. I take it you didn't catch the Call for National Salvation rally Sunday afternoon?"

Whitcomb shook his head. "I was on the phone all day with the Middle East," he said. "You can add everyone embroiled in this Third Temple controversy to the Goose List, by the way, Cynthia," he added, tapping her note pad.

"They don't appreciate your mediation efforts, sir?" Cohn asked.

"The Israeli government used to," Whitcomb said wryly. "I don't think they do anymore. Of course, Rabbi Salomon never did."

"In my judgment, sir, it's a waste of your effort," Vaughn said. "The Middle East is one of those permanent no-win situations for U.S. Presidents."

"Perhaps," Whitcomb said, his voice taking on a dark edge. "But it's also the powder-keg most likely to kick off World War III. Anything I can do to help blow out matches is worth the effort."

"I understand the inherent dangers of the situation, sir," Vaughn said, a little too stiffly. "I'm merely suggesting that the people involved will have to find their own solutions."

"I agree," Whitcomb said. "But one of the biggest stumbling blocks is the question of security guarantees, and at the moment we're the only kid on the block who can make promises like that with any hope of making them stick."

He looked back at McPherson. "So what's Reverend Lane's problem with me this week?"

"The usual," McPherson said. "You're a traitor to the Founding Fathers, a blot on the American landscape, and your UN policies are starting us on the road to a one-world government and Armageddon."

Whitcomb snorted gently. "If we don't give the UN some real teeth to go with all the peacekeeping roles we've saddled them with, he's likely to see more local Armageddons than he can stomach." He threw a look across the table at Vaughn. "Very likely starting with the Middle East. A UN security guarantee would be a lot easier for most of the parties over there to swallow than one issued from Washington."

"Maybe your whistle-stop tour will finally get that point across to the people," Duvall said.

"I hope so," Whitcomb said ruefully. "So far, nothing else has. Any words of support for Reverend Lane from the other right-wing groups?"

"Not so far," McPherson said. "You can bet they're privately cheering him on, though."

"Well, keep an eye on him," Whitcomb said. "He may be completely sincere in his concerns, and Lord knows I half agree with him every time Secretary-General Muluzi delivers himself of one of his West-baiting tirades. But we've all seen the kind of trouble that can come when inflammatory rhetoric percolates into the shallow end of the gene pool. The last thing any of us want—including, I dare say, Reverend Lane—is another Oklahoma City."

"Amen," Vaughn murmured.

Whitcomb threw a quick look around the table, then nodded. "That should do it for today. Thank you all for coming, and I'll see you next Wednesday."

Amid the general rustle, McPherson collected his papers back into his briefcase and headed out the door.

"Wait up, Frank," a voice came from behind him.

He turned to see Cohn hurrying to catch up. "Larry," McPherson said. "Early enough for you?"

"Quite, thank you," Cohn said, puffing slightly as he came up. Sixty years old and more than a little overweight, he'd more than once been referred to as a coronary waiting for a convenient opening in the man's schedule. "And thanks so much for making the first twenty minutes of it a waste of time," he added.

"Hey, you got to eat your danish in peace for a change," McPherson pointed out as they continued down the hall. "Besides, the President made it three minutes till, remember?"

Cohn grunted. "Right. I forgot. Speaking of which—or of whom— what do you think of our Fearless Leader?"

McPherson glanced behind them. General Vaughn was just leaving the conference room, ramrod stiff as always; behind him through the open door he could see Whitcomb and Duvall still conferring at the table. "Specify topic."

"The perverse pride he takes in this Goose List of his," Cohn said. "He seems to almost gloat over the fact that he's making enemies hand over fist."

McPherson shrugged. "At least you always know where he stands," he said. "Unlike certain other governmental tap dancers we could both name. My father used to tell me that if you didn't have any enemies you weren't making your position clear enough."

"My father used to tell me never to stand next to someone who's throwing manure at an armed person," Cohn countered. "I can't help wondering when one of his geese is going to get tired of lobbing verbal grenades and try the real thing."

"That thought *has* occurred to me," McPherson admitted. "But I don't know what to do about it except stay on our toes."

"Mm."

"You don't agree?"

"No, I agree," Cohn said. "I just . . . something's in the wind, Frank."

McPherson cocked an eyebrow at him. "You know something I don't?"

"Nothing concrete," Cohn said. "But I've got a gut that's been in Intelligence work since the Carter administration. That gut doesn't feel right about things this morning."

"Maybe it was that last danish."

Cohn threw him a glare. "I'm serious."

"I know," McPherson soothed him. "And I respect your gut and its hunches. I'm just not sure what we can do about it other than what we're already doing."

"Me, neither," Cohn conceded, turning his glower on the Secret Service agents ahead, lounging with deceptive casualness near the elevator to the underground garage. "I just wanted you to be on the alert. Maybe talk to your buddies in the DEA and NSA—they always pay more attention to you than they do me."

"A strange fact, but true," McPherson agreed. "Okay, I'll make some calls."

"Thanks."

The Secret Service men passed them out, and a few minutes later McPherson was back on the slush-covered streets of the capital, fighting yet another wave of morning traffic. He and Cohn had locked horns frequently throughout their respective careers, and there had been many times he considered the older man to be the epitome of pompous assdom.

But McPherson's own Federal government experience only dated back to the second Reagan administration, and he wasn't about to dismiss even vague Cohn hunches out of hand. The very first thing on the morning's agenda, he decided, would be to make the calls the other had suggested. After that, he would pull up the latest status reports and go over them with a finer-tooth comb than usual.

He swore under his breath as a Ford Explorer swerved into the street two cars ahead, nearly taking off a BMW's bumper as its tires hit a patch of ice. And it had looked like such a peaceful week, too.

02

IT HAD BEEN over an hour since the Pakistani container ship *Rabah Jamila* had left its dock at the Vietnamese port of Da Nang. Sitting cross-legged on his cot in the twenty-foot-long cargo container that would be his home for the next few days, Eleven rocked back and forth with the rhythm of the jostling waves and decided odds were good they had cleared the harbor and were in the open sea.

Though he could certainly be wrong about that, given the almost total lack of sensory cues inside the container. Ten would know; he was the expert seaman of their two-man team. But Ten was in the next container over, and the general had given them strict instructions to avoid using their radios unless absolutely necessary. With the *Rabah Jamila* cruising serenely along, and no one from the crew bursting into his hideaway to demand some answers, chatting with Ten hardly qualified as absolutely necessary.

Or rather, chatting with Choi. Rhee chatting with Choi.

Choi. Rhee. He ran the names through his mind again. Unfamiliar names. Totally unlikely names.

Still, that's what was printed on the forged South Korean military IDs they were carrying, so he might as well get used to thinking of himself and his partner that way. Particularly since they would eventually be playing those roles for the captain and crew.

He smiled to himself in the darkness. The absurdity of the whole thing was almost tangible, the sheer brazenness of it even more so. Neither he nor Ten looked the least bit Korean, and even with the full-face masks they would be wearing there was a good chance some sharp-eyed crewman would notice. And on top of that, the South Korean forgeries they carried weren't even all that good.

But the general had assured them that this would work. So far, the general had never been wrong about such things.

Besides, absurdity and brazenness had already taken them farther than any reasonable man would have thought possible. At the back of Eleven's container, its thick protective casing bolted securely to the wall and floor, was the tactical nuclear weapon the general's men had spirited out of India's newest weapons development lab.

How the general had pulled that one off he didn't know, and was pretty sure he didn't want to. Still, if that other group could manage their part of this master prestidigitation, he and Ten could certainly manage theirs. Pride alone dictated that.

He grimaced. No, not pride. Survival. Theirs, and that of the country they all loved.

A soft sound of grinding metal snapped him out of his thoughts. Silently, Eleven got up from his cot and crossed to the other side of the container, taking care that the long suppressor on his shoulder-slung Heckler & Koch MP5 submachine gun didn't clang into the supply locker or the holding tank for his portable toilet.

The sound changed pitch as the drill bit finished off the outer metal shell and started through the interior padding. Flicking on a low-level finger light, Eleven waited.

A moment later the bit broke through, scattering flecks of padding into the air. It withdrew, and a thin metal tube poked tentatively through the opening. Eleven pulled it all the way through, exposing the flexible coax cable that had been snugged inside it. He pulled through enough of the cable to give himself plenty of slack, then connected the end to the jack in his headset.

"Clear?" Ten's voice came in his ear.

"Clear," Eleven confirmed. "Are we out of the harbor?"

"Feels like it," Ten said. "Check your exits."

"No need," Eleven said. "I'd have known if they'd loaded anything on top of me."

"The plan says we check," Ten said. "I'll tell you when to start improvising."

"Yes, sir," Eleven sighed, swiveling the MP5's muzzle back out of the way and crossing to the ladder fastened to the wall by his cot. The slender, meter-long testing wand was secured beneath the cot's frame; pulling it out, he climbed to the ceiling and eased the wand around the light-blocking baffles and up through one of the concealed ventilation holes.

As expected, the wand was unobstructed for its entire length. "Clear on top," he announced, resisting the temptation to deliver his report in formal parade-ground intonation.

"Clear on top," Ten echoed his own situation. "Check sides."

The port and starboard sides, to Eleven's complete lack of surprise, were blocked, with the adjoining containers no more than a few centimeters away from his. The bow end was clear, which meant his little mobile home had been placed at the front end of the stack of containers as planned. The aft end, though, was a surprise. "Stern's clear," he reported, frowning as he waggled the wand around, searching for the next container over. "There's nothing there."

"Mine's blocked," Ten told him. "The container that was supposed to be behind you must have been canceled at the last minute. Just as well you checked."

"Indeed," Eleven agreed politely, though offhand he couldn't see any reason why he would need to use his container's stern exit instead of simply going out through the top when the time came. "What now?"

"I'll deploy the scanner antenna," Ten said. "Might as well see what this ship's normal radio chatter sounds like. After that I'll set the GPS antenna and get a position reading."

"Be sure to plug the scanner into the phone so I can hear, too," Eleven reminded him. "Anything you want me to do?"

"Go ahead and tape down the phone line. After that, you're off duty."

"Right," Eleven said, snagging the roll of black electrical tape from his small tool kit and stepping over to the point where the line entered the container. It was really an unnecessary refinement; with the containers stacked two deep here on the *Rabah Jamila*'s deck, and his and Ten's containers on the top layer, there wasn't much chance anyone walking the deck would see the faint light that might leak out around the line.

But Ten was right. The plan was running smoothly, and at this point improvisation was neither necessary nor desirable. "How about a game of chess?"

"You're on," Ten said. "Give me fifteen minutes."

Fifteen minutes later, with the reading lamp over his cot bathing his quarters in a soft glow, Eleven sat with his small magnetic chess board balanced on one knee. Ten fancied himself an expert at the game, he knew. Perhaps sometime in the next few days Eleven could take that opinion down a step or two. "Ready?" Ten asked.

"Ready," Eleven said. "Pawn to king four."

~

The phone rang, dragging McPherson out of a deep sleep.

Beside him, his wife Sally muttered something and rolled over. Rolling the other direction, McPherson snagged the handset, focusing on the bedside clock as he did so. Two twenty-eight. He'd been asleep a grand total of twenty minutes. "Yeah, McPherson," he muttered.

"Cynthia Duvall," came the crisp voice of the President's NSA advisor. Far too crisp and alert for this hour of the morning, he thought sourly. The woman must be a vampire. "The President would like you at the White House at seven o'clock tomorrow morning."

The sleep-induced cobwebs abruptly vanished. Tomorrow was Thursday; and Whitcomb invariably reserved Thursday mornings for the Cabinet. "Of course," he said. "Can you tell me what the meeting's about?"

There was a pause as Duvall no doubt checked the monitor that watched for eavesdropping on the line. "We received a message from New Delhi an hour ago," she said. "It appears they've lost a tactical nuke."

"Lost?" McPherson echoed. "What do you mean, *lost*?"

"All they'll admit right now is that the weapon is missing," Duvall said. "Regardless, the President feels we need to discuss the situation."

"The President is right," McPherson agreed grimly. "I'll be there."

THE
SECOND
DAY

03

"THE DETAILS OF the theft itself are still spotty," CIA Director Cohn said, sorting through his stack of papers and selecting one of them. "The Indian government isn't even sure when exactly the weapon was stolen, let alone who might have done it. A dummy casing had been left in its place, and it wasn't until someone went through taking the daily radiation readings that they found out it was empty. At which point they went instantly into ape-sh—ah, panic mode."

"The unusual military activity you mentioned yesterday?" President Whitcomb asked.

"Yes, sir," Cohn said. "New Delhi's got an assumed window of opportunity for the theft, and they're working to narrow it down. We've alerted our ambassadors and top overseas military commanders to keep their ears to the ground, but so far nothing."

"And that's as far as I want the news to go for now," Whitcomb said. "We want to keep this as quiet as possible."

Across the table from Cohn, Logan cleared his throat. "I agree, Mr. President, that we certainly need to find this thing," he said. "But at the same time, I think we're rather literally making a mountain out of a molehill. At last count there were over a hundred Russian nukes still missing; and those are strategic warheads, not piddling tactical jobs like this one. Besides, I see no evidence that the Indian nuke has anything whatsoever to do with U.S. interests."

McPherson threw a sideways look at Vaughn and Cohn, noting the contemptuous set to both men's mouths. Clearly, Logan was completely missing the point, him and possibly Duvall, too. Just as clearly, Vaughn and Cohn were anxious to explain it to them.

Whitcomb offered Cohn first serve. "Larry? You want to take that one?"

"Yes, sir," Cohn said, nodding to the President before turning back to Logan. "Let's take your questions in order, Spence. First of all, yes, the Russians have quite a few missing nukes. But just because they don't know where they are doesn't mean *we* don't know where they are. In point of fact, we have tabs on most of them, or at least know who the countries and groups are who have them."

"And how could you possibly know that?" Duvall scoffed.

"Because most of the current owners bought them outright on the black market," Vaughn rumbled. "That means large money transfers, and we've become quite adept at tracking large money transfers."

"So have we," Logan said, a bit testily. "If you know where they are, why haven't you gone after them?"

"Two reasons," Vaughn said. "First, because we don't have the manpower to hit all the locations at once. The minute we started an operation like that everyone we didn't hit in the first wave would punch the panic button and squirrel the things away where we couldn't easily get to them."

"Or might use them," Cohn added pointedly.

"Or might use them," Vaughn agreed. "And second, because as Mr. Cohn just said, quite a few are currently owned by sovereign nations who bought them as insurance policies against unfriendly neighbors. I presume you're not suggesting the United States launch an invasion against, say, Turkey or Greece?"

Logan made a face. "Point taken."

"Point not yet complete," Cohn countered. "You seem to think that the missing nuke being tactical instead of strategic is a good thing. In actual fact, it's precisely these lower-yield weapons that are the *most* likely to be used."

"I don't follow," Duvall said, frowning.

"The more devastating the weapon, the more certain the massive retaliation following its use," Cohn told her. "You fire off a twenty-megaton warhead and vaporize two hundred fifty square miles of someone's real estate, and they *will* hunt you down—absolutely guaranteed. If they can't find you personally, they'll take it out on your nation or ethnic group or funding partners."

"Whereas with a tactical weapon, the victims won't be nearly so mad," Vaughn said. "Oh, they'll still hunt you down—we showed that after 9/11—but it won't be the feeding frenzy it would be with a larger warhead."

"All of which means your average wild-eyed fanatic would be more tempted to give a small weapon a whirl," Cohn said. "And the fact that they passed over whatever strategic weapons were at Raipur in favor of a tactical tells me they *do* intend to use it."

"Yes," Duvall said, and for the first time since the meeting began McPherson could see some genuine concern behind her eyes. About damn time. "Yes, I see."

"Good," Cohn said. "Then let me add one more unpleasant consideration into the mix. Because this particular weapon was stolen instead of purchased, there's no paper or contact or money trail for us to follow. In other words, unlike those strategic weapons Spence mentioned, *we have no idea who has it.*"

"Uh-oh," Logan murmured.

"Exactly," Cohn said. "Furthermore, let's not forget the scale we're working with. When I call the warhead small—when you call it piddling—we're not talking bottle rockets. A point-two-kiloton weapon still has the explosive yield of two hundred *tons* of TNT. Imagine that stacked up against the White House fence."

At the head of the table, Whitcomb stirred. "I believe we have the threat adequately defined," he said. "Cynthia, you've talked to New Delhi most recently. What exactly do they want from us?"

"They started by asking us to go back through our satellite data," Duvall said. "See if we could spot the theft vehicle leaving the Raipur facility with the nuke."

"They were joking, I trust," Cohn said. "We don't have nearly enough satellite coverage of that region to pull off a stunt like that."

"Yes, I did explain that to Minister Rao," Duvall said. "He wasn't very happy about it."

"Who's Minister Rao?" Logan asked.

"Home Affairs," Duvall said. "He's been put in charge of coordinating the search with us."

"I'll bet he was thrilled," McPherson murmured. "After all the rhetoric over their nuclear program, asking us for help has to gall them no end."

"Which just shows how badly they want the weapon back," Whitcomb pointed out. "I gathered from our earlier conversation that they're near panic over the possibility that an Indian weapon might be used against some foreign capital."

"Which brings us to our possible target list," Cohn said. "And to answer your final question, Spence: no, I don't think the nuke is headed this way. But that doesn't mean U.S. interests won't be affected. Quite the contrary."

"Cynthia, let's start at the top of Jameson's preliminary work-up," Whitcomb said. "What's the likelihood the weapon is intended for use inside India itself?"

"Reasonably low," Duvall said, opening a three-ring binder with the State Department seal on the cover. "New Delhi's got their usual level of political tension, but there isn't any abnormal intrigue or rhetoric coming from the opposition."

"What about Jammu and Kashmir?" Vaughn asked. "That region's been an on-and-off hot spot for decades, and it's been grabbing a lot of press lately."

"That's mostly due to their new unofficial spokesman," McPherson said. "Tahir Kazi. The media always gives a blip of interest when there's fresh blood on the scene."

"Mr. Jameson does mention Dr. Kazi specifically," Duvall said, turning over a page. "He reminds us that Kazi's a very determined and charismatic man, and that historically that's a dangerous combination."

"Let's not jump to conclusions," Whitcomb said mildly. "So far Kazi's advocating only peaceful solutions to the Kashmiri situation. Besides, Jameson's already granted him a visa to speak at the UN's human rights conference, so he can't be *that* worried about the man."

Cohn snorted. "Wait till Kazi sees just how little world attention a UN platform gets him. He's likely to be a tad disappointed."

"Unless he plans to use that platform to declare holy war against India," Vaughn said darkly.

All heads turned to the general. "You know something we don't, General?" Whitcomb asked.

"Just observation and gut-level feelings, sir," Vaughn said. "With most of the world's ethnic, religious, and other splinter groups screaming for attention, it's getting harder and harder for any of them to stand out of the crowd." He gestured toward Duvall's binder. "Imagine how far out you'd stand if you punctuated your demands for independence with a nuclear blast in downtown Delhi."

"It would be suicide," Logan declared. "For his people as well as him."

"Maybe he thinks they've got nothing left to lose," Vaughn countered. "Maybe he's right."

There was a moment of silence around the table. "All right, that's one possibility," Whitcomb said. "What's next on Jameson's list?"

Reluctantly, McPherson thought, Duvall looked back down at her folder. "There's Pakistan and China," she said. "Both have nukes of their own, of course, but there are various border grievances some splinter group might think they can remedy the quick way. Alternatively, the Indian government or some segment thereof could itself be behind a border operation, and have cooked up the whole stolen-nuke idea to push the blame off on person or persons unknown. Finally, either the Pakistanis or Chinese might have decided they want a closer look at the kind of work India's turning out these days."

"That takes care of the major players on the subcontinent," Whitcomb said. "Who's next?"

"A whole smorgasbord of local unrests," Duvall said, shaking her head as she leafed through the binder. "We've got new or long-standing minority problems in Sri Lanka, Myanmar, Thailand, Cambodia, and the Philippines."

"Not to mention North Korea," Vaughn said.

"Jameson devotes an entire page to North Korea," Duvall said. "There are also a handful of small but sophisticated anti-government groups in Japan. Remember the subway poison-gas attacks?"

"All too well," Whitcomb said soberly. "Is there more?"

"Much more," Duvall assured him. "Heading the other direction, we've got Somalia, the Sudan—most of Africa, actually—plus the Basques, Northern Ireland, much of central Asia, and large tracts of the Balkans. And of course, there's always the Middle East."

"Iran," Cohn said.

"And Iraq, Syria, and Turkey," Vaughn added. "Also known as the Kurdish problem."

"The Kurds take up another full page of Jameson's report," Duvall said. "Mustafa Dagli has been whipping them up lately, and there are signs the local governments are starting to get extremely annoyed with him. Then there's Rabbi Salomon and the Third Temple crowd threatening to put a match to the whole Muslim world."

"Salomon's also scheduled to speak at the UN conference," Logan pointed out.

"Dagli and a Kurdish delegation will be there, too," Whitcomb said. "Turkey's already threatened to walk out if they're allowed to speak."

"I understand Reverend Lane plans to attend, too," Duvall added. "Protesting out front, no doubt. He and the Turks should make for interesting TV coverage."

"No doubt," Whitcomb said. "So which of these potential powder kegs does Jameson consider our front-runner?"

"Mr. Jameson currently has no idea," Duvall said. "His analysts hope to have a probability chart worked up by the end of the day."

"Handy," Logan growled. "Especially since the bomb's probably already arrived at its detonation point."

"Certainly if they took it out by air," Cohn said heavily. "Possibly even if they went overland if it's headed to one of their neighbors. The trick will be to track its route before the fireworks start."

"Then we'd best get to it," Whitcomb said. "Larry, I'd like you to take over Cynthia's liaison with New Delhi. We'll need all the data they can pull together: air freight lists, shipping manifests, rail information, car rental records. If it moves without using feet, we want to know about it."

"Minister Rao and I have already discussed that," Duvall said. "They should be downloading everything later this morning."

"Good," Whitcomb said. "Frank, since the Bureau isn't directly involved with this, I'd like your people to help out with some of the data consolidation and analysis work."

"We can certainly do that, sir," McPherson said. "However, I don't agree that the Bureau isn't necessarily involved. The U.S. mainland might not be the intended target; but on the other hand, it might. Certainly yesterday's Goose List included plenty of people mad enough to park Larry's two hundred tons of TNT out there by the fence."

"I don't think any of them are *that* mad at me," Whitcomb said. "But I suppose you're right. Very well. Along with helping with the analysis, you can also put together your own threat assessment and potential target list."

"Yes, sir," McPherson said. "What about your whistle-stop tour? That was supposed to start tomorrow."

"And so it will," Whitcomb said. "Is there a problem?"

"I'm thinking you might want to consider canceling it," McPherson said. "Or at least postponing it a few days."

Whitcomb shook his head. "The timing is too important, Frank. I need to build as much support for the UN as I can prior to the conference. A little jawboning from me, plus the stories of human rights' atrocities we'll be hearing at the conference, might be enough to create the momentum in Congress that the UN so desperately needs."

"Yes, sir, I understand that," McPherson said. "But—"

"But even more important is the principle of the thing," Whitcomb continued. "I can't change my schedule every time there's a crisis somewhere in the world. I have complete confidence in all of you, and you certainly don't need me looking over your shoulders in order to do your jobs. I can keep up with things just as well from Air Force One as

I can from here. If for some reason you need my participation you can always get to me through Cynthia."

McPherson looked down the table, again noting Vaughn's compressed lips. Clearly, the general didn't like the President running off at a time like this any better than McPherson did.

But Whitcomb had his mind made up, and there was no point in arguing with him. At least, not now. "Yes, sir," he said.

"Good." Whitcomb said. "You'd best get to it, then. Good luck."

~

The sun had long since been swallowed up by the Santa Cruz Mountains rising in the distance behind Angie Chandler, but the security lights ringing the Sand/Star Technologies grounds were more than adequate for her to see the coil of razor wire topping the perimeter chain link fence. She gazed with distaste at the fence and its unpleasant new crown as she let her car coast up to the gate and the softly lit guardhouse beside it. The razor wire had been added three weeks ago, in response to some vague and nameless threat her husband James had been equally vague about, and in Angie's mind it did a decided disservice to a place that already looked too much like a prison. It evoked half-remembered childhood memories of the quiet but tense journey as her family slipped across the border from the Chinese mainland into Hong Kong twenty-eight years ago.

Little in the way of specific images remained of that night, but she vividly remembered her pregnant mother snatching her upstart four-year-old's hand as she reached out toward the curiously shiny spider web they were passing.

The night duty officer was waiting outside the door of his booth as she rolled to a stop and slid down her window. "Good evening," she said, nodding politely and trying hard not to see him as a border guard. She didn't recognize this one, but most of the Sand/Star security people she'd met seemed pleasant enough. "Angie Chandler, to see Dr. James Chandler in Building D."

"Good evening, Mrs. Chandler," the guard said, nodding back and offering her an electronic notepad. "Would you sign in, please?"

She took the stylus and wrote her name on the pad, feeling her usual twinge of nervousness as she did so. They used versions of these things everywhere these days, and she'd signed in on Sand/Star's system a hundred times without incident. But she could never quite shake the feeling that, sooner or later, her scrawl was going to land outside the computer's built-in tolerances and be declared a forgery. She didn't know what would happen then, but her mental image involved hooting alarms, flashing lights, and large men in security uniforms.

She finished writing and handed back the pad and stylus. No alarms or lights went off, and the guard merely nodded. "Thank you," he said as the gate swung open in front of her. "Have a good evening."

"Thank you," she said, closing her window and easing on the gas. At least it wasn't raining, which was the normal state of affairs in the Bay Area in January. Rainwater couldn't do those electronic pads any good.

Building D was one of the smaller structures of the Sand/Star complex, a building that had been further subdivided into a warren of small facilities for minor researchers, underfunded projects, or for what James called "crapshoot ideas": concepts which probably wouldn't pay off at all but would reap tidy sums if they did. In the three years James had worked here Angie had often wondered which category his Tarnhelm project fell into. Possibly all three.

Most of the building's parking lot was empty, but a glance at the scattering of cars that remained showed her that all six members of the project were still here. Pulling in beside Dr. Wendell Fowler's beat-up Ford Bronco, she headed to the main door. Another uniformed guard at a reception desk inside the lobby buzzed her in; another scrawl on an electronic pad, and she was on her way to James's third-floor complex.

She opened the door to the main lab area to find what her mother would have referred to as a four-man whirlypit. In the center of the room, folded haphazardly over four lab tables pushed together, was a mass of thick black cloth; black, but with an odd luminescence where the overhead fluorescent light struck the edges of its folds. On different sides James's three lab techs were hunched over the mass on stools, examining the material with a variety of instruments. Circling the whole group like an impatient vulture was Dr. Fowler, scowling and muttering under his breath as he glared at his tablet, scrolling through pages with quick swipes of his fingers. None of the lab techs looked very happy, either.

"Have I come at a bad time?" Angie asked hesitantly, pausing just inside the doorway.

"No, no, come on in," Fowler said, his glare still on his tablet. "James and Barbara are in the office—he'll be out in a sec. Damn it all. Jack, are you sure it isn't there?"

"If it is, it's hiding," Jack Burke growled, moving a device like an oversized magnifying glass slowly over his section of the cloth. "No breaks at all."

"Ah-ha!" Ramon Esteban called abruptly, leaning closer to the material. "I got it. Here it is, Wendell."

Fowler was already at his side, peering over his shoulder. "Give that man a cigar," he said. "Better yet, give him a patch kit."

"Got it," Scott Kingsley said, getting up from his stool and crossing to a crowded equipment table against the wall. Slapped down in the middle of the equipment, Angie saw, were two half-eaten pizzas and three two-liter bottles of soda. "Evening, Mrs. Chandler," Kingsley added, throwing her a friendly grin. "How's the world of high finance?"

"Fine, thank you," Angie said, walking up to the mound of cloth, an odd sensation in her throat. So here it was. After months of experimentation, aggravation, headaches, and blind alleys, here it finally was. "Is this the Cloak?"

"This is it," Fowler said proudly as he came to her side. "This is Mama Bear, actually—Papa Bear and the two Baby Bears are in there." He pointed to the open door leading into the group's main office, where Angie could see a shoulder-high stack of similar material piled in a corner. "They're finally ready to go."

"And in the traditional nick of time, too," Burke added, reaching over his shoulders for a long stretch. "After everything James went through to get the Army to come take a look, it would have been highly embarrassing to have to postpone the demo."

"And it works?" Angie asked, the odd sensation taking on a twinge of unreality. "It really works?"

"Sure does," Fowler said, sounding like a proud father. "No, go ahead—you can touch it. It won't break."

Carefully, Angie ran her fingertips down the material. Despite its almost satiny sheen, the cloth's texture was hard and cold and rather stiff.

"Maybe we could fire it up and give her a private show," Esteban suggested. He was digging into the black surface with something that looked like a dentist's probe as Kingsley stood over him holding a set of long, thin fibers.

"Better yet, come to the demo tomorrow," Fowler invited. "The Army people will be here for James's presentation at ten, and we'll then head out to the Calaveras Reservoir site about eleven. Come for all or part of it."

Angie gazed at the cloth. She could do it, she knew. They weren't *that* busy at the bank, and after having spent most of her evening there trying to get the new computer system up and running they definitely owed her. Anyway, it wasn't like loan approvals were a matter of life or death.

They most certainly weren't something of massive historical importance. But to see the first public demonstration of her husband's creation . . .

Behind her, the door to James's private office opened, and she turned to see him stroll out into the main lab, an almost idiot grin on his face.

His arm draped casually across Barbara Underwood's shoulders.

The sense of history in the making vanished in a puff of green-edged smoke. "Hello, James," she said quietly.

His eyes focused on her. "Oh, hi, hon," he said. For another second his arm stayed where it was. Then, a little too hastily, he let it slide off Barbara's shoulders back to his side. "What are you doing here?"

"We had to work late," she said, her face warming. Dr. Barbara Underwood was, according to James, an absolute genius at optics and software development, exactly the qualities the project had needed when he'd taken her on four months ago.

Unfortunately, she was also everything Angie wasn't: tall, blonde, vivacious, well-endowed. And Caucasian.

A flood of suppressed memories rose to the surface. The first-grade bully who'd saved his chief animosity for her. The more subtle high-school prejudices she'd had to endure despite laws that were supposed to stop such things. Her parents' not-so-subtle warnings that a marriage outside her own kind was doomed to failure. "I thought you might be done and we could drive home together," she finished awkwardly.

"Sorry, but I don't think I'm getting out of here tonight," James said, leaving Barbara's side and coming over to her. "There's still way too much paperwork that has to be organized before the demo."

"I see," Angie murmured.

James hesitated, then took her hand. "Come here," he said, pulling her toward the office. "Wendell, as soon as you're finished checking Mama Bear, fold 'er up and start on Papa Bear. Hopefully, he won't have sprung any new leaks."

"Right," Wendell said, crossing to where Barbara and Burke were talking quietly together as they worked on the leftover pizza. "Let me know when you're finished there, Ramon."

James led Angie into the office, stopping just inside the door. "I know this has been a strain for you," he said in a quiet voice, taking both her hands in his. "And I know I've been something of a stranger lately. But it'll all be over soon. I promise."

"I know," Angie murmured. Behind him, the surface of his huge metal desk was nearly invisible beneath the mass of scattered papers and Cloak test equipment, with the humming workstation and the four laptops rising out of the chaos like islands in a sea of flotsam.

But Angie's attention wasn't on the desk or its contents. It was, instead, on the military cot in the back of the office. The cot where James had spent the night more times than she cared to remember over the past few weeks.

Sleeping. Alone. Or so he'd said.

"Dr. Chandler?"

She turned, annoyed at the interruption but at the same time welcoming it. Kingsley was standing outside the office, a mostly-eaten slice of veggie pizza in his hand. "Sorry to intrude," he apologized. "I just wanted to warn you there are only two slices of pepperoni left, in case you wanted to get to them before Ramon does."

"Thanks," James said. "No, wait, don't run off. You told me once you could handle an eighteen-wheeler, right?"

"Three summers driving for my dad when I was in college," Kingsley confirmed. "Why?"

"I made arrangements to borrow one, on the assumption that we'd be ready," James said, letting go of one of Angie's hands and digging a set of keys from his pocket. "Number 4686, out at the shipping building's main loading dock. Can you go get it?"

"Sure," Kingsley said, taking the keys. "Do I need a note for the gate guard to bring something like that in at this time of night?"

"You shouldn't, but I'll give him a call and let him know," James said. "If you can maneuver it into the receiving dock, that would be great. Otherwise, just park it anywhere. We'll load the Cloaks aboard later. Oh, and our cards won't open the loading dock door, so if you park there you'll have to come back around to the front to get back in."

"Right," Kingsley said. "Angie, was it raining when you came in?"

She shook her head. "No."

"Well, that won't last," he said, stuffing the last of the pizza into his mouth. "Le' me gra' my coat," he added around the mouthful, "'n I'll be ri' back."

He headed back across the lab, circling around the pile of Cloak material on the tables and snagging a brown paper towel from beside the pizza boxes as he continued on into the far office.

"So you're going to stay here all night?" Angie asked. She tried to lift her eyes to her husband's, but somehow wasn't quite able to get past the vicinity of his chin.

He sighed. Rather theatrically, she thought. "Don't do this, Angie," he warned. "I can't deal with it right now."

She hesitated, feeling her resentment wavering. He had indeed been under a lot of pressure lately. And the reality of a scientist's life was something she'd known she was getting into when she married him.

From behind her came a whiff of subtle perfume. "Only one slice of pepperoni left, James," Barbara said, her voice bright and cheerful and as all-American as the rest of her. "Hello, Angie. How are you?"

"Just leaving," Angie said, a flash of fresh resentment yanking her back from the brink of wifely understanding as Barbara turned back to the lab tables. No, of course he didn't have time to deal with her now. "I'll see you tomorrow, James."

"Angie—wait. Please."

She turned away without answering. Wendell was standing behind Esteban, blocking the most direct route out of the room. Grimacing, Angie turned the other direction, taking the long way around the lab tables. She glared at the remnants of the pizza as she passed it, resisting the urge to sweep that last slice of pepperoni onto the floor and smash it under her shoe. Finishing her circle, she slipped through the doorway and escaped out into the deserted hall. None of the others, as near as she could tell, had even noticed she was leaving.

And not once had James called out to her.

The guard downstairs checked her out, and the one at the gate did likewise. Somewhere along the way she cooled down; and by the time she was driving down the private road she realized with embarrassment that she'd acted like a child in there. Never in their six years of marriage had James given her any reason to suspect he was cheating, and working late hardly qualified as proof now. Even when he was working late with someone like Barbara Underwood.

But the house would still be empty when she reached it tonight. So would their bed.

Ahead in the distance, the stoplight where the Sand/Star drive intersected the highway was red. She let the car coast toward it, trying to decide what to do. It was nearly eight-thirty, the evening already half gone. A right turn and another half hour on rain-slicked roads would take her to their modest house up in Castro Valley. A left turn and a ten minute drive would take her in toward San Jose proper and Greenleaf Center Mall, where her bank branch was located. The branch where she would have to show up for work in eleven and a half hours anyway.

A group of flashing red lights to her left caught her eye, and she looked to see two police cars and an ambulance tearing north along the highway. They blew past her intersection in convoy and disappeared over a low hill to the right, the reflection of their flashing lights fading into the night. An accident somewhere that direction, obviously. If it was on or near the highway, she could probably add another half hour to her travel time home.

Ahead, the light turned green, and with sudden decision she spun the wheel left. Her dress would stand up to another day of wear, especially if she threw a sweater on over it, and there were toiletries and a change of underwear in the emergency bag James insisted they carry in case they got trapped away from home by an earthquake or mudslide. And of course, she always had her needlepoint with her in case there was nothing good on TV. A motel room would be no less lonely than her house, and it would save her the long commute in the morning.

She would get a late supper, relax for what was left of the evening, and get as good a night's sleep as she could have alone. Maybe take one of the sleeping tablets Dr. Bates had prescribed to help with all these long nights without her husband. She didn't like the things, but she had to admit that they worked. As long as she took it before ten o'clock, she shouldn't be groggy when she woke up.

And when she got to work in the morning, she would inform Nora that she'd be taking off at nine-thirty, possibly for the rest of the day. If she was going to put up with Tarnhelm's aggravations, it was only fair that she be there for its triumphs, too.

With that settled, she shifted to the right-hand lane and accelerated to the speed limit, or rather as much above the speed limit as she figured she could get away with. And tried to decide whether she was in the mood for Chinese, Thai, or Italian.

04

FOR A LONG moment Eleven lay motionless on his cot, staring into the darkness of his sea-going apartment, wondering what had snapped him awake. He could hear nothing through the container's sound insulation; certainly there was nothing to be seen.

He checked his watch. Just after three in the morning.

And then suddenly it clicked. The faint but pervasive vibration beneath him was gone.

The *Rabah Jamila* had stopped.

He was crossing the container toward the hook holding his headset when he heard the soft call-up buzz from it. He snagged the headset and slid it in place with one hand, scooping up his MP5 with the other. "What's happened?" he demanded. "Are we supposed to be stopped?"

"In the middle of the Taiwan Strait?" Ten growled back. "Not likely. It's either engine trouble or we've run into pirates."

Eleven swore under his breath. Not even two days into the voyage and already a complication had reared its ugly head.

Still, piracy was hardly unknown in these waters, and the plan did take this kind of contingency into account. They should be all right.

Provided they lived through the next ten minutes. "What's the move?"

"We assess the situation," Ten told him. "Get geared up and switch to radio."

"Right."

Three minutes later Eleven was ready, clothed in full night camouflage outfit with gloves and pullover head mask, with a compact night-vision monocular over his left eye and the radio headset snugged over his left ear. His suppressed MP5 was slung over his right shoulder, a suppressed Walther P5 riding his right hip. Spare magazines, flares, and grenades lay close to hand in hip pouches. "Ready," he said.

"Go out your stern exit," Ten instructed. "I don't want either of us popping up top until we find out if someone's walking the containers."

Eleven worked the stern latches, and with a soft pop the hidden exit swung open. Swinging the MP5 around behind his back where it would be out of the way, he drew the Walther and eased outside.

As his earlier probe had suggested, there was no container immediately aft of his. There was no wind, at least not in this container-sized pit, and only a handful of stars were showing through the mostly cloud-covered sky. For a moment he stood where he was, looking around the handful of container tops within his view and listening hard. Somewhere off to starboard was the engine noise of an approaching ship; closer at hand, also to starboard, he could hear muted voices. One of the voices rose in volume and gave what sounded like a sharp command.

A command that was definitely not in Urdu.

There was an access ladder built into the side of the container to his left. Keeping the Walther ready, he climbed cautiously up to where his head was even with the top of the overall container level. From his new vantage point he could see there were two figures walking across the tops of the containers. They were about eighty meters aft of his position, silhouetted against the superstructure lights behind them, looking slightly hunched over. Both carried large flashlights, pointed downward.

"Two men approaching," he murmured. "Eighty meters aft. Looks like they're reading the container markings."

"Checking out their prize," Ten said. "What else?"

"Ship and voices to starboard," Eleven said, sliding up into a prone position on top of the container. Keeping an eye on the approaching figures, he crawled across that container and the two beside it to the starboard edge of the stack and looked down.

There were two groups of people on the deck, gathered around the accommodation ladder about ten meters aft of his position. One group, six in number, were clearly members of the crew, standing tautly ready with the necessary gear for tying up the dark fishing boat rapidly approaching from that side. The other group, three of them, were standing a few meters forward of the crewmen holding shotguns on them.

"Three pirates holding six crew," he murmured to Ten. "Looks like they're bringing a fishing boat alongside. Pirates are Asians, probably Chinese."

"How many on the fishing boat?"

Eleven peered into the darkness, concentrating on the green image being fed to his left eye. "One in the wheelhouse, seven or eight on deck, all armed. From the size, I don't think there could be more than another five or six below deck."

"Cargo capacity?"

"Not worth mentioning. They must be planning to take the whole freighter."

"Sounds like it," Ten agreed. "Put the crew on the fishing boat and tow it off the main shipping lane, then set it adrift or machine-gun the lot of them."

"Probably," Eleven said. "Is it time yet to start improvising?"

"Funny," Ten grunted. "No choice but to ride to the rescue. A couple of days early, but there's nothing for it. Actually, the fact they're Chinese may work in our favor."

"Or else we could let the pirates take the ship and work a deal with them afterward," Eleven suggested as the idea suddenly struck him. "That might work even better."

"Or it might get our heads blown off," Ten said tartly. "No, we take them now."

"Fine. What's the plan?"

"It would be nice if we knew where all of them were," Ten said. "I'd hate to have to do a door-to-door through the whole superstructure—"

"Hold it," Eleven interrupted, peering aft. A large group had just come into view at the stern end of the ship, hands on their heads in classic prisoner style, another armed threesome behind herding them forward. He gave the captives a quick count: fourteen. "The rest of the crew is on their way forward," he confirmed. "Three more Chinese playing sheepdog."

"Excellent," Ten said with grim satisfaction. "Unless they've left someone in the wheelhouse, that means they're all bunched together on deck. How very convenient. Where are our two treasure hunters?"

Eleven looked at the men walking the containers. "About sixty meters back now," he reported. "Still seem oblivious."

"Let's make that condition permanent," Ten said. "Watch them; I'm coming out."

Eleven holstered his Walther and swiveled his MP5 up to point at the men. Behind him came the soft snick of Ten's topside exit popping open. He glanced over his shoulder, saw the long muzzle of Ten's Galil sniper rifle come out of the hole like a periscope going up, then swing down to point at the approaching pirates.

The Galil's suppressor was a top-notch design. From the deck below, Ten's two shots were probably completely lost in the engine noise from the approaching fishing boat. The first treasure hunter dropped without any reaction; the second had just enough time to swing his light toward his dead companion before going down himself.

"Get ready," Ten ordered, the second word half grunted as he hauled himself out of his container. "I'll check port, then find a crossfire position. Don't shoot yet unless you're spotted."

He took off at a crouching jog aft, angling to his right toward the ship's port side. Eleven shifted his attention back to the deck, watching the approaching *Rabah Jamila* crewmen and the fishing boat and trying to estimate their relative arrival times. Ideally, the crewmen would get to the ladder first, before the boat could be tied up. That would bring all the pirates together into nice one-two punch range without them having the option of joining forces.

And then he heard a shout from the fishing boat. One of the Chinese on deck was jumping up and down, jabbing an emphatic finger repeatedly toward the top of the containers. Eleven looked where he was pointing just as Ten skidded to a stop at the edge of the starboard container twenty meters aft and dropped onto his stomach.

"Take the boat," Ten snapped, the order punctuated by the soft crack of his Galil as he fired toward the deck.

Eleven didn't need any prompting. The men on the fishing boat were scrambling to get their guns lined up on Ten, but so far Eleven himself seemed to have escaped their notice. Flicking the MP5 to three-shot burst, he lined up the muzzle on the leftmost Chinese and squeezed the trigger.

The pirate jerked like a kicked monkey, his reflexive shotgun blast booming harmlessly into the air as the 9mm slugs tore his chest apart. The man next to him went the same way as Eleven swung the MP5 methodically across the boat's deck, while the third man in line had just enough time to gape in astonishment before he joined them. The fourth was diving for cover when he died, with the fifth through eighth pirates making it to safety ahead of the MP5's sweep.

Safety, of course, being a relative term. Eleven shifted aim and put a burst through the wheelhouse window, then dug into a hip pouch for one of the three grenades he'd brought up top with him. Ten wouldn't be happy if he spent them with too free a hand; the grenades and ammunition both had been appropriated with considerable difficulty from a closely guarded military base, and the two of them were under strict orders not to waste either. Under the circumstances, this probably qualified as proper use.

From below a new sound joined in the cacophony of noisy but ineffectual shotgun blasts: someone on the fishing boat had apparently found a rifle. Arming the grenade, Eleven hurled it sidearm toward the boat, keeping his head as far down as he could. His aim was perfect, the grenade shattering what was left of the wheelhouse glass as it dropped inside. "Grenade away," he warned into his mike as he ducked back and flattened himself on top of the container. Out of the corner of his eye he saw Ten do likewise.

The grenade went off with a most satisfying blast. The sound faded away, the screams of the injured replacing gunfire as the main source of noise from that direction. The fishing boat's midsection was burning briskly, Eleven saw as he eased an eye over the edge of the container, and the vessel was no longer under power.

The fire could be trouble. It would be visible all the way to the horizon, and the last thing they needed right now was a visit from curiosity seekers. But that problem was easily remedied. Calling another warning to Ten, he armed a second grenade and lobbed it into the stern of the crippled ship. Again he ducked back, wondering briefly whether the crewmen on the deck below were taking any damage from either the blasts or the gunfire.

The second grenade went off as noisily as the first, igniting another fire behind it. But from the way the boat was now listing it was clear that neither fire would be above the waves for much longer. Shuffling a few centimeters further forward, Eleven looked down at the *Rabah Jamila*'s deck.

The pirates were still holding out, but it was a lost cause. Four of the six were lying in pools of their own blood, while the other two crouched beside the containers were firing blindly up at Ten's position from the relative safety of a pair of unwilling human shields. Two of the other crewmen were tearing desperately aft, while the rest had evidently decided their most prudent course was to hit the deck right where they were.

At least, Eleven hoped that was what they were doing stretched out that way. If they'd instead been caught in the gunfire, the plan was going to get a lot trickier. All the more reason to wrap this up as quickly as they could.

With the two remaining pirates' full attention on Ten, their backs were completely unprotected. Shifting forward a few more centimeters, Eleven clicked his MP5 to single shot and lowered his sights.

Ten seconds later, it was all over.

"That takes care of that," Eleven breathed into the sudden silence. "Or does it, you think?"

"Better make sure," Ten grunted, hauling himself to his feet and heading aft over the containers. "I'm going to check the wheelhouse. You might as well get down there and start sweet-talking the captain. While you're at it, see if he knows of any crew or pirates still on the loose."

"Got it." Slinging the MP5 around his back again, Eleven found the container ladder on the starboard side and started down.

The crew's traditional Pakistani hospitality had suffered greatly in the past quarter hour or so, and Eleven reached the deck to find himself facing three of the late pirates' shotguns. "Which of you is the captain?" he called, ignoring the shotguns and the nervous crewmen holding them and hoping his rather broken Urdu wasn't too broken for them to understand. "The captain, please?"

An older man behind the semicircle of shotguns lifted a hand a few centimeters. "I'm Captain Syed," he said. "Who are you?"

"Important questions first," Eleven said. "Are there any pirates or crewmen unaccounted for who might be hiding elsewhere aboard the ship?"

In the fading firelight of the sinking fishing boat he could see the suddenly tight expression on Syed's face. "Why do you ask?"

"If there are more pirates, my partner is on his way to shoot them," Eleven explained patiently. "If there are more crewmen, my partner would like to *avoid* shooting them."

"I see," Syed murmured. "Yes, all my men are here. The pirates' sweep was quite thorough."

"There were eight of them," one of the crewmen offered. "Four in each of two rowboats. They linked the boats together with a rope, and when we struck the rope they came alongside—"

"There are only six here," someone else cut him off, looking around at the carnage. "There are two more elsewhere."

"They were on top of the containers," Eleven told him. "They've been dealt with. Excuse me."

He pressed the microphone closer to his mouth, not because it was necessary but to show the Pakistanis he was talking to his partner. "All clear, but check the superstructure anyway," he told Ten in fluent Korean. It was one of only ten sentences he could be fluent with in that language, but of course Syed wouldn't know that. "Now, Captain Syed,

I need a word with you," he said, switching back to his broken Urdu. "In private, if you please."

He gestured toward the bow of the ship. The shotguns wavered a moment, then reluctantly gave way as Syed stepped calmly between them and walked forward. Eleven fell into step beside him and together they moved fifteen paces away from the others before Syed stopped. "This is far enough," the captain said, turning to Eleven. "First of all, I want to know who you are."

"My name is Lieutenant Rhee," Eleven told him, pulling his ID wallet and a small flashlight from his tunic and handing them over. "South Korean Special Warfare Command."

"Indeed," Syed said, frowning as he opened the wallet and peered closely at the card. As if, Eleven thought with amusement, the man actually knew what a real one looked like. He peered back up at Eleven, as if trying to match the Korean face on the ID with the face mask confronting him, apparently gave up the effort, and handed the wallet and light back. "And what, may I ask, are you doing aboard my ship?"

"Our unit was tasked with transferring a special cargo to our Taipei embassy," Eleven told him. "As part of that effort—"

"Taipei?" Syed frowned. "We're not scheduled to go to Taipei."

"We planned to offload the cargo at sea before we left Taiwanese waters," Eleven said, struggling to keep up with the rapid-fire Urdu and wishing the captain would slow down. "As part of that effort, my partner and I were assigned to ride with the cargo in case of attack along the way."

He gestured toward the fishing boat, now nearly under water. "It was just as well we did."

Syed looked at the boat, his frown deepening. "But those were just ordinary pirates. These waters are filled with them."

Eleven gave a snort. "If you believe that, you're a fool. A fool who will certainly not survive their next attack."

"You think there will be another?"

"Most definitely," Eleven assured him grimly. "This first attempt was disguised as a pirate raid in case some of your people survived. It failed because they didn't expect us to be aboard. They won't make that mistake twice."

Syed looked again at the smoldering remains of the fishing boat, exhaling raggedly. Eventually, Eleven knew, it would occur to him to wonder why the attackers hadn't abandoned their pirate masquerade as soon as the stowaways appeared and produced heavier weaponry. But for the moment he was still too shaken by the near loss of his ship, and still too awed by the man with the automatic weapons and South Korean ID.

With luck, those thoughts and the accompanying doubts wouldn't surface for another couple of days.

"What do you propose to do?" Syed asked at last.

"The simplest plan would be to call in the rest of our unit," Eleven said. "But such a blatant show of force would erase any lingering doubts our enemies might have that the cargo is in fact aboard the *Rabah Jamila*."

"Is that a bad thing?" Syed asked. "Why do we care if they know where it is as long as they stay away?"

"Because they *wouldn't* stay away, that's why," Eleven said, letting an edge of contempt into his tone. "It would merely lead to an escalation of force on their side, with the *Rabah Jamila* caught in the middle." He lowered his voice. "And sooner or later, one side or the other would decide that a draw was preferable to a loss."

Syed drew himself up; and in that moment, Eleven knew he had him. At least for now. "My ship and crew are in your hands, Lieutenant," he said firmly. "Tell me what to do."

"First, you and I will get the ship underway," Eleven said, looking back at the little clumps of crewmen silently watching the conference. "While we do that, the rest of your crew will treat any wounded you have."

"Yes," Syed murmured. "Your enemies, of course, will be searching for us."

"They will be searching for the *Rabah Jamila*," Eleven said. "But that won't be the name of this ship much longer. Among our supplies we have self-adhering sheets that can be placed over the ship's name and markings. We also have a Panamanian flag for you to fly."

"I see." Syed hesitated. "They'll still know our heading, though."

"They'll know our *original* heading," Eleven corrected. "That's now changed. Our mission has been compromised, and our best hope is to try to reach South Korea ahead of them."

Syed's mouth dropped open. "What? But we're scheduled for Tokyo and—"

"Your schedule will be irrelevant when the *Rabah Jamila* lies on the bottom of the sea," Eleven cut him off harshly. "We head for Pusan harbor, or we all die. Those are your choices."

Syed looked back at his crew. "Understood," he muttered.

"Now you're being wise," Eleven said approvingly. "Have you any weapons aboard?"

"We have three rifles," Syed said. "They're locked in my cabin."

"Well, now you have more," Eleven said, gesturing at the crewmen nervously fingering their captured shotguns. "Not very useful for distance work, but if our enemies try to board us again they'll be in for a surprise. We'll check them for booby-traps, and then you can lock them up with your rifles. Some of your men can handle firearms, I trust?"

"Enough of them can," Syed said. "I'll inform our head office of the change in plans."

"You'll do no such thing," Eleven said flatly. "Are you mad? We travel under complete radio silence from now on."

"But—"

Eleven cut him off with a lifted hand. "I understand how difficult this is," he said, letting some understanding into his voice. "But no radio message is private—surely you know that. Even satellite conversations can be intercepted. With modern direction finders, even a single message could bring them to us like a pack of wolves."

Syed made a face, but nodded. "I suppose you're right."

"Of course I'm right," Eleven said. "Don't worry, you and your company will be more than adequately compensated for your trouble when we reach Pusan." He smiled slyly. "And if your head office suffers for a few days under the belief that you've been taken by pirates, imagine their joy and relief when you turn up alive and well. Surely there are one or two of them who deserve some sleepless nights, eh?"

Syed managed a wan smile in return. "One or two, yes," he conceded. "Very well, Lieutenant. Let me show you to the wheelhouse."

~

It had been nearly two in the morning when the last of the techs, Burke, had finally given up and toddled off for home. Now, an hour later, yawning hard enough to snap jaw muscles, James Chandler poured himself another cup of coffee and reached for the sugar. This last pot was decidedly on the bitter side, and he hadn't yet figured out whether it was because Esteban had made it or whether his taste buds were simply out of whack from tension and three weeks' worth of screw-ups in his eating and sleeping habits.

But the preliminary work was finally over. The military people would be here at ten, and he and the Cloak were absolutely, positively going to knock their khaki socks off. Twelve hours from now, give or take an hour, and he would forever be done with the days of begging Tarlington and the board for more funding. Despite their polite skepticism and, no doubt, private amusement, his approach had indeed proved workable. The Sand/Star crapshoot philosophy was about to pay off.

And the name James Chandler was about to go into the history books.

He gazed across the lab, leaning his suddenly weary body against the edge of the table. Barbara was seated at the center work area, half lying on the Papa Bear Cloak she and Wendell were supposed to be folding up to put into the semi parked downstairs. He wondered where Wendell had gotten to, then spotted a foot stretched out past one corner of the lab table. Wendell must have decided to take a nap, he decided, though it couldn't be very comfortable down there on the floor. Barbara had had a better idea, sacking out on the Cloak itself.

He sipped at his coffee again, noticing vaguely that the cup seemed to be getting heavier. Dr. Barbara Underwood. The same given name, Esteban had pointed out, as the patron saint of engineers and architects.

She'd certainly lived up to that heritage. Tonight's work alone would guarantee her a prominent spot in that future encyclopedia listing.

A programming genius, and a really nice person besides. A shame Angie seemed to have taken a dislike to her. But that would change. She just needed to get to know Barbara better, that was all. Maybe the three of them could go rent a couple of Angie's parents' cabins at Tahoe sometime. He and Angie could teach Barbara how to fish.

He started suddenly. In a single instant the room had twisted crazily, and it took a minute of careful thought to realize he was now lying on the floor, gazing at his cup and the puddle of coffee around it. There was a sort of throbbing in his cheek and head, but no real pain. He must be more tired than he thought.

But that was okay. The Army guys weren't due until . . . he couldn't remember, exactly, but he knew it wasn't for a while yet. He would take a little nap, then get up and get the Cloaks ready. Yes. That's what he would do.

Closing his eyes, he drifted off to sleep.

~

Setting up the satellite uplink took several minutes, and it was several minutes more before the general came on. "Yes?"

"Eleven, sir," Eleven identified himself, glancing at the container tops around him. Pure reflex; there was nothing he would be saying that would be dangerous for an eavesdropping crewman to overhear. "We've changed course for Pusan."

There was a short silence, long enough for Eleven to wonder if the freighter's gentle rocking had disrupted the connection. "You're two days early."

"Unavoidable, sir," Eleven told him. "We had an incident with pirates. Chinese, by the looks of them."

"You've dealt with the problem?"

"Thoroughly," Eleven confirmed.

"Bodies?"

"In the sea," Eleven said. "Scattered among the wreckage of their ship."

"Yours?"

"Renamed and on secondary track."

"The captain?"

Eleven smiled, remembering the long and often heated discussion that had taken place among the Pakistanis after the renaming and reflagging work had been finished and he and Ten had retired again to their seagoing apartments. It was a conversation the two of them had listened to with great interest by means of the Russian FSB listening devices Ten had scattered around during his sweep of the ship's living areas. "Not happy, but willing to go along."

"Very well," the general said, his tone dismissing the unexpected change in plans with the calmness of a strategist who has all possible contingencies already mapped out. "Make certain you're ready when he decides to stop cooperating. I'll alert Twelve to move into quick-response position ahead of you. You'll of course inform him at once of any course changes."

"Yes, sir," Eleven said. "How are matters proceeding there?"

"According to schedule," the general said. "We'll be ready when you reach the rendezvous point." The general's tone darkened. "Make certain *you* are likewise ready."

~

With a suddenness that always meant trouble, Madison Talbot snapped fully awake, his hand darting automatically for the holster hanging underneath the nightstand shelf as he scanned his darkened bedroom for unexpected company. He had a grip on his Glock 22 before his brain caught up with the fact that it was the warbling cell phone and not an intruder that had awakened him. Blinking a couple of times, he let go of the gun and snagged the phone, looking at the softly glowing blue numbers on his clock as he did so. Ten minutes to six. The phone cut off in mid-warble as he thumbed it on. "Talbot."

"It's Nate," San Jose detective Natal Delgado's familiar voice came. "We've got trouble at Sand/Star."

Talbot had already thrown off the blankets. "What sort?" he asked as his feet slapped down onto the cold floor.

There was a barely audible sigh. "James Chandler and two of his colleagues have just been found in their lab by the cleaning crew. Dead."

Something squeezed hard at Talbot's gut. "Murdered?"

"That, or they got a really bad pizza," Delgado said grimly. "Can you get down here?"

Talbot flipped on a light and headed for his closet. Damn, and damn, and damn again. "I'm on my way."

THE
THIRD
DAY

05

By seven o'clock the Building D parking lot was awash with cops, medical examiner types, and enough vehicle-mounted flashing lights to start a dance club. Talbot drove carefully through the gauntlet and parked his car in an unobtrusive spot near the rear. For a wonder, the ubiquitous TV camera crews weren't in evidence, and he wondered whether Delgado had deliberately frozen them out or if they were just sleeping in this morning. His badge got him through the standard police receiving line at the various doors and elevators, and at last he was ushered into the third-floor Tarnhelm lab.

The bodies had already been removed, with only tape outlines showing where they'd been found: two on different sides of the pushed-together tables in the center of the room, the third over to one side by a table decorated with a coffee maker, three mostly empty soda bottles, a couple of pizza boxes, and assorted scientific hardware. Open doors at opposite ends of the lab led to adjoining offices, the one on the left much larger than the one on the right. He caught a glimpse of Delgado through the smaller office door, and maneuvered his way that direction through the fingerprint and sample collectors.

"Nate," he greeted the other as he stepped into the office, giving the room a quick once-over as he did so. The cramped space was dominated by a large paper-strewn desk with an expensive-looking computer workstation on it; an older man in rumpled clothing was seated in front of the latter, pounding away at the keyboard. Flanking the desk were a pair of file cabinets and a small drafting table, with a coat tree holding a windbreaker and overcoat tucked into a corner by the door. Stretched out in the back, looking rather out of place, was an old army cot.

"About time," Delgado said, glancing at his watch. "Car trouble?"

"You forget how early East Bay traffic gets started," Talbot countered. "What have you got?"

"So far, precious little," Delgado said. "This is Dr. Theodore Tarlington, in charge of this division of Sand/Star. Doctor: FBI Special Agent Madison Talbot."

"Special Agent Talbot," Tarlington said, not looking up as he continued assaulting the keyboard. His hair was as rumpled as his clothing, and his face had a sheen of sweat and a slightly greenish tinge. Early-morning murders apparently didn't agree with him.

"Dr. Tarlington," Talbot said, nodding politely. "What are we looking up?"

"He's trying to access Building D's security records," Delgado said. "We've got the gate guard from last night on his way in to pull the complete record for the whole complex—the various shifts are staggered, and he went off duty at four. Right now, I'm mostly interested in who in this building went home when."

"Here it is," Tarlington said, leaning forward. "The final checkouts, anyway. Looks like everyone except the six in this room were out by seven p.m. Of those six, two of them—Ramon Esteban and Scott Kingsley—signed out of the building close together, at one-thirty-five and one-thirty-six this morning. The door openings were at one-thirty-six and one-thirty-eight."

"When did they check through the gate?" Delgado asked.

"That's not in this file," Tarlington said. "The gate guard will have to pull that up."

"What about the third tech?"

"Jack Burke," Tarlington said. "He signed out twenty minutes later, at one-fifty-five, and opened the door within the same minute."

"Got it," Delgado said, making some pigeon scratches in his notebook. "Was the door opened any time after that, either with a card or from the desk?"

"Yes," Tarlington said, frowning at the display. "It was opened once, at three-fifteen. No sign-out, though."

"What was the downstairs guard doing at the time?" Talbot asked.

"Propped up in a stall in the first-floor restroom, drugged to the eyebrows," Delgado said grimly. "The obvious suspect is the coffee pot down there. We're having it checked."

"Same drug that killed the scientists?"

"Doesn't look like it," Delgado said. "For one thing, he's still alive, though he's under observation at the hospital while he sleeps it off. For another, the trauma marks indicate his brew took effect a whole lot faster than the stuff the scientists got."

Talbot nodded. "Inevitably."

"Why inevitably?" Tarlington asked.

"You can't take out a group of people with anything fast-acting unless they all take it at the same time," Talbot explained. "Otherwise, the balloon goes up as soon as the first one keels over. On the other hand, there are lots of good reasons for knocking out a trained guard as fast as possible, especially when he's got access to panic buttons. What about the guard our sleeping warrior replaced? Is he all right?"

"He was as of fifteen minutes ago, when we hauled him out of bed," Delgado said. "The shift change downstairs was midnight, and he said he drew his last cup of coffee from the pot around eight o'clock."

"Four hours before the shift change, and an hour *after* everyone except the people in this lab left the building," Talbot noted. "That's handy. So our poisoner could have drugged the pot at any point after that."

"Assuming he knew the evening guard's habits," Delgado agreed.

"What do you mean?" Tarlington asked. "What habits?"

"His coffee-drinking schedule," Talbot said. "If he followed a more or less strict regimen of knocking off caffeine at eight, say, it would give the poisoner a larger window of opportunity than if he sometimes had his last cup at, say, ten or eleven."

"Right," Delgado said, scribbling more notes. "So we need to know how consistent he was, and who in this room might have known it."

"In this room?" Tarlington echoed, looking aghast. "Surely you're not suggesting one of their own lab assistants did this to them."

"Who else?" Talbot countered. "You said yourself no one else was in the building."

"Well, I mean—" Tarlington floundered. "Maybe it was one of the cleaning staff. Or a visitor from outside. It *has* to be someone from outside."

"We'll check out that possibility," Delgado assured him. "Thank you, Doctor. You can go home now if you'd like."

"Thank you." Tarlington leaned back wearily. "If it's all right, I'd rather go to my office and work up a press release."

"Sure, go ahead," Delgado said. "We'll call if we need anything more. Leave that workstation on, if you would."

Tarlington hesitated, then nodded. He stood up and headed out through the main lab, his shoulders slumped.

"Not a happy camper, is he?" Talbot murmured.

"Not very," Delgado agreed. "I trust you noticed the curious timing here. The last lab assistant signs out just before two, with the guard presumably awake and kicking. An hour and a half later, when our unknown Mr. X either comes in or goes out, he's apparently not there to wave his magic pen and sign-in pad at him."

"The question being how Mr. X got the door open," Talbot said. "Either he had a card to swipe in with, which means a Sand/Star employee, or else someone in here opened the door for him."

"Right," Delgado said. "According to Tarlington, the cleaning crew came in about midnight. But since they work in pairs they're likely to all have alibis for the three-fifteen time slot. Another possibility, I suppose, is that one of the three victims opened the door."

"What, after he'd downed the poison but before he dropped dead?" Talbot scoffed. "That doesn't make a lot of sense."

"I agree," Delgado said. "Which leaves us the option that Mr. X slipped in earlier while the door was open anyway, with the guard either distracted or in the washroom. The three-fifteen opening would then be Mr. X going out."

"Leaving him the problem of getting through the gate," Talbot said. "Over the fence, maybe?"

"Not likely," Delgado said doubtfully. "There are supposed to be sensors woven into the chain, and there's razor wire on top. Still . . . Greer?"

A large plainclothes cop poked his head around the door. "Yes, sir?"

"Get a team out checking the perimeter fence," Delgado ordered. "Look for signs someone might have sneaked over or through it last night."

"Got it," Greer said, and vanished again.

"We need a look at that complete security list," Talbot commented. "And we need to talk to the techs. I presume they're on their way?"

"They should be here any time," Delgado said, stepping out of the office into the lab. "Something else I want to show you."

"You didn't say where the poison was in here," Talbot commented as Delgado led him through the milling evidence-gatherers toward the lab tables.

"Probably the coffee," Delgado said. "The lab's working on it, but the stuff smelled funny when I sniffed it."

"Our poisoner has a one-track mind," Talbot said. "I don't suppose the doors of this suite are locked during the day or evening."

Delgado shrugged. "We'll ask the techs, but Tarlington said most of the people in this building tend toward the casual end of the paranoia spectrum. Apparently," he added in a slightly bitter tone, "nothing secret or of military importance was being done in here."

"Yeah," Talbot said. "Right."

They stopped beside the lab tables. "You'll find this particularly interesting," Delgado said, pointing to two of the tape outlines. "The ME's preliminary check of Chandler and Fowler showed head and shoulder trauma marks where they fell onto the floor before they died."

He pointed to the third outline. "But Underwood has no such marks. What she *does* have are pressure marks on her left cheek and arm that indicate they were pressed together a short time before she died."

Talbot eyed the stool beside the outline. "As if she was sitting with her upper body lying across the tables?"

"That's my guess," Delgado agreed. "Furthermore, the way she was positioned on the floor looked to me like someone pulled her off and laid her more or less gently down there."

He lifted his eyebrows. "Which either means they didn't want her falling with a thud that might draw attention . . . ?"

"Or else she was lying on something they wanted," Talbot finished the sentence.

Delgado nodded. "Very good. We'll make a police detective of you yet."

"I may have to take you up on that offer one of these days," Talbot warned, surveying the scene. So Mr. X's goal had been the Cloaks. Big fat hairy surprise. "What's happening upstairs on this?"

"I've called Garcia," Delgado said. "He'll be coming down later. As far as your presence on the case is concerned—" He raised his eyebrows. "I don't suppose you want to get Lyman out of his morning shower for this."

"Not especially," Talbot said. "We'd better wait until his second cup of coffee."

Delgado made a face. "Under the circumstances, you should probably rephrase that."

"Probably," Talbot conceded.

"Lieutenant?" the door guard called, poking his head inside. "The lab assistants are here. Kiyohara's got them down in the cafeteria. First floor."

"Thanks." Delgado gestured to Talbot. "Shall we go have a chat?"

"Let's," Talbot agreed. "You might want to offer them something to drink, too. See if any of them happens not to be a coffee drinker."

"Way ahead of you."

~

The three lab techs were seated at one of the cafeteria tables, huddled together like children at midnight who've watched one hack-and-slash movie too many. All of them had the same rumpled look Dr. Tarlington had exhibited earlier, and if anything looked more miserable even than he had. There was a steaming cup in front of each of them, and the aroma of vending-machine coffee pervaded the air, but it was unclear whether any of them had even touched their drinks. Three uniformed cops, probably the ones who'd rousted them out of bed and driven them here, sat casually at other tables nearby, paying close but unobtrusive attention to the soft and probably rather brittle conversation.

They looked over in unison as Delgado pushed open the door and he and Talbot stepped into the room, their faces taking on the deer-in-the-headlights look Talbot had seen so often before. "Good morning," Delgado said, putting on his best the-policeman-is-your-friend smile. "I'm sorry to drag you all out of bed, especially after such a late night. And especially when I have bad news for you."

"What sort of bad news?" one of the techs demanded in a quavering voice. He was Hispanic, late twenties, with bright eyes that darted nervously around the room as he spoke.

"Let's have some introductions first, shall we?" Delgado said. "I'm Detective Lieutenant Natal Delgado of the San Jose Police Department. This is Special Agent Madison Talbot of the FBI."

All three sets of eyes bugged on that one. "FBI?" one of the other techs echoed. He was tall and blond, with chiseled features and deep blue eyes, and a heritage as obviously north of the Alps as the Hispanic's was south of the Rio Grande. He was also slightly younger than the Hispanic, probably no more than twenty-seven. "What in the name of God—?"

"Your turn, now," Delgado interrupted him smoothly. "You are—?"

The blond man grimaced. "Jack Burke," he said.

"And you?" Delgado asked the Hispanic.

"Ramon Esteban," he said.

"And you?" Delgado asked, shifting his attention to the third man, a medium-height-and-build type with light brown hair and eyes to match.

"Scott Kingsley," he said. Of the three of them, Talbot decided, Kingsley had the best control of himself, though perhaps it was just the experience of age. He was probably in his early thirties, which gave him at least six years on Esteban and a good ten on Burke. "So what *is* going on?"

"There was some trouble upstairs, I'm afraid," Delgado said, casually pulling over a chair from the next table and sitting down facing them. He had a tendency toward the dramatic, Talbot knew, which could sometimes be useful. "Early this morning, as best we can tell."

"What sort of trouble?" Burke demanded suspiciously. "Come on, it's too early in the morning for games."

"Fine," Delgado said. "Doctors Chandler, Underwood, and Fowler have been murdered."

Their reactions were of almost text-book quality. Esteban's mouth dropped open, his eyes widening with shock. Burke's breath went out of him as if he'd been punched in the stomach. And Kingsley, for all his surface calm, went visibly pale.

Burke found his voice first. "What are you talking about?" he demanded. "They—no. They can't be."

Delgado shook his head. "I'm sorry."

"But that's crazy," Kingsley breathed. "Why would anyone do something like that?"

"That's what we're here to find out," Delgado said. "Let's begin with a recap of yesterday's activities. I want to know what you did, where you went, who else was in the lab—everything. Which of you arrived first?"

Kingsley swallowed visibly. "I did," he said. "I mean, of us three I did."

"And when was that?" Delgado asked.

"Around eight-thirty," Kingsley said. "The sign-ins can give you the exact time if you need it. Dr. Chandler and Dr. Underwood were already here, working on the big workstation in Dr. Chandler's office. Dr. Fowler arrived a few minutes after I did. I'd just finished making a pot of coffee and he made a beeline for it."

"And the other techs?" Delgado asked, his face not showing any reaction to the mention of coffee.

"Uh—" Kingsley looked at his companions. "Jack, I think, got in a little before nine. Ramon was later, about nine-thirty."

"I had to drop my niece off at school," Esteban put in. "My sister's sick and her husband's out of town. Dr. Chandler knew I was going to be on a strange schedule this week."

"That's right, he did," Kingsley confirmed. "Anyway, this was the last day before our demo tomorrow. Today, I mean. We hit the lab tables right away and started the final equipment check."

"Tell me about this demo," Delgado invited.

Again, Kingsley looked at his companions. "I don't know if I should," he said uncertainly. "It's not exactly a secret. But . . . "

"This is a murder investigation, Mr. Kingsley," Talbot reminded him mildly. "And Dr. Tarlington has already told us there's no top-secret work in this building."

Burke snorted. "That's because Tarlington is an idiot," he said contemptuously. "He wouldn't know a revolutionary breakthrough if it snatched him aboard an alien spaceship and took organ samples."

"Easy, Jack," Esteban said warningly.

Burke hunched his shoulders as if chilled by a sudden draft. "Sorry," he muttered.

"That's all right," Delgado soothed. "I know this is a lot to have dropped on your plate first thing in the morning. Tell me about the project, Mr. Kingsley."

Kingsley glanced at the others again, then shrugged slightly. "It's called a Cloak," he said. "You can drape it over yourself or a machine gun emplacement. Or a whole military camp, for that matter, if you've got one big enough."

"And?" Delgado prompted.

Kingsley seemed to brace himself. "And it makes you invisible."

The three listening cops straightened up a bit. "Really," Talbot said, putting a note of skepticism into his voice.

"You don't believe us," Kingsley said without rancor. "That's fine. Tarlington never believed us either. But we've got four Cloaks upstairs, all ready to go. If you want, we can show you."

"They *are* still there, aren't they?" Esteban demanded suddenly. "Oh, God. Is that why they were killed? For the *Cloaks*?"

Delgado looked over at Talbot. "We don't know yet why they were murdered," he said. "But the Cloaks do seem to be missing."

For a long moment the room was silent. Talbot watched the techs closely, trying to evaluate whether they were reacting more strongly to this shock than they had to the news of their colleagues' murders. Esteban seemed more sandbagged, Kingsley less, Burke about the same. By itself it meant nothing; rapid-fire revelations hit different people in different ways. But right now, every data point was useful.

Delgado gave them another few seconds before clearing his throat. "Let's continue with yesterday. You all arrived between eight-thirty and nine-thirty and got to work."

"Right," Kingsley said. "Right. Well, first thing on the agenda was to start checking the Cloaks for the demo. We ran through the two Baby Bears pretty quickly—"

"The what?" Delgado interrupted.

"Baby Bears," Kingsley said. "We made up three different Cloak sizes, which we named Papa Bear, Mama Bear, and Baby Bear."

"We had two Baby Bears," Esteban added.

"Right," Kingsley nodded. "The Baby Bears were designed for personal use, big enough for one or maybe two men to crouch or lie beneath. Mama Bear was big enough to cover a couple of tanks or a helicopter, and Papa Bear could handle a hundred-foot Quonset hut."

"That's what we were going to do with it, in fact," Burke said. "The climax of the demo was going to be to make the Quonset hut over at Calaveras Reservoir disappear."

"Sounds like a David Copperfield special," Talbot murmured.

"Go ahead and laugh," Burke bit out. "But as soon as we make up another Cloak—" He broke off, looking back at Delgado. "The fabrication equipment's still there, isn't it? Or did they take that, too?"

"We don't know what else is missing," Delgado told him. "As soon as they've finished sweeping the room we'll let you run an inventory."

"I'm a little confused," Talbot said. "You had a Quonset hut-sized Cloak already made up for the very first demo? Seems a little excessive."

"We already knew the technique worked," Kingsley explained. "The fabrication machine Jack and Dr. Fowler put together assembles half-meter-wide strips of the material, and can make them whatever length you've got base fabric for. It's no harder to turn out fifty strips than it is to make one."

"The only thing that gets trickier with size is getting the optical interfaces hooked up," Esteban said. "That, and programming the computer to handle the extra input. Doctors Chandler and Underwood handled most of that."

"That's why we had four of them, actually," Kingsley said. "We needed two Baby Bears to test the theory and see how they might interact—diffraction or interference problems; that sort of thing. We had to make up Mama Bear to see how the larger size affected programming and response time. Papa Bear—" He shrugged. "I suppose we did that one just for the hell of it."

"It wasn't at all for the hell of it," Burke insisted, throwing Kingsley an annoyed look. "Dr. Chandler was determined to make this a real test, something that would make the Army sit up and take notice. It's one thing to make a computer workstation disappear. It's something entirely different to do it with a whole Quonset hut."

"Still sounds excessive to me," Talbot said. "But then, I'm not trying to pitch an idea to the Army. All right, so you checked out the Baby Bears."

"Right," Kingsley said. "Like I said, they went real fast and without any trouble. We finished them about—" He looked at the others questioningly. "What, one and three o'clock?"

"The first was closer to one-thirty," Esteban said. "I remember because Dr. Chandler went out into the hall to talk to Tarlington just before we finished, and Tarlington always seems to wander our part of the building about that time."

"And the second was definitely at three," Burke added. "Ramon headed out to pick up his niece just after we got Mama Bear spread out on the table."

"Right," Kingsley said with a nod. "So it was just after three o'clock that we started on Mama Bear."

"What about lunch?" Talbot asked.

The three techs looked at each other. "Did we have lunch?" Esteban asked.

"I don't think we did," Kingsley said. "We've skipped a lot of lunches lately. Too busy getting this wrapped up."

"So there was never any time when the lab was empty?" Delgado asked.

"None." Kingsley was positive.

"Where did you put the Baby Bears when you were through with them?"

"They were stacked on the floor in the main office," Kingsley said. "Over in one corner."

"Were they in your sight the whole time?" Talbot asked.

"Well, no, not really," Kingsley said. "Though anyone who walked into the office would have seen them. Why?"

"I'm wondering if anyone could have gotten to them besides the six of you."

"I doubt it," Kingsley said, forehead furrowed in thought. "None of us ever uses the door between the office and hallway, so it's usually locked."

"I suppose someone could have unlocked it, though," Burke added. "There are a few master keys floating around."

"We'll check on that," Delgado said. "So you started on Mama Bear a little after three o'clock. When did you finish?"

"Not until, oh, about eight," Kingsley said. "Some of the kinesthetic sensor fibers had come loose, and it took us forever to find out where."

"We got it just about the time Angie Chandler dropped in," Esteban said.

Talbot felt himself straighten just a bit. "Mrs. Chandler was here yesterday?"

"Yes, but she didn't stay long," Esteban said. "Ten minutes, tops. I think she came to see if Dr. Chandler was ready to go home. He wasn't, so she left."

"And went home?" Delgado asked.

Esteban shrugged. "I suppose."

"And she left the lab after eight o'clock?"

"The check-outs can tell you," Esteban said. "I'm pretty sure it was after eight, though."

Delgado nodded. "All right. Continue."

"After that we went to work on Papa Bear," Kingsley said. "There were no problems, and we wound up leaving about—let's see. Ramon and I left the lab together about one-thirty. I don't know when Jack took off."

"It was about two," Burke said. "Maybe a little before."

"You signed out with the guard?"

Kingsley shook his head. "He wasn't at his desk when Ramon and I went through, so we just signed ourselves out on his pad."

"Wait a minute," Burke said, frowning. "He wasn't there when I signed out, either."

The three looked blankly at each other, a group expression Talbot could well sympathize with. If the guard had already been knocked out and disposed of before two o'clock, then the window of opportunity was suddenly a lot wider than he and Delgado had thought. "I assumed he was in the john," Burke said.

"So did we," Kingsley said. "Remember, Ramon? I even made a joke about him and me having to stop meeting like this before I went in."

"Yes, I remember," Esteban confirmed, his face having the pinched look of someone braced for more bad news. "Was he killed, too?"

"No, just put to sleep," Delgado said. "He's at the hospital, but should be okay."

"Let's back up a minute," Talbot said. "Mr. Kingsley, you said you went to the washroom after signing out?"

"Yes," Kingsley nodded. "I'd drunk too much soda that last hour and didn't feel like holding it for the drive home."

"And you didn't see him in there?"

Kingsley glared at him. "You really think I would have seen him and not said something?" he demanded.

"No, of course not," Delgado soothed.

"I didn't exactly go around looking under the stall doors, you know," Kingsley added, still sounding offended.

"Of course not," Delgado said again. "Did you wait for him inside, Mr. Esteban?"

"No, I went out to get my car started," Esteban said. "His was outside the fence, over at the shipping building, and I was going to give him a ride."

"I left it there earlier when I brought the semi in," Kingsley added.

Delgado frowned. "Semi?"

"Yes," Kingsley said, frowning in turn at his reaction. "Dr. Chandler sent me to get it about eight."

"And you left it here by the building?" Talbot asked.

"Yes, parked along the north side," Kingsley said, blinking suddenly. "That's right—it wasn't there when the cop brought me in. I didn't even think about that."

Delgado had his phone out and was punching a number. "I don't suppose you remember the license."

"No, but the cab was number 4686," Kingsley said. "And it had 'Sand/Star Technologies' plastered all across the sidewalls."

"Close enough," Delgado grunted, holding the phone to his ear. " . . . Batista? APB out on a Sand/Star Technologies semi; cab number 4686. Has the gate guard arrived yet? . . . Let me know when he does."

He slid the phone back into his pocket. "I think that'll be all for now," he told the techs, getting up. "I'd like you to wait, if you don't mind, in case we have other questions."

"You'll need to take inventory upstairs anyway when the lab folks are finished," Talbot added. "Oh, one more thing. Mr. Esteban, you said you left during the Mama Bear test between three and three-thirty to go get your niece; and you, Mr. Kingsley, just said you left at eight to bring in the eighteen-wheeler. Did you happen to go outside the fence at all during the day, Mr. Burke?"

"No," Burke said. "No, wait, yes I did. I went out to get the pizzas and sodas about five."

Talbot nodded. "Thank you. Well, make yourselves comfortable, or as comfortable as you can. We'll let you know when you can go upstairs."

He and Delgado headed out, leaving the techs to their coffee, broodings, and imaginations. It was, Talbot knew, an unpleasant combination. "Well, at least we know now how Mr. X got in without the guard lifting an eyebrow," Delgado growled as they walked down the hallway. "He was already well past eyebrow-lifting capability."

"Mr. X, and half the damn alphabet if they'd wanted," Talbot pointed out. "Each of the techs was alone for a minimum of a minute on their way out. A whole busload of people who knew what they were doing could have made it inside while the door was open."

"Certainly Burke had opportunity," Delgado agreed. "But Esteban and Kingsley left together. How could Esteban know Kingsley was going to hit the head on the way out?"

"Maybe he'd been the one keeping Kingsley's cup filled upstairs," Talbot said. "Or maybe he had an excuse of his own ready and just didn't have to use it. At this point I'm not ready to rule any of them out. Them *or* Angie Chandler."

"Funny you should mention her," Delgado said darkly. "I had Poole make the next-of-kin calls, and he told me he talked to Mrs. Chandler at home. He offered to have a driver pick her up and bring her here, but she declined, saying she could do it herself."

"I hope you didn't take her word for that."

"Matter of fact, I already had a car on the way to her place," Delgado said. "They reported she wasn't home."

Talbot frowned. "When did they get there?"

"Three minutes after Poole hung up," Delgado said. "And this at a quarter to six in the morning. Show me anyone who can get out of bed, get dressed, and be in the car in three minutes."

Talbot chewed at his lip. "They're sure she was gone?"

"They leaned on the bell for ten minutes," Delgado said. "And her car wasn't in the garage."

"In other words, she wasn't in bed when Poole called," Talbot said slowly. "She was dressed, packed, and ready to go."

"Sure looks that way," Delgado agreed. "Unfortunately, by the time I got both reports and put them together, it was already after six-thirty. I've put out an APB on her car, and we're working on getting a search warrant for her house."

"Grounds?"

"Suspicion of foul play," Delgado said. "They could probably go in right now, but I'd rather we had our ducks here properly lined up first."

"Probably a good idea," Talbot said. "What now?"

Delgado shrugged. "Not much else we can do until they finish upstairs or the gate man gets here and pulls up the security files. I think I'll go see how the perimeter check is going. However our Alphabet Gang got in and out of the building, they first had to get through the fence."

"I'm betting they came in through the gate," Talbot said.

"Probably," Delgado agreed. "You want to come watch?"

"Thanks, but I'll stick with kibitzing your people in here where it's warm." Talbot looked back toward the cafeteria. "Or maybe I'll chat some more with our friends back there."

"Okay. See you later."

Delgado continued on down the hallway toward the main door, pausing briefly to exchange some words with the cops on duty before the Sand/Star man at the desk buzzed him out. Talbot watched until he had disappeared around the corner, then turned and headed back toward the cafeteria.

But he didn't go any farther than the first recessed doorway. There, out of sight of either the cops behind him or any of the cafeteria squad who might happen to step out into the hallway, he pulled out his phone and punched in a number. Special Agent in Charge Paul Lyman would probably be out of his shower by now, but he certainly wouldn't have finished his first cup of coffee yet. Not really a good time to call him.

The conversation was short. When it was finished, Talbot put the phone away and retraced Delgado's steps toward the exit. The detective could slog around the fence all he wanted; Talbot was more interested at the moment in the more immediate landscape surrounding Building D. One small patch of it in particular.

Zipping up his coat, he nodded at the cops and Sand/Star man as he passed them, and strode out into the California morning.

06

GREENLEAF CENTER WAS a small shopping mall, as Bay Area malls went. Laid out in an unimaginative rectangle in the center of a wrap-around parking area, it had only a single corridor and two floors, with the top floor given over to such low walk-in-traffic businesses as insurance agents, Armed Forces recruiters, and real estate centers. It had two anchor stores—a Macy's and a Pottery Barn—a small Bank of America branch near the middle of the long corridor, three fast-food places, a modest sit-down restaurant, and the usual assortment of shoe stores, jewelers, and knick-knack purveyors that seemed standard at neighborhood places like this.

And as of one month ago, it had also had its very first detective agency.

Standing down on the main floor, leaning his weight against one of the decorative pillars as he eased his stiff left leg, Adam Ross gazed up through the second-floor railing at the modest sign painted on the frosted glass of his office door. *Wellington Security and Investigations,* it said in large letters; below, just readable from down here if you had particularly good eyesight, were the words, "Adam Ross, Investigator."

For four weeks now, that sign and office had been the source of decidedly mixed feelings on his part. On the one hand, it felt very apple-pie entrepreneurial to have his own place, with a shingle on the door and everything. His father had been a Chicago cop, marching shoulder to shoulder in step with the rest of the force, and if he'd been alive he would undoubtedly have looked at that door with an embarrassing degree of paternal pride.

On the other hand, Ross had to face the rather ego-bruising fact that in those same four weeks he hadn't had a single legitimate case walk in through that door.

There'd been a few inquiries, of course. Pre-divorce stuff, mostly, one spouse looking for dirt on the other, with either dollar signs or homicide lurking behind their irises. There'd been a couple of even more distasteful requests, including a couple of breaking-and-entering jobs and even one thinly-disguised invitation for him to contract for a murder.

But none of that was why he'd set up shop here, and he'd eased all of them out the door with a combination of excuses, contract provisos, and astronomical rate quotes. The would-be murderer he'd sent packing in no uncertain terms, and had followed it up with an anonymous phone call to the San Jose Police.

He lowered his eyes to the brightly lit bank directly beneath his office and a pair of bustling employees working behind the glass panels that sealed it off from the rest of the mall. It wasn't quite eight o'clock yet, and like most of the other stores the bank still had an hour to go before opening time.

Even so, the mall was hardly deserted, a phenomenon that never ceased to amaze him. Aside from the growing trickle of employees arriving to set up shop, there were a fair number of senior-aged walkers taking advantage of the low population density to take their morning exercise out of the chilly rain that had started streaming down outside. Two of the four eateries were open, as well, the sit-down place catering mainly to those same seniors and others with no jobs or schools to rush off to, while the McDonald's serviced those in more of a hurry.

And soon, if he was lucky, among the people wandering into view along the corridor to his right would be Angie Chandler.

He'd spotted her his first day here, watching from this exact spot as the painter lettered the sign on his door. She'd been in one of the smaller offices in the back of the bank, one of those the tellers pointed you to if you came in inquiring about a loan. He knew that, because as soon as she'd returned from lunch that afternoon he'd gone in and made just such an inquiry.

After that, with the ice broken, he'd contrived to run into her at least once a day, twice if he could manage it, usually as she left or returned from lunch or break. Once he walked out the eastern door with her at quitting time, and made careful note of where she'd parked her car. Spot-checks on the following days showed she always used the same general area of the lot.

And through all those chats, he'd learned quite a bit about the lady.

She was first-generation Chinese-American, having come to America with her parents from the mainland via Hong Kong in the days before the British turned that venerable colony back over to Beijing. She had two younger siblings, a brother living in Minneapolis and a sister in LA, and her parents managed a group of houses and apartment complexes in Monterey and the Bay Area. Both sets of grandparents were still alive in China, the paternal pair in Loyang, the maternal pair in Canton. She had no particular accent that he could detect, but at least in the semiformality of their conversations there had been a deliberation about her speech and manner that he concluded was probably as much her cultural upbringing as it was anything ethnic. She had a quiet passion for needlepoint, and her office was decorated with several examples of her work.

Ross had always found Asian women easy on the eyes; but Angie's exotic looks were also deepened by a down-to-earth manner and bearing reminiscent of the homespun Midwest girls he'd grown up among. It wasn't a combination he'd run across very often, though to be fair he didn't know many Chinese women as well as he was getting to know Angie.

She also had a wedding band on her left hand. But you couldn't have everything.

His watch beeped: eight o'clock. Rather, five minutes till, since he always set his watch fast. Angie should be coming along the corridor any time now.

He let his eyes drift around the mall . . . and as he did so, he spotted something he hadn't noticed before. Four men had taken up positions, two each, on two of the benches set against decorative plant islands twenty yards on either side of the bank's entrance. They were facing opposite directions down the long hallway, their faces toward the mall's two main entrances, their backs to Ross, their eyes ostensibly buried in newspapers.

And all four were wearing knitted gray stocking caps.

An unpleasant tingle ran up the back of Ross's neck. It was certainly chilly enough outside for hats of some sort not to be out of place. But it was also pouring down rain, and in his experience stocking caps were next to useless under those conditions unless you wore a poncho over them or had an umbrella. As far as he could see from where he was leaning, none of the loiterers had either.

He pushed himself away from his supporting pillar and strolled casually down the hallway toward the eastern end of the mall. It might mean nothing; simply four men who happened to favor the same unlikely type of cap taking up what looked like stake-out positions. Even if it did mean something, maybe all they intended was a bank robbery. It might have nothing whatsoever to do with Angie Chandler.

He didn't believe it for a second.

He passed the eastern pair, throwing a single casual glance that direction as he went by. It didn't do much good; both readers had their newspapers held high enough to cover everything but their eyes. The eyes were dark, he noted, with the small amount of skin he could see between newspaper and the neatly rolled cap rim also reasonably dark.

Still, the glance hadn't been a complete waste of effort. Both sets of dark eyes had likewise flicked to him as he passed, a return glance that had looked more like a professional once-over than simple curiosity.

And there wasn't a single poncho, hooded jacket, or umbrella in sight.

With their obvious vigilance a second glance on his part would have been risky. He continued past, walking as quickly as he could without looking obvious about it. He couldn't see any more gray stocking caps between him and the mall's eastern entrance, but that didn't mean anything. Maybe whoever was down at this end of the mall was working a different color scheme.

He was still fifty feet from the entrance when four white-haired and walking-shoed senior women came in, laughing and chattering together as they shook water off their windbreakers. Right behind them, likewise shaking out her plain black umbrella, was Angie Chandler.

Ross picked up his pace, throwing a quick look around him. There was no reaction to Angie's arrival that he could detect, but that didn't mean any more than the lack of gray caps did. He would hardly expect them to jump up and down, shouting and pointing excitedly. Wincing at the stress the unplanned exercise was causing his left leg, he unzipped his jacket nearly to the waist and kept going.

With her view partially blocked by the group of seniors, Angie didn't see him until he was practically on top of her. "Mr. Ross," she said, a flicker of surprise touching her face at his sudden appearance. "You're in a hurry this morning."

"But never in too much of a hurry to spend a few minutes with my favorite banker," he said with a gallantry he wasn't especially feeling as he reversed course and fell into step beside her. Beneath her white cardigan was the same dress she'd worn yesterday, which implied she hadn't been home last night. There were all sorts of possibilities there, none of them pleasant. "How are you this fine, wet morning?"

"I'm fine, thank you," she replied in the semiformal tone she always seemed to take with him. "And you?"

"I'm just ducky," he said, glancing over his shoulder. Between the arriving employees and the exercise crowd, it was impossible to tell if anyone was following them. "That was my sister's perennial rainy-day joke," he added. "Just ducky. Get it?"

"I think so, yes," she said, smiling with obvious amusement. "Your sister's sense of humor is a worthy match for your own."

"That sounds suspiciously like an insult," Ross said, putting a little pout into his voice. Ahead, in the distance, the gray stocking caps had come into view, still poking up above their newspapers. No obvious reaction; perhaps they hadn't spotted Angie behind the four seniors still in front of them.

But that moment of grace was about to come to an end. The group of women had finished their preliminary chatting and were spreading out to begin their morning exercise. In about two seconds, Angie would be completely exposed to view from that end of the mall.

"I assure you I didn't mean it that way," Angie said, still sounding amused.

"I'm still offended," Ross insisted, looking around for inspiration. Just ahead on the right was the McDonald's, its cloud of early-morning customers buzzing around it like moths at a streetlight. With the mall entrance far behind them, and most of the other stores around them still closed, it was their best shot. "The least you can do by way of apology is to have a cup of coffee with me."

"I really can't," she said, even as he took her arm and steered her toward the smell of coffee and Egg McMuffins. "Please—I can't."

"One cup," he said, keeping her moving and watching the gray caps out of the corner of his eye. Distantly, it occurred to him that if he was guessing wrong he would not only look like a complete and blithering idiot but would be leaving himself open to charges of harassment, assault, or even kidnapping.

"Mr. Ross—"

"Half a cup, then," he said, bypassing the end of the line and aiming for the gap at the far side of the serving counter. "Come on. Please?"

"I have to get to work," she insisted firmly, propriety finally overcoming social politeness as she dug her heels into the floor tile. "Please let go."

"Sorry," Ross said, digging in heels of his own. With his fifty-pound advantage, his heels won. "We don't have a choice."

"What are you talking about?" she demanded, prying at his fingers with her other hand, her eyes starting to look genuinely scared. He was now all but dragging her along, and the customers were starting to take notice. "Please—I don't want to cause a scene—"

"Too late," he said, letting go of her arm so fast she nearly lost her balance as his hand dove inside his jacket. Thirty yards away, all four of the gray-capped loiterers had abandoned their posts and were coming toward them at a fast walk, their feet moving in step with almost military precision, their right hands concealed inside their now neatly folded newspapers.

And as Ross had suspected, those weren't gray stocking caps they were wearing. They were gray ski masks, now pulled down over their faces. Ross got a glimpse of dark eyes and skin through the eye and mouth openings; and then he had his Glock 19 out of its holster and was tracking on them.

They were fast, all right, faster than he cared for at all. In perfect unison they jumped wide of each other, taking themselves out of any chance for a quick four-shot, throwing their newspapers aside as they did so.

And suddenly there were four handguns pointed in his direction.

"Move!" he snapped, taking a long step in front of Angie and shoving her behind him toward the gap in the counter. There wasn't time for further instruction; and anything he could have said would have been lost anyway in the ear-shattering boom as one of the guns out there opened fire.

There was a scream from somewhere behind Ross, barely audible in the multiple echo from that shot, and instantly covered up anyway by the double thunderclap as his Glock spat out return fire.

Not at the gunmen, unfortunately—there were too many bystanders behind them for him to risk that. His shots were instead targeted at one of the decorative plant islands, this one a yard or so off the nearest gunman's left. At this point all he could do was try to make them flinch, break the flow of their attack, and hope he and Angie had enough of a lead to beat them outside.

They flinched, all right, dropping reflexively into combat crouches as their guns tracked him. He fired one more shot into the planter and then ducked after Angie.

She hadn't gotten far, either stunned paralysis or the natural hesitation of people not to violate invisible boundaries having hung her up right at the counter. Ross charged straight through the opening, all but scooping up the slender woman as he reached her. No one tried to stop them, the only two counter girls who hadn't automatically hit the deck staring like stricken gargoyles at the scene. Angie didn't make a sound as they charged through the cooking area and over, around, or through the startled staff back there. They turned sharply past what looked like a giant freezer, Ross hit the service door at a full run, and a second later they were out in the cold morning rain.

"Back here," Ross ordered, yanking Angie to the side and pushing her down behind a large dumpster as he leveled his Glock at the door closing behind him. Surely their pursuers were too professional to charge blindly out through a closed door; but then, maybe they would expect Ross to be professional enough not to think they'd do anything that stupid.

"What's going on?" Angie asked, panting like someone at the end of the Boston Marathon as the panic reaction started to hit. "What were—you were *shooting* in there!"

"They started it," Ross pointed out mildly. Someone should have come through that door by now, he decided, if they were coming at all. They must be going for a flanking maneuver instead. "Where's your car?"

"My car?"

"Your car," he repeated. "So we can get the hell out of here."

"But you were shooting and—" She broke off abruptly, and he risked a glance at her face. Her eyes were wide and terrified as they stared up at him, but her mouth had settled into a hard, thin line. A fast recovery, all right. Maybe too fast. "It's over there," she said, pointing to their left. "Around the corner of the mall."

"About where you usually park?"

The wide eyes narrowed, and the tight lips twitched. "Yes. You know where that is, don't you?"

"I walked you out once," Ross reminded her, blinking water out of his eyes as he scowled at the mostly empty expanse of wet blacktop around them. It was going to be a hell of a long hike to her car, with no cover to speak of the whole way.

His car was marginally closer. But not close enough, not by a long shot.

And long shots were exactly what they were likely to get here. Still no movement at the McDonald's door. A flanking maneuver, for sure, with him and Angie at the wrong end of the duck shoot.

Down at the far end of the mall, directly between them and both of their cars, two ski-masked gunmen came charging out through the glass entrance doors, scattering a group of teenagers who'd been about to go in.

The number of options dropped to exactly one. "Come on," he snapped, grabbing Angie's hand and charging toward an old Lincoln twenty yards away just pulling into a parking space.

For a moment he felt her full weight on his arm as she fought to get her feet moving. Then she was up to speed, and the drag eased. So far, she was following his lead without argument. He only hoped she'd keep it up until they were out of immediate target range.

A pair of shots boomed from behind them. Angie gasped, and Ross threw a quick look at her, fearing the worst. But while her eyes were starting to go crazy again, her white sweater was still white. No hit. Not yet.

The Lincoln was still idling as they reached it, the elderly woman behind the wheel staring wide-eyed at the two men inexplicably shooting off guns her direction. It was doubtful she even noticed Ross and Angie coming from her right side until they'd rounded the rear and Ross had wrenched the driver's door open. "Move over," he ordered, bracing the butt of his gun on the top of the car for a quick two-shot at the gunmen running toward them.

Perhaps his deliberately missed shots inside the mall had made them overconfident, or perhaps the wet pavement simply didn't allow for the necessary rapid maneuvers. Whatever the reason, they dodged too slowly; and for one of them, it was the last miscalculation he would ever make. Ross's first round caught him squarely in the center of his chest, and he spun half around on suddenly rubber legs to sprawl face first onto the blacktop. His partner threw a quick glance at him; and suddenly there was a stuttering hail of shots whistling past Ross's head and shoulders.

"Damn!" he snarled, ducking back into the car. Peripherally, he saw that Angie had the back door open and was diving in; the driver, too, had come unstuck from her paralysis and was scrabbling across the worn leather bench seat in a mad dash for the passenger side. Ross dropped into her place, flinching as a pair of bullets blasted through the windshield and rear passenger window, cursing again as his right thigh slammed against the steering wheel. Dropping the Glock into his lap, he hauled the gear shift lever to drive and floored it.

The car lurched into motion with all the power and acceleration Ross would have expected from a Detroit flagship land cruiser. He spun the wheel hard to the left, turning away from the remaining gunman—

And twisted partially back the other way as he caught a glimpse of two more blazing guns spattering lead at him from the other direction. Where and how they'd gotten out of the mall he couldn't tell, but it didn't matter now. Swinging wide toward the back end of the parking lot, he roared the car away from them, twitching in sympathy with every shot that thudded into the car's body or sent fragments of glass scattering through the interior.

"You can have the car," the elderly woman said, her quavering voice muffled by the seat her face was pressed into. "Just let me out. Please."

"Don't worry, Ma'am, we don't want you or your car," Ross assured her, fumbling a moment before he located the wiper switch and turned it on. The blades stumbled a bit on the bullet holes, washing extra surges of water into the car with each pass. The gunfire had stopped, he noted as he turned to follow the edge of the parking lot, and he risked a quick look over his shoulder. The remaining gunmen had given up their pursuit and were running back toward their fallen colleague, possibly to pick him up and escape, more likely to pick him up, stuff him into a vehicle, and come charging for a rematch. "We just need a short ride," he added to the woman. "Sorry about your car."

The white head came cautiously up a bit. "Are you a policeman?"

"Just a Good Samaritan trying to keep this lady alive," he said. "Angie? You okay?"

"I think so," her voice came from the back seat, trembling almost as much as the old woman's. "What's going on?"

"We'll sort that out later," Ross told her, his full attention on the parking lot as he came around the final corner of the building and in sight of his car. There was no sign of the gunmen anywhere that he could see.

Which wasn't really surprising, considering that the lot was now rapidly filling up with cops. Two cars were already parked by the east entrance, with three more scorching pavement that direction, lights flashing but sirens off.

Time for him and Angie to fade into the sunset. Sunrise. Whatever.

"Here we are, Ma'am," he said, letting the Lincoln roll to a stop beside his rented Ford Taurus and hoping like hell the cops kept their eyes on the mall. "If you don't mind, I'd like you to stay where you are until you hear us drive off. After that, scoot on over to the cops over there and tell them what happened."

"I didn't see anything," she insisted quickly. "Not a thing."

"Tell them everything," Ross insisted firmly, throwing the car into park and retrieving his gun from his lap. "We're the ones those men were shooting at, and we want them caught as much as you do. Come on, Angie."

"Wait a minute," she protested as he got out. "Shouldn't we go to the police, too?"

"Not here," Ross said, pulling open her door and taking her arm again. "Some of our playmates might still be lurking around waiting for us to show ourselves."

She shivered violently as he helped her out of the Lincoln and into his car. Somewhere along the way, he noticed, she'd lost her umbrella.

They were a block away from the mall before she spoke again. "I think it's time you told me what this is all about," she said, her voice still tense but under control. "Who were those men? Why were they shooting at you?"

He threw her a quick frown. "They weren't shooting at *me*, Angie. At least, I don't think so. They were shooting at you."

"That's ridiculous," she said, some of her control slipping. "I'm not somebody anyone would want to kill. You're the private eye—it has to be you."

Ross shook his head. "Sorry, but no. I was hanging around near the bank for at least five minutes before you showed up. In fact, I walked right past two of them, with my back wide open. If they'd wanted me, they could have done it right there."

"But I'm just a bank loan officer," she protested. "People are upset about the banking business, but surely—" She broke off. "A foreclosure?" she asked in a suddenly small voice.

"You told me your husband was a scientist," he said. "Could it have something to do with him or his work?"

"I don't see how," she said. "I'm just a wife, not a scientist. Unless," she added in a suddenly thoughtful tone, "they were trying to kidnap me."

"If they were, they took a huge risk throwing that much lead around," he pointed out.

"Or maybe I was right about them shooting at you," she countered. "Maybe they *were* kidnappers and didn't want you interfering."

"Too late," he murmured, keeping his voice neutral. That wasn't the way he would expect competent kidnappers to behave, and if he was sure of anything it was that this bunch was competent.

But at the same time, there was a nugget of possibility wrapped up in her suggestion, and he couldn't afford to dismiss it out of hand. "It was still a big risk if they wanted you alive."

"Then I give up," she said, annoyance momentarily displacing her fear. "Anyway, if they wanted something from my husband, they should have taken it up with him, not me."

Ross sighed under his breath. "Let's stop here a minute," he suggested.

He pulled into a Denny's lot and took a parking space near the back, leaving the car idling. "I take it you didn't listen to the news this morning," he said, turning to face her.

Her face had gone rigid. "No," she said. "I didn't . . . what is it?"

Ross caught her hand and held it tightly. It felt icy cold. "I'm sorry, Angie," he said gently. "Someone got into your husband's lab last night. He and two of his colleagues were murdered."

For a long moment he thought she was going to faint. Her eyelids fluttered, her mouth slightly open, her lower lip visibly trembling. Her initial silent gasp turned into a series of short, shallow breaths. If the shock didn't get her, he thought distantly, the hyperventilation might.

Her first words, predictably, were denial. "No," she breathed. "You're wrong. You're lying."

He shook his head. "The news broke a few minutes before you got to the mall. That's why I was waiting to see you. I'm very sorry."

She turned away from him, blinking against the tears. Her cultural upbringing, fighting against the expression of such emotion in the presence of a stranger. "What happened?" she asked, her voice sounding dead. "How did he . . . ?"

"The report didn't say." He hesitated. "I hate to ask you questions, Angie, especially at a time like this. But the cops will if we go to them, so you might as well—"

"What do you mean, *if*?" she cut him off, a faint spark of life coming back into her voice. "My husband's dead. I have to go to him."

"Of course," he soothed her. "I'm just saying they'll want to know some things. Like why you didn't go home last night."

"Why I—" She broke off, her eyes going suddenly cautious. "What makes you think I didn't?"

"You're wearing the same outfit you wore yesterday," he said, waving at her dress with his free hand. "It's the first time in a month you've done that."

She suddenly seemed to realize he was holding her hand and pulled it away. "You must have been watching me pretty closely," she said accusingly.

You have no idea. "Yes, I have," he said aloud. "For the same reason I've tried to chat with you as often as I can, and the same reason I took you away from those gunmen just now. I like you, Angie, and I want to help you."

"Why?" she demanded.

"Like I said: I like you. But I can't help if you don't level with me. Where did you spend the night? And were you with anyone?"

Her eyes flashed twin mortar rounds at him. "How *dare* you imply such a thing?"

"I didn't mean it that way," he hastened to assure her. First her voice, and now life had come back into her eyes. Again, recovering quickly. "I simply wondered if you spent the night with a girlfriend or something."

"I was alone," she said, only slightly mollified. "I had a—well, it wasn't a fight, really. It was what James calls a unidirectional argument. I was mad at him, but he wasn't mad at me. Probably didn't even know I was upset."

"What was it about?"

"It was stupid," she said, tears welling up in her eyes again. "One of the people on his project is a woman. I guess I was . . . " Her voice faded away.

"Jealous?"

She looked away again. "You said two other people were also killed," she said. "Did the report mention their names?"

"Wendell Fowler and Barbara Underwood," he said. "I take it Dr. Underwood was the woman you mentioned?"

"I saw them all last night," she said, her voice suddenly dead again. "I saw them, and stomped out, and went to a motel. Oh, God—they're going to think *I* did it. Is that what they think? Do they think I did it?"

"Hey, hey," he said, catching up her hand again and giving it his best reassuring squeeze. "Let's not jump to conclusions. They said it happened early this morning—you probably weren't within miles of the place at that time. Right?"

She took a deep breath. "No, I left last night about eight."

"There you go, then," he said. "Did you pay for the motel with a credit card?"

"Yes, of course."

"Then we'll be able to pull up a time stamp for the transaction," he said. "That'll prove when you were there. There's also a good chance the desk clerks will remember you checking in last night and then out again this morning." He turned back to the wheel. "Come on, let's get out of here."

"Where are we going?" she asked as he swung the car toward the exit. "We have to go to the police, don't we?"

"Let's wait on that for now," he said, sneaking into the traffic flow ahead of a panel truck that was just a shade too far back from the car ahead of it. "I'd like to make sure first that our pals with the ski masks haven't anticipated us and taken up positions near the police station."

"How could they be there already?"

"We don't know how many of them there are."

"Oh."

"In the meantime," he went on, "you're wet and cold and need of a change of clothing. I'll get you to a hotel and let you take a shower while I scare up a temporary wardrobe."

"I'd rather go home," she said, her voice suddenly weary. "Can't you just take me home?"

Ross shook his head. "Not a good idea. If they know where you work, they certainly know where you live."

She shivered. "God, this is a nightmare," she murmured. "What do they want with me?"

"I don't know," Ross said. "But we'll figure it out. Until we do, our primary job is to keep you alive and well."

"So you're going to take me to a hotel."

"Yes," Ross said, deciding to ignore whatever nuances might be lurking beneath the words. "For now, it's the safest place."

"I suppose," she said, and fell silent.

Which was just as well, Ross decided as he maneuvered through the crowded streets, trying to watch all directions at once, painfully aware that there was no way in all this traffic that he would know if they were being followed.

Equally aware that there was no way he could know who exactly he was sharing his car with.

Because all that talk earlier about motel keys and time-stamps and alibis had been complete nonsense. Angie could easily have checked in and then headed straight out again to commit a murder. Even if she hadn't, in an age of professional hit men even ironclad personal alibis didn't amount to much.

And adultery, real or imagined, was still considered a first-class motive for murder. Especially when both parties to the alleged affair died together.

It would be at least a forty-five minute drive to the hotel he had in mind. Perhaps those things would occur to her before they got there. If not, he was eventually going to have to bring them up.

He could hardly wait.

~

The general had hoped Angie Chandler would stay in the Denny's parking lot a little longer. But her new white knight protector was too smart for that. Long before the strike team could gather and position itself for a second try, the dark red Ford was once more on the move.

Still, eventually the woman would have to come to a stop. As long as he didn't lose them in the traffic, his team would get a second chance.

He scowled. A second chance. By all rights, they shouldn't have needed more than a first. Every possibility, every variant had been anticipated and prepared for.

Except the possibility that some stranger would come out of nowhere and ruin it.

Who was he? That was the big question pressing against the general's mind. Who was he, and why was he sticking his neck out for a total stranger like Angie Chandler?

The general had no answers. But he needed them, and fast. What he'd said back home about the crucial aspects being under their control had been true enough, but this was one he hadn't anticipated. Until they could tie it off, it had the potential to become the loose end that would unravel the carpet.

Right now it was all balanced on where the red Ford was heading. If the white knight was going to ground, the general would have time to assemble his limited forces for that second chance. If he was instead taking her to the police, they wouldn't have the luxury of preparation time. In that case, the general would most likely have to do this himself.

And the instant complication of performing a murder on the police's own doorstep wasn't one he particularly cared to add to the mix.

But that branching was not in his hands, and he could only watch as the path was laid out before him. Drifting back another car length, he continued his quiet pursuit.

07

THE COP STANDING guard by the Greenleaf Center's outer door stiffened to attention as he caught sight of the man approaching him. "Sir," he said briskly.

"Officer Gable," San Jose Police Chief Orlando Garcia grunted, reading the man's nameplate as he walked toward him. "Who's in charge here?"

"Sergeant Ng, sir," Gable said, pulling the door open for his superior. "He and his partner were first on the scene."

Garcia grunted again. "Thank you," he said, stifling the urge to say something more scathing as he brushed past the man. Parade-ground posture always looked so ridiculously affected to him, all the more so when you were standing in the middle of a rainstorm. But decorum and parade-ground nonsense was what they taught cops these days, and it wasn't any reason to jump down the kid's throat.

Besides, maybe it was just his mood, or the rotten start this morning was already off to. An early morning triple murder at a high-visibility local corporation wasn't enough—oh, no, not here. No, he had to get the report of a gang flash before he could even get to Sand/Star to look over that situation.

The damn gangs, tying up his time for nothing. And not just his, either. Ng would probably be snarled in here for hours, taking statements and supervising evidence collection, instead of being out there showing some police presence on the streets. All because some gang still on a crash-high from last night couldn't blow their wad on their own turf.

What they needed, he decided blackly, was to get those clone experiments going that he was always reading about in the Sunday papers. Clone a few of his best cops and get rid of the deadwood, and he could have a force that could stuff this sort of crap straight down the perps' throats.

And while they were at it, maybe they could de-clone some of the perps. They'd forfeited their right to live anyway, most of them, as far as he was concerned. De-clone the worst of that crowd, and this town would be a decent place to live.

It would never happen, of course. The ABA would have a cow at the very thought of real justice for those bastards. The ACLU would probably have a hippo.

He spotted Ng over by a McDonald's, taking notes as an old woman talked and gestured with the jerky movements that came from having been too close to the action. A dozen feet behind the woman, a pair of EMTs were crouched over a young man lying near the counter, the bright red blood scattered around mute evidence that he'd been even closer to the action than the old woman had. Gathered around the scene was the crowd of gawkers that showed up at every disaster.

If he was lucky, some of them might be eyewitnesses who could actually shed a little light on what had happened. Most of them, he knew from long experience, were simply ghouls.

There was nothing he could do for the wounded man except stay out of the EMTs' way. Saying a silent prayer for him, he headed instead toward Ng. The old woman he was talking to was pretty short; but even so, she had a good inch on Ng, who Garcia had always considered too short to project the kind of strong authority a cop needed. Maybe when they cloned him they could add in another six inches of height somewhere.

Ng spotted him and quieted the woman with a touch on her arm. "This is Police Chief Garcia," he said, gesturing toward him. "Sir, this is Mrs. Elaine Hawthorne, who was just arriving at the mall when the incident occurred. She's been telling me that she saw the gunmen, and that the apparent targets of the attack—a man and a woman—briefly commandeered her car."

Garcia frowned. *Targets*? "I thought this was a gang pop-off."

"Yes, sir, that was the initial assessment," Ng said. "It seems to be a bit more complicated."

Garcia shifted his attention to the woman. "What did all these people look like?"

"As I've already told Officer Ng, I don't know," she said, sounding a little annoyed. "The gunmen were all wearing ski masks. The man who took my car was youngish, probably in his thirties, but he pushed me aside so fast I really didn't get a look at his face. I never did see the woman."

"How do you know it *was* a woman, then?" Garcia asked.

"I heard her voice," she said. "And as I told Officer Ng, the man called her Angie."

Well, that was something, Garcia thought sourly. There couldn't be more than a hundred thousand Angies in the greater Bay Area. Piece of cake. "Did either of them mention *his* name?" he asked.

"I don't think so," she said. "It happened so terribly fast."

Garcia nodded, suppressing a tired curse. That was the way of the world, sure enough. Nine times out of ten they didn't want to get involved; and when they *were* willing, nine times out of ten they didn't know anything useful. "Is there anything else you *do* remember?" he asked with all the politeness he could muster.

She drew herself up to her full five foot six. "As a matter of fact, there is," she said. "They left in a dark red Ford sedan."

Garcia blinked. "You saw it?"

"Of course I saw it," she said. "How do you think I know what kind of car it was?"

"Of course," Garcia said hastily. Beside her, Ng wasn't quite suppressing an amused smile. Everyone in the whole department loved it to pieces when he got in trouble. "I just meant—thank you for your cooperation. I don't suppose you got the license?"

"The first part was 4DAL," she said, still clearly miffed by the implied insult to her eyesight or memory or both. "He told me to stay down until they drove off. By the time I thought it was safe to look, I couldn't read the rest. The windows were wet, you know. Oh, and I'm pretty sure he was the one driving."

"I already have the rest of her statement, sir," Ng put in, finally coming to his rescue. "She'll need a copy of the report for her insurance company."

"Fine," Garcia said. "Thank you for your help, Mrs. Hawthorne. We'll contact you if we need anything more."

She nodded curtly and strode off toward a bench, pulling out a small cell phone as she went. "That Lincoln's been in her family for years," Ng commented. "Once she got over her fright, she was mad straight through at what they did to it."

"Good for her," Garcia said shortly. "What about the shooting victim?"

Ng shrugged fractionally. "The EMTs say he's got a pretty good chance," he said. "He seems to have been waiting in line and got caught in the crossfire. Bullet in the abdomen."

Crossfire. That was interesting. "What else have you got?"

"Quite a bit," Ng said, flipping back a few pages in his notebook. "There were four gunmen, or at least four who got involved. The male target apparently shot one of them outside during the pursuit, just before he and the female commandeered Mrs. Hawthorne's car. After the targets drove out of range, the other three went back and retrieved the one who'd been shot. They all got into a late-model white Chrysler and took off."

That explained the two cops Garcia had seen outside crouching over an otherwise unremarkable section of wet blacktop. Probably a waste of time—they'd be hard pressed to get a decent blood sample in this rain. "Anyone happen to get the license?"

"We got a partial," Ng said. "We're running the possibilities. And I've got an alert out to area hospitals, too."

"Good," Garcia said. "Now the interesting question: did the target nail him with one of their guns, or did he have one of his own?"

"His own," Ng said, pointing toward a large planter with two more cops working at it. "He lobbed three shots at them in here—all of them lodged in that planter. It's not clear who fired first, but we've got at least one witness who says it was the target."

"He identify himself as a cop?"

"No, sir, just as a Good Samaritan."

Garcia sniffed. "That and five bucks will get you an espresso. Any descriptions?"

"The male target was Caucasian, mid-thirties, roughly six foot, with neatly cut dark brown hair, wearing black pants and a dark green jacket," Ng said. "The female was Asian, not much over five feet, with black shoulder-length hair, wearing a white sweater and flowered dress and carrying a black umbrella. We found the umbrella outside." He paused. "And as you just heard, the man called her Angie."

Garcia eyed him. "You say that like it's significant."

"It could be," Ng said, his voice going a little grim. "It turns out that the B of A branch down the way has an employee named Angie Chandler, who hasn't shown up for work yet."

"And?"

"Angie Chandler is the wife of Dr. James Chandler," Ng said. "Rather, the widow of the late Dr. James Chandler. Of Sand/Star Technologies."

And finally it clicked. "Bloody hell," Garcia murmured, looking around with new eyes. "You're sure?"

"I called Delgado over at Sand/Star," Ng said. "From the description, I'd say chances are good she is indeed the Angie who was involved here."

And who was now missing in action. "What about the man?" he asked. "Who's this clown she drove off with?"

"There we're a little less certain," Ng said. "But there's a PI who set up shop about a month ago in the spot above the bank. The bank employees we've talked to say he's been dropping in on her and chatting every chance he got. None of them saw him this morning, but we've got the mall manager checking the security cameras to see if they got a clear picture."

"And of all the people hanging around a mall at eight in the morning, a PI is the one most likely to be carrying," Garcia said. "I want a warrant to search his office."

"Done," Ng said. "Judge Dreyfus gave us a telephonic, with the paperwork on the way. Davison and Harper are already inside."

Garcia nodded. "Let's get on those vehicles, then. I want some speed records set in pinning them down. Any other evidence?"

"The rounds our presumed PI fired into that planter," Ng said. "It also appears the gunmen were concealing their weapons inside newspapers before they opened fire. We're dusting them."

"Good," Garcia said, looking at his watch. He still had to put in the appearance at Sand/Star that he'd promised Delgado, and he'd better do that before the media got hold of the story. If they hadn't already. "I'm going up to Sand/Star—"

The radio at Ng's shoulder crackled. "Sergeant, this is Davison up in the PI's office," a voice came. "You're going to want to see this."

Davison was waiting for them at the office door, copying the information on the outer door into a notebook. "Chief," he said, flipping the book shut. A cop from the older school, he didn't bother to come to attention. "Come take a gander at this."

He led them through the small anteroom and into the office proper. There they found Harper crouched in the corner, a coax cable in his hand as he probed with a pocket knife at the rug where the end of the cable vanished into the floor. The other end led to a small desktop TV. "We found this cable," Davison said, gesturing to it as he stepped over to the desk. "Given that there's a perfectly good cable outlet not three feet away, I wondered why he'd wired his TV into the floor."

He swiveled the TV around to face them. "Take a look."

Garcia felt his jaw tighten. On the screen was a slightly distorted bird's-eye view of a desk equipped with a computer workstation and a neat stack of paper, with two guest chairs on the far side. "The bank?"

"Yep," Davison said grimly. "Looks like he tapped into their own security camera setup. We may need to tear up part of the floor to find out how he did it."

"Any idea whose office that is?" Ng asked.

"Ten to one it's Angie Chandler's," Garcia muttered.

"That's the one," Davison confirmed.

Garcia and Ng looked at each other. "The guy's a stalker," Ng said.

"Or was casing the bank," Garcia growled. "Harper, stay here—I want the mall manager's permission before you go digging. Davison, get on the horn to Wellington Security's corporate HQ and see what you can find out about this Adam Ross character."

~

There were many cities in the country, Ross knew, where rush hour traffic traveled almost exclusively one direction in the morning and the opposite direction at night, giving a traveler moving against the flow a relatively easy time of it.

The Bay Area, unfortunately, wasn't one of them. From the moment he and Angie left the Denny's, they were as snarled in traffic as everyone else in sight. Interstate 880, once he managed to get onto it, was nearly as packed as the surface streets, with the additional bonus that many of those still on the road were late for work and accordingly driving like maniacs. Ross kept to an inside lane, away from the worst of the land rockets, adjusting the Ford's defrost level to keep the windows as steamed as safe navigation would permit. If there were people cruising the highways this morning looking for a car containing a Caucasian man and Asian woman, there was no point in making it easy for them.

Angie spent most of the trip slumped against the door, her face turned to the window where he couldn't see it. She probably didn't say a dozen words to him the whole time, most of those coming within the first mile when he noticed her shivering and pulled into a Seven-Eleven to grab two cups of coffee and a cheap gray vinyl hooded windbreaker. She'd put on the windbreaker, pulling up the hood as instructed without comment. Her coffee still sat cold and untouched in her cup holder.

Finally, they were there.

~

"It's not exactly the Waldorf-Astoria," Ross commented as he closed the door behind them and set down the flat-bottomed gym bag he'd brought in from the trunk of his car. "But it'll do."

"It's very nice," Angie murmured, looking around the hotel room as she put her purse down on the end of the bed. It was a good two steps up from the sort of places she and James had usually been able to afford to stay.

And yet, Mr. Ross had seemed to think nothing of pulling out high-denomination bills from his wallet to pay for a room like this. The same Mr. Ross who'd never seemed to have any work to do back at the mall. The same Mr. Ross who always seemed to have plenty of time to chat with her, or to wait around the bank entrance for her to return from lunch, or to walk her out to her car.

"At least for now," Ross said. "No, no—stay away from the windows."

"I just wanted to see what kind of view I had," Angie said, stopping obediently halfway to the wide windows lining the far wall. "You said no one followed us."

"I don't think anyone did, but there's no point in taking chances," he said, moving in a low crouch to the curtain pulls and closing the translucent inner curtain. The slight limp she'd noticed at their first meeting had become more pronounced, and it turned his crouching walk into something almost comical. Distantly, she wondered whether the strain of the morning's activities had aggravated an old injury or whether it was something to do with the rain and humidity.

"That's better," he said, straightening up. "When the plan is to crawl into a deep hole, it's not smart to pop up every so often and wave."

"You make it sound so appealing."

"It beats the hell out of the hole our friends at the mall would have left us in," Ross said bluntly.

Angie shuddered. "You're right. I'm sorry."

"It's okay," Ross said, stepping close and taking her hands. "You're new to this."

Angie looked up into his face, his closeness uncomfortable. Her husband wasn't even in his grave yet. And what exactly did she know about this man, anyway?

Almost nothing, she realized suddenly. For all the conversations they'd had—conversations *he'd* drawn her into—he'd said remarkably little about himself. They'd always talked about her. "And you're not?"

she asked, forcing herself to leave her hands in his. "New to hiding, I mean?"

He shrugged. "I've had what used to be known as a checkered career," he said, stroking the backs of her hands gently with his thumbs as he held them. Again, she forced herself to not pull away. "Sometimes I've been the chaser, sometimes I've been the chasee. If you know what I mean."

"I think so." She shivered again, only half acting, freshly aware of the fact that she was alone with an armed stranger.

And that this elegant room he'd gotten for them had only a single king-sized bed.

"The first rule of hiding is that sneezing is as bad as waving," he added briskly, finally letting go of her hands. Instead of stepping away, though, he moved to her side and slipped an arm around her shoulders. "What you need is a hot shower," he announced, turning her around and leading her toward the bathroom. "Or a hot bath. Whichever you prefer."

Something cold seemed to close around her heart. No—surely he didn't mean what she thought he meant.

"And while you get all toasty warm," he went on, letting go of her shoulders and snagging a pen and note pad from the writing desk, "I'll go get you a new wardrobe. You'd better write down the relevant sizes if you want it all to fit. Shoes, too—the ones you're wearing are a mess."

She took the pad and began writing, her emotions swirling from relief to embarrassment back to suspicion again. Had she misinterpreted his intentions right from the beginning? Or had she nailed them correctly, and he'd simply picked up on her reaction and done a quick backpedal?

"I'll need to borrow your phone, too, in case you need me while I'm out," he said, walking to the bed and gesturing to her purse. "May I?"

"I'll get it," Angie said, joining him by the bed and picking up the purse. She didn't want him holding her hands, and she certainly didn't want him rummaging through her things. She found the phone and handed it to him, slipping the purse's strap over her shoulder as she resumed her writing.

"Thanks," he said, tucking the phone inside his coat and going around her to retrieve his gym bag. "You should be fine here for the couple of hours this'll take," he went on as he dropped the bag on the bed and unzipped it. "Even if they somehow managed to track us here, there are over two hundred rooms they'd have to go through to find you."

"What about the front desk?" Angie asked, watching as he laid out a polo shirt and pair of slacks, thinking wistfully about her own emergency bag sitting in the trunk of her abandoned car.

"They won't give out room numbers to strangers," Ross said, zipping the bag closed and setting it out of the way on the back part of the writing desk. "At least, they're not supposed to. If I need to call you, I'll let the phone ring twice, hang up, then call right back. If you don't get that signal, don't answer."

"All right," Angie said. "Is it all right if I call out?"

"Absolutely not," Ross said firmly. "Who in the world would you want to call, anyway?"

Angie felt her face harden into lines familiar from her occasional fights with James. "My parents," she said, just as firmly. "They'll have heard about James by now. They're going to be worried about me."

"Oh," Ross said, and she had the minor satisfaction of seeing him look embarrassed. "I'm sorry, but it's not safe to call from here."

"Why not? They can't tap into the phone if they don't know we're here, can they?"

"No, but they could tap in from your parents' end," Ross pointed out.

Angie felt her breath catch in her throat. No. He wasn't implying—

He must have seen something in her face. "No, no, I'm sure they're not after them," he said hastily. "Besides, the police are probably all over your parents by now trying to find out where you've disappeared to."

"Oh," she said, some of the weight lifting. But only some of it.

"If it'll make you feel better, you can give me their number and I'll call them while I'm out," he offered. "I can at least let them know you're all right."

"No, that's okay," Angie said. "I guess I can call them later."

"Right." Ross hesitated, as if trying to think of something else to say, then simply nodded. "I'll be back as soon as I can. Double lock the door behind me and don't go out. No room service, of course. If you get hungry or want something to drink, the minibar's over there. I'll call you on my way in—same signal I just gave you—and let you know when to unlock the door for me. And remember not to answer the phone unless it's my signal."

"I understand."

"I'll be back soon," he said again. Easing open the door, he looked both ways down the hallway, then slipped out.

For a long moment Angie stared at the door. Then, wearily, she walked over and fastened the deadbolt and security loop. Things were happening too fast. Too fast for her to understand. Too fast for her to absorb.

She suddenly realized she was shivering again. Ross was right; pneumonia wouldn't get her anywhere. Going into the bathroom, she turned on the water to the tub and began to pull off her wet clothing.

Yes; that was it. It was all happening too fast. The gunmen at the mall—Ross—the news of her husband's death—and now here she was, hiding out on the top floor of a luxury hotel. Much too fast.

Was that why she hadn't yet cried for James?

Because she hadn't. Why hadn't she? She *had* loved him, hadn't she?

Time. She simply hadn't had time yet for such feelings to come. The first she'd heard of James's death, after all, had been right on the heels of the mall thing, when she was already badly shaken up. And of course she'd only had Ross's word for it. You couldn't trust a stranger with news like that.

Except that midway through their drive a news report had confirmed that Ross had been telling the truth.

So why hadn't she cried? Had she been afraid of showing emotion in his presence? Were propriety and proper behavior really that important to her?

The roaring water in the tub was sending up clouds of steam by the time she finished undressing. She added some cold water to the flow and stepped in. Closing the curtain, she pulled up the diverter knob.

The water burst out of the shower head, splashing over her shoulders and back with the unpleasant shock of too-warm water on too-cold skin. She straightened up, closing her eyes as she turned around, letting the spray hammer at her face. It was a familiar, homey feeling; the feeling of a thousand other showers that had driven away the chill of California winter mornings.

The feeling of the other shower she'd had this morning, not three hours ago. The shower she'd taken when all was still right with the world, when she was happy and contented with life.

When she'd still had the husband she loved.

And suddenly the barriers of fear and denial—and yes, damn it, propriety—crumbled into dust, and all the anguish and misery and grief finally came pouring through the gap.

With the hot water streaming over her, she sank to her knees on the hard porcelain and sobbed like a baby.

08

THE MEN WITH the fingerprint powder and little plastic bags had departed, and Delgado had just brought Talbot and the three techs back to the scene of the crime when Chief Garcia finally made his promised appearance.

From the look on his face, Delgado had the feeling that the morning was about to get even less pleasant than it already was.

"Delgado," the chief greeted him tersely. "What have you got?"

"Three dead scientists," Delgado said, mentally editing his preliminary report down to the essentials. That was definitely not the chief's chit-chat face. "Poison suspected, probably in the coffee. Guard downstairs also drugged, not fatally, probably to allow perps to make off with valuable experimental equipment. Preliminary check of the fence shows no sign of a break-in."

Garcia grunted, eying Burke and Esteban as they continued their search through the lab's cabinets under Talbot's casual-looking supervision. "We talking CTH?"

CTH: close to home. Department slang for a murderer well known to his victim. "Probably, though non-CTH hasn't been entirely ruled out."

Kingsley appeared from the main office, crossed the lab without even looking at the cops, and vanished again into the smaller office. "How did all this experimental equipment make it out of the compound?" Garcia asked.

"In about the most straightforward way you can imagine," Delgado said, flipping to the notes of his brief interview with the night gate guard. "Dr. Chandler had one of his assistants drive a semi in last night and park it by the building."

"What for?"

"They were supposed to take their equipment to a remote test site this morning," Delgado explained. "The perps simply loaded the equipment aboard a few hours early and drove it right out."

"Where the hell was security during all this?"

"The driver was made up to look like Dr. Chandler," Delgado said. "The disguise didn't have to be all that perfect, given the gate guard was looking up into the shadowy cab of an eighteen-wheeler."

"How'd he get inside the compound in the first place?"

"We're still working on that," Delgado said. "I've got a couple of theories."

Garcia scratched his cheek. "What about that pad gizmo I had to sign in on when I got here? This guy a competent forger as well as a look-alike?"

"Not necessarily," Delgado said. "He pulled the pad up into the cab to sign it, out of sight of the guard. He may have had some way to electronically gimmick the thing."

"And of course the guard didn't think to look in the trailer itself."

"As a matter of fact, he did," Delgado said, putting the notebook away. "Both when Kingsley brought it in and when the look-alike drove it out. He claims it was empty both times."

Garcia's eyes drilled into him. "I thought you said a truckload of valuable equipment was stolen," he said in that tone he always used when he'd caught a subordinate in an error. "Where was it, stuffed in the cab?"

Delgado hesitated. "Actually—"

He was saved the need for a reply by Kingsley's reappearance from the small office. "Looks like they left all the documentation, Lieutenant, but they took the programmed laptops," he reported. "That means all four Cloaks are operational."

"What about that prototype you mentioned?" Delgado asked.

"It's still here," Burke put in, peering into one of the cabinets. "We should be able to run it off the workstation, if you want to see it."

"Definitely," Talbot said. "How about you and Kingsley setting it up while Esteban finishes the inventory?"

"All right," Burke said, running a quick eye up and down Garcia but making no comment. "Come on, Scott."

The two techs headed together into the small office, Talbot tagging along behind them. "Next question," Garcia said, lowering his voice to a murmur and jerking his head at Talbot's back. "What's *he* doing here?"

Delgado braced himself. Chief Garcia and the FBI did not work and play well together. "I asked him to stop by."

"Since when are local murders Bureau business?"

"They're not," Delgado said. "But Sand/Star has a lot of government contracts, and I thought it would be a good idea for someone to at least be here as an observer. Just in case we made a connection."

"Did you?"

"Not yet," Delgado conceded.

Garcia was right, of course. Talbot's presence was a breach of protocol, and the chief should have unloaded both barrels on those grounds alone.

But to Delgado's surprise, Garcia merely stood there, giving his subordinate a penetrating gaze that was more disconcerting in its own way than a plain-vanilla outburst would have been. "I'll give Lyman a call as soon as he lands at his desk," he said. "See if he'll assign Talbot to you."

Delgado consciously relaxed his shoulders. He'd expected to need considerably more diplomacy. "Thank you, sir."

"No problem," Garcia said, the intensity of that gaze not easing up a single watt. "As it happens, the Bureau may wind up in the game anyway. I just came from Greenleaf Center Mall—"

He broke off at a muffled trilling from inside his coat. He pulled out his phone and flipped it open. "Garcia . . . Already? Nice work. Let's have it . . . well, well—imagine my surprise. Has Davison checked in yet? . . . And?...Imagine my surprise on that one, too . . . Yes, you'd better. Hang on—let me find something to write on."

He slapped at his pockets. Delgado dug into his pocket for his notebook; Kingsley, passing through the lab again, got there first, snagging a pen and multicolored sticky-pad cube from a niche by the office door and dropping them on the table in front of Garcia. "Okay," Garcia said, nodding Kingsley his thanks. "Go."

For a few seconds he scrawled on the top sheet, one of the last two remaining pieces of impossibly brilliant yellow before the pad gave way to a layer of equally vibrant red, another of cheerful blue, another of bright pink, ending in a base layer of lime green.

Even without the lab's background of death, Delgado thought, the color scheme would have struck him as obnoxious. Under the circumstances, it bordered on the obscene.

Garcia finished writing and peeled off the top sheet. "Fine," he said into the phone. "Put out an APB, and alert whoever's at the house to watch for them . . . probably not, but you never know. And keep on that getaway car."

He closed the phone and put it away. "That was Ng," he said. "As I was saying, the Bureau may be getting in on this anyway, because it looks like Dr. Chandler's widow may be the murderers' next target."

"What?" Esteban demanded, the word echoed in almost perfect unison by Burke, who had just emerged from the smaller office.

"You heard me," Garcia growled, alternating his attention between the two techs. Kingsley returned from the large office, a thick notebook in hand, and the chief's attention went into a three-way split. "A group of unknowns took a shot at her on her way to work this morning. She made it out with the help of a PI who'd just moved into the mall."

"Lucky for her," Esteban murmured.

"Maybe not," Garcia said. "Thing is, the guy doesn't seem to exist."

Delgado glanced around, saw identical startled frowns on all three techs' faces. "What do you mean?" Burke asked.

"He's not on the state's PI list," Garcia said. "And the driver's license he used for his rental car has an entirely different name than the one on his office shingle."

He handed Delgado the yellow sheet. Two names—Adam Ross and Charles Sullivan—were scribbled at the top, followed by a California license plate number and an Iowa address. "That's him and his car," Garcia said. "Or at least, his car. Make sure Sand/Star and your people at the fence have that license, too. Hard to believe he'd come here, but you never know."

"Right," Delgado said, pulling out his phone. "Mr. Kingsley? How's it going?"

"We're almost ready," Kingsley said. "If you and—ah—?"

"Chief Garcia," Garcia introduced himself gruffly.

"If you and Chief Garcia would like to join Special Agent Talbot in the other room, we'll collect the rest of the gear and be right in."

"So what exactly are we here to see?" Garcia asked as he and Delgado crossed to the small office.

"A demonstration of the experimental gear that was stolen," Delgado told him.

Garcia looked pointedly at his watch. "Fine."

The preparations weren't quite as complete as Kingsley had implied. The techs continued bustling back and forth for several minutes between the office and lab, going in and out for notebooks, portable hard drives, and a thick cable with a computer connector at one end and another connector that looked handmade at the other. Picking a moment when all three techs were out of the office, Delgado called the cop at the Sand/Star gate and relayed the description of Ross's rented Ford and its license number, along with a thumbnail summary of the incident at the mall.

After that, all he could do was stand between his colleagues, a human buffer zone between Garcia and Talbot, and cultivate his patience.

It was apparently too early in the growing season for Garcia to have any patience to cultivate. He looked at his watch four times before the techs finally gathered around the workstation, and twice more as they alternately consulted their notebooks and manhandled the keyboard.

Through it all Talbot remained silent, apparently unaffected by either the long wait, the news of Angie Chandler's vanishing act, or Garcia's rather rude lack of acknowledgement of his presence.

Or maybe he was bothered by all three, and just didn't show it.

"Okay," Esteban said as they finally finished their preparations and lined up along both sides of the desk flanking the workstation. "As we said, this was just the prototype, so it won't be perfect—"

"Get on with it," Garcia growled.

"Yes, sir," Esteban said hastily, holding up a square piece of black cloth about two yards on an edge. "This is the Cloak."

He turned it around like a stage magician preparing to do a trick, and Delgado saw that the homemade connector had been plugged into a receptacle in the back of the cloth. The cable's other end disappeared around behind the workstation. "As you can see, it's tied into the computer. Now, what happens is—"

"Why don't you just show us?" Talbot put in mildly.

"Oh. Sure." Esteban draped the cloth over the top of the workstation, smoothing it down as best he could. Lifting the front edge, he tapped for a moment on the keyboard, lifted the edge higher to check something on the screen, then lowered it and smoothed it out again. "It'll take a few seconds," he said, stepping back.

Delgado tapped his watch into stopwatch mode and started it running.

The seconds ticked by and nothing happened. Out of the corner of his eye he saw Garcia starting to shift his weight between feet, a sure sign he was rapidly reaching his patience break point. On his other side, Talbot seemed perfectly relaxed.

Then, with no fanfare or warning whatsoever, the black cloth and workstation both vanished.

Garcia's breath went out in an explosive huff. "What the *hell*?" He stepped forward and reached out toward the apparently empty section of desk where the workstation had been.

"No, don't touch it," Burke said. "If you do, it'll have to resample."

"Let it," Garcia said. His probing fingers reached the point where the black cloth had been—

As suddenly as it had vanished, a section of the Cloak reappeared.

Garcia's fingers twitched back as if he'd hit a live wire. "This is nuts," he murmured, leaning carefully forward to look at the section of black cloth apparently hanging in midair. "This is *nuts*."

Belatedly, Delgado realized he'd forgotten the stopwatch. He clicked it off and looked at the display. Just over a minute since he'd started it. Just under a minute, then, for the Cloak to have done its magic.

"It's fiber optics, isn't it?" Talbot asked. "You've got the light from one side of the Cloak being piped around through the cloth to the other side."

"That's the basic concept," Burke said. "But it's a lot more complicated in practice. For one thing, that kind of simple pass-through technique only works for a single vantage point. If you want it to work from all angles, you have to make sure each observer gets the proper image."

"So how's that done?" Garcia demanded.

"Basically, what we do is create a picture directly on the Cloak's surface," Esteban said. "The fibers feed a complete global image into the computer, which takes it and sorts it out into the proper directions and angles. It then takes the light and sends it to a set of interlocking, facet-planed LCs on the surface."

"A set of what?" Delgado asked.

"Facet-planed liquid crystals," Esteban said.

"The idea and design are proprietary," Burke said, a little stiffly. "So's the manufacturing technique. We can't discuss any of that."

"I trust you haven't forgotten we're talking a murder investigation here," Garcia said, his voice deepening with official weight. Midway through his sentence, the black section of the Cloak winked out again.

"This has nothing to do with that—" Burke began.

"It's all right, Jack," Kingsley put in diplomatically. "We can give them the general idea without going into details. Remember that Jack said you could only do a straight pass-through for one specific observer direction. The facet-planed LCs allow the light to be split off into different directions so that each observer direction gets the proper light pass-through."

"Sounds tricky," Talbot said.

"That's why it's proprietary," Burke said, clearly still not happy with the direction the conversation was going.

"If you'll take a couple of slow steps to the side, you'll see how it works," Esteban added.

Carefully, Delgado eased his head to the side. The image on the surface of the Cloak stayed as it was, moving slightly out of synch with the background, and for a fraction of a second he could tell where the cloth's surface was as the relative movement gave him something for his eyes to latch onto.

He moved another inch; and suddenly the image was lined up again with the wall behind it, and the half-imagined surface vanished.

Beside him, Garcia muttered something under his breath. "And this works whatever direction you go?"

"Pretty much," Esteban said.

"What about the section of the desk top underneath it?" Delgado asked. "How's the Cloak getting that image?"

"There's a sampling strip beneath the inner edge," Kingsley said. "The computer can extrapolate the desk top from that."

"Of course, if you're sitting on something more complicated, you need to do more than just take a sample," Esteban added. "The programming scheme for the Mama and Papa Bears includes the ability to store a complete ground image. You basically use a digital camera to take six specified views of the terrain where you want to park your tank or whatever and feed all of them into the computer. A standard 3-D modeling program takes over and maps out the image and contours for the Cloak."

"Then all you have to do is move your tank onto that spot and throw the Cloak over it," Kingsley said. "The Cloak does its standard sampling for the side views and draws on the stored 3-D record for the underside."

"Sounds so simple," Delgado commented, shaking his head.

"In theory, it is," Kingsley agreed. "It's the real-world mechanics and electronics that were a bear to figure out. That's one reason Dr. Chandler wanted all our ducks in a row before we demonstrated it for the Army people. The theory isn't much use if you can't demonstrate that it works."

"Which is where our thieves missed a bet," Burke said, jerking a thumb back toward the lab. "They may have gotten the Cloaks and laptops, but they didn't take either the LC fabricator or the assembly machine."

"Small wonder, given they weigh about half a ton each," Esteban murmured. "Would have had a mass hernia attack."

"Regardless, they're going to find out pretty soon that they only have half the story," Burke insisted. Distantly, Delgado wondered if the young man was really so completely without humor, or whether the morning's revelations had simply knocked it all out of him. "They can study the LCs forever without figuring out how to make them."

"Seems to me I remember overhearing Dr. Chandler talking to Dr. Underwood about trapdoors in the programming, too," Esteban said. "They may not even have half of what they came for."

Kingsley shivered. "I wonder if that means they'll be back for the rest."

"If they do, we'll be ready for them," Garcia promised grimly.

Delgado threw a sideways glance at Talbot, found the other looking back at him. Did the thieves' only partial victory imply that none of the three techs had been the inside man? "You said this was a prototype," he said, looking back at the techs. "What's the difference between this and the ones that were stolen?"

"The final versions were equipped with the kinesthetic sensor fibers Scott mentioned earlier," Esteban said. "Those let the computer know where there are folds or wrinkles in the Cloak so that it can compensate."

"Obviously, the programming had to be completely redone for that," Kingsley put in. "Dr. Chandler and Dr. Underwood have been working a lot of nights lately. Especially lately," he added, his voice suddenly sounding a little odd.

"Something?" Delgado prompted.

"No," Kingsley said, a little too hastily. "Anyway, along with reprogramming for the corset—that's what Dr. Fowler called the kinesthetic frame—they also found some shortcuts for making the sampling procedure faster."

"How much faster?"

The techs looked at each other. "I'd say the Baby Bears could go active in ten seconds or less," Esteban hazarded. "I don't remember ever actually timing them."

"I know Papa Bear could go in less than three minutes," Burke offered. "On our last big test Dr. Fowler made a joke about this being the world's biggest egg timer, but that we would always undercook it."

"And Mama Bear would have been somewhere in the middle," Kingsley concluded.

"What happens if you try moving with a Cloak over you?" Delgado asked.

In answer, Kingsley reached over and tapped the Cloak. As with the last time it was disturbed, a section of the black material instantly reappeared. "Obviously, we haven't been able to crack that problem," he said. "It wasn't important, though, for this first test. Once the project has more funding—"

He broke off, lips compressing briefly. "The project, hell. The three of them *were* the project. I don't know what's going to happen with this now."

For a long moment there was silence. The lull lasted until the visible section of Cloak winked out again. "This is all fine and dandy if everything holds still," Garcia said. "But what if something nearby is moving?"

In answer, Esteban stepped to the desk and waved a hand slowly behind the Cloak. It looked perfectly normal. "Do that again," Delgado said, leaning a little closer.

Esteban did so. Even watching carefully for discontinuities, Delgado couldn't see any. "How fast can you go before the sampling can't keep up?" he asked.

"Reasonably fast," Esteban said. "I don't know if anybody did any official experiments."

"The newer ones can also handle faster movement than the prototype," Kingsley put in.

"So what's the difference between something moving past the Cloak and the Cloak itself moving?" Garcia asked. "Seems to me to be six of one and half a dozen of the other."

"You'd think so, but it's not," Burke said. "In essence, it sort of comes down to the Cloak's awareness of where it is. You get it set and it can handle changing light patterns around it just fine. You start it moving, though, and its entire frame of reference goes completely crazy."

"When Ramon waves his hand behind it, the rest of the landscape is still stationary," Kingsley added, gesturing toward the Cloak. "Only the data from the moving hand has to be changed. But when the Cloak itself moves, *everything* changes, and all at once."

"The software can't handle it and basically shuts down," Burke said. "You saw how the prototype goes black when it's touched. Same thing happens to the others when you try to move them."

"It's going to take sheer brute-force computing power, I expect," Esteban said. "That, and faster clock speeds. Give the industry four or five more product generations, and we should have a crack at it."

"We might have, anyway," Kingsley muttered.

There was another short silence. "Well, thank you for the demonstration," Garcia said at last. "And your cooperation."

"So what happens now?" Kingsley asked.

"Unless Lieutenant Delgado needs you for anything else—" Garcia looked questioningly at Delgado.

"No, we're finished for the moment," Delgado confirmed. "You can go home if you'd like. Just keep yourselves available in case we have more questions."

"All right." Kingsley looked at the Cloak. "Uh—"

"Just leave it running," Talbot said. "I'd like to study it a little longer."

Kingsley hesitated, then nodded. "Sure. Just turn off the workstation when you're done."

"You'd better lock the Cloak away somewhere, too," Burke added.

"Don't worry," Delgado assured him. "This whole place is going to be locked down for quite a while."

The techs shambled from the room, all three looking suddenly very tired. Small wonder, considering everything they'd been through. "I suppose I'd better go talk to director what's-his-name," Garcia said. "Tarlington. You know which office he's in?"

"Actually, he headed over to Building A just before you got here," Delgado said. "He was meeting with the board and senior staff in the main conference room over there."

"Okay." Almost grudgingly, Delgado thought, the chief nodded to Talbot. "Special Agent Talbot."

"Good day, sir," Talbot nodded back.

"Not likely." Garcia took one more lingering look at the desk, shook his head, and strode from the room.

Delgado turned to Talbot. "So how deep exactly would you say the kimchi is on this one?"

Talbot shook his head as he stepped up to the desk and crouched down in front of it, peering at the Cloak. "Pretty damn deep," he conceded. "You believe this thing?"

"I wouldn't have if I hadn't seen it," Delgado agreed soberly. "So which of our fine upstanding lab techs do you think iced their bosses?"

"I'm not convinced that it *was* one of them," Talbot said. "All their reactions to your death announcement looked pretty authentic to me."

"Drama schools teach that kind of authenticity."

"They don't teach how to make your face go pale."

Delgado nodded. "Yes; Kingsley. Well, if not one of them, then who? The security readings show Angie Chandler was the only other one here at the right time to spike the downstairs coffeepot."

Talbot poked gently at the Cloak. Once again, a small section appeared, this one not much larger than his fingerprint. "There's the downstairs guard," he pointed out. "He could have set everything in motion and then drugged himself."

"How did he spike the lab's coffee without anyone remembering he'd dropped in?"

"Point," Talbot conceded. "I didn't check earlier—was the coffee up here in cans or pouches?"

"Pouches, both here and downstairs," Delgado said. "I suppose the guard *could* have slipped a poisoned package into the lab's supply sometime before last night. Trouble is, how could he control when it was used?"

"He couldn't, unless he poisoned all of them," Talbot nodded. "But unless he did the switch just before the last pot was brewed—"

"And everyone was still here at that time," Delgado put in.

"Right," Talbot said. "Unless he did it then, they would have keeled over much earlier in the day."

"I suppose he could have come in after all the techs had gone," Delgado offered thoughtfully. "Chatted with the scientists and poisoned the coffee then."

"Pretty risky," Talbot said. "You said the cleaning crew was already working the far end of the hallway by then, right?"

"And going semi-randomly in and out the doors down there," Delgado agreed. "I'll have Greer ask if they saw anyone wandering the halls after Burke took off at two a.m. We'll confiscate all the rest of the coffee pouches, too, and give 'em a look."

"Good," Talbot said. "You'll want to do a background on the guard in any case, but I'm guessing he's clean. We also have Dr. Tarlington in here at one-thirty in the afternoon."

"Which is way too early."

"Right, but he might have learned then that the Cloaks were ready to go," Talbot said. "He might have a way of gimmicking the doors to sneak in unannounced."

"What about the gate guard?"

Talbot straightened up again. "Maybe Tarlington's got a private entrance," he said. "I suppose we should wait and see what the lab boys come up with before we start rushing off in all directions. Who's the M.E. going to be on this one?"

"Probably Barry," Delgado said. "He was here at the scene, so he'll probably take it."

"Competent?"

Delgado shrugged. "Reasonably so."

"I suggest you impress on him that he do a thorough job on the autopsies," Talbot said. "And I mean *really* thorough."

"I'll do that," Delgado promised. "Unfortunately, there's one slight problem with sitting on our hands until we have all the facts."

"Our little early-morning fracas at Greenleaf Center," Talbot agreed sourly. "That one had better be my first priority."

He lifted the edge of the Cloak, bringing most of it back to visibility, and reached under to the workstation's power switch. There was a click, and the entire Cloak appeared as the quiet hum of the cooling fans wound down. "You might not want to get quite so involved just yet," Delgado warned as the two of them headed for the door. "At least not until the chief has officially borrowed you."

"I'm already involved, thank you," Talbot growled as he stepped into the lab. "Another fine mess you've gotten me—"

He broke off. "What?" Delgado demanded, hand going automatically for his gun as he shot a quick look around the empty room.

"The notepad," Talbot said quietly. "The one your boss wrote the license number on."

Delgado looked at the table. The sticky-pad was still there, right where he and Garcia had left it.

Except that where a single sheet of yellow had been showing, the pad had now inexplicably turned lime green.

Or, rather, not so inexplicably. "It's upside down," he said.

"It is indeed," Talbot agreed, stepping over to the table. "I wonder why." He picked up the pad and turned it over.

It was immediately apparent why. The single yellow sheet that had been on top of the pad was gone, leaving the first sheet of the red layer showing.

The two men looked at each other. "I'd say someone wanted that license number," Delgado said.

"Looks that way," Talbot agreed, setting the pad down the way he'd found it and heading for the door. "I think I'll skip the mall and head over to the Chandlers' house. Garcia said you had people there?"

"I'll give them a head's-up," Delgado said, pulling out his phone.

And then Talbot was gone. "Yes, indeed," Delgado murmured to himself as he punched in the number. "Another fine mess we've gotten us into."

09

It was just after twelve thirty when Talbot finally made it in to the office. By all rights, certainly by all expectations, Special Agent in Charge Paul Lyman should have been out to lunch at that time.

He wasn't. He was waiting for Talbot.

And he was loaded for bear. A twelve-foot Kodiak bear.

"Nice of you to drop by," he greeted Talbot darkly as the agent stepped through the door into the squad room. He couldn't have been standing there the whole morning, Talbot knew; clearly, someone downstairs had tipped him off. "Join me in my office."

Silently, they walked through the squad room toward Lyman's office. None of the men and women working or eating at their desks, Talbot noticed, paid them the slightest attention. Either Lyman hadn't ranted enough about this to draw anyone's notice, or else he'd ranted so much that everyone was carefully keeping his or her head down.

Sometimes deductive logic was a big help.

They reached Lyman's office and went inside, Lyman closing the door behind them. "So," he said, sitting down behind his desk and waving Talbot to the line of three identical chairs facing it. "I hear you want to join the San Jose Police Department."

"Yes, sir," Talbot said, easing carefully into the center chair. One of these chairs had a horrendous and utterly disconcerting squeak, and Lyman was forever switching them around to throw his subordinates off stride. "Temporarily, of course."

"Uh-huh," Lyman grunted, leaning back in his chair. "And what exactly are your interest and involvement in this case?"

"Sir?"

"Interest, as in you're questioning suspects before you're even officially on loan," Lyman said. "Involvement, as in Lieutenant Delgado called you practically before he called his own chief."

"Ah," Talbot said, choosing his words carefully. "Actually, there's nothing mysterious about it. Delgado and I have consulted on a couple of previous cases, and we've always worked well together. So when there was trouble at an important research facility in his jurisdiction, particularly trouble that might have national implications, I was the obvious one to call."

"And you didn't think it worth calling in yourself?"

"As I said, there was only the potential for national implications," Talbot said. "Until we knew for sure, I didn't want to bother anyone else with it."

"Part of my job is to be bothered with things like that," Lyman reminded him tartly. "Chief Garcia and I don't agree on a lot of things, but one of the things we *do* agree on is not liking it when our subordinates play their cards under the table where we can't see them."

"I understand, sir."

"Good," Lyman said. "So let's see your cards."

"Sir?"

"There's something you're not telling me," Lyman said, turning his gaze up to full shrivel power. "I want it. Now."

Talbot lifted his hands innocently. "You've got all of it, sir," he said, his mind kicking onto afterburners. "Lieutenant Delgado asked me in on a case he thought the Bureau should be involved in, that's all. Now that we know it does indeed have Federal implications, we naturally want our presence to be official. Hence, Delgado's request and Chief Garcia's phone call."

For a long moment Lyman just gazed at him. "This is why McPherson kicked you out of D.C., isn't it?" he said at last. "This kind of passive insubordination."

"I meant no insubordination, sir," Talbot protested. "Passive or otherwise."

"You remind me of my kid sister when we were little," Lyman went on. "She had a lot of your same style: the same innocent look, the same 'gosh-shucks' humility. When she couldn't finagle Mom's permission to do what she wanted, she usually just did it anyway. When she got caught, she pulled such a terrific remorseful groveling act that she usually got away with only token punishment. Drove me crazy."

"You're lucky, sir," Talbot said. "My sister used to deliberately get in trouble and then throw me the blame."

"That *is* why McPherson exiled you out here, isn't it?" Lyman persisted. "Insubordination? Something to do with the Clarkston kidnapping case last summer?"

"You'd have to ask Director McPherson about that," Talbot said politely.

"I have," Lyman said, making a face. "He won't tell me."

"Playing his cards under the table," Talbot said, nodding knowingly. "Don't you just hate that in a superior?"

"You've got a smart mouth, too," Lyman said. "Fine—keep your little secrets. It's not *my* career. Fill me in."

"The three scientists were apparently murdered in order to get hold of the fruits of their recent work," Talbot said, breathing a little easier. There'd been the potential for a real mine field on this one, but he'd apparently made it through intact. "Specifically, they wanted four Cloaks of invisibility.

Lyman's eyebrows lifted. "Cloaks of *what*?"

"You heard me right," Talbot assured him. "I know; it sounds like something out of Grimm's Fairy Tales. I wouldn't have believed it either, except that the lab techs demoed a prototype version the thieves left behind."

"And?"

"The thing works, sir. Damn well."

Lyman shook his head. "Hell in a handcart," he muttered.

"At least," Talbot agreed. "Still, it's not as bad as it could have been. For one thing, the Cloaks can't keep up with any sort of movement, so we're not looking at the ultimate stealth fighter."

"Do they make you invisible to radar, too?"

"No," Talbot said. "Actually, they only affect visible light, so stealth aircraft are out anyway. The thieves also skipped out without the equipment to manufacture more of the stuff, and the techs say you can't reverse engineer it. If we can recover these four Cloaks we may be able to tourniquet this particular technology hemorrhage before it gets started."

"Unless they plan to come back for the rest of it," Lyman pointed out.

"Already thought of that," Talbot said. "Delgado's putting a guard setup together."

"What about the techs themselves?" Lyman asked. "They must know how to make the things."

"To varying degrees, yes," Talbot said. "Actually, it's when you start looking at the techs that things start getting murky."

Lyman eyed him. "Let me guess. An inside job?"

"Very much so," Talbot said grimly. "There could conceivably be other players, but at least one of the techs absolutely has to be involved."

"Give me the rundown."

"They spent the workday before the murder doing a final equipment check," Talbot said. "After each of the Cloaks was done, it was folded up and piled with the others in an office off the main lab. Sometime after one of the two smaller Cloaks was finished, one of the techs left the compound with it, probably in the trunk of his car, and gave it to one or more accomplices outside the fence."

"How did he get it out of the lab?"

"He slipped it out the window before he left," Talbot said. "I found a spot beneath one of the office windows where something had hit the ground. The Cloaks are heavier than they look, and a folded one in particular leaves marks. The necessary programming could have been smuggled out weeks earlier and loaded onto the thieves' own laptop."

"I don't suppose any of the techs stayed inside the compound the whole day?"

Talbot shook his head. "All three left exactly once, either that afternoon or evening."

Lyman snorted. "Figures. Go on."

"Whoever it was delivered the Cloak to his buddies before returning to the lab," Talbot said. "When Kingsley went outside the fence to get the semi from the loading area, the rest of the group was already inside the trailer, hidden underneath their new Cloak."

"Or else Kingsley was the one who delivered it to them," Lyman pointed out.

"Possibly," Talbot said. "But as I said, each of the other two could have done the same thing earlier in the day."

"Except that the gang then wouldn't have known which trailer to hide in."

Talbot shook his head. "Unfortunately, Chandler reserved the semi the day before. It would have been simple for any of the techs to pull up the record."

Lyman gave a little grunt. "Okay, then, let's try this. You said the things don't work when they're moving. So unless the gate guard is in collusion, how come he didn't see anything?"

"Because by the time he got around back and swung the door open the semi would have stopped bouncing long enough for the Cloak to do its stuff," Talbot said. "So that's how the gang got in. After that, all the tech had left to do was sprinkle potions into coffee pots, hide the drugged guard before anyone could stumble on him, and make sure he was alone in the foyer long enough to let in the accomplices lurking by the outside door."

"Couldn't he have let them in when he disposed of the guard?" Lyman asked.

"He could have, but he didn't," Talbot said. "The door time-stamp records didn't show any unaccounted-for openings. A shame, actually—one of the other techs might have remembered someone being out of the lab at that time. As it is, all we've got is the guard's disappearance, and that could have happened any time after midnight."

"All three techs were wandering in and out the whole time, I suppose?"

"They were drinking a lot of coffee and soda up there," Talbot reminded him.

Lyman grunted. "Right. Any inside cameras?"

"None," Talbot said. "This was Sand/Star's lowest-security building, and the card-keys and guards were considered adequate. Plus the outer fence, of course."

"Amazing what people consider adequate," Lyman said contemptuously. "Go on."

"That's basically it," Talbot said. "The accomplices hid from the cleaning staff until the scientists were dead, then loaded the Cloaks into the semi and took off. The driver was made up to look like Dr. Chandler, who of course hadn't checked out yet, and he had something to gimmick the sign-out pad with. Everyone and everything else was in the trailer, again underneath one of the Cloaks, so that when the guard took another peek inside all he saw was empty space."

"You've put out an APB on the semi, of course."

"No need," Talbot said. "It's been found three miles north of the Sand/Star grounds. The rain's obliterated most of the tire tracks, but Delgado's people say it looks like the Cloaks were transferred to a panel truck. They're going over the semi now, but I'm not expecting much."

"So the damn things could be in Mexico by now."

"Or almost anywhere else in the world if our friends had a fast plane on hand," Talbot agreed. "Somehow, though, I don't think they've left the country. If it was foreign espionage, or even the domestic industrial variety, why didn't they take the manufacturing equipment?"

"Maybe they didn't know they needed it."

Talbot shook his head. "No. Whichever tech is involved would have told them what they needed to have the complete set."

Lyman picked up a pen and began fiddling with it. "Unless it's a double-cross," he suggested. "Possibly while the inside man angles for a larger payoff."

"Interesting," Talbot said thoughtfully. "That one hadn't occurred to me."

"It's actually unlikely," Lyman conceded, "considering what it would take to steal anything else from that lab now. Simpler to assume they don't need the equipment because the inside man's already given them the blueprints."

"They say none of that stuff is missing," Talbot said. "Of course, like the laptop programming, it could have been duplicated and smuggled out before last night. It still bothers me, though."

"I presume you have a gut sense about what's going on," Lyman said. "Let's hear it."

"Frankly, I'm still a little overwhelmed by the possibilities this thing opens up," Talbot admitted. "Assassination, for one thing. Shoot some prominent figure from a rooftop, then wrap up under a Cloak off in a corner and take a nap until the search dies down. Maybe a bank job, or some other sort of robbery, or your proverbial fly-on-the-wall corporate or governmental eavesdropping. Anything your fictional invisible man could pull off, these guys can now do."

"Mm," Lyman said, setting down the pen again. "All right. What do you need?"

Talbot shrugged. "Unless we want to call in the National Guard for a door-to-door search—"

"Which we don't."

"—which probably wouldn't do any good anyway," Talbot continued, "what we need right now is some serious information crunching."

"Let me guess," Lyman said, his tone suddenly dark. "You want Hanna Swenson."

"If I could, sir."

Lyman was glaring again, this time with the voltage turned up a couple of notches. "I don't know if it's occurred to you, Talbot," he said, "but just because Swenson arrived on the same plane from Reagan National that you did doesn't give you any special claims on her time."

"I know that, sir," Talbot said humbly. "And I know I do ask for her a lot. But I need someone who can pull a huge amount of information together fast, and who can sort out the good from the bad from the ugly. The Jigsaw Girl's the best there is."

"How about if I give you Anderson and Chiang instead?" Lyman offered. "Swenson's up to her ears in satellite tracking data right now on an interstate smuggling ring."

"That's perfect," Talbot said. "One of her first jobs would be to sift through satellite photos to see if she can pick up the truck they transferred the Cloaks to. It's a long shot, but we could get lucky."

"Chiang's good at satellite analysis, too."

"But more important would be the job of backtracking the three techs," Talbot continued. "They're the best handle we've got on this. The faster we can pull that handle, the better our chances of recovering the Cloaks before the media get hold of it."

Lyman sighed. "You really have to meet my sister someday, Talbot," he said. "You two would get on like a chemical factory fire. Fine—you can have Swenson."

"Thank you, sir."

"Save it," Lyman growled. "You'd just con her into working for you after hours anyway, and the lady needs her sleep. Now get out of here."

"Yes, sir." Talbot stood up and stepped to the door.

"One more thing," Lyman called after him.

Talbot paused with the door halfway open. "Yes?"

Lyman was gazing at him with a look Talbot didn't at all care for. "Garcia said Dr. Chandler's widow has been kidnapped. How come you didn't mention that to me?"

"I thought it a bit premature, sir," Talbot said, feeling his pulse start up again. So he hadn't cleared the verbal mine field after all. "All we know for sure is that there was gunfire at Greenleaf Center this morning, and that she was spirited out by a man who had opened a PI office there."

"A man running under an assumed name," Lyman said pointedly. "And who disappeared with her instead of dropping her at the nearest police station. None of this seemed worth mentioning?"

"She may have been too rattled to go to the police right away," Talbot suggested. "He may have taken her someplace where she could calm down. Or he may have wanted to go to ground for a while to cool any pursuit."

"Or he may have something else in mind," Lyman said. "Something involving the theft and murders."

"Perhaps," Talbot said. "On the other hand, we don't even know which one of them the gunmen at the mall were shooting at. Maybe he's the one in trouble, and he just hasn't found a convenient place yet to lose her."

"It's a puzzle, all right," Lyman agreed evenly. "You'd better get it sorted out, hadn't you?"

"Yes, sir." Talbot took one final look at his superior's face, then made his escape out the door.

It hadn't been an encouraging look, he decided as he retraced his steps back across the squad room. A man didn't rise through the ranks to head up an FBI office by being an idiot, after all.

And for all of Lyman's talk about Talbot having been exiled out here, the San Francisco office was hardly the Bureau's dumping ground for incompetents and malcontents. Lyman was a lot sharper than even most of his agents realized, with a hell of a lot of experience under his belt. He could evaluate people and situations with a glance, and he could spot evasion a mile upwind.

Talbot's failure to mention Angie Chandler had been a serious mistake. But it was too late to do anything about that now. Besides, whatever suspicions Lyman might be nurturing, he couldn't possibly know anything for certain. With a little luck, Talbot could get this tied up before that line was crossed.

With a little luck, and a lot of Hanna Swenson. Picking up his pace, he headed for the stairs. She was going to be thrilled to hear about this one.

~

It had started to rain again as Captain Billingsgate trudged up onto the *Tasman Venture*'s deck where First Mate Chung was waiting. "This had better be good, First," he warned, pulling his collar more tightly around his neck. "I was holding a full house, and I *know* Jackson was bluffing."

"Yes, sir," Chung said, offering Billingsgate his binoculars as he pointed just off the freighter's starboard quarter. "There—about thirty meters distant."

Billingsgate squinted. There was something floating in the gently swelling sea out there. Pressing the binoculars to his eyes, he focused in.

It was a human body.

No. It was three human bodies.

The rain was suddenly forgotten. "Get us in closer," he ordered. "Padmic and Manducci into the boat. I want those bodies out of the water. Move, mister."

It took nearly half an hour and a little fancy maneuvering on Manducci's part, but in the end the three bodies were laid out on the *Tasman Venture*'s deck.

Or at least, what was left of them. The sharks and scavengers had not been kind to the deceased.

But they'd left enough. They'd left more than enough.

"There," Billingsgate said, gesturing as he squatted beside the bodies. "And there and there. Bullet wounds, too close together for single fire. We're talking a machine gun with burst capability, lads. Nine millimeter rounds, too, or I'm a frog."

"Bloody pirates," Chung muttered uneasily. For a freighter the Tasman Venture's size, pirates were a constant worry.

"Maybe," Billingsgate said, rubbing one of the remaining scraps of material thoughtfully between his fingers. "But these don't look like seaman's togs to me. I'm thinking these *were* the pirates, and it was someone else fed 'em the big end of the mushroom for a change."

"Like who?" Padmic demanded. "Who around here carries automatic weapons?"

"Unless you think they took on a military ship by mistake," Manducci added sarcastically.

"You don't know the half of it, lad," Billingsgate rumbled. "You see here, and here? That there's the marks of grenade shrapnel."

"Come off it," Manducci sniffed. "How could you tell *that*?"

"Twenty years in the Royal Navy, that's how," Billingsgate huffed. "Five'll get you ten there are fragments in the bone here, too. All you want to do is dig it out."

Padmic made a retching sound. "No thanks. Who'd want to do a bloody job like that?"

"Chap I know in Taipei, for one," Billingsgate said, standing up again. "First, get us back underway, and try to coax another knot or two out of her if you can. I'll go see if I can raise him."

He headed off toward the radio room. "What about them?" Chung called after him.

"Throw a tarp over 'em and leave 'em be," Billingsgate called back. *Urgent but quiet*, the message had read, the one Glassey had sent out to his contacts in the region. *Report any and all unusual activity esp. involving terrorist, rebel, or paramilitary forces*. Machine-gunned bodies, Billingsgate thought dryly, ought to fit that category. *Strict confidentiality imperative*. Well, it was as confidential as Billingsgate could manage. Once they hit land all of Southeast Asia would know, but for the moment it was just him and his crew.

And then had come the best bit, the bit that made it all worth the effort and delay and having dead bodies lying on his deck.

Substantial bonus for information leading to resolution of situation.

Typical vagueness on Glassey's part, and of course nothing at all about what was really going on. But the important part was as clear as a Singapore club dancer's brassiere. There was money involved; and *substantial bonus* were two of Billingsgate's favorite words.

He flicked some water off his chin and picked up his pace a bit. Yes, Glassey and his friends at the American CIA would be very interested in this bit of news. Very interested indeed.

10

IT WAS NEARLY four-thirty in the afternoon by the time Ross finally returned.

He'd been gone over five hours. Angie knew that because she'd been counting those hours over and over. It had been long enough for her to finish her shower and get dressed in the shirt and slacks Ross had left her. The idea of wearing his clothing made her skin crawl, but the thought that she might be caught wearing nothing but a towel when he returned was even worse. She was dressed before she was even completely dry.

After that she sprawled tiredly on the bed, watched some TV, and sampled the slightly stale and seriously overpriced delicacies from the minibar. The local news channels were stale, too, endlessly recapping the stories of the Sand/Star murders and the mysterious shootout at Greenleaf Center with nothing new to add.

At about hour three she'd given up on the TV and pulled out her needlepoint. But it had reminded her too much of the life that had been shattered that morning, and she had soon put it away again. After that there had been little to do but think, cry, and, as her enforced solitude began to stretch out, worry about Ross.

A dozen times in those final two hours she picked up the phone to call him. A dozen times she put it back down again. If he was all right, there was no point in bothering him. If the gunmen had found him, there was equally no point.

But now, at last, he was back. "About time," she said reproachfully as she double-locked the door behind him. "I was getting worried."

"Sorry," Ross apologized, dumping his armful of bags onto the bed. "This isn't my usual kind of shopping, and it took longer than I expected. I hope the selection's okay."

"I'm sure they'll be fine," Angie said, frowning as she ran an eye over the bags. Either he'd included a sleeping bag and parka in his gift pack, or else he hadn't been kidding when he'd talked about buying her a new wardrobe. "Just how long are you expecting us to be on the road, anyway? Or in this room?"

"Oh, it's not just clothes in there," he assured her, dropping into one of the chairs with a tired huff. "There are also shoes and toiletries, plus a collapsible suitcase to carry it all in. Never hurts to be prepared, you know."

"No, of course not," Angie said, digging gingerly into the bags. From what she could see, his taste in women's clothing didn't seem too bad. "You didn't answer my question."

"Which one? How long we're going to be the chasees?" He shrugged. "I don't know. Like I said, it never hurts to be prepared."

He waved at the bags. "As to how long we're staying here, about five minutes longer than it takes you to pick out something and get dressed in it. It's going to be dark soon. Time for us to be gone."

Angie studied him out of the corner of her eye as she gathered up the bags. With her concern for his safety this afternoon, all those ominous questions about who this man was and what he wanted with her had faded into the background of her thoughts. Now, with him back safe and sound, those questions were back, too. "You still don't want to go to the police?"

"Not until we're sure we've lost our playmates," Ross said. "And even then, I'm thinking we should go to some police department outside the Bay area."

A police department outside the Bay area. A long ride alone together through the darkness of night. "Perhaps," she murmured.

"But we can sort that out later," Ross went on. "Get changed and let's hit the road."

"All right," Angie said. Collecting the last of the bags, she headed into the bathroom.

She made a point of locking the door behind her.

~

"Anything?" the general asked into his phone.

"Negative, One," Two's voice came back, sounding faintly disgusted. "He got into the elevator alone; but from the pauses on the lobby display, it looks like he hit every floor button on his way up."

The general stared out of the car window at the tall structure of the Chancellor Hotel looming across the parking lot from him. This man was smart, all right. Maybe too smart. He was certainly becoming inconvenient.

Unfortunately, there wasn't time in the plan for inconvenient people. In just over forty-eight hours he and most of his team needed to be in southern Oregon. Three days after that, assuming Ten and Eleven out in the western Pacific were able to hold to schedule, they would enter into the riskiest part of the entire operation.

Angie Chandler had to be dead by then. At least, according to Hooker she did.

Which brought up another disturbing question. Hooker had already expressed considerable anger that what he'd expected to be a simple act of corporate theft had turned into a triple murder. It was a rather curious reaction, the general thought, considering that it was Hooker's own words that had sealed the scientists' fates.

But the fact remained that he was angry. Could this trouble with Angie Chandler's new protector be his response to what he considered a betrayal of their deal? Had Hooker inserted someone into the operation to protect Mrs. Chandler, either out of pity or some less noble motive? It was unlikely, but it was possible.

Still, when all was said and done, it didn't matter who the man was. There was too much at stake for loose ends. "Then we do it the hard way," he concluded. "There are seven occupancy floors, you said?"

"Yes, sir," Two said. "We can't cover all of them, at least not on the first pass."

"No need," the general said. "Our opponent would never take the lowest and most vulnerable floor. Send the others to the top six floors; report via radio when in position."

"Yes, sir."

The phone clicked off, and the general switched on the family-band radio on the seat beside him, leaving the microphone live but turning the speaker volume all the way down. The top floor, he decided, making a private bet with himself.

Three minutes later, everything was ready. "Stand by," the general said into the radio, reminding himself that this particular means of communication was about as secure as shouting across the Chancellor's parking lot. But the danger was minimal if they were careful what they said and stuck with their numerical identification system. "Single click means move, double means mark."

He got acknowledgements from each of his men, then keyed on his phone again and punched for the hotel's front desk. "Chancellor Hotel," a young woman's voice came.

"Hello, I have some friends who are supposed to meet me there," the general said. "Could you see if they've checked in yet?"

"Certainly, sir," the woman said. "Their names?"

"Adam Ross and Charles Sullivan," the general told her, giving the name that had been on the man's office door and the one that Hooker said was on his driver's license. "I don't know which one reserved the room."

"We have a Charles Sullivan who checked in this morning," she informed him. "Shall I ring his room?"

"Yes, please—that would be great."

"Certainly." There was a click, and the phone began to ring. The general poised a fingernail over the radio's microphone . . .

"Hello?" a cautious male voice answered.

"Mr. Sullivan, this is the front desk," the general said, giving a sharp tap on the microphone. "Our system just flagged a discrepancy with your payment. Can you confirm which credit card you used?"

"I didn't use a credit card," Sullivan said. "I paid in cash."

"Cash, sir?" the general asked, trying to sound puzzled as he listened closely. Nothing yet. "Let me check that . . . no, it's still coming up flagged. Do you happen to remember who exactly you dealt with?"

"The name badge said Richie," Sullivan said, his caution starting to give way to annoyance. "And he made enough song and dance about it to have lasted you people for the rest of the week."

"Yes, sir," the general said. Was that music he was starting to hear now from the other end of the connection? "I do apologize for the inconvenience." Yes; it was definitely music, the volume rising as the boom box in the hallway outside came ever closer. "Unfortunately, Richie has already gone home for the day, and I still have this flag to deal with."

"Richie doesn't have a phone?"

"It shouldn't be necessary to call him," the general said. "Do you happen to have your receipt available?"

"Hang on, I'll get it," Sullivan said, sounding thoroughly irritated now. There was a faint shuffling of papers, an interesting counterpoint to the music swelling in the background. Military music, he could tell now, with a definite marching beat.

That was Six's tape, which meant that the general's guess about the top floor had been right. He held his breath, straining his ears, hoping their quarry would continue to hunt silently for his receipt for just a few more seconds.

"Got it," Sullivan came back. "Which number do you want?"

"Just a moment, sir, the computer's frozen up," the general said. For another second the march continued to get louder; and then, abruptly, it began to drop off again.

Marking the spot where Six and his boom box passed by Sullivan's door.

"Here we go," the general said, tapping twice on the radio microphone. In the background the music was fading away as Six continued down the hall. "Can you read me the number on the receipt?"

Sullivan did so. The general listened with half an ear, gazing at the line of windows beneath the hotel roof line and wondering idly if they were on this side of the building or the other. "Yes, sir, I see the problem now. It's all fixed. I'm sorry for the inconvenience. Good evening."

"Yeah, 'bye," the other growled, and hung up.

The general hung up, too, then punched in Two's phone number. "It was the march," he said when the other answered.

"Yes, sir," Two said. "That makes it either 822 or 823."

"Have Six put the boom box in the stairway and go back to listen for signs of life," the general ordered, pushing open his door and checking his gun. "The others are to move to their designated positions. As soon as I'm there, we'll take them."

~

Carefully, Ross set the phone back into its cradle, the distant sound of warning bells clanging in the deep recesses of his brain. There was no reason for the hotel to be having any trouble with his bill. He'd already gone through all that when he'd first checked in with cash in hand and a steadfast refusal to put down a credit card as guarantee.

Which meant that that call had been something else.

The gunmen?

It had to be. Question was, what had the call gained them? As far as he knew, they'd never heard him speak before, so they couldn't have been after voice identification. Had they expected Angie to answer the phone, and simply had this smoke screen prepared in case she didn't?

"Is it the Fourth of July already?" Angie asked, coming out of the bathroom dressed in one of the outfits he'd bought her, the borrowed shirt and slacks folded over one arm.

"What?" Ross asked.

"The parade in the hallway," she explained. "Didn't you hear it?"

He frowned at the door. "Parade?"

She sighed. "It was a joke," she said tiredly. "It was just someone with a boom box playing Sousa."

And suddenly it clicked. "Your stuff all packed?" he demanded as he heaved himself out of his chair and drew his Glock. "Good. Throw those things in my bag and get your coat on."

"What is it?" Angie asked, the fatigue abruptly gone as she shrank back from him with suddenly widened eyes.

"I think they've tagged us," he said, motioning her back as he peered through the door's peephole. "Be quiet."

For a moment there was nothing. Then, through the floor he felt the faint vibration of approaching footsteps. A man appeared from the right, his image distorted by the fisheye lens, and stopped at the room directly across the hall. Cupping his hand around the peephole, he peered closely at it.

"Damn," Ross muttered under his breath as he pressed his face even closer to the door. That cute little music-in-the-hall trick of theirs could only narrow the search to these two particular rooms, and now they were hoping to cut the possibilities down to one by seeing which room was occupied. Too late to turn off their lights; Ross could only hope his face would block enough of the telltale leakage through the peephole.

A moment later, the searcher turned around and repeated his experiment on their room. Ross held his breath, gazing at that intense face and trying to commit every line to memory. The man looked vaguely Hispanic, though with the peephole's distortion and the low hallway lighting his ancestry could as easily have been anything from Spanish to Greek to Arabic to Iranian. In the complicated melting pot that was the Bay Area's population, he could be practically anything.

He seemed to stand there a long time before finally moving out of view toward the right, the direction of the stairway thirty feet away at the end of the hall. Ross waited until the vibration of his footsteps had died away before turning to face Angie, making sure to cover the peephole with his hand. She was still standing by his bag, frozen in the process of repacking his clothes. "Grab the bags," he whispered. "We're heading out."

She nodded quickly, stuffing in his things and zipping the bag closed. She pulled on her jacket as she crossed again to the bathroom, emerging with her new suitcase. She grabbed his bag with her other hand and nodded again.

"Stay behind me," he murmured, easing the locks off as quietly as he could. Opening the door, he crouched down and stuck his head out looking to the right.

There was the quiet *crack* of a suppressed gun, and above him a splatter of wood and plaster erupted from the spot where his head would have been if he'd been standing straight up. He dropped to the floor onto his side, catching a glimpse of a single ski-masked figure crouching inside the half-open stairway door as he brought his Glock into firing position.

The gunman was quicker, dodging to the side into the protection of the stairwell, leaving Ross's shot to ricochet loudly off the metal door. Ross fired twice more, twisting his head around for a quick look the other direction. No one was visible yet, but that wouldn't last long.

He looked back, just in time to brush back the first gunman with another shot as the other came to the door for another look. For a second he considered rushing the man, but crossing thirty feet of open space would be a high-exertion way of committing suicide.

But he couldn't just leave him at their back, either. "Get the minibar open," he ordered, putting three rounds into the ceiling just in front of the door and sending bursts of disintegrated acoustic tile fluttering down. "Dump all the liquor onto one of the pillows."

He put two more rounds into the ceiling and then swiveled his gun around the other direction. Unlike the gunman, his Glock wasn't suppressed, and unless the backup forces were deaf they knew the jig was up. Some discouraging fire was clearly called for.

Still, he couldn't risk innocent lives by firing blindly down the hall and hoping no one stepped out of his room at the wrong time. Lifting his aim, he sent three rounds at the ceiling as far down the hallway as he could see, at the point where the other hallway branched off at an angle from the elevator alcove.

He'd expected to get more acoustic tile dust drifting down there. What he got instead was a sudden and impressive spray of water. Apparently, he'd hit one of the feeder pipes for the emergency sprinkler system.

Perfect.

"Here," Angie's voice called from behind him, dimly heard through the ringing echo of the gunshots in his ears. The soggy pillow she was thrusting at him reeked of a dozen types of alcohol.

"Great," he said, taking the pillow with his free hand and tossing it into the center of the hallway between them and the stairway. "Take this," he continued, handing her his old Zippo lighter. "Grab that HBO guide by the TV, light it, and throw it on the pillow."

He fired two more rounds into the ceiling near the stairway, giving silent thanks he'd chosen a room on the top floor. He wasn't sure if the Glock's rounds would penetrate the floors here, but having no one above them meant one less thing to worry about. "Then grab the bags and get ready to run to the elevators," he added.

He swiveled back and added one more shot into the ceiling by the waterfall, finishing off the magazine. He was pulling another from his belt pouch when the flaming booklet arced over his head and dropped onto the pillow. There was a whoosh of blue flame—

And as the pillow stuffing caught, the hallway began to fill with dense white smoke.

"Go!" Ross snapped, jamming the magazine into the gun and releasing the slide as he heaved himself to his feet. He sent two more rounds through the smoke toward the stairway door as Angie dashed past him, the bags bouncing against her hips, then turned and ran after her, clenching his teeth against the sudden sharp pain in his left leg. He caught up with her ten yards down the hall and shifted to a sideways run, his Glock pointed forward and his backup HK Compact in his left hand pointed backward as he tried to watch both directions at once.

Midway through their mad dash the smoke detectors in the hallway kicked in, and once again they were running through a rainstorm, this time to the accompaniment of a blaring fire alarm. Ross could only hope the other guests on this floor would continue to show good sense by staying in their rooms instead of rushing out to see what all the commotion was about. All he needed right now was a bunch of innocent bystanders to contend with.

And then they were to the elevators and the intersection with the other hallway. Ross peered through the cascading water from the shredded pipe as he shoved Angie across the open area toward the relative shelter of the elevator alcove.

The other hallway was deserted, and they made it to the alcove without incident. "Elevator?" Angie asked, punching the call button without waiting for an answer as Ross slammed shoulder-first against the wall beside her.

"Won't work—fire lockdown," Ross said, peering carefully around the corner. The other hallway was still deserted, and as he looked the other direction toward the fading cloud of smoke he could see that the first gunman was also nowhere in sight.

The warning bells were going off in his brain again. These people had gone to considerable effort to track them down, and they'd already demonstrated they wanted at least one of them dead. Probably both of them.

So where were they?

"Stairs?" Angie asked. "There's a set right there." She started toward the door.

"No," Ross said, grabbing her arm.

"But—they're—" she protested, waving back toward the room they'd just left.

"They're not there anymore," Ross told her, glancing around as he slipped his HK back into its belt holster at his right hip, keeping the Glock handy. Still no one in sight. "They know the elevator will be locked down, and they're waiting for us in the stairways a floor or two down. No cover, nowhere else to go. Fish in a barrel."

"So what do we do?"

"The same thing we were trying to do when we first got here: go to ground," Ross said, taking her arm again. "Let's hope it works better this time."

Skirting the edge of the waterfall, he retraced their steps toward the smoke at the far end of the hallway. Instead of continuing on that direction, though, he stopped two doors from the elevator lobby, his backup electronic key in hand. Another quick glance both directions as he slid the plastic into the lock, and they were inside.

"No lights," Ross warned as he eased the door silently closed behind them. "They'll have people watching. There's enough light coming in from outside for us to see by."

"Where did this room come from?" Angie breathed, her voice starting to tremble with reaction.

"I arranged it earlier," Ross said, wiping the water off his face with his sleeve. "On my way out to do the shopping."

"They didn't find it odd that you wanted a second room?"

Ross shrugged, thinking quickly. "The arrangements weren't quite so formal," he improvised. "I've done a little hotel desk clerking in my time, and I know how their key-coders work. I took advantage of some momentary inattention to cut myself an emergency bolthole."

"So what now?"

"First, we get into some dry clothes," Ross told her, making his way to one of the two beds and stretching out on top of it, wincing as he eased his bad leg into a more comfortable position. "You first—go ahead and change in the bathroom. After that, we leave the lights off, ignore anyone who knocks, and pretend very hard to be an empty room."

"Even if it's the police?"

"Especially if it's the police," Ross said firmly. "Anyone can rent a police uniform at a costume shop, you know."

"Oh," Angie said soberly.

"Don't worry, no one's likely to come in," Ross hastened to reassure her. "Even when the real police come up here looking for clues and witnesses, they'll just knock on the doors. Most of their attention will be concentrated on the other end of the hall and our old room."

Angie sighed, a wispy sound in the darkness. "How long do we wait?"

"As long as it takes," Ross said. "In the meantime, let's see if we can figure out what the hell is going on."

~

It was three hours before the police cars began to turn off their flashing lights and drive away. Sitting in his car at the far end of the lot, the general stared across at the Chancellor, drumming his fingers on the steering wheel.

Damn these two, anyway. They'd already cost him more time than they should have, far more than any reasonable man could have predicted. And still they were at large, a ticking time bomb waiting to go off.

His phone rang. "One," he said tersely. "Anything?"

"No, sir," Six's voice came, sounding as disgusted as the general felt. "But unless they somehow got past Two in the lobby, they're still inside."

"Then they're still inside," the general said. "And they have to come out sometime."

"Yes, sir."

"You sound uncertain."

"I was just wondering if all this is worth the effort, sir," the other said. "How do we know she hasn't already told the police everything?"

"We don't," the general conceded evenly. "And if she has, this is indeed a waste of effort. Still, from what Hooker said, it doesn't sound like she's even spoken with them yet, let alone said anything damaging."

He gazed out the windshield. "You just keep watching that door. Sooner or later, they have to surface."

~

"But this doesn't make any sense," Angie protested quietly, sitting in the room's desk chair and gazing out at the lights of the city beyond. "Why would anyone want to kill me?"

"I don't know," Ross said from the bed, a lighter outline against the dark bedspread. "And frankly, I think you're the only one who can figure it out."

Angie shook her head in frustration, the damp ends of her hair slapping against her cheeks. She'd been over it a million times since the mall, and was still no closer to an answer than she'd been then. "They're psychos," she said. "They killed my husband, and now they want to kill me."

"No," Ross said. "Whatever else they are, they're not psychos. Remember, they didn't kill the Sand/Star reception guard. Why not? Answer: they didn't need to. They just needed to get him out of the way, so they knocked him out. No, they have a solid reason for why they think they need to kill you. Or me. Or us."

"But it doesn't make sense," Angie repeated. "I hardly know a thing about the Tarnhelm project. Certainly none of the technical aspects."

"Maybe they just think you know something," Ross suggested. "Or maybe you know something but don't realize it."

"If they worried about people who know things, why aren't they going after Burke and Esteban and Kingsley?" Angie argued.

"Maybe they are," Ross said. "But there's a problem. The police know one of the techs poisoned the lab's coffee pot. If his buddies now knock off one or both of the others . . . you see?"

Angie nodded. "Yes," she said. "Unless they decide he's a liability and take him out, too."

"They could," Ross agreed. "In fact, if they're smart, they will."

"I guess it doesn't pay to work with murderers," Angie murmured, frowning into the darkness. She'd been listening to the news off and on all afternoon, watching the details of the crime gradually emerge.

Yet, here was Ross, spouting information even CNN didn't have, or at least wasn't reporting.

Where was he getting it from?

"No, it doesn't," Ross agreed. "One other possibility I've been toying with is that they're trying to frame you for the murders, and these attempts are geared to make you look like an inside person they don't need anymore."

A chill ran through Angie's body. "In which case, they won't stop until I'm dead."

"They may keep trying," Ross said. "Doesn't mean they'll succeed."

The room went silent. Ross shifted his left leg off the pillow it had been propped up on, bending the knee experimentally. Angie watched the procedure, wondering again what was wrong with that leg. Was it something congenital? Arthritis, maybe? Or was it some kind of injury?

She suppressed the impulse to ask. There were a lot of things she still needed to know about this man, but personal questions like that would imply a level of friendship she didn't feel and definitely didn't want.

"Let's try a new tack," Ross said as he laid his leg back down. "Could your husband have left something behind somewhere that could shed light on all this? Information about threats against him or the project, maybe, or suspicions about one of the techs?"

"I suppose," she said doubtfully. "But wouldn't something like that be at the house or his lab?"

"If it was, it's long gone by now," Ross said. "No, I'm looking for a long shot here, some place neither the cops nor the murderers would think of. Any ideas?"

Angie chewed at her lip, trying to think. Where else did James ever go these days? He probably hadn't even left the lab for meals in the past six weeks. Mostly he ate in the cafeteria or sent the techs for carry-out.

Six weeks. "There could be something in one of my parents' rental cabins near Tahoe," she offered. "James and I spent a weekend there about six weeks ago."

"Did he bring any of his work with him?"

Angie grimaced. "Of course he did."

"I'm sorry," Ross said. To Angie's mild surprise, he actually did sound sorry. "You game for a road trip?"

She took a deep breath. A long ride with a stranger through the darkness of night. "I guess so."

"That's the spirit," Ross said, heaving himself up from the bed. "Let's do it."

"You think it's safe to go out?" Angie asked. "I thought you'd decided they know what our car looks like."

"Probably," Ross said, stepping to the door. For a moment he stood with his ear pressed against it, then stepped back and pulled Angie's cell phone from his pocket. "Just means we have to do something clever."

~

A cab was waiting with its engine running as Ross led the way through one of the Chancellor's fire exits. The driver had clearly been well briefed, and took off across the lot practically before Angie had the door closed beside her.

A short drive took them to a large parking structure. There, at Ross's orders, the driver spiraled up to the third level, paused for a handful of seconds, then spiraled back down again. Midway through the maneuver Ross had Angie lie down on the floor with their bags as Ross stretched out on the seat.

They proceeded back to the street, and within a few minutes repeated the maneuver in a different structure.

Angie watched the play of lights on the car ceiling as they returned to the street, wondering what the remarkably taciturn cabby was making of all this. It wasn't until they were working their way up their third parking structure that it suddenly occurred to her that with both passengers out of sight of his mirrors there was only one likely conclusion for him to jump to. Her cheeks warmed; and she was just trying to figure out what to say about it when Ross called for a halt and pushed open the door.

Thirty seconds later they were out in the exhaust-laden air of this latest parking garage, standing beside their bags as the driver headed back down toward the street. Thirty seconds after that, they were hunched down in the front seat of a parked Chevy Blazer. Ross gave any potential pursuers a few more minutes to disappear into the night after the cab, then headed out behind a pair of departing minivans.

"What happens when the cab picks up another fare?" Angie asked as Ross turned the Blazer east.

"He's supposed to visit two more parking garages before he resumes his normal life," Ross told her. "Hopefully, this little exercise will string out the opposition enough that we'll only have one tail at most to worry about. Over the kind of distance we're talking about, a single tail should be easy to spot."

"Yes," Angie murmured. A long ride alone together through the darkness of night . . .

"The big question is whether they'll anticipate us," he went on. "Was it common knowledge around the lab that you and James sometimes used your parents' rentals?"

"I don't know," Angie said. "But even if they did, they won't know which one we went to this time. My parents have several cabins in the

Tahoe region, and we didn't even know which one would be vacant until we got there."

"You wouldn't happen to have a key, would you?"

"Are you going to need one?" Angie countered.

"Not really, no." Ross dug in his coat a moment, came up with her cell phone. "Speaking of parents, if you want to call them now you can. Make it quick; just a reassurance that you're all right. *Don't* tell them where we're going."

"Don't worry," Angie said, taking the phone from him and wondering a little at her sudden change of mood. She'd gone through a whole range of emotions since this morning, hitting peaks and valleys she normally didn't get in six months of normal life. From panic and numbness she'd gone through anguish and despair and fear, then bounced straight to terror and near panic again.

But all that was over now. Someone had cold-bloodedly taken her husband from her, and by God she was going to do whatever it took to find those responsible and bring them down.

She punched in her parents' phone number and waited for the connection. It felt good to be angry. A lot better than being scared. She just hoped she could hold onto the feeling a little while longer.

~

Between the heavy Friday night get-away-day traffic, a light but road-slicking snowfall that began as they hit the foothills, and a missed turn while Angie was dozing, the trip took far longer than Ross had expected. It was nearly three in the morning when the Blazer finally rolled to a stop in front of the darkened cabin.

Angie had fallen asleep again. Opening the Blazer's door as quietly as he could, Ross slipped out.

She was awake when he returned a few minutes later, her hands rubbing restlessly together. "I was starting to wonder if you'd run away," she said as he opened her door.

"Sorry," he apologized as he collected their luggage. "I wanted to have a look around before we went in."

"And?"

"Looks clear. Come on—I've got the door open and the heat turned on."

The cabin was only marginally warmer than the outside air. But the heater was a good one, and by the time they'd closed the curtains, turned on the lights, and made up the bed the temperature had become almost cozy.

There was only the one bedroom, Ross had noted on his first pass through the place. But the living room couch looked comfortable enough.

"What about you?" Angie asked as Ross finished with the final pillowcase.

"What about me?" Ross asked, looking at her as she stood beside the dresser and her open suitcase. There was a tightness about her eyes, he could see, a tension that seemed to deepen whenever she looked his direction. Clearly, she still had doubts.

"I mean where are you going to sleep?" she asked, her voice carefully neutral.

"The couch, of course," Ross said, as if there'd never been a question about that. "You can have first crack at the bathroom, if you want to brush your teeth," he added, choosing a blanket from the stack on the closet shelf.

"I'm too tired," she said, her posture wilting noticeably. She really *had* been worried about the sleeping arrangements. "I'm just going to turn in."

"Good idea," Ross said, heading toward the living room with his pillow and blanket. "Pleasant dreams."

"No," she said quietly. "I don't think so."

"I guess not," Ross conceded. It had been a stupid thing to say. "See you in the morning."

She locked the bedroom door behind him, the bolt sliding into place with an unexpectedly loud and totally unsubtle click.

All for the best, from Ross's point of view. Should Angie suddenly decide to come out, the loud bolt meant he would have a half second's warning. Considering what he had planned for the next hour or so, that could be useful.

He went around the cabin first, double-checking the locks on the doors and windows and making sure no light showed through the curtains. After that he pulled out his toiletry pouch and arranged the various items on the shelf above the bathroom sink, managing in the process to stretch his normal five-minute bedtime routine to nearly three times that. Next, he unpacked his gym bag, stacking the clothing on one of the chairs in the breakfast nook. By the time he was finished with everything, nearly half an hour had passed.

With luck, Angie was sound asleep.

Taking the empty gym bag with him, he settled onto the couch, propping up his bad leg on his folded blanket. Reaching into the bag, he carefully peeled back the inside flap that covered the thick supportive base and pulled out the miniature digital video recorder hidden there.

The recorder was old, with a capacity of only four hours, and he'd left Angie alone this afternoon for more than five. Still, unless she'd spent an inordinate amount of time in the bathroom out of range, there ought to be more than enough here. He ran the recording forward to the point where she came into view, freshly showered and wrapped in a towel, and settled down to watch.

11

ELEVEN HAD HOPED to get two days' grace out of Captain Syed's fear and naïveté. He'd more cautiously estimated they might get one.

In actual fact, they got one and a half.

"He's on to the home office," Ten said into his earphone in the vaguely distracted voice of someone trying to listen to one conversation while carrying on another. "Telling them all about our pirate encounter."

"And about us, I suppose?" Eleven asked, slipping a couple of extra magazines for his MP5 into his belt pouches.

"Definitely about us," Ten agreed. "You know, from the way they were talking together yesterday I expected them to crack soon, but I thought we'd at least get a few more hours out of them. At least until nightfall."

Eleven glanced at his watch. Just after four, with a couple of hours until full dark. "It's close enough," he said, snagging his pullover mask. "In fact, it may work out better this way. I presume he's just asking them to contact Seoul?"

"Actually, he's not even suggesting they go to Seoul directly," Ten said with a snort. "He wants them to try someone at the Karachi consulate. The fool."

"Then we should have all the time we need," Eleven decided.

"Right. Ha—listen to this: he's telling Syed to check the shotguns we gave them, to make sure we didn't sabotage them."

Eleven smiled tightly. "I'm glad Syed and not this other one was in command of this ship. I'll call Twelve and then get to the bow. You roust the captain and send him forward."

It took several minutes for Eleven to finish his preparations. By the time he reached the bow, the shadow ship was visible on the horizon.

He was picking out gun positions when he heard the sound of running feet behind him. A moment later Captain Syed came stumbling to a halt beside the forward-most container, panting heavily, a set of binoculars bouncing against his chest. "What is it," he managed between breaths, looking wildly around the sea. "Sergeant Major Choi said your enemies had returned."

"Indeed they have," Eleven said harshly. He gestured out at the yacht-sized vessel off the port bow, now visibly approaching the *Rabah Jamila* under the heavy clouds. "I wonder how they knew where to find us."

"That?" Syed asked, frowning. He raised the binoculars to his eyes, struggling to hold them steady against his heavy breathing. "But surely, Lieutenant—"

"Our enemies are aboard," Eleven cut him off, pushing the binoculars away from Syed's eyes and glaring at the other through his mask from point-blank range. "I repeat, I wonder how they knew where to find us."

Syed seemed to shrink inside his jacket. "I—that is—"

"Spare me your lies," Eleven said coldly. "You disobeyed me. Despite my warnings and my direct orders you used the radio."

He jabbed a gloved finger toward the approaching ship. "And *that* is the result. I trust you're proud of yourself, *Captain.*"

Syed swallowed hard, gazing at the approaching ship as if it were a sleeping tiger he'd been instructed to tiptoe past. "What do you want us to do?"

"I first want you to start obeying me," Eleven said. "Even then, our odds will not be good. We'll need your men up here—all of them—with their weapons. *Move.*"

There might have been a flicker in Syed's eyes at the mention of the guns, a ghost of remembrance of his home office's warning concerning them. But the ship out there was getting closer, and Syed was clearly a man used to obeying orders if they were loud enough. Without another word he turned and scampered back the way he'd come.

He wasn't gone long. Within ten minutes he was back with all but two of his crew, all of them brandishing weapons. "We've just received a radio message," Syed gasped, even more out of breath now than he'd been earlier. "They say they have a medical emergency aboard and need our assistance."

"Typical," Eleven grunted contemptuously. "Bold, yet stupidly transparent. Choi will deal with it."

"Shouldn't he be here?" one of the crewmen asked anxiously, peering around the edge of the foremost container at the distant vessel, fingering his shotgun nervously. "You and he are the professionals."

"Sergeant Major Choi knows his business," Eleven told him. "He and the remaining crewmen will stay on the bridge: the others to handle the ship, he to watch for submarines."

Syed's eyes widened. "*Submarines*?"

"You're not playing with children, Captain," Eleven reminded him darkly. "Now, quickly, we must get into position. Choi has instructions to keep our port bow to them, so we'll set up here on the starboard side where we'll be out of sight until they're in range. I'll show you where to stand."

It took another five minutes to get the crewmen into position. The shadow ship, as per Eleven's instructions, maintained its distance, staying visible but too far away for anyone to get a good look at it.

Syed still had enough wits left to notice that. "What are they waiting for?" he asked, peering around the corner of the foremost container as he and the final two crewmen took up kneeling positions there. Eleven had been most careful with the positioning of these three: they were the ones carrying the *Rabah Jamila*'s rifles. "Why don't they come nearer?"

"Perhaps there's no need," Eleven suggested, turning to look back at the line of crewmen standing or kneeling nervously alongside the containers behind him. All of them looking his direction, all of them waiting expectantly for the professional from South Korean Special Warfare Command to tell them what to do.

All of them concentrating so much on him and their own fears that they were completely oblivious to the fact that Ten was now walking silently up behind them, MP5 at the ready. "Perhaps," Eleven continued, "they have already done their part."

Syed frowned up at him. "What do you mean?"

"This." Eleven swiveled the muzzle of his MP5 to point at the bridge of Syed's nose. "Lower your guns. Now."

The look on the Pakistani's face was priceless: a flicker of open-mouthed disbelief followed immediately by the sharp embarrassment of having been duped by a man he'd been warned about not half an hour earlier. "What's the meaning of this?" he demanded. Not really expecting a response, Eleven knew, but driven by what was left of his pride to at least sound like he wasn't a fool.

"I said put down your weapons," Eleven called out toward the line of crewmen, who were all now looking rather like beached fish themselves. "All of you. Or you will be shot."

One of them, braver or stupider than the others, snapped his shot-gun up and pulled the trigger. There was a loud snap from the firing mechanism, but nothing more.

A second later the crewman's stricken expression was lost to view as he and most of the others threw themselves flat on the deck in response to the overhead burst from Ten's MP5. "The next burst will kill someone," Eleven said mildly as the sound died away. "Captain?"

"You heard him," Syed ordered harshly, slipping his own rifle sling off his shoulder and slapping the weapon onto the deck. "Put them down."

There was a multiple clatter as the crew obeyed, some of the guns landing with a quick staccato as they were dropped like burning coals, others with a muffled clink as they were more carefully lowered. "I was warned you might have sabotaged those weapons," Syed murmured bitterly.

"Yes, I know," Eleven said. "I was listening. Get your men on their feet, hands behind their heads, fingers laced together. You've seen American crime movies—you know the procedure."

"What did he do to the two on the bridge?" Syed asked as he straightened up. "I heard no shots."

"There were none," Eleven assured him. "Your men were simply handcuffed somewhere out of the way. We have no need to kill any of you. Certainly we have no interest in doing so."

Syed snorted. "Of course not."

"If we wanted you dead, we could have slaughtered you any time in the past two days," Eleven reminded him. "Fortunately for you, you've already served your purpose." Which wasn't entirely true, of course. But Syed didn't need to know that. "You'll simply be put into storage while we continue on our way. I believe one of your holds will have enough space to hold your crew in relative comfort."

There was a subtle implication in the words, and Syed caught it immediately. "Only my crew?" he asked, his face going a little gray.

"You're the captain," Eleven said. "You of course will be offered better accommodations. Now move."

"You won't get away with this," Syed warned, his voice still a little uncertain as he walked stiffly toward the stern. Each little clump of crewmen fell sullenly into step alongside him as he passed. "My office knows about you. They'll be sending ships and planes."

"Let them," Eleven said, keeping a respectful distance from the Pakistanis and watching warily for the sudden appearance of a knife.

"As long as they don't reach us for another three hours, they're welcome to come get you."

~

"Sir?"

Lieutenant Mick Wiesnewski looked up from his desk, his face falling naturally into the flat, expressionless mask that he'd found was his best response to Joneser and his heavy-handed sense of dishumor. If this was another of his insulting Polish jokes—

But for once Joneser wasn't grinning that idiot's grin of his. His face was pinched and intense, his earphone pressed hard against the side of his head. "I'm picking up a mayday, sir," he said. "Freighter in trouble."

"Really," Wiesnewski said, getting up from his desk. If this was Joneser's latest variant of a joke setup, he told himself firmly, he would have the other up on charges. You didn't joke about emergencies, not in the U.S. Marine Corps. Certainly not on Okinawa, and especially not under the watch of Lieutenant Mick Wiesnewski. "Got a location?"

"Pulling it now, sir," Crenshaw called from across the room, hunched over his board. "Signal's pretty weak."

Wiesnewski felt something stirring in his stomach. Crenshaw never joked. Maybe this wasn't one of Joneser's gags after all. "ID?"

"They identify themselves as the *Rabah Jamila*," Joneser said. "Pakistani, en route to Tokyo. They say they've got boarders—"

He broke off, fiddling with his board. "Well?" Wiesnewski demanded, glancing at the window but seeing only his own reflection against the outside blackness. Seven o'clock and full night out there, with a hundred miles of low cloud cover. A rotten time for an emergency.

"The signal just cut off," Joneser said tightly. "Just the name, some-thing about being boarded . . . hold it."

He pressed the headset harder to his ear. "Got something else. Sounds like code."

"Run it through the computer," Wiesnewski ordered, turning to Crenshaw. "Crenshaw, did you get a fix?"

"Yes, sir," Crenshaw confirmed. "This new signal . . . it's coming from the same place."

"You sure?"

"Dead sure, Lieutenant," the other said. "Got a solid triangulation from Kadena. Butler's doing a confirmation now."

"Punch it up," Wiesnewski said, coming up behind him and looking up at the display. "Where is it?"

"Right there," Crenshaw said as a glowing spot appeared on the display. "About thirty degrees forty north, one-twenty-five degrees ten east. Five hundred sixty klicks from here, maybe four-eighty from Kagoshima. The middle of freakin' nowhere."

"Well, pass it on to Tokyo," Wiesnewski ordered, scratching his chin. "See what they want to do about it."

"Yes, sir."

Probably not much, Wiesnewski decided regretfully. Not much anyone could do, actually. Whatever was happening out there, it would be long over before a ship could get to them.

And no matter how loud anyone sang about the shores of Tripoli, no one sent the Marines out after pirates anymore.

Still, he hated to just sit by and let another freighter get screwed over. The damn pirates were getting too bold as it was.

From behind him came a startled curse. "I'll be damned in butter," Joneser said. "Lieutenant—computer says that new signal is Chinese military code."

"What?" Wiesnewski crossed back to him. "You must have screwed up."

"I did not," Joneser insisted, waving the printout at him. "See for yourself."

Wiesnewski snatched the paper out of his hand and gave it a quick scan. Damned if he wasn't right.

"Crenshaw, double-check that fix," he ordered, heading for his desk. "Joneser, tell me you had the recorder going when this all started."

"'Course I did," Joneser growled, still not mollified. "Still do."

"Good," Wiesnewski said, scooping up his phone and punching for the command center. This ought to be worth at least a fly-by.

Pirates and Pakistani freighters might not be Marine business. But Chinese military operations definitely were.

~

" . . . not all the track length will be visible through the cloud cover," Cohn was saying to a half dozen young men and women as McPherson walked into the CIA's main satellite analysis room. "But there may be enough. Give it a shot."

The group broke up, the analysts scattering back to their desks, leaving Cohn standing alone glaring down at a clipboard. There were far too many people here, McPherson decided as he walked toward Cohn, for ten minutes after four in the damn morning. They looked far too awake, too. Kids. "You're up early," he commented.

Cohn looked up, the glare lingering for half a second before the face registered and his expression smoothed a bit. "Actually, I'm up late," he corrected, rubbing the stubble on his cheek. "The first twenty-four hours of an investigation are the most important, you know."

"We're well past that marker already," McPherson reminded him.

"We do what we can." Cohn gestured to McPherson. "You've already shaved, so *you* must be up early."

"Couldn't sleep," McPherson said. "Anyway, as someone once said, we can sleep when we're dead."

"Ben Franklin, paraphrased," Cohn identified the quote. "I used to have a partner who'd memorized every sleep quote in Bartlett's. Used to drive me crazy on stake-outs. Here's another one: the more you sleep, the less you live."

McPherson grimaced. "That one could easily apply to the current situation. What was that about tracks? Checking on train traffic?"

"It's a long shot," Cohn admitted. "But if the thieves weren't in any hurry to get out of India, there's a lot more anonymity in bulk transport. That might have seemed a better deal to them than the convenience of a private car or plane."

"Or a stolen military truck," McPherson said.

Cohn snorted. "Yeah, I saw that reference," he said. "If you ask me, Rao's jumping at shadows on that one. People steal military vehicles all the time. There's no reason to think this particular vanishing act's connected to the bomb."

"Still, Rao thought it important enough to put into his report."

"That report was two pounds of data in a one-pound bag," Cohn sniffed. "He put everything in there but his own shoe size. Personally, I think New Delhi's setting us up to take the fall if we don't find the bomb before it goes boom. Did your analysts get in okay yesterday, by the way? I never made it down there to check."

"Yes, Atkinson's got them settled in," McPherson said. "I appreciate you finding space for them."

Cohn waved a hand. "Better to have as many people under one roof as possible. Makes for faster communication. What is it, Evans?"

McPherson turned to see a young man in vest and shirtsleeves coming toward them with a piece of paper in his hand. "This just in from Taipei, sir," he said, offering the paper. "Don't know if it means anything, but a freighter captain found some bodies floating in the Taiwan Strait that had apparently run into machine-gun fire."

Cohn took the proffered sheet and gave it a quick look. "Possibly grenades, too," he said, passing the paper to McPherson. "Do we have a list of recent ship traffic through that area?"

"Right here," Evans said, holding up a flash drive. "Who wants it?"

Cohn glanced around the room. "Give it to Heuval," he said, pointing. "Have her look for anything that could have made it from India to that point since the bomb disappeared."

"Right." Evans headed off.

"It won't be anything big," McPherson pointed out, doing a quick calculation in his head. "It must be eighteen hundred nautical miles from any east Indian port to Singapore, and at least that much back up to where these bodies were found. To get there in three and a half days would be crowding, what, thirty-six knots. That's pretty good for a major freighter."

"A fast yacht, then," Cohn said. "Or a military ship."

McPherson frowned. "Are you suggesting someone's military could be involved in this?"

"Why not?" Cohn countered. "Stealing a nuke requires certain basic skills. A working knowledge of military procedure would be one of them."

"Yes, but there's a big difference between getting a team together to sneak into a weapons facility and having your own naval ship on hand to take out on a pleasure cruise."

"A matter of degree only." Cohn held up a hand. "Let's hold off on this argument until we have some reason to think we've got a connection. In that part of the world it could just as easily be pirates or even a summary execution."

With grenades? McPherson thought. But he kept the thought to himself. Anyway, Secretary Jameson's State Department odds makers figured the bomb was probably headed for the Middle East.

"Do you know if the NSA's made any headway on the commercial and charter air transport end?" Cohn asked into the silence. "Logan was going to liaise with them on that one, but I haven't had a chance to touch base with him yet."

"I talked to him this afternoon," McPherson said. "They've pretty well figured out which ones the thieves *didn't* use. Of course, that assumes New Delhi's window is accurate. If they're off by a few hours as to when the nuke disappeared, things get more complicated."

"To the tune of probably twenty additional vectors per hour," Cohn agreed. "Too bad the thieves didn't leave a body or two lying around on their way out. We'd have had a lot better handle on their timetable."

"Good enough reason not to do it," McPherson said. "Certainly anyone planning to detonate a nuke isn't likely to worry about an extra death or two along the way."

"So you think Vaughn was right? That they're actually going to fire it?"

"I wish I didn't," McPherson said soberly. "But I can't see it making sense any other way. There haven't been any ransom or blackmail demands, no front-page news releases by frothing terrorist or separatist groups trying to scare the world spitless. What else is there?"

"No ransom or blackmail demands we know about, anyway," Cohn corrected. "If *I* were head of a government who'd gotten that note, I sure wouldn't be announcing it to the world at large."

"Point," McPherson conceded. "Though between your people and the NSA's satellite monitors, you'd think we'd have picked up something if it were out there. I wonder if the Indians have told anyone besides us."

"Rao implied they hadn't," Cohn said. "He could have been fudging the truth, though. I'll ask him point-blank next time we talk."

"Sir?" one of the analysts called, lifting a hand. "I think I may have something."

He had a large-scale satellite image on his display by the time they reached his side. "Satellite view of the Sambalpur region, light-enhanced," he identified it. "About a hundred fifty miles from the Raipur facility. That's the Hirakud Reservoir there to the northwest. This shot was taken four hours after Delhi's presumed time of the theft."

He manipulated his mouse and clicked a couple of times, and the view zoomed in. "This looks to be a local airstrip near the reservoir," the analyst said. "You'll notice there's a plane sitting there waiting to take off."

"A corporate jet, no less," Cohn commented. "Can you clear up the image any?"

"The scrub's running now," the other said, tapping the screen. "What I'm most interested in is right here, beside the plane to the north."

The computer beeped, and he tapped a few keys. The image dissolved slightly, then came into sharper focus.

"I'll be damned," Cohn said, leaning over the analyst's shoulder. "Looks like Rao's missing army truck."

"Or one of a hundred other trucks in the region," McPherson reminded him. Still, he could feel a cautious excitement starting to mix with the coffee in his bloodstream. "Wasn't the army out in force by then combing the countryside?"

"That's the point, sir: they weren't," the analyst said, pointing to the photo's time stamp. "According to the report, they didn't discover the bomb had been stolen until nearly half an hour *after* this picture was taken."

"He's right." Cohn straightened and raised his voice. "Evans?"

"Yes, sir?" the other called back from across the room.

"Get New Delhi on the phone," Cohn ordered. "Have Minister Rao check on whether there were any authorized military vehicles in the Hirakud Reservoir region at zero plus four. And get the name of that airstrip and find out if there was anyone on duty that night."

"Right."

"I doubt there would be anyone there after dark," the analyst said. "The place doesn't look like it's set up for night flights."

"It's still worth checking," Cohn said. "Can you tell what kind of jet that is?"

"The computer's working on an ID," the analyst said, his fingers stuttering over the keyboard. "There we go. A Cessna 525 CitationJet."

"How much clearer can you get that photo?" McPherson asked. "If we can get the number, we can track it."

The analyst leaned closer to the screen. "Probably a little dicey at this angle," he warned. "But it won't hurt to try."

"When's the next set of shots?" Cohn asked.

"About twenty minutes later, I think," the analyst said. "I don't know who's got that group."

"They're over here," a young woman at a console two rows over spoke up. "You said a CitationJet, Cliff?"

"Right," the analyst confirmed.

"Okay," she said. "We're on it."

The minutes ticked by. McPherson spent the first few of them walking back and forth between the two stations until he realized the analysts were flipping through their photos and working their magic computer scrubbers too fast for him to follow anyway. Giving up, he crossed the room to the huge map of the Indian subcontinent that had been put up on one wall and tried to work through the possibilities in his mind. The truck had taken the bomb east, assuming they were on the right track here. But at that point the plane could head any direction it wanted. It could turn northwest, toward Pakistan or Iran, or northeast, toward China.

Or due east toward the Taiwan Strait . . .

"Got it," one of the analysts called. "One Cessna CitationJet, just approaching Durgapur."

"Which direction is that?" McPherson asked.

"East-northeast of Sambalpur," the analyst said. "Looks to be bypassing Calcutta and making for the Bangladesh border."

"Got it," McPherson said, locating the spot on the map and heading back to join Cohn. "Looks like China after all."

"Or a transfer to someone else," Cohn said. "I can't see the Bangladeshis frothing to get into the nuclear race." He frowned across at the map. "On the other hand, there's another potential hotspot that general direction we haven't considered."

McPherson followed his line of sight. "Tibet?"

"Exactly," Cohn said. "Someone might have decided it was time to take matters beyond UN speeches and bumper stickers."

"Um," McPherson said, rubbing his chin. "I wonder if the Dalai Lama's going to be at the UN human rights conference."

Cohn's eyebrows lifted. "Are you suggesting he might be involved with nuclear terrorism?"

"We haven't been above suggesting Reverend Lane or Rabbi Salomon might be involved," McPherson pointed out. "Or Kurdish Moslems or Kashmiri Sikhs, for that matter. The world has become a strange place."

Cohn wrinkled his nose. "Granted," he admitted. "It wouldn't be the first time some noble leader's more unstable followers have gone off the deep end."

"Sir?" Cliff spoke up. "I've got the photo scrubbed as clean as it's going to get. It's not absolutely clear, but I think we can get a good approximation of the plane's number. It's also got a fairly distinct color scheme: red overall, with a yellow tail and a wide yellow stripe along each side."

"Good," Cohn said, heading to his side. "Feed everything to Evans for transmission to New Delhi, and get Logan to pull in the NSA. Let's see if we can track him."

~

Their yacht was nearly a hundred nautical miles from the *Rabah Jamila* and heading more or less toward Okinawa when Eleven heard the distant rumble of the plane. "There they go," he commented to Twelve, peering through the ship's rigging at the clouds. No sign of lights, but at the jet's distance that wasn't unexpected. "Earlier than I expected."

"Some risk-taker must be on duty tonight," Twelve said. "Usually they're more cautious these days about spending aviation fuel. I'll go get the fish."

He disappeared below. "Well?" Eleven asked, turning to Thirteen, standing beside the charcoal grill he and Twelve had set up on the ship's fantail, just over the starboard engine. "What are you waiting for?"

"I'm just wondering if this is such a good idea," Thirteen said, gesturing toward the coals with his lighter. "This and the heater both. They're going to put out infrared beacons that'll shine for miles."

"That's the point," Eleven pointed out patiently. "Would you rather that plane spotted us on its way home and found a sailing yacht with hot engines?"

"My point is that if we don't light it he might not even notice us," Thirteen countered. "The only reason he's out here is to have a look at the *Rabah Jamila.*"

"And when the *Rabah Jamila* doesn't respond to his hails, he's going to do a spiral search or else call in help," Eleven said. "Sooner or later someone will spot us. So stop arguing, stick with the plan, and light it."

Clearly still not happy, Thirteen obeyed, touching the flame from his lighter to the edge of the grill. With a *whoosh* the fuel-soaked briquettes caught, sending blue-yellow flames blazing up nearly chest high. "If he doesn't see that, he shouldn't be flying without a cane," he grumbled. "Now what?"

"We prepare the rest of the stage," Eleven said, finishing knotting the fancy yachtsman's scarf around his neck and reaching for the almost gaudy jacket that went with it. "Twelve? Where are those fish?"

"Here," Twelve called back, emerging from below with a plate of raw fish, cleaned but otherwise whole, and a set of grilling utensils. He had put on a jacket that was even gaudier than Eleven's. "I caught them myself this afternoon, so they're even appropriate for these waters if anyone bothers to investigate."

"They won't," Eleven said with a snort, crossing to the open-air space heater sitting over the portside engine and cranking it to full power. "Put your jacket on, Thirteen, and sit down over there."

The three of them were nearly finished with their meal before the plane's lights appeared against the black cloud cover, moving their way at a high rate of speed. "Easy," Eleven murmured as he sliced off another bite with his fork. "Ignore him unless he makes a second pass. If he does, wave. We're idle yachtsmen on holiday, remember."

But the jet wasn't even that interested in them. It roared past half a kilometer to starboard, then disappeared again into the darkness. "That was almost too easy," Thirteen commented suspiciously as the rumble of engines faded away.

"They'll be sorry later," Eleven assured him. "Twelve, when's the next satellite pass?"

The other pulled his laptop from beneath the seat and keyed for the program. "There are two coming up that will have a view of us," he said. "The first is in twenty minutes, the second in thirty-five."

"Unless they've retasked something," Ten warned.

"They may do that later," Eleven said. "Probably not yet."

"So we go?" Thirteen asked.

"We go," Eleven confirmed, throwing a critical gaze skyward. "But slowly, very slowly. Those clouds look like they could be partially broken up by then, and we don't want unexpected progress setting off any alarms. Set course for Yaku as planned, and we'll pose for a few more photos."

"Right," Thirteen said. "Two fish left, gentlemen. Who wants them?"

THE
FOURTH
DAY

12

BUILDING D HAD a double security team on duty when Delgado arrived just after eight-thirty Saturday morning. They checked his ID carefully before releasing him to go upstairs, where the two guards outside the Tarnhelm lab door repeated the scrutiny. The two cops Delgado had assigned, in contrast, were nowhere to be seen.

But then, they weren't supposed to be seen. Delgado was rather hoping the thieves would try again.

The main lab, when he was finally allowed in, was surprisingly well populated. Director Tarlington and the three Tarnhelm techs were there, seated around the large central lab table arrangement with five other scholarly-looking men and two equally distinguished women. A dozen different folders and schematics were spread out in front of the group.

"Detective Delgado," Tarlington greeted him. "What can we do for you?"

"Director," Delgado nodded in return. "I'm sorry, I didn't mean to interrupt your meeting. I had a question about the Cloak and wondered if I could get someone to fire it up for me again."

"Certainly," Tarlington said, gesturing to Kingsley. "Set it up for him, Scott, will you?"

"Sure," Kingsley said, pushing back his chair and crossing to the office.

"How's the investigation progressing?" a silver-haired man with piercing blue eyes asked.

"We're putting things together," Delgado said. "Dr.—?"

"Stryker," the other identified himself. "Chairman of the board." He waved a hand around the table. "Which, to anticipate your next question, consists of the other men and women here."

"We thought this would be the best place to discuss Tarnhelm's future," Tarlington added.

"What's there to discuss?" Delgado asked. "The thing obviously works."

"The issue isn't whether to keep going, Detective," Stryker said solemnly. "The question is who will take over the project, and how many of the original team will continue to be involved. If any."

Delgado looked at Burke and Esteban. Both had standard corporate-neutral faces in place, but it didn't take any detective skill to see the resentment smoldering beneath the surface. "Aren't they the logical core for any new team?"

"I was under the impression they were considered suspects in yesterday's unpleasantness," Tarlington reminded him.

"One of them may conceivably be involved," Delgado acknowledged. "That leaves two who aren't."

"When you sort it out, be sure to let us know," Stryker said, his smile about two frog hairs away from being patronizing. "In the meantime, if you'll excuse us . . . ?"

"Of course," Delgado said, nodding as he backed toward the office. "Sorry for the intrusion."

Kingsley was seated at the workstation as Delgado closed the office door behind him. Unlike the other two techs, he was definitely not wearing his corporate face. "Almost ready," he said.

"Thanks." Delgado pulled over a chair and sat down. "Insult to injury, eh?"

"What?

"Yesterday's shock being followed by today's," Delgado said. "Can't be much fun having to sit there and watch them take your project away from you."

Kingsley threw him a glower. "Yeah, thanks to you," he growled. "It was your big fat idea that one of us was involved."

"Who else could have done it?"

Kingsley started to speak, apparently thought better of it, made a face, and changed his mind back again. "I don't want to point fingers," he said. "But Angie Chandler was here, too, you know. And from what I'm hearing, she's disappeared."

"Yes, she has," Delgado said, wondering which of his men was talking about things like that in Kingsley's presence. "Her motive for the murders?"

"She's Chinese," Kingsley said. "First generation, with both sets of grandparents still there. Has it occurred to you that maybe the Chi-Coms put pressure on her?"

"It's occurred to us, yes," Delgado said. "Special Agent Talbot's looking into it."

"Oh," Kingsley said, looking a bit flustered now that his prepared tirade had been punctured in mid-launch. "I just thought—well, that you should know about that."

"I appreciate it," Delgado said. "We about ready?"

"Yeah, all set," Kingsley said, unfolding the Cloak prototype and draping it over the workstation. "Okay, it's running."

"Thanks," Delgado said. Pulling out a flashlight, he reached over and turned off the overhead lights.

"What are you doing?" Kingsley asked.

"I've been running through the theft scenario in my mind," Delgado said, making his way gingerly toward the desk. As his eyes adjusted, he found there was enough light coming under the door for adequate navigation. "Given the Cloak's sampling delay time, I wondered what would have happened if the gate guard had shined a flashlight into the back of the semi."

"You could have just asked and saved yourself a trip," Kingsley said. "But be my guest."

They sat in silence until the black shadow that was the Cloak vanished into the other shadows of the wall behind it. Delgado twisted his flashlight to its tightest beam, aimed, and flicked it on.

The beam went straight through the Cloak as if it wasn't there, illuminating the wall behind the workstation. He turned the light off, then back on again, with the same result.

"It's pure light, you see," Kingsley said. "No visual pattern the computer has to deal with. So it basically goes straight through the fiber optics, hits the distant landscape, and reflects back through again."

"Yes, I see," Delgado said, trying one last time before stepping back and turning on the overhead lights. As with the flashlight, the fluorescents came on to show an apparently empty desk. "Well, so much for that approach."

"Actually, there *is* a slight delay in the beam as the light wends its way through the computer and the software has a quick look at it," Kingsley added. "But it's measured in microseconds. Way too fast for you to notice."

"I guess that makes sense," Delgado said. "Thanks."

"No problem." Kingsley's gazed thoughtfully at the detective. "This wasn't any late-night theory. The gate guard said he *did* shine a light in, didn't he?"

"As a matter of fact, he did," Delgado said, inclining his head toward the other. "But I like to check these things myself. Who do you think they'll give the Cloak project to?"

"Some big name," Kingsley said disgustedly. "That's how it works in this business."

"Pretty annoying?"

"What do you think?" Kingsley retorted. "I've been working on this for nearly a year, and Jack and Ramon aren't far behind me. We put in as much sweat and blood as any of the scientists did."

"Not quite as much blood, of course," Delgado murmured.

Kingsley reddened, but was clearly not going to get sidetracked. "The point is that they owe us the chance to finish what we started," he insisted. "But you watch. They'll go outside the lab for this one, sure as hell they will. Stryker's practically salivating over the chance to dangle this over Silicon Valley and see who he can poach."

"If it makes you feel any better, I think it's more likely he'll get to watch the government spirit the whole thing off to the Nevada desert," Delgado warned.

"Not a chance," Kingsley said firmly. "Not with Stryker and Tarlington manning the barricades. They might agree to moving it to Building A, where there are fifty more security hoops to jump through. But if you think they'll let someone just walk away with a breakthrough like this, you're crazy."

"Of course, someone just did exactly that," Delgado pointed out.

Kingsley dropped his gaze to the desktop. "You know what I mean."

"Sure." Delgado gestured to the cloak. "I'm a little confused, though. You call it a research project, not a manufacturing or marketing project. But the research is basically finished, isn't it? The Cloak works. What else is there to do?"

"Depends on whether you want an expensive parlor trick or something practical," Kingsley said. "For starters, you already know you can't move with it, so that part still has to be figured out. There's the problem that if whatever's underneath the Cloak radiates heat you can still use infrared detectors to pick it up. Dr. Chandler wanted to experiment with baffles or short-term insulators in the material, and Dr. Fowler had this really wild idea about actually programming out infrared emissions."

"How?"

"No idea," Kingsley admitted. "I couldn't follow half his explanation, and the half I could sounded lunatic. Even by Fowler's standards." He started ticking off fingers. "Then there's the question of radar absorption if you want to use Cloak technology for stealth planes. Along with simple movement, we need to find if there's a theoretical limit to sampling and refreshing speed—if you can make them fast enough, you might be able to Cloak a chopper and get even the blades to disappear. Research into fiber optic wavelength profiles might find us something that'll handle infrared like it does visible light and solve half the heat problem right there. You want more?"

"No, no, you've made your point," Delgado conceded. "Thanks for your time."

The group around the table didn't seem to notice as Delgado slipped across the lab toward the door, though he was mildly surprised they didn't put their conversation on hold until he was out of earshot. There were dozens of corporate types, he knew, who would give their golden parachutes to eavesdrop on a high-level board meeting like this.

Maybe someone was.

He paused at the door, glancing around the room with new eyes. Over in the back corner, for instance, in that apparently empty space under the work table. Someone could be sitting there under a Baby Bear Cloak, taking down every word they said.

No—that was ridiculous. Whoever it was would have had to get through locked doors and a whole array of freshly alert guards. Even an invisible man had his limitations.

Unless he'd been there all the time, hiding under the Cloak since the murders. Sitting quietly, watching and listening as the cops bustled about collecting their evidence.

Which of the board members, he wondered, had suggested it be held here? He took half a step back into the room.

And stopped. No, that was even more ridiculous. His people had been over this room from top to bottom, including the whole floor. Unless he was hanging from the overhead lights, there was no invisible man hiding in there.

He left the lab, mentally shaking his head. This case was going to make him paranoid yet.

He had just been passed through the gate when his phone rang. Pulling it out, he flicked it on. "Delgado."

"Garcia," the chief's familiar growl came back. "Where are you?"

"Just leaving Sand/Star," Delgado told him. "I wanted to confirm part of the gate guard's story with the prototype Cloak. It checks out."

"You find out anything else?"

"Sand/Star's board is discussing how to proceed with the project. Informed opinion is that the current lab techs are going to be frozen out of the reorganization."

"A motive there, you think?"

"Could be," Delgado agreed. "If one of the techs suspected the higher-ups would give the project away once it showed promise, he might have been inclined to go looking for a better deal elsewhere."

"We need to do some serious background checks on those three."

"Talbot's on it," Delgado said. "He's got the Bureau's best analyst digging through their records. If there's anything there, she'll find it."

"Good," Garcia said. "That'll leave us free to concentrate on Mrs. Chandler and her abductor."

"We're sure it's an abduction, then?"

"It's been twenty-four hours now since she vanished with this Ross person," Garcia reminded him. "Any legitimate protector should have brought her in long before now." He paused. "But then, he's hardly a legitimate protector."

"You mean because he's not California licensed?"

"I mean because he's not licensed anywhere," Garcia said. "Ng's run the list. There's no Adam Ross or Charles Sullivan with his description licensed as a private investigator in any of the fifty states or Canada. And just for good measure, the Sullivan driver's license is also a phony."

"Doesn't necessarily mean he has any designs on Mrs. Chandler."

"If you think that, you need to go to Greenleaf Center and take a look at his handiwork," Garcia countered. "He did a very professional job of tapping into the bank's security setup. And, I might point out, he ignored all the cameras aimed at the vault or cashiers and went straight to the one in her office. No, he's had his eye on her for a long time. We need to drop a load of bricks on him, and fast."

Delgado grimaced. This was all they needed. "Can't argue with that," he conceded. "I'll get some people on him."

"No need," Garcia told him. "Ng's already requested the job, and I've given it to him."

"Really?" Delgado asked, frowning. "Ng's not a detective."

"Not yet," Garcia agreed. "But I've been wanting to move him up. He's already put in a lot of time on this, and he really wants to nail the guy."

"I thought you didn't like your people getting personally involved in cases."

"He's professionally involved, not personally," Garcia said. "Correct me if I'm wrong, but aren't you the one who wanted all the help you could get? At least, that was the excuse you spun when you wanted to borrow Talbot."

"I didn't mean it that way, sir," Delgado said. "I'd be happy to have Ng aboard."

"That's more like it," Garcia said. "Teamwork—I love it. Anyway, Ng's going to go after Ross, which will leave you free to concentrate on Mrs. Chandler. Check with parents and siblings, see if there's any place she might have suggested they hole up. Ross has probably shown his true colors by now, but he might still be playing Sir Galahad and letting her think she's got some control of the situation."

"Yes, sir," Delgado said. "I'll make some calls as soon as I get back to the office."

"Good. Oh, there's just one other thing."

Delgado sighed. The chief must be watching his *Columbo* DVDs again. "Yes, sir?"

"This business of Mrs. Chandler's whereabouts yesterday morning," Garcia said. "How is it you let her get from her house to her office without at least a brief stopover here first?"

"We didn't, sir," Delgado said. "Rather, she didn't. It appears now that Poole didn't speak to her at her home that morning after all."

"Then who *did* he speak to?" Garcia demanded. "The maid?"

"Probably the murderers."

There was a long silence. "The murderers," Garcia said at last. "So they've got a woman on their team? Or can't Poole tell the difference between soprano and baritone?"

"I'm guessing they used a voice changer," Delgado said. "It's not Poole's fault—he had no idea what Mrs. Chandler's real voice sounds like."

"You've checked the house, I presume?"

"Yes, sir," Delgado said. "No forced entry—probably a lock pick—and no mess left behind. If they were looking for something, they did an extremely tidy job of it. In retrospect, it looks like they went there for the sole purpose of killing her."

"And to take messages."

"It was a risk, but one they had to take," Delgado said. "If we hadn't gotten hold of her at home, we would have sent someone to intercept her at her bank. I can hardly blame them for not wanting a police presence at the scene of their planned murder."

"You should have sent someone anyway."

"Agreed," Delgado said. "But at the time, none of us realized she was in danger."

Garcia grunted. "So someone sat around waiting for your call, played the shocked widow for Poole, then high-tailed it out the back door."

"Basically," Delgado said. "Meanwhile, more of the gang staked out Greenleaf Mall."

"So where *was* she that night?"

"Probably a motel," Delgado said. "We're checking on that."

"Which means, aside from everything else, we released the name of one of the victims prematurely," Garcia said sourly. "She hadn't actually been contacted at the time."

"True," Delgado said. "Under the circumstances, I hardly think that'll be a major consideration."

"You never know what some people will consider major," Garcia said heavily. "Listening to the news is a hell of a way to find out your husband's been murdered."

"Yes, sir," Delgado said. "I'm sorry."

"Save your apologies for Mrs. Chandler," Garcia said. "I'll expect you to have some leads on her by this afternoon."

"Yes, sir," Delgado said. "I'll get right on it."

~

McPherson was on the phone in his temporary CIA office, trying to catch up on the burgeoning backlog of regular FBI business, when the call came to meet Cohn in the satellite room.

"Got two interesting bits of news for you," the CIA director said, handing him a printout. "First of all, we've got a possible make on our pirate killer. Freighter named the *Rabah Jamila*, Pakistani flag, en route from Karachi to Tokyo. Our projections put it in approximately the right place at the right time."

"And you're getting the *right time* part how?" McPherson asked, scanning past the *Rabah Jamila*'s stats to the CIA analysis. "Autopsy reports?"

"Right," Cohn said. "We picked up the bodies with a chopper and had Taipei do a quick check. From exposure, blood readings, and whatever the hell else they look for, they figure the victims died on Friday between midnight and six a.m. local time."

McPherson tried to remember what time zone the Taiwan Strait was on. But he'd been up since three a.m., and his brain wasn't up to it. "How much is that in American?"

"Forty hours ago," Cohn said. "Plus or minus three. Backtrack the currents from where the bodies were found, and the *Rabah Jamila*'s projected course nails it pretty damn close."

"Awful lot of 'ifs' in that," McPherson said, handing back the printout. "So how does this relate to the problem at hand?"

"That's the interesting part," Cohn said, taking his arm and walking him toward the wall which had earlier held a map of the Indian subcontinent. That map had now been replaced by one showing all of eastern Asia, from India to Japan. "Follow me on this one. The *Rabah Jamila* left Karachi in Pakistan, made a stopover in Colombo, and nine days ago docked in Vishakhapatnam, the closest major port to the Raipur nuclear facility. They left a day later, heading for Da Nang and then Tokyo."

"Which means they left Vishakhapatnam four days before the nuke was stolen," McPherson reminded him.

"Maybe," Cohn said. "Maybe not. Do we—or the Indians—really *know* when the nuke disappeared?"

McPherson shrugged. "They say they do."

"They *say* they do," Cohn echoed. "But all right, let's assume the nuke disappeared exactly when they said it did. Question: who took it, and how did they enter the country?"

"We're talking India here, Larry, not downtown Tehran," McPherson pointed out. "You don't exactly have to sneak in."

"You do if you're carrying equipment for breaking into a high-security facility," Cohn said. "We got Rao's preliminary report on the entry method an hour ago, and it was damn sophisticated. And it did not use the sort of stuff customs ordinarily waves through."

"Fine," McPherson said. "I temporarily concede the point. So why pick on the *Rabah Jamila* instead of any number of other ships?"

"Keep following," Cohn said. "The *Rabah Jamila* picks up, say, an al-Qaeda group or a Japanese radical commando team and its equipment at Colombo—we know a couple of those groups have been working with Tamil rebels in the north of Sri Lanka. They head to Vishakhapatnam and put them ashore, then continue on their scheduled route toward Tokyo. En route, they run afoul of pirates; but since not all the radicals went ashore in India, there's still plenty of military hardware aboard and people who know how to use them. Exit, one pirate gang."

"Why wouldn't all the radicals have gone ashore?"

"Because the ship is headed for Tokyo," Cohn said. "And Japan may very well be the target."

"And you figure this why?"

"Because we've tracked down the CitationJet's number," Cohn said. "It appears that it, too, is heading straight across China, also bound for Tokyo."

"The Chinese are letting them?"

"Why not?" Cohn said sourly. "It's their plane."

McPherson shook his head. "You've lost me."

"It's one of Zhardi Manufacturing's corporate jets," Cohn explained. "One of their senior members was in southern Iran for a meeting with some Mideast oil executives. Their filed flight plan was from Bandar-e 'Abbas on the Strait of Hormuz to Varanasi, India, about four hundred thirty miles southeast of Delhi. A quick refueling, then on to Chongqing, Shanghai, and Tokyo. The NSA's got people tapping into the various airport computer records to check the actual landing and take-off times."

He waved at the wall map. "Obviously, they made an unscheduled stop at the Hirakud Reservoir along the way."

"To pick up a nuke?"

"So it would seem."

McPherson shook his head. "I'm sorry, but this doesn't make any sense at all. What would the Chinese want with an Indian nuke in Japan?"

Cohn sighed. "As you suggested in the wee hours this morning, Frank, the world has become a very strange place. My current guess is that we've got a weird ménage à trois going between Japanese radicals, some faction of the Chinese government or military, and possibly someone in the Middle East, as well."

"This gets worse by the minute," McPherson growled. "What are everyone's motives?"

"The radicals' motive for setting off a nuke is obvious," Cohn said. "Destabilization of the Japanese government, a basis for future extortion demands—the usual laundry list. The Chinese may be hoping that the fact that it's an Indian bomb will frost-kill the current medium-warm relationship between Tokyo and New Delhi. Or maybe they want to see the West's reaction to something like this for future reference, or they might just want to see how Indian nukes work in the field."

"Or the government may not be involved at all," McPherson pointed out. "This could be some cozy game being played by Zhardi Manufacturing."

"That's another possibility," Cohn agreed. "I've got people looking over Zhardi's finances and investments to see if they stand to gain from Japanese chaos."

"And your Middle East connection?"

"Their motives are even less obvious than Beijing's," Cohn admitted. "I don't know. But like I said Wednesday, there hasn't been a really good attention-grabbing terrorist act lately, and maybe someone misses the headlines. Of course, as I also said, we're only guessing at Middle Eastern involvement. The Iranian connection could be purely because it was a convenient way to get Zhardi's CitationJet where it would head home through India at the right time."

McPherson looked at the map again. "So where's the Zhardi jet now?"

Cohn hissed between his teeth. "That's part of the problem," he said. "As I said, its original flight plan had it scheduled for Tokyo, but at the moment it's still on the ground in Chongqing. The airport records indicate engine trouble."

"You're sure the plane is actually there?"

"Oh, it's there," Cohn assured him. "We lost it in cloud cover for the next satellite pass after those two photos you saw this morning, but after that we had clear sailing and were able to track it pretty much the whole way to Chongqing."

"How about during the time the *Rabah Jamila* was in Da Nang?"

Cohn smiled tightly. "Great minds, Frank. Yes, I also wondered if it could have changed course after the Durgapur photo and headed for Vietnam. But no, we've got photos of it in the air the whole time the freighter was in harbor."

"So you definitely think they have the nuke?"

"Or they're a complete decoy," Cohn said. "Remember my point a minute ago that the nuke might actually have disappeared several days before the Indians missed it?"

"Yes," McPherson said. "I didn't buy it then, either."

"Fine—don't buy it," Cohn said. "But rent it for a minute. Assume the nuke disappeared before the Indians missed it, however that particular sleight of hand was performed. Now instead of putting a raiding party ashore, the *Rabah Jamila* is actually there to pick up the prize and part of the commando team, while the rest stay behind to fake an infiltration a few days later."

"And this gains them what?"

"It gains them us running around like idiots looking for an exit vector in the wrong time frame," Cohn said. "The Zhardi plane makes an unscheduled stop at the Hirakud Reservoir to help bolster that false perception. Meanwhile, the *Rabah Jamila* steams its way up the Southeast Asian coastline without a single glance being thrown its direction."

McPherson rubbed his chin. It was not, he had to admit, nearly as crazy as it sounded. "Until they have the bad luck to run into a pirate gang."

"Right," Cohn nodded. "And even that wouldn't have fazed them if someone with a keen eye hadn't spotted the bodies and phoned it in."

"Mr. Cohn?" someone called from a desk across the room. "Phone, sir—Minister Rao."

"Put it on speaker," Cohn instructed as he and McPherson headed that direction. "Want to make a small wager he's calling to say the nuke disappeared four days early?"

McPherson smiled tightly. "Sorry. My mother won't let me bet real money."

In retrospect, it was a bet he should have taken. "We have new information for you," Rao's clipped voice came from the speaker. "We've checked with all military bases and commanders, and the army truck you photographed near Sambalpur was not authorized to be there at that time. Almost certainly it was the one reported stolen."

"Thank you, sir," Cohn said. "That would appear to confirm that the plane it rendezvoused with is involved somehow."

"Indeed," Rao said. "We've also uncovered one other piece of information that may or may not mean anything. Five days before the theft there was a security disturbance at the Raipur facility."

"What sort of disturbance?" Cohn asked.

"It seemed unimportant at the time, merely a guard jumping at shadows," Rao said. "Everything was found to be in order afterwards."

"Including the nuclear weapons?"

"Those were the first things checked," Rao said, his dry voice going a little drier.

"And you're absolutely certain they were all still there?" Cohn persisted.

"Do you doubt my word?" Rao demanded, his voice going from dry to frosty. "Or is it merely our competence that you hold in question?"

"Neither, sir," Cohn said with a quiet sigh. McPherson suppressed a smile—Cohn hated having clever theories explode in his face. "We were simply wondering if the actual theft could have taken place earlier than everyone thought."

"Interesting you should bring up that question," Rao said, apparently mollified. "We've also been wondering if this disturbance was in fact a failed attempt to infiltrate the facility. Working on that assumption, we've done some further checking, and have discovered that a Pakistani ship named the *Rabah Jamila* was conveniently in Vishakhapatnam harbor at that same time."

McPherson and Cohn exchanged glances. "I'm not sure I see the significance," Cohn said, his voice carefully neutral. "Why pick up on this particular ship?"

"To begin with, as I said, it is Pakistani owned and operated," Rao said. "The Pakistanis have a long history of unfriendliness."

"I understand that," Cohn said. "But surely Pakistani ships dock in Indian harbors all the time."

"There are other circumstances," Rao said, starting to sound huffy again. "It was scheduled to load eight containers, yet the records show it picked up only six. The other two were mysteriously not available."

"Have you backtracked the paper on them?" McPherson asked.

"Who is that?" Rao asked.

"FBI Director Frank McPherson," McPherson identified himself.

"Ah," Rao said. "No, we've not yet finished that task. At the moment they appear to be legitimate, but I do not believe they will ultimately be found to be so."

"I see," Cohn said. "Interestingly enough, our own investigation has also turned up the *Rabah Jamila*'s name, though from a different angle."

"Indeed," Rao said. "From which angle is this?"

"It involves a possible pirate incident in the Taiwan Strait," Cohn said. "Bodies were found—"

"Pirates?" Rao sounded startled. "Are you certain?"

"Not yet, no," Cohn said. "But in those waters it's a reasonable assumption."

"Perhaps," Rao said thoughtfully. "Though in the Taiwan Strait there is also the possibility of direct Chinese involvement."

Privately, McPherson raised his evaluation of this man a notch. Here he and Cohn had only just started wondering about a Chinese connection, and Rao was already well along that track. Not a bad bit of extrapolation for a career politician.

Of course, Rao was a career politician in India, with the whole weight of that region's history on his shoulders. Maybe he saw Chinese involvement under every rock.

"That is a possibility, sir," Cohn acknowledged cautiously. "However, until we have more information we don't want to focus too strongly in any one direction."

"You're right," Rao said reluctantly. "Still, I strongly suggest that you consider the *Rabah Jamila* to be at least peripherally involved."

"We're considering everything," Cohn promised.

"Very well," Rao said. "I believe you also wanted us to search for information about the CitationJet that appeared in the photos with the stolen truck?"

Someone appeared at Cohn's side and slipped a piece of paper into his hand. "Yes, sir, we did," he said as he skimmed down the paper. "Our records show it touching down for refueling at Varanasi at approximately—"

"Just a moment, sir," Cohn cut him off. "I've just been handed a message from General Vaughn at the Pentagon. Four hours ago a Marine station on Okinawa picked up a distress call from a ship identifying itself as the *Rabah Jamila*."

"What?" McPherson demanded.

"The transmission was weak, but they implied they were under attack from boarders," Cohn continued. "Then a new signal originating from the same location began, this one in what appears to be Chinese military code."

Rao muttered something under his breath. "I knew it. The Chinese and Pakistanis are working together."

"Sounds more like a falling-out to me," McPherson murmured.

"It does, doesn't it," Cohn agreed, skimming down the page. "Anyway, the Navy scrambled a P-3 Orion from Kadena as soon as they got the signal. There was no one on deck, and no answer to repeated hails."

"Any vessels nearby?" Rao asked.

"Some other freighters on the same route, but nothing within ten miles," Cohn said. "Vaughn's got the U.S.S *Vincennes* on its way for a closer look."

"What are the Chinese doing?" McPherson asked.

"They apparently also picked up the transmission," Cohn said, "and unlike us, they probably know what it said. One of their Jiangwei-class frigates, the Anqing, has left Shanghai on an intercept course. Looks like it and the Vincennes will get there at roughly the same time."

"And what has the *Rabah Jamila* been doing through all this?" Rao asked.

"Not responding, and heading a shade west of due north at full speed." Cohn looked at McPherson over the top of the paper. "Best guess is that it plans to come around Changsan-got and make for Namp'o."

McPherson felt his throat tighten. North Korea. "This could get awkward."

"To put it mildly," Cohn growled. "Minister Rao, we'll have to call you back."

"Of course," Rao said. "Please keep my government informed."

"We will," Cohn promised.

He broke the connection. "So what now?" McPherson asked.

"I'm going to call the President," Cohn said, scooping up the handset. "He's, where, Miami today?"

"Right." McPherson checked his watch. "He may be in the middle of one of his speeches right now."

"I don't care what he's in the middle of," Cohn said, punching in a number. "The *Rabah Jamila* is Pakistani and in international waters. If the President can get the Pakistanis to give us sole boarding authorization, we may be able to keep the Chinese off for a while."

"Unless Rao's right about Pakistan and China working together."

"In which case we'll get a very quick refusal out of Islamabad," Cohn said. "And that would tell us something, too, wouldn't it?"

"True," McPherson said, looking at the wall map. "While you do that, I think I'll head over to the Pentagon and check on the situation."

"Good idea," Cohn grunted. "Hello—this is CIA Director Cohn. Get me the President."

He was still holding as McPherson slipped out.

13

AFTER THE LATE night and the harrowing day that had preceded it, Ross decided to let Angie sleep in as late as she could. But she was up before nine, sneaking past him—or so she probably thought—to the bathroom. Ross, already awakened by the click of her lock, waited until he heard the shower running before dragging himself off the couch and starting a search of the kitchen cabinets. By the time Angie emerged from the bathroom, still damp but fully dressed, he had a rudimentary meal ready. "Morning," he greeted her, pouring a second mug of instant coffee. "Sorry about the fare, but coffee and cereal seems to be the only breakfast stuff this restaurant stocks. Creamer or sugar?"

"Just sugar," she said, crossing the living room to the table. There was a strange set to her expression, Ross noted uneasily, a dreamlike quality to her movements and voice. He hoped it was just lack of sleep and not some fresh state of denial.

"Sugar it is," he said, tearing open one of the little packets and dumping the contents into her coffee. "How'd you sleep?"

"Fine," she said, sitting down across from him. "As well as could be expected. You were up late last night."

He forced himself not to react. Could there have been some way for her to have seen his private video show? An inconvenient knot hole in the pine paneling, perhaps? "A little," he said, keeping his voice casual as he handed her the mug. "Did I keep you awake?"

"I was awake, but it wasn't you," she said, taking a sip from her coffee and picking up one of the boxes of cereal. "I didn't sleep well the last time I was here, either."

"What exactly did you do?" Ross asked, glad for an excuse to get back to the main topic. "I know skiing's big here. Did you do any of that?"

"A little," she said. "James mostly stayed inside and worked while I went out alone."

"Where did he work? Here at the table?"

"No, usually on the couch. He liked to slouch back with the computer on his lap. Said it helped him think."

"Then that's where we start," Ross said, taking a last sip from his coffee and standing up. "You take the couch. In fact, you take all the furniture. I'll check the walls. Look for any nooks or crannies where he might have slipped a flash drive or some papers."

"And if we find something?"

"Then maybe we'll know why the thieves are trying so hard to kill you."

~

The projection from the helos had been that the Vincennes and Anqing would arrive at the *Rabah Jamila* at the same time, about half past midnight. Damned if the helos hadn't been right.

It was cold out on the *Vincennes*'s deck, with a typical winter wind accompanied by a typical winter drizzle. But Lieutenant Commander Billy Nagano didn't even notice the weather. His full attention was on the lights of the Chinese frigate sitting out there beyond the dark bulk of the *Rabah Jamila*. At last check the *Anqing*'s guns weren't exactly pointed at the *Vincennes*.

But they weren't exactly pointed away, either.

"What the hell's going on up there, anyway?" Seaman Rawlings muttered from beside him, ducking his head out from under their group's token shelter to look up toward the *Vincennes*'s bridge.

"Take it easy, Rawlings," Nagano said. "The captain knows what he's doing."

It was the proper thing for an officer to say, and he fervently hoped that he meant it. Captain Brossmann was a fine officer and an excellent commander and no doubt a credit to his parents as well. But what he was doing up on the bridge right now came under the heading of diplomacy, and in Nagano's respectful opinion the captain didn't have the diplomatic skills God gave crabgrass. Particularly not in the middle of the night.

And unless he could pull an extra supply of patience and suaveness out of a secret locker somewhere, there was going to be trouble. Because the *Vincennes* had orders to board that freighter out there, and the *Anqing* apparently had orders not to let them. And however the argument went, it was going to be Lieutenant Commander William Nagano, also a fine officer and a credit to his parents, who was going to be crossing to that freighter under Chinese guns.

Ensign Javits appeared around a corner and squeezed back into his place under the shelter. "Nothing, sir," he puffed, handing back Nagano's nightscope binoculars. "I checked out everything you can see from here. Nothing's moving on that freighter."

"Thanks," Nagano said, grimacing. And *that*, of course, led to Daily Worry Number Two. Whoever was aboard that freighter, who had yet to show their faces, could very well be lying in wait for whoever finally came aboard. And after crouching in the dark and rain for the past hour, they were likely to have restless trigger fingers.

"Heard something interesting up on the bridge," Javits went on. "Someone said the radio's reporting President Whitcomb cut short a speech in Miami an hour and a half ago and hasn't been heard from since. CNN figures he's off somewhere being sick over the sausage he had at breakfast."

"Sounds like a CNN analysis," Nagano said, some of the tension easing in his chest. So Whitcomb was already on top of this, was he? That was automatically a good sign. Whatever you thought about the President's UN politics—and everyone aboard the *Vincennes* had an opinion one way or the other—there was no denying the man had a twenty-four-caret golden larynx and the political savvy of a snake charmer.

"Hope that means he's doing all the talking instead of the old man," someone else commented. "Maybe we'll get out of here without kicking off World War III."

"Let's keep a civil tongue," Nagano chided mildly. "Unless we want ourselves on permanent guard duty."

"I just want to get this show in the water," Rawlings muttered, shivering violently.

Nagano peered out at the Chinese lights rising and falling with the waves. "Patience, gentlemen," he said. "Patience."

~

General Vaughn snorted. "No," he said. "With all due respect to a fellow professional, absolutely not. The Chinese and Iranians in bed with Japanese radicals? Not a chance in hell."

McPherson shrugged, most of his attention on the large-screen TVs showing the satellite-transmitted images from the Vincennes. To him they looked uniformly dark and fuzzy, and could only hope that Vaughn and the other military people conversing quietly or talking urgently on phones were getting more from the view than he was. "Larry has a tendency to jump into the deep end of the grand conspiracy pool," he conceded. "Still—"

"What still is there about it?" Vaughn retorted. "For all their public harmony these days, Beijing and Teheran don't trust each other any farther than either of them could throw an oil derrick. And nobody wants Japan destabilized. The whole idea is ridiculous."

"Well, then, *you* explain it," McPherson challenged, suddenly tired of trying to defend someone else's theory.

"The most likely explanation is playing itself out right now," Vaughn said, gesturing toward the displays. "I'm guessing the whole thing is a North Korean power play, pure and simple. Everything else we're running into is either coincidence, a deliberate red herring, or the product of fevered imagination."

"A power play to what end?" McPherson asked.

"Full nuclear capability, of course," Vaughn said. "Pyongyang has been lusting after that for the past sixty years."

"I was under the impression the North Koreans had both tactical and strategic nukes already on their soil."

"On their soil is not the same as ownership," Vaughn reminded him. "Those are in carefully constructed bunkers, under the close watch of Chinese advisers. You ever hear of a deer gun?"

"I presume you don't mean a standard hunting rifle."

Vaughn shook his head. "It's a class of little single-shot guns. They're dirt cheap, not much more than stamped metal with a firing mechanism attached, usually distributed wholesale to resistance groups that you want to support but don't have the funds or supply pipeline to properly arm. A deer gun's sole purpose in life is to let a guerrilla kill an enemy soldier and trade up to a proper rifle or handgun."

"Okay," McPherson said, nodding. "I *have* heard of them, just not by that name. And your point?"

Vaughn waved again at the displays. "I think that's what this Indian bomb is to them: a tool to blast their way into a cluster of bunkers and get their hands on a whole bunch of Chinese tactical nukes."

McPherson felt his eyebrows go up. "Or accidentally vaporize them."

"Oh, it would have to be done carefully," Vaughn agreed. "But with proper placement it should be quite doable."

"I'll admit that's one scenario that hadn't occurred to me," McPherson said. "You want to give me the whole rundown?"

"Nothing to it," Vaughn said. "A group of North Koreans swipe a nuke, and however they manage it they smuggle it aboard *Rabah Jamila*, along with some caretakers probably posing as members of the crew. They're steaming happily northward when they're hit by pirates and have to reveal themselves to the rest of the crew in order to beat them off."

"Shocking the hell out of them."

"With their cover blown, they now have to kill or lock everyone else up," Vaughn went on. "But a day or two later one of the prisoners gets loose, or else they missed someone in the general massacre, and he makes it to the radio room. They nail him, but it's too late—he's already sent a mayday. At that point they either panic or else realize the Marines are on the way and they have no choice but to kick full revs toward home."

"What about the Chinese code message?"

"That's the really troubling part," Vaughn said. "There's always been a faction of the Chinese military that favors using the North Koreans as surrogates in operations where the Chinese can't afford to have an official presence of their own. Could be this faction has decided to take matters into its own hands."

"North Korean mercs with nuclear weapons," McPherson murmured. "There's a cheery thought."

"Fortunately, it looks like we were fast enough off the chocks to contain the problem," Vaughn said. "We've had the freighter under constant surveillance since the Navy P-3 did that first recon, and no one's gotten off."

"I thought it took the P-3 an hour to get there," McPherson pointed out.

"Forty-six minutes," Vaughn corrected. "But it did a complete sweep of the area, and there were only two other freighters that a boat from *Rabah Jamila* could have gotten to in that time. We're watching them, too."

"How about a seaplane or submarine?"

Vaughn shook his head. "*Rabah Jamila* was already pulling over twenty knots by the time the mayday was sent," he said. "Transferring anything at that speed, in those seas, would have been extremely tricky. Anyway, radar showed nothing but the P-3 in the air, and the P-3 itself checked for subs."

McPherson looked at the TV images. "I wish you'd boarded it before the Chinese showed up."

"We probably should have," Vaughn conceded. "But there's no place for a helo to safely set down, and under the circumstances Admiral Eskin didn't want to rappel people in without heavy guns standing by to back them up. Can't say I blame him."

McPherson shook his head. "This is getting too complicated. We're sitting on a potential international incident with the Chinese, and we don't even know what that ship's significance is."

"I know," Vaughn agreed darkly. "I get the feeling someone's having way too much fun pulling our chains. I just hope our whiz-kid analysts can unravel this mess before something goes down." He eyed McPherson thoughtfully. "I hear you've got a pretty crackerjack analyst of your own on staff, don't you? Swanson or Swenson or something?"

McPherson grimaced. "Swenson. Hanna Swenson."

"That's right," Vaughn nodded. "I remember her report on the Livermore situation to our Wednesday group a few months back. She working on this?"

"Actually, no," McPherson said, looking back at the monitors. "She was transferred to the San Francisco office."

He could feel Vaughn's eyes on him. "And you haven't called her back?"

"We *do* have other people," McPherson said, the words sounding more than a little defensive in his ears.

"As good as Swenson?"

"Good enough," McPherson said stubbornly.

The silence stretched out a little too long. "You have a problem with the lady," Vaughn said at last. It wasn't a question.

"Let's just say she comes with awkward memories."

"So do half the people in this room," Vaughn said acidly. "What does that have to do with anything?"

McPherson grimaced. "Well . . . "

"Up to now I can maybe see your point," the general said, the disapproval in his tone moderating only fractionally. "We had a stray nuke headed for the Middle East or Indonesia or wherever. Fine—offshore stuff isn't your job. But now we've got a brand new game going. That ship was heading for North Korea, and if Pyongyang's involved you can bet your rear echelon any nukes they manage to collect won't stay there long. You want to guess who's at the top of North Korea's short list these days?"

"All right, all right," McPherson said, conceding defeat. "Fine, I'll call her in."

"Good." Vaughn hunched his shoulders, settled them back down. "And you'd better get used to this," he added. "If the UN gets the kind of military power they want, this sort of thing could become a bi-weekly exercise."

"What sort of thing?" McPherson asked, frowning.

"Wayward nuclear weapons," Vaughn told him. "You give a few tactical nukes to the UN and half of them will vanish from the shelves the first day they're there."

"I don't think anyone's suggesting we give them nuclear weapons," McPherson said. "That's certainly not what President Whitcomb has in mind."

"I don't know what the President has or hasn't got in mind," Vaughn countered. "But you try listening to Muluzi's speeches sometime. I mean *really* listening to them. The man wants to go down in history as the Secretary-General who made the UN a nuclear power."

"General Vaughn?" a man wearing colonel's eagles called across the room, his hand cupped over a phone. "Line four, sir."

Vaughn picked up the phone at his elbow and punched the proper button. "Vaughn."

For a minute he listened in silence. McPherson watched the monitors, mentally running through some of the possible consequences of a North Korea with full nuclear capability. Would Pyongyang try to set itself up as a major terrorist sponsor? Given the current regime's hatred for the West—and for most of the rest of the world, for that matter—it was a distinct possibility. And with an arsenal of tactical nukes to draw on, they could sponsor some truly terrifying acts.

In which case the United States might well find itself at war again on the Korean peninsula. He tried to think back on the wartime histories he'd read, and the FBI's role in those conflicts. There would be spy rings to break, saboteurs to find and stop, intel to process, and sheep-and-goat separation to be done between legitimate protest organizations and foreign based incitement groups.

Only this time it would be with the threat of nuclear weapons lurking in the background.

"Thank you." Vaughn set the phone back into its cradle. "That was Duvall," he told McPherson. "The President's worked out a compromise with the Pakistanis and Chinese. *Vincennes* and *Anqing* are both going to send landing parties aboard, which will search the ship together. Our people will be wearing helmet cams, so we'll be able to watch the whole thing."

"Looks like they've already started," McPherson said, nodding toward the monitors. "I wonder what it's like to see a bullet coming straight at you."

"I wouldn't wonder about that too loudly if I were you," Vaughn warned grimly. "There's a very good chance you're about to find out."

~

"Talbot?"

Talbot paused with one foot on the first step of the stairway, to see Lyman bearing down on him from the direction of his office. "Hello, sir," he said. "I'm surprised to see you here on a Saturday."

"You have no idea the hours I work, do you?" Lyman growled. "Glad I caught you. I just got a call from McPherson. He wants your Jigsaw Girl on the next plane to D.C."

Talbot felt his throat tighten. "What for?"

"No idea," Lyman said. "Need-to-know, and I apparently don't. Must be something big, though. She's supposed to report to him in Langley, which means the CIA's also involved."

"Did you happen to mention that we had something big of our own going on here?"

"I gave him a quick thumbnail," Lyman said. "He suggested that a man of your extraordinary abilities should be able to handle it alone."

Talbot grimaced. "He's too kind."

"Yes, he clearly holds you in high esteem," Lyman said with only a trace of sarcasm.

"Fine," Talbot said. "I'm on my way up to see Hanna anyway. I'll give her the news, get a quick summary of what she's got so far, then send her on her way."

"Uh-huh," Lyman said, eying him with far more discernment than Talbot cared for. "You won't mind if I tag along?"

"Not at all, sir," Talbot said politely, starting up the steps again.

Hanna Swenson's station was in a back corner of the analysis room, a rather impressive U-shaped workspace she'd created by pushing three standard-issue desks together and filling in the U's corners with a pair of spare printer carts to give her more horizontal surface to work with. Neatly arranged across the desks were two computer workstations and a laptop, a printer/fax machine, a portable light table with magnifier, a flatbed scanner, and what looked to be about thirty cubic feet of file folders and other neat stacks of paper.

Seated in the midst of the controlled chaos, looking for all the world like a petite, determined spider in her web, Swenson was hunched over one of the workstation keyboards tapping diligently at the keys. She glanced up as Talbot and Lyman approached, her determined expression softening into half a smile. Talbot rather hoped the smile was for him. "Hello, Mr. Lyman; Madison," she greeted them, peeling off two file folders from the top of one of her stacks. "I was just about to call you, Madison. I've finished the preliminaries for Scott Kingsley and Jack Burke."

"Good timing," Lyman said. "I just got a call from D.C.—"

"Let's see what she's got first," Talbot said, handing Lyman the Kingsley folder and flipping open the Burke one.

He could feel Lyman's eyes on him. But the other didn't say anything, but merely opened his folder and started reading.

Swenson had, if anything, surpassed herself, Talbot decided as he took a quick overview run through the folder. She'd had the assignment for little more than a day, yet had already pulled together Burke's whole life history. Elementary and secondary education, college, previous employment experience, current bank and credit card information, affiliations and professional associations—

He paused as a name suddenly caught his eye. "Well, well," he murmured. "Reverend Lane."

"Reverend *Kirkwood* Lane?" Lyman asked, looking up.

"That's the one," Talbot confirmed. "Burke's a member of his extended flock."

"Interesting," Lyman said, peering over Talbot's shoulder.

"That's not all," Swenson said. "I pulled up Burke's tax returns, and for the past two years he's listed significant donations to Lane and his church."

"Isn't that illegal?" Talbot asked. "I thought Lane wasn't tax exempt anymore."

"Yes, but he didn't give up that status until last April," Lyman said. "Gifts up until then were okay."

Talbot eyed him. "You sound like someone who's been following Lane pretty closely."

"What I sound like is someone who was assigned to check into the man's activities," Lyman countered. "Accusations had surfaced that he was fronting for some right-wing terrorists, and we were told to check it out."

Talbot frowned down at Swenson, got a similar puzzled look in return. "I never heard anything about that."

"This isn't the Hoover era, you know," Lyman reminded him darkly. "Poking into loud or politically unpopular groups is frowned on by our various Congressional watchdogs. One has to be careful about such things."

"I suppose," Talbot said. "I take it the investigation came up empty?"

Lyman shrugged. "People like Lane attract a diverse following, and his fan club has its share of dangerous nuts. Lane himself seems clean, though. Is this everything on Kingsley?"

"That's all I've been able to pull up," Swenson said. "The man's led a rather dull life."

"Except for a bankruptcy three years ago," Lyman said.

"A bankruptcy?" Talbot asked, frowning. "What for?"

"For going into debt, dear," Swenson said sweetly.

"*Thank* you," Talbot said. "I meant what got him into it?"

"The usual trouble with credit cards," Lyman said. "Doesn't seem to be gambling or medical, if that's what you were wondering."

"It was," Talbot said. "How's he doing now?"

"Seems to be handling his finances just fine," Swenson said. "His salary and known expenditures are right in line."

Talbot nodded. "What about Esteban?"

"I've just started on him," she said. "So far, nothing's jumped out at me."

"And nothing's going to," Lyman said. "As of right now, you're off the case. Put anything you've collected on Chiang's desk and get packed for D.C. McPherson wants you back there right away."

Swenson blinked. "Me?"

"Let's hold on a second," Talbot said. "First of all, sir, whatever Director McPherson has, this Cloak thing is important, too. Furthermore, just between you, me, and the printer, the CIA is terrible about consolidating their data. Chances are they won't even be ready for Hanna until Monday at the earliest. We can keep her here until tomorrow afternoon, put her on a plane, and have her at Langley bright and chipper and ready to go first thing Monday morning."

"Sounds like a wonderfully logical compromise," Lyman said. "Why don't you call McPherson and suggest it?"

"He won't even miss her," Talbot said. "Really. Monday morning—"

"He said now, Talbot," Lyman cut him off. "*This* now, not some vaguely future now. Swenson, get your stuff on Chiang's desk and go home and pack."

"Give her another half hour to work," Talbot cajoled. "I'll make the reservations while she does, then drive her to her apartment to pack. My overnight bag's already in my trunk, so we can just head from there to the airport and—"

"Wait a second," Lyman interrupted him, frowning. "What do you mean, your bag? You weren't invited to this party."

"I need Hanna to pull these pieces together," Talbot said. "If you won't let her stay here until tomorrow, at least let me have her on the flight. She can use the on-board Internet to pull up Esteban's records. When we get to D.C., I'll deliver her to McPherson, turn around and take the next flight back."

Swenson lifted a hand. "Excuse me—"

"Are you insane?" Lyman demanded. "You can't tap into sensitive systems from a commercial plane. Security considerations alone dictate that."

"No, you can do it," Talbot insisted. "I saw it done once by a senior CIA official. All it takes is the proper seat positioning, a laptop screen filter, and the basic scrambling system already on Hanna's computer. Absolutely secure access and retrieval."

"Excuse me," Swenson tried again. "Do I get any say in this?"

"No," Talbot said. Her eyes flashed at him; he ignored it. "Look, sir, I can be back tomorrow morning. You won't even miss me."

"I already don't miss you," Lyman retorted. But he was weakening.

"I'll even pay for my own ticket," Talbot wheedled.

Lyman sighed, shaking his head. "You and my sister," he growled. "Fine; do whatever you want. Just make sure you get Swenson to D.C. Tonight."

"Thank you, sir," Talbot said. "I'll have the reservations set up before she finishes here."

"Yeah." Lyman looked down at Swenson. "What about that alleged PI Mrs. Chandler ran off with? Anything on him yet?"

Swenson looked at Talbot, the fire still smoldering in her eyes. "Special Agent Talbot told me to concentrate first on the lab assistants and the theft."

"San Jose's handling the preliminaries on Ross," Talbot put in quickly. "I thought the theft should be our first priority."

"The theft is not our business," Lyman said, frowning. "The reason the Bureau is involved with this—the *only* reason—is because of the kidnapping angle."

"Lieutenant Delgado also asked us in," Talbot reminded him mildly.

"That's beside the point," Lyman said, his glare taking on a suspicious edge. "I want the Cloaks recovered as much as you do. But I also have charter considerations to answer to. If I let you get on that plane tonight, you'd damn well better spend from about Colorado Springs eastward tracking down Ross."

"Yes, sir," Talbot said humbly. "I will."

Lyman let the glare linger another moment, then looked back at Swenson. "Good luck, Swenson," he said. "Whatever's got McPherson climbing a tree, clean it up for him and get back as soon as you can."

"I'll do my best, sir," Swenson said.

"And have a safe trip." Lyman favored Talbot with one final look, then stepped past him and stalked across the room and left.

"So I don't get any say in this, huh?" Swenson demanded frostily.

"Don't get upset," Talbot soothed. "I just didn't think this was something you needed to get in the middle of."

Swenson's expression didn't change. "You know, other women might be offended by that kind of patronizing attitude," she said. "But I happen to know you better than that. If you don't want me in the middle, the middle's about to become an unpleasant place to be."

She crossed her arms across her chest. "So tell me, Madison dear: what have you got up your sleeve that's about to make the middle an unpleasant place to be?"

"Me?" Talbot asked, radiating innocence. "What could I possibly have up my sleeve?"

"I don't know. I hate to think."

"I made a promise," Talbot said firmly. "And I fully intend to do everything in my power to keep it. You concentrate on collecting your data while I book us a flight, okay?"

Her expression didn't change, but she unfolded her arms. "Okay," she said. "Sure."

~

They searched *Rabah Jamila*'s working areas and accommodations first, moving from room to room, corridor to corridor, with the exaggerated caution that helped keep a man breathing in situations like this.

They found no one. The ship's engines had been set on full, the autopilot engaged, the course set to clear Paengnyong Island and Changsan-got and put the ship firmly into North Korean waters. Nagano shut the engines down as per orders, and as the deck vibration died beneath their feet they continued their search.

Nagano's first worry, that of working with the Chinese, turned out not to be the problem he'd expected. The lieutenant in charge of their group kept a good balance to the operation, not always letting the Americans take the riskiest point positions but at the same time not trying to sneak ahead where they could check things out without anyone looking over their shoulders. More than once Nagano wondered if the sterling cooperation was due to Whitcomb's powers of persuasion or whether in the hours since *Rabah Jamila*'s mayday the Chinese had had time to analyze that coded message and had found something suspicious in it.

It was as they went below that they first heard the knocking.

At first it was so faint that Nagano thought it was something from the machinery, perhaps the cooling of heat-stressed engine parts or even an echo of their own footsteps. But it persisted, and as it grew louder Nagano was finally able to make out the somewhat sloppy attempt to beat out a Morse SOS. Still mindful of the ambush possibilities, they followed the sound.

They found *Rabah Jamila*'s crew in one of the holds. Cold, hungry, and furious, but otherwise unharmed.

"—and then they locked us in there," the ship's first mate said, waving a hand downward in the direction of their recent incarceration, the motion sloshing a few drops of steaming tea from his mug onto the mess room floor. "Except for Captain Syed—we didn't even know if he was still alive until you found him. They banged around for a while, and we could hear one of the cranes operating from about five o'clock until nearly six. We could hear their ship tied up alongside, too."

"How do you know it was a ship?" Nagano asked.

"The captain saw it," the mate said patiently. "I told you that."

"You said he saw it approach," the Chinese lieutenant put in. "You didn't say whether it tied up alongside."

"It did," the mate said, gesturing toward the ship's starboard side. "We were right beside the accommodation ladder, and we could hear the ship bouncing against our side. Metal against metal. The sound is unmistakable."

Nagano nodded. "What happened then?"

"As I said, the crane stopped a little before six, and we could hear nothing more from the deck. Then the engines increased speed, and the banging of their ship against our side grew louder. That went on for an hour. Then there was one final bang, and after that nothing. That's how we knew the other ship had gone."

"Did you notice what time that was?" the Chinese lieutenant asked.

"A few minutes after seven o'clock."

Nagano and the Chinese lieutenant exchanged glances. Immediately after the mayday and coded transmissions. "Could you hear the other ship's engines?" Nagano asked. "Either before or after it left?"

The mate shrugged. "Madra thought he heard an engine just before the banging ceased," he said. "But I did not, and he may have imagined it. Our own engines were making considerable noise."

"I understand," Nagano said. "I was wondering if it could have been a metal plate or something banging against the side that you were hearing."

The mate shook his head. "No."

"I meant like something hung over the side," Nagano persisted. "Something to make you think there was still a boat there."

The mate drew himself up. "It moved in time with the swell," he said stiffly, a man whose professional seamanship has been called into question. "It did not move in time with the wind."

"How could you tell how the wind was going from inside a hold?" the Chinese asked.

"I have sailed with this ship for ten years," the mate said, drawing himself up even taller. It wasn't that much of a difference. "I have sailed on other seagoing ships for twenty years more. Even in a ship this size you can tell. It was most definitely floating alongside us."

"All right, fine," Nagano said hastily. "The ship came in and tied up about four-thirty and didn't leave until seven. Did you or anyone else besides Captain Syed see it?"

The mate lifted his hands, palms upward. "I had a brief look before we were taken prisoner. But it was distant, and I had no binoculars. I saw no detail. I do not believe any of the others did, either."

"But the captain *did* have binoculars."

"Yes."

Nagano gestured to *Rabah Jamila*'s captain, sitting in indignant silence at the mate's side. "Will you ask him to describe it?"

"Certainly."

The two Pakistanis conferred quietly in Urdu. Beside Nagano, the Chinese lieutenant murmured something into his headset. "You getting all this, Captain?" Nagano asked into his own headset, just to keep from feeling left out.

"Such as it is," Brossmann's deep voice growled in his ear. "Is it just me, or does this whole story not make a hell of a lot of sense?"

"It's not you, sir," Nagano assured him. "Wait a second."

The first mate had finished his conversation and turned back. "It was a mega yacht," he reported. "Monohull, single-level wheelhouse, perhaps forty meters long, white with red trim."

"Ask about rigging," Brossmann ordered.

Nagano put the question, and there was another brief conference. "None," the first mate said. "He saw the vessel very clearly. There was no mast or sail."

"So much for that," Brossmann muttered. "The Marine recon flight spotted a forty-meter boat, but it was a fully-rigged sailboat. Bunch of idle yachtsmen types sitting out under the stars grilling fish on the fantail."

"Commander?" Javits's voice cut in tautly. "You'd better come see what the Chinese found. Number Three hold, port side."

Nagano looked around the room. In the last couple of minutes, while he hadn't been paying attention, the Chinese lieutenant had somehow slipped quietly out of the room. "Rawlings, take over here," he said, and headed out.

He found a small group waiting in the Number Three hold when he arrived, including Javits and the Chinese lieutenant.

All of them loosely gathered around the bundled sticks of dynamite attached to the hull.

"That *is* a bomb, isn't it?" Nagano asked. He was trying to sound casual, but the words came out with more of a croak than he'd planned.

"Sure as hell looks like one to me," Javits said. His voice didn't sound much calmer than Nagano's. "Zhou thinks so, too."

Nagano focused on the Chinese officer kneeling beside the mechanism wired to the dynamite, looking closely but not touching anything. "Zhou knows bombs, does he?"

"He is an explosives and demolitions expert," the Chinese lieutenant said quietly. "My commander has authorized him to defuse the device."

"Captain?" Nagano asked urgently.

"It's all right, Billy," Brossmann said. "They've sent me his credentials, and he looks to be as good as anyone we've got here. Besides, he's already on the scene. You might want to consider pulling your men back to a safer position, though."

Nagano looked around. None of the Chinese were making any move to leave. "Thank you, sir," he said. "We'll stay."

The next few minutes more than made up for the boredom of the first hour of the search. But once again, in retrospect, it turned out to something of an anticlimax.

A very curious anticlimax.

"Interesting," the Chinese lieutenant murmured, translating as Zhou pointed to various spots on the now defused bomb. "This bomb should have gone off a long time ago. The timer was set for two hours, and the detonator did indeed activate."

"Really," Nagano said, an odd feeling in the pit of his stomach. "So why didn't it go boom?"

"He does not yet know," the lieutenant said. "A flaw somewhere in the mechanism. He will need to bring it back to *Anqing* for analysis."

"Captain?" Nagano asked. "Should I let him take it?"

"Go ahead," Brossmann said. "But we'll want someone there to observe the disassembly. I'll set it up with their captain."

Nagano nodded. "At least now we know why they didn't bother to shoot the crew. They weren't expecting them to be alive much longer anyway."

"Which could be a lucky break for us," Brossmann pointed out. "If they were expecting to send *Rabah Jamila* to the bottom, they may have been careless about leaving other things around."

"Maybe something that'll implicate Pyongyang directly?" Nagano suggested.

"As far as I'm concerned, they're implicated already," Brossmann rumbled. "South Korean Special Warfare Command, my butt."

"Yes, sir," Nagano said. "You want us to take a look?"

"No, better not," Brossmann said. "We need people with the training and equipment for this sort of thing. You said the captain knows where the stowaways were hiding?"

"Up in the forward deck group of containers," Nagano said. "He's not sure exactly which ones."

"Close enough," Brossmann said. "Put a cordon around that general area. No one's to go near it."

"You'll want to run that past *Anqing*," Nagano warned, glancing down at the sidearm at the Chinese lieutenant's hip.

"I will," Brossmann grunted. "And while you get the cordon set, I suggest you finish your sweep below decks. The hijackers might have left a second bomb for insurance."

Nagano smiled tightly. "Yes, sir. I believe the Chinese are already on the job."

~

One of Swenson's most endearing characteristics—or one of her most annoying flaws, depending on your point of view—was her tendency to so completely immerse herself in a project that she lost track of time. That single-mindedness had occasionally driven Talbot nuts; this time, however, it was going to work to his advantage. He gave her the half hour of work that he'd bargained out of Lyman, then let the minutes stretch out nearly a half hour more before finally calling her attention to the clock and reminding her it was time to go.

He took his time getting to her apartment, though he took care to make it look like he was hurrying. All of it was wasted effort—with Swenson busy sorting through the most recent batch of downloaded files on her laptop she might not have noticed if he'd pulled off the street and parked for an hour.

Swenson was experienced enough to have an overnight bag already tucked away in a corner of her closet. But with the indefinite time frame of McPherson's recall order Talbot insisted she include a more complete wardrobe. Her packing, unfortunately, took less time than he'd hoped, and within a quarter hour they were on the highway again heading for the airport.

"What are we booked on?" Swenson asked as Talbot wove into the left lane to get around a Lexus puttering along at barely the legal speed limit.

"It's a Delta flight," Talbot told her. "I've got the number in my notebook. I just hope they've got seats left."

"What are you talking about?" Swenson frowned. "I thought you made reservations."

"I tried to," Talbot said. "It turns out that every flight between the Bay and D.C. is booked solid."

"In *January*?" she said. "You're kidding."

Talbot lifted a hand, palm upward. "Don't ask me. Maybe the cherry trees are blooming early this year. All I know is that this is the last flight available until tomorrow night. If we can get it."

Out of the corner of his eye he could see her staring hard at him. "The last flight until Sunday night," she said, her voice deeply suspicious. "How terribly inconvenient."

"Hey, I did my best," Talbot protested. "I really did. You know how hard it is to get last-minute airline tickets."

Reluctantly, he thought, she turned her face away and settled back into her seat. "Of course," she murmured. "We'll just have to hope this flight has seats."

It didn't.

"So that's it?" Swenson said in a voice of strained calm as they stood in front of the Delta flight board. "None of these other flights have seats?"

Talbot shook his head. "I'm sorry."

"United is booked, too?" she persisted. "And Virgin, and Alaska, and American?"

"I tried everything," Talbot said. "I'm sorry, Hanna, but there's just no way we can do this."

"Uh-huh." She folded her arms across her chest and glared up at him. "So what do you suggest we do now? Wait—let me guess. As long as I'm stuck in town for the rest of the weekend anyway, why don't we go back to the office and I can spend the next twenty-four hours digging up files and compiling data for you before I disappear back to D.C.?"

"You wound me," Talbot said, trying to look hurt. "What kind of slave driver do you take me for? No, I was thinking more along the lines of getting you a nice hotel room here by the airport and you could work from there. Certainly not a full twenty-four hours, either. You have to eat and sleep sometime."

"And what do you think McPherson is going to say about this?"

"If this project of his was that critical he'd have had a chartered plane standing by for you," Talbot pointed out. "Twenty-four hours are not going to make or break it."

Swenson sighed. "You're going to get me fired, Madison," she warned. "And you're going to get *you* reassigned to collecting brass at the D.C. firing range."

"You're way too valuable to fire," Talbot assured her quietly. "As for me . . . this Cloak case is important, Hanna. If having you on the job an extra day helps break it, then it doesn't matter what they do to me afterwards."

She stared at him, an odd expression on her face. "This case has become personal, hasn't it?"

Talbot grimaced. "Sometimes you're too smart for your own good," he said. "Are you with me or not?"

"With you, I guess," she said, giving him a faint smile. "Why not, since I can't get out of California anyway?"

"Thanks," he said, picking up her bag and turning back toward the exit. "I'll make it up to you somehow."

"You can start by promising me a decent dinner once I'm set up in the hotel," she said, falling into step beside him.

"You will have the most magnificent meal available in the entire San Francisco area," Talbot promised.

"Yeah," Swenson said. "Sure."

14

THEY SPENT THE rest of the afternoon searching the cabin. In the end they found what Angie had always expected them to find.

Nothing.

"Well, that's it," she said, collapsing wearily onto the couch. "Unless he wrote something on the walls in invisible ink, there's nothing here."

"I guess so," Ross agreed, easing down onto one of the dining table chairs. Even before they'd started the day's activities Angie had noticed he was favoring his left leg more than usual, and several hours of walking, crouching, squatting, and crawling hadn't improved matters any. It couldn't be something congenital, she decided as she watched him, not with just a single leg affected. It must have been an injury. "Still, dead ends are part of the detection process."

"James used to say that about science, too," Angie murmured, gazing down at the tips of her shoes. *His* shoes, rather, the ones Ross had bought her. "I don't think I could get used to watching my time and effort go down the drain that way."

"It can be frustrating," Ross acknowledged. "But negative information is still information. In this case, we now know they're not after you because there's something you have that they want."

"So why *are* they after me?"

Ross shrugged. "It has to be something you know. Either something they want to know, or something they don't want anyone else knowing."

"Or maybe they're just psychos," she said, a shiver running through her. "They just like killing."

"No," Ross said, his tone emphatic. "They didn't kill the reception guard or the gate guard. They only kill when they think they need to."

"So why James and the others?" Angie demanded, her voice suddenly breaking. "For the damn Cloaks? The damn, damn Cloaks? Things? Money?"

With a sigh, Ross got up and walked over to her. "There's something big going down here, Angie," he said quietly as he sat down at her side. "Something that involves the Cloaks themselves, as they are right now. Maybe they killed James because he knew something important about them."

Angie turned her face away, wanting to move to a different chair but sensing that wouldn't be a good idea. "Like what?"

"Maybe how to jam their operation," Ross suggested. "Or how to see through them, or how to screw up their programming. Very likely it's the same thing they think you know."

The cheeks beneath Angie's dribbling tears went stiff and hard. How did this man know so much about what had happened on that awful night? How did he know about the guards, and drugs?

How did he know so much about the Cloaks?

"That's what we have to concentrate on," Ross continued. "You stopped by the lab that evening. While you were there, you saw or heard something that made them decide you were a threat."

"Why does it have to have been that night?" she asked, trying to keep her voice steady. "Why not something James might have told me earlier?"

"Because the thieves were on Sand/Star's grounds when you showed up," Ross said. "If they'd already been planning to kill you, they could have done it as you left the building."

And he didn't want her going to the police, either. "I see," she said, shivering again.

"Hey, it's okay," he said, patting her shoulder reassuringly. "You're safe now."

"If you say so."

"I definitely say so," he said firmly. "The point is that whatever happened that night, they didn't find out about it until later, after they'd talked to their inside man." He hesitated. "In fact, they probably dropped by your house sometime in the early hours of the morning. Your decision to go to a motel probably saved your life."

"Lucky for me," she murmured.

"Maybe lucky for all of us." Out of the corner of her eye she saw his arms go outward in a wide stretch. "I don't know about you, but I'm starved. Are there any good restaurants around here?"

"There are a few places down the road," Angie said carefully. The first wisps of a desperate plan were beginning to form in her mind. "I think I'd rather eat in, though."

"Fine with me," Ross said, getting to his feet. Even in the past couple of minutes his leg seemed to have stiffened up considerably. "We'll need supplies, though. Unless you're a whiz with corn flakes."

"I was thinking about spaghetti," Angie said, standing up beside him. "There's a little grocery store in town."

"Sounds good," Ross said, almost hiding a smile.

Almost, but not quite. "What's funny?" Angie demanded.

"Sorry." He gestured to her. "It just struck me odd for a second—a Chinese lady making spaghetti. Though I don't know why it should, come to think of it. The Chinese invented pasta, didn't they?"

"That's a myth," she said shortly. "The Italians had it long before Marco Polo."

"Really," he said, sounding impressed. "You learn something new every day. Shall we go?"

"Maybe I should go by myself," Angie suggested, gesturing to his leg. "It would give you a chance to put that leg up for a while."

"That's okay," he said, heading toward the dining room chairs where they'd hung their coats. "I could use the fresh air."

"If you're sure you can handle it," Angie said, feeling a hollowness in her stomach that had nothing to do with her own gnawing hunger. Could he have sensed her sudden doubts? "Would you rather go alone?"

"We should stick together," he said, pulling on his coat and picking up hers. "Come on, let's go."

~

The last page came to a halt on Swenson's screen, and with a tired sigh she hit the save key. "Okay," she called to Talbot as he lay on the bed, his head and shoulders propped up on a pile of three pillows. "I'm ready. Get your feet off my bed."

He looked up, lowering the report he was reading, a mildly questioning expression on his face. "Ready for what?"

"Dinner," she said, waving at her laptop. "I've finished the data blitz on Esteban, and you promised me the best dinner in San Francisco."

"Ah," he said, his forehead furrowing slightly. "How does a room service Reuben sound?"

"Pretty chintzy," Swenson said, letting her voice drop into theatrical-ominous range. "You promised, Madison. I want to go out."

"Two hours ago you wanted a Reuben."

"Really," she said scornfully. He wasn't pulling this one on *her*. "And where is it, may I ask?"

He lifted his eyebrows. "You ate it."

For a moment she just stared at him. Then, slowly, she followed his pointing finger to the low dresser across from the bed.

Sitting beside the TV were the remnants of a room service delivery. And now that she thought about it, her mouth *did* rather taste like sauerkraut and Russian dressing. "Not again," she groaned.

"Again," he confirmed, putting the folder aside and getting off the bed. "It's really extraordinary to watch. Entertaining, too."

"I'll bet it is," she growled, thoroughly disgusted with herself. She'd expected him to try to weasel out of his promise. Instead, she'd weaseled out of it for him. "Did I at least enjoy it?"

"Hard to tell, but you did almost smile once or twice before it vanished," he said, coming over to the writing desk where she sat. "You really need to work on your global awareness."

"Starting with the six feet immediately around me?"

"Something like that. What did you find on Esteban?"

"About the same as I did on Kingsley and Burke," she said, pulling up her summary. "He's led a slightly more exciting life than Kingsley—he got hauled in twice as a kid for heaving rocks at police car windows. But he straightened up when he hit high school and hasn't been in trouble since. His brother didn't make the curve quite fast enough, unfortunately. He's in San Quentin for armed robbery."

"Any connections with fringe groups, like Burke with Reverend Lane?"

"Nothing on file," she said, passing over the question of whether Lane really belonged in the fringe-group category. "On the other hand, none of this may actually mean much."

"Oh? Why not?"

"Well, the Consolidated Data Base was being snotty," she said, "so while I was waiting I decided to check out the lists of known industrial spies."

"On the assumption that our boys may have hired themselves a pro," Talbot said, nodding. "I was going to suggest you try that after you finished with Esteban. Any names jump out at you?"

"As a matter of fact, one did," she said, pulling up the appropriate file. "Guy who calls himself Hooker. Ring any bells?"

"No," Talbot said. "Should it?"

"Not necessarily," she said. "He's been operating for about three years, at least under that alias, and during that time has managed to siphon high-tech secrets out of Lockheed, Fairchild, and Molex."

"Impressive. We have a description?"

"Nothing useful," she said. "For one thing, he changes faces like other people change socks. He's also an accomplished hacker, with a talent for getting into computer files and either changing or appropriating them."

"Appropriating, as in identity theft?"

"Exactly what I wondered," Swenson said, waving at the screen. "There may very well be another Ramon Esteban somewhere out there—a real one—working in happy obliviousness at Sun or Intel while Hooker temporarily uses his identity. Or there could be a real Kingsley, or a real Burke."

"Like this case wasn't messy enough," Talbot grumbled. "I don't suppose there's any way of knowing when Hooker started on his most recent job?"

"No idea whether he even *is* on a job," Swenson said. "But it does look like he dropped out of sight somewhere between twelve and eight months ago."

"Did he, now," Talbot said, digging out his notebook and leafing through the pages. "Eight to twelve months . . . damn."

"What?"

"Yet another brilliant thought run off into the ditch," Talbot said, scowling at the notebook. "Turns out that's the same time Tarnhelm kicked into high gear and picked up all three of the techs. Kingsley was transferred from another project at Sand/Star eleven months ago, while Esteban was poached from Hewlett-Packard two weeks later and Burke was hired straight out of Stanford grad school a month after that."

"Normally, I would say that would leave Burke out," Swenson said. "You can't very well attend classes and steal Lockheed blind at the same time. But given that Hooker might simply have borrowed his identity for the moment—" She shrugged.

"Yeah, but Burke also *looks* like he's only twenty-five," Talbot pointed out, scratching his cheek. "Maybe there's an angle there we can use. Can you get Lockheed's or Fairchild's security people on the line and see if anyone remembers Hooker being particularly boyish looking?"

Swenson arched her eyebrows. "On a Saturday night?"

"Oh. Yeah," Talbot said, looking at his watch. "No, I guess not. Monday morning, then."

"By Monday morning I'll be in D.C.," Swenson reminded him pointedly. "Speaking of which, I'd like to know how you came to the conclusion that there were no seats to D.C. open until tomorrow night."

His eyebrow twitched. "Why do you ask?"

"Because while the CDB was being snotty I also took a minute to check out the airline websites," she said. "There were lots of seats available."

"But not the ones I needed to keep my promises," he said in that innocent voice that always meant trouble. "I told Lyman that if he let you work on this on the plane I'd make sure no one was peeking over your shoulder. Remember?"

"Vividly," she said. "What does that have to do with anything?"

"Well, obviously, there are only certain places in a plane where I can guarantee that kind of security," he said. "Specifically, we need two seats together at the back of one of the sections; first class, business, or coach. Unfortunately, those seats weren't available."

Swenson glared at him. "And of course, when Sunday night rolls around and you've gotten the weekend of work out of me that you wanted in the first place, there's no reason for you to fly to D.C. at all. So suddenly we only need one seat, we don't care where in the plane it is, and like magic the whole world opens up again."

He pursed his lips. "Something like that."

"And you don't think Lyman and McPherson are going to see through that?" she demanded. She should have known it was something like this. She should have *known*. "Damn it, Madison, you are going to get us both in such deep fertilizer we'll grow mushrooms."

"You're okay, Hanna," he assured her quietly. "You acted in good faith—"

"Until now."

"Until now," he admitted. "But this was my doing. You were completely innocent. It'll be me standing in front of the fan when the eggs hit, not you."

"And this is supposed to make me feel better?" she countered angrily. Earlier, with her head in the computer, this airline data had registered as nothing more than an interesting factoid to pursue. Now, back up again for air in the real world, the emotional reaction was kicking in with a vengeance. How *dare* he put her in a position like this? "You know, I never believed the rumors that you made McPherson so mad he kicked you as many time zones away as he thought he could get away with. I'm starting to wonder if there might not be some truth there, after all."

"I'm sure I don't know what you're talking about," Talbot said. "If McPherson was mad at me, wouldn't he have simply fired me?"

"I don't know," Swenson said, eyeing him suspiciously. The words were reasonable enough; but they came a little too quickly, and were oiled with a little too much glibness. "You tell me."

His eyes wandered off to a corner of the room. "There are reasons I'm out here," he said. "Call it a gentlemen's agreement."

"Uh-*huh*," Swenson said, not buying it for a minute. "What exactly was it you gentlemen agreed on?"

He spread his hands, all innocent again. "It was no big deal. Besides, it worked out okay for you, didn't it?"

"Me?"

"Sure," Talbot said. "You used to grouse all the time about D.C. weather, winter in particular, and wished McPherson would turn you loose more often so you could visit your family in Oakland. And here you are."

She felt her eyes narrow. "Are you saying that part of this gentleman's agreement was to get me transferred out here?"

His lip twitched. "I may have mentioned you weren't happy in D.C."

"And it didn't seem worth mentioning to me?"

"You *are* happier here, aren't you?"

"That's not the point," Swenson insisted. "I don't appreciate people poking their fingers into my career without my knowledge. You or anyone else. You got that?"

"Yes," he said humbly. "You're absolutely right. I'm sorry."

For a few seconds she continued to glare at him. But he was impossible to be mad at when he went into that beaten-puppy act of his. "Just don't do it again," she said with an exasperated sigh. "What do you want me to do next?"

"Were you able to pull up the police report on the Greenleaf Center incident?" he asked.

"Yes," she said, marveling cynically at his instant transformation from whimpering puppy to confident FBI agent. No lingering shame or repentance, no indication whatsoever that she'd just called him on the carpet and verbally slapped his muzzle. He'd gotten what he wanted, had quickly and efficiently defused her annoyance, and now it was back to business. If McPherson really did hate his guts, he probably had excellent reasons to do so. "They came up with nothing."

"Nothing?"

"Well, mostly nothing," she amended. "No unaccounted-for fingerprints on the newspapers the gunmen used to hide their guns—the report suggests they may have used the old rubber-cement-on-the-fingertips trick. The slugs they fired were 9mm, probably Brownings, so far untraced. The ballistics match some of the rounds found at a noisy fracas at the Chancellor Hotel up in Oakland later that afternoon."

"Murder attempt number two."

"So it would seem," Swenson said. "Let's just hope there isn't a murder attempt number three."

"Oh, I'm sure there will be," Talbot said grimly. "These people are nothing if not persistent." He tapped a finger thoughtfully against his lips. "Let's try something completely different. See what you can pull up about recent funerals in the Bay area."

She blinked. "Funerals?"

"Our friends have a freshly deceased body they need to dispose of," he reminded her, "and they don't strike me as the sort to dump a comrade down a canyon. If you were in that situation, what would you do?"

"Probably dig a shallow grave out in the hills."

"And if they did, we're out of luck," Talbot agreed. "But what else might you do?"

Swenson nodded in sudden understanding. "I might hold a private ceremony at someone else's grave site before it's filled in," she said. "I hadn't even thought of that one."

"Probably a long shot, but it's worth a try," Talbot said. "Did you dig up anything else interesting?"

"Just the fact that Dr. Chandler and your friend Nate Delgado knew each other," Swenson said. "I was profiling the three murdered scientists on the chance that one of them was Hooker's inside man and got double-crossed. I found a reference to a case eight years ago where Delgado brought Chandler in as an expert witness."

"In Sacramento," Talbot said, nodding. "Before Chandler started with Sand/Star and Delgado moved to San Jose."

Swenson frowned. "You already knew about that?"

"Just the basics," Talbot said. "It's why Delgado wanted the Bureau in this thing right from square one. There was a bit of a personal edge."

"I'm told that's a dangerous edge for law enforcement officers to have," Swenson warned pointedly.

Talbot smiled faintly. "Relax, there's nothing personal about my fervor on this case," he assured her. "I've just thought through more of the implications than everyone else has."

"Such as?"

"Such as the question of why the Cloaks were stolen *now*," he said. "Delgado talked to Kingsley this morning, and Kingsley said there's still a lot of work yet to be done. If Hooker was the man involved—hell, if *any* professional thief was involved—why blow his cover now instead of waiting until there was something more valuable to steal? And why kill the creators of the thing?"

"Maybe he thought the Army was about to take over the project and he'd be out in the cold."

"According to Kingsley, Sand/Star would have fought tooth and claw to keep it," Talbot said. "Shouldn't he at least have waited until they'd lost the tug-of-war before pulling the ripcord?"

"Okay, but all sides would have insisted on tighter security from that point on," Swenson pointed out. "Maybe he was afraid he wouldn't be able to get the Cloaks out later. Or that his false identity wouldn't stand up to any extra scrutiny."

"The second is a possibility," Talbot acknowledged. "But the first point brings up a new problem all its own. Namely, why steal the Cloaks in the first place?"

"What do you mean?"

"The manufacturing machine wasn't stolen, but the schematics for making it could have been," Talbot said. "The Cloaks' programming could have been stolen, and in fact we assume they had at least a rudimentary version of it. So why bother with the Cloaks themselves *and* the laptops needed to run them?"

"Maybe he needed a demo to show his buyer."

"He didn't need all four Cloaks for that," Talbot pointed out. "Besides, the perfect demo was there for the taking, tucked away in one of the cabinets where it probably wouldn't have been missed for weeks. And again, why kill the scientists?"

Swenson gazed at her computer screen. "I don't know," she said at last. "It doesn't make sense."

"Not if what they want is the Cloak technology," Talbot said. "It only works if what they want is the Cloaks themselves. And they want them now. Not later, but now."

"They have something planned," Swenson said slowly. "Some crime. And they need the Cloaks to pull it off. We need to alert the rest of the law-enforcement community."

"I wish we could," Talbot said. "But that might just make the whole situation worse. For one thing, ninety percent of them will think it's a gag. For another, news like this could stir up the whole foreign espionage community. All we need is to turn this thing into a multinational Easter egg hunt . . . " He trailed off, his face going rigid.

"Madison?" Swenson prompted carefully.

He took a careful breath. "Hanna, where's President Whitcomb right now?"

"Somewhere on his big speaking tour, I think."

"He's in Miami," Talbot said in a graveyard voice. "Or en route to Denver for his Sunday appearances. Then it's Monday in Seattle, Tuesday in Dallas . . . "

"Oh, God," she breathed. "And Wednesday at the Moscone Center. You don't think . . . ?"

"Why not?" Talbot said darkly. "For that matter, why not Denver, or Seattle, or Dallas? All you need to move the damn thing is a panel truck."

For a moment the silence hung in the air like a cloud of cigarette smoke. "I'd better get back to work," she said at last.

"Yeah," Talbot said, crossing to the bedside phone. "While you do, I'll give the Secret Service a call. Hopefully, *they* won't think it's a gag."

~

The grocery store was small but surprisingly well stocked, as befit a small-town place which also catered to a steady stream of vacationers and tourists. Angie had been inside on previous trips, and had a fairly good idea of how the shelves were laid out. With Ross in charge of pushing the cart, she moved up and down the aisles collecting the necessary ingredients for the spaghetti sauce James had always loved. Occasionally she sent Ross to retrieve a spice she'd forgotten, or to choose a wine, or to see whether they had fresh parmesan cheese and a proper cheese grater.

It was on one of those errands, as she and the cart were momentarily alone, that she quietly slipped her vial of sleeping pills out of her purse into her coat pocket.

Fifteen minutes and thirty-six dollars later, they were on the road again. Halfway there, picking a moment when Ross was looking to his left in preparation for a turn, she tucked her purse beneath her seat.

Her spaghetti sauce was a fairly complicated one, but she'd made it often enough that she knew the recipe by heart. Ross offered to help, but the kitchen was her domain and she limited his participation to opening cans and filling the spaghetti pot with water. She'd hoped he would go away for a while, perhaps out for a walk, but he merely settled down on the couch with his leg propped up.

It was as the sauce was simmering, the spaghetti nearly cooked, and the French bread in the oven that she pretended to notice her purse was missing. As expected, Ross volunteered to go rescue it.

He was gone less than a minute. But it was enough time for her to crush one of her sleeping tablets between the wheels of the can opener and hide the powder in a folded napkin. A few minutes later, as she ladled the sauce onto the plates of spaghetti, she added the powder onto his serving. A sprinkle of parmesan to cover up anything odd in the texture, and dinner was served.

The meal was a quiet affair. Angie didn't feel like talking, and after the obligatory compliments on the meal and a few attempts to get a conversation going Ross took the hint.

"What's our next move?" Angie finally broke the silence as they cleared the table.

"I think we've gone as far as we can on our own," Ross said, peering at the level in the wine bottle. Neither of them had had more than a single glass, and for a tense moment Angie wondered if he was going to find her lack of interest suspicious. If there was anyone in Tahoe who should want to get lost in an alcoholic stupor, it was her.

But he merely resealed the bottle and put it back on the sideboard. "Tomorrow morning we break camp and head back to San Jose."

Angie frowned. Going back to civilization should be the last thing on this man's mind. No, it had to be a ruse, something to lull her into a false sense of security. "I thought you didn't trust them."

Ross yawned, the action seeming to take in his entire face. "I don't," he said. "But we're at a blind alley here, and there aren't a lot of other options."

He yawned again. This time, his shoulders and chest got into the act, too. "Sorry," he apologized when he could speak again. "It's not the company. Really."

"It's been a busy couple of days," Angie reminded him, faking a yawn of her own. "I'm about ready to turn in myself."

"Right." He squinted at his watch. "Seven-thirty. Definitely time for bed."

"Don't be snide," Angie reproved him, putting the last plate in the dishwasher. "I can still remember when seven-thirty was my bedtime."

"Not being snide," Ross said, yawning again. "Actually sounds pretty good."

"You'd better get to the couch before you fall over," Angie warned. "Go on, I'll finish up here."

"Okay," he murmured, shuffling over to the couch and collapsing into a horizontal heap. Angie watched out of the corner of her eye, wondering uneasily if the performance was perhaps too good to be true. Was he on to her, and merely faking sleepiness to see what she was up to?

He stirred, and in almost slow motion drew his gun from beneath his jacket and slipped it under his pillow. Then, with a deep sigh, he adjusted his shoulders and hips against the cushions and lay still.

Angie took her time, fiddling quietly with the dishes, putting spices away in the cupboard, washing off the table and counter tops. Ross's breathing remained slow and steady the whole time. If he was faking, he was doing a good job of it. Finishing her cleanup, she turned out all the lights except a small one over the sink and went back to the bedroom.

Five minutes later, her new wardrobe packed in her new suitcase, she was ready to go.

Ross didn't move as she tiptoed to the couch. He'd put the Blazer's keys in the left rear pocket of his slacks, she'd noted earlier. Setting her teeth, her pulse thudding painfully, she eased two fingers into the pocket and carefully worked the keys toward the opening.

He didn't move at her touch. Didn't react in any way. She kept at it, feeling her arm beginning to tremble, and after what seemed like an hour the ring finally came clear, the keys jangling together like a dropped tambourine before she could stifle them.

There were half a dozen in all, and for a moment she considered taking the whole bunch and seeing what the police could make of them. If one of them was to the Tarnhelm lab, then they would have a solid connection.

But that would be way too convenient. Also way too stupid on Ross's part. Besides, right now all she wanted was to get away from here. She separated out the Blazer's keys and put them in her side pocket, leaving the rest of the keys on the floor beside the couch.

Now came the really tricky part. Bracing herself, she reached to his other back pocket, where the bulge of his wallet pressed against the material. She'd seen enough TV crime shows to know that using her credit cards would be an engraved invitation for anyone who could tap into the system to come and get her.

That meant she needed cash. And at the moment there was only one place to get it. If Ross wasn't working with the killers, she could pay him back later. If he *was* one of the bad guys, this was nothing but poetic justice.

The wallet was harder to extricate than the keys. But Ross's complete lack of reaction to her probing gave her confidence, and after a minute she had it free. His bankroll was smaller than she'd hoped, only about two hundred dollars. She took it all; then, with a pang of conscience, put back one of the twenties.

Aside from the money, the wallet was surprisingly empty, containing only a driver's license and a single VISA card. Again mindful of the made-for-TV movies, she pulled the license out for a closer look.

She felt her breath catch in her throat. Tucked away in the slot behind it was another plasticized card. An Iowa driver's license made out to a Charles Sullivan.

With Ross's picture on it.

For a moment she stared at the license. Then, almost unwillingly, she set it down and slid the VISA card out of its slot. It, too, had a twin hidden behind it. Like the Iowa license, this VISA was made out to Charles Sullivan.

Carefully, she replaced the Iowa license and credit card back behind their California counterparts. She'd wondered all evening if Ross could possibly be working for the killers, for God only knew what reason.

But through it all she'd clung desperately to the hope that her suspicions were wrong, an artifact of panic and tension and this horrible sense of helplessness. The hope that the whole nightmare was in fact no more than it seemed on the surface, and that Ross himself was the Good Samaritan he claimed to be. The hope that she had an ally and friend in him, and wasn't completely alone in the world.

But Good Samaritans didn't have two completely different identities.

And she was indeed all alone.

She gazed down at the sleeping man, starting to tremble again. A kaleidoscope of images flashed through her mind: his arrival in the office over her bank; his immediate zeroing in on her there; his knowledge of her usual parking place at the mall; his fortuitous appearance as people started shooting, and his willingness to offer her his protection.

And her completely reflexive and unthinking willingness to go with him.

Ross's main gun was under his pillow with his full weight on top of it, not a job she was willing to tackle even with him drugged. But she'd seen at the hotel that he also had a second gun. Keeping a wary eye on the sleeping man, she began to search.

She found it almost at once, at the bottom of the otherwise empty gym bag sitting beside the TV. She pulled it out gingerly, wincing at the unexpected weight. She'd never fired a gun in her life, and wasn't even sure where the safety catch was. Still, there were only a couple of levers on the side. If it became necessary, she should be able to figure it out. Reaching into the bag again, she felt around to see if there were extra bullets hiding in a corner somewhere.

She paused, an odd shiver brushing past her mind. Something was wrong here. She felt around some more; and then, all it once, it struck her. The base of the bag was thick. Nearly an inch thick, in fact.

An inch thick?

She picked up the gun and bag and carried them beneath the single kitchen light still burning. It took only a minute for her to find the tabs nestled up against the inner sides of the bag and to use them to pull up the top of the hidden compartment.

She stared into the open space, her muscles tightening with shock and revulsion. Inside was a digital recorder, with a camouflaged lens pointed out one end.

Angie looked back at Ross, feeling like she was going to throw up, the image of that bag flashing to view as it sat so innocently on the desk at the hotel room. Sitting there as she walked around naked after her shower.

So her instinctive discomfort at being alone with him had been dead on target. He was a stalker. A voyeur. A pervert. Maybe a rapist.

She picked up the gun, suddenly glad of its weight in her hand. For a moment she considered taking the bag and checking out the playback once she was far away from this place. But no. She already knew what was on it.

The Blazer was icy cold. She pulled the door only partially closed, not wanting to risk the sound of a slam, and turned the key. In a made-for-TV movie, the dark thought occurred to her, the engine would refuse to turn over, making just enough noise to wake up the enemy sleeping inside.

But this was no movie. The Blazer started right up, and three seconds later the all-weather tires were crunching through the crust of snow. Half a mile away she stopped to close the door properly, and she was on her way.

She still didn't know exactly where she was going. But she would think of something.

THE
FIFTH
DAY

15

BURKE WAS WEARING a bathrobe when he finally opened the apartment door. A bathrobe, slippers, and an annoyed scowl. "For God's sake, Delgado," he grumbled, peering bleary eyed at his visitor. "It's seven o'damn clock in the morning. Don't you guys keep regular hours?"

"This coming from a lab tech who doesn't remember when he last ate lunch?" Delgado countered. "Anyway, we all have to work when the work's there. May I come in?"

The bleary eyes narrowed. "Why?"

"I have some questions," Delgado said. "If you'd prefer, I can wait here while you dress and we can go down to the station."

Burke's mouth puckered, but he moved back from the door, rubbing his eyes with one hand as he gestured inside with the other.

"Thank you." Delgado stepped inside, taking in the room with a single glance. It was a typical post-college bachelor pad: cheap second-hand furniture in sharp contrast with the shiny TV, computer, and surround-sound system. "I'm surprised you're still in bed," he commented as Burke closed the door behind him.

"Sunday's my day to sleep in," the other grunted, scratching his head vigorously as he walked past Delgado to a dark blue couch and flopped down onto it. "My *only* day."

"Ah," Delgado nodded, choosing a green-plaid recliner positioned at an angle to the couch. "My mistake. I thought you might get up for Reverend Lane's early broadcast."

Burke didn't bat an eye. "I get it later from his website," he said. "That better not be all you came here for."

"What better not be all I came here for?"

"To find out if I watch Reverend Lane." Burke's lip twitched sarcastically. "Or have you already checked with my friends and family?"

"We did better than that, actually," Delgado said. "The IRS says you've been quite generous to the Reverend and his cause."

"I'm glad you approve," Burke bit out, his face darkening. "What gives you the right to go poking around my tax files?"

"A triple murder and the search warrants that go with it," Delgado told him. "Don't worry, it's all properly legal."

"By whose definition?"

Delgado shrugged. "Legal is legal, Mr. Burke. You want the murderer caught or not?"

"Don't cloud the issue," Burke growled. "If all you want is to catch criminals, turn America into a police state. You're halfway there as it is."

Delgado sighed. "Look, I'm not here to discuss political ethics, and I don't care who you listen or donate money to. All I want is the people responsible for this crime. The puppet and the ones pulling his strings."

Burke eyed him suspiciously. "So what, you think Reverend Lane is involved? Just because you don't like his politics?"

"Lane's politics are irrelevant, too," Delgado said. "There are some who consider his exhortations to be on the edge of sedition, but—"

"Dictatorships talk about sedition," Burke interrupted. "Democracies recognize the people's right to change their government if it isn't doing its job."

"At the ballot box."

"Or otherwise," Burke countered. "We learned that from Washington, Franklin, and Madison."

"Perhaps," Delgado said. "A Cloak could be very useful for a group of patriots pitted against an oppressive government. Or they might be more concerned with keeping Cloak technology out of UN hands."

"So you are accusing him of being involved," Burke insisted. The words were still belligerent, Delgado noted, but a note of caution had appeared in his tone.

"Not necessarily," Delgado said. "Certainly not the Reverend himself. But rhetoric like his attracts all sorts. Someone might have taken it on himself to read between the lines and offer him a belated Christmas present." He cocked an eyebrow. "Unless you want to defend *all* of Lane's followers."

"No, there are nuts everywhere," Burke conceded reluctantly. "So why didn't this patriot destroy the whole lab? Killing the scientists doesn't do much if the data's still there."

"Maybe he thought the Cloaks weren't of any serious use," Delgado said. "An expensive parlor trick, as Mr. Kingsley put it. He may have thought the project's future was all that needed to be cut off."

Abruptly, Burke got to his feet. "If you're going to charge me with murder, do it," he said stiffly, drawing himself up to his full height.

"I'm not accusing you of anything, Mr. Burke," Delgado said mildly. "I'm just exploring possibilities."

"That's not what it sounds like at this end of the room," Burke insisted. "It sounds more like you're trying to railroad Reverend Lane, and me along with him."

"We're trying to solve a crime," Delgado said, letting his voice go cold. "For that we need motive, opportunity, and method. We've got opportunity and method. We need motive. You want to work with me to try to eliminate political fervor from that list, or not?"

For a moment Burke continued to glare. Then, reluctantly, he sat down again. "Fine. What else do you want to know?"

"Tell me about Angie Chandler."

Burke's lip twitched again. "About time you started paying some attention to our missing link. What do you need?"

"First of all, do you have any idea where she might run if she was in trouble? Family, friends, favorite hideaways—anything?"

Burke scratched an unshaven cheek. "I think her parents live in Monterey," he said, "and I seem to remember a brother or sister somewhere else in California. Friends or hideaways, no idea."

Delgado nodded. "Next question. Do you know if she went anywhere near the coffee pot during her visit Thursday evening?"

"Nope," the other said, shaking his head. "I mean I don't know. I wasn't paying attention to her."

"Too bad," Delgado said regretfully. "It would have been nice to eliminate her as a suspect."

"You should talk to Scott Kingsley," Burke said. "He was the one with google-eyes for the lady."

"What do you mean?"

"Well, I mean, he liked her," Burke said, sounding slightly flustered, as if he'd let out a secret that wasn't his to talk about. "Thought she was cute. I mean, she *was* cute—*is* cute—and Scott has kind of a roving eye. He tried to hit on Dr. Underwood, too, but she wasn't having any of it."

"Sounds risky," Delgado said. "It's considered bad form to hit on your boss's wife."

"Oh, I don't think it went anywhere," Burke said hastily. "Angie wasn't the sort to buy into stuff like that, and I think Scott knew it. He settled for staring at her from afar."

"Still risky," Delgado said, watching Burke's face closely. "Even if Mrs. Chandler wasn't interested, that doesn't mean her husband wouldn't notice and take exception. Unless, of course, there was a reason he wasn't noticing things like that."

The reaction wasn't big. But it was definitely there. "Yeah," Burke muttered. "Well . . . yeah."

"You have something else to add?" Delgado prompted. "You have an obligation to give me any facts pertaining to the case."

Burke squirmed in his seat. "I guess it's not really a secret," he said at last. "Not really a fact, either. More of a rumor."

"I'll settle for rumors," Delgado said. "Let's have it."

Burke squirmed again. "Well . . . it could be that Dr. Chandler wouldn't have noticed if his wife was fooling around because he and Dr. Underwood . . . well, they'd been spending a lot of time together lately. A *lot* of time."

"All of you have been spending a lot of time together," Delgado reminded him. "You had a project up against a deadline."

"I know that," Burke said, sounding suddenly annoyed. "That's not the kind of work or time I'm talking about. The two of them would go off into that office of his and spend hours alone. Dr. Fowler wouldn't let any of us bother them, even if there was something we really needed to ask. He'd come up with the answer himself or else call them on the phone."

He leveled a finger. "And there were a lot of times, especially in the last three weeks, where the two of them would be working when we left for the night and still be there when we arrived the next morning."

"I see." For someone who'd seemed reticent to bring up the subject, Burke had warmed to it with amazing speed. "Of course, Dr. Underwood *did* live only half a mile away from the Sand/Star gate. She could easily have gone home and come back while the rest of you were out. And Dr. Chandler had that cot."

"Yeah, he had that cot, all right," Burke agreed. "That's one of the things that got us thinking about it in the first place."

"Mm," Delgado said noncommittally, deciding to pass for the moment on who exactly the *us* referred to. "Do you know if Mrs. Chandler shared these same suspicions?"

The blue eyes suddenly went wary. "I don't know. Why? You looking for a motive again?"

"Looking for a motive still," Delgado said. "And jealousy has a long history in that role."

Burke snorted. "Jealously and political fervor. You're all over the map with this, aren't you? Besides, I thought we'd decided the motive was gain."

"The thieves were definitely after the Cloaks," Delgado agreed. "But the inside man or woman could have had an entirely different reason for throwing in with them."

The eyes were still wary. "So now you think Angie did it out of jealousy?"

"Or one of you three could have done it, for a reason we haven't yet considered."

"Such as?"

"Dr. Tarlington dropped by the lab the afternoon of the murders," Delgado reminded him. "Kingsley told me yesterday that he and Dr. Stryker sometimes use high profile projects like Tarnhelm to poach people from other companies."

"More like *often* than *sometimes*. So?"

"Maybe one of you overheard Tarlington and Chandler planning to dump you and bring in new talent," Delgado said. "Maybe that same person thought you'd have a better chance of keeping your jobs if you were the only ones who knew how the Cloaks worked."

"And what, made a couple of phone calls, ordered some poison, and lined up a gang of thieves on half an hour's notice?" Burke countered. "Come *on*, Delgado."

"Oh, it clearly wasn't set up the day of the murders," Delgado agreed. "But Esteban said Tarlington tended to wander around that same time every day. It could be that the plan to dump the three of you was initiated weeks earlier."

"In that case, why not just steal the software and sell it somewhere? Why bring murder into it?"

"Maybe the murders weren't intentional," Delgado said. "Maybe the thieves told the inside man the stuff he was putting into the coffee was the same knock-out drops he'd nailed the downstairs guard with."

"Or maybe it was Tarlington who did it," Burke shot back. "You ever think of that? He's the only one who gains anything by knocking off the scientists. He now gets to recruit *six* new people, not just three."

"How did he get in without the guard signing him in?"

"You think there's only one door into the building?" Burke scoffed. "There are four of them, plus the loading dock."

Delgado frowned. "I was told there was only the one door that operates after hours."

"Technically, yes," Burke said. "The others are locked down, and they set off alarms all over the compound if they're opened. But the loading dock doesn't have an alarm. You just need a special card and code."

"Interesting," Delgado murmured. Talbot, he remembered, had suggested early on that Tarlington might have a private way into the building. "Who would have those?"

"The people who work there, obviously," Burke said. "They usually go home at five. Tarlington and the other supervisors have master cards, but I don't know if they work on the dock."

"We'll look into it," Delgado promised. "Just two more questions and I'll let you get back to bed. First, you said you didn't think Kingsley had made any headway with Dr. Underwood. Why do you think that?"

Burke shrugged uncomfortably. "Like I said, Scott fancies himself a ladies' man. He's not the type to score and not brag at least a little about it. Besides, Dr. Underwood was still married, wasn't she?"

"Legally, yes," Delgado said. "But she's estranged from her husband."

"Did you check his alibi?" Burke asked, an edge of sarcasm in his voice. "If you're still looking for traditional motives."

"He was in Boston at the time," Delgado said. "Besides, how would he have gotten into the lab?"

"Maybe he's working with Tarlington." Burke waved a disgusted hand. "Never mind. Forget him."

"Don't worry, we're checking everyone, including Mr. Underwood," Delgado said. "Final question. From what you said earlier about Mrs. Chandler being a missing link, I gather you know she's vanished. How did you find out?"

Burke was looking wary again. "Why? Is it a secret?"

"It's not exactly something we want to broadcast across the greater Bay Area," Delgado said. "How did you find out?"

Burke made a face. "Ramon told us Friday morning," he said reluctantly. "After the prototype demo, after you shooed all of us out of the lab."

"How did *he* find out?"

"I don't know," Burke growled. "Why don't you ask him?"

"I will," Delgado said, getting to his feet. "Thanks for your time."

"Sure," Burke said sourly. "Don't slam the door on your way out."

~

Kingsley was jogging toward a corner convenience store when Talbot caught up with him. "Mr. Kingsley," he called through the open window of his car, slowing down to pace the other. "I wonder if I could have a few words with you."

"It's Sunday, friend," Kingsley puffed, not breaking stride as he pulled off his headphones and draped them around his neck. "A day of rest the world over."

"Not for the crooks it isn't," Talbot said. "Therefore, not for the cops, either."

"You guys need a better union," Kingsley said, slapping the door of an archaic-looking phone booth at the side of the store as he passed it. "Here's a phone. Why don't you call in sick or something?"

"Thanks, but I need the overtime," Talbot said. "You going to be ready for a break soon?"

"Serious runners never need a break," Kingsley said, pointing toward a bus stop bench two blocks ahead. "But if you insist. There at the bench."

Talbot had parked the car and was sitting on one end of the bench by the time Kingsley reached him. "I thought running was passé these days," he commented as the other collapsed onto the other end of the bench. "Health clubs and celebrity workouts are the *in* thing."

"Can't stand them," Kingsley panted, wiping his forehead on his sleeve and pulling a garishly decorated water bottle from its belt loop. "Too crowded. Give me an early-morning sidewalk any day."

"You do this every morning?"

"When I can," he said, taking a long drink. "Lately I've been lucky if I could manage three times a week. What can I do for you?"

"We're looking for Angie Chandler," Talbot told him. "Thought you might have some idea where to start."

Kingsley sniffed. "Have you tried the Chinese consulate?"

"So far we haven't found any evidence of Chinese involvement," Talbot said. "Besides, she appears to have been kidnapped." He cocked his head. "You *did* know that, right?"

"Yeah, I heard rumors," Kingsley said. "If you ask me, that whole thing was staged to cover her vanishing act. For my money, she's either in the consulate or a hundred miles outside U.S. waters."

"Could be," Talbot said, keeping his voice neutral. "Any other suggestions where we might look for her?"

Kingsley shrugged. "She's got parents in Monterey. You could check there. Aside from that, I haven't the foggiest."

"Okay," Talbot said, standing up. "Thanks."

"Is that it?" Kingsley asked, frowning up at him. "You came all the way out here just to ask me that?"

"That's it," Talbot assured him. "Unless, of course, you want to tell me about your relationship with Mrs. Chandler. The off-hours one, I mean."

Kingsley snorted. "I wish. Sorry, Talbot, but if you're looking for scandal, you're out of luck. Not that I couldn't have pressed the matter. I'm pretty sure her husband was fooling around with our lovely and talented Dr. Underwood."

"Really," Talbot said. "What makes you think that?"

"A guy can tell when a woman's getting regular service," Kingsley said, his tone an odd mixture of sage wisdom and locker-room crudeness. "Barbara had that look. Angie didn't. It's that simple."

"And you're sure it was Dr. Chandler who was servicing her?"

Kingsley made a face. "Go check our work schedule. You tell *me* if she had time to see anyone on the outside."

"There were other men on the inside," Talbot reminded him. "You, for instance."

"Yeah, well, it wasn't for lack of trying," Kingsley said ruefully. "But that lady came equipped with a three-foot speed bump as far as I was concerned. I guess she was one of those one-man women. One man at a time, anyway."

"Could it have been one of the other techs?"

Kingsley shook his head. "Not a chance. Jack was too young for her, and too pure and noble to touch a married woman anyway. Ramon was too Hispanic, if you know what I mean. No, it had to be Dr. Chandler."

"How about Dr. Tarlington?"

Kingsley gave him an odd look. "What do you do, work for the *Enquirer* on the side? What does this have to do with anything?"

"Jealousy and betrayal are two of the classic motives for murder," Talbot pointed out.

"You want to talk jealousy, you should talk to Jack Burke," Kingsley said. "He's the one who's big on that theory. Besides, I thought you'd already decided that stealing the Cloaks was the motive."

"Nothing says a crime can't have two motives," Talbot said. "Especially when there's more than one person involved, as there is here. Sometimes these things get pretty twisted."

"I suppose," Kingsley said, with the air of a debater conceding a point. "My money's still on Angie. Though that's not to say she wasn't forced into it."

"Of course not," Talbot agreed. "Speaking of her, did you happen to notice whether or not she went near the coffee pot that evening?"

Kingsley frowned in concentration. "She didn't while I was there," he said slowly. "But I left the lab before she did, when I went out to get the semi. You'd have to ask one of the others what she did after that."

"I'll do that," Talbot said. "Thanks for your time."

"Yeah, no problem," Kingsley said, getting to his feet and swinging his arms experimentally. "And you really *should* get a better union."

"Have a good run," Talbot said.

He returned to his car as Kingsley jogged off. Fiddling with his keys and his notebook, he managed to postpone starting the engine until Kingsley had turned a corner and disappeared. Then, making a U-turn, he headed back the way he'd come, coasting to a halt beside the convenience store they'd passed earlier.

For a moment he sat in his car gazing through the window at the muted security lights in the back. The name spelled out in neon tubing in the front window was similar to one of the national chains but not an exact match. That, plus the small house connected in back, indicated a mom-and-pop operation.

A conclusion further bolstered by the hours card he finally spotted on the angled window beside the door. No twenty-four-hour operation here—the place was open seven to seven on weekdays, eight to ten on Saturdays, and eleven to seven on Sundays. If Kingsley ever wanted a drink on his early morning runs, he concluded, he'd better make sure his water bottle was already filled.

He looked at his watch, estimating driving times. Delgado should be nearly to Esteban's place by now. Once he finished there, the two of them would be getting together to compare notes. Copies of Swenson's impressive collection of data were on Lyman's and Garcia's desks. Swenson herself, unfortunately, had politely but firmly put herself on an early-morning plane for Washington.

Shifting back into drive, Talbot pulled away from the curb and headed toward the coffee shop where he was to meet Delgado. Things were starting to come together, though how exactly the pieces would wind up fitting was still up in the air. Especially as one of the biggest pieces steadfastly refused to surface.

Where the hell was Angie Chandler?

~

Esteban shook his head as he shoved a last corner of cinnamon toast nervously into his mouth. "I'm sorry, Lieutenant," he said, the words punctuated by crunching. "I have no idea where Angie might have gone. I just hope she's okay."

"That goes for all of us," Delgado said.

"All except whoever was shooting at her," Esteban said. "You any closer to figuring out who those guys were?"

"Afraid not," Delgado conceded. "We also haven't been able to dig up anything on this Adam Ross character she left with."

"It makes you wonder," Esteban murmured, turning to look out his kitchen window. "If they're after her, maybe they're after us, too."

"I don't think so," Delgado said. "Right now the three of you are more valuable to them alive."

Esteban shivered. "You mean they might kidnap us?"

"I doubt it," Delgado soothed. "If that's what they wanted, they could have taken you the night of the murders, when no one was expecting trouble. No, you're useful mostly because keeping you alive means there's only a one in five chance that any of you is the poisoner. Criminals like having crowds to hide in."

"Wait a minute," Esteban said, frowning a little harder. "Three of us techs; but you said one in five. Who are the other two?"

"Angie Chandler's one," Delgado said. "Your colleagues seem convinced she's involved."

"Yeah, I know," Esteban said, an edge of contempt in his voice. "Jack thinks it was jealous rage. Scott's convinced she's a mole for the Chinese."

"Motives come in all shapes and sizes," Delgado said. "The problem with Mrs. Chandler—one of them—is that no one saw her go near the coffee pot the night of the murders." Delgado lifted his eyebrows. "Unless *you* happened to notice something?"

Esteban grimaced. "Actually . . . yes, I did," he said reluctantly. "On her way out she went the long way around the tables we'd pushed together into the middle of the room. Going that direction, she had to pass by the table with the pizza and soda and coffee."

Delgado felt himself straightening a bit. "Did she pause there?" he asked, trying to keep his voice steady. If she had in fact had opportunity . . . "Or did her hand get anywhere near the pot?"

Esteban shook his head. "I don't know," he said. "I was working on Mama Bear at the time and just happened to glance up and see her walking that direction. But then I looked back down again. I know she didn't change direction and circle around behind me the other way, but that's all."

"Was there anyone near you who might have seen more?"

Esteban gave him a bitter smile. "Sure. Doctors Fowler and Underwood. Big help, huh?"

"There's a lot of that in this business," Delgado said philosophically. "I understand you're the one who told your fellow techs that Mrs. Chandler had gone missing. Mind telling me how you knew?"

Esteban lowered his eyes guiltily. "I guess I eavesdropped. A little."

"You *guess*?"

He winced. "I mean, I did. Eavesdrop. While you and Garcia and Talbot were waiting for us to get the Cloak demo ready. I was pulling one of the notebooks from a cabinet near the office, and I overheard you telling the gate people what had happened at the mall and the kind of car she was in."

"So having heard all that, you naturally trotted off and spilled the beans to your friends?"

"It wasn't like that," Esteban protested, managing to look both shocked and offended. "I wouldn't have said anything, except that Jack caught me listening and wanted to know what was going on. I shushed him and said I'd tell him later."

"Later being when?"

"After we all left, while you and the others were still in the office," Esteban said. "He hit me up as soon as we were in the elevator. And of course Scott wasn't about to be kept out of it, either."

"So you told them," Delgado said, letting his voice harden a bit.

Esteban winced. "I guess I shouldn't have, should I?"

"No, you shouldn't," Delgado said. "Next time you overhear something that wasn't meant for you, we'd all appreciate it if you'd keep it to yourself."

"Yes, sir, I will," Esteban said humbly.

"And if you hear something that *should* be passed on to us, we'd be just as grateful if you'd do so at once," Delgado continued.

"I haven't heard anything," Esteban insisted quickly. "Really."

"I wasn't implying you had," Delgado said. "I'm not keeping you, by the way, am I? You look like you're ready to go out."

"No, I'm all right," Esteban assured him. "I'm just meeting my parents and sister for lunch. After that—" His mouth compressed briefly. "We're going to see my brother."

"The one in San Quentin?"

Esteban nodded. "You know all about that, I suppose."

"Yes," Delgado said. "How's he doing?"

Esteban shrugged. "How well does anyone do in prison? All right, I suppose."

"It's pretty rough, isn't it?"

"It's hell," Esteban said bluntly. "I could have been in there, too, you know, if I hadn't gotten my head squared up. It's a scary thought."

"So I gather," Delgado said. "I suppose you'd do about anything to get him out, eh?"

"If there was anything I could do—" Esteban broke off, his face going rigid. "No," he said through suddenly stiff lips. "Not what you're thinking."

"What am I thinking?"

"Don't you put words in my mouth," Esteban snapped, his dark face darkening a little more. "I didn't kill them."

"Okay," Delgado said, keeping his voice calm. "Wasn't implying you did."

"Yeah, right," Esteban muttered, clearly not mollified. "Are we done yet?"

"Just one more question," Delgado said. "You seemed rather nervous when you answered the door. Any particular reason for that?"

"You mean aside from the obvious?" Esteban retorted. "A cop knocking on your door two days after a murder?"

"Aside from the obvious, yes," Delgado said. "Like for example, maybe Burke called to warn you he'd spilled the beans about your eavesdropping in the lab?"

Esteban exhaled between his teeth. "You've got us pretty well figured, haven't you?"

"Part of my job," Delgado said. "I've dealt with tight-knit groups like yours before. You tend to keep close tabs on each other, especially when you're under stress."

He gestured at Esteban. "Same pattern as you telling them about Mrs. Chandler's abductor. Which you knew perfectly well you shouldn't."

"I know." Esteban made an attempt at a smile. "Don't worry, I've learned my lesson."

"I'll hold you to that," Delgado warned, moving to the door. "Thanks for your time."

16

SATURDAY NIGHT HAD gone a little better than the night before. But only a little, and McPherson was long past the age where he could easily bounce back from two nights in a row of clocking less than four hours of sleep. Sunday morning had come all too quickly, and now as he sat in Cohn's office it was rather like reliving that mother of all hangovers during his sophomore year of college that had finally driven him to permanently swear off alcohol.

Cohn, to his certain knowledge, had had even less sleep than he had. Despite that, and despite the man's seven extra years and thirty extra pounds, he looked a lot better than McPherson felt. That was the really irritating part.

But at least the preliminary report from the *Rabah Jamila* was beginning to hammer this thing into some kind of sense.

Maybe.

"So it looks like North Korea," he commented, looking through the papers Cohn had given him.

"Yes," Cohn said. "It does, doesn't it."

McPherson frowned. Cohn's face wasn't visible as he stood at the window gazing out at the dirty clouds that hung over the equally dirty snow below. But there had been something in his voice . . . "You're not happy with that?"

The other shrugged. "The evidence seems conclusive," he conceded, turning from the window to the coffee pot on the table beside it. "It was like Little Pyongyang in those containers: North Korean cots, North Korean field rations, North Korean clothing—"

"Yes, I saw the list," McPherson said. "So the conclusion is that the nuke is heading to North Korea. May actually be there by now, in fact."

"Possibly," Cohn said, refilling his mug. "On the other hand, Admiral Eskin is doing a good job of surveillance and interdiction of ship traffic heading that direction. The other possible vector, the Zhardi CitationJet, still hasn't moved from Chongqing."

"Though the nuke could have gone overland from there," McPherson pointed out. "Either all the way to North Korea or to another waiting plane."

"That's possible, too," Cohn said, coming back to his desk and hitching himself up onto a corner facing McPherson. "We're sifting through Chinese air traffic records, but so far there's no clear vector for the nuke to have taken."

"What about those three other freighters the Navy tagged? I didn't see any references here."

"Two of them have allowed us to board, but the searches aren't finished," Cohn said. "The third—the Indonesian one—is still refusing. I understand the President's still talking to Jakarta."

"We're sure those three were the only ships close enough for the stowaways to have transferred to during that forty-six-minute window?"

Cohn shrugged. "So it would appear."

McPherson eyed him. "You know, you don't seem very enthusiastic about this. What's the problem?"

"Basically, that I can't make it hold together." Cohn waved a hand in invitation. "Why don't you reconstruct it for me? Maybe I'm missing something obvious."

"The stowaways came aboard the *Rabah Jamila* at Da Nang," McPherson said slowly, thinking through each word as he watched for the logical quicksand Cohn obviously thought was in there somewhere. "The captain, crew, and manifest all agree that's where those two containers were loaded. They were surprised by pirates in the Taiwan Strait, blew them away, and convinced Syed they were South Koreans with a mission. Any problems so far?"

"One or two," Cohn said. "But go on."

"Syed finally broke radio silence and called home. The stowaways had the radio room bugged and knew the jig was up, so they took over the ship. They locked the crew in a hold, sent out a fake distress call, left a bomb behind to cover their tracks, then transferred to the yacht Syed saw."

"And then vanished."

McPherson grimaced. "Something like that."

"Okay," Cohn said. "Question: was the nuke aboard the *Rabah Jamila*?"

"I don't know," McPherson said. "Until we have a clear vector for it from Raipur to Da Nang, I hesitate to say it was. On the other hand, if this was nothing but a diversion, it's been one hell of an impressive one."

"Agreed," Cohn said, nodding. "That's the way Vaughn's reading it, too, or at least that's the tone I get from his report. Putting aside the critical question of where the nuke actually is, that still leaves us with two big questions. Number one: where is the yacht now?"

McPherson shrugged. "Probably the bottom of the East China Sea."

"Why?"

McPherson frowned at him. "What do you mean, why? Because they were already aboard another ship, or submarine, or seaplane, and didn't need it anymore."

"Except that Vaughn says there weren't any seaplanes or submarines in the area at the time."

"Maybe something slipped in without the surveillance planes spotting it."

"Maybe," Cohn said. "But again, why sink it? Who knew to even give it a second glance?"

"Well . . . " McPherson took a long sip from his cup. The coffee didn't seem to be helping today. "Try this. The yacht took them to another ship. Maybe a different freighter than the three the Navy tagged, because the yacht could travel a lot faster than a dinghy or longboat from the *Rabah Jamila* itself."

"Good so far," Cohn encouraged. "So then why sink it?"

"Because its presence would have shown us where they went," McPherson said. "They knew we'd be out there pretty quick and would take a look at any ship close at hand."

Cohn gave him a brittle smile. "Exactly," he said. "Which brings us to question number two. *Why did they send that distress signal?*"

McPherson gazed into the other's intense eyes. "That," he said quietly, "is a damn good question."

"It made a certain amount of sense before," Cohn went on. "We assumed it was someone from the crew who sent the mayday, with the boarders subsequently overpowering him and sending a message of their own to the Chinese. But now we know the crew didn't get anywhere near the radio room before they were locked up. Ergo, both signals had to have been sent by the stowaways. Why?"

McPherson looked out at the dark clouds. "They wanted us out there," he said slowly. "That's the only explanation. Us and the Chinese both."

"I agree. But again, why? Especially since they already had a bomb set to send the ship to the bottom?"

"Maybe that's why," McPherson suggested. "If they could convince us the nuke was aboard, we might think it went down with the ship. That would also explain why they didn't bother to clean up the evidence they'd left behind in the containers."

"Then you're saying the Chinese CitationJet was a feint," Cohn said. "And you must also be saying that the nuke actually disappeared from Raipur five days before the Indians thought it did, hidden in one of the containers that was loaded at Vishakhapatnam."

"That's not entirely impossible," McPherson pointed out. "Remember, Rao said it was only when they took radiation readings that they realized the bomb casing was empty. What if the original thieves left a radiation source inside the casing big enough to fake the proper readings? In that case, what the Indians thought was the actual theft was in fact a second team infiltrating for the purpose of removing the decoy source."

"Interesting thought," Cohn murmured, frowning into his coffee cup. "If that's true, there's not a chance in hell of tracking the bomb."

"Actually, I don't think that's very likely," McPherson confessed. "I just bring it up for completeness. From Rao's report it didn't sound like anyone even penetrated the weapon storage area during the first security disturbance."

"At least not that they know about," Cohn said with a snort. "So with the sinking of the *Rabah Jamila* we were supposed to believe that the nuke had disappeared? Joy and rapture all around, and everyone relaxes until the thing goes off somewhere?"

"I can't think why else they would make sure both we and the Chinese were there to watch the ship sink," McPherson said. "In fact, it may be that the Zhardi CitationJet has its own set of evidence pointing to the *Rabah Jamila* for Beijing's benefit. I wish I knew what the Chinese knew."

"We'll see what we can find out." Cohn leaned forward slightly. "Let's try something different. You game for a dip into the grand conspiracy pool?"

McPherson felt a tingle run through him. How in hell could Cohn know . . . ? "Grand conspiracy pool?" he asked politely.

"Don't bother," Cohn advised, favoring McPherson with a slightly brittle smile. "I'm well aware of my reputation among you more down-to-earth, reality-based sorts. But you have to admit that flights of fancy do occasionally get you where you want to go."

"I don't have to admit anything when my head feels like this," McPherson said. "But go ahead."

"Try this," Cohn said, gazing intently at McPherson. "Assumption: the stowaways never intended that bomb to go off."

McPherson felt his eyes narrow. "You're not reading your own reports, Larry. That bomb stayed in one piece purely through the grace of God and a single faulty wire."

"Or perhaps through a carefully disabled wire and far less divine intervention," Cohn countered. "No, wait, think about it. It's solely because it didn't go off that we have all this wonderful evidence of North Korean involvement. Evidence that, as you pointed out, any terrorist or merc worth his salt should have destroyed before jumping ship."

"We already knew North Korea was involved," McPherson reminded him. "Syed's call home, remember?"

"No, Syed said they were *South* Korean agents," Cohn corrected. "It wasn't until we got into those containers that we had any proof of a North Korean connection. Supposed proof, anyway."

McPherson pursed his lips. This wasn't nearly as ridiculous as it sounded. "And the yacht?"

"We know Syed saw it," Cohn said. "Got a very good look at it, in fact. Knowing that he'd be describing it to us, since they knew the bomb wasn't going to go off, they went ahead and scuttled it to make us waste time looking for it."

McPherson drained the last of his coffee. "So instead of wanting us to think the nuke went down with the *Rabah Jamila*, they really want us to think North Korea is involved when it isn't?"

"It just gets more and more complicated, doesn't it?" Cohn conceded. "Frankly, I have no idea which direction to jump. The one thing that *is* clear is that whichever way this goes, we've wound up spending the bulk of our attention on East Asia."

"Yes, I've noticed that," McPherson said. "You think the nuke may actually have gone the other direction?"

"Or somewhere less obvious," Cohn said. "Vaughn's theory about using a tactical nuke as a deer gun to get hold of bigger nukes is a disturbing one. The Chinese aren't the only ones with nuclear arsenals outside their borders."

McPherson nodded soberly. "We are, too."

"Or they could take a trip to Israel or South Africa," Cohn added.

"Or Pakistan or China."

"Or India itself."

"Now, wouldn't *that* be cute?" McPherson said thoughtfully. "All this sound and fury, just to draw everyone's attention away from India."

"And we already know whoever's behind this does enjoy playing cute," Cohn pointed out. Behind him on the desk the phone rang, and he reached over to tap a button. "Yes?"

"Minister Rao is on line three, sir," the secretary's voice came over the speaker. "He wants to discuss the report you sent him."

"Thank you," Cohn said, throwing a look at McPherson as he hopped off his corner and circled back to his chair. "This should be interesting," he said, sitting down and pushing a button. "Cohn."

"Good morning, Mr. Cohn," Rao's firm voice boomed. Like Cohn, he sounded a lot more alert than McPherson felt. Unlike Cohn, of course, he had a reasonable excuse: it was only early evening in New Delhi. "I've finished the report you sent two hours ago."

"And your conclusions?"

"It's distressingly incomplete," Rao said bluntly. "I trust you have an update since it was prepared?"

Cohn made a face at McPherson across the desk. "I'm afraid not, sir," he said. "We still haven't finished searching the possible transfer vessels. For that matter, we're still searching the *Rabah Jamila* itself. It's possible that the stowaways jumping ship was simply more misdirection."

"And that the weapon is still aboard the ship?" Rao asked thoughtfully. "Interesting. If true, that would imply Japan was the ultimate destination, not North Korea."

"Possibly," Cohn agreed. "At this point I'm not ready to commit to any particular destination or target. Bear in mind that we still don't even know what the *Rabah Jamila's* true involvement is in all this."

"Its involvement is with the weapon," Rao insisted. "Perhaps its purpose was to allow the Chinese to look like innocent bystanders by offering them an opportunity to cooperate with you. You said the CitationJet which took the weapon from India is still in China, did you not?"

"Yes, it is," Cohn confirmed.

"Do we know where the *Rabah Jamila* is headed after Tokyo?" McPherson asked, a sudden thought striking him.

"I'd have to check," Cohn said.

"It is bound for Petropavlovsk-Kamchatski," Rao said, sounding suddenly thoughtful. "That is an interesting possibility, Director McPherson. You think the weapon will be taken by plane to Tokyo, then reloaded aboard the *Rabah Jamila* there for further transport?"

"Possibly," McPherson said. In point of fact, he hadn't gotten nearly that far in his own thinking. But now that Rao mentioned it, it made a certain lopsided sense. "With the *Rabah Jamila* having just gone through the wringer, who'd give it a second glance?"

"While meanwhile, we're still busy looking at Japan and the Korean Peninsula," Cohn rumbled.

"Perhaps," Rao said. "What of this sailing yacht, the *Eureka*, which your Navy plane saw in the region of the *Rabah Jamila* that night? Could it be involved?"

"I don't see how," Cohn said. "For one thing, it was fully rigged for sailing, while the yacht Captain Syed saw wasn't. More importantly, we have satellite photos of it both before and after the incident, and it was never closer than eighty miles."

"What if it were traveling under power? Most sailing yachts also have engines."

"Still no chance," Cohn assured him. "The *Eureka* is a displacement monohull, and that kind of ship can't do more than twenty or twenty-five knots, no matter what kind of engines it's got. The design simply doesn't allow for higher speed."

"Yes," Rao murmured. "Of course, that assumes the Pakistanis are telling the complete truth about the incident. Would it be possible for representatives from my government to speak directly to the captain and crew?"

"That would be up to them," Cohn said. "The ship's back on a slow course for Tokyo while we continue our search, but it should arrive in port in a couple of days. If you'd like, I'll ask the President to see if he can arrange things with the Pakistani government."

"I would appreciate that," Rao said. "One question still remains. If not to the yacht the Pakistani captain claims he saw, where exactly did the stowaways go?"

"That's another good question, sir," Cohn acknowledged. "There were three freighters close enough for them to have transferred to in the time allotted, but so far none of them has shown evidence of such a move. We know which other ships were in the area, and have them under surveillance. If necessary, we'll broaden our search to them."

"I want these men found, Mr. Cohn," Rao said firmly. "They are our only direct link to the organization plotting against us."

"We'll find them," Cohn promised.

"Good," Rao said. "Please keep me informed of further developments."

"Yes, sir," Cohn said. "Good-bye, Minister."

There was a click as Rao hung up. Cohn keyed off from his end, then turned back to face McPherson. "He's getting impatient."

"I don't blame him," McPherson said. "What's our next move?"

"We keep doing what we're doing," Cohn said with a sigh. Suddenly he didn't look nearly as fresh as he had a few minutes ago. "We search ships, examine satellite photos, dig into communications, and patrol the sea."

He turned to gaze out the window. "And I think I'll have them take another look at the *Rabah Jamila* bomb."

~

It was, Angie thought morosely as she stared out through the gauzy motel curtain, like being trapped in Act II of a badly done play. A play where the writer couldn't think of anything else to do, so simply wrote the same scene over again while stalling for time.

It had started with another long ride through the rain and snow with strangers, this time on a bus instead of in a car with Ross. Another roller-coaster emotional ride, again starting with limp relief at having gotten away, this time from Ross instead of mysterious gunmen, followed by a slow buildup of quiet dread and fear, this time from the realization that any of the other passengers on her bus could in fact be one of those same gunmen.

Now another motel room, plainer than the one Ross had taken her to. Another motel window for her to stare out of as she, like her imaginary playwright, stalled for time.

What was she going to do?

It had seemed so simple on the drive to Reno. She would ditch the Blazer, take a bus back to San Jose, and turn herself in to the police. Certainly they would understand the situation and why she hadn't come forward sooner.

But somewhere between the cabin and the Greyhound station the simplicity had started to break down. The gunmen had been waiting for her at the mall, and Ross had suggested they might also be waiting at the police station. Clearly, they couldn't cover the whole Bay Area . . . but what if they were covering whichever one she went to? Could the police really protect her against further attack?

Of course, maybe Ross had exaggerated the danger so he could make sure she didn't leave him. But if that was all he wanted, why hadn't he cut and run the minute the shooting started? Why had he stuck it out at the risk of his own life? Surely the chance to secretly record her after a shower wasn't worth *that* much to him.

By the time she reached Reno her resolve had eroded enough that she'd bought a ticket to her parents' town of Monterey instead of San Jose. The Monterey police weren't involved in this, she reasoned, and should therefore be safe to approach.

But as the bus lumbered its way through the night, it occurred to her that cops talked to one another, particularly those on murder investigations. The Monterey cops could be as pure as Florida orange juice, but if the gunmen were monitoring police communications, the wrong word to the wrong cop in the South Bay would get her killed.

She hadn't slept on the bus, despite the desperate fatigue that had pulled at her eyelids like ten-pound ankle weights. Every time one of the other passengers twitched in his sleep, or tried to strike up a conversation, or got up to go to the tiny bathroom behind her the adrenaline would flood into her bloodstream like an instant double espresso, sending her heart racing and her hand groping for the stolen gun buried at the bottom of her purse. It was a wonder she hadn't accidentally shot anyone along the way, including herself.

By the time the bus pulled in a little after eight thirty in the morning, she was so physically and emotionally exhausted that even issues of life and death hardly mattered anymore. She'd taken a cab to a motel near the highway, waited until the driver was out of sight, then trudged to a different motel two blocks away. She'd checked in under a fictitious name, paid for one day with some of Ross's cash, and was asleep almost before she was fully on the bed.

She had awakened four hours later to a sore back, a mouth that tasted like something had crawled in there and died, and a brain only marginally more functional than it had been the night before.

Now, gazing out the window, she still had no idea what to do.

She looked at her watch. One-thirty. She wondered if Ross was awake yet. Those sleeping tablets were pretty powerful, she knew from recent experience. Coupled with his overall fatigue, he could very well still be asleep.

She sighed. None of this was making sense. She needed help. She needed advice.

She needed her dad.

She turned away from the window and crossed to the token writing desk and the beige motel phone waiting there with its list of fees and dialing instructions. Ross might have been a liar and scum, but he'd been right about one thing: line phones could easily be tapped and traced. Instead, she scooped up her bag and dug out her cell phone. The battery was starting to run low, and the charger was of course back at her house. But there ought to be enough power for at least one more call. She turned it on, pausing as she searched her memory for her parents' own cell phone number.

In her hand, the phone trilled.

She jerked, nearly dropping it. Who in the world—?

It trilled again, the display indicating a blocked number. Bracing herself, she tapped the switch. "Hello?"

"Angie, it's Adam," Ross's voice boomed in her ear. "Thank God. Listen—don't hang up—"

She jabbed the button hard enough to crack a nail, cutting him off in mid-sentence. She jabbed again, this time turning the phone off completely, and threw it onto the bed. For several minutes she stood there staring at it, shaking uncontrollably even as she berated herself for her completely ridiculous overreaction. Who else had she thought it could be?

By and by the shaking stopped, taking with it every trace of the cautious hope she'd been trying so hard to talk herself into. She still needed to talk to her parents, needed it more than ever now. But the desk phone was still out, she couldn't stand to even touch the cell, and the thought of going out in search of a pay phone—if there were even any around anymore—was suddenly terrifying.

At least in the daylight. Yes, that was it. She would wait until it was dark and then go make her call. She'd waited this long. A few more hours wouldn't make a difference.

Besides, it would give her a chance to try to catch up on her sleep. And maybe do some thinking.

~

The usual stack of paper was sitting on Garcia's desk when he arrived for what his wife liked to call his weekly it's-my-day-off-but-there's-work-to-be-done-anyway session. Sunday after lunch, with the shift out on the streets and an insulating layer of command personnel on duty, was his only opportunity to catch up on all the reading he was supposed to have time for during actual duty hours.

Today, naturally, he had a bumper crop. Not only was the autopsy report in on the Sand/Star murders, but there was an annoyingly tall stack of paper with "FBI" stamped all over it. Scowling at the latter pile—Carlita would be furious if he wound up missing dinner with their son and daughter-in-law over this—he picked up the autopsy report and started to read.

He was only on page two when he groped for his phone and punched in Delgado's cell number.

The other answered on the second ring. "Delgado."

"Garcia. I just got the cause of death report on the Sand/Star scientists. Potassium, nice and neat and unobtrusive. Only it wasn't in the coffee. It was injected."

"Really," Delgado said, suddenly sounding very interested. "Where?"

"A vein in the ankle," Garcia told him. "Very small hypo, with the skin abraded afterward to try to hide the mark. Almost worked, too."

"It must have taken awhile to inject a lethal dose," Delgado said. "I assume they weren't taking an active interest in proceedings at the time?"

"You assume correctly," Garcia agreed, flipping another page and scanning down it. "That's where the coffee tampering comes in. It was drugged with the same chloral hydrate the desk guard got, except that their dose was smaller so that it wouldn't take effect as fast. And that *was* ingested."

"Interesting," Delgado said. "So the person we've been calling the poisoner actually did nothing but put them to sleep. It was the second crew, the ones who took off with the Cloaks, who did the dirty work."

"And then dumped the drugged coffee and brewed up a fresh pot to throw us off track," Garcia said. "There was no chloral hydrate left in the pot—they cleaned that out thoroughly—but Barry found traces of it in the sink."

"Good job," Delgado said. "I didn't think Barry had it in him."

"I think your make-damn-sure-it's-complete-or-it's-your-butt suggestion had something to do with it," Garcia said. "You should raise your voice to the staff more often."

"I'll remember that," Delgado said. "I should point out that it was Special Agent Talbot who had that hunch and suggested I press the point."

Talbot. It figured. "Thank him for me when you get a chance."

"Actually, he's right here," Delgado said. "You want to thank him yourself?"

Garcia scowled. But fair was fair. "Put him on."

There was a brief pause. "Talbot."

"Garcia. I just wanted to tell you your hunch and suggestion panned out."

"Yes, I got the gist from Nate's side of the conversation," Talbot said. "Very enlightening. Have you had a chance yet to look over that material I sent you?"

"Not yet," Garcia said. "Why, does this throw it out the window?"

"Just the opposite," Talbot said. "My researcher came up with a professional industrial spy who might be involved. The major flaw in that theory was that professionals of his class never commit violence if they can avoid it, and murder is absolutely out."

"Unless his buyer gave him the poison and told him it was harmless."

"That's the assumption I've been working under," Talbot agreed. "But I've never been happy with it. Given his record, Hooker should be smart enough not to simply take someone's word for that. Now, it makes much better sense."

"Glad we could oblige you," Garcia said dryly. "Where does that leave us?"

"It leaves us with a single motive for the crime," Talbot told him. "It's very unlikely now that the murders were done out of jealousy or revenge."

"You going to tell the techs they're off the hook, at least for the murders?" Garcia suggested. "It might make this Hooker more inclined to come forward and make a deal."

"I'd rather wait on that," Talbot said. "I think we're close to figuring out which one did it, and he may be more inclined to sell out his buyers if he still thinks he's facing a murder rap."

"Just make sure you talk to Delgado before you take any action," Garcia warned. "It's still his case, you know. Anything else?"

"We have a few interesting developments," Talbot said. "Nothing we're ready to put into a report yet."

In other words, he wasn't going to share his marbles with the rest of the playground. Garcia made a face, remembering now why he didn't like working with these people. "Let me know when you are."

"You could always start with the other material I gave you," Talbot suggested helpfully.

"Good-bye, Talbot." Without waiting for an acknowledgment, he hung up.

He had taken the first page off Talbot's stack when there was a tap on the door. He looked up, prepared to be further annoyed, to find Sergeant Ng looking in. "Come in," Garcia called, beckoning.

"We've got a lead on Angie Chandler," Ng said as he stepped inside the office. "I think she's in Monterey. *And* I think she's ditched Ross."

Garcia set down the page in his hand. "Fill me in."

"You'll remember we found Ross's car abandoned in the Chancellor Hotel lot after that eighth-floor shooting spree," Ng said. "On the assumption he'd need another vehicle in a hurry, I checked all the rental places for both his Ross and Sullivan aliases. We were lucky: he didn't have a third name handy, and we nailed him. I put out an APB on the Blazer he rented; and on a hunch I called a cop I know in Reno."

"Why Reno?"

"Mrs. Chandler's parents manage some rental properties near Tahoe," Ng explained. "Anyway, they spotted the Blazer this morning near the Greyhound station, and one of the late-night clerks remembered Mrs. Chandler buying a ticket for Monterey." He held up his index finger. "*One* ticket. According to the schedule, she hit Monterey about eight-thirty this morning."

Garcia looked at his watch. "And not a peep out of her since then," he said. So much for Special Agent Talbot and his casual dismissal of her as a suspect. Innocent people were usually quick to call the police when they were in trouble. "We have anyone in Monterey?"

"No, sir," Ng said. "I'd like permission to go down there myself. Talk to the parents, maybe see if I can shake something loose."

"Assuming all three of them haven't headed for the high grass by now," Garcia said. "Go ahead. Take Harper or Davison with you. If the parents are still in town, you might want to keep an eye on them."

"Yes, sir," Ng said, his voice taking on a grim edge. "Who knows? Ross may even show up."

"We can hope," Garcia agreed. "You had any luck yet tracking down his identity?"

Ng shook his head. "We got a partial print from the phone in their room at the Chancellor, but it wasn't nearly complete enough. I sent it in anyway, but I'm not expecting anything."

"Keep on him," Garcia ordered. "Sooner or later he'll slip up. I don't want you more than ten minutes behind him when he does."

"Don't worry," Ng promised. "I'll make it eight."

"Good man. I'll call Brayman in Monterey and let him know you'll be in his jurisdiction."

"Thank you," Ng said, stepping back to the door. "I'll call as soon as I know anything."

He left, and Garcia reached for his phone. So Angie Chandler was in Monterey. Delgado would definitely be interested in this one.

He paused with his hand on the phone. No. They didn't actually *know* she was in Monterey, after all. No reason to interrupt whatever cozy conference Delgado and Talbot were having.

Besides, if he called now Talbot would probably just ask why he hadn't read the damn FBI report yet. No, Ng was on it, and Ng was a good man. Time enough to call Delgado when there was something to tell him.

Grunting once under his breath, he got back to his Sunday reading.

17

FROM THE OFFICE off the Lees' living room came the trilling of the phone; and for what was probably the hundredth time in the past two days Six pricked up his ears as he squinted into the fiber optic eyepiece strapped over his left eye. In the fisheye image he saw Angie Chandler's mother snatch up the phone with the same cobra-like pounce she'd shown on all the previous calls. "Seahawk Properties," she said, an edge of tension coloring the rote cheeriness.

Six watched closely. But even with the distorted view he could see her posture sag a little. "Yes, sir, we do," she said, the hidden fire vanishing and leaving only the rote cheerfulness behind. "We have cabins in both the Tahoe and Yosemite areas . . . "

Six tuned out the recitation, silently cursing Angie Chandler, her parents, and the ill fortune that had had him sitting here in the Lees' living room for the past forty-eight hours.

Sitting here in the narrow space between the sofa and the corner, just behind the floor lamp. In plain sight.

Six still found the whole thing utterly bizarre. He understood the theory all right, at least as far as the general had been able to explain it. And he'd insisted on a demonstration before agreeing to this insanity.

But he hadn't really, truly believed it. Not until Mrs. Lee came downstairs Saturday morning, casually reached to within an arm's length of his face to turn on the lamp in front of him, and gone into the adjoining office without a flicker of reaction.

Theory and lab demonstrations were all well and good, but it was under field conditions that new equipment performed or failed. And under field conditions this Cloak device was performing flawlessly.

There was a warning twinge from his right calf, and he eased it to a new position before it cramped up on him. Not that the setup here didn't have its own set of problems, of course. The fiber optic spy line had to be small enough to escape detection as it peeked coyly from under the edge of the sofa. That severely limited his range of vision. Of more continual concern was the lack of space and air he had available under here. The metal framework they'd rigged up for the Cloak to rest on, which Two had dubbed the birdcage, meant that he at least didn't have the Cloak resting on him like a child reading at night beneath the blankets. But the atmosphere was stifling, and the extra heat coming from the laptop under the edge of the couch added to the discomfort of the overwarm house.

And of course, the complete lack of dining and sanitary facilities meant that he was effectively on a sunrise to sundown fast. But he was a soldier, accustomed to hardships. It would all be worth it when Angie Chandler finally showed up, as the general was convinced she eventually would. As for the daily fast, he could just pretend he was celebrating Ramadan.

Six smiled wryly at the thought. Imagine him, of all people, on a Ramadan regimen.

Mrs. Lee finished her conversation and hung up the phone. It was nearly four o'clock, and if the Lees stuck with yesterday's schedule they would close down their office at 4:30, prepare and eat dinner, read or watch TV until eight, then move upstairs for more reading and an eleven o'clock bedtime. With the start of the work week tomorrow, Six rather hoped they would go for an earlier bedtime. It had been a long day, and he was hungry.

The phone rang again. Again the cobra pounce of her hand— "Seahawk Properties."

Once again, Six waited for the sag of her shoulders. Instead, it was like someone had yanked a marionette's strings. "Angie!" Mrs. Lee gasped, jumping halfway out of her seat. "Oh, darling, where are you?"

There was a long pause, and Six silently cursed the fact that all of their Russian FSB listening devices were halfway around the world with Ten and Eleven. It would be interesting to know what she was telling her mother.

Interesting, but not vital. Sooner or later she would show up here, and then they would have her.

"I don't know what to tell you, darling," Mrs. Lee said. "Your father's out on a maintenance call, but I know he knows some of the people there. I'll talk to him when he gets back, and we'll figure something out . . . No, not since Friday afternoon. We told them we hadn't heard from you, and they left. But listen, dear—we already have a plan going. After you called Friday night, your father pulled a thousand dollars out of the bank and—"

She broke off as, from Six's left, the front doorbell rang. "Just a minute, there's someone at the door," Mrs. Lee said, her voice suddenly quiet as she got up and crossed left through the archway into the foyer and out of Six's view. "It's the police," she hissed, as she made a hurried reappearance. "Call me back in an hour, all right? Good-bye, darling." She dropped the handset into its cradle and retraced her steps back to the door.

Muttering a curse under his breath, Six got a grip on his gun and forced himself to relax. He heard an opening door and soft voices, male and female. The door closed again and the voices drew nearer, the words becoming understandable. "I'm afraid my husband isn't home right now," Mrs. Lee was saying as the group came into the living room. There were two officers, Six saw: a large Caucasian and a smaller one he tentatively tagged as Vietnamese.

"That's all right, Mrs. Lee," the Vietnamese said as the two officers walked past Six and seated themselves on the couch. To Six's annoyance, one of them set his foot down directly in front of the fiber optic cable, completely blocking his view. "We stopped by to tell you we think your daughter's in the Monterey area."

Six would have given a lot to see Mrs. Lee's face right then, to see how good she was at feigning surprise. "Are you sure?" she asked. "How do you know?"

"She arrived by bus this morning from Reno," the Vietnamese said. "The Monterey police are checking motels, but it occurred to us that she might not have needed one."

"What do you mean?" Mrs. Lee asked, the puzzlement in her voice almost painfully counterfeit in Six's ears.

As it clearly was to the Vietnamese's. "This is no time for games, Mrs. Lee," he said firmly. "If you know where your daughter is, you need to tell us."

"I'm sorry, Sergeant," she said, her voice low. "I'm afraid there's nothing I can tell you."

"Have you heard from her at all?" the other officer put in. "Has she phoned or sent any messages?"

"There's nothing I can tell you," Mrs. Lee repeated.

There was the faint sound of shifting cushions, and Six could imagine the officers looking at each other. "There are people trying to kill her, Mrs. Lee," the Vietnamese said, his tone quiet and earnest and sincere. Much better at this sort of thing, Six thought cynically, than Mrs. Lee was. "They've already made at least two attempts on her life."

"There's also the matter of the man she left Greenleaf Center with," the second officer added. "Our efforts to identify him have come up completely blank."

"What do you mean?" Mrs. Lee asked, some genuine puzzlement in her voice.

"We haven't been able to identify him," the Vietnamese explained. "The point is that he may be as much of a danger to her as the other group."

"But she's not with him anymore," Mrs. Lee blurted out. "I . . . you said she came here alone."

"Actually, we didn't," the Vietnamese said quietly. "What else did your daughter tell you, Mrs. Lee?"

There was a long, awkward silence, and once again Six cursed the bad luck that Angie Chandler continued to bring to this mission. Now, with the Vietnamese's suspicions confirmed, there was no way he would leave the house unwatched. If the woman was fool enough to show up here, the police would grab her before she got into killing range.

And if that happened, Six would just have to make sure no one had a chance to talk to her. The cops, or anyone else.

Predictably, it was the Vietnamese who broke the silence. "Mrs. Lee, I don't know why you're afraid of us, but it's obvious that you are. Please understand that we really are on Angie's side. All we want—*all* we want—is for your daughter to be safe."

"I'm sorry, Sergeant Ng," Mrs. Lee said, her voice trembling but firm. "There's nothing I can tell you."

There was another, shorter pause. "All right," the Vietnamese said. There was a creaking of cushions beside Six, and suddenly his field of vision was clear again. Mrs. Lee was seated in a chair across from the couch by the office door, her hands clenched tightly together, her face that of the stereotypical impassive Asian. "If you should change your mind," the Vietnamese added, stepping over to her and handing her a card, "here's where you can reach me. Thank you for your time."

Mrs. Lee took the card without comment, and the two officers left the room. There was the sound of the door opening and then closing behind them.

Then, and only then, did Mrs. Lee finally break down.

Six watched her cry for a while, feeling an uncomfortable mix of embarrassment and impatience. If Angie didn't phone soon, there was a good chance Mrs. Lee would take the call upstairs out of his hearing.

But all he could do was wait. Laying his gun carefully on the floor beside him, he picked up his radio and silently turned it on. The others would soon be leaving the Bay Area for their mission to the north, and the general would want an update before they left.

Keeping one eye and half an ear on Mrs. Lee, he began tapping out Morse code.

~

The guard at the door checked Hanna Swenson's temporary badge with what she thought was way too much scrutiny. But finally she was allowed into the CIA satellite analysis room.

She spotted McPherson at once, looming over the consoles manned by a pair of hapless-looking FBI analysts. "I don't accept that, gentlemen," he was saying, his voice the deep rumble of doom she'd nearly forgotten after all her months in San Francisco. "It's either on the ground at Chongqing or it's left. Either way, we should be able to locate it. So locate it."

He glanced up and caught sight of Swenson. "About time. Where have you been?"

Swenson opened her mouth, preparing her carefully rehearsed mix of truth and obfuscation— "Never mind," McPherson interrupted his own question, taking her arm and steering her to an unoccupied station. "I need you to locate a plane that left the Hirakud Reservoir region in India, flew to Chongqing in China, and now seems to have vanished. Hang on, I'll get you the file number."

"Yes, sir," Swenson said politely, calling up the Current Project Directory and keying in a search for "Hirakud" and "Chongqing" as he shuffled through his paper collection. Unlike Talbot, McPherson never just gave her an assignment and let her run with it. He always offered embellishments or advice or bunny trails he thought would be useful for her to hop along. Simpler to locate the background herself and just get to work.

She found the data trail and started skimming through it. The original data and satellite photos were referenced, and she went back and sifted through those as well. Vaguely in the background she was aware of McPherson reading off numbers and file names that she'd already found. Somewhere along the way he apparently wandered off.

An hour later, she called him back over. "I need a clarification," she said. "Do you want the plane that left India or the one that landed in China?"

He gave her an odd look. "What do you mean? They're the same plane."

She shook her head. "No," she said. "The one at the reservoir was phonied up."

McPherson looked around the room. "Evans, go get Cohn," he called to someone. "Go ahead," he said, looking back at Swenson.

"It's a good job," she said, pulling up the original reservoir photo, aware that all conversation around her had ceased. "They're both CitationJets, of course, but I'm guessing the yellow trim on this one is a set of adhesive sheets. The number's fake, too, obviously designed to match the other plane's."

"How do you know?" McPherson asked.

"Here's the other picture," Swenson said, pulling the in-flight photo onto a split screen. "You can see the ripples here and here where the yellow sheet's starting to come loose."

"Those ripples disappear if you scrub the picture," someone objected.

Swenson looked up, mildly surprised to find a small crowd had gathered. "That's why I didn't scrub them," she said. "Sometimes technological tricks are more damaging than useful."

"Amen, sister," someone else muttered.

"Quiet," McPherson growled with the kind of disgust that could only come from seeing hours of work go down the drain. It was a sound and a feeling Swenson knew quite well. "But we tracked that plane from Bandar-e 'Abbas all the way across the Indian subcontinent."

"Losing it in the clouds and landscape a few times," Swenson reminded him. "I took a quick look at the photos, and I'd guess the real CitationJet was somewhere near Patna when the reservoir photo was taken. The fake then headed up toward an intercept with the real one's route, making sure you got one last photo before its camouflage stripped away, then changed course and headed to points unknown. The interval between satellite passes is just long enough to pull that off without it being obvious. Can I ask what we want it for?"

McPherson smiled thinly. "The Indians are short one tactical nuclear weapon. Headed for God only knows where, but possibly aboard that plane. You think maybe you can find it for us?"

Swenson swallowed, Talbot's casual and off-handed dismissal of this job flashing through her mind. "I'll see what I can do, sir."

Three hours and hundreds of satellite photos later, she had it.

"There," she said, rubbing her left temple with one hand as she tapped the spot on the screen with the other. The long flight, jet lag, and all this detail work had given her a splitting headache. But it was worth it. "That curly bit of yellow wrapped around the top of that tree is one of the CitationJet's side stripes."

"I'll be damned," McPherson said, leaning close over her shoulder as he peered at her screen. His breath smelled like stale coffee, with a hint of body odor behind it. How long, she wondered, had he been here? "You sure it's not something else?"

"What else in nature comes in that shade?" the older man beside McPherson put in. CIA Director Cohn, she tentatively identified him, though she had no recollection of him arriving in the room.

"Yes, I'm sure," Swenson told McPherson, pulling up another photo from half a mile away. "Because *that*, I think, is the other one."

"She's right," McPherson agreed, straightening up and turning around. "Someone put a mark at eighty-nine degrees thirty-three point seven minutes east, twenty-two degrees two point nine minutes north, and do an extrapolation."

Swenson turned, too, and for the first time noticed the giant map on that wall. Talbot was right: she really needed to work on her global awareness. The point was duly marked, the extrapolation duly made—

"Well, well," McPherson rumbled. "Would you look at that. Straight to Da Nang."

"Is that significant?" Swenson asked.

"Very," Cohn said grimly. "Roberts, get some people on this. Backtrack whatever photos we've got and see if it goes to Da Nang or somewhere else. Try to pull a number off one of the photos if you can."

"Yes, sir," one of the analysts said, scooping up some papers and heading across the room.

"And as for you," Cohn added, looking down at Swenson, "good work. I wish you'd been here sooner."

"She should have been," McPherson pointed out, giving her an odd look. "I specifically told Lyman yesterday afternoon that I wanted her here right away."

"I was working on another case," Swenson said carefully. "An important one, which I couldn't in good conscience leave in the middle."

"More important than a wayward nuke?" Cohn demanded.

"I wasn't told the nature of the situation," Swenson said, forcing herself to stand up to the heat she could feel radiating her direction. Talbot's contention that she was too important to fire ran fleetingly and unconvincingly through her mind. "If I'd known, I certainly would have dropped everything."

"Never mind that now," McPherson said. "What's important is that we finally have a solid vector to the *Rabah Jamila*. Larry, why don't you set Swenson up somewhere and let her get up to date on everything?"

Cohn was still glowering, but he nodded. "Sure. Come on, I'll find you a quiet corner."

"If I may, sir," Swenson said, lifting a finger. "It's been a long day, I've got a headache, and it's already seven o'clock. I'll do much better if I could get to a hotel and grab a few hours of sleep first."

"We need you now," Cohn insisted. "None of us has had much sleep lately, either."

"I don't function well on no sleep, sir," Swenson said firmly, her eyes on McPherson. "If I'm going to be of any use, I have to be able to function."

Cohn drew himself up. "Look, *Ms.* Swenson—"

"Forget it, Larry," McPherson said, stopping him with an uplifted hand. "Swenson doesn't wilt under official glares. Besides, she's right. When she's on top of things she's a dynamo. When she's not, she's useless."

"Thank you, sir," Swenson said humbly. "I want to do the best I can."

"Uh-huh," McPherson said, eyeing her. "Talbot's been giving you lessons, has he?"

"Sir?"

"Never mind," McPherson grunted. "Larry, we can fix her up with quarters somewhere in here, can't we?"

"I suppose," Cohn said.

"That way," McPherson added blandly to Swenson, "you can take the files with you. In case you wake up in the middle of the night and want something to read."

"That's a good idea, sir," Swenson said. "Thank you."

"No problem," McPherson said. "Rafferty? Go find Ms. Swenson a room."

~

It had been a long day, Ross reflected as he drove slowly through the pools of light down the quiet Monterey street. A day full of backtracks, dead ends, and long drives, complicated by the lingering haze that Angie's farewell Mickey Finn had left draped over his brain like a discarded beach towel. Now, as his watch beeped the ten o'clock hour, he'd come to probably the trickiest part of the whole day: talking to Angie's parents.

Their house was just ahead, sitting on a corner lot surrounded by an impressive expanse of grass and an even more impressive scattering of decorative shrubs. Not bad, he decided, for an immigrant family who'd arrived from Hong Kong a couple of decades ago with nothing but the suitcases they were carrying.

At least he wouldn't have to wake them up. Though the downstairs was uniformly dark, he could see a light shining through one of the upstairs curtains.

Unfortunately, the Lees weren't the only ones still up. One of the cars parked along the street had two shadowy figures sitting in it.

Cops.

He continued past them, going another two blocks before turning down a side street and circling back toward the rear of the house. The stakeout car had a good angle on the front and north side of the house, as well as a view of the main approaches to the rear. But the entire back of the house should be out of their sight. If there wasn't a second car, he might be able to get in the back door unseen.

And remaining unseen was definitely high on his priority list. The San Jose cops probably had his face plastered across central California by now. The last thing he wanted was to be dragged off for a cozy little Q and A at the Monterey station.

He pulled his car to the curb a block away from the house and took a minute to collect various necessities from the back seat. Making sure not to slam the door behind him, he continued on foot, keeping to the shadows as much as possible and stopping every so often to study his surroundings with a small set of night-scope binoculars.

For once the universe was working in his favor. There was indeed no second stakeout car. Sloppy, really, but the whys and wherefores could wait for another day. Right now, he needed to focus his full attention on how to get across the back lawn without being spotted by the cops who were on duty.

A suitable distraction should do the trick. Slipping into a convenient shadow beside a thick street-side bush, he pulled a hunting slingshot from his pocket and flipped the arm brace into position. On the opposite corner from the Lees' house, on the far side of the cop car, was a small place, currently closed, with a sign *Catskills Deli* in the window. Settling the slingshot into his left hand, he pulled a small steel ball from another pocket, gauged the distance and angle, and let fly.

The first shot was low, hitting the sidewalk and bouncing up into the wall. The second was perfect, nailing his target window dead center.

The alarm that went off was quieter than some Ross had heard. But in the quiet stillness of the night it might as well have been a tornado warning siren.

The cops were probably very good cops. But they were only human. In his binoculars Ross saw them turn toward the sudden noise, heads bobbing as they searched the shadows for the would-be impulse shopper. One of them produced a searchlight and flicked it on, sending a dazzling beam sweeping across the front and sides of the deli.

With their attention pointed the wrong direction, and their night vision shot to hell on top of it, Ross gathered his feet under him and sprinted across the lawn.

He made it to the back door without any shouts or other obvious signs that he'd been spotted. For a minute he crouched there, catching his breath and listening. Aside from the wailing burglar alarm there was nothing. Putting the slingshot away, he got out his lock picks.

It was a forty-second job to get the door open, and it only took that long because the doorknob lock turned the opposite direction from the deadbolt and it took him a couple of tries to figure that out. Easing the door open, he slipped inside.

As he'd already noted, the Lees had closed down their lower floor for the night, with the only illumination coming from the faint ribbons of streetlight leaking in around the edges of the curtains. For a dozen heartbeats Ross stood with his back to the door, letting his eyes adjust and again listening for indications that his entry might have been noticed. To his right was the kitchen, to his left a sort of TV room, and straight ahead through an archway and past a couple other rooms he could see all the way to the front door. Just to the left of the front door was the stairway leading to the upper floor.

Ross grimaced. This was not going to be pleasant, even if his sudden appearance in their bedroom didn't give either of Angie's parents a coronary. But it had to be done. Squaring his shoulders, he headed forward.

He was stepping through the archway when he heard a faint sound behind him.

His first thought was that he had run afoul of one of the Lees on a late-evening refrigerator raid, and that the last thing he wanted to do was make things worse by jerking guiltily like a burglar caught in the act. But even as he thought it through, trained reflexes took over.

He skipped a half step forward and spun around, dropping into a low crouch.

The move probably saved his life. He caught just a glimpse of the dark mass as it whipped past his face with a soft whoosh, swiping through the air where the back of his neck had been a fraction of a second earlier. The figure behind the movement was little more than a dark silhouette, but it clearly wasn't either of the Lees.

The hand with the blackjack was starting to come back for a second try as Ross lunged for the moving wrist. But the darkness and his lack of balance were against him, and he was forced to jerk his head to avoid catching the weapon across his temple. The move threw his balance off even further, and he had to move his feet quickly to keep them beneath him.

His assailant leaped after him, the blackjack swinging downward this time. Again Ross's backward motion saved him from a concussion as the weapon swished past his face. This time he succeeded in catching the arm as it passed. Holding on with both hands, he kicked his right foot up into the assailant's lower abdomen and collapsed his other leg beneath him, letting his momentum roll him onto his back.

The traditional, if somewhat flashy, stomach toss always worked in movies: sending the attacker flying spectacularly over the hero's head to crash against the distant landscape. But the few times Ross had tried one in the real world he'd had mixed results.

This time, unfortunately, it didn't work at all. With only the one-point grip on his assailant's arm, the other's balance on Ross's right foot was only marginal, and the man was quick enough to take advantage of that. Rolling sideways in mid-throw, he dropped, full weight, onto Ross's torso.

Ross grunted with the impact, retaining enough presence of mind to keep his grip on the other's arm. As the man started to slide off, Ross locked his legs around his, preventing him from rolling away.

And with the other's face now only inches away, he was finally able to make out some detail of the silhouette he was fighting with.

Not that there was much detail to be had with a full-face ski mask. In the dim light he couldn't tell what color it was, but he would have given long odds that it was gray.

And with that, the game plan had suddenly changed. "About time," he muttered, putting some impatience into his voice. "Where have you guys been hiding? I've been looking all over for you."

The assailant's struggle to free his right arm seemed to falter. "What?"

"You heard me," Ross said. "I'm ready to make a deal. But you can't make a deal with someone you can't find."

The dark eyes behind the mask were steady on his face. "What kind of deal?"

"You want Angie Chandler," Ross said, letting go of the other's hand and unlocking his legs. It was a risky move, with a fair chance that his reward would be a slap on the head with the blackjack. But he had to show some good faith if he hoped to get a hearing.

"You killed my friend," Ski Mask said. The voice was flat and cold, the sort of voice a venomous snake might use.

"Yeah, sorry about that," Ross said. "But hey, you were all shooting at me, and I didn't know what the hell was going on. Now I do."

"And?"

"You want Angie Chandler," Ross repeated. "I know where she is."

Ski Mask seemed to consider that . . . and in the silence Ross heard a creak of wood from the ceiling above them.

The masked head jerked up; and suddenly the man had rolled off Ross and lurched to his feet. "Come," he whispered urgently, backing across the room toward a couch against the side wall. "Quickly."

Ross got up and followed. More creaking could be heard now—something in the brief fight must have caught the Lees' attention. Ski Mask reached the far end of the couch and stopped by a small shadow in the corner that in the dim light looked like a camper's dome tent, only smaller. "In here," he told Ross, gesturing to the dome. The gesturing hand, Ross noted, had somewhere along the way stashed the blackjack and drawn a small handgun. "Quickly."

The dome consisted of some kind of dark cloth lying over a cage-like metal frame, and it was exactly as small as it looked. It took Ross a few seconds to get himself inside and seated cross-legged at the back of it. Ski Mask was scrambling in even before he was settled, facing Ross so closely as to be practically sitting in his lap. Jamming the muzzle of his gun warningly up under Ross's chin, he reached behind him to pull the cloth down over their entrance, slid a finger under the couch beside them and tapped something that made a clicking sound. "Not a sound," he breathed into Ross's face.

Ross gave a truncated nod. From his left he could hear the rhythmic sound of footsteps descending the stairs. Ski Mask probed briefly under the edge of the couch with his free hand and came up with an eyepiece connected to a fiber-optic thread. A moment later the distinctive click of a light switch came from the room; simultaneously, a faint ring of light appeared on Ski Mask's face around the edge of the eyepiece.

Ross frowned as a second set of footsteps descended the stairway, trying to figure out what the hell was going on. The first footsteps had moved past the dome tent to the archway now, pausing to the sound of clicks from another pair of light switches. Weren't the Lees surprised to find a tent in a corner of their living room?

And then, with a jolt of adrenaline, he suddenly got it. This wasn't ordinary tent nylon he was sitting under.

It was one of the stolen Cloaks.

A chill ran up his back as the searchers continued walking back and forth through the house, completely oblivious to the intruders' presence. Angie had told him about the Cloak's capabilities, but it had been easy to listen politely while privately marking it down to exaggeration or hype.

Now, for the first time, he believed it.

The search went on another few minutes. Then the lights began to go off, and he heard the footsteps go back up the staircase. A few more creaking boards from the ceiling as the Lees returned to their bedroom, and silence again descended on the house.

Ski Mask set the eyepiece aside. "You wonder how that was done, don't you?" he murmured in Ross's ear.

"Not really," Ross said, striving to sound casual. "Angie told me about the Cloaks."

The other grunted. "You spoke of a deal."

"Right," Ross said, starting to nod before he remembered the gun was still pressed up under his jaw. "Bottom line: I'm tired of getting shot at. I stuck with it this long mainly out of curiosity. You seemed so serious about taking her down, way out of proportion—"

"The deal," the other cut him off impatiently. "What is the deal?"

"A straight trade," Ross said. While the man normally had only a slight accent, this last comment had come out with something more pronounced, as if irritation had caused him to lose a little of his control. Interesting. "I give you Angie Chandler. You let me walk away."

"Really." The pressure against his chin seemed to waver.

"I also get twenty thousand dollars," Ross added.

The pressure was suddenly back. "You must be joking."

"I never joke about money," Ross assured him.

"What makes you think she's worth that much to us?"

Ross shrugged as best he could without moving his jaw. "You've spent a lot of time and effort trying to track her down," he pointed out. "I figured there was something you needed to get these Cloak things to work, but I see I was wrong about that. But you *do* still want her. Under the circumstances, twenty thousand seems a very fair deal."

"Mrs. Lee told the police she came to Monterey without you," Ski Mask countered. "Why should I believe you know where she is?"

"She *thinks* she came to Monterey without me," Ross corrected, giving the other a smug smile that was probably a waste of effort in the darkness. "The Sir Galahad approach was a dead end, so I decided to give her more leash." He shrugged again. "She's ripe for the picking. The question is how badly you want her."

For a minute Ski Mask didn't speak. "Only our leader can make such a bargain," he said at last.

"Fine," Ross said. "Let's go see him."

"Impossible," Ski Mask said. "He's not in the area."

"So we drive back to San Jose," Ross said. "Nothing I like better than a scenic drive, especially when there's money at the end of it."

"It would be a longer drive than you know," Ski Mask said dryly. "He's considerably north of San Jose."

Ross sighed theatrically. North of San Jose, eh? "Well, *that's* useful," he growled. "So how do we proceed?"

"There are two options," Ski Mask said. He looked through the eyepiece again, then lowered it and slid his hand under the couch. A few tapped keys on what Ross realized now was the Cloak's laptop, and he reached behind him to push the material aside. "You could take me to her right now, accepting my word that we'll pay whatever my leader considers fair."

Ross shook his head. "Sorry. Option two?"

"We find a place for you to wait comfortably for his return," the other said, backing out into the living room. "Come."

Ross stretched his legs carefully out through the cage's opening, wincing as his bad leg twinged. Just as carefully, he rotated himself half over into pushup position and backed out on hands and knees.

Ski Mask waited until Ross was out, then readjusted the Cloak material and turned it back on. Even in the dim light it was eerie to watch the dome quietly vanish in front of them. They went out the back door, Ross locking it behind them at Ski Mask's orders.

A marked police car was sitting in front of the Catskills Deli now, its red and blue lights strobing across the neighborhood. It made getting across the lawn a little trickier, but they made it to Ross's car without raising the alarm.

Halfway down the block, picking a convenient spot in the middle of a shadow, Ski Mask frisked him, relieving him of his Glock and the slingshot. Three minutes later he was driving toward downtown Monterey, the muzzle of his own gun pressed firmly against his side. "Where to?" he asked.

"I'll direct you," the other said. "It's not far."

"And then?"

"You'll see."

"Uh-huh," Ross said. "You *did* say I'd be waiting comfortably, right?"

The other shrugged. "You'll see."

18

ANGIE HAD THE cab drop her off three blocks from the oceanside rental house her father had specified in their brief conversation half an hour ago. She waited for its taillights to disappear down the street, then started to walk.

It was a long three blocks. The ground was uneven and the street lamps few and far between. Even if she'd had a flashlight she wouldn't have dared use it. She nearly lost her balance several times as she stepped into shallow pits and potholes, one of those times twisting her ankle painfully.

On top of it, the darkness seemed to be filled with a hundred menacing shadows and a thousand strange sounds, things she'd never noticed when she used to come here on cleanup duty when she was a teenager. By the time she reached the house her hands were shaking so hard it took her two tries to get the mailbox open.

The thick envelope was there, apparently untouched. She scooped it up, closed the mailbox, and continued walking, her legs shaking now as much as her hands as she waited for the shouts of triumph or, worse, the sound of the shot that would send her sprawling to the ground in a pool of her own blood.

But there was nothing but the same thousand strange noises. She went one more block just to make sure, and then ducked under a wide bush on one of the other rental house's lawns where she used to play hiding games with her brother and sister when she was little.

With typical foresight, her father had added a small flashlight to the envelope's contents. Angie cupped it in her hand, letting just enough light through for her to read the note.

Dear Angie,

A.J. and Sarah are in the Caribbean for a couple of weeks and we're watching their house. You can stay there. Call whenever you want or leave a note in one of the other rental mailboxes. I'll check them every day. I'll talk to people here and see what can be done.

Help yourself to anything in their freezer, we can replace it later. We love you, honey.

Dad

The rest of the envelope was filled with two rubber-banded stacks of twenty-dollar bills and a key on a small ring.

She turned off the light and put it and the envelope in her coat pocket, feeling more hopeful than she had since she'd gotten on that bus in Reno. The Kimballs' house was only a ten-minute walk away, and if she hadn't been spotted so far chances were good that none of her pursuers were anywhere around. Once she was in the house, she should be safe.

With visions of one of the Kimballs' thick steaks dancing seductively in front of her eyes, she ducked out from under the bush and headed again through the night.

~

Ski Mask's target address was close, all right, at the edge of the Alvarado business district only a couple of miles from the Lees' house. But it was quickly evident that his and Ross's ideas of comfort differed considerably.

The building was the remains of one of the discontinued-item discount places that had sprung up like Presidential hopefuls over the past few years. This one had apparently neglected to build enough profit margin into its operation. All that was left was a hollow building, a few display racks too beaten up to bother with, assorted pieces of paper and plastic, and leftover cleaning equipment scattered randomly across the incongruously cheerful vinyl floor.

Arranged at systematic intervals, the apparent reason for Ski Mask's choice of this location, were a dozen two-foot-thick ceiling support pillars.

Ski Mask led the way to one of the pillars near the back, well removed from any idle eyes that might happen to glance through the grimy front windows. Handcuffing Ross's hands in front of him, he had his prisoner sit with his back to the pillar and secured him to it with a half dozen strands of PVC cable, wrapping them snugly around his waist with just enough slack to allow him to breathe.

"This is your idea of comfortable, huh?" Ross asked as Ski Mask moved down to his feet, tying them together at the ankles with another PVC cable. "I'll bet you don't get visitors very often."

"Be thankful I give you the benefit of the doubt," Ski Mask said as he stretched out the other end of the cable to the next pillar back and fastened it there, tightening the knots with the pliers of a fold-up multitool. "Would you find being dead more comfortable?"

"Not really," Ross conceded.

His prisoner adequately trussed, Ski Mask went through Ross's pockets, relieving him of everything except his handkerchief and some loose change. With his treasures in hand, he headed to the front of the store, presumably to examine everything in marginally better light. Ross couldn't see him from his angle, but faintly across the empty space he heard the unmistakable beeps of a number being punched into a cell phone. He strained his ears, hoping to eavesdrop, but between Ski Mask's quiet voice and the echoes bouncing off the empty walls, he couldn't make out a single word. He couldn't even tell whether or not it was English.

The conversation went on far too long for a simple report that the field troops had started to take prisoners. He wondered uneasily if there was an argument going on as to what to do with him, and if so, which side was winning.

The conversation ended. There was some puttering around, again outside Ross's range of vision, and then Ski Mask reappeared holding a small cardboard box. "The commander has agreed to speak with you when he returns," he growled, setting the box on the floor beside Ross. "Here are food and water."

"Thank you," Ross said cautiously. Ski Mask's tone was not that of a man who'd just won his side of an argument.

Ski Mask grunted and stepped over to a dented wringer bucket. He gave it a kick, sending it rolling to just within Ross's reach. "Here are your sanitary facilities."

"Again, thank you," Ross said, eying the bucket. A nice gesture, but it was going to be a very tricky operation to use it in the manner suggested. "Any idea when your commander will be back? Not prying, you understand, just curious."

Ski Mask stepped over to him and removed his handcuffs. "And then we shall see," he said, "what shall be done with you."

He regarded Ross in silence another few seconds. Then, returning the cuffs to his pocket, he picked his way back through the debris to the back door they'd entered through and left.

Ross took a deep breath, or as deep a breath as he could strapped to the pillar. He was alive, undamaged, and in a far better position than he could reasonably expect to be.

But there was no guarantee how long those pleasant conditions would last. If Ski Mask and his buddies caught up with Angie before the commander got back, their next visit would probably include a bullet in the head. Even if they didn't find her, the commander's first question would be for her location. Unfortunately, that was one Ross currently had no answer for.

Either way, he needed to get out of here.

He took a minute to size up the situation. His pockets had been emptied of everything that might have been useful in cutting the cables, including his pocket knife and nail clipper. A little experimentation with the strands binding him to the pillar showed he wasn't going to be breaking them with his bare hands. Obviously, his cell phone was also missing.

On the plus side, Ski Mask had left his hands free. With a little luck and ingenuity, maybe Ross could make him regret that decision.

The ration box contained an unimaginative selection of foil-encased snack bars and plastic water bottles. The bucket with its attached mop wringer looked promising, with gears that might be capable of cutting or grinding down the PVC. But a quick examination showed that the wringer part was jammed, the gear system immobilized. Probably why it had been left behind in the first place. The pillar was slender enough for him to reach around and feel the knots, but Ski Mask hadn't left him much to work with there, either. Not only had he pulled the knots pliers-tight, but he'd gone ahead and cut the ends off, leaving nothing to grab hold of.

There was the ceiling sprinkler system, of course, and the associated fire alarm system might still be connected. But Ski Mask had taken his lighter. Even if he hadn't, Ross couldn't think offhand how he could get a flame within reach of the sensors. The vinyl flooring consisted of long sheets, not individual tiles he might have been able to pry up.

And then, as his fingers searched the pillar for some break or rough edge, he happened to look toward the front of the store as a car made a turn that sent its headlights sweeping across through the windows.

On the floor, not five feet away, something flashed a metallic glint.

The headlights passed, and the murky twilight again descended. Ross peered toward the object, trying to figure out from the faint shadow what it was. No luck; the thing was too small and the lighting too dim. It was also well out of reach.

But there was the wringer bucket beside him. And the wringer bucket's long handle.

It took some maneuvering to get the bucket into position, and some serious straining against the PVC to get the handle in reach of the unknown object. His first attempt to reel it in nearly pushed it out of reach, and it took more straining to get a second grip on it. The next try scraped it those critical two inches closer; and after that the rest was easy. Hoping like hell he hadn't just retrieved a gum wrapper, he pulled it within reach and picked it up.

It was a nail clipper. Specifically, it was *his* nail clipper.

For a long minute he held the cool metal nestled against his palm, staring at it with the same set of emotions as a mouse who's just noticed an odd spring-loaded contraption wrapped around the bit of cheese lying on the kitchen floor. Ski Mask hadn't dropped the clipper on his way to the front of the store. Ross had watched him closely, and he was positive nothing had fallen from the man's hands.

Which meant he'd dropped it on his way back. But why bring it back in the first place? Why not simply leave it up there?

There were only two reasons Ross could think of. One, Ski Mask had intended to steal the clipper and had accidentally bobbled it while manhandling the food box. Two, he'd dropped the clipper there because he was following orders.

Ross smiled. So Fearless Leader was being cute. Rather than attempting to beat Angie's location out of him, they were going to try letting him escape and hope he led them to their quarry.

If that didn't work, they could always go back to the beatings later.

The clipper wasn't strong enough to take a full PVC cable at once, but by nibbling away at the edges Ross was able to work his way through each strand. Fifteen minutes later, his thumbs aching with the strain, he was free from the pillar. Another three minutes and his feet were loose, too.

The rest of his pocket stuff was lying beneath a piece of crumpled paper. Everything was intact, including his wallet and money, which was a surprise right there. Apparently, the stakes these guys were playing for were big enough that a couple hundred dollars wasn't worth the trouble of stealing.

The street seemed quiet as he checked out the view through the front windows. There were still cars driving by, one every half minute or so, with a dozen vehicles parked in the lot across the street. Several of the latter, he suspected, contained shadowy figures gazing his direction. Unless Ski Mask had left his car conveniently parked out back with the keys in the ignition, they would be expecting him to head off on foot.

First step, therefore, was to arrange some transportation.

Ski Mask had left Ross's cell phone with the rest of his gear. Ross smiled, and dropped it into his jacket pocket. With the proper equipment cell calls could be monitored, and this bunch undoubtedly had the proper equipment. Communication with the outside world would have to wait until he could buy a burner or dig up a pay phone somewhere.

The metal display racks were lighter than they looked, and it took only a few minutes to move half a dozen of them to the front windows. He flipped them over onto their backs and laid them on the floor, so that they stretched across the whole expanse of glass but were out of sight beneath the window level. Next was a methodical tour of the store, collecting everything that would burn. Between the scrap paper, cardboard boxes, and cleaning rags there was quite a lot, and it took several minutes for him to bring it all up to the windows and arrange it on the racks. The rear storage area yielded a real prize: two half-filled bottles of flammable cleaning fluid, which he squirted evenly across his impromptu bonfire setup.

And with that, his own little spring-loaded contraption was set. All he needed was a mouse with a taste for the cheese he would be setting in the center of it. Positioning himself at one end of the windows where he had a good view down the street, he pulled out his lighter and got ready.

Two minutes and three passing cars later, he spotted his mouse: a city police car pulling out of a side street a block away and turning his direction. Flicking the lighter, he touched it to the end of his bonfire.

The paper and rags blazed up with a *whoosh* that would probably have singed his eyebrows if he hadn't already been sprinting toward the back of the store. He threw open the door and charged into the night air, half expecting one of Ski Mask's buddies to be hanging around and fully intending to bowl him over if he was. But there was no one. Glancing around—Ski Mask had not, in fact, left his car conveniently parked back there—he ducked into the narrow alleyway at the side of the store and headed for the street.

The two cops were out of their idling vehicle by the time he rounded the corner, the light bar strobing red and blue, the driver standing outside his door snapping orders into his radio as they both stared at the conflagration behind the windows. "Oh, God—thank God," Ross gasped as he charged toward them, pointing frantically back into the alley. "God—my son's still in there! You have to help me!"

"Your what?" the nearer and younger of the two cops demanded. "Your *son*?"

"We were cleaning," Ross gasped, stumbling and dropping his shoulders as he reached the cop. Reflexively, the kid reached out to catch the distraught man clearly on the verge of collapse. Ross obliged by sagging into his arms, still gesturing toward the alley. "Buyer coming tomorrow. Something exploded—gas maybe—Danny's still in there. Come on—back door."

He lurched upright and made as if to head back into the alley. "No," the young cop said firmly, shifting his grip to Ross's upper arm. "It's too dangerous."

"Let me go," Ross demanded, fighting feebly. "We can't leave him in there."

"I'll get him," the older cop said, already halfway to the alley. "Where was he?"

"In the front—right up in the front," Ross called, gesturing wildly toward the windows.

"Is the back door unlocked?"

"Yes," Ross said. "I'll show you."

He started to break away from the young cop, who tightened his grip even more. "You stay put," he ordered. "We'll get him out."

"What are you talking about?" Ross insisted, struggling harder. "I have to go to him."

"Stay with him, John," the older cop ordered, and disappeared around the corner into the alley.

"I have to go," Ross moaned, sagging again in the cop's grip. They were brave men, all right—from out here, Ross's window display looked like a pyro's dream date. "I have to go," he repeated pleadingly, turning to face the young cop and putting his hands on the kid's shoulders as if to emphasize his case. "I've got to . . . " He broke off with a gurgle, rolling his eyes up and letting his knees buckle beneath him. The cop shifted his grip in response, grabbing Ross's torso.

For his compassionate trouble, he got Ross's elbow full in the solar plexus.

The cop folded over with an agonized cough that sounded about as reproachful as a cough could. "Sorry, friend," Ross murmured, catching the kid across his left arm as he chopped the side of his neck with the other. Relieving the unconscious man of his gun, he dumped him unceremoniously onto the back seat, closed the door, and got in the front.

Just in time. He'd barely slid behind the wheel and shifted into drive when he caught the reflection of flashing lights approaching from down the winding street. Behind him, a car parked half a block down the street turned on its headlights.

Grinning tightly, Ross stomped on the gas pedal and peeled out.

He met the approaching fire trucks a block away, roaring past and then making a hard U-turn just behind them, killing all his lights as he made the turn and paralleling the rearmost truck in the currently unoccupied parking lane. In his mirror he saw the car that had been tailing him roar past, missing him completely in the glare of the fire trucks' lights, and disappear around a curve in the road. At the next driveway heading off to the right—a bar parking lot—Ross pulled off and coasted to a stop between two parked cars.

He covered three blocks at a fast walk, taking alleys where he could and keeping to the shadows as much as possible. In one of the alleys he ditched his jacket and empty shoulder holster in a convenient dumpster, transferring his borrowed gun to his waistband beneath his shirt.

It was only a little after eleven and even in the middle of winter there was a fair scattering of people walking the streets, locals moving between clubs and bars or hardy visitors determined to sample the Monterey night life despite the off-season chill. Stuffing his hands in his pockets, keeping watch for more of Ski Mask's buddies, Ross concentrated on blending in.

Two blocks more brought him to a downtown hotel. He checked in under the name Charles Dickens with a desk clerk who seemed more than half asleep, put down a cash deposit and got a key, and headed back out again, ostensibly to go park his car and pick up his luggage.

Instead, he walked down the street toward the neon lights of a bar. In the distances he could see glimpses of flashing red lights. John the Cop's partner, he reflected, was probably very unhappy with him right now.

The bar's handful of patrons were sitting around watching some late-night sports recap on the wide-screen TV. Ross ordered a beer he didn't especially want, took a couple of sips while he checked out the place, then headed back toward the rest rooms. Pay phones were becoming a thing of the past, but he was in luck—there was still one here, tucked into an alcove between the restroom doors. Glancing around to make sure no one was watching, he picked up the receiver and punched in 911.

"911," a brisk female voice came almost at once. "Please state the nature of your emergency."

"It's a warning," Ross said, dropping his voice an octave and putting a double handful of angry surliness into it. "Catskills Deli has screwed me over for the last time. They've asked for it, and now they're gonna get it."

"What do you mean, sir?" the voice asked, the cool professionalism not even denting.

"I mean boom," Ross snarled, checking his watch. His location would have come up instantly on her screen, and it wouldn't take long to relay it to the cops roaming the neighborhood. "If you've ever wanted to roast marshmallows over a bonfire of rotten pastrami, this is your chance."

"Am I to understand you've set an incendiary device, sir?"

"Bet your boobs, lady," Ross growled. "Ya got thirty minutes till the big boom."

He dropped the phone back into its cradle and was out on the street five seconds later, walking leisurely back toward his hotel. He was a block away, pressed into a shadow beside a hardware store, when the flashing lights converged on the bar.

He waited until the cops had charged in, and then continued on his way, getting to a different street as soon as he could. Only once did he have to duck out of sight as an unlit cop car came barreling past without even pausing. It probably hadn't occurred to them that troublemakers brazen enough to hijack cop cars and phone in bomb threats—and they would certainly assume the two incidents were unrelated—would also not be stupid enough not to have backup transportation.

Though to be fair, between the store fire, the fuss he'd created at Catskills Deli with his slingshot, and the bomb threat he'd just phoned in, this had already become an unexpectedly hectic night for the local police. Under the circumstances, a certain degree of carelessness could be forgiven. Especially when the carelessness worked in his favor.

He reached his hotel without incident, slipped in without attracting attention from the desk clerk, and climbed the steps to his third-floor room. Locking the door behind him, he collapsed onto the bed. A long, tiring day for him and a long, frustrating night for Monterey's Finest. It seemed a fair enough exchange.

At least his day was almost over. The cops', sadly, had only begun.

Staring at the ceiling, Ross shook his head. Between Greenleaf Mall and the Chancellor Hotel he already had the San Jose and Oakland police royally pissed. Now he could add Monterey to the list.

But there was nothing he could do about it. Ski Mask had undoubtedly gone back to his living-room vigil, and Ross had no intention of leaving the Lees sitting innocently there in the man's line of fire. If the cops knew what they were doing, the first thing they would do in the face of a bomb threat would be to evacuate the neighborhood.

Hopefully, Ski Mask wouldn't open fire on cops who were simply moving the Lees temporarily out of their house, certainly not with backups presumably standing ready to follow them to their new quarters.

On the other hand, once they were safely out of the house . . .

He peered at his watch. No, he wasn't quite done for the day. He would give the cops another hour, maybe two, and then he would take a stick to the anthill one more time. Hopefully, the police wouldn't be so sick already of anonymous calls that they wouldn't listen.

All of this assuming, of course, that Angie Chandler didn't show up before the bomb squad moved in.

He swore tiredly at the ceiling. He hated lying here doing nothing, but at the moment he didn't have a lot of other options. Alone and on foot, he wouldn't have had much of a chance against Ski Mask's people even if the entire Monterey County law enforcement community wasn't after his hide. All he could do was hope that Angie and her parents had worked out some scheme that didn't involve her sneaking home in the dead of night.

If they had, he needed to figure out that plan and get to Angie before Ski Mask did. Until then, all he could do was stay put and let the various search parties run themselves in circles. Hopefully someplace other than where he actually was.

In the meantime, the *on foot* part needed to be remedied.

He pulled his borrowed gun from his waistband and slid it under the pillow where it wouldn't dig into his ribs. Then, rolling over toward the nightstand, he snagged the phone.

THE
SIXTH
DAY

19

THE SECURITY COUNCIL meeting began promptly at eight o'clock Monday morning.

Or at least, it was eight o'clock for the men and women assembled in the White House conference room. For the President, across the country in Seattle, it was only five.

Which was probably why on the large secure-circuit TV monitor that had been set up behind his usual chair he looked drawn and tired. "Well?" he demanded. "What do we have? Mr. Cohn?"

"Not as much as we'd like, Mr. President," Cohn said, punching up a copy of the latest data on his laptop and keying for coded transmission to the President's suite at the Sheraton Towers. "The inspection team has found traces of secondary radiation on the inner back and floor of one of the two containers the hijackers were using. That would seem to confirm they did indeed have the weapon with them."

"Or else all they had was a pound of plutonium in a cardboard box," Whitcomb countered. "This could still be just a feint."

General Vaughn cleared his throat. "It's not quite that simple, sir," he said. "The radiation profile has been analyzed, and it's consistent with a point two kiloton weapon in the kind of casing the Indians were using. I'm told that gives us a ninety percent probability that the weapon was in that container."

"We should have more to say in a day or two," Cohn said. "We're transferring both containers and their contents to the FBI lab for a complete inspection."

Whitcomb waved a hand, the fingertips briefly crossing the bottom of the screen. "Fine," he said. "At this juncture the point's not worth arguing." His glare hardened. "What is worth arguing is how the hijackers were able to disappear so thoroughly after they jumped ship."

"We know now that they transferred to the yacht Captain Syed saw," Cohn said. "Several of our satellite photos clearly show it tied up alongside the *Rabah Jamila*."

"What time was that?" Whitcomb asked.

"The last photos were taken at five-twenty, local time," Cohn said. "The crane the crew said they heard can be seen operating at that time. It appears to be holding something, but the object is small and the crane's framework is obscuring enough of the shot that we can't positively identify it."

"Transferring the nuke to the yacht?"

"That's the most likely assumption," Cohn said. "Unfortunately, by the next pass the clouds had moved in over the whole region, and we got nothing more until the Navy P-3 did its flyby two and a half hours later. By then, the yacht had disappeared."

"And where exactly did it go?" Whitcomb demanded.

"We don't know," Cohn conceded. "Using the top speed for that type of yacht, we've come up with five different freighters they could have reached in the forty-six minutes between the time of their final transmission and the P-3 flyby."

"That's an overly generous window, too," Secretary of Defense Norris put in. "Even if it was specially prepared, a yacht that size would take some time to scuttle. Certainly if you didn't want debris floating around afterward."

"There was no debris," Vaughn added. "We've checked the entire area."

"You've interrogated the various ship crews?" Whitcomb asked.

"Yes, sir," Vaughn said. "No one saw or heard anything, no one saw a yacht or small boat of any sort, and there doesn't seem to be any way they could have sneaked aboard any of the freighters unseen."

"Unless they had an agent in one of the crews," Whitcomb pointed out.

"We're looking into that," Cohn said. "But so far it seems unlikely. We're also in the process of searching the five freighters themselves."

"Could the hijackers have gone to ground inside another container?" Whitcomb asked. "You can't possibly have checked all of them yet."

"No, that search is still ongoing," Cohn confirmed. "Since we know the containers they were using on the *Rabah Jamila* had phony registrations, we've obtained loading manifests for the five freighters and are backtracking each container."

"In the meantime, of course, none of the ships will be allowed any-where near land," Vaughn added.

Whitcomb made a face. "So who have we added to the Goose List with *that* one?"

"The shipping companies involved are Indonesian, Taiwanese, and Canadian," Cohn said. "They are, of course, uniformly furious."

"What about their governments? Tony?"

"No one's exactly happy about it, Mr. President," Secretary of State Jameson said. "So far they're holding their tempers, though all three have made it clear they expect full explanations to be forthcoming."

"Which of course there won't be," Whitcomb said heavily. "How long can you keep patting their shoulders without actually saying anything?"

Jameson shrugged. "As long as I have to."

"Good," Whitcomb said. "General, how fast can you get the ships cleared?"

"We're moving as quickly as we can, sir," Vaughn assured him. "There are ten more inspection teams assembled and on the way to lend a hand."

"Frankly, though, I think we could turn them loose at any time," Cohn said. "We backtracked their courses over the past few days, and they weren't anywhere near the *Rabah Jamila* until just before the hijackers' Mayday transmission. They're almost certainly just five random ships that happened to be in the wrong place at the wrong time."

"It could have been planned to look that way," Cynthia Duvall's voice came from somewhere off camera. "We know these people like to play those games."

"Granted," Cohn said. "But in this particular instance, I don't think so. The stowaways had no way of knowing when the *Rabah Jamila*'s crew would grow suspicious enough to call home, which is what precip-itated the actual hijacking. They needed to have their transport standing within quick reach at any time after the pirate attack."

"That's a good point," Norris said thoughtfully. "Especially when you look at the yacht's behavior."

"Right," Cohn said. "The satellite photos show it paralleling the *Rabah Jamila* at a distance of about thirty miles from the time the freighter left Da Nang harbor. Shortly after the pirate attack, it moved to within ten miles and stayed there until after the hijacking, when it moved in."

"And then vanished," Whitcomb said.

Cohn's lips puckered briefly. "Yes, sir."

There was a moment of awkward silence. "There was another ship in your report," Whitcomb asked. "The one the P-3 spotted. Could that be the missing yacht?"

"No, sir," Norris said. "It was an entirely different type of ship, a fully rigged sailboat. It's not likely Captain Syed would have missed that on a yacht heading straight toward him."

"Besides which, we've been able to track that one," Cohn added. "They left Manila two days before the *Rabah Jamila* put into Da Nang and have been moving leisurely toward Japan since then."

"You have photos?"

"Quite a few, yes," Cohn assured him. "Including some both before and during the hijacking incident. In the couple of hours between the time the clouds moved in and the P-3's flyby it moved just about the distance we would have expected, along the course it had been following."

"Have you backtracked its ownership?" Norris asked.

"We're working on that now," Cohn said. "But we're not expecting to find anything significant."

"Then the hijackers must have transferred to a submarine or seaplane," Whitcomb concluded. "Did either North Korea or China have anything in the area?"

"Not that we can find," Norris said. "The problem is that the data doesn't show any planes or subs at all in the region."

"Then the data is wrong," Whitcomb said flatly. "The hijackers didn't go to all that work and effort just to sink into the ocean and drown. They got away somehow. I want to know how."

The men and women at the table looked around at each other. "I'm sorry, sir," Norris said for all of them. "We'll keep checking, but so far what they've done seems impossible."

"Mm," Whitcomb rumbled. "It occurs to me, ladies and gentlemen, that they seem to have a rather complete knowledge of our procedures. Up to and including where our satellites are at any given time."

"Unfortunately, most terrorist and paramilitary groups also know that, sir," Norris said. "We're in the process of retasking two of them to give us better Pacific coverage, though. That may throw them off stride."

"Rather a waste of time if the bomb's already in North Korea," Whitcomb reminded him acidly. "Or Japan, or China."

"I don't think it's in North Korea, sir," Logan spoke up from beside McPherson. "We've stepped up our telecommunications surveillance, concentrating on official traffic between China and North Korea.

There's no sign of the increased level we would expect to see if Beijing suspected Pyongyang of having a stolen nuke."

"Assuming the Chinese even know we're dealing with a stolen nuke," Whitcomb pointed out.

"They know now," Vaughn assured him. "Their team was standing in the container with ours when the radiation readings were being taken."

"What if the Chinese and North Koreans are in it together?" Duvall asked. "In that case there wouldn't be any reason for the long conversations you're looking for."

"Unfortunately—or maybe fortunately—that doesn't track," Jameson said. "If China wanted the weapon, for whatever reason, why send it via Vietnam? They could have just slipped it across the border and been done with it. There's also no reason for them to help North Korea obtain a tactical nuke, certainly given the cool political climate between them at the moment."

"Unless it's a breakaway Chinese faction allied with Pyongyang," Logan added. "But again, in that event the rest of the Chinese government should be melting the phone lines trying to find out what's going on. As I said, that isn't happening."

Whitcomb rubbed the side of his face. He was tired, McPherson realized suddenly, and not just because of the early hour. McPherson hadn't had much time for news in the past few days, but the bits and pieces he'd caught had indicated that public reception to the President's tour wasn't as enthusiastic as the other had hoped. Having a UN with genuine military clout was apparently more important to Whitcomb than McPherson had realized.

Briefly, Vaughn's warning about a world full of wayward nukes flashed through his mind.

"What about the *Rabah Jamila* itself?" Whitcomb asked. "Any chance the crew or owners aren't as innocent as they seem?"

"Minister Rao has indicated similar suspicions," Cohn said. "We're checking their backgrounds, but so far we haven't found anything out of the ordinary."

"There are a few oddities in their testimony about the trip itself, though," Vaughn said. "The crew state they were put in the hold a little before five o'clock that evening, except for Captain Syed, who was taken to his office after the others were locked up and forced to open his private safe."

"What was in there?"

"Mostly official shipping papers," Vaughn said. "Syed said the hijackers gave the contents a cursory examination without taking anything, then took him below and handcuffed him to the pipe where the boarding party found him. That was right at five, two hours before the hijackers sent their transmissions."

"What were they doing for those two hours?"

"That's the question," Vaughn said. "Transferring the weapon from their container should have taken a maximum of half an hour, which jibes with the satellite photo of the moving crane. The setting of the destruct bomb shouldn't have taken more than ten minutes unless they had to assemble it, in which case we're talking maybe another half hour. That leaves a minimum of an hour unaccounted for."

"Any idea what they were doing?"

"We thought they might have set a backup bomb, but we haven't found one," Vaughn said. "It could be that they had to deal with another container, perhaps one that wasn't as easily accessible as the other two."

Whitcomb rubbed his cheek again. "Could they have moved the weapon and themselves into a third container after they sent their mayday?"

"That's one possibility," Norris acknowledged. "It has the chutzpah of hell, but would explain how they managed to vanish so completely. In that case, the yacht would have been a pure red herring, probably scuttled to confuse matters."

"Or they could have spent the time waiting for their real transport to arrive," Jameson suggested. "The sub or seaplane no one spotted. Or maybe they were just waiting for full dark and making sure there was enough cloud cover in place."

"I see." For a moment Whitcomb was silent, his eyes moving around the table, pausing briefly on each of them. A neat little trick, McPherson thought with a touch of fatigue-driven cynicism, particularly since the positioning of the camera made the operation more than just a matter of simply looking at each image where it appeared on the President's own TV monitor. He wondered how long Whitcomb had had to practice that one before he got it right. "I know you're all doing your best," he said when he'd finished his visual survey. "But we're going to need more. I'll expect you to know where the weapon is within the next twenty-four hours, and to have recovered it within the next forty-eight."

It was a dismissal. "Yes, sir," Jameson said for all of them. "We'll keep you informed."

"Thank you," Whitcomb said. "Good luck." He reached off-camera, and the TV screen went black.

There was an instant shuffling of papers and the hum of quiet conversation. "Forty-eight hours," Logan muttered.

"We can do this," Vaughn said firmly from across the table as he collected his own papers. "We have to."

"That extra hour really bothers me," McPherson said, tapping his fingers gently on the wooden surface in front of him. "General, I presume your people have been all over the *Rabah Jamila*'s radio. Could it have been rigged to send a canned message with a one- or two-hour delay?"

Vaughn shook his head. "There were no recorders anywhere near the transmitter that could have been used."

"How about something wired in from behind?" Logan suggested. "A recorder hidden in the wall or floor or even in another room?"

"No," Vaughn said. "We specifically checked for that. There was nothing connected to the radio."

"A second transmitter, then," Logan persisted. "Something hanging off the aft rail where it could fall into the ocean when it was finished."

"Doesn't look like it," Cohn said, coming around the end of the table to join in the conversation. "We've done a preliminary spectrum profile of the transmissions. We're still refining it, but so far it looks like everything came from the same radio in the same location."

"What's a spectrum profile?" Logan asked. "I don't think I've heard of that before."

"Sort of the radio equivalent of a voiceprint," Cohn said. "By breaking down the various factors that affect a signal—transmitter, transmission line, antenna, position of the antenna relative to nearby absorbing or reflecting objects, and so on—we can form a composite image that's unique to each transmission system. Radio astronomers have been doing a version of it for years; we've just taken it a step further. It's still a bit experimental, but so far seems to work."

"And you're sure both signals came from the main *Rabah Jamila* transmitter?" Logan asked, clearly not yet willing to give up his two-radio theory.

"Ninety percent sure, yes," Cohn told him. "When the final analysis comes back I expect to be in the ninety-eight-plus range."

Logan made a face. "So what you're saying is that someone had to be physically there to send the messages," he said reluctantly. "Either the hijackers themselves—" He raised his eyebrows. "Or Captain Syed."

"He's the obvious suspect," Cohn agreed. "Separated from the crew early on and restrained only by a set of handcuffs, which he could have put on himself. And we have only his unsupported word that he was put in there shortly after his crew."

"Problem is, he's a little *too* obvious," Vaughn pointed out. "And far and away too easy. I don't believe it for a minute."

"Still, these people enjoy leading us around by the nose," McPherson said sourly. "I presume we're checking him out?"

"Already in the works," Cohn said. "I don't believe it either, but at the same time we can hardly afford to ignore the possibility. General, you might want your people to have another talk with the *Rabah Jamila*'s crew. Make sure none of them could have slipped out of the hold while they were supposedly locked in."

"I'm sure that's been asked, but I'll have someone double-check," Vaughn said, making notes on his pad. "Assuming Minister Rao's people have finished their own third degree by now."

"He got permission to talk to the crew?" McPherson asked, frowning. "I hadn't heard that."

"Yes, about two hours ago," Cohn said. "Sorry—you were busy with something and then I forgot to mention it to you."

"I get the impression he's half convinced the Pakistani government itself is behind the theft," Vaughn added.

McPherson looked over at the door, where Jameson and Norris were just leaving, talking quietly together as their staffs trailed behind them like obedient puppies. "That's what's really killing us here. Not knowing who we're up against."

"We may not know who they are," Logan said. "But we've narrowed the list of who they aren't. We've tracked most of the top tactical planners in the largest terrorist and paramilitary organizations, and all of them seem to be sitting at home."

"They could be running things by remote control," Vaughn pointed out.

"Not without at least occasionally talking to the field troops," Logan said. "We've got a lid on their communications, and so far we haven't picked up anything even remotely promising."

"What's the next step?" McPherson asked.

"We move on to foreign governments and official military forces," Logan said. "Concentrating mostly on fringe factions, rogue leaders, and so on. We'll probably start with number one on the Goose List and work our way down." He cocked an eyebrow toward McPherson. "I trust the Bureau is doing likewise with our home-grown nutcases?"

"We're checking them out," McPherson assured him. "So far, nothing."

"The man behind this is too good not to be known," Vaughn said. "Sooner or later, we'll find him."

For a long minute Whitcomb stared unseeing at the blank TV screen, his thoughts a molasses turmoil of frustration and concern swimming its way upstream through the fatigue of too many days with too little sleep and too many meetings with too much polite resistance. This whole thing was getting out of hand. *Way* out of hand.

"You really think we can retrieve it in two days?" Cynthia Duvall's voice sliced across his reverie.

He turned away from the TV, shaking his shoulders in a gesture he'd picked up in childhood in imitation of his beloved cocker spaniel Speedy. "Not a chance in the world," he told her soberly. "Frankly, I think it'll be one hundred percent pure luck if we even know what country it's in before the new owners set it off."

Duvall was silent a moment. "There must be some reason behind it," she said at last. "Some very strong, very important reason."

"I'm sure there is," Whitcomb agreed. "But that doesn't necessarily mean we'll understand it."

He waved a hand past the watchful Secret Service agent at the window toward the scattered lights of Seattle glittering in the wall of darkness outside. "We can talk all we want about global villages, Cynthia," he said quietly. "But the truth is that there are far more differences dividing humanity than there are uniting us. Cultural differences, ethnic differences, religious differences, and none of the groups trust any of the others to make decisions that will affect their lives. They especially don't trust *us* to do it."

"Hence, the need for a United Nations that can make those decisions in global consensus and enforce them the same way," Duvall said, smiling lopsidedly. "Yes, I know the speech."

"Sorry," Whitcomb apologized, smiling back. The smile made his face feel even more tired. "Sometimes I have to preach to the choir to convince myself that this is the path we need if our world is going to survive."

"I warned you not to listen to Reverend Lane's speech last night," she chided. "I don't think any of your critics get under your skin the way he does."

"I'm a professional politician and a statesman," he said, putting a note of dignity into his voice. "Critics do *not* get under my skin." He shrugged. "Still, I'll concede that Lane is a boil on the butt of humanity."

"All boils eventually get lanced," she reminded him, consulting her watch. "That prayer breakfast is when, eight o'clock?"

"Yes," he said, turning to the softly humming computer set up beside the TV. "Should give me enough time to catch up on the material they just sent."

"You'd do better to take a nap," she said, a note of disapproval in her voice. "You've been running yourself ragged."

"Stop nursemaiding me," Whitcomb grunted, stifling a yawn. "That's what I have a wife and a chief of staff for. On the way back to your room, ask Perkins to send up a fresh pot of coffee, will you?"

"I'll call him instead," she said, stepping over to a table and picking up one of the suite's phones. "A couple of hours should give me time to get through that material, too."

"Mr. President?"

Whitcomb turned the other direction, to see the head of his Secret Service squad standing at a respectful distance, hands folded in front of him. "Yes, Ron, what is it?"

"We'd like you to wear the turtle today, sir."

Whitcomb felt his lips compress. The turtle was the deceptively thin-shelled body armor suit of ceramic, graphite fiber, and Kevlar III, custom molded to fit his body and virtually undetectable beneath normal street clothing.

It was state-of-the-art protection. It was also hot, claustrophobic, and considerably heavier than it looked. "I had no idea Seattle had become so dangerous in the past few hours."

Ron shrugged microscopically. "Orders from Washington, sir. Apparently, they got a warning from a San Francisco FBI agent that there might be an assassination in the works."

"Really," Whitcomb said, feeling his forehead wrinkle. Threats and lunatic ravings were all part of the Presidential package these days, something the Secret Service had learned to take in stride long before Andrew Whitcomb had moved his legal pads into the Oval Office. An order to wear the turtle implied something more concrete than simple crank email. "Anyone we know?"

"If anyone's got details, they're not giving 'em to me," Ron said, the corners of his mouth tightening. "All they said was there's been some kind of high-tech theft, and that Special Agent Talbot's gut says the thieves may be gunning for you."

"I see," Whitcomb murmured. "What do we know about this agent?"

"Checked him out myself," Ron said. "Seems to be clean. Better than clean, actually—on paper, at least, he's a damn good agent." Another barely visible shrug. "I can't speak for his gut."

"Still, guts do play an important part in this business," Whitcomb conceded. "I suppose it would make everyone happier if I kept mine inside where they belong."

Ron acknowledged the small joke with an equally small smile. "Yes, sir, it would."

"Fine," Whitcomb said, bowing to the inevitable. "Tell Mr. Larson to call me an extra fifteen minutes early, will you?"

"Yes, sir."

Ron turned and glided away. "Just what we needed," Whitcomb commented, swiveling his chair back around toward Duvall.

"It could be worse," she said, deadpan. "They could be ignoring you completely."

He smiled wryly. "Thank you, O voice of encouragement." He turned to the computer and punched up the first of the new files. "Come on, let's get through this."

~

The black-suited man eased the freshly unlocked door open a crack and lobbed in the small canister he'd been carrying. There was a muffled *poof*; and suddenly the interior of the Lees' house was roiling with a billowing cloud of CS powder.

The S.W.A.T. team was through the door in three seconds, their MP5 submachine guns held high. Simultaneously, the searchlights outside snapped on, sending their brilliant beams through the windows and lighting up the dust cloud like the inside of a camera flash. Clutching his more modest Smith & Wesson 4046, hoping like hell the full-face mask he'd been fitted with wouldn't pop its seal, Sergeant Ng moved in right behind them.

The sweep of the house took only a few minutes. Ng spent most of the time crouched behind the Lees' office desk, his gun trained on the empty space between the living room couch and the wall, blowing sweat out of his eyes and muttering curses against Detective Delgado for putting him in this ridiculous position in the first place.

"Clear," the S.W.A.T. leader's voice came in Ng's earphone, cutting through the terse combat chatter from the rest of the squad. "Ng, this is Benson. You copy that?"

"Yes," Ng confirmed, feeling more than ever like an idiot. "I guess it was a false alarm."

"I guess it was," Benson said, sounding disgusted. "Waste of a perfectly good MPG-120; and they're going to be hours cleaning this stuff up. I hate anonymous tips."

"Yeah," another of the team chimed in. "No offense, Ng, but your buddy Delgado has tofu for brains. He should have smelled something rancid when this jerkface hauled him out of bed instead of just calling us directly."

"The man said he called him because cops don't have trap-and-trace systems in their apartments," Ng pointed out, rising cautiously from his partial concealment as the dust-obscured figures of the team began to gather in the living room. "Whereas you might have them on your 911 line."

"If we don't, we ought to," Benson growled. "I'd give Vegas odds this is the same S.O.B. who called in the phony bomb threat on that deli across the street."

"Brilliant deduction, skipper," one of the others grumbled. "This guy got a grudge against the whole neighborhood?"

"I don't know," Ng agreed, starting across the open floor toward the near end of the couch, the end beside the floor lamp. If the intruder warning had been nothing but flatulent air, this other part had to be even more so.

But Delgado had thought it worth checking out, so check it out he would. If anyone came out of this looking like a complete idiot, it was going to be Delgado, not him.

He'd thought his movements and intent were sufficiently unobtrusive to avoid notice or at least comment. But then, this *was* a S.W.A.T. team. "Where are you going?" Benson demanded. "Don't tell me you're *buying* this fairy tale?"

"Delgado's doing the buying, not me," Ng said sourly, crouching down beside the end of the couch.

"Right," someone said sarcastically. "You're just taking delivery."

Ng reached under the couch, trying to ignore the wisecracks reddening his ears. Yes, Delgado was going to look like a prize idiot. But he, Ng, had already sewn up the first runner-up slot.

His fingers touched something. Plastic. Slightly warm plastic, in fact. Sliding his fingertips along the smooth edge, he found the corners. Setting down his gun, he shifted to a two-handed grip on it and eased the edge out from under the couch.

It was a laptop computer, humming indifferently away, its display swung open nearly a full one-eighty degrees to allow it to fit in the limited space while still giving access to the keyboard. Precisely as

Delgado's early-morning caller had predicted he would find it, in fact. Ng pulled the computer the rest of the way out, aware that the desultory conversation around him had faded away. Mentally crossing his fingers, he pressed the power switch. There was a faint clunk as the computer's hard drive shut down.

And without any fuss or fanfare a four-foot-high dome appeared in the empty space behind the floor lamp.

"What the *hell*?" Benson breathed.

Ng nodded silently. Delgado had told him about this Cloak thing on the phone, but Ng had put it down to either technobabble or else some strange bee buzzing in Special Agent Talbot's shorts.

And he'd been right there, he realized suddenly, a hollow sensation twisting into the pit of his stomach as he stared at the dome. Saturday afternoon, barely a day and a half ago. He'd sat on that very end of the couch, pressing Mrs. Lee for information on her daughter, while someone sat beside him listening quietly to every word. If that someone had felt like popping a couple of cops that day . . .

He shook off the paralysis and picked up his gun. Given that no one had yet opened fire, it seemed likely that the duck blind was empty. Still, someone really ought to confirm that. Lifting up the edge of the Cloak, he looked underneath.

No one. Aside from a piece of discarded snack bar wrapper half tucked under the supporting framework's back edge, the area beneath the Cloak was completely empty.

"I guess there *was* someone in here," Benson grunted, his tone that of a man trying desperately to swim his way to the surface after having been thrown into the deep end of the pool. He'd been even less prepared for this magic act than Ng had.

"I was sitting next to him Saturday afternoon," Ng said, heaving the front edge of the Cloak up over the top of the framework. The material was heavier than it looked. "I wonder why he didn't come back."

"Probably scared off by everything going on across the street," Benson said. "Or maybe he followed the Lees after we took them out."

"Maybe," Ng said. "Well, whatever happened, he's long gone. Let's get this tagged and bagged and get back to work."

20

SWENSON HAD WORKED until nearly two a.m. the night before, but as usual woke at six-thirty Monday morning anyway. She spent ten minutes attempting to get back to sleep, gave up and hit the shower, and was back at her station by seven, punching her keyboard with one hand and eating CIA-issue donuts with the other. At least the CIA-issue coffee was strong and hot.

The donuts were gone, the coffee in her cup had long since sunk to room temperature, and she was quietly going mad from an apparently never-ending stream of Indonesian container background checks, when a familiar voice shoehorned a welcome reprieve into her concentration. "Hey, Swenson. I didn't know you were back."

"Hey, Banderlaine," she said, smiling up at him. Prematurely white-haired, and with nearly thirty years of Bureau service under his belt, George Banderlaine had inevitably picked up the nickname "Gramps" sometime in the past decade. Swenson had made it point to never call him that, and as a result the two of them had gotten along well during her time in D.C. "I'm not really back. McPherson called me in to help with this nuke thing."

Banderlaine shook his head. "It's a mess, isn't it? What are you working on, container backtracks?"

"That, and a nervous breakdown."

"It could be worse," Banderlaine said. "I just spent ten hours with the CIA's spectrum profile group analyzing the transmissions from that Pakistani freighter. At least you get a new container to look at every fifteen minutes."

"The *Rabah Jamila* transmissions?" Swenson asked. What little remained of her interest in Indonesian paperwork vanished like the last kibble at a dogfight. "What did you find?"

"Not what you're hoping," he said. "The transmission definitely came from their main radio, and there's a ninety-eight percent probability that the mayday came from a live person instead of a tape."

"Rats, mice, and little vermin," Swenson growled. "How did you get the number that high?"

"Because the follow-up message, the one in Chinese military code, *was* on tape," he told her. "Same transmitter, but definitely not live. There are clear differences in background sounds, freq-intensity profiles—you know the drill. Did you know we'd cracked the message, by the way?"

"No," Swenson said, not particularly interested one way or the other in the message itself. She'd been working on various theories on how the hijackers had slipped away earlier than the evidence indicated. But all of them had started with the assumption that both transmissions had been canned.

"Well, actually it wasn't us," Banderlaine amended. "The Indians cracked it, but they sent us a copy. The hijackers were identifying themselves as Chinese military couriers who'd come under attack by South Koreans and needed immediate military backup."

"Doesn't sound like a story they expected to stand up for long," Swenson said, still annoyed with reality for messing up perfectly good theoretical work.

"Agreed," Banderlaine said. "Odds are that by the time the *Anqing* got out there Beijing already knew the whole thing was a setup. Probably why they were so cooperative."

"Probably," Swenson said. "It was the same voice on both the mayday and coded signal, I suppose?"

"Funny you should mention that," Banderlaine said, eying her curiously. "The coded signal itself was digital, of course; but there was a short verbal section first alerting Shanghai to prepare for an incoming message. And it was not the mayday voice."

Swenson frowned. "*Not* the mayday voice," she repeated thoughtfully. "That's interesting. I wonder why."

Banderlaine shrugged. "Could be one of the hijackers was in charge of getting the message organized while the other one sent the fake mayday."

"But why?" she asked. "They couldn't have been rushed. By all estimates they had a whole hour to spare."

"Maybe the estimates are wrong," Banderlaine suggested. "Maybe something went south with the weapon transfer or the self-destruct bomb, something that ate up that extra hour. Matter of fact, we *know* something went wrong with the self-destruct."

"Maybe," Swenson murmured, gazing off into space. So one of the hijackers was definitely aboard until the mayday was sent. But only one of them.

Or maybe neither of them? "Have you done a voiceprint analysis on the mayday yet?" she asked.

"You're thinking Captain Syed," Banderlaine said, nodding sagely. "Yes, that's the current theory upstairs, too. We're trying to get a good sample of his voice for comparison."

"What's stopping you?"

"The Indians still have the whole crew locked away being questioned. I hear the Pakistani government's lodged a protest with New Delhi, claiming they've gone from reasonable interrogation to harassment."

"Could be," Swenson said, her mind already running in four different directions. "Let me know what happens."

She thought he said "sure," and walked away, but the world around her was already a hazy blur. Only one of the two hijackers was aboard at the end . . .

The Indonesian cargo data was still on her screen. With the touch of a key she returned it to cyberspace. A few keystrokes more, and she had pulled up the last satellite photo they had of the partially cloud-obscured *Rabah Jamila* with the yacht tied up alongside. A quick check along one of the links showed the yacht's identity and ownership still hadn't been determined.

That was interesting, too. Not to mention suspicious. If the yacht was simply going to be sunk, why make it so hard to trace? Why not just steal a boat, disguise it if necessary, and go on from there? And where had that second hijacker gone after making the transmissions? Sub or plane, like everybody thought but which all the evidence argued against? Or had it been a fanatic-style suicide, complete with self-burial at sea?

She didn't have the answers. But they were there, she knew. Buried somewhere in the data or the photos.

Draining the last of her cold coffee, she set out to find them.

~

The transmitted coordinates from the GPS locator had led the ship to a spot in the Pacific about three hundred kilometers north of Midway

Island. With the transceiver in one hand and his own GPS in the other, Eleven waited until the readings were nearly identical before signaling for a halt.

"We here?" Twelve called, joining him on the bow and peering ahead of them.

"So it would seem," Eleven said. Handing him the GPS, he keyed in a command on the transceiver, trying hard not to let his misgivings show. The general had assured him this technique was perfectly straightforward and as foolproof as anything could possibly be.

But the general wasn't the one sitting on a stolen nuclear weapon in a high-tech boat that had insufficient fuel left to make it even to Midway, let alone civilization. Mentally crossing his fingers, he pressed the transceiver's send key.

For a dozen heartbeats he saw nothing. And then, perhaps thirty meters off their port stern, there it was: the flash of a slow-cycle strobe, brilliant in the early morning sunlight.

"There it is," Twelve said triumphantly.

"Yes," Eleven murmured, glancing at the clear blue sky overhead as Twelve scrambled back below. The winter cloud cover had been their ally for much of this trip, shielding them from view from satellites and high-flying aircraft alike. Now, just when they were about to engage in the most suspicious-looking activity they'd attempted since leaving the East China Sea, the clouds were naturally nowhere to be seen.

Not just the most suspicious activity, but also with the ship itself in its riskiest configuration. But there was nothing for it but to carry on, and trust that once again their opponents wouldn't notice anything until it was too late.

At forty meters long, the ship wasn't as maneuverable at low speeds as Eleven might have liked, and he found himself drumming his fingers impatiently on the handrail as the ship wallowed its way toward the slender, sea-colored plastic tube sticking half a meter out of the water. But Twelve and Thirteen were good at their jobs, and within a few minutes they had the ship in position. Two minutes after that, they had the rest of the tube out of the water and secured to their fuel tank intake. Another command on Eleven's transceiver, and the pump connected to the inside of the 30,000-gallon fuel bladder floating serenely a meter below the ocean surface sputtered into action.

And with the general's assurances once again proved correct, it was now a matter of waiting patiently for the bladder to transfer its contents into the thirsty tanks.

Out here in the middle of the Pacific. Under a cloudless sky. In front of the whole damn world.

Thirteen, at his side, was obviously thinking the same thing. "How long is this supposed to take?" he asked, shading his eyes from the morning sun and doing a slow sweep of the horizon.

"The general said between thirty and sixty minutes," Eleven told him. "Depending on how empty our tanks are and how full we want them to be."

Thirteen nodded, running a finger inside the collar of his uniform shirt as if the material was stinging his neck. "I think we should have some of our props up here," he said. "At least try to look busy."

Eleven nodded. "Go ahead."

They had moved a pair of large and impressive looking boxes onto the fantail, and the bladder was probably half empty, when Thirteen spotted the approaching ship on the northwestern horizon.

"Looks like a bulk carrier," Twelve said, peering through his binoculars. "The *Shimizu Nakama*, if I'm reading it correctly. Unless it changes course, it ought to pass a couple of kilometers north of us."

"Keep watch," Eleven ordered, picking up one of the long poles wired to the starboard box and trying to stifle the sense of foreboding gnawing at him. They'd come within sight of a dozen other ships on this leg of their journey, and each time it had been simply a matter of slowing down to a reasonable speed for a vessel of their size and profile until the interloper was safely out of sight, then continuing on at a slightly altered course. This encounter was almost certainly going to fall into that same category.

But on none of those other occasions had they been tethered to a large underwater fuel bladder. A fuel bladder that had no business being in the middle of the ocean at all.

And on none of those other occasions had they been masquerading as a ship of the United States Navy.

From behind Twelve came the crackle of the radio and a brief bit of chatter, unintelligible from Eleven's place on the deck. "They're hailing us," Twelve reported tightly. "They want to know if we're having trouble. Do you want me to respond?"

"Not yet," Eleven said, shading his eyes casually toward the distant freighter. Damn these helpful busybodies, anyway. "Let them get close enough to see the probe equipment. Maybe they'll realize we're working here and go away."

There was another burst from the radio. "I think we'd better respond," Twelve pressed. "Looks to me like they've already changed course a few degrees toward us. If we don't talk to them, they may decide to come alongside."

"All right, all right," Eleven said, bracing the probe on the rail and crossing to the companionway stairs. Picking up the microphone, he tapped the key. "This is United States Navy LCU 1618," he said. "Commander Peter Durand speaking. Is there a problem, *Shimizu Nakama*?"

"This is First Officer Fukuda," a deep, no-nonsense voice came back. "Are you in trouble?"

"Not at all," Eleven said. "We're on detached service with NOAA, doing some deep oceanic research."

"Then you may have trouble you do not realize," Fukuda warned. "How long since you've run your screws?"

"About half an hour," Eleven said, frowning. This was more than mere busybodiness. "Why?"

"It looks to me like you've moved up against something," the other said. "Perhaps an abandoned drift net. I can see the outline."

A hard fist clamped around Eleven's heart. "Really," he said, trying to keep his voice steady as he peered over the port side. As the fuel bladder emptied, it was supposed to sink deeper into the water until they disengaged the hose and sent the whole thing to the bottom.

Instead, contrary to all promises and alleged design specifications, it had actually drifted closer to the surface. As each of the long swells passed over it, Eleven could see its edges break the surface.

And with the sun low in the eastern sky, the *Shimizu Nakama* was apparently seeing it quite clearly.

"There certainly wasn't anything there when we stopped," he continued. "I'll go take a look."

He handed the microphone back to Twelve and returned to the deck, feeling sweat gathering beneath his uniform collar despite the chill morning air. "The bladder's bobbing," he told Thirteen tersely as he headed for the port rail. He didn't need a closer look, but Fukuda clearly had glasses on them and he had to make all of this look realistic. "They think we've snarled ourselves in a drift net."

Thirteen cursed, setting down his probe and joining Eleven at the side. "What do we do?"

"Tell them they're right, of course," Eleven said, gazing out at the bobbing fuel bladder. "And count ourselves lucky that they came up with an explanation instead of us having to make up our own and hoping they believe it. Keep looking as if you're trying to figure out its extent."

He headed back below and retrieved the microphone from Twelve. "There's a net there, all right," he said. "Lucky for us you spotted it before we started the engines."

"That was my thought," Fukuda said. "Do you need assistance clearing it away?"

"Thanks, but we can handle it," Eleven assured him.

"Are you certain?" Fukuda asked, sounding doubtful. "I've seen screws tangled in nets. It's not always easy to clear them."

"I can imagine," Eleven agreed. "But as I said, we haven't run our engines, so there shouldn't be any tangling to deal with. And of course, we have divers aboard. I'll send one down for a better look."

"Very well, then," Fukuda said. "Good luck, Commander."

"Good sailing to you," Eleven said. "Thanks for your concern."

The radio went silent. "Keep an eye on them," he instructed Twelve as he headed back to the deck.

Thirteen was still peering over the rail. "Looks like they're veering off," he reported.

"Good," Eleven said. "Go see how full the tanks are."

"You thinking we may pull out before we're completely full?"

"I'm thinking we may pull out as soon as the *Shimizu Nakama* is over the horizon," Eleven said bluntly. "The next ship along may not be so gullible."

"Good point." Thirteen pushed off the rail and headed for the companionway.

"And after that," Eleven called after him, "let's figure out a way to make sure the damn thing sinks when we're done with it."

~

McPherson had spent the entire morning and far too much of the afternoon in Langley watching the various analysts come up with labor-intensive results of exactly zero. Just before three he managed to sneak back to FBI Headquarters and his own office in hopes of getting a little actual Bureau business done.

He got a whole hour before the nuke once again intruded.

"Director McPherson, this is Minister Rao," the Indian's crisp voice came in McPherson's ear. "I wanted you to know that we've made some progress tracking the recent movements of the *Rabah Jamila*'s Captain Syed."

"Yes, Minister, I'm listening," McPherson said, suppressing the impulse to tell him to write it up and email it to him. Rao sounded as tired and edgy as McPherson felt, and there was nothing to be gained by irritating the man. "Shouldn't you be giving these reports to Mr. Cohn?"

"I'm told Mr. Cohn is taking a nap and cannot be disturbed," Rao said stiffly, clearly offended that anyone would bother with something as inconsequential as sleep at a time like this. "At any rate, my request more properly falls within your province."

"Very well," McPherson said with a silent sigh. "Go ahead."

"Captain Syed has made several highly interesting ports of call during the past six months," Rao said, the sound of rustling paper in the background. "Among them were Jaffna in Sri Lanka five months ago, your own San Francisco three and a half months ago—" he paused dramatically "—and Bandar-e 'Abbas in Iran, only three weeks ago."

McPherson felt an unpleasant tingling on the back of his neck. The Chinese CitationJet that had provided a decoy for the smugglers' plane had started its trip in Bandar-e 'Abbas.

Current theory at the CIA was that the Chinese plane was merely an innocent bystander. On the other hand, maybe it wasn't. "Did he meet with anyone there?"

"We're still seeking those details," Rao said. "But it seems likely. Still, there are other possibilities. Can you assemble a report on the distant relatives Syed claims to have visited in the United States? All are designated as resident aliens. I can email you a list."

"We'll do what we can," McPherson said. "But if they've behaved themselves there won't be much on them. You have my email address?"

"Yes," Rao said. "I'm sending it now."

"Good," McPherson said. This one, at least, he could dump on Homeland Security instead of spending Bureau personnel on it.

"Have your people made any progress on their analysis of the radio transmissions?" Rao continued.

"They finished this morning," McPherson said. "It does appear that at least one of the hijackers was still aboard the freighter when the mayday was sent."

"Are you certain it was one of the hijackers?"

McPherson frowned. "Who else could it have been?"

"Possibly Captain Syed, perhaps using a voice-altering device. From your own report, it's clear his movements after the hijacking cannot be verified."

"Yes, we noticed that, too," McPherson acknowledged reluctantly. Either Rao's thinking was running remarkably parallel to his and Cohn's, or else someone in the department was feeding New Delhi data and theories under the table. "Which reminds me. I understand your people still have the crew tucked away out of circulation."

"I instructed my investigators to be thorough," Rao said, not sounding the least bit defensive. "Thoroughness requires time."

"And voiceprint analysis requires that we get a clear recording," McPherson countered.

"Ah," Rao said. "Yes, I understand. I'll instruct them to permit you access."

"You may have to do more than that," McPherson said, feeling a fresh stirring of annoyance. He would *permit* them access? "I also understand the Pakistani government has lodged complaints with both of our governments over their treatment."

Rao's contemptuous snort came through as crystal-clear as only modern communications satellites and fiber optics could make it. "Does one permit a probable criminal to depart simply because his attorney demands it?" he countered. "I think not."

"I think probable criminal is a bit strong," McPherson warned. "Unless you have information you're holding back."

"This is a matter of instinct, Director McPherson, not information," Rao said, his voice gone all stiff again. "The understanding of years of bitter rivalry between our two peoples. I *know* Islamabad is involved, as surely as I know that whatever their ultimate goal, the international embarrassment of our nation is a part of it. You did know, did you not, that the plane that carried the weapon to Vietnam was Pakistani-owned?"

McPherson blinked. "No, I didn't," he said. "When did that come in?"

"My office sent it to Mr. Cohn nearly five hours ago," Rao said, sounding surprised. "Did he not receive it?"

"I'm sure he did," McPherson said. "I probably just haven't kept up."

It was the wrong thing to say. "Haven't kept up?" Rao demanded. "A crisis of global importance, and you haven't *kept up*? Tell me, Director McPherson: just how seriously is President Whitcomb taking this matter?"

"Very seriously indeed," McPherson said hastily, silently cursing both Rao and himself, and not necessarily in that order. "But my duties are to address threats within U.S. borders, and this matter doesn't come under that mandate. There are other matters that do, and I have to budget time to deal with them."

Rao took a deep, audible breath. "You're right," he conceded with clear reluctance. "Forgive me. It's easy to forget that this is an attack on our sovereignty and prestige, not yours." He paused significantly. "At least, for now."

The man knew how to play his audience, McPherson had to admit. Typical politician. "I take your point, Minister," he said. "I'll get someone on this right away."

"Thank you," Rao said. "I'll look forward to the results. Good-bye."

"Good-bye." McPherson hung up the phone. Then, scowling, he punched in Cohn's number.

"Director Cohn's office; Evans," a brisk voice answered on the second ring.

"FBI Director McPherson," McPherson identified himself. "I understand we have information on that CitationJet the smugglers flew from Sambalpur to Da Nang."

"Yes, sir, it was in this morning's report."

"Summarize, please."

"Property of Makrani Ltd," Evans said. "It was in for routine maintenance in Lahore and someone borrowed it."

McPherson pursed his lips. With the assistance, perhaps, of either Makrani or the Pakistani government? "How hard would a theft like that have been?"

Evans snorted. "I don't know. Harder than walking off with an Indian nuke?"

"Point," McPherson conceded. "Anything new with the other plane, the Zhardi one?"

"Still on the ground in Chongqing," Evans said. "We've pulled the airport records, and the engine trouble appears to be legit. Of course, you'd expect it to appear that way regardless."

"Any unusual communication traffic in or out of Chongqing?"

"Logan says no," Evans said. "Between that and Beijing's cooperation with the *Rabah Jamila*, I think we can pretty well scratch official Chinese involvement."

McPherson toyed with a pencil on his desk. "Leaving us what? Pakistan and North Korea in bed together?"

"Stranger things have happened," Evans said. "Maybe the lab people will turn up something in those containers."

"Maybe," McPherson said. "Any other highlights in that report?"

"The bomb the hijackers left in the *Rabah Jamila* was definitely foiled by a faulty wire in the triggering mechanism," Evans said. "We still don't know whether the break was deliberate or accidental. We've also dug up the paper trail on the *Eureka*, the sailing yacht the Navy P-3 spotted the night of the hijacking. The trail led us back to a well-known and respected boat-building company in Singapore."

"Do we know what kind of speed it can make?" McPherson asked.

"About par for a displacement hull," Evans said. "The engines can pull maybe fifteen to twenty knots. Of course, in a good wind, with the rigging up, it could do a lot better."

"I don't remember the report saying the rigging was up," McPherson said, thinking back.

"It wasn't," Evans agreed. "And there wasn't a lot of wind, either. The thing's put in to shore, by the way."

"Really? Where?"

"Yaku Island, due south of the main Japanese island group, about eighty miles from Kagoshima. It's tied up in a small inlet on the southwest side of the island."

"You're sure it's still there?"

"According to the satellite and high-flyover photos it is," Evans said. "Admiral Eskin said he'd go in for a ground-level look as soon as he can shake someone free from freighter search duty."

"Long-range photos don't impress me nearly as much as they used to," McPherson grumbled. "Not with this bunch."

"I'll remind the admiral of that," Evans promised. "Oh, and those bugs they found in the *Rabah Jamila*'s living areas were definitely Russian. Probably FSB—we're still checking."

"Terrific," McPherson growled. "So now we've got a possible Russian connection."

"Could be," Evans agreed. "Moscow's trying to trace them."

"Anything else?"

"Mostly negative search results," Evans said. "Nothing pressing."

"Okay," McPherson said. "Thanks."

"No problem. Good-bye, sir."

McPherson dropped the phone back into its cradle and looked across the room at the faceted crystal wall clock his wife had given him for his birthday five years ago as a not-so-subtle reminder that even vitally important government officials needed to come home occasionally.

The hands stood at four-fifteen. Outside on the streets, the crush of rush hour traffic would already have started. No point in even trying to leave now until at least six.

Keying for his email, he pulled up Rao's list of Syed's relatives, scowling as he ran his eyes down the list. Rao was clutching at straws on this one.

Still, McPherson had been in law enforcement long enough to know that every lead, even the absurd ones, had to be chased down.

So he would pass the list on to DHS and be done with it. After that, he would have a good hour and a half to concentrate on Bureau business until the streets cleared enough for him to head home. With the freighter searches still slogging along, the Zhardi jet still on the ground, and the sailboat tied up on a river, nothing else was likely to happen today.

21

ROSEBURG WAS A small town in the southwest corner of Oregon, nestled among the forests and hills and straddling both the meandering Umpqua River and the straighter strip of pavement that was Interstate 5. It was the kind of small, isolated town that so many people seemed nostalgic for these days, Captain Daniel MacMillan Hamilton thought as he flew his AV-8B Harrier II+ beneath the heavy cloud layer in a wide curve around the town. Even people who'd never lived in such a place. Especially people who'd never lived in such a place.

"Not like Yuma, eh?" the voice of his wingman, Lieutenant Carl Olsen, came in his headset. "Look at all that greenery. Bet they don't have to limit their showers to thirty seconds a pop."

"Probably nothing to do there *but* take showers," Hamilton countered with the automatic superciliousness toward small towns that was required of someone born and raised in the heart of Manhattan. "Places like that roll up their sidewalks at eight p.m."

Still, he had to secretly admit that growing up among all those climbing trees might have been nice.

"I could live with that," Olsen commented. "At least for a week or two. There's the airport—north end of town."

"Looks like we've already got a crowd waiting," Hamilton commented, peering out the cockpit at the knot of people visible at the airport's south end. "Let's do it."

The airport was tiny by Hamilton's standards—hell; by *anyone's* standards—consisting of a single north-south runway and a group of hangars scattered around the southwest corner. Between the hangars and the runway was a fair-sized parking area, open in the center, with two sets of small plane tiedowns at the north and south ends.

Standing just outside the largest of the hangars, peering up at the incoming Harriers, were three men: one in civilian clothing, one in Marine dress uniform, and one in full Air Force regalia. A hundred meters south of them, clustered between the south-end tiedowns and a chain link fence and behind a red-rope barricade, were the two hundred or so curiosity seekers he and Olsen had spotted from the air. "This must be the place," he commented, setting the Harrier into its approach and rotating the vectoring nozzles down to hover stop. "I see the Air Force is here, too. Let's show him how it's done."

Hamilton was normally pretty good with his landings anyway. With Air Force brass watching, he was doubly so, and had the satisfaction of setting the Harrier down sixty feet from the hangar with hardly even a bump. Olsen, he was sure, had been just as careful.

He shut down the engine and fired up the plane's auxiliary power unit. By the time he'd popped the canopy and climbed down, the three-man reception committee had arrived. Ducking under the Harrier's nose, he stepped up to them and came to attention. Olsen, with perfect timing, reached his side at precisely the same time. No doubt about it, they were definitely showing the Air Force how it was done.

"Gentlemen," he said, delivering his best parade-ground salute to the Marine major and Air Force general. "Captain Daniel MacMillan Hamilton, U.S. Marine Corps Attack Squadron 513. My wingman, Lieutenant Carl Olsen."

"Major John Avendon, retired," the Marine officer responded, returning their salutes. "Welcome to Roseburg, gentlemen."

"Thank you, sir," Hamilton said. "It's good to be here."

"The pleasure is ours," Avendon said, gesturing to the civilian to his left. "May I present Roseburg mayor Peter O'Donnell? He was the driving force behind this whole memorial project for the late General Clarke."

"How do you do, sir," Hamilton said, nodding to him.

"A pleasure, gentlemen," O'Donnell said. "I'm so very glad we were able to work around your scheduling problems and make this whole thing happen."

Hamilton felt his forehead wrinkle slightly. *Their* scheduling problems?

"And this is General Lionel Kalil," Avendon continued before Hamilton could say anything, gesturing to the Air Force officer on his right. "He came to Roseburg specifically for this service."

"Gentlemen," Kalil said. His voice was measured and deep, with the slightly odd intonation and sing-song flavor that Hamilton had always associated with foreign-born types for whom English was a second language. His face was a match for his voice: slightly darkened Latino or South Asian skin accentuated by white hair, a neatly trimmed beard, and piercing green eyes. Most Air Force officers Hamilton had met had been pretty nondescript, but Kalil more than made up for it. "I knew General Clarke quite well," the general continued. "In addition, Captain, I believe I also served with your current C.O., Colonel Abrams, in Afghanistan."

"I'm sorry, sir, but I believe you've been misinformed," Hamilton said politely, most of his brain still working on Kalil's green eyes and that odd scheduling comment of O'Donnell's. "Our C.O. is Colonel Raymond Broderick."

"Oh?" Kalil's forehead wrinkled. "My apologies. I wonder who I'm thinking of."

"There's a Colonel Abrams at Yuma, sir," Olsen offered. "But I believe he's with MACS-7."

"Yes," Kalil murmured. "Well, no matter."

A movement behind the three men caught Hamilton's attention: a short, wiry man in mechanic's coveralls hurrying toward them from the open hangar door. "Excuse me," he said as the reception committee turned toward him. "Which one of you is Lieutenant Olsen?"

"I am," Olsen said.

The man hooked a thumb over his shoulder toward the hangar. "Phone call for you, sir—a Colonel Broderick. Urgent and personal, he said."

Hamilton caught Olsen's eye, saw his own puzzlement mirrored there. "He asked for me specifically?" Olsen asked.

"That's what he said," the mechanic confirmed. "Urgent and personal, for Lieutenant Olsen."

"Yes," Olsen said, still frowning. "Major?"

"By all means, find out what he wants," Avendon said. "Don't worry, there's some slack in our schedule."

"I'll show you where you can take it," the mechanic offered.

"Thank you," Olsen said. "Excuse me."

With the mechanic in the lead, the two of them headed back to the hangar, turning into one of a row of offices Hamilton could see just inside the main door to the left. "I hope it's nothing serious," O'Donnell commented, turning back.

"Probably something to do with one of his kids," Hamilton assured him. "They're always breaking or spraining something. Mr. Mayor, may I ask what you meant by that comment just now about our scheduling problems? I was under the impression that it was *you* who had scheduling problems."

O'Donnell frowned. But before he could speak, General Kalil gave a delicate cough. "I'm afraid the confusion is my fault," he said. "Tell me, Captain, what's your philosophy concerning dying for your country?"

Something with lots of cold feet landed on Hamilton's spine. "What do you mean, sir?" he asked carefully.

"Exactly what I said," Kalil said. "Have you any wish to needlessly sacrifice your life, here and now, in the name of patriotism?"

The other two men were staring at Kalil now, too. Avendon's expression was hardening like fast-setting concrete as he began to catch on to what was happening, while O'Donnell still looked merely bewildered. Kalil hadn't moved, his untroubled green eyes locked on Hamilton, his empty hands hanging at his sides. "Are you threatening me, sir?" Hamilton asked.

"Not necessarily," Kalil said. "There's no reason anyone has to die today. Not you, not the young lieutenant in the hangar, not these gentlemen here—" he inclined his head slightly toward the crowd gathered behind the rope barricade behind him "—not any of those innocent civilians. All we want are your planes."

He shrugged microscopically. "Still, if you insist on playing the tragic hero, we can oblige you. Your decision."

Some outraged comment was clearly called for, Hamilton thought distantly. The fact that none of them made one implied that Avendon and O'Donnell were as floored as he was.

"You've got guts, I'll give you that," Hamilton managed at last. "May I ask how exactly you intend to pull this off?"

Kalil favored him with a smile that didn't touch his eyes. "In other words, what should you tell Colonel Broderick when he asks why you meekly surrendered instead of leaping upon me and wrestling me to the ground?"

"Something like that," Hamilton said through teeth clenched to keep them from shaking as adrenaline surged through his bloodstream. He could do it, he knew. Whatever weapon Kalil might have, there was no way he could draw it before Hamilton could get to him. And once he had him . . .

"You might wish to look at your chest," Kalil said mildly. "Just about there," he added, pointing.

Hamilton looked down . . . and as he did so, his dramatic plans evaporated like drops of water on a hot engine casing.

Hovering directly over his heart was the bright red spot of a laser targeter.

"You'll notice how steady the beam is," Kalil went on calmly, sounding for all the world like a flight instructor describing some subtle detail of an avionics system. "That implies that, if called upon to shoot, he would be unlikely to miss."

"Yes," Hamilton murmured, sweeping his fingers slowly across the beam as if trying to brush it away, hoping Kalil wouldn't figure out his true purpose for the action. If he could figure out the direction of the beam and locate the gunman, he might still be able to jump Kalil and use the man as a shield.

"You other gentlemen are also being targeted, of course," Kalil said, looking at Avendon and O'Donnell. "As I'm sure you can see."

Hamilton looked at them, the stomach-acid taste of defeat rising into his mouth as he spotted the two red dots now hovering on their chests, as well. His own gunman, he figured, was positioned somewhere just past the north corner of the hangar where Olsen had gone.

But lasers trained on Avendon and O'Donnell meant there were two others somewhere at Hamilton's back.

Which meant there was no blind spot where he would be out of range. No chance of using Kalil as a shield.

Assuming, of course, the snipers were good enough and confident enough to shoot him off Kalil's back . . .

Kalil might have been reading his mind. "You could probably jump me, Captain," he said. "But my men could easily put you down before you did me serious damage."

"A good trick," Hamilton said, glancing casually around behind him across the expanse of tarmac and runway beyond. The nearest cover in that direction were some buildings and trees probably half a mile away. "Especially at that distance."

"I don't know what the hell you think you're doing," Avendon growled, apparently only now finding his voice. "But if you think you can get away with this insane—"

"Be silent, Major," Kalil said quietly. Quietly, but with an edge to his voice that made Avendon sputter to a halt. "This isn't about you. You and Mr. O'Donnell will do as you're told or you will die. Captain Hamilton is the man under oath to his nation, responsible for his plane and his life and his comrade's life."

His eyes shifted back to Hamilton. "He's the one," he added, "who will decide whether or not this day ends in bloodshed."

For a long moment Hamilton stood silently, staring at Kalil, trying to gauge the man's determination and figure out what his own duty called for. If Olsen had still been here beside him, he might have risked some sort of action, counting on his wingman to back him up or make it to the safety of his Harrier where he could call for help. But Kalil had been smart enough to split them up.

Out of the corner of his eye he could see the milling crowd, the people gazing at the awesome warplanes as they waited patiently for the pilots to finish with the pleasantries and go on with their exhibition. The breeze faltered a bit, and in the relative quiet he could hear children's voices mixed in with the deeper rumble of adult conversation.

And with a sinking feeling he realized which way his decision had to go. He was a Marine, with the sworn duty to sacrifice his life if and when called upon to do so. But it was clear his death here would serve no purpose. Kalil surely had men standing by who had the training and skill to fly a Harrier. Even if he nailed Kalil, the planes were as good as gone. Whether or not Hamilton himself was lying on the tarmac in a pool of his own blood.

Whether or not Olsen and two hundred of Roseburg's civilians also lay in pools of blood.

"Major Avendon is right," he told Kalil quietly. "You can't possibly get away with this."

"We shall see," Kalil said, gesturing toward the hangar. There was no triumph in his voice or face, no gloating that Hamilton could detect. There wasn't anything personal in this, he realized, no twisted game the man was playing with the Marines in general or him, Hamilton, in particular. Stealing a pair of Harriers was just a job. "This way, please."

He led the way toward the hangar. The red spot stayed steady on Hamilton's chest, and after a few steps he again waved a finger in front of it to confirm its direction. Eventually, he knew, the north corner of the hangar had to cut off the hidden gunman's line of sight, effectively putting that weapon out of commission.

Though of course there would still be the two snipers at his back to deal with.

They reached the hangar and walked in beneath the vertically-folding door, finally moving out of sight of the civilians at the south end of the field. Hamilton half expected Kalil to whip out a gun now that the need for subterfuge was over; but the man merely gestured toward the row of offices where Olsen had disappeared. Olsen himself was nowhere in sight, but the mechanic who'd brought the phone message was waiting expectantly beside one of the half-open doors. He had taken off his coveralls, revealing a good imitation of a Marine flight suit.

And as Hamilton half turned around toward the north, he saw that the red spot on his chest was still there.

He stared at the dot, a hard knot settling into his stomach. Something was wrong. He had checked the sniper's vector—had checked it a dozen times—and it should have been blocked off long before they entered the hangar. The only way for that laser to still be on him was if the sniper was inside the hangar itself.

But that was impossible. The north end of the hangar was empty, with only a stool, a small pump, and a breadbox-sized electronics monitor scattered around the otherwise bare concrete floor, plus a half dozen large tool chests against the far wall. There were no planes awaiting repair, no stacks of equipment someone could be crouching behind, not even any conveniently placed piles of rubbish. The rafters spanning the hangar overhead were bare and empty, uninterrupted by cranes or storage boxes. There was literally no place a sniper could hide.

Which meant there was no sniper.

A sudden rage swirled up inside Hamilton like backwash sewage. So it was nothing but a con game. No snipers, just a couple of laser targeting systems hidden in one of the tool boxes and kept pointed at him by remote control.

And if there were no gunmen . . .

"In there, gentlemen," Kalil said.

Hamilton turned back toward the fake general, taking a deep breath as he and the others moved toward the door the mechanic was standing beside. All right. Avendon and O'Donnell probably hadn't caught on yet. But his side was still up by three to two. If he could take out the mechanic, the other two ought to be able to handle Kalil. He continued to walk, letting his path drift slightly toward the mechanic . . .

Once again, Kalil might have been reading his mind. "There are, of course, *four* gunmen," he said conversationally. "Do you require a demonstration, Captain Hamilton?"

Hamilton stopped short. Slowly, he turned half around, waving his hand in front of the red dot pinned to his chest, feeling like an idiot. Of course it wasn't the same dot as before. It couldn't be. From somewhere outside, a fourth sniper had simply picked him up as he moved out of range of the first.

But for the grace of God, and Kalil's pointed comment, he would have died right there.

He turned back, a fresh surge of acid taste burning his mouth. "No," he said quietly.

"Good," Kalil said. "In here, please."

The room they'd chosen was a small office with no windows and only the one door. Another man in a Marine flight suit was already inside, duct-taping Lieutenant Olsen's ankles to the leg of a massive wooden desk. Olsen's wrists were already secured; above the strip of tape over his mouth his eyes were seething. He looked up as Hamilton appeared, the rage in his face turning to something closer to disgust. Hamilton could hardly blame him.

It took only a minute for the flight-suited men to secure the newcomers. The mechanic gave a final tug to Hamilton's wrist bonds, straightened up, and nodded to Kalil standing in the doorway. "Hamechiz hazer ast," he said briskly.

To Hamilton's surprise, a flash of anger flicked across Kalil's face, the first genuine emotion he'd yet seen from the man. *"Engelisi harf bezan, ahmaq,"* he all but snarled.

The pilot flinched as if he'd been struck. "Yes, sir," he murmured.

For another heartbeat Kalil held his eyes. Then, he dropped his gaze to Hamilton.

Hamilton held his breath, striving to look as innocent and stupid as he could manage with half his face covered by duct tape. The mechanic's thoughtless words were a clue to their identity, possibly the only clue they were going to get. If Kalil realized that—and if he realized that Hamilton realized that—he might decide to end the day in bloodshed after all.

The innocent look worked. Kalil's lip twitched and he looked away, visually checking each of the bonds. "That will do," he said, gesturing to his men and moving out of the doorway as they filed from the room. "Good day, gentlemen," he added, throwing the prisoners an ironic salute. "My apologies for the inconvenience."

He left, closing the door behind him. Like fish at the bottom of a boat, Hamilton's three fellow captives instantly began flopping around, grunting wordless curses as they fought to free themselves.

Hamilton didn't bother. Kalil's men were too competent to have done a halfway job, and he had no doubt that fighting against the duct tape would be a waste of effort.

Besides, he had a far more important task right now. The foreign words had been incomprehensible to him; but even incomprehensible words could be memorized. *Hamechiz hazer ast engelisi harf bezan ahmaq,* he ran the phonemes over in his mind, burning them into his synapses. *Hamechiz hazer ast engelisi harf bezan ahmaq. Hamechiz hazer ast engelisi harf bezan ahmaq.*

Through the door came the familiar sound of Harrier engines rev-ving up. Olsen growled in his throat, and for a moment the writhing ceased as everyone paused to listen. The roar became louder, and then fell off slightly as the planes lifted off the tarmac. The pitch changed as the pilots eased from vertical into horizontal flight, then faded rapidly away. A moment later, all was again silent.

So Kalil's men did indeed know how to fly the damn planes. Distantly, Hamilton wondered what the watching crowd had made of it all.

Olsen grunted again. As if on signal, the trio's frantic efforts resumed.

Hamilton stayed as he was, concentrating on the voices ringing in his mind. *Hamechiz hazer ast engelisi harf bezan ahmaq. Hamechiz hazer ast engelisi harf bezan ahmaq.*

~

The Harriers had disappeared over the hills to the west, and the crowd had finally drifted away, disappointed or confused but apparently not suspicious.

Time to go.

For a few seconds the general stood by the open hangar door, methodically scanning the airport grounds for lingering onlookers. But everyone had either gone home or headed for the cemetery where the memorial service was supposed to take place. For their sake, he hoped the rain in those heavy clouds held off a little longer.

Gently, he tapped the tiny microphone hidden beneath his shirt and the civilian jacket he'd changed into. "Eight, Nine: all clear."

For a moment nothing happened. Then, with a suddenness he still found startling, a flat expanse of black cloth with two large lumps beneath it abruptly appeared in the center of one of the patches of grass on the far side of the runway. The lumps moved, one end of the cloth flipped up, and Eight and Nine crawled out, their Galil sniper rifles in hand. Taking both rifles, Eight crossed the tarmac at a quick jog, handed them to the general, then headed back to assist Nine with the task of gathering up the Cloak. A couple of minutes later they were back, the folded material held between them like a heavy tarp.

"Well done," the general said as they slipped under the door into the hanger and relative safety from prying eyes. "How did the system work?"

"Perfectly, sir," Eight said as they set the Cloak down. "I was worried that extending the scope forward with fiber optics would ruin the resolution, particularly at that range. But the image was quite adequate."

"How did the profile look from this end?" Nine asked. "Did we have the Cloak draped over enough of the barrel?"

"Yes," the general confirmed. "The few centimeters of suppressor and scope extension I could see looked like bits of discarded tubing in the grass. I'm quite certain our two Marines never saw a thing."

"A successful test, then," Eight said.

"Indeed," the general said. "The technique should work equally well in the city."

"Any word about Three and Four, sir?" Nine asked.

"Not yet," the general said, consulting his watch. It had been fifteen minutes since the stolen Harriers had lifted off. "They should be down by now, and possibly concealed. Two is monitoring the military frequencies, and he would have informed me if the alarm had been raised. As long as the search holds off until their engines have cooled, they should be safe." He gestured to Eight and handed Nine his rifle. "Eight, get the van. Nine: backstop."

The two men crossed to the hangar's rear door, Eight heading outside for the rented van they'd parked discreetly behind one of the nearby buildings, Nine taking up a watchful post just inside the door. The general turned back to the front of the hangar, again checking for bystanders or belatedly suspicious police. While he'd told Captain Hamilton the truth about not wanting the day to end in bloodshed, he wouldn't hesitate a moment if such bloodshed became necessary.

Fortunately, it didn't. Eight pulled the van to the door, and a minute later he and Nine had loaded the medium-sized Cloak and rifles into the back. "Seven: clear," the general said into his mike.

Across the hangar, the section of concrete floor behind the pump turned into their small Cloak. Seven flipped the edge of the black cloth over his shoulder and stood up. The empty beer can that had been lying on top of the pump casing came up with him, still wrapped around the muzzle of his suppressed rifle.

Three minutes later they were off the airport grounds and heading for the highway. Sitting in one of the back seats, listening to the post-operation chatter, the general set to work removing the false beard, wig, and theatrical putty that had subtly but effectively disguised his features. One more hurdle had been overcome, and the pieces of this mission continued to fall neatly into place.

With one exception. One single, glaring, potentially devastating exception.

Angie Chandler.

It was apparently a common thought. "Sir, has there been any news from Six?" Nine asked from beside him.

"Not since early morning," the general said, aware that the conversation in the front seats had ceased. "As far as I know, he's still driving around Monterey looking for her."

"He wasn't able to get back into the house?"

"I told him not to try," the general said. "The raid will have left a considerable amount of CS residue behind. The Lees won't be back until it's been cleaned up."

Eight snorted. "A gift from Ross, no doubt."

"No doubt," the general agreed. "Though I think our friend may have outsmarted himself for once. If the police hadn't been roving the neighborhood over his bomb threat, Six might well have returned to his post. If he had, the subsequent raid would have left him either dead or a prisoner. As it is, all we've lost is one of the Cloaks."

"Which is going to be a major problem," Eight said darkly.

"A problem, but not a major one," the general said. "The plan can be adjusted."

From behind the wheel, Seven rumbled something under his breath. "You know, sir, I'd have given long odds that no one could lose Six that easily, especially starting out on foot. Ross is good. Suspiciously good."

"Suspicious is definitely the word for it," the general agreed. "The more I think about it the more I'm convinced he's tied in with Hooker."

"But if Hooker's turned on us, why hasn't he gone to the police?" Nine pointed out.

"With what?" the general countered. "A story about a disembodied voice and email address hiring him to drug some scientists?"

"It would at least get him out from under the murder charge," Nine pointed out.

"Only if they believed him," the general said. "*And* only if they catch us. If not, he'll still be the one charged with murder, and he must surely know that. No, all he can do is stay low and hope they can't put together enough evidence to arrest him."

"I still don't understand how Ross fits in," Seven said. "If he's working for Hooker, they must think keeping Angie Chandler alive gains them something. But what?"

Carefully, the general peeled off the putty at his jawline that had given him an extra chin. "I don't know," he said, wadding the putty into a ball and dropping it into a bag at his feet. "I first thought it was a slap at us for killing the scientists, Hooker trying to force us to waste time tracking her down. But it's gone too far for that. He must see her as insurance of some sort."

"A fourth suspect, perhaps?" Eight suggested. "Having been there that evening, she might qualify."

"Perhaps," the general said. "But it strikes me as too shallow for a man of Hooker's reputation."

"Perhaps she's a different sort of insurance," Seven offered slowly. "Since we want her dead, and since he knows the same secret she does, keeping her out of our hands may be his way of making sure it's not worth the effort for us to shut *him* up."

"Yes, I thought of that," the general said. "That one does sound more like Hooker. But it still doesn't hold together."

"Could Ross be nothing more than the innocent bystander he appears to be?" Nine suggested.

"No," the general said firmly. "He's too clever, his presence at the mall was too convenient, and he's stayed with her too long. No, he's involved. Either with Hooker or someone else."

"Maybe Mrs. Chandler herself?" Seven suggested.

"Then why did she ditch him?" Eight countered.

"We only have Ross's word that she did," Seven pointed out. "The story he spun for Six might have been pure fabrication."

"No," the general said. "The police said the same thing to her parents that afternoon."

"Does it really matter who he is?" Nine growled. "The woman still has to be eliminated. If Ross gets in the way, I say we take them both."

"Agreed," the general said, popping out the uncomfortable green contact lenses that had masked the natural darkness of his eyes. "I'd prefer to first learn what his role in all this is, but that may end up being a luxury we can't afford. If the opportunity presents itself, we'll take it."

Eight grunted. "Hopefully before the weapon arrives."

"Most definitely," the general said grimly. "I won't risk bringing the weapon ashore until she's been silenced."

"That could be awkward," Nine warned. "The ship's only two days out."

"If I may suggest, sir," Eight offered, "Nine and I could get another vehicle and return to Monterey while you and Seven rendezvous with the others. You shouldn't need all of us there until the weapon arrives."

Staring over Seven's shoulder at the road ahead, the general came to a decision. "Yes, Six will need help," he said. "Two, Three, and Four can watch over the Harriers alone. The rest of us will return together to Monterey." He considered. "With a stop first in San Jose."

"For a chat with Hooker?" Nine asked.

"No, he's surely being watched," the general said. "So we'll return the favor with a watch on Detective Delgado. If and when someone locates Mrs. Chandler, she'll certainly be brought to see him. Seven, before you get on the highway you'll need to find a secluded place where we can change plates and decals."

"Yes, sir," Seven said. "May I ask what we're going to do about Hooker?"

The general gazed at the road ahead, through the raindrops beginning to appear on the windshield. "We shall see," he said softly. "We shall see."

22

THE LATER AFTERNOON clouds had begun to blow away as Lieutenant Jason Flanders maneuvered his bright orange Coast Guard HH-65A Dolphin helo over the tiny Oregon community of Lakeside, a few miles in from the roiling Pacific Ocean.

Clouds or not, sunlight or not, his search area was still coming up the way it had all afternoon.

Empty.

"Coast Guard Twelve to Nexus," he said into his helmet mike, banking slightly as he eyeballed a group of trees clustered at the western edge of one of Tenmile Lake's many arms. Was there a flicker of color in there? "I'm at the northern boundary of my area. Still negative."

"Coast Guard Twelve, acknowledged," Colonel Belford growled. As the Marine officer coordinating the search, he apparently felt it his duty to growl at all non-Marine personnel who'd been pressed into service. "Give me your location."

"Tango Oscar three five," Flanders read off his map grid, easing a few meters down for a better view. It would be a real kick if on a routine check-in he could casually announce that he'd found the missing Harriers.

But it was just a dilapidated trailer tucked in there among the firs. "Requesting instructions," he added.

"Yes, yes, I know," the colonel said. "Hold on."

The radio went silent. Immediately after the first frantic scramble, Flanders remembered, the colonel's voice had been sharp and angry, full of the controlled professional fury the Marines liked to think they had the market cornered on. Now, two hours after the Harriers had vanished, with everything on the West Coast that could fly out searching for them and not even a whiff of a lead in sight, the man just sounded frustrated.

Flanders could sympathize. To lose a pair of fighter planes in broad daylight—and in full view of two hundred witnesses, yet—had to be embarrassing in the extreme.

"Coast Guard Twelve, have you searched all the way to the coast?"

"I've taken it as far as I have to," Flanders assured him. "Most everything west of 101 is scrub and sand dune. No chance they could have stashed the planes there."

Coast Guard assurances were apparently not good enough for the Marines today. "Ever hear of camouflage netting?" the colonel shot back. "You go look at everything in your sector, and I mean everything. You don't stop until the ocean is under your rotors, and not even then if you can still see the bottom. Understood?"

"Understood," Flanders said, suppressing a sigh. He wasn't sure where exactly this command post was set up, but it was clear the colonel had no idea what the plant life was like on the Oregon coast. He *had* had some experience with camouflage netting, thank you, and there wasn't a chance in hell he could miss something the size of a fighter on the dunes with this kind of low-level search.

But they were Marine planes, and the Marines were in charge, and Flanders didn't have any other plans for the day. "Continuing search pattern."

Giving the trees one last lingering look, he turned the big helo around and headed west.

~

"There were at least seven of them," General Vaughn growled, handing copies of the hastily assembled report around the conference room table. From the simmering blaze in his eyes, McPherson thought distantly, it was a wonder the paper didn't catch on fire. "Possibly more, though the pilots only saw three."

"Were the planes armed?" Logan asked.

"No," Vaughn said. "But anyone who can steal a Harrier probably knows how to load 25mm cannon rounds, too."

"What about witnesses to the theft itself?" McPherson asked.

"What the hell was there to witness?" Vaughn bit out. "Two men get out of the planes, two men get back in and fly off."

"I was wondering if anyone spotted anything unusual in the flying itself," McPherson persisted. "Something that might have marked the pilots as unfamiliar with V/STOL aircraft."

Vaughn shook his head. "There were a lot of former Marines in the crowd. Not a big surprise, given it was a Marine general's memorial service. We've talked to seven of them so far, and they all say the take-offs were textbook perfect. On top of that, all the beacons and fancy little location transponders we have aboard for exactly this sort of situation were apparently quite efficiently disposed of." He hissed out a breath between clenched teeth. "Two Radar Birds. *Damn*, this is embarrassing."

"Would you rather Hamilton and Olsen had sacrificed their lives fighting the inevitable?" Cohn countered. "Would that have salved your wounded pride any?"

"Trust me, they'll wish they *had* died by the time Broderick gets done with them," Vaughn said icily. "He's going to flense them straight to the bone."

"If I were you, I'd shelve the righteous indignation and stop taking this personally," Cohn said, clearly not in any mood to be conciliatory. "You and the rest of the Pentagon. This gang has been leaving egged faces everywhere from Pakistan eastward, and it just happened to be our turn. Deal with it."

"What makes you think it's the same gang?" Logan objected. "There's no evidence this is connected to the Indian nuke."

"Check out page four," Vaughn told him, flipping over to that page in his own copy. "The debriefing of Captain Hamilton. One of General Kalil's men slipped up when they'd secured the Marines and he thought it was in the bag. "He said, 'everything is ready'; to which Kalil said, 'Speak English, you fool.' Notice what language that exchange was in?"

"Yes, I can read," Logan said impatiently. "Hamilton claims it was Farsi. But he could have been mistaken."

"Hamilton isn't claiming anything," Vaughn said. "He doesn't even know the language. All he did was memorize the sounds. The linguists took it from there."

"And what, you're making a connection with the Indian nuke because that Chinese CitationJet started from an Iranian port?" Logan asked. "I thought we'd decided that plane had nothing to do with the theft."

"You can decide whatever you want," Vaughn said. "I'm not ready yet to let them off the hook. The fact remains that the Chinese jet ran interference for the theft plane, and I still find the timing suspicious."

"So they said a couple of sentences in Farsi," Logan said. "The crewmen on the *Rabah Jamila* claimed the hijackers spoke Korean. So which are they, Korean or Iranian?"

"Why can't they be both?" Cohn suggested. "We've discussed the possibility the Chinese were involved, and Minister Rao is ninety-percent convinced the North Koreans are working with Pakistan on this. Why not an Iranian-North Korean effort?"

"Or it could be nothing but a matched set of red herrings," Logan argued. "Anyone can memorize a few sentences in another language."

"Speaking of suspicious timing," McPherson said, glancing through the report, "I'm confused as to why the Harriers were in Oregon today in the first place. I see a reference here to a planned memorial service for General Clarke, but it says the service wasn't supposed to take place until June, the anniversary of Clarke's death."

"We're still sorting that one out," Vaughn said. "It appears that about three weeks ago the Roseburg organizers received a series of phone calls saying that the 513th was going to be shipped out to Afghanistan in early February. At the same time, Colonel Broderick at Yuma got a similar series of calls saying that, due to family conflicts, they were going to need to move the memorial service up to January."

"More cuteness," Cohn put in. "Certainly sounds like our nuke gang's signature."

"It does, doesn't it?" Vaughn agreed. "At any rate, by the time all the dust settled, the service had been moved to today. Now we know why."

"What about the planes themselves?" McPherson asked. "You can't fly tactical fighters around without leaving some kind of trail."

"Maybe not, but they're making a damn good try at it," Vaughn said. "For starters, they stayed at treetop height, so there's no radar record of them. We have a few satellite photos where they broke briefly from cloud cover that show them heading a few degrees north of west, but most of the time they were out of sight."

"Infrared?" Logan asked.

"Too much cloud interference," Vaughn said. "Once the alarm was given and we got a low-level search going, IR detectors were brought into play. But by then the engines were probably too cool to show up anyway, certainly if they'd been shielded or force-cooled."

"What about the locals?" Cohn asked. "I know that's not a heavily populated region, but a fighter blowing past ought to draw *some* attention."

"It's a question of gathering and codifying the reports," Vaughn said. "We've got people fanned out all over the Coast Ranges, plus telephone contacts with the more remote ranches and farms. Eventually, we should be able to pin down their route."

"The question being whether we can do it in time," McPherson murmured.

"That's one question," Vaughn said heavily. "The other being, in time for *what*."

There was a moment of silence. "Let's assume for a moment that the two thefts are related," Cohn said slowly. "Question: what do two Harriers have to do with a stolen nuke in the East China Sea?"

"Assuming the nuke is actually there," McPherson pointed out. "As far as I know, we still don't know how it got off the *Rabah Jamila*."

"Especially since we have no solid proof it was ever aboard in the first place," Logan seconded. "Residual radiation notwithstanding."

"It was there," Vaughn insisted, the glint back in his eye again. "And they *did* get it off."

"Fine," Logan said, waving a hand impatiently. "In that case, we're back to Larry's question. What do Harriers have to do with the nuke?"

"Could be a diversion," McPherson suggested. "For the past few days all our attention has been focused on the western Pacific. Maybe things were getting too hot for them."

Logan shook his head. "The Roseburg rescheduling started three weeks ago," he pointed out. "If it was a diversion, that means they knew that far back they would need us diverted at this particular moment."

"Which isn't impossible," Cohn said thoughtfully. "We already know they run on tight numbers and like to leave puzzles littering the road behind them. If they knew, say, that they'd be moving the nuke today, they could have staged this to keep our satellite people looking the wrong direction."

"If that's what they want, they're getting it," McPherson said. "I've already sent most of my satellite people back to the Bureau to help with the search. Yours are back home, too, aren't they, Spence?"

Logan nodded. "That could very well be the plan," he conceded. "They distract us, while at the same time throwing in another Iranian red herring."

"I'm not convinced it *was* a red herring," McPherson said.

"Then why didn't they kill everyone when they knew they'd been overheard?" Logan countered.

"Maybe they didn't think anyone could remember the words," Cohn said. "But it's not worth arguing at this point. We're still a long way from eliminating any possibilities."

Vaughn cleared his throat. "There's one other reason they might have wanted a Harrier," he said. "Possibly it's to be the delivery system."

McPherson felt something tighten in his throat. "I didn't know the nuke was packaged for dropping."

"It wasn't," Vaughn said. "But they might be able to rig a droppable casing. Hell, they don't even have to drop it. They could just fly it to the target and detonate it inside the plane. Suicide mission, but so what?"

"But why steal a plane from *us*?" Logan objected. "There have to be others closer to their target."

"Why use an Indian nuke?" Vaughn countered. "New Delhi thinks the perpetrators want to embarrass them. Maybe they want to embarrass us, too."

"Some embarrassment," Logan muttered. "So how do they get the Harriers out of the country?"

"Maybe they're already gone," McPherson said. "There are freighters running up and down the coast all the time, and today was no exception. Maybe that's why they specifically wanted Harriers, so that they could land in a confined space."

"Unlikely," Vaughn said. "We've been in contact with all the ships along the Oregon, Washington, and northern California coasts. With only three exceptions, every ship was in view of at least two others during the critical hour, and all of them had people on deck."

"You're checking the exceptions?"

"Search parties are already aboard." Vaughn paused. "The other possibility is that they don't need to get the planes out of the country because they plan to use them right here. Them, and maybe the nuke."

Logan swore softly. "Someone out there must *really* be mad at us this time."

"So it would seem," Cohn said grimly. "Let's get busy and figure out who the hell he is."

~

Angie had had a good meal the night before: one of A.J.'s extensive collection of specialty steaks, microwave defrosted and cooked on the built-in kitchen grill. A session with Sarah's collection of vanity supplies had followed, at the end of which time her long black hair had become a tightly coiled bun of light brown. She'd experimented some with makeup, too, deciding what would work best to camouflage her face. Then, with fatigue dragging at her eyelids, she had fallen into bed.

She'd intended to sleep in as late as she could, hoping to catch up on her rest now that she finally had a safe place to stay. Instead, she'd awakened at six sharp with her heart pounding and a terrifying sense of imminent danger.

All nerves and delayed reaction, of course. As she'd watched the bedroom shades slowly brighten with the approaching dawn she'd tried to persuade herself of that.

But the pep talk hadn't helped. All through her quick shower and quicker breakfast the feeling had persisted that this house, which she'd counted on so heavily to be her fortress while she thought things through, was no longer safe. Perhaps it had never been safe.

As the electric cuckoo clock in the kitchen had chirped its brainlessly cheerful announcement of the seven o'clock hour, she'd slipped through the back door and out into another bleak California morning.

She'd spent the morning browsing the waterfront shops with the rest of the off-season visitors and the scattering of locals who hadn't already grown bored with the scenery. Along the way she bought tinted fashion sunglasses, a scarf to help conceal the length of her newly colored hair, and a new coat to replace the one Ross had given her.

Lunchtime came and went, with her stomach too tense to eat. Her theory was that no one would expect a fugitive to be wandering the streets acting like a tourist, and so far it seemed to be working. Still, with every cruising police car that went by, or every friend of her parents who strolled past without a second glance, she seemed to die a few more inches.

At four o'clock she finally called it quits. She hadn't been discovered, at least as far as she knew, but at the same time she hadn't gotten anywhere, either. There were still killers on the loose who had murdered her husband, and from the lack of news she was able to glean from radio and newspapers, it looked as if the police weren't making any headway.

It was time for her to have a go at it.

The waterfront bars and restaurants were only sparsely populated at this hour of the afternoon, but a little hunting turned up a corner tavern named Peg Leg's near the Breakwater Cove Marina that had managed to attract more than its share of business. The interior was divided into a central bar plus two long wings running parallel to the streets outside. One of the side areas was equipped with tables, the other with booths. Selecting a booth near the back of the latter area beside one of the smoked-glass windows, she ordered a glass of white wine and pulled out her cell phone. The battery was almost dead, but the conversation should be short. Mentally crossing her fingers, she punched in the Tarnhelm group's phone number.

It was answered on the third ring. "Lab D-327," Esteban's familiar voice said.

Angie took a deep breath. "Ramon, this is Angie Chandler," she said, keeping her voice low.

"Angie!" he all but gasped. "What in—are you all right? We've been worried sick about you."

"I'm all right for now," she assured him. "But someone's trying to kill me."

"I know," Esteban said grimly. "The police are going nuts trying to find you. That private eye who's been hanging around you? Watch out—he's a fake."

"Don't worry, Mr. Ross is long gone," Angie said. "But I'm just getting in deeper, and I don't know what to do."

"Call the police," he told her firmly. "They're the only ones who can help."

"Are you sure they can be trusted?"

"Sure," he said. "I mean, I suppose so. Why shouldn't they be?"

"I don't know," Angie said, trying to sound as woebegone as she could. "I don't know anything anymore."

"Look, why don't you give Lieutenant Delgado a call," Esteban urged. "I've got his card right here . . . yeah, here it is."

He read off the phone number. "I think you can trust him," he added. "I do."

"I don't know," Angie said. "I'm still scared. And starving, I haven't eaten since yesterday. Maybe it'll be easier to think when I've got some food in me."

"Sure," Esteban said. "Where are you?"

It was the question she'd been waiting for. "Monterey," she said, gazing out the window at one of the seafood restaurants halfway down the block and across the street. "A seafood place called the Windjammer. I just ordered dinner."

"Okay, but make it fast," Esteban warned. "You shouldn't be out in the open like that."

"I'll be careful," she promised. "Thanks, Ramon. Maybe I'll call this Lieutenant Delgado after I eat."

"Okay," Esteban said. "If you need anything else, just call."

"Thanks," Angie said. " 'Bye."

She clicked off and closed the phone as, with perfect timing, her order arrived. If Esteban was innocent, then she was simply going to have a quiet glass of wine by herself. If he was the man who had murdered her husband, in league with the men who were trying to murder her, there should be some interesting activity down the block soon.

Taking a sip of wine, she settled back to watch.

The minutes ticked by. A number of people moved in and out of her view, most of them tourist looking, none of them showing the sort of urgency she would expect from hunters who'd suddenly gotten wind of their prey. Eight minutes after her call a middle-aged couple wandered into the Windjammer, but again in a leisurely fashion. A foursome came out of the restaurant a few minutes after that, stood for a while on the sidewalk apparently discussing their next move, then headed off together toward the marina.

Across the bar the bell attached to the door tinkled its announcement that another late-afternoon drinker had arrived. Angie glanced over—

And felt her throat freeze.

It was Ross.

23

WITH A FINAL click of her mouse, the last picture dissolved from Swenson's screen, joining the rest of the photos in its proper place in the sequence she'd spent the afternoon digging out and lining up. A long and tiring process, but worth it. Well worth it. Now all she needed to do was corral McPherson or Cohn or one of the other higher-ups—

"Finished?"

She spun around, nearly sliding off her chair in her surprise. McPherson was sitting right behind her, not three feet away, his feet propped up on a vacant desk and a coffee cup in his hand. "You startled me, sir," she said reproachfully. "What are you doing back there?"

His eyebrows lifted slightly. "Waiting for you to finish this analysis that's going to knock my socks off," he said mildly. "As you asked me to do when I last passed by half an hour ago."

Swenson felt heat flow into her cheeks. "I didn't."

"You did," he assured her. "You don't remember, do you?"

"Not a bit," she confessed, thoroughly embarrassed. It was one thing to go blank on someone like Talbot. In fact, Talbot usually deserved it. It was something else entirely to do it to the head of the whole Bureau. "I'm sorry, sir."

"Don't worry about it," he said, waving the apology away as if swatting at a fly hovering in front of his nose. "It's been a madhouse the past few hours, and it's been kind of relaxing to just sit here and do nothing."

"Yes, but I've kept you from other work," Swenson said, dimly aware that he was letting her off the hook and that she was perversely arguing the point. "More important things."

"All that's coming in right now is negative information," he said. "No one needs me sitting there for that." He gestured at her screen.

"Besides, you sounded excited, and an excited Jigsaw Girl is always worth listening to. You said something about sleight of hand?"

"Yes, sir," Swenson said, turning back to her keyboard and punching for the first photo in her lineup. She didn't remember saying that, either, but it was an apt description. "You remember our problem—well, one of them, anyway—is figuring out just what happened at the end aboard the *Rabah Jamila*."

"Right," McPherson said, hitching his chair up to her side. "I remember that photo."

"I think we're all familiar with it by now," she agreed ruefully, gazing at their best satellite shot of the yacht tied up alongside the *Rabah Jamila*, a photo that had been scanned and studied and analyzed and enhanced half to death. "This shot was taken at four-thirty-seven Friday afternoon, local time, shortly after the crew was locked below, but before Captain Syed was taken to his private cell."

"Allegedly taken there, anyway," McPherson said. "The lab's still running his latest voiceprint sample against the transmission."

"It's going to come up negative," Swenson told him. "I think we'll find it happened just the way he said. The only reason they locked him up separately was to make us think he might be an inside man."

"Okay, but if Syed didn't send the Mayday you're going to have to explain how the hijackers vanished into thin air during their forty-six-minute window," McPherson warned. "I trust you're not going to suggest the yacht was a James Bond special that converts to a submarine."

"Actually, you're not that far off," Swenson told him. "I got to thinking about what the crew said about hearing the yacht's hull bouncing against the starboard side of the ship until seven o'clock. Usually you avoid metal-to-metal contact between ships—you use rubber fenders or hang old tires there instead. But that doesn't make as much noise as metal-on-metal would. The yacht was tied up on their starboard side, and the crew was locked into a hold on the starboard side, and right beside the accommodation ladder. Coincidence?"

There was the creak of chair springs as McPherson straightened up. "You're saying they wanted them to hear the yacht?"

"No, they wanted them to *think* they were hearing the yacht." Swenson punched up the next photo. "This is the *Rabah Jamila* at about five-forty, or at least what you can see of it through the clouds and with the sun almost gone. This is our last even partially clear photo before it takes off and heads north at high speed, which according to the crew's testimony will happen in about twenty minutes. You can see—sort of—that the yacht is still there, and that the crane is poised either coming or going over it."

"Finishing the nuke transfer," McPherson said. "Right. And?"

"Something interesting." Swenson touched the yacht with the eraser end of her pencil. "You'll notice the yacht has drifted back a bit since the previous shot. Not more than a few feet, and not past the ladder. As if a line tying it to the freighter has been loosened a little, either preparatory to casting off or to facilitate the crane's operation. On the assumption they are about to leave, I ran over it with a fine-tooth comb—"

"Wait a minute," McPherson said. "That *they* are about to leave? Both of them?"

"Sorry, I meant just the yacht and one of them," she corrected. "The other one will stay aboard another hour to let the yacht put some distance between it and the freighter."

"With a random slab of metal bobbing alongside so that the crew would think the yacht was still there?" McPherson suggested. "Interesting theory. It still leaves us two major problems, though."

"Where the yacht went, and how the second hijacker got away," Swenson said, nodding. "I think I can answer both of them. Second hijacker first. As I was saying, I went over this photo with a fine-tooth comb. Against the *Rabah Jamila*'s hull, just clear of the yacht now that it's shifted, I spotted this."

She tapped for the next photo, and there was another creaking of springs as McPherson hitched his chair a little closer. "Clear as mud," he commented.

"I know," Swenson apologized. "As I said, the sun's almost gone, and the light's coming from the wrong side of the ship anyway. Leaves this side pretty much in shadow. I enhanced it as much as I could."

"Probably why they tied the yacht on that side in the first place," McPherson grunted. "Looks like a bunch of cylinders inside a framework. What is it, some kind of cluster bomb?"

"I don't think so," Swenson said. "What it is—at least what I think it is—is an array of scuba tanks."

There was a moment of silence. "You're joking."

"Not at all," Swenson assured him. "I know it sounds crazy—"

"Not sounds, Swenson," McPherson corrected her. "Is. In case you hadn't noticed, that ship is over a hundred fifty miles from anything that qualifies as dry land. What did he do, swim all the way to Shanghai?"

"As a matter of fact, he didn't even have to lift a flipper," Swenson said. "Remember what's about to happen: the *Rabah Jamila*, steaming for all it's worth toward North Korea, is going to send a pair of transmissions that stir up a hornets' nest in both the U.S. and China. Where is all that attention going to be focused?"

"On the *Rabah Jamila*," McPherson said, scratching his chin as he gazed at the screen. "And the hijacker knows that. So he just . . . jumps overboard?"

"He just jumps overboard," Swenson confirmed. "Maybe lowers himself down on a rope after untying his oxygen cluster from the deck rail so that he won't make a splash. He's in a full dry suit, undoubtedly heated and probably with a full-head helmet so he's got access to food and water. The cluster will be rigged with buoyancy gear, of course. He sinks down twenty feet or whatever he figures will keep him safe from passing ships, and just drifts with the current."

McPherson shook his head. "It's so damn simple. By the time the Navy P-3 gets to the scene, the freighter's already fifteen miles away from him. Not a chance in the world they would spot him."

"And with him just floating quietly, there's nothing for the P-3's sonar buoys to pick up, either," Swenson pointed out.

"Sure isn't," McPherson said, sounding thoroughly disgusted now. "And, of course, by the time the *Vincennes* and *Anqing* arrive, everyone's a hundred miles away from what they're really looking for. You know, that's a good enough reason right there for them to have fired off that Chinese code."

"What do you mean?"

"That got our attention focused solidly on the *Rabah Jamila*," McPherson explained. "Which in turn effectively defined our search area. I assume you've followed up on this."

"Yes, sir, I did," Swenson said. "The mayday was sent about seven p.m., local time. I had some Navy people calculate the currents for me, then tracked along that path." She tapped a key, calling up the next photo in her file. "This is seven fifteen the next morning, a little over twelve hours later."

"Well, well," McPherson said sourly. "A nondescript fishing boat out for some early-morning angling. What a surprise."

"Note especially right here," Swenson said, pointing to a spot southwest of the fishing boat. "Watch as I flip between this shot and the next one."

The flicker of light was small, but for Swenson it had been clear enough. Apparently it was for McPherson, too. "A strobe light," he identified it. "Sitting on—what's that, a small buoy?"

"Yes," she said. "Along with the strobe light support, the shadows indicate another, thinner object that could be a short-range transmission antenna. I'm guessing that at an agreed-upon time our hijacker let the buoy float up to the surface, where it took a GPS fix and transmitted his coordinates to the recovery boat."

"With the strobe light there to guide them in," McPherson said. "Do we see them pick him up?"

"Unfortunately, no," Swenson said, running quickly through the next series of shots. "We do have the boat sitting beside the buoy for over an hour, though."

"Waiting for him to go through decompression," McPherson murmured. "I wonder what the schedule is for twelve hours submerged. Depends on how deep he was, I suppose."

"I don't remember the tables," Swenson pulled up the last of the series. "And finally, we have this one, where the boat's turned around and is heading for home."

"And the buoy's gone," McPherson said. "Any chance of tracking the boat?"

Swenson shook her head. "It was headed into Nagasaki when I lost it in the clouds. No idea where it docked; and that was over forty-eight hours ago. They'll be long gone by now."

"Damn." McPherson hissed out a breath. "I wish to hell you'd been here Saturday, Swenson. Maybe you'd have caught this fast enough for us to have nailed them."

"Yes," Swenson murmured, a pang of guilt twisting through her gut. She could have been here then. *Would* have been here if Talbot hadn't conned her into staying in San Francisco those extra sixteen hours.

If he hadn't conned her, and if she hadn't willingly gone along with it. She knew the kind of stunts Talbot pulled. She could have figured out the scam a lot earlier than she had.

"Nothing we can do about it now, though," McPherson went on briskly. "All right, one hijacker accounted for. Tell me about the other one."

"Yes, sir," Swenson said, listening hard to his voice as she pulled up the first photo again, wondering why was he taking her small act of mutiny so calmly. Saving his wrath for Talbot? "What we have to do now is take a close look at that yacht. We know the specs for that type of craft: top speed of twenty-five knots, range of maybe a thousand miles, etc., etc. None of which anyone has paid much attention to until now, since everyone's convinced it was scuttled."

"And you're convinced it wasn't?"

"Why bother bringing it along if they were just going to sink it?" Swenson pointed out. "To bring Hijacker Two his scuba setup? They could have had that stashed away in one of their shipping containers."

"How about providing an excuse to get the crew out on deck where they could get the drop on them?" McPherson suggested.

"That may be part of it," Swenson agreed. "But they could have done that some other way. No, the only plausible reason I can see for the yacht is for it to take Hijacker One and the nuke off the *Rabah Jamila*."

"I'd love to buy that," McPherson said. "Unfortunately, we're faced with the fact that it *did* disappear."

"Did it?" Swenson countered. "Remember, we know now that the yacht didn't have a forty-five-minute window before the P-3 got there, but an hour and forty-five minutes. That extra sixty minutes makes a big difference."

"It makes a difference of twenty-five miles for that kind of boat," McPherson said, shaking his head. "Not enough."

"Maybe it is," Swenson said. "I once heard a magician say that there were three ways to make something disappear: hide it, destroy it, or change it into something else."

"Hiding is out," McPherson said. "The P-3 searched the area thoroughly. You've already said you don't think it was destroyed. So what did it change into, a whale?"

"Close," Swenson said, pulling up one of the aerial photos of three idle yachtsmen lounging around their fish grill. "What exactly do we know about this other yacht that was in the area that night?

"The *Eureka*," McPherson identified it. "Just about everything, actually. Brand new ship, fresh off the line, built by one of the most prestigious custom shipbuilding companies in Singapore. We've talked to the management, the builders themselves, and everyone else we could find. It's your basic plain-vanilla displacement-hull sailing yacht. No supercharged engines, no secret hydrofoils, no special modifications of any sort."

"Could it have picked up such upgrades later on?"

"Not a chance," McPherson said firmly. "It was launched only seventeen days ago; and except for the inevitable cloud problems, we've been able to backtrack its entire course. There's been no time when it was close enough to any port for that kind of work. Even if it was, a monohull simply can't manage high speeds without becoming unstable. Trust me."

"Oh, I do," Swenson assured him. "Anyway, I looked it up myself." She cocked her head. "But suppose that instead of a displacement monohull we had a racing catamaran?"

"But it isn't a racing cat."

"No, *this* one isn't." Swenson keyed back to the photo of the yacht alongside the *Rabah Jamila*. "But what about this one?"

McPherson's eyes darted to the display, back to her. "I can't wait to hear this," he said, leaning back in his chair and crossing his arms. "Go ahead."

"Here's a closer view of our bandit yacht's bow, suitably scrubbed," Swenson said, pulling up another picture. "Again, the sun's on the *Rabah Jamila*'s far side, so it's mostly in shadow. But I think you can see enough."

She called up another enhancement. "False color infrared image," she identified it.

"That scale looks different than usual," McPherson commented, leaning forward to peer at the tiny numbers and equally tiny color-coded blocks at the bottom of the photo.

"I've exaggerated it beyond the usual false-color range," Swenson explained. "I know that's frowned on, because it can lead to artificial constructs, but in this case I think it'll be useful."

"Caveats noted. Go on."

She tapped the yacht's stern with her pencil. "The stern's the hottest, naturally, because of the engines. From there forward it grades more or less properly for a mostly aluminum deck and cabin structure."

She shifted her pointer. "But now note the color change between the bow and the midsection and the similar difference between the central area and both the port and starboard sides. *And*, more importantly, the rather sharp defining lines in all cases."

"Yes, I see," McPherson said. "And you don't think it's an enhancement construct?"

"No, sir, I don't," Swenson said. "I ran a computer analysis on it. The heat differences are compatible with the central part of the ship being made of aluminum and the side and bow pieces being made of rubber."

For a moment the humming of her computer's cooling fan was the loudest sound in the room. "Rubber," McPherson said at last, his tone flat. "As in . . . ?"

"As in inflatable add-ons," Swenson said. "I think what we've got here is a racing cat made up to look like a monohull yacht."

"Now, wouldn't that be a kick?" McPherson murmured, staring hard at the image on the screen. "The crazy thing is that I can see it. The twin hulls would be there and there, with the cabin sitting between them . . . Yes, it fits. The damn thing fits."

"And once we know they've got a racing cat, the rest is easy," Swenson went on. "With a top sprinting speed of sixty or seventy knots, it would have plenty of time to rendezvous with the *Eureka* a hundred miles away, bring over whatever crew, and then sink it. Sink the *Eureka*, I mean."

"And then reconfigure itself to take its place," McPherson said. "Tricky."

"Sure, but remember the cat could be loaded to the gunwales with neat gadgets and equipment," Swenson reminded him. "It's the *Eureka* that's so squeaky clean you could brush your teeth with it. And because it's so clean, once they've made the switch they can sail off to wherever their destination is, totally in the clear."

"Or go someplace nice and quiet where they can leisurely transfer the bomb to a totally unknown vehicle," McPherson said. "Upriver on a small Japanese island, for instance."

"Is that where it is?"

"As of the last satellite pass," McPherson told her, sounding decidedly annoyed. "So we were right all along about one of the ships being scuttled. We were just wrong about which one."

Swenson nodded. "Another magician once told me that by the time he says the words *watch carefully*, the trick's already done."

"You must have hung around magicians a lot when you were a kid."

"Don't knock it," Swenson said. "That's what got me started with this business of putting puzzle pieces together."

"In that case, the nation owes them a debt of gratitude," McPherson said. "What *I'd* like to know is why the rest of my people can't figure out stuff like this."

"I'm sure they would have eventually," Swenson said, with a smoothness born of long practice with such diplomacy. More than once her odd talent had ended up disjointing the noses of superiors and fellow analysts alike. "It's only been a couple of days since all this happened. We don't even have all the raw data in yet. I just happen to have a knack for sideways thinking."

"We're glad you're on our side," McPherson said. "So when the crew heard the yacht bouncing against the *Rabah Jamila*, what they were actually hearing was the scuba array framework?"

"Right," Swenson said. "The yacht itself can't make any metal-on-metal sounds—the only part of it that's touching the *Rabah Jamila* is this glorified inner tube of theirs. Probably the main reason they put the array between them and the freighter."

"Also makes it trivial to cast off the yacht without making any noise the crew might notice," McPherson added. "The bumping sound never changed because it was never anything *but* the scuba framework in the first place."

"Right," Swenson said. "And tucked up under the portside inflatable the way it was, it would also be out of sight of passing satellites."

"Right." McPherson shook his head. "Who the hell *are* these guys, Swenson?"

"I don't know," Swenson said. "But you'd think a style like this would make them easy to identify. There can't be too many people out there who prefer rapiers to thirty-pound sledgehammers."

"One would think," McPherson said ruefully. "Cohn and Logan have been running tactical profiles, but as far as I know they haven't found any likely contestants."

"A new player?"

"Or an old one getting back into the game," McPherson said grimly. "Whoever he is, he's got this kind of precision sleight of hand down cold. Just one more reason to think he's behind the Harrier theft this afternoon."

Swenson frowned. "There was a Harrier theft?"

McPherson gave her an odd look. "You didn't hear? I thought Evans made a general announcement before I pulled out the rest of the Bureau people."

Startled, Swenson looked around. He was right: the room was practically empty, with only a handful of CIA analysts scattered around at various workstations. "Sorry, but I don't even hear things when *I* say them."

"I'd forgotten that," McPherson said, his tone and face going suddenly dark. "The Marines lost a pair of Harriers this afternoon in southwest Oregon. A small group of armed thieves got the drop on the pilots at a memorial service and basically just flew off with their planes. With no one in the crowd even remotely aware of what had happened, I might add."

Swenson felt her mouth drop open. "Now, *that's* chutzpah."

"Chutzpah may not be quite the right word." McPherson gestured toward her screen. "The pilots overheard one of the thieves say something in Farsi."

"Iran," Swenson commented thoughtfully, gazing at her screen. "Have you noticed, sir, that every time these people make a move someone new gets dragged into the tangle? We start out with an Indian nuke carried by a Chinese jet—only it wasn't Chinese—to a Pakistani freighter, where two men claiming to be South Koreans transfer to an unknown ship while we're watching a decoy yacht that came out of Singapore."

"Don't forget that the disguised CitationJet transferred the nuke to the *Rabah Jamila* in Da Nang," McPherson reminded her. "That brings in Vietnam."

"Plus a Chinese code message, a lot of North Korean stuff left aboard the freighter, and the fact that the Chinese jet had been flying back from Iran," Swenson concluded.

"And you may or may not have heard that the CitationJet they actually used was stolen from a Pakistani company," McPherson growled. "Still, what did you expect? They can't have the evidence sitting nicely packaged on their doorstep before they make their new toy go boom. What better way to confuse things than to spread the guilt around as much as possible?"

"I know," Swenson said slowly. "But I don't think that's all there is to it."

"Meaning?"

"I don't know," she admitted. "Do we have any idea where the nuke is headed?"

McPherson made a face. "Up until a few hours ago I would have bet heavily on the Far East: Japan, Taiwan, or somewhere on the Korean peninsula. Now, with this Harrier incident, I have a bad feeling it's headed our direction."

"Possibly," Swenson said. "But why? None of the countries implicated so far has any serious reason to nuke us. Except maybe Iran or North Korea. Is there something going on in international politics I don't know about?"

"Not unless I don't know about it either," McPherson said. "And while I don't see any of the possible players being mad enough to nuke us, none of them qualifies as our best friend, either."

"Do we know *anyone* who might be this mad at us?"

McPherson snorted. "Half the time we don't even know where the knotholes are until they pop out of the woodwork. No one's declared holy war lately, but that means nothing. We've got a bunch of anniversaries coming up, including Waco, Oklahoma City, and the first

World Trade Center bombing. But that might not mean anything either. Bottom line: your guess is as good as mine."

Swenson sighed. "In that case, we'd better get in some better guessers."

"I'll see what I can do," McPherson said. "Meanwhile, you keep poking at it. Like you said, you've got a talent for this sideways thinking."

He got to his feet, swinging his chair around and rolling it back to the desk he'd borrowed it from. "And while you do that, I've got a few cages to rattle," he added. "Admiral Eskin said he would try to send someone to check out the *Eureka*. I think I'll suggest he do more than just try. They're undoubtedly long gone by now, but they might have left some clues behind."

"Yes," Swenson said. "It should be interesting to see who gets implicated this time."

"Yeah," McPherson warned her wearily. "But sooner or later we have to run out of smoke layers and hit something solid. They can't hide forever."

"I hope not," Swenson said, rubbing her eyes. "What do you want me to do next?"

"Get some sleep before you fall on your keyboard," McPherson advised, running a critical eye over her. "How long since you've eaten?"

"It's been awhile," she conceded, suddenly aware of a hollow feeling in her stomach. "And I could probably use some sleep, too."

"Better get it while you can," McPherson warned. "I have a feeling that starting about ten minutes from now things are going to be heating up again around here. We need to backtrack the satellite photos of the *Eureka*'s mooring site and try to figure out what kind of vehicle they're in now. I've got a bad feeling they went with a seaplane or helo, in which case they could have the nuke tucked cozily away anywhere in the damn world by now."

"That's not a happy thought," Swenson murmured.

"You have a gift for understatement," McPherson said. "Now get out of here. Don't come back for at least eight hours."

"All right," Swenson said. "You sure you can do without me that long?"

"The Bureau was doing just fine before you came to work for us, and we'll do fine after you go. So go."

"Yes, sir."

McPherson nodded and headed toward the duty desk at a brisk walk. Swenson watched his back as he went, wondering distantly how long it had been since *he'd* eaten or slept.

She was suddenly too tired to care. Sending her files back into their folders, she eased up out of her chair, wincing as her entire musculature complained about the sudden movement. Come to think of it, eight hours of sleep sounded pretty good right now.

24

FOR WHAT SEEMED like an eternity Angie sat motionless in her booth, her pulse hammering in her neck like a deranged woodpecker, staring in horror and disbelief as Ross took another step into the bar, letting the door swing closed behind him. *No,* she pleaded silently with the universe. *Not him. Not now.*

But the universe ignored her plea. Ross stepped to the archway leading into the other room and stood there with his back to her as he gazed inside. Then, turning back, he shifted his attention to the bar itself, and she could see by the subtle movements of his eyes and face that he was giving each of the patrons there a long, careful look.

When he had finished with the bar, Angie knew with the certainty of death, he would be coming into this section.

And he would find her.

Run! The frantic command flashed like sheet lightning through her mind. But there was nowhere to go. Ross was blocking the front door, and the emergency exit was too far away for her to get to before he spotted her, especially since it would mean coming out of the partial concealment of her booth.

But she couldn't just sit here like a frightened rabbit watching a wolf wandering towards her. Ross wasn't looking for a good seat to get drunk in. He was looking for her. And booth or not, hair dye or not, brand new fashion-tinted glasses or not, he was going to find her.

She remembered her gun.

Her purse was on the seat beside her. Carefully, trying to keep her movements imperceptible, she groped the zipper open and dug into the purse, pushing past the wallet and phone and keys until her fingers closed on the cold metal grip.

Ross had finished his examination of the bar and was walking slowly toward her, his eyes methodically searching each booth as he reached it. Clenching her teeth, Angie braced herself.

And as his gaze shifted to one of the booths on the far side of the aisle she yanked the gun clear and jumped into the center of the aisle. Jabbing the weapon toward him in the two-handed grip she'd seen people use on TV, she filled her lungs. "Freeze!" she barked.

Or at least she tried to bark it. Tried to make it strong and firm and confident. Instead, the word came out as little more than a loud squeak. Ross jerked as if he'd been kicked, his head twisting around toward her. "Angie!" he said, taking a step toward her.

"Don't move!" she snapped. "Don't *move!*"

He took one more step before he obeyed. "It's all right, Angie," he soothed, holding his empty hands palms outward toward her. "I'm on your side." He took another step—

"Stay there!" she demanded, her muscles trembling with strain and emotion.

And with the terrifying realization that even though she was the one holding the gun, it was Ross who was in control. It was Ross who was calm and alert and ready to take advantage of any slip or sign of weakness on her part. It was Ross who could undoubtedly read her face and body language like a fifty-foot billboard even as he remained a total mask to her.

And in that single, awful moment in jellied time she knew that if she was going to survive she would have to shoot him.

All other conversation in the bar had been swallowed up by a gaping silence, the patrons staring in open-mouthed astonishment at the confrontation. "Angie, listen to me," Ross said, his tone that of a patient father trying to quiet an unreasonably upset child. "I know you don't understand all that's happened—"

"Don't I?" she cut him off. "You lied to me from the start. Your name isn't Adam Ross, it's Charles Sullivan. I saw your other cards."

"I can explain all that," he said. "If you'll just let me—"

"Like you can explain why you snatched me out of the mall?" Angie shot back. "And then talked me out of going to the police?"

"I also saved your life," he reminded her. "Twice."

"So you could get me up to the cabin," she accused him.

"Did I bother you at all up there?" Ross asked in that same soothing tone. "Did I assault you or threaten you or even harass you?"

Her muscles were trembling even more violently now, and she had to clamp down hard on her teeth to keep them from clattering. He sounded so convincing, so calm and polite and so damn reasonable. She could feel her resolve draining away into uncertainty like a ridge of sand in a tidal backwash. "You taped me after my shower," she snarled, playing the last card she had left. "I found the recorder in your bag."

If the revelation shocked him, it didn't show. "I wasn't recording *you*," he said, still completely calm. "I was recording your phone."

The words were so unexpected that they caught her flatfooted. "What?"

"I had to see if you called anyone while I was gone." His eyes flicked sideways, as if suddenly aware of the strangers listening in. "Just give me a chance to explain."

He started to take another step toward her. "Stay *there*!" she shouted, jabbing the gun at him again.

"Listen to the lady, pal," one of the men standing at the bar spoke up in a voice that sounded like a tractor trailer changing gears. "Sammy, call the cops."

"Yeah, okay," the bartender said. He was just a kid, probably no more than a few years past legal drinking age himself. His expression was that of someone in way over his head but determined not to show it in front of his elders. "You just stay put, Mister," he added, staring unblinkingly at Ross as he sidled toward the cash register at the center of the bar.

"That won't be necessary," Ross said, turning toward him.

With his back to Angie, all she could see was the subtle movement of his right shoulder and arm as he reached inside his jacket. But it was enough. "Watch out!" she shouted. "He's got a gun!"

The kid goggled for a split second. Then, abruptly, he ducked down, his hands scrabbling somewhere beneath the bar. He jerked upright again; and suddenly there was a shotgun pointed at Ross's face. In the dark silence the *ka-chunk* as he worked the pump was as loud as a double thunderclap.

Ross became a statue, his moving arm and shoulder freezing in mid-grope. Staring at the back of his head, Angie wondered fleetingly what his face looked like at that moment, whether it was angry, or chagrined, or just plain scared.

Slowly, he turned his head part way around toward her . . . and she saw that he was as calm as ever.

A fresh jolt of fear churned through her stomach. If there was ever a man who should be worried, it was Adam Ross. And if he believed he was still in control, it was because he had a plan in mind.

Something, if past history was any indication, that would be quick, smooth, and violent. Something a kid as inexperienced as the bartender would likely not even see until it was too late.

And she was the only one who could keep it from happening.

By shooting first.

She took a deep breath, trying to work up the courage to pull the trigger—

"As I was going to say," Ross said, looking back at the bartender, "go ahead and call. But instead of the cops, call *this* man." His shoulder twitched again, just slightly, and Angie winced as his right hand came clear of his jacket.

But instead of a gun, he was holding a business card. A card that even from here she could see had the FBI logo stamped across it. "FBI Special Agent Madison Talbot," Ross continued, laying the card on the bar in front of the kid.

He looked again at Angie. "My former junior partner."

~

The silence in the room subtly changed color. The direction of reality shifted rather more violently. "You're lying," Angie heard herself say as if speaking though a long tunnel. "It's a trick."

"It's no trick," Ross assured her. "I couldn't tell you the truth before. Now I can. I can tell you everything." He took another step forward. "But first we have to get out of here."

The spell abruptly vanished. "No," she said, abruptly remembering the gun in her hands and jabbing it toward him for emphasis. "I'm not going to go anywhere with you."

"You called Ramon Esteban," he said as he took another step forward, and another. "Burke and Kingsley were there, too, which means that all three of them know where you are. Whichever one is the murderer will have tipped off his friends by now; and at least some of those friends are already in the area. We have *got* to get out of here before they arrive."

He stopped, finally, a long pace away from the end of her gun. Angie stared into that mask of a face, aware that her arms were trembling again. "I can't," she whispered. "I can't trust you anymore."

"Angie, they want to kill you," he said, some of the calm cracking as a note of urgency entered his voice. "They're *going* to kill you if we don't leave."

She tore her gaze away from the intensity of those eyes. The rest of the bar's clientele had silently moved in to watch the drama, grouped in a rough semicircle between the bar and the doorway alcove. Some of them had brought their beer mugs along, as if they'd wandered in on some impromptu sports event. The bartender was still holding his shotgun, but its tip had sagged to point at the floor somewhere behind the bar as he stared at the business card Ross had put in front of him. "And what if you're with them?" she countered. "I don't even know who you are anymore."

A muscle twitched in Ross's cheek. "Suppose I can prove I'm on your side," he offered. "Would you go with me then?"

She clamped her teeth together, uncertainty tearing at her. "How?" she challenged, trying to stall for time. "Anyone can print up a fake FBI business card."

He smiled faintly. "That they can," he agreed.

And without a whisper of warning, his left hand flashed forward like a striking rattlesnake, grabbing the barrel of her gun and with a single flick of the wrist twisting it out of her grip. Simultaneously, he turned halfway back around toward the bar, darting his now empty right hand back under his jacket.

And before the bartender could do more than gasp, Ross's gun was pointed at his chest.

The color of the silence changed again, this time to complete and utter black. "Take it easy, Sammy," Ross said quietly. "Lay the gun on the floor. Then straighten up—slowly—and take two steps back. The rest of you, stay as you are."

The bartender's face had gone the color of a mud puddle as he silently obeyed. Angie, with a flash of foolhardiness born of shame and desperation dived for her gun. Without even looking, Ross twitched it out of her reach. "Now," he said conversationally, taking a long step back where he could keep his attention on the group of open-mouthed men and women by the bar and still see Angie out of the corner of his eye. "I count . . . twelve of you. Sammy makes thirteen and you, Angie, make fourteen, which means I have enough rounds in my Glock alone to kill everyone in here. That doesn't even count the rounds in the HK."

"I should have shot you," Angie stuttered, shaking so hard now she could hardly get the words out. "I should have shot you."

"You still had the safety catch on," Ross told her. "Is there any reason I should bother luring you into my car? Wouldn't you agree I could just go ahead and kill you right here and now?"

Angie looked across at the other patrons. She hadn't noticed before that there were two women among the men. "I'll go," she whispered. "You don't need to kill anyone else."

"Good," Ross said briskly.

And to her astonishment he lifted his gun muzzle to point at the ceiling. "I hope that's good enough," he added, flipping the other gun over and offering it back to her, butt first. "Because frankly, I'd rather not face down Sammy's shotgun again. Those things make a mess."

Angie stared at him, looked down at the gun he was holding out to her, looked up at his face again. "*That* was your proof?"

His lip twitched into something that was almost a smile. "I can do better when we get to San Jose," he promised. "But there's no time now. Please, Angie."

She took a deep breath. "All right," she said, reaching out and taking the gun. He was right: the safety catch *was* still on. She wasn't sure whether she felt relieved or stupid. "Let's go."

~

Duty came in many different shades, San Jose Police Officer Shana Donahue reflected as she let her patrol car coast to a halt by the care-taker building at the Sunlight Glade Cemetery. There was standard police duty, of course: to serve and protect, catch the bad guys and put them behind bars. Then there was what she liked to call subpolice duty, where the odd jobs like rescuing wayward keys locked inside car trunks got listed. And there was dumb duty, which included benevolent fund raiser variety acts and virtually all departmental paperwork.

Then there was *really* dumb duty, a category sparsely occupied, but still the perverse aspiration of the participants in after-hours cop-and-bull sessions. In her five years on the force, Donahue had never yet pulled a job that her colleagues had been willing to allow into the Really Dumb category.

Until now, she thought as she got out of the car. In fact, they might have to start a brand-new category for this one.

An elderly man in dirt-stained coveralls came around the corner just as she reached the door. "Help you, officer?" he asked, his voice rich with the clipped tones of a lifetime spent in New England.

"Yes, sir," Donahue said, readying herself for another entry in today's series of strange looks. "Are you the caretaker?"

"Yes, ma'am," he said, nodding. "Jeremiah Smith. What can I do for you?"

"I'm investigating a possible irregularity in a burial sometime in the past four days," she said, the words lining up with the ease of far too much practice. "In particular, the possibility that a second body might have been added to one of your graves before it was filled in."

Smith was actually something of a disappointment. "Nope," he said, his wrinkled face not reacting in the slightest.

"Not even a possibility?" Donahue pressed, wondering if she was losing her touch. Maybe shock value didn't work on Northeasterners. "You surely don't hang around each grave the whole time between the end of the service and the time you fill it in."

"Sure do," he said without rancor. "Me or one of the boys. Ever' time."

"And you've been there after each service since Friday morning?"

"Ever' time," he repeated, putting just the slightest bit of extra emphasis on the words.

"Are there any areas of the cemetery that someone else might deal with?"

"Nope," Smith said.

"Did you notice any strangers loitering around after any of the services?"

"They're all strangers," Smith said. "Sometimes they stay awhile. Then they leave."

"And nothing unusual has happened in the past four days?"

"Nope."

And that was that. "All right," she said, nodding to him. "Thank you for your time, Mr. Smith."

"No problem."

He didn't seem inclined to further conversation, so Donahue nodded again and returned to her car. The clipboard with the complete Bay Area cemetery, mausoleum, and crematorium list—all ten glorious pages of it—was on the seat beside her, and she took a moment to put a check mark beside Sunlight Glade. Seventeen down, God alone knew how many to go.

She could only hope that the FBI clown who'd come up with this brilliant idea had a complete set of hemorrhoids of his own. Really painful ones.

Seventeen down. Time to tackle number eighteen.

~

Thirty-three years in police work, Chief Garcia mused as he stood beside Special Agent Lyman's desk, and he had never before been quite as mad at a subordinate as he was at this particular moment. Delgado had committed the unforgivable sin of deliberately keeping him in the dark on a vital police matter, and he was absolutely going to make sure the detective regretted it for the rest of what was left of his miserable career.

The single grain of consolation in the whole mess—and it was one hell of a small grain—was that Lyman was even madder than he was.

"I swear to you by God and His angels," Lyman ground out in a voice like doom incarnate, "that I am going to have you busted to dog catcher on Guam."

He jabbed a finger toward Ross. "And him? *Him*? What the *hell* did you think you were doing pulling him into this?"

There was a moment of silence, the first such gap in the tirade since Lyman had launched it five minutes ago. Talbot moved into the opening with the skill of someone who's learned which of his boss's questions are rhetorical and which ones aren't. "We were asked to do a friend a quiet favor, sir," he said, pitching his voice in the soft, reasonable tone that always drove Garcia up a wall when he was already mad. The fact that it was directed at Lyman and not him made it just barely tolerable. "Events simply got ahead of us."

"Events simply got ahead of you," Lyman repeated, his voice flat. "Seems to me you and Mr. *Ross* were *driving* a lot of those events. Not to mention letting us waste our time chasing shadows." He shifted his glare to Ross. "Or should I say *ghosts*?"

Ross gave a little shrug. "As Special Agent Talbot said, sir, he was asked for a favor. I was available."

"I'll just bet you were," Lyman snarled. "Who the hell was this quiet favor for?"

"Dr. James Chandler," Talbot said.

There was another momentary silence. Apparently, that hadn't been the answer Lyman was expecting. "Chandler," he repeated.

"Yes, sir," Talbot said. "I can explain."

For a moment Lyman eyed him, and Garcia took advantage of the gap to give each of the men a long, appraising look. Talbot had the calmness of a man who was used to being in official trouble, which Garcia didn't find the least bit surprising. Delgado was considerably less at ease, either because of the unfamiliar locale or because he knew he was next in line to get his paint blistered. That would be Garcia's job, and he was looking forward to it. Ross, or whoever the hell he was, stood between them, his face as impassive as Talbot's. Gazing at that smooth expression, Garcia made a mental note to save back some of what he'd been planning to dump on Delgado to deliver to Ross when it was his turn.

"I'm listening," Lyman said, leaning back just slightly in his seat. "Let's start with why you were in the kind of favor-granting mood that inspires you to bring a civilian troublemaker into Bureau business."

"It actually started with me, sir," Delgado spoke up. "About six weeks ago, Dr. Chandler came to me with concerns that someone was trying to steal the Cloak project."

"Why didn't you file a report?" Garcia asked.

"He asked me not to." Delgado's lip twitched. "Because the most likely suspect was his wife."

Lyman's eyes narrowed a bit. "Why did he think that?"

"One night when he was working late at the lab he tried signing onto the Internet on his personal account," Delgado said. "The system informed him he was already signed on. He did some poking around and discovered that someone was using his account to send coded emails."

"Where to?" Lyman asked.

Delgado shook his head. "We were never able to figure that out. Whoever was doing it knew how to cover his tracks. But Dr. Chandler did a comparison between the various project milestones and the times the coded messages went out and was convinced someone on the inside was keeping someone else informed of their progress."

"Couldn't it have been one of the people on the project instead of his wife?" Garcia asked. "One of the techs could have gotten hold of his account data."

"We're pretty sure now that's what happened," Delgado agreed. "But Dr. Chandler couldn't ignore the fact that his wife was the only one that he knew for sure had access."

"I might mention that he never thought she would do such a thing except under duress," Talbot put in. "But with her grandparents living in China, he thought Beijing might have pressured her into spying for them." He hesitated just a fraction too long. "And there were other considerations."

"Which was why he begged me to investigate as quietly as possible," Delgado said. "I told him there were limits to what I could do off the record, but that there was someone who might be able to act with fewer official constraints."

"Enter Special Agent Madison Talbot," Lyman said sourly. He turned his glare onto Ross. "And friend."

Talbot gave a small shrug. "Ross touched base with me a few months back. When Detective Delgado brought me Dr. Chandler's request, I thought he would be the perfect man for the job. We set him up in that office above Angie's bank and he tapped into the camera system so he could see if she was sending any covert emails from work."

"I thought the messages were going out at night," Garcia said.

"Some did, but others went out during the day," Delgado said. "We never did find a pattern."

"Which was probably deliberate," Talbot said. "I also spoke to Dr. Stryker at Sand/Star about beefing up their security, but as far as I know the only thing he did was have razor wire put on top of the fence."

"Our unofficial status on this didn't exactly impress him," Delgado said. "Anyway, Ross watched Angie for a month, keeping track of her computer usage and also getting to know her. He already had that Charles Sullivan identity from—well, you know—and used it to blur the paper trail in case someone tried tracking him down."

"Such as officers of the San Jose Police Department?" Garcia asked pointedly.

"Yes, sir," Delgado said, wincing. "At any rate, Ross concluded that Angie wasn't the one we were looking for. We'd given Dr. Chandler the good news, and were gearing up for a more official investigation elsewhere when he and his colleagues were murdered."

For a moment the word hung in the air like a black curtain. "Go on," Lyman prompted.

"Detective Delgado called me and we went to the scene of the crime," Talbot said. "The murders didn't make sense to either of us—industrial thieves never go in for violence, especially not murder. Clearly, there was something else going on. The techs told us Angie had dropped by the lab that evening, and when I heard that she'd apparently taken off early that morning I wondered if Ross might have miscalled it. I was still tied up at the lab, so I called to see if he could intercept her at the bank."

"And if she *did* show," Ross added, "I was to take another stab at figuring out whether she was innocent or just a very good actress."

"At which point the whole thing stops making even partial sense," Lyman said. "Once the shooting started and you knew she was in the clear, why didn't you bring her in?"

Ross made a face. "Because the mall shooting didn't prove anything of the sort," he said. "They might have been trying to kill her; but if she was working with them they might have been trying to shoot *me* off her back. I decided my best play was to act the brave maverick hero and see if she would try to lose me or buy me off."

"Hence, giving her a few hours of alone time in a hotel room," Talbot said.

"Right," Ross said. "With a recorder going to see what she did with those hours."

"Meanwhile, we know what the killers used the time for," Lyman said sourly. "Gathering for round two."

"Having conveniently gotten his tag from that damn sticky-note impression," Garcia muttered, feeling his face warming. An incredibly boneheaded mistake, and that one had been all his.

To his annoyed surprise, Ross came to his rescue. "If it makes you feel any better, sir, that wasn't how they found us. In fact, it turns out that stealing that note was an incredibly risky bit of uselessness. There was no way the gang could have canvassed the whole Bay Area that quickly, which implies they already knew where we were. Probably tailed us from Greenleaf Center." He gestured at Lyman. "Though you're right, they did need some time to pull their attack together. The point is that Angie *didn't* call anyone while she was alone, which again strongly implied that that she was in the clear."

"What if she'd simply walked out on you?" Lyman asked.

"For the first two hours after I left the room, I'd have followed her," Ross said. "For the three hours after that, while I was out wardrobe shopping, Special Agent Talbot was watching from a room he'd rented down the hall from ours. Unfortunately, he'd already left by the time the attack came."

"And when the dust settled you decided to go on a road trip?" Lyman asked.

"Angie said they'd been in Tahoe a few weeks earlier," Ross said. "I thought Dr. Chandler might have left something behind. Detective Delgado used one of the department's undercover cabs to help us get to the new vehicle I'd rented and we headed out."

"I assume you didn't find anything?" Lyman asked.

"Unfortunately, no," Ross said. "At that point, having already watched the hotel recording, I decided it was time to tell Angie who I was and bring her back here." He made a face. "Unfortunately, somewhere along the line she picked up that there was something wrong and spiked my dinner."

"He called me the next day after he woke up," Talbot said. "I got him another car, and he came back here to help us look for her."

"And you know the rest," Ross said.

"Why didn't you come in right when you got back?" Garcia asked. "We could have put the manpower we were wasting looking for you into looking for her."

"Maybe I should have," Ross conceded. "But I assumed that anyone looking for me would also be looking for her, so that wouldn't change things that much." He hunched his shoulders. "Besides, I was the one who'd lost her. It was my job to fix that."

"No, *your* job was to stay the hell out of the way," Lyman growled. "Which you're going to start doing as of right now."

Ross looked sideways at Talbot. "Actually, I don't think I can do that quite yet."

"Oh?" Lyman asked, something very unpleasant lurking beneath the word. "Why not?"

"Because frankly, sir, you still need me," Ross said evenly.

"Do I, now," Lyman said darkly. "The way *I* see it, between lying to us and working behind our backs you've managed to waste four days of our lives. And with nothing to show for it."

"That's not entirely fair, sir," Talbot said, a bit reproachfully. "For one thing, we have one of the Cloaks back. We also know that the group is small, a dozen people at the most."

"How do you figure that?" Garcia asked.

"Because the man I ran into in the Lee house was alone," Ross explained. "Logically, he should have gone straight back to his stake-out after he left me tied up and put someone else in charge of tracking me after I got loose. Instead, he never got back before my bomb threat locked down the neighborhood. Also, the ease with which I lost them after my escape implies he was probably the *only* one on me."

"Which seems odd, given their interest in Mrs. Chandler," Talbot said. "If they had so few to spare for such an important job, it follows that the rest of the group was off on some other job."

"Hence, your call to the Secret Service," Lyman said, nodding. "Don't look so surprised—of *course* they called to check up on you. I gather from what they said that you didn't specifically mention the Cloaks?"

Talbot shook his head. "I was afraid any perceived crazy-talk would cloud my credibility. I stayed with vague references to hidden gunmen and camouflaged bombs."

"Someone should lay out the full story for them now," Garcia said. "Whitcomb's going to be here in two days."

"I know," Lyman said heavily. "At least now we can give them a demo of what they're up against."

"Thanks to Ross," Talbot murmured.

Lyman glared at him, then shifted the glare to Ross. "How exactly do you think you're going to be of use to us?"

"For one thing, I've got a feel for the gang," Ross said. "How they think, and how they operate. For another, I've made direct contact with them."

"You think they're going to listen to you after your Houdini trick?"

"I wasn't talking about negotiation," he said calmly. "I was talking about bait."

For a moment the room was silent. "We'll see," Lyman said. "Before we go down that road, we still have to figure out which of the techs is working with them."

Talbot cleared his throat. "Actually, sir," he said, "I already have."

~

Carefully, Sergeant Osgood eased the Rigid Inflatable Boat around the rocks surrounding the unpronounceable river flowing down out of the hills into the East China Sea, swearing almost equally unpronounceable Japanese curses under his breath. He would far and away have preferred to hit the river at slack tide, when the bar would have been safer to cross. But the Pentagon had said *now*, and when the brass got this kind of burr up their butts there was no shutting them up until you did what they wanted.

So up the river it was going to be. With or without the proverbial paddle.

"Rocks ahead, starboard," Pvt. Chillsworth announced from his spotter's position in the bow.

"So what else is new?" Osgood grumbled, turning the tiller a fraction to avoid them. They could at least have given him a decent boat—if a damn forty-meter sailboat could get in here, a Marine LCPL landing craft sure as hell could, too. But no, some desk-warming paper-pushing alleged expert said the water wasn't deep enough for a real boat, so his team was stuck sailing through the Pacific in this damn thirty-foot motorized life raft.

A sudden scraping on the RIB's underside startled him out of his private grousefest. "Chilly, you mallet-head," he barked. "You're supposed to be *watching* for those damn rocks."

"I am," Chillsworth retorted. "What, you need me to warn you about the bottom, too?"

Osgood frowned, peering ahead. The bottom? What the hell was the bottom doing this far out? "What's our depth?"

"Shallow enough to see the sand," the other called back. "You want numbers?"

"Never mind," Osgood grunted, easing back the throttle a bit.

It was worse than he'd expected, but better than it could have been. He got them across the bar and headed up the river, which was pretty damn near as shallow as the approach had been. Way too damn shallow for a forty-meter yacht to negotiate.

One of the other Marines was clearly thinking the same thing. "There's no way that frigin' boat got in here," he muttered to Osgood. "Not unless they brought their own water."

"And one hell of a squirt gun to lay it down with," Osgood agreed tightly. Ahead, the river curved slightly to the right. According to the reconnaissance photos, the Eureka should be just around that curve. "Let's get ready, Marines."

There was a brief shuffling of cloth and muffled metallic clinking as the squad shifted from Alert Mode to what the major liked to refer to as Damn-Sure Alert Mode. Reaching to his hip, Osgood undid the safety strap on his holster and got a grip on his sidearm. They negotiated the curve and swung around the trees.

It was there, all right, right where the reconnaissance guys had said, as big and fat and sassy as you could want. A complete forty-meter yacht, its mast waving gently in the breeze

There was only one small problem. It wasn't a boat. It was a balloon. A huge, contoured, inflatable raft, bobbing like a big rubber cork along the side of the river.

"I'll be damned," Chillsworth said, sounding awed. "Look at that. They've got a bigger tubby toy than we do."

"Cork it," Osgood growled. "We're going in for a look. Stay sharp—they might have left a reception committee."

He didn't know what all this froth was about, who they were chasing or why they were searching freighters and islands and fishing boats.

But one thing he was sure of. Whatever was going on, whoever was on the other team had just scored a point.

Steering them cautiously toward the huge float toy, he reached down to the radio beside his left foot. The Pentagon was going to love this one.

THE
SEVENTH
DAY

25

"A BALLOON," COHN growled, sounding as disgusted as McPherson had ever heard him. "A damn rubber balloon. Why the *hell* didn't someone catch this earlier?"

"Because the damn rubber balloon looks just like a forty-meter yacht from the air and no one bothered to go in for a closer look," McPherson growled back. He wasn't any happier about this than Cohn, but flailing around looking for a scapegoat was just going to waste more time. "This isn't exactly our first clue that this gang knows what they're doing."

"Fine," Cohn said, tossing the report onto the duty desk and looking around the satellite room and the weary CIA analysts. "We're still going to be the laughingstock of the intelligence community. Assuming this doesn't trigger World War III and no one's laughing at anything anymore. Your people still sifting through West Coast photos?"

McPherson nodded. "Whitcomb gave the Harrier search priority."

"How convenient for somebody," Cohn said darkly. "Right now, I'm ready to give odds they ditched the Harriers in the ocean, and that all they ever wanted was to siphon off our people into a snipe hunt."

"I wouldn't put anything past them," McPherson had to concede. "Still, there is a bright side to this. The fact that they went to all the trouble to create a fake ship for us to watch implies they haven't transferred the nuke anywhere else since it left the *Rabah Jamila*. That means it's still aboard their gimmicked racing cat."

"A ship we know has already had at least two configurations," Cohn reminded him. "What makes you think it doesn't have a third, a fourth, and a fifth?"

"I'm sure it does," McPherson agreed. "On the other hand, there's a limit to what you can do to a hundred and twenty feet worth of ship.

You can't turn it into a rowboat or six-hundred-foot tanker, for instance. We know its basic size and shape, and there can be only so many ships in the Pacific that fit that description. All we have to do is find it."

Cohn grunted. "That assumes they haven't anticipated we would follow this line of reasoning. In that case, they might still have transferred the nuke to another vessel, sunk the cat in deep water, *and* left the blow-up toy to make us think we're still looking for the cat. In which case, it *could* be on a rowboat or six-hundred-foot tanker."

"Director McPherson?" one of the senior CIA men—McPherson couldn't remember his name—appeared at his elbow holding a sheaf of papers. "Email printout for you."

"Thank you," McPherson said, taking the papers.

"What is it?" Cohn asked.

"The lab report on the *Rabah Jamila* containers," McPherson said, skimming down the first page and flipping to the next one. "We were right about all the North Korean stuff in there. Looks like it was all the genuine article—"

He broke off as something completely unexpected caught his eye. "What?" Cohn demanded, craning his neck to see.

"Swenson was right—they've implicated another country," McPherson murmured, pointing to the spot on the page. "China, North Korea, Pakistan, Vietnam, Iran; and now—"

"*Israel*?" Cohn breathed, almost hissing out the word.

"Why not?" McPherson said, flipping to the details. "Some of the clothing they wore during the pirate attack was still in the containers, complete with powder residue from the rounds they fired. Impurities confirm the rounds were Israeli manufacture."

"Israelis usually use Uzis," Cohn pointed out. "The Pakistanis all agreed that they carried MP5s."

"They also said one of them had a long sniper rifle," McPherson reminded him. "Unfortunately, no one got a good look at it."

"Maybe we can do an end run," Cohn said, stepping around the side of the desk and snagging the phone. "Let's have someone take another look at the bodies they fished out of the Taiwan Strait."

He got a connection and started delivering orders. McPherson moved a few steps away, his eyes drifting to the world map dominating one wall. The Israelis had their own tactical nukes. Why would they want an Indian one? To embarrass New Delhi? Unlikely. Israel had no particular quarrel with India at the moment, certainly no more than they had with anyone else. This Third Temple flap had Moslems up in arms all over the world, but a mostly Hindu nation like India shouldn't care all that much.

Abruptly, his thoughts froze in place.

"They're going to check," Cohn said, coming up beside him. "Probably won't be much residue left after that long an immersion, but you never know. They're still working on backtracking the shrapnel from the grenade."

"We need to get the radiation experts back in," McPherson told him, his eyes still on the map, his voice sounding distant in his ears. "Find out if they can figure out how long the nuke was inside the container."

"Meaning?"

"Meaning maybe they started by sending the bomb east, but now they're taking it back west."

There was a short silence. "You know where it's going?"

"I don't *know* anything," McPherson said. "But if the Israeli connection isn't just another red herring . . . what do you think would happen if someone set off a tactical nuke beneath the Temple Mount in Jerusalem?"

"My God," Cohn muttered. "With all the fault lines under there? You'd take out every piece of architecture bigger than a storage shed."

"Including the Dome of the Rock," McPherson said. "Conveniently opening the way for Rabbi Salomon and his Third Temple."

"And putting a match to the whole Islamic world in the process," Cohn said. "Hell."

"Certainly a damn good approximation of it," McPherson said. "That would also explain why they took a tactical instead of something bigger."

"They want to demolish the mosques, not vaporize the mountain." Cohn hissed between his teeth. "When is Salomon due to give his UN speech?"

"Opening ceremonies are this Friday at seven p.m.," McPherson said. "I don't know if any of the invited speakers will be doing anything that night or whether the first ones are on tap for Saturday."

"Salomon may not even show up until Saturday after sunset," Cohn pointed out. "I don't know what the Orthodox position is on non-religious meetings on the Sabbath."

"Someone had better find out," McPherson said. "On the other hand, he may figure that announcing the way has been cleared for the Third Temple might sanctify the meeting as a religious session."

"Maybe," Cohn agreed reluctantly. "Let's be careful not to go off half-cocked. This Israeli connection could be just as much sand as all the others have been."

"Agreed," McPherson said. "Regardless, you'd better alert the analysts not to limit their focus to the Pacific."

"I'll do that," Cohn promised. "And I think I'll have someone do another check on that Chinese CitationJet. See if maybe it's decided to turn around and head west."

~

The drive down from Roseburg had been a long one, and the van hadn't reached San Jose until a little after midnight. Eight and Nine had promptly stolen a pair of vehicles parked on a residential street, then switched plates with two others parked in a different part of town.

At precisely five minutes after six o'clock in a black California pre-dawn morning the general dropped the proper number of coins into the pay-phone slot and made the call.

Hooker answered on the second ring. "Yes?"

"Any news?" the general asked, peering closely at the meter on the device he'd hooked to his pay phone. The light stayed green: no tap on the line.

"Lots," Hooker said darkly. "What's it worth to you?"

"Come now, Hooker," the general chided him mildly. "I thought we were professionals here. We've already paid a fair price for your services."

"My services don't include holding the bag for three murders," Hooker countered. "Last time we talked you promised to get me off the hook for those."

"I will," the general promised. "Truthfully, though, the police should already have everything they need to clear you of that particular crime."

"Then why haven't they said anything?" Hooker growled. "No, you'll have to do better than that."

"Very well," the general said. "If they haven't cleared you of the murders in the next twenty-four hours, I'll send an anonymous email pointing out the relevant evidence."

There was a pause, filled only with the faint sound of Hooker's breathing. "Good enough, I suppose," he said at last. "Here's the news: Angie Chandler has finally surfaced."

The general gripped the phone tightly. "Where is she?"

"I don't know where she *is*," Hooker said. "But I know where she'll be. She wants me to meet her at ten o'clock this morning at Golden State Mall."

The general felt his eyes narrow. "Golden State Mall," he repeated, looking at Seven.

"Four floors," Seven murmured. "Full atrium spanning each of the four wings. Large parking lot, isolated from the surrounding streets by drainage ditches—"

The general stopped him with a nod. "I know the place," he told Hooker. "She called you personally?"

"Yes," Hooker said. "Relax. I know it sounds a lot like yesterday's call to the lab, but it's not. She didn't call the cops after that—she doesn't trust them. But she thinks now that she has a handle on what you want from her."

"Which is . . . ?"

The general could almost hear Hooker's snicker. "She wants me to bring a flash drive with the manufacturing specs," he said. "She says she remembers James talking about some coded sequencing in the electrical system designed to keep anyone from making a duplicate of the machine. The two of them discussed possibilities for the coding, and if she sees the specs she thinks she can figure out how to unsnarl it."

"I see," the general said. "And she told you all this, did she? Especially the part about not calling the police yesterday?"

"You are the nervous one, aren't you?" Hooker said snidely. "Relax—she doesn't suspect me."

"And she said all this on a tapped line? I presume your home phone *is* tapped."

"Yes, it is; and no, she didn't," Hooker said. "Give her a little credit. She called the bar I was having a late drink in last night—must have followed me from the lab. I had my clicker with me, and the line wasn't tapped."

"I see," the general said, staring out through the glass wind shelter of his phone booth. He didn't like this, not at all. It was far too easy, far too convenient. "And it was her suggestion you meet at this mall?"

"Relax," Hooker said again. He had a fondness for that word that the general was starting to find annoying. "She never mentioned the place by name, even on the clear line. She described it as the place where she ran into me a few weeks back buying a box of chocolates. Look, you're the one who claims she's such a threat. You want to hit her or not?"

"Yes, indeed," the general said quietly. "Where exactly are you meeting her?"

"Well, *she's* going to be on the top level by the Godiva's," Hooker said. "It's in the north wing, a few stores down from the Sears. *I'm* not going to be anywhere near the place."

"Why not?"

"Why *not*?" Hooker echoed. "Are you nuts? I've got enough trouble without being at the scene of another murder."

"We need you there, Hooker," the general said.

"Why? To hold your hand?"

"To draw her to the atrium railing."

There was a long pause. "You're going to push her over?"

"You will be waiting for her beside the railing near Godiva's," the general said evenly. "She'll naturally come over to you there. We'll do the rest."

"You're scumbags," Hooker said, his voice a mixture of contempt and nausea. "You know that? What if I say no?"

"Then the email I'll be sending the police won't clear you, but will instead detail your full involvement in the crime."

"You do that and I'll sing," Hooker threatened. But there was a note of fear beneath the anger. "About *everything*. You want me to do that?"

"Of course not," the general said. "Just as you don't want to be the one in police custody after the rest of us are long gone. I've noticed that police the world over have the unpleasant habit of venting their anger and frustration upon the bird in the hand, even when that bird has had only a minor role. Am I wrong?"

"Is that why you killed the rest of them?" Hooker demanded. "To keep me from talking?"

"We killed them for the same reason we have to kill Mrs. Chandler," the general reminded him. "Too much knowledge."

"And me?"

"Your silence is guaranteed by your status as accomplice to murder," the general reminded him. "Theirs was not. Need I say more?"

Hooker sighed. "No."

"Then you'll be there?"

"I'll be there."

"Good," the general said. "Don't worry. I'll make certain you aren't blamed for this one."

"You'd damn well better."

"Trust me," the general said. "We'll see you in a few hours."

There was a loud thud, and the connection was broken. "Long conversation," Seven commented.

"Too long," the general agreed, turning on his prepaid phone and punching in Eight's own cell number. "He may be thinking about turning. Perhaps has already done so."

There was a click from the phone. "Yes?" Eight's voice said.

"Status report."

"He's on the move," Eight reported. "Left home at approximately five ten and went to police HQ. Emerged at five forty-five in a car with three others, all in plain clothes. Currently heading west on Stevens Creek Boulevard."

"Map," the general murmured. "Stevens Creek."

Seven held up the map. "Here," he said, pointing.

The general nodded. To his regret, but his complete lack of surprise, Detective Delgado was heading straight for Golden State Mall. "Confirm departure timing."

"Five forty-five," Eight repeated. "Wait a moment, he's pulling over. Looks like they're heading into the Golden State Mall parking lot."

"Break off pursuit," the general ordered. So his gut-level sense had been right. Hooker, pressured beyond his capabilities, had cracked under the strain. He'd made a deal with the police to betray them.

"Yes, sir," Eight said. "Orders?"

"Scorched earth," the general told him. "Rendezvous with Nine and clean the backtrack. Six, Seven, and I will deal with Hooker and the woman."

"Yes, sir," Eight said, his voice sounding grim. "Backtrack will be cleaned."

"Out," the general said, and hung up.

"Too bad," Seven murmured.

"But necessary," the general said. "Tell me, what are the mall's atrium railings like?"

"About waist high," Seven said, his eyes unfocusing slightly as he thought. "Maybe a bit higher. It's a single horizontal brass bar six or seven centimeters in diameter, with vertical supports anchoring it to the floor every meter or so."

"What about the open gaps?"

"Covered by Plexiglas panels, anchored to both the horizontal and vertical bars. Over the top will work best."

"Agreed," the general said. "Come. We have four hours to make our preparations."

~

Swenson woke up with a bad taste in her mouth, a throbbing pulse in her neck, and the horrible feeling that she'd had a grip on something vital and then somehow lost it.

She looked around the room, her brain taking a slow moment to remember where exactly she was. Right: Langley—a stolen tactical nuke—

She looked at her watch, and to her embarrassed chagrin saw that it was already past noon. She'd had McPherson's eight hours of sleep, all right, and then some. She took a quick shower, dressed and brushed her teeth, and grabbed an apple from the stash of fruit she'd brought last night from the cafeteria. By twelve-thirty, she was back in the analysis room.

The room was only half full, the FBI people either still chasing those wayward Harriers or else off-duty. Sipping at a mug of freshly brewed coffee—if nothing else, the CIA was great at keeping their coffee urns filled—she pulled up a summary of the past twelve hours.

Her analysis of the double reverse boat switch was in there. Logged in only a couple of hours later was the news that the disguised racing cat they'd thought was sitting quietly in a Japanese island river was in fact a decoy.

Coming in barely an hour after that was a double reverse of their own: Cohn had ordered the search area widened from the North Pacific to the entire Asian theater.

She pulled up the referenced evidence, the FBI lab report on the containers and the CIA's analysis of it, wincing as she skimmed through it. When she'd wondered aloud to McPherson which country was next in line to be smeared, she hadn't expected the hijackers to take her quite so blatantly at her word.

And the idea of a stray nuke rattling around the Middle East—*anywhere* in the Middle East—was unnerving in the extreme.

She looked at the world map on the wall. She didn't believe this supposed Israeli connection for a minute, any more than she believed any of the other theories she'd heard since arriving here. There were certainly enough hot spots in Asia, and she knew the CIA and Pentagon were looking carefully at all of them.

But as far as she was concerned, there was only one place in the world that could inspire the kind of anger and hatred that could drive so elaborate a plan, with such a devastating payoff waiting at the end.

The United States.

A map of the Pacific and a computer course mapping program were the first step, plotting out for her the most direct routes between the spot where the catamaran had left the *Rabah Jamila* and the major port cities on the West Coast. Racing catamarans, she'd learned from her admittedly limited research, could pull speeds of anywhere from thirty knots to seventy or eighty. But the faster the speed, the more fuel the engines gulped, and the more frequently the ship would have to stop for refueling.

The most straightforward approach would be to put into ports along the way. Under the circumstances, she couldn't see them going anywhere near land if they could possibly avoid it. Particularly since most of the likely ports were under U.S. control.

Which suggested they had an alternative refueling arrangement set up, something which had to have been in place well before the *Rabah Jamila* was commandeered. All she had to do was figure out what that arrangement was.

It took nearly half an hour to program the retrieval system to pull up the satellite photos she wanted in the order she wanted them. But once that was done the rest was relatively easy. Keying for the photos taken Friday as the hijackers abandoned the *Rabah Jamila*, she began scanning along her course projection for Seattle. The simplest refueling option would be a tanker ship, probably disguised as something else, either waiting near the hijackers' course or moving in for a rendezvous at a predetermined place and time. She tracked east as far as the Aleutians, tagging each possible ship as she went, then pulled up the next set of photos and repeated the procedure. Sooner or later, she would find a ship that was spending more time than it should along the projected course.

And if it wasn't hanging around the Japan-Seattle route, then perhaps it was waiting for a ship bound for Portland, or San Francisco, or LA.

Sipping at her coffee, she kept at it. And tried to block out the mental image of a nuclear mushroom cloud floating above Jerusalem.

26

NINE-FIFTY.

Already the Golden State Mall was comfortably packed with shoppers. More than comfortably, Talbot thought uneasily as he gazed out through the copper-sheathed security windows that filled the narrow space between the tops of the fourth-floor shops and the domed skylights arching over the atrium. There were hundreds of people on this floor alone, most of them moving purposefully along on their errands, but a good number just lazing around window shopping. Occasionally, someone would glance up toward the skylights, probably checking to see if the heavy gray clouds had started to dump their load of rain yet.

Nine-fifty-one.

The cops were in place, forty of them, all in plain clothes and most on the third and fourth levels. All nearby elevators and escalators were guarded, as were the escalators in the middle of the Sears store that sealed off this end of the mall.

There were cops out in the parking lot, too. Most were sitting in unmarked cars, looking as casual as cops on a stakeout ever looked, watching the people filing in and out and ready to seal off the entrances the second they got the call. Four others were sitting in idling semis at the far ends of the lot, a last line of defense between the mall grounds and the safety of the street in case whoever showed up was able to get past everyone else.

Directly beneath Talbot's window, at the center of all this tense and hopefully invisible activity, waited Angie Chandler. Ten feet away from her, as tense and quiet as everyone else, stood Ross.

Nine-fifty-two.

"What about the Godiva's itself?" he asked Delgado, standing beside him and murmuring last-minute positioning instructions into his mike. "Is there a service door into the storeroom?"

"It's covered," Garcia, on Talbot's other side, answered instead. "You always this nervous in the field?"

"I am when people's lives are on the line," Talbot countered, probably more harshly than necessarily. "We know they're going to try to kill her. Probably her and Ross both."

He expected Garcia to take offense at the tone. Rather to his surprise, the other didn't. "They're as safe as we can manage," he reminded Talbot mildly. "You know that. There are ten cops right there, on hair triggers and good to go."

Talbot took a deep breath. He and Lyman had begged Angie to give this meeting a miss and let Ross take her place. Garcia had taken it a step farther, threatening to lock her away as a material witness.

But she'd insisted. She was the one the killers were after, she'd pointed out, and they were unlikely to come out of hiding just for a shot at Ross. Besides, if she didn't show, there was every chance they would keep hounding her until they *did* find her. Better to have it out here, she'd argued, than on the street where the situation wouldn't be so well controlled.

"Not to mention Ross himself," Garcia continued into Talbot's thoughts. "Sometime after this is all over, I'm going to have to sit you down and hear his whole story."

"Sure."

"If it makes you feel any better, I hate the waiting, too" Garcia said wryly. "As long as we've got a minute, how about filling in the gaps in the logic chain? I was on the phone when you laid it out for the others."

He was trying to distract him, Talbot knew, now that everything was in place and worrying wouldn't gain anyone anything. Still, he was just as glad to have the mental break. "It started with the notepad in the lab," he said. "The one you wrote Ross's license number and car description on. You tore off that sheet and gave it to Nate. Then, while we were in the office waiting for the Cloak demo, one of the three techs swiped the next sheet down."

"So he could pull off the information via the indentations," Garcia growled. "I'm still kicking myself for that one."

"Don't," Talbot assured him. "As Ross said, it didn't affect the attack on him and Angie. What it *did* do was flush out our man. As it happened, the sheet you wrote on turned out to be the second to the last of the yellow ones in the color scheme, which meant he was forced to take the last yellow. He knew that if any of us spotted it, the sudden change in color from yellow to red would be a dead giveaway of what had happened. But he assumed his associates needed that information, and he had to take the risk."

"You sure he was even thinking along those lines?"

"Positive," Talbot said. "He tried to hide what he'd done by turning the pad upside down. But the change to lime green was just as noticeable, and Nate and I caught it immediately."

"He should have just taken the whole pad and been done with it."

"He probably figured it was too thick to fit into any of his pockets without the bulge showing," Talbot said. "Remember, the other techs were wandering in and out of the room, and trying to shoehorn a whole pad into your pocket is a lot more obvious than just peeling off the top sheet. I suppose he could have taken the sheet and hidden the rest of the pad in a drawer, but I'm guessing he never had a clear enough window to do that. He certainly didn't want to get caught with the pad in his hand, no matter what he was doing with it. Everyone was on edge, and there might be awkward questions."

"So he took the top sheet," Garcia said. "What does that tell us?"

"For starters, it immediately took Angie off the hook," Talbot said, letting his gaze sweep across the mall again. Still no sign of Hooker. "Not entirely, I suppose, since she still could have been part of it. But it meant that one of the techs was definitely involved."

"The question being which one."

"A question that was finally answered two days ago in our Sunday morning interviews with the suspects," Talbot said. "Although it took me awhile longer to put the pieces together. Nate found out that Esteban had eavesdropped at the lab while he was phoning the description of Ross's car to the gate guards. Burke apparently caught Esteban at it, got a quick thumbnail sketch of what was happening, and when all three of them left the office they nagged the details out of him."

"Sure, but we already knew one of the techs was involved," Garcia said. "How does this narrow anything down?"

"You miss the crucial point," Talbot said. "Esteban overheard Nate give out the license number, so he didn't need to take the yellow sheet. Even if he'd already taken it, he could easily have put it back. It was a sticky pad, so there would have been no problem reattaching it. Similarly, Burke knew that Esteban had overheard the information, and even though he didn't have the details he would have known he could get them from him after they left. Which only leaves—"

He broke off as Delgado tapped his arm. "Report from the northwest door," the other said quietly. "Kingsley has just entered the building."

Talbot took a deep breath. "Right."

"Over a lousy yellow sticky pad sheet," Garcia said, shaking his head.

"It's always the little things, isn't it?" Talbot agreed soberly. "But there it is. By the time Kingsley even knew Esteban had the data on Ross's car, they were already in the elevator heading down and it was too late for him to put the sheet back."

"So *is* he really Scott Kingsley?"

"More or less," Talbot said. "Though a better way to say that might be that Scott Kingsley is really Hooker. At least, no one's found any other Scott Kingsley yet whose identity Hooker might have stolen. Hooker probably creates a fresh identity like this out of whole cloth every time he starts a new job, complete with all the computer records necessary to make the identity look real. If we'd tried sifting through actual paper trails, of course, the house of cards would have collapsed. But there wasn't time to get that going."

"Sand/Star should have done that themselves."

"Agreed," Talbot said. "But most people don't bother with paper trails these days, especially for the low-security setup he was in."

"So he was the one sending the coded email."

"Coded email going out, phone calls coming in," Talbot said, nodding. "Kingsley's regular early-morning run took him past a market that was closed at that hour but had a convenient phone booth outside. He used those whenever possible, I assume, because you can spot a tap on a land line easier than you can on a cell call. If his buyers wanted to get hold of him, all they had to do was make a call to that booth when he was passing it."

Garcia grunted. "The timing gets tricky."

"Unless they plant someone in the area to watch the booth and signal when he gets close," Talbot said. "That approach had the added advantage of allowing the signaler to watch for tails or other surveillance. That's why I didn't want anyone in the immediate area this morning. The last thing we could afford was a tip-off."

"I still wish we could have listened in," Delgado said. "It would have been nice to know what their plan is."

"Too risky," Talbot said. "As I said, a man of Hooker's expertise would have had gadgets to warn him about line taps or electronic surveillance. Probably all of it packed into the bottom of his water bottle.

And with his headphones turned outward and his music blaring away, a spy-ear dish would have been useless, too."

He grimaced. "Besides, we know what their plan is. It's to kill Angie Chandler."

"He must have had some pretty good snooping equipment of his own," Garcia commented thoughtfully. "He had to be keeping close tabs on what was happening with the project. Even the private stuff he wasn't supposed to know."

"He was up to date, all right," Talbot said. "But I think he had a simpler method than listening at keyholes. I can't prove it yet, but my guess is that he was bedding down with Dr. Underwood."

Garcia's jaw dropped slightly. "You're kidding."

"Why not?" Talbot countered. "She and her husband were separated, and she was probably lonely. A perfect opening for a smooth operator like Hooker."

"The real capper was his effrontery at suggesting Dr. Chandler was the one having the affair with her," Delgado said. "Not only did it give Angie a motive, but it also deflected any hints we might dig up about Underwood's private life."

"They guy's a prince, all right," Garcia growled. "I'm looking forward to a quiet chat with him down at the station."

Nine fifty-nine.

"There he is," Delgado said, pointing toward the wide walkway on the far side of the atrium. "Greer, you got him? Okay, stay sharp. And keep back—he's not the one we want. Smitty, move back and cover that escalator."

Half listening to the one-sided conversation, Talbot watched as Kingsley worked his way through the milling crowd and circled around in front of the Sears to their side of the atrium. As he rounded the corner, he moved to the edge of the walkway by the brass railing, as if trying to avoid the denser traffic near the store windows and entrances.

"Kiyohara, anything at your end?" Delgado asked.

"Is there?" Talbot asked.

"Not yet," Delgado reported. "I hope we didn't scare them away."

"They want Angie dead," Talbot reminded him.

Angie had spotted Kingsley now and was weaving carefully through the shoppers toward him. Ross was on the move, too, moving at a pace that would get him there before Angie. Kingsley caught the other's movement, and for a second he seemed to falter. Then, lip visibly twitching, he plowed on ahead.

"Hail, hail, the gang's all here," Garcia muttered. "Okay, you bastards. Show yourselves."

~

Angie Chandler was heading hesitantly toward the railing and the sheer four-story drop beyond. Watching her out of the corner of his eye, Six suppressed a smile as he set a can of pralines and two crisp twenty-dollar bills on the counter. The police here were so unimaginative, from the men loitering near the escalators right down to the perky young couple standing not ten feet away from him, gazing out through the shop window as they pretended to discuss the best sort of chocolates to bring to a dinner party.

Still, even obvious leopards were dangerous, and not to be taken lightly.

The sales girl returned with his change and his pralines, the latter now encased in a fancy plastic bag. He smiled as he took the change, the normal creasing of lips and cheeks feeling strange and wooden beneath the unaccustomed beard and facial makeup. Stuffing the coins and bills into his pocket, he turned toward the door, pausing long enough to open his new Godiva's bag and put the small Radio Shack bag he'd come in with inside it. A perfectly normal consolidation move, he knew, one that wouldn't even attract attention, let alone comment. By now, Angie Chandler and Hooker would have reached their positions by the rail.

Time to go.

He left the store, pausing again outside the door to reach into his now combined shopping bag, rummaging around a moment as he tore off the can's cellophane wrapping, worked off the lid, and brought out one of the pralines. The targets were there, all right, he saw as he popped the delicacy into his mouth: Hooker leaning casually on the rail with one elbow, Mrs. Chandler standing much more stiffly a meter or so away from him.

And to Six's mild surprise and eternal satisfaction, they weren't alone. Standing at Mrs. Chandler's side, his back to the railing, was Ross.

Again Six smiled. But this time the smile had an edge to it. Ross had killed one of his comrades at the Greenleaf Mall, and the bastard's Monterey escape had shamed him in front of his commander.

Mrs. Chandler would be business. Ross would be personal.

Five meters behind Mrs. Chandler was a trash receptacle, nestled out of the way beside one of the thick white columns supporting the high roof. Rummaging again in his bag, Six headed casually toward the trash can, pulling out part of the torn cellophane wrapper and ostentatiously wadding it up in his hand. He reached the trash can, aware that a multitude of police eyes were undoubtedly trained on his back, and tossed the cellophane wad into the opening. Out of the corner of his eye he saw Ross turn slightly toward him, and wondered if the man had guessed who he was.

Not that it mattered. It was far too late for suspicions now.

Trying to look as innocently oblivious of the world around him as he could, Six pulled out another praline. Setting it between his teeth, he leaned slightly forward and rummaged again in his bag, as if putting the lid back on the can. Under cover of the movement, he worked the handcuffs hidden in his left sleeve partially down to where he could palm the lower cuff in his hand. He straightened up again and turned toward the trio having their quiet discussion at the rail, and with his right hand he drew the pistol he'd had hidden in the Radio Shack bag.

Centering the weapon on Mrs. Chandler's back, he fired twice.

~

Even fifty feet away and behind glass, the two gunshots sounded as loud as pipe bombs. "There!" Garcia snapped, jabbing a finger at the man in the blue windbreaker as Angie's back exploded in a sickening splash of brilliant red. "*Damn* it all!"

"Move in!" Delgado ordered.

~

Angie Chandler's back exploded in a burst of blood, the force of the impacts jerking her forward toward Hooker. Automatically, the other reached out to catch her, his eyes wide with disbelief, his face twisting in horror. Six looked away from the gruesome sight, the quiet twinge of guilt at having just shot an unarmed woman vanishing as he lined up the muzzle on Ross. The other was in motion, stepping toward Six and twisting his body as if trying to get between the gun and Mrs. Chandler.

Too late for her, and now too late for him. Again Six fired twice, and had the satisfaction of seeing the shock on Ross's face as his chest also exploded in red. He bounced backward off the railing and slid down onto the clean white tile. Around him, the sedate milling of the crowd disintegrated as screaming shoppers dropped flat on the floor or scrambled madly over each other trying to get away.

All of them, that is, except the watching police. They would be running the opposite direction, trying to reach him. But their very concealment within the crowd now worked against them, slowing their advance as they pushed their way forward.

Shifting his aim one last time, he lined up his gun on Hooker.

The traitor, still holding Mrs. Chandler's limp body, saw it coming, and his eyes bulged wider still. But he had betrayed them to the police, and Six felt no compunction as he fired two final times. Hooker jerked and collapsed, dropping Mrs. Chandler's body and falling on top of it.

Dropping the gun, Six slapped his left hand down onto the brass railing. The handcuff concealed there snapped around the cylinder and locked solidly in place.

And with his left hand as a support and pivot point, he vaulted sideways over the rail and hurled toward the distant floor below.

~

Even as the first wave of police broke through the scattering crowd and charged forward, the gunman vaulted over the railing and disappeared. "Bloody hell!" Garcia gasped. "He jumped!"

"He's on a wire," Delgado said sharply. "First floor—who the hell's on the first floor?"

Talbot didn't wait to hear the answer. Dodging around Garcia, he raced to the narrow staircase and charged down it, popping open the discreet door beside the Godiva's and emerging onto the walkway.

A dozen guns spun toward him, turned away again as the cops spotted the luminescent "FBI" on his windbreaker. "He went over the railing," one of them called uselessly.

"I know where he went," Talbot snarled back, sprinting to the edge. "Seal the mall. *Now!*" He dodged around the two EMTs already crouched over the blood-splattered figures and leaned over to look. Below him, the rope connected to the railing was swaying gently back and forth.

The murderer was gone.

~

The harness and friction brake they'd rigged up worked perfectly, and Six came to a solid but not uncomfortable stop among the startled shoppers on the first floor. Even as his knees bent to absorb the shock of landing, he had his switchblade out, and with a quick slash through the nylon rope he was free.

Armed only with his knife, he could have been stopped easily. Instead, the crowds stood transfixed or flinched away as he shoved his way through them and dodged beneath the walkway out of sight of the watchers above. A second later, he had blended in among the more distant mass of people still looking wildly around them for the source of the gunshots and screaming. Sheep.

But there were wolves in their midst, he reminded himself as he walked along as quickly as he could without making it look like he was hurrying. Most of the police had been on the third and fourth levels, but they would be racing downward to join forces with the backups guarding the exits. He had only a few minutes of grace before they sealed down the mall and began an all-out search.

Fortunately, those few minutes were all he needed.

The McDonald's was three stores from his landing point, and as he brushed past the startled counter workers and cooks he paid note to the fact that it had been Ross who'd taught them this trick. Wherever his shade now resided, Six hoped he appreciated the irony. Slipping out of his blue windbreaker and tossing it aside, he pushed open the rear service door.

The rain was still holding off. In the distance in both directions armed men were sprinting from parked cars toward the mall's entrances, but so far they didn't seem to have noticed him. With perfect timing Seven was just pulling up. Popping open the passenger door, he jumped in.

~

"Seal the entrances," Delgado snapped into his microphone as he slammed open the door and charged out into the chaos of the fourth-floor walkway. The EMT's were nearly as bloodstained as the three on the floor, he could see now, as they worked feverishly away.

There was nothing he could do here. Turning, he sprinted for the elevator.

"Possible make," a crisp voice reported in his ear. "A man exiting one of the service doors on the east, midway between the northeast and north-central entrances. Burgundy late-model Ford is picking him up."

"Cut him off," Delgado ordered as he reached the elevator. One of the cops was holding the car, and he ducked inside. "And get those damn semis in place."

~

Six had apparently been wrong about the police not noticing him. Even as Seven pulled away from the service entrance he spotted a car veering out of a parking spot near the northeast entrance. A fraction of a second later his guess was confirmed as a hand tossed a flashing light up onto the roof. "They're coming," he warned.

"I know," Seven replied, twisting the car into one of the parking lanes and gunning the engine. "Looks like the trucks are on the move, too."

"Trucks?" Six asked, frowning as he looked around. He spotted them immediately: big highway trucks, pulling ponderously across the parking lot exits.

"They arrived after you went in," Seven explained. "Clever, eh?"

"In a heavy handed sort of way," Six agreed. Heavy handed, but still a smart move. With the parking lot isolated from the surrounding streets by low concrete curbs, a formidable drainage ditch, and an extra half-meter of vertical separation between the two areas, no one was likely to get a vehicle out except through those now blocked exits.

The direction Seven was now taking them was even more intimidating. The lane of the street closest to them was a maze of orange cones and brightly striped barriers with flashing orange lights, where members of the San Jose Streets Department were in the process of digging random holes in the pavement. Six had driven alongside that lane earlier on his way into the mall, and while he couldn't see what the point of the operation was, it wasn't a lane he would want to try to cross after dealing with the concrete and moat.

Fortunately, he wouldn't have to.

Behind them, the police car skidded into their lane, its driver managing the high-speed turn without slamming into any of the parked cars. He had friends now, too: three more flashing lights had joined in the pursuit, angling in from other parts of the mall.

But all were coming from the mall itself, Six noted, with none moving in from further out in the lot. He did a quick estimate of distances and intercept times and permitted himself one final smile. The end of the lot was rushing up toward them, the moat and concrete the last barrier between them and freedom.

~

"They're heading for the edge of the lot," the voice reported tightly in Delgado's ear as the elevator reached the first floor. "They're going to try to jump to street level!"

"Not a chance," a cooler voice cut in. "Not in that thing. We've got 'em."

Right, Delgado thought darkly as the doors opened and he raced toward the exit. *Sure we do.*

~

Seven waited until the last second before slamming on the brakes. Maybe waited a split second too long, Six thought, wincing as the nose of the car twisted up then sharply down as the wheels hit the curb and went over, the grille slamming with a crunch into the wall of earth and concrete beyond. "It's not our car," Seven reminded him philosophically as he snapped off his seat belt and shoved open the door.

Six did likewise, then turned to look. The four pursuit cars were nearly on top of them, no more than fifty meters back, splitting apart in an encircling maneuver as they screeched to a halt. From behind him, up at street level, another set of screeching brakes joined into the cacophony.

Because he was listening for it, Six heard the soft *chummpf.* A small canister arced over their car and dropped onto the pavement between them and the approaching police.

And with a brilliant flash the canister erupted with heat and fire and a billowing cloud of dense smoke.

Six didn't wait to see any more. Ducking out of the car, he dodged around the open door and scrambled up to the street above. The general was waiting there, his car deftly inserted into one of the few sections of undamaged pavement left. Six caught a glimpse of the spent single-shot grenade launcher as the other tossed it into the drainage ditch.

Then he and Seven were at the car and the general was thrusting a second launcher at him. "Upwind," the other reminded him.

Six turned his face into the wind and fired at a spot perhaps five meters away. Again there was a flash and burst of smoke, this cloud softer and gentler than the red phosphorus they'd used to block the police.

But it was just as thick. Even as Seven yanked open the rear door, the wind blew the smoke into a concealing cocoon around them.

~

"Damn!" one of the cops snarled as Delgado charged out into the cold morning air. "What the—?"

"Back up—*back up!*" someone else cut in urgently. "That's red phosphorus. Burns like hell."

"Get away from it," Delgado ordered, craning his neck to look toward the expanding cloud at the far end of the lot. He had just a glimpse of a car sitting up at street level between two of the orange barriers before the phosphorus smoke screen rose high enough to block his view. "Can anyone see them?"

"Richards—northeast lot," another voice chimed in. "I can. Oh, hell—they've laid down another smoke screen over themselves. We've got collisions. Traffic's going nuts."

"Get some cars up there," Delgado ordered, making for one of the police cars idling beside the curb. "Move those semis—we've got to block the street before they just drive away. Where the hell is the chopper?"

"Coming up and over," a new voice put in as Delgado jumped into the front seat and jammed the gearshift lever into drive. "We've got the smoke screens in sight. What are we looking for?"

"Dark-blue full-size car in the south-bound lane," Richards answered. "Looked like a late-model Buick, but I couldn't tell for sure before the smoke rolled in."

"Get ready to watch it roll out again," the chopper pilot said grimly. "I'm going in."

"Watch yourself," Delgado warned, accelerating across the lot toward the southeast exit, the one that would get him out onto the street ahead of the escape car. The semi blocking that access was starting to back out of the path now, and out of the corner of his eye he saw two more unmarked squad cars racing from different directions to join him. With luck, maybe they could get ahead of the Buick before it made its break for freedom.

That moment would probably be coming sooner than the murderers had anticipated. Overhead, the chopper came to a halt directly over the second smoke cloud. With casual disregard for his own safety and whatever FAA regulations applied, the pilot dropped straight down.

The smokescreen had been drifting south in response to the northerly breeze. Now, suddenly, it was like something inside a high-speed blender. The cloud flattened and bulged outward in the downdraft from the chopper blades, tendrils of it flying in all directions.

There it was: a dark-blue Buick, sitting in the torn-up lane between a pair of barriers.

Empty.

The murderer and his accomplices were gone.

27

DELGADO CURSED, SWINGING out of the lot and up onto the street. He accelerated hard toward the Buick—going the wrong way, but of course all southbound traffic had come to a sudden crunching halt behind the Buick when the smoke canister went off. He braked to a halt a dozen yards away, slammed the lever into park, and shoved open his door. As he drew his gun, the other cars arrived, stopped beside and behind him in street-blocking positions. "Lieutenant?" one of the cops called.

"Cover me," Delgado ordered. Bracing himself, he slid out from behind the relative protection of the car and headed forward, squinting against the downdraft from the chopper.

He'd been wrong about the car being empty. Its occupants were long gone, but the package sitting on the dashboard more than made up for it. "They left us a going-away present," he called into his radio, his chest tight as he stared at the collection of red sticks and the small mechanism holding it together. "Looks to be a bomb."

"Get out of there," Garcia's voice called sharply. "Winslow, get that chopper up."

"Easy," Delgado said, leaning forward for a closer look at the wires disappearing beneath the dashboard as the helicopter lifted away. "I don't see a timer, so it probably won't go off on its own. But it's wired into something under the dashboard, probably the security system. They've also added a bunch of suction-cup breakage sensors to the windows. My guess is that messing with the car will set it off."

Garcia cursed feelingly. "Smith, Kelsey, get a team together and block off traffic in both directions back at the cross streets," he ordered. "U-turn all the cars already inside the box. We don't want anyone getting nervous and bumping the Buick on their way out."

"Better yet, route them all into the mall parking lot," Delgado suggested as a sudden thought struck him. "Away from the booby trap, but someplace where we can search them."

"You think the killer's in one of those vehicles?"

"He has to be *somewhere*," Delgado pointed out. "Winslow, Harrington, did either of you see anything?"

"I didn't," the chopper pilot said.

"Me, neither," the observer added hesitantly. "But that cloud was pretty big, and spread damn fast. Someone might have sneaked out the east side before we got over there."

"Jawarski, get your squad checking the businesses on the east side of the street," Garcia ordered. "And throw a cordon around the area—they may try to steal a car."

"Or already have one standing by," Delgado said, giving the Buick one last look as he backed away. "We'll want to block all those parking lots, make sure no one gets out."

"Right," Garcia ground out. "If we're going to be unpopular, we might as well be unpopular with the whole damn city. Come on, people—move it."

~

The detective—it was Delgado himself—backed away, looking rather pathetic as he waved his gun at basically nothing. Pathetic, even comical, Six decided as he squinted through the fiber optic eyepiece. He hadn't been able to hear more than bits and pieces of the conversation, but it was clear that the police had not a single clue as to what was going on.

Seven, sitting stiffly beside him beneath the collapsible framework that filled much of the interior back seat space, was obviously thinking the same thing. "Not very smart, are they?" he murmured.

"They're smart enough," the general put in quietly from the driver's seat before Six could answer. "The first reaction of trained men in an unexpected situation is always to fall back on standard routine. Given sufficient time, they'll pause and think things through. We simply have to make sure not to give them that time."

"Yes, sir," Six said. Personally, he still thought the police were just stupid. "How long?"

"Fifteen minutes," the general said. "Just long enough for them to shift their focus elsewhere. Six, tell me what you can see at the mall. Seven, try to locate the helicopter."

"Yes, sir," Six said, setting the windshield eyepiece back into his lap and selecting the one connected to the right-hand-window suction cup. Making their spy-line system look like a set of breakage sensors had been a stroke of genius on the general's part. Not that the police were likely to appreciate it.

Given the fish-eye distortion and the distance between them and the mall, Six wasn't sure exactly what he was supposed to see. Their first smoke screen, the phosphorus one, had dissipated, leaving more cops standing around waving their guns uselessly. "Helicopter's off to the east," Seven reported. "Seems to be hovering."

"Can you see where they've blocked off traffic behind us?" the general asked.

"Looks to be at the last cross street," Seven said, changing eyepieces. "Yes, they're directing traffic away from this section. They're also directing the southbound traffic in here with us out through the northbound lanes."

"They're doing the same at this end," the general said. "Five minutes, and the way ahead of us should be clear."

Six smiled. The police would block the northbound lanes ahead of them, of course. But with the southbound traffic already blocked behind them, there would be no reason to do anything more with the southbound lanes. Once the rest of the trapped traffic had been cleared out, there would be nothing between them and the anonymity of the city but the barrier across the other half of the road. The cops manning that barricade would probably be too stunned as they drove past to even draw their guns.

Then, at the mall entrance, Six caught a flicker of new movement.

"Keep an eye out for a police truck," the general continued. "We'll need to move before the bomb squad arrives."

"Something's happening at the mall," Six reported. "Looks like they're bringing out a body bag on a stretcher."

The atmosphere beneath the Cloak went suddenly tense. "How many?" the general asked.

"One so far," Six said, squinting into the eyepiece and silently cursing the distortion.

"Any sign of an oxygen tank?" the general asked. "Or an IV, or other life-support equipment?"

"None that I can see," Six said. "Two ambulances are pulling up. Here comes a second stretcher . . . and a third. Body bags, all of them. They're loading them into the ambulances."

He heard the general's long, tired sigh. "Then the final question mark is gone."

"Assuming she didn't talk," Seven cautioned.

"She didn't," the general said. "I'm convinced she never realized the significance of what she knew. But in time she might have. We couldn't afford to take that risk."

"No, sir," Six said, vaguely surprised that the general seemed to feel it necessary to justify his actions.

Still, Six had felt the same twinge of guilt as he pulled the trigger. Perhaps the general was simply making sure his men fully understood the reasons for the order they'd just carried out. "Not with Hooker, either," he added.

"Hooker earned his own execution."

"Of course," Six agreed.

"Let's hope *he* didn't talk, either," Seven muttered.

"Again, he didn't," the general said. "That knowledge was his only bargaining chip. He wouldn't have given it away so quickly. Now, he never will."

"Yes, sir," Six said. "The ambulances are pulling away. Not running with lights."

"There's no need to hurry," the general said. "The morgue is always open."

~

The ambulance pulled away from the curb; and with a harsh ripping sound that sounded like it was right in her ears, someone pulled open the zipper of Angie's body bag. She opened her eyes, squinting against the light, to find Talbot leaning low over her, swaying a little as the ambulance made a turn. "You okay?" he asked.

Angie closed her eyes again. What kind of answer was there to a question like that? What kind of answer could there be when you'd been scared, then terrified, then in agony, then literally face to face with what had happened back there?

What could you say after you'd lain in someone else's blood and your own vomit?

"Sure," she said, her voice sounding as dead as her soul felt. "I'm fine."

"I'm sorry, Angie," he said quietly. "Sorry for all of it."

Almost involuntarily, she opened her eyes again. There'd been an unexpected edge of pain in his voice, an emotion she wouldn't have expected in a professional like Talbot.

She hadn't been mistaken. The pain was visible in his face, too. "Going in there was my idea," she reminded him, feeling an obscure need to offer comfort. "It's not your fault."

"Unfortunately, it's *all* my fault," he said. "Someone once said that sooner or later in this business you run into someone cleverer and stronger and more ruthless than you are. Whoever these guys are, they beat me hands down on at least two of the three."

"Not necessarily," came a muffled voice from the other stretcher, the words accompanied by the ripping of another body bag zipper. "They've been clever enough," Ross continued, working his way awkwardly out of the bag and into a sitting position. The sight of his blood-soaked shirt made Angie want to throw up again, even knowing it was fake. "But we haven't exactly been slouches in that department, either." He thumped his chest.

"Yeah, right," Talbot growled. "Except that those vests were fifty percent luck and thirty percent the grace of God and the Secret Service. Did you hear what Barry said about those slugs?"

"It was hard to miss," Ross said grimly. "Teflon-coated expanders, cop-killer variety. Guaranteed to punch through bullet-proof vests like they were cardboard."

Angie stared at him, feeling the blood draining from her face. "But—"

"Standard bullet-proof vests, that is," Ross hastened to add. "That's what that plaster-mold procedure last night was all about. Lyman talked the Secret Service into fitting us with a set of the same turtle things the President wears when there's extra danger. Uncomfortable, but they work."

"Yes," Angie murmured. "A shame you didn't make one for Scott."

The look on Talbot's face made her immediately wish she hadn't said that. "Sorry," she said. "I didn't mean that the way it sounded."

"Yes, you did," Talbot said. "And you're right. That was my fault, too."

"It was as much mine as yours, Madison," Ross put in. "Don't forget, I backed your argument that if they wanted to kill him they'd have done so already."

"Fine; so we're both idiots," Talbot countered. "Pretty cold comfort."

"He must also have thought they wouldn't kill him," Angie pointed out. "Otherwise, he wouldn't have shown up."

Talbot shrugged. "Maybe."

Angie leaned up onto one elbow, not an easy maneuver in the form-fitting armor she was wearing, and looked around the ambulance. The thought of Kingsley's body in here with her was suddenly chilling. "Where is—you know? The—?"

"It's in the other ambulance," Talbot said. "I didn't think we wanted . . . Anyway, there wasn't enough room for all three of you in here."

"Speaking of realism, we're sorry about the body bags," Ross put in. "But these guys would certainly have had a spotter in the crowd. We needed them to think they succeeded."

"I understand," Angie said. Which wasn't to say she'd liked the idea, then or now. Being zipped up inside a body bag was about as gruesome a sensation as she'd ever experienced, just one step shy of being sealed in a casket. "What happens now?"

"You're going into hiding in an FBI safe house," Ross said. "Your parents are being officially notified of your death right now, and privately told that you're all right."

"You put Ng on that?" Ross asked.

Talbot nodded. "He'll drive them up here for identification of the body and the rest of the official hoops. After that, they'll go into seclusion for a period of mourning, probably at the same safe house. Something similar is being done with your brother and sister."

Angie felt her throat tense up as a horrible thought struck her. "You said identification of the body. Does that mean I'll have to—at the morgue—?"

"No, no," Talbot assured her hastily. "That's all just for the benefit of the media. Your parents will basically go into a room with Ng and Chief Garcia, and a little while later they'll come out."

"And while they're doing that, we'll be sifting through Hooker's private papers," Ross added. "Looking for his insurance policy."

"His what?" Angie asked, frowning.

"The stuff shady people tuck away to keep the bedbugs from biting, if you get my drift," Ross explained. "Notes, important documents, damning evidence. Hooker's bound to have left something like that behind."

"Not that it matters," Talbot said with a sigh. "I got a call while you were being loaded into the body bags. Kingsley's apartment is currently going up in smoke."

"Hell," Ross murmured. "Anyone hurt?"

"I don't know," Talbot said. "Hopefully, most of them are at work, and it sounded like they've kept the blaze confined to Kingsley's end of the building. But any dirt he's got on his buyers is long gone."

"Someone cleverer and stronger and more ruthless," Ross murmured. "Maybe you were right."

"Certainly on the ruthless part," Talbot agreed darkly. "Did Hooker say anything useful before the shooting started?"

"Nothing worth listening to," Ross said. "Mostly just asking Angie if she was all right and who the hell I was. You can listen to the tape later—"

"Hold it," Talbot interrupted, digging out his phone and flipping it open. "Talbot. What is it?"

For a long minute he listened in silence. Angie watched him, her throat tightening again as his face slowly went rigid. "Sure," he said at last, his voice low. "Thanks."

He closed the phone and turned to gaze at the back of the ambulance, and for a half second Angie had the sense that he was about to hurl the phone against the doors as hard as he could.

The moment passed, and he slipped the phone back into his pocket. "That was Delgado," he said, turning to Ross. "It seems our booby-trapped Buick just took off, sailed straight past a collection of dumbfounded cops directing traffic, and vanished into the mists."

Ross's jaw dropped. "You're joking. How did they get back in—? Oh, *damn*."

"What?" Angie demanded, looking back and forth between them. "I don't understand."

"They didn't have to get back into the car," Talbot told her bitterly. "They never left it. They were inside the whole time, under one of the Cloaks."

Angie winced. "Oh, no."

"Oh no is right," Ross agreed ruefully. "Damn it all. I'm not used to thinking this way."

"Neither are the rest of us," Talbot said. "Nate was right there with me when the techs showed us the prototype, and it still didn't occur to him to wonder if someone might still be in the car. We've grown up believing what our eyes tell us, and it's not easy to break that way of thinking."

"I presume they gave chase?" Ross asked.

Talbot snorted. "Such as they could, and for all the good it'll do. The cops were scattered all over the place, and the chopper was off watching them search the nearby buildings. By the time they had anything organized, the Buick was long gone. They're still looking, but my guess is they changed cars the minute they were out of sight."

Ross muttered something under his breath. "Who *are* these guys, anyway?"

"I don't know, but we'd better figure it out fast," Talbot said grimly. "I'm thinking maybe I should give Hanna a call."

"Hanna Swenson?" Ross asked. "I thought you said she was pulled for some other project."

"She was," Talbot said. "Maybe I can finesse a couple hours out of her anyway."

"McPherson won't like that," Ross warned.

"Only if he catches me," Talbot pointed out. "But first things first." He looked back at Angie. "We head to the morgue, take you and Ross inside, then sneak you out the back way and get you to the safe house."

Angie braced herself. "Both of us?"

Talbot's lip twitched. "It's a big house," he assured her. "You won't even have to see him if you don't want to."

There had never been a time in Angie's life when she'd felt less like smiling than she did right now. But just the same, and with a supreme effort, she managed a small one. Ross deserved that much. "That wasn't what I meant," she said. "Mr. Ross has been very good to me, even when I didn't know it."

"Thank you," Ross said, managing a small smile of his own in return, a smile she could tell was as much an effort for him as it had been for her. The world wasn't exactly going well for him at the moment, either. "Meanwhile, we have got to get a handle on these damn Cloaks. There has to a way to detect them. Radar, sonar, infrared—something."

"I agree," Talbot said. "In fact, I'm convinced that's what the scientists knew that made it necessary to kill them. Some way to penetrate the disguise."

"Angie?" Ross invited. "Any ideas?"

She shook her head. "I'm only the wife. The widow," she corrected herself quietly. "I know just the basics of how they work. You need Jack or Ramon for that."

"That's not a bad idea," Ross said. "Matter of fact, it's an excellent idea."

"It is indeed," Talbot said, pulling out his phone. "They can experiment on the Cloak Ng recovered from your parents' house. We'll find them a secure lab somewhere and get them working on a countermeasure."

"Assuming our killers don't get to them first," Ross warned.

Talbot's face was carved from stone as he punched numbers on the phone. "Yeah," he said quietly. "Let's definitely assume that."

28

MCPHERSON WAS CHOKING down yet another CIA cafeteria meal, and hating every bite, when the call they'd been expecting for several hours finally came through.

"Do you have actual confirmation of a meeting?" Cohn was asking as McPherson slipped into his office.

"Not yet," Minister Rao's voice replied from the phone's speaker. The man was finally starting to sound as weary as the rest of them, McPherson noted with a certain perverse satisfaction. About time. "But we do have confirmation that Barez was in the city the same time. We're still searching for proof of actual contact, but in my own mind I feel there is no doubt that they did, in fact, meet."

"Who's Barez?" McPherson murmured as he slid into a chair in front of Cohn's desk.

"Joshua Barez," Cohn said. "One of Rabbi Salomon's top aides, who was apparently in Bandar-e 'Abbas three weeks ago."

McPherson hissed between his teeth. "The same time Captain Syed was there."

"Who is that?" Rao asked. "Director McPherson?"

"Yes," McPherson confirmed, raising his voice loud enough to be clearly heard. "Do we know why Barez was in Iran?"

"Ostensibly, to meet with representatives of the Iranian Jewish community," Rao said. "However, I don't think we need ask the true reason for his visit."

McPherson frowned at Cohn. "I didn't know there *was* an Iranian Jewish community."

Cohn shrugged. "It isn't big, but it does exist."

"Its very smallness makes the leaders easy to locate," Rao said. "Our people have already interviewed two of them, both of whom say they were unaware Barez was even in Iran. Certainly neither was invited to any such Jewish meeting."

"What do Salomon's people say?" McPherson asked.

Rao sniffed audibly. "You think we're fools enough to ask them?"

"He's right," Cohn agreed. "If they're involved, we don't want to tip them off that we know about it."

"What do you mean, if they're involved?" Rao countered. "We have Barez scheduled to meet Iranian Jews, yet not doing so. We have Captain Syed and the *Rabah Jamila* in harbor at the same time. What other reason could there be except for the one to exchange final instructions with the other?"

"Maybe Barez wasn't supposed to meet with *all* the Jewish leaders," Cohn suggested. "Or maybe the two you talked to were just being cautious. In their position, I certainly wouldn't go blabbing about my recent activities in front of strangers. Especially when those activities concern a man my host country considers a dangerous radical."

"On the other hand, we do have the powder residue in the hijackers' containers," McPherson pointed out. "That at least points that direction."

"The what?" Rao asked. "What is this?"

Cohn looked pained. "I forgot to tell you," he confessed. "The lab found gunpowder residue on the hijackers' clothing that could be traced to Israeli manufacture."

"And you didn't think this might be useful for me to know?" Rao demanded.

"I forgot," Cohn repeated, starting to sound a little annoyed. "You called to discuss the results of your military personnel search, and I simply forgot. All right?"

There was a moment of frosty silence from the other end. "I see," Rao said at last, his tone as chilly as the silence. "So once it is proven that the weapon will not directly endanger United States territory, you lose interest in the proceedings."

"No one said we weren't interested, Minister Rao," Cohn said, clearly trying to be soothing. "If we weren't interested, we wouldn't have already shifted so many or our analysts to searching possible vectors into Israel."

"Much as we might wish it were otherwise," McPherson put in, "events in the Middle East often impact U.S. interests far more than events much closer to home. If the weapon is headed for Jerusalem, be assured we want it stopped."

"The problem is that, indirect indicators aside, we have no real proof it's going there," Cohn said. "So far our satellite and ground route investigations have come up dry."

"Then your efforts must be redoubled," Rao urged. "The weapon is indeed heading for Jerusalem. I'm convinced of it. If it's not stopped, I fear it will spark a war such as none of us has ever seen."

"Look, we need to calm down," Cohn urged. "We agree this is serious. But this group has already thrown so much dust in our eyes that I don't want to commit any more resources to a Middle East snipe hunt until there's more proof the weapon is going there."

"I see I am dealing with the wrong people," Rao said stiffly. "Very well. Thank you for your time."

"Minister Rao—"

There was a loud click. "Great," Cohn muttered, punching off the phone. "Nothing like dissension in the ranks to brighten a dull afternoon."

McPherson cocked an eyebrow at him. "You forgot to tell him about the powder residue?"

"I am *not* getting old," Cohn insisted, glaring across the desk.

"I never said you were," McPherson protested.

"No, but you were thinking it."

"You just need more sleep," McPherson said, wondering how in the world they'd gotten into this. "Men our age can't keep running on four hours a night without starting to pop a little at the seams."

"We can sleep when we're dead," Cohn muttered.

"Sure," McPherson agreed. "Can we get back to the problem at hand? What did he mean about dealing with the wrong people?"

"He's already threatened twice to go over my head to the President," Cohn said sourly. "Maybe this time he really means it."

McPherson winced. "Ouch." He glanced at his watch. "What do you think? Ten minutes?"

"I'll give him five," Cohn said, leaning back tiredly in his chair. "You know how twitchy Whitcomb gets on matters involving the Middle East."

McPherson nodded. "Rao's line about it sparking a war like we've never seen could have come straight out of one of our Wednesday meetings."

"Exactly," Cohn agreed. "We'll get our marching orders soon enough. Meanwhile, anything new on the Harrier hunt?"

"Not as of this morning," McPherson said. "We've been talking to rural witnesses, and it looks like the planes flew pretty much due west after they left Roseburg. But tracking along that line has so far come up empty. I'm beginning to wonder if you were right about them ditching the planes in the ocean or a convenient lake."

"It seems incredible that anyone would go to this much effort just for a diversion," Cohn said, shaking his head. "But stranger things have happened."

"Some of them this very week," McPherson agreed ruefully. "I checked the UN schedule, and Salomon's main speech isn't until nine o'clock Sunday morning. But each of the invited delegates also has five minutes during the Friday night opening ceremonies to introduce themselves and give a thumbnail of their particular group's plight."

"Mm," Cohn said. "If I had to guess, I'd guess he'll save any announcements for the Sunday slot. Gives him more time to set up and then plead his case, not to mention a wider window for the boys in Jerusalem to push the plunger while he's on stage."

"That would be my guess, too," McPherson agreed. "At the same time, if they sense too much heat coming in their direction, in the form of Israeli commandos, say—"

"Or the majority of the Arab world."

"—they could always move the timetable up to Friday," McPherson finished. "Either way lets Salomon make his Third Temple announcement with a maximum of exposure."

"And a maximum of dramatics," Cohn said heavily. "That gives us somewhere between seventy-six and a hundred fourteen hours."

McPherson grimaced. That wasn't a lot of time. "What's the plan?"

"We find the damn thing, that's what's the plan," Cohn growled. "I'll make sure the Pentagon has an alert out to all military commanders in the Middle East. We'll want to coordinate with the Israelis, Saudis, Iraqis, and anyone else we're on speaking terms with at the moment. If the weapon's really on the way, *someone* must have heard something."

"I don't know," McPherson murmured. "I'd still rather have at least a plausible vector before we start poking our stick into all those anthills."

Cohn shook his head. "No time for that. We'll have to try to nail it along the way." He grimaced. "To which end I'm also going to recommend that the Pentagon continue the search for their missing Harriers on their own, while your satellite and analysis people get back over here to Langley. There's a lot of ground to cover between India and Israel."

McPherson frowned. "Are you saying we should give up on the Pacific search? I'm still not convinced the *Rabah Jamila* was a feint."

"Neither am I," Cohn conceded. "But I'm guessing that's going to be the de facto result. Like it or not, we have a finite number of resources, and Whitcomb will likely insist we throw most of them at Israel."

His intercom buzzed. "Mr. Cohn, Cynthia Duvall is on line three," the secretary announced.

"Thank you," Cohn told her, glancing at his watch as he reached for the phone. "Four minutes. A new record." He lifted his eyebrows questioningly. "Care to make any bets as to what she's going to say?"

McPherson snorted. "No, thanks."

~

The Seattle course projection had come up dry. So had the Portland one, and the San Francisco one, and Swenson was just getting ready to start on the LA area when a sudden thought occurred to her.

A tactical nuke set off in the middle of San Francisco harbor would certainly make a satisfying bang. But if the target wasn't one of the major West Coast cities, then the thieves would want to bring the weapon ashore quietly and without fuss to be transported elsewhere.

And for that, one of the smaller coastal towns would be a much more reasonable entry point.

There were, unfortunately, any number of coastal ports capable of handling a forty-meter catamaran. Running her eye along her map of the coastline, trying to judge which ports were close enough together to have similar vectors from southern Japan, she got to work.

She was tracking the route to Crescent City when she spotted something odd: a bulk carrier changing course toward what appeared to be an old 1600-Class Navy utility landing craft.

The LCU didn't look much like a racing catamaran, of course, and not at all like a luxury yacht. But it was roughly the right size, and that made it worth a closer look.

She'd pulled the freighter's name from one of the photos, and was in the process of collecting the rest of the relevant data when she vaguely heard someone calling her name.

She looked up to find McPherson standing over her. "Hello, sir," she said, trying to look at him and her display at the same time. "I'm sorry I was late this morning. I overslept."

"That's all right," he said, pulling over a chair and sitting down. "Any luck?"

"Maybe," she said, reluctantly letting her fingers come to a halt and turning her full attention on him. She hated being interrupted in the middle of something, but he had that settled look that made it clear he wasn't just passing by. "I found a small ship and a freighter having a close conversation."

"How close?"

"I've got a shot of them coming to within a kilometer of each other," Swenson said, closing her data window and pulling up her best photo. "I'll have to check the timing, but they may have had enough time to come alongside each other, do a fuel transfer, and separate again before the next satellite pass."

"Or even easier, just hand off the nuke," McPherson said, rubbing his chin.

"You're right," Swenson said, feeling a little chagrined. Her attention focused on the catamaran, she'd missed that possibility. "That would take a lot less time, too."

"With good seas and the right equipment, about ten minutes," McPherson said. "What do we know about the two ships?"

"The computer says the smaller is a 1600-class LCU," she said, tapping the image with the end of a pencil.

"A Navy ship?" McPherson said, frowning.

"More likely one that was surplused to a private buyer," Swenson said. "The 1600s are thirty to forty years old, and the computer says a lot of them were sold when the upgraded versions started being deployed. The angle was too steep for me to pull any identification, either a name or number. Maybe the next pass will have a better shot."

"The freighter?"

"The *Shimizu Nakama*," she identified it, putting the data window back up. "Japanese registry, currently on its way to Coos Bay, Oregon, for a load of wood chips."

"Mm," McPherson said. "And we're sure that actually is the Shimizu Nakama?"

"Point," Swenson conceded. "That's the name printed on the stern; but then, the *Rabah Jamila* was running under a different name for a while, too."

"Either way, it's worth a closer look," McPherson said. "I'll talk to Vaughn, see if he can get a ship or chopper freed up to take a run out there. You'll also want to backtrack both ships." He paused. "I'm afraid you'll be on your own for that part."

Swenson glanced around the room. It was more crowded than it had been earlier, but was hardly filled to capacity. "Is everyone on break?"

McPherson shook his head. "We've picked up some more indicators that the nuke is on its way to Israel. The decision has been made at the highest levels to treat the *Rabah Jamila* as a feint and concentrate our efforts on tracking the other direction."

Swenson felt her chin sag. "We're going to drop it? Just like that?"

"Just like that," McPherson said heavily. "I'm not happy with the decision, either. But as I say, it came from the top."

"So we're just going to leave the whole West Coast undefended?"

"Not at all," McPherson assured her. "All major ports have been alerted and ordered not to allow any forty-meter ships to dock until their background records have been checked and their bona fides established."

He gestured toward the wall map. "In addition, we're setting up a cordon of warships, augmented by choppers, subs, and land- and carrier-based planes, to check ships heading eastward."

"There's a lot of ocean out there to watch," Swenson pointed out.

"I know," McPherson agreed. "And the search for those missing planes is still drawing off a lot of resources. But unless we can borrow the Canadian Air Force—and I understand Whitcomb is talking to Ottawa about that—we'll have to make do with what we've got." He nodded back toward the door. "In a few minutes Cohn will be making the official announcement on the change in focus."

"Okay," Swenson said, trying to read his face. "But you said *I* was going to be tracking down these ships?"

McPherson's lips puckered. "One of your few failings, Swenson, is that you often get so wrapped up in your work that you don't hear instructions like that." His eyes drifted away. "I think it's likely you'll miss hearing this one, too."

"I see," Swenson said, trying hard to choke back a smile.

She apparently didn't try hard enough. "What's funny?" McPherson demanded, his full attention snapping back to her again.

She hesitated. But there was no way around it. "I was just appreciating the irony, sir," she confessed. "I presume this is the same sort of under-the-table massaging of orders that got Madison Talbot kicked out to San Francisco in the first place."

"Talbot's talent for getting his own way had nothing to do with it," McPherson said stiffly. "If everyone in the Bureau who ever creatively interpreted orders got sent to the West Coast, the weight would have sunk California a long time ago."

"Really," Swenson said, frowning. She would have placed long odds that that was what had so irritated McPherson. It was certainly what irritated Lyman. "Then what *did* he do?"

"It was personal, and none of your business," McPherson said, getting up from his chair. "You just concentrate on figuring out where those ships came from and where they're going."

He strode away without waiting for a reply. "Yes, sir," she murmured after him. Taking a deep breath, she swiveled back to her computer, positioned her fingers over the keys—

"Hanna Swenson?" a new voice said.

With a sigh, Swenson looked up again. "Yes?"

A middle-aged woman stood there, who Swenson vaguely remembered seeing running the duty desk when Cohn and his second-in-command were both absent. "Phone call for you," she said. "A Madison Talbot in San Francisco. You can take it at the desk—line five."

"Thank you," Swenson said, slipping out of her chair and making her way through the workstations to the duty desk. Picking up the phone, she punched for line five. "Swenson."

"Hi, Hanna, it's Madison," Talbot's voice came back, sounding as weary as McPherson had looked. "Still in Langley, I see."

"Hello to you too," Swenson said. "Funny you should call. Director McPherson and I were just talking about you."

"Glad *something's* funny these days," Talbot said. "I just wanted to let you know that the Cloak theft case has been solved. Sort of."

" 'Sort of?' "

"Turns out Kingsley was our man," he said. "We haven't proved yet that he was your industrial spy Hooker, but I think it probable that he was."

"What about Angie Chandler?"

"We got her back," Talbot said. "The group that's been trying to kill her thinks they succeeded. Unfortunately, they smoked Hooker at the same time; and they really *did* get him."

Swenson winced. "Doesn't sound pleasant."

"The technical term is fiasco," Talbot said bitterly. "And to make the morning complete, they even got away. We had fifty cops on the scene, and they still slipped straight through our fingers. With a little help from the Cloaks."

"Well . . . at least Angie's safe," Swenson said, searching for something encouraging to say.

"Only for the moment," Talbot said. "We need to nail this gang, and we need to nail them now."

Swenson stiffened with sudden premonition. "Don't say it," she warned.

"We need you, Hanna," Talbot said, his voice low and persuasive and utterly sincere. "These people are clever and inventive, with a tactical genius in charge who likes going for finesse whenever possible instead of brute force. Nothing like the typical gang or industrial spy ring. But they're too good not to have left footprints *somewhere*."

"You've got ten other analysts at your beck and call," Swenson countered. "Any one of them can do this."

"But none of them can do it fast enough," Talbot said. "They've got something in mind for the Cloaks—I'm sure of it. And the clock's ticking."

"We've got clocks here, too," she reminded him. "That's why I was hauled back, remember? I can't just drop everything and sift your sandbox for you."

"I understand that," he said, his voice going even more reasonable and persuasive. "But there are occasional slack times in every operation—"

"Not this one," Swenson cut him off. "Sorry, dear, but you're on your own."

His sigh was clearly audible, and just as clearly designed to trigger guilt feelings. Clamping her teeth together, she resisted the reaction. "All right," he said. "I'll have everything we know about them loaded onto my computer sometime in the next hour, including the report on this last action of theirs and as much of their M.O. as we've been able to put together. You know how to access the file, if you happen to have any spare time."

"My spare time for the next month is already spoken for," Swenson told him. "But thanks for the offer."

"Okay," he said calmly. "I'll let you get back to work, then. Take care."

She grimaced. "You too. 'Bye."

She dropped the handset back into its cradle, glaring at it for a moment before getting up and returning to her desk. The man was infuriating, and the fact that he always stayed so calm made it even worse.

If he would only get a little mad at her it would be easier to brush him off. But he knew her buttons far too well.

Of course, he knew *everyone's* buttons too well. Maybe that was why he'd been kicked out of D.C.

But she couldn't bother with Madison Talbot right now. Not his personality, his foibles, his cases, or his Cloaks. She had a nuke to find.

An hour later, when she surfaced to go get more coffee, it occurred to her that Cohn must surely have made his announcement by now. McPherson had been right; she'd missed it completely.

THE
EIGHTH
DAY

29

It was still the middle of the night, a good three hours till sunrise, when First Officer Fukuda was awakened with the news that a United States Naval helicopter was standing off the *Shimizu Nakama* and very much wanted a word with him.

Captain Uematsu was already in the wheelhouse when he arrived, gazing dispassionately out at the helicopter lights pacing the freighter perhaps five hundred meters to the south. "Do we know what this is about?" Fukuda asked, stepping to the captain's side.

"We encountered a ship Monday morning while you were on duty," Uematsu said, giving his first officer the same sort of look he'd just been giving the distant helicopter as he offered him the radio microphone. "They want to ask you a few questions about it."

Hiding a grimace, Fukuda took the microphone. "This is First Officer Fukuda," he said. "How may I help you?"

"Two days ago your ship had a close approach with a ship about three hundred kilometers north of Midway Island," a brisk military voice came over the thudding of rotors in the background.

"Yes, we did," Fukuda said. "It was a U.S. Navy utility landing craft."

"Navy," the voice said, the tone half statement, half question. "Not a private craft?"

"The captain identified himself as a Naval officer," Fukuda said. "And the LCU had the number 1618 across its bow."

There was a brief silence. "Tell us about the incident."

"There's little to tell," Fukuda said. "I observed it was unmoving and wondered if it might be in trouble. On closer observation, I noticed the signs of a drift net alongside it. Knowing what that can do to a screw, I ordered us closer and radioed to see if they needed assistance."

"Did they?"

"No," Fukuda said. "I was informed they hadn't run the screws recently, and that they furthermore had diving equipment that would enable them to clear away the net before it could cause damage. With those assurances, I resumed course and left."

"Did they say why they were just sitting there?"

"The captain said they were doing oceanic research."

"How close did you get?"

Fukuda thought back. "No nearer than half a kilometer. I couldn't determine the full extent of the net and didn't wish to snarl our own screws."

"Is there anyone else aboard who can confirm that distance?"

Fukuda gazed out at the lights, the hairs on the back of his neck starting to tingle. What was going on here, anyway? Some kind of smuggling case? "Mr. Hamaguchi was on duty in the wheelhouse," he said slowly. "I also remember noticing at least two other crewmen on deck, though I would have to make an inquiry to find out which ones. Shall I have the rest of the crew awakened?"

There was another pause. "Maybe later," the voice said. "What exactly did you see in the water beside the yacht?"

Fukuda frowned. "I told you: a section of a drift net."

"Describe it."

Fukuda waved a hand helplessly. "A section of a drift net," he repeated. "It was a faint contour in the water that was clearly not a function of waves or wake or shadow."

"Were there any buoys?"

"Not that I saw, no."

"But you *are* sure it was a drift net?"

"Of course," Fukuda said, some heat creeping into his voice. This was getting ridiculous. "What else could it be?"

His answer was silence. "Have you any other questions?" Captain Uematsu asked into the pause.

"Not right now," the pilot said. "We'll let you know if we need anything more. Thank you for your cooperation."

And with that, the helicopter banked sharply away and headed back toward the south. "*Shimizu Nakama* out," Fukuda murmured, gazing at the receding lights as he set down the microphone. "What do you make of that?" he asked.

Captain Uematsu snorted. "With Americans," he said, "who can tell?"

~

Cohn tapped off his office speakerphone, breaking the satellite link to the helo. "Ball's in your court, Swenson," he invited. "What else could it have been?"

"I don't know," she said, poring over the keyboard of Cohn's computer, flashing through satellite photos too quickly for McPherson's eyes to follow. The view made him slightly dizzy, and he shifted his gaze to her fingers. "I'm trying to find a good view."

"No chance of a closer look at the Shimizu Nakama, I suppose," McPherson said.

"None," Cohn said flatly. "At least not while it's in the middle of nowhere. We were lucky to get Vaughn to even agree to a flyby, and if the *Decatur* hadn't been in helo range we wouldn't even have gotten that. Everything we've got in the eastern Pacific is moving into position along the U.S. coast."

"Here we go," Swenson announced, her fingers coming to a halt. "This should be our best angle. Let's see . . . "

Her fingers began to move again, slowly and deliberately now, and the image on the screen began to change, sometimes subtly, sometimes dramatically. "I'm trying different mixes of IR and visible light," she explained as she shuffled through the options. "Also trying various contrasts and enhancements."

"What did you find out about the freighter itself, Frank?" Cohn asked.

McPherson shrugged, watching the screen as the image did its complex optical dance. "I talked with the owners, and that's exactly where the *Shimizu Nakama* is supposed to be. Fukuda, Uematsu, and that other crewman Fukuda mentioned, Hamaguchi, are all listed on the crew register. Looks clean."

"Which means this is probably just another snipe hunt," Cohn said sourly.

McPherson didn't answer. Considering the executive order they were all supposed to be working under, it was not only a snipe hunt, but a snipe hunt being run on extremely thin ice. Vaughn had asked some pointed questions as to how all this related to the Israel search, and if Duvall found out they were diverting resources there would be hell to pay.

"There," Swenson said suddenly.

McPherson blinked away the gloomy thoughts and focused on the monitor. "Where?"

"That outline," she said, tracing a squarish shape on the photo with the end of a pencil. "Roughly rectangular."

"I'll be damned," Cohn said, leaning over Swenson's shoulder. "You see it, Frank?"

"I think so," McPherson said, his brain trying to resolve the faint dots and line segments into a coherent shape. "Doesn't look like a drift net to me."

"It's not," Cohn said tightly. "It's a fuel bladder. Thirty to forty thousand gallon capacity, looks like."

"What's a fuel bladder?" McPherson asked, frowning.

"A sort of do-it-yourself gas station," Cohn said. "You can drop them in the ocean from a ship, submarine, or even a cargo plane. They just float there, usually slightly submerged, until you need them."

"Okay, right—I remember hearing about them now," McPherson said. "So our disguised catamaran's been refueling?"

"Definitely," Swenson said, tapping the screen again. "See right here, coming up the side? That's a fuel line connected to the bladder."

"Yes," McPherson said, gazing at the photo. For the first time in days, or so it seemed, his mind was actually starting to function. "Which means the nuke's still aboard."

"Or else they transferred it to the *Shimizu Nakama*," Cohn reminded him. "Or to some other ship Swenson hasn't found yet."

"No," McPherson said. "A fuel bladder means the LCU is definitely involved—that's now a given. The only question is where the freighter fits in. If it's an innocent passerby, then Fukuda is telling the truth about the encounter, and they're in the clear."

"And if it's not so innocent?"

"Then either it picked up the nuke from the yacht or it didn't," McPherson said. "If it did, then Fukuda's job should have been to focus our attention on the LCU so that we would leave him alone to bring the weapon into port. Conversely, if Fukuda *doesn't* have it, he should have tried to draw our suspicions to himself."

"But he did neither," Swenson murmured thoughtfully.

"And either would have been dead easy to do," McPherson said. "Was this photo from one of the usual satellites or a retasked one?"

"I think one of the retasked ones," Swenson said, pulling up the tag. "Yes, it was."

"Then they couldn't know we'd have this shot," McPherson said. "So let's assume my logic is correct and find that LCU. Hanna?"

"At the time of the refueling it was headed more or less toward Eureka, in northern California," Swenson said, closing down the photo and pulling up a map of the Pacific with various great circle routes marked on it. "This one right here," she said, pointing to it.

"Can you find it?" McPherson asked. "Bearing in mind it has at least three configurations that we know about."

"I can find it." Swenson looked up at McPherson. "The question is whether I can find it fast enough. It made better time to that fuel bladder than it should have, which means its top speed is higher than even a standard racing cat is supposed to have."

"How much faster?" Cohn asked. "Could it already be through the Navy's cordon?"

"It could," Swenson agreed soberly. "Especially now that we know it can masquerade as a Navy ship. It's entirely possible that it could make landfall sometime this morning."

McPherson glanced at his watch, did a quick calculation. "About an hour to dawn on the West Coast," he muttered. "Perfect time to come ashore. Any idea what the weather is like out there?"

"I can check," Cohn said. "You planning to call the Coast Guard?"

"And the Navy, and the Air Force, and all three West Coast National Guards," McPherson said, sliding off the corner of the desk where he'd been sitting. "The minute that thing hits territorial waters, I want it stopped."

"I hope you realize the trouble you're opening us up to," Cohn warned. "Everyone you're talking about sending after the cat is already busy either with the cordon or the Harrier hunt. If the yacht is a feint, Whitcomb is going to skin us alive."

"It's not a feint," McPherson said grimly. "A feint would be taking over the *Rabah Jamila*, scattering red herrings, then heading east for a nice quiet cruise to Hawaii. There'd be no need for them to go farther than that, especially since they should have guessed that by now we'd have picked up on Syed's alleged connection with Rabbi Salomon."

"Besides, if it was a feint, Fukuda would definitely have tried to make us suspicious," Swenson added. "Suspicious of both him and the LCU."

"And if the *Shimizu Nakama* isn't involved?" Cohn countered.

"Then the LCU crew themselves should have tried to look more suspicious," Swenson said.

"Exactly." McPherson gestured toward the computer. "You saw the size of that fuel bladder. No mistake—they're making for the mainland."

"I'll get the weather report," Cohn said quietly, moving toward the door. "After that, I think I'll make some calls of my own."

"I'll go with you," McPherson said, following him. "Swenson, you stay here. Find us that cat."

~

Dawn had arrived, and off in the eastern sky the sun had risen over the Coast Ranges.

Theoretically, anyway, Jason Flanders thought as he sipped at his coffee in the North Bend, Oregon, Coast Guard station and gazed out at the flat gray clouds that stretched across the sky from horizon to horizon. A typical coastal January morning, except that the rain had turned to a gentle mist instead of still pouring down in buckets. In a couple of hours the clouds would probably blow away, there would be a couple of hours of nice weather, and then the next batch of clouds would roll in and rain on them again.

It was, in short, lousy weather for hunting missing planes. He wondered if the thieves had taken that into account when they'd planned this job. Probably.

But lousy weather or not, pitiful visibility or not, he had his orders. Ten more minutes, and he and the new Marine spotter they'd saddled him with would be heading up in his HH-65.

"Flanders?" a familiar voice called from the door.

Speak of the devil. "Be with you in a minute, Feldman," Flanders said, taking another sip of his coffee and pointedly not looking in the other's direction. Gung-ho at seven-thirty in the morning was very hard to take, especially when Flanders himself had been up at five looking over maps and weather reports and checking out his bird.

Sergeant Feldman didn't take the hint. In the twenty-four hours of their association thus far, Sergeant Feldman had never yet taken a hint. "I've got our search assignment," he said, his brisk footsteps accompanied by the sound of crackling map paper. "It's up in the hills between Hood Mountain and Bingham Mountain, just north of Powers."

"Yes, I've looked at the map," Flanders said as the other sat down beside him.

"You know the area?"

"We don't get much call for air-sea rescues twenty miles inland," Flanders told him. "But as it happens, yes, I know the area."

"Good," Feldman said. "Then let's go."

Flanders gestured toward the alleged sunrise. "I also know that with weather like this on the coast, Powers is probably going to be socked in with mist and low clouds for the next hour or more."

"So you're saying there's no point in obeying our orders?" Feldman asked coldly.

"I'm saying there's no point in rushing madly off into the wild blue," Flanders said patiently. "You take another look at the maps and let me finish my coffee, all right?"

"The colonel said we were to be in the air by oh-seven-thirty," Feldman insisted, dropping his hand to his waist and tapping the grip of his holstered sidearm with the backs of his fingers.

It was about as silly and unsubtle a threat as Flanders had ever seen, and he was half inclined to laugh in Feldman's face just to see what would happen.

But he restrained himself. He and his Coast Guard buddies might believe the Harriers were long gone, buried at sea or bundled up on a flatbed and rolled out of the state, but the Marines were still deadly serious about this search.

And for all he might also think that the name *jarhead* was a perfect description, insulting one to his face was probably not the smartest way to start off a rainy morning. "Fine," he said instead, draining his cup and standing up. He tossed the cup in the trash and turned toward the door.

He paused, peering through the mist-fogged window. A car was just pulling in through the front gate, heading toward the waiting HH-65s. He squinted, trying to see if it had a government license plate, but there was too much glare from the headlights.

Feldman was obviously thinking along the same lines. "If that's Major Donnerman wondering why we're still here," he warned, "it's your butt, not mine."

"Isn't it always?" Flanders muttered.

"What was that?"

"Never mind," Flanders said. Another fine way, he thought glumly, to start a rainy morning.

Pulling his cap low over his eyes, Feldman dogging at his heels, he headed out to meet the visitor.

~

With the perversity Swenson should have expected by now, the cat was no longer headed towards Eureka.

Her fingers stuttered across the computer keys, over to the mouse, back to the keys, pulling up photo after photo, switching between visible and infrared as she tried to pierce the stubborn winter clouds. But it was no use. Somewhere a few hours after its encounter with the *Shimizu Nakama*, the cat had changed course.

"Take it easy," a voice said quietly.

She looked up in surprise. She hadn't even realized that McPherson had come back into the room. "I've lost them," she said, the words hurting her throat.

"I know," McPherson said. "It's all right. You'll find them again. You've done it before."

Swenson shook her head, frustration curling her fingers into fists. "It's different this time. I don't have the whole ocean to play with anymore."

"All the more reason to take it easy," McPherson said. "You know how these people think. Take a deep breath, focus your mind, and tell me where they're *likely* to have gone."

Swenson turned back to the computer, the unexpectedness of McPherson's calm pep talk stilling the majority of the butterflies circling her stomach. Offhand, she couldn't remember the FBI Director ever acting so fatherly toward his subordinates.

He was right. She *did* know how these people thought. Or she certainly ought to by now.

So how exactly were they thinking this time?

"North," she said slowly, her fingers starting to move on the keyboard again. "They want a quiet place to land, which means avoiding everything from San Francisco south. So they'll have veered north."

McPherson said something else encouraging sounding, but she didn't really hear it. The most likely tracks north were between Eureka and the Colombia River . . .

She didn't know how long she worked. The clouds on the tracks north of Eureka were as bad as they were on the more southerly ones, and it was a matter of painstakingly sifting through the photos and seeing what she could see. The most recent predawn shots were useless, with clouds covering virtually the entire northwest coast. But if she could get something from a few hours ago, maybe on infrared . . .

And then, with dramatic suddenness, she had them.

"There," she said, jabbing a finger on the screen. Jabbing a little too hard, in fact, the impact sending a sharp twinge of pain up her fingernail. She barely noticed. "This infrared engine signature. We've got two clear photos from the same pass, and this thing is going way too fast for anything but a hydroplane or a racing cat. It has to be them."

"How fast *is* it going?" Cohn demanded from her other side.

Swenson hadn't heard him come in, either. "Hang on," she said, checking the scale and doing a quick calculation. "Good God—it's hauling a hundred knots."

"Destination?" McPherson asked, punching a number into his phone.

"Unless they've changed course again, the southern Oregon coast," she said, pulling up a detail map and running an extrapolation. "Somewhere between Humbug Mountain and Cape Blanco. Possibly Port Orford."

Cohn was punching numbers into his desk phone. "ETA?"

Swenson swallowed. "Twenty minutes," she said. "Maybe less."

"In that case," McPherson said tightly, "we'd better hurry."

~

The car pulled up near the HH-65s and rolled to a stop. Flanders picked up his pace a bit, reaching it just as the driver and passenger stepped out. Feldman had been right to be worried, he saw with a sinking feeling; both newcomers were in uniform, the passenger wearing the eagles of a full colonel and carrying a large briefcase. "I'm Lieutenant Flanders, sir," he identified himself as they turned his direction. "May I help you?"

"Colonel Kalil," the officer replied. His voice was rich and deep, the voice of a man used to being obeyed without question. "Either of these helos ready to fly?"

"This one is, sir," Flanders said, frowning. Kalil. Why did that name sound familiar? "The other can be ready in a few minutes."

"Good," Kalil said briskly. "There's an emergency, and I need to commandeer it. You'll give my pilot the necessary clearance."

"Yes, sir," Flanders said, trying to blink the mist out of his eyes. There was an odd sort of stiffness to the colonel's face. "I'll need some authorization."

"Are you deaf, Lieutenant?" Kalil demanded, his voice raising in volume and lowering in pitch. "I told you this is an emergency. We don't have time for paperwork."

"Lieutenant?" someone called from behind Flanders.

Flanders turned around. Seaman Randolph was running toward them across the pavement, a piece of paper clutched in his hand. "Or perhaps the paperwork has already arrived," Kalil added.

Randolph splashed his way to a halt beside Flanders and Feldman. "Priority orders from D.C., sir," he panted, thrusting the paper into

Flanders's hand. "You're to fly to Cape Blanco to try and intercept an incoming ship that—"

He broke off, his suddenly wide eyes focused on something behind the others. Frowning, Flanders turned back toward Kalil.

To find himself staring down the muzzles of two handguns.

And with that, the name finally clicked. "Oh, hell," he breathed. "Kalil."

"Correct," Kalil said evenly. The earlier dramatics had vanished from his voice, leaving something cold and flat in their place. "There's no need for any of you to die this morning. You—Marine—take out your sidearm with the forefinger and thumb of your left hand and lay it on the ground."

"You want my weapon?" Feldman snarled. "Come get it yourself."

Kalil's eyes flicked to Flanders. "Lieutenant Flanders, remove his gun," he said. If he was angry or even annoyed by Feldman's defiance it didn't show. "Carefully."

Swallowing, Flanders stepped around behind Feldman to his right side and gingerly reached his left hand into the Marine's holster. He could feel Feldman trembling with anger and pumping adrenaline as he eased the Beretta out, making sure to hold it with forefinger and thumb as ordered. He took another half step forward and started to lean over in preparation for laying the weapon on the pavement.

And with a convulsive jerk, Feldman snatched the gun away from him.

There was nothing Flanders could do. But in that terrible fraction of a second he tried desperately to do something. His reactions were too slow to twitch the gun out of Feldman's reach, his two-fingered grip too weak to hold onto the weapon. He swung for the Marine's gun arm, trying to push it aside, realizing even as he did so that if Kalil and his man had hair-trigger reflexes knocking Feldman's gun aside would condemn the Marine to death without even the chance of taking one of the enemy with him. But even that point turned moot as Feldman dropped to one knee, out of Flanders's flailing reach, and lifted the gun toward Kalil.

The shot came from behind Flanders; and it was so quiet and unremarkable that for the first half heartbeat he wasn't even sure it had been a shot. Feldman jerked forward, his gun snapping up as his back and chest erupted in blood. Beside Flanders, Randolph yelped, a high-pitched sound that was well on its way to becoming a scream before he abruptly choked it off. Feldman pitched forward onto the ground and lay still, his gun clattering from his fingers, his blood mixing with the shallow pools of water.

For a long moment no one moved. Then, feeling like a man in the middle of a nightmare, Flanders turned slowly and looked behind him. His eyes flicked across the landscape, searching for the sniper.

There he was, lying in the mud and shadows beneath a delivery van parked on the street outside the station. His suppressed rifle was still pointed at the little knot of people.

Flanders turned back around. Kalil was watching him, his own face expressionless above his gun. "I warned him," he reminded Flanders quietly.

"A suppressed gun," Flanders heard himself say. The words sounded distant in his ears.

"There's no need to wake up the whole neighborhood," Kalil pointed out.

It was as if someone had flipped a switch. Suddenly, the haze of shock clouding Flanders's mind was gone, flash-burned to ash by the sudden burst of anger over the sheer uncaring callousness of that remark. A man had just *died* here, shot down in cold blood—

He clamped down hard on the fire. "What do you want?"

"I told you," Kalil said. "Your helo."

"Take it," Flanders said. "Choke on it."

Kalil nodded in an abbreviated bow, and without another word brushed past Flanders and Randolph and headed for the helo. His companion was more cautious, walking sideways as he followed, his eyes and gun trained on the two Coast Guardsmen. A waste of effort, Flanders thought with contempt, so long as the sniper still had them in his sights.

"What do we do now?" Randolph asked, his voice trembling almost too much for Flanders to understand.

"We wait," Flanders said, his anger growing hotter as he watched the two hijackers disappear into his helo. "We wait until they're gone."

"Wh—what then?"

Flanders didn't answer. The blades began to spin, the engine revving up and down as the pilot checked the systems. Then, with the smooth touch of someone who knew what he was doing, the HH-65 lifted off the pavement. Twenty feet up it paused and rotated southwest. Then, with its nose dipping toward the ground, it headed toward the open sea.

Flanders was on his knees a second later, kneeling in the bloody water beside Feldman as he checked for a pulse. But he didn't expect to find one, and he was right. He threw a smoldering glance toward the sniper, only to find that sometime in the past thirty seconds both the gunman and the van had gone. Tracking down the street, he caught just a glimpse of the vehicle as it disappeared around a curve.

"Call the cops," he ordered Randolph, getting back to his feet, the wet trouser legs sticking unpleasantly to his shins. "Give them a description of that van, and warn them the guy inside is armed and dangerous. Then get on the horn to Command and tell them the same guys who stole the Harriers now have a Coast Guard helo."

Without waiting for an answer, he sprinted toward the second helo. "Wait a second," Randolph shouted after him. "What about you?"

"That's my helo," Flanders shouted back, the anger burning white hot now. A dangerous condition to make important decisions in, but at the moment he didn't give a damn. "I'm going to get it back."

30

TEN MINUTES LATER, Flanders was in the air.

The other HH-65, twelve minutes ahead of him, wasn't visible through the mist and low clouds. But Flanders knew that lead wouldn't last. If Kalil was headed for the incoming ship Randolph had mentioned—and he couldn't believe there wasn't a connection between the two events—they would eventually have to slow down. And then he would have them.

He was passing Cape Arago when the radio crackled to life. "Lieutenant Flanders, this is Colonel Belford," the Marine search coordinator said into his headset. Still growling; but at least this morning he had something real to growl about. "What's your status?"

"Passing Cape Arago heading southwest," Flanders reported. "In pursuit, I believe, of the people who took your Harriers."

"So I understand," Belford grunted. "You have visual on them?"

"Not yet, sir," Flanders said, scanning the horizon. "But it's damn hard to hide in Coast Guard orange. I'll find them."

"When you do, watch yourself," Belford warned. "They won't take kindly to being followed."

"Understood, sir. I trust there's backup on its way?"

"You've got enough backup coming to start a war and win it," Belford said darkly. "There are fighters and helos scrambling from Portland, Seattle, San Francisco, and two offshore carriers. The Portland group should be about four minutes behind you—"

"Hold it," Flanders cut him off sharply. Was that a flicker of orange ahead?

It was. "Got 'em," he said, lowering the helo's nose and increasing his speed. "About a mile offshore, maybe three miles north of the Coquille River mouth."

"Is there a boat there with them?" a new voice cut in.

"Checking, sir." Flanders peered through the mist. There was indeed something else out there. Just a little closer . . . "Yes, sir, there is," he announced. "It's—damn, it's a Navy boat. Cyclone-class Patrol Coastal, I think."

"The *Squall*?"

"Uh—" Flanders peered harder. "Could be. I can't make out the full name, but it does start with an S."

"That's it," a new voice said grimly. "We've just learned that a ship masquerading as *Squall* penetrated the cordon about an hour ago. What are they doing?"

"The helo's hovering over the stern," Flanders said. "Correction: it's landed on the stern."

Someone swore. "All right, Lieutenant, here's the situation," the new voice said. "This is General Eldridge Vaughn, JCS Intelligence Coordinator. There's a high probability that a stolen nuclear weapon is aboard that ship. Under no circumstances do we want it getting *off* the ship. Do you understand?"

Something cold splashed across the heat of Flanders's rage. "Yes, sir."

"Backup will be there in three and a half minutes," Vaughn continued. "You need to keep that helo buttoned up until then. Can you do it?"

"Yes, sir." Flanders said. "In fact, maybe I can button them up permanently."

"What are you going to do?" Colonel Belford asked.

"I'm going to sit on it," Flanders told him, pulling for a little more altitude. "Trade my landing gear for his blades. If I can get above him, they won't even be able to shoot at me without taking out their own helo."

"Do it," Vaughn said. "But watch yourself."

"Yes, sir," Flanders murmured. The ship and HH-65 were dead ahead now, no more than a mile away. Another minute and he'd be in position on top of them.

He didn't get that minute. He got maybe five seconds before the world suddenly exploded in sound and fury and chaos and wind.

And as his helo spun and tipped crazily toward the ocean two hundred feet below, he found himself fighting for his life.

"Flanders?" someone shouted in his ear. "Flanders!"

Flanders didn't answer, his full attention on the battle to bring his bucking helo under control. He had nearly succeeded when a second hurricane blast again sent him spinning and sliding toward the water.

But this time, at least, he got a glimpse of the source of the attack. Even as he renewed his battle for stability, a jet fighter flashed past overhead, its backwash shaking the helo like a child's rag doll.

"Flanders!"

"I've found your missing Harriers," Flanders managed as the shoreline spun past dizzyingly in the distance. "I can't get near the ship—the Harriers are trying to splash me."

"Hang on, Flanders," Vaughn said. "Three more minutes."

"Yes, sir," Flanders said between clenched teeth. He'd regained some measure of control now, or at least was flying more or less level. The shoreline was directly ahead, which meant he'd been turned completely around. Putting the HH-65 into a wide circle, he started back.

The other helo was still sitting on the ship's stern three hundred yards away. Between it and him, just settling into hover mode like a pair of angry eagles guarding their nest, were the Harriers.

For a moment he stared at them in fascination and dread. He'd never seen Harriers in action except in movies, and had always subconsciously believed that half of what they could supposedly do was the result of cinematic special effects.

But this was real, and those planes were indeed hovering like seagulls riding an ocean wind. The blast from their engines churned the air beneath them into a swirl of heat haze, reducing Flanders's view of the ship and helo behind them to a smudge of orange against a smudge of white and gray.

And while there might indeed be enough firepower on its way to start a war, for the moment the only force the United States had on the scene was him.

He took a deep breath. This was no longer merely futile. It was suicidal. But he was a military man, and he'd sworn a military oath. And this most definitely came under the category of enemies foreign or domestic. Visually picking out a slot beneath the Harriers, knowing full well they would never let him get anywhere near that close, he got a grip on his throttle.

Without warning, the plane on his right abruptly broke from formation, shifting from hover to full flight as it veered sharply off toward the north. "What the hell?" he muttered.

"What?" Belford demanded.

"One Harrier away," Flanders said. "Heading—" he craned his neck "—northeast, looks like. Repeat: one Harrier heading northeast. Going like a scalded bat."

"On its way to intercept the National Guard F-15s," Vaughn said. "Guard Wing Commander, you copy that?"

"Yes, sir," another voice put in. "Is it still below the clouds?"

"Yes, but it's climbing," Flanders said.

"Okay," the commander's voice came. "We're on it."

"What about the other one?" Belford asked.

The second Harrier was still holding position between him and the splotch of orange and gray. "It's drawing a line in the sand," he told the colonel.

"The helo?"

"Still on the ship," Flanders said, peering ahead. "I can't see what they're doing. Best guess is that they're transferring the weapon. Orders?"

"Hold position and wait for the cavalry. And let us know if the helo takes off."

~

"Bandit helo sighted offshore near Coquille River," Ground Control's voice came through Captain Jack Galway's helmet, the words filtered through the roar of the engines shoving his F-15 through the air at full thrust. "Be advised that a second HH-65 is also on the scene."

Galway grimaced. Leave it to those Coast Guard weenies to make a tricky situation trickier. Now, instead of just splashing anything that moved that was orange, his National Guard task force would have to figure out which of the helos was the right target. "Acknowledged," he said, looking down at the rippled mat of sunlit clouds below and trying to calculate the proper moment to drop his planes through them onto the deck. They were still a good three minutes away from the target zone, but with the enemy below the clouds and sitting so close to the ground that even their pulse-Doppler radar was iffy, they were effectively flying into the situation blind. Not a good position to be in.

There was a click as Ground Control patched in a new frequency. "—northeast, looks like," an unfamiliar voice said nervously. "Repeat: one Harrier heading northeast. Going like a scalded bat."

"On its way to intercept the National Guard F-15s," the Pentagon general on the line—Vaughn—put in. "Guard Wing Commander, you copy that?"

"Yes, sir," Galway said. "Is it still below the clouds?"

"Yes, but it's climbing."

"Okay," Galway said. "We're on it."

He clicked back to group frequency. "All right, gentlemen, put 'em on the deck and get ready for company." Without waiting for a response, he started down into the clouds.

"Picking up a spike," one of the others said suddenly. "What the hell? Sir, incoming Harrier pilot has ejected. Repeat, pilot has punched out."

"*What*?" Galway threw a glance at his own instruments as he dropped through the bottom of the cloud layer into clear air again. "Ground, can you confirm?"

"Confirmed," Ground Control said, sounding as bewildered as Galway felt. "We have a visual from the North Bend airport. Pilot has ejected approximately four miles north of the Coos River. Bandit Harrier continuing on heading zero-thirty, presumably on heading hold system."

Galway stared out his canopy, the underbelly of the cloud layer rolling past just over his head. Sudden engine trouble? Or did the bandit just not have the stomach for a fight with anything better equipped than a Coast Guard helo? Or was this a feint to draw off his group?

His radar beeped. "Got him," he reported, peering at the blip that had appeared on his head-up display. "Bandit Harrier should be on your scopes."

"Confirmed," Ground Control acknowledged.

"We have visual," Galway added. There it was, coming their direction and still climbing. No engine trouble that he could see. In fact, the damn thing was running full throttle. A second later it disappeared up into the cloud layer. "We've lost visual," he said, switching his attention back to the radar. The Harrier was still burning along toward them on its original heading. "Instructions?"

"Oh, hell," Belford said suddenly. "The thing's heading straight for Portland."

Galway's stomach twisted. "You think they're trying to splash it there?"

"What else?" Belford said. "General?"

Overhead, above the clouds, the runaway Harrier flashed past. "Instructions?" Galway repeated urgently.

"Take it down," Vaughn ordered.

"You heard the man," Ground Control confirmed.

"We're on it," Galway said, throwing the F-15 into a hard turn and kicking in his afterburners. If it was a feint, he thought blackly, it had worked like a charm. Someone else would now have to take care of the unfinished business on the coast. "Let's go, gentlemen."

~

"Guard group is veering off to splash northbound Harrier," Belford said. "Secondary backup now six minutes from your position. Repeat: six minutes and counting."

Terrific, Flanders thought blackly. "That's going to be about five minutes too long," he told the colonel bluntly. The ship was still being obscured by the Harrier's belly jets, but in the water beneath the plane Flanders could see the ripple pattern that meant the helo had increased power to its blades. "Bandit helo is preparing to lift."

"Can you stop it?" Belford asked.

"No, sir," Flanders said, his heart thudding in his throat. Even as he spoke, the splotch of orange began to move. "Helo's lifting now."

"And you can't get to it?"

It was probably just anger and frustration he was hearing in the colonel's voice, Flanders knew. God knew there was enough of both to go around. But out here alone, the only man standing between terrorists and the people he'd taken an oath to protect, all he could hear was accusation. "No, sir," he said. *All enemies, foreign and domestic . . .* "But I might be able to at least take out the Harrier. I doubt he'll be expecting me to ram him."

"Out of the question," General Vaughn said firmly. "Stand down."

Flanders took a deep breath. "Sir—"

"That's an order, Lieutenant," Vaughn said, his tone leaving no room for argument. "Get to shore and put down. Now."

The other helo had settled into place behind and a little to the right of the Harrier during the argument, both of them facing Flanders.

And with a mixture of relief and regret he realized that even if he now deliberately disobeyed Vaughn's order, it was too late to have even a chance of stopping them. "Yes, sir," he sighed. Twisting the stick, he turned around toward shore.

And as the land came into view, something caught his eye. Two somethings, in fact, shooting up from low-level concealment behind the coastal ridges and blistering the air behind them as they headed his direction.

"There you go, Flanders," General Vaughn said softly. "Surprise."

"Hello, General Kalil," a new voice snarled onto the frequency, a voice edged with bitterness and grim anticipation. "In case you're monitoring this frequency—and of course you are—this is Marine Captain Daniel MacMillan Hamilton. Remember me?"

~

Hamilton was sitting in the Roseburg Airport hangar that was operating as makeshift headquarters for the Marine investigation unit, glowering at yet another set of negative reports, when the scramble call came in. The team had two fully armed Harriers on hand, standing by against the day when they found the stolen jets, and he was in the cockpit of one of them practically before the echo of the alert had faded away into the hills.

By all rights he shouldn't have been there, of course. It wasn't his plane, he wasn't assigned to flight duty, and on top of that he was still under investigation for the loss of his own Harrier. But none of that mattered to him.

It didn't matter to Major Johnson, either. He took one look at Hamilton's expression and wordlessly pointed him to the fighter. The plane captain who'd preflighted the Harrier didn't even bother to look at his face.

With one of the group's other pilots, a Lieutenant Hofstetter, flying wingman beside him, he took off over the hills, heading for the coast at full throttle and not giving a tinker's damn whether they rattled the civilians below or not. With no military aircraft supposedly closer than Portland, this little wild card ought to come as an unpleasant surprise to Kalil and his men.

Major Johnson and General Vaughn knew it, too. Johnson had phoned in word of the Roseburg response instead of acknowledging the scramble via radio; and Vaughn, the old fox, had likewise made sure it stayed off the air.

The flight across the Coast Ranges was like a simulation exercise nightmare, except that it was real, with no reset available if he screwed up. The tree-covered hills loomed up in front of them, grabbing at his plane as he hugged the ground as closely as possible, not wanting Kalil's forward spotters to get even a glimpse of the incoming fighters until it was too late. He shot over small towns and smaller ranches, dodged between hills and through narrow river valleys, and more than once scraped the underside of his Harrier on the treetops. The early-morning Umpqua River Valley sunlight changed to fog, then to low clouds, a brief clearing, and then to low clouds again.

Almost before he expected it, he topped the last ridge and saw the Pacific Ocean stretching away before him. There, dead ahead, was the standoff between the Coast Guard HH-65 and the Harrier. *His* Harrier.

Smiling tightly, he flipped his radio switch. "Hello, General Kalil," he said. "In case you're monitoring this frequency—and of course you are—this is Marine Captain Daniel MacMillan Hamilton. Remember me?

"You have my plane. I want it back."

~

It was as unexpected a development as Flanders could have looked for, on a morning that had already seen far too many surprises crammed into the same shopping bag. Where this particular pair of fighters had come from, how Hamilton had come out of nowhere back onto the scene, and what had happened to Belford's damn six-minute-and-counting time-table he couldn't begin to guess. All he knew, or cared about, was that the incoming planes were a welcome addition to the game plan.

It was quickly evident that his surprise at Hamilton's appearance was shared by the pilot of the stolen Harrier. Flanders was able to swing his helo completely back around before the other even reacted, and when he did it was to shift abruptly from hover to full forward flight. With its vertical thrust platform knocked out from under it, the plane plunged toward the ocean for a few heartbeats before it built up sufficient forward momentum to regain adequate lift. Rising sharply, tracing out a half loop beneath Flanders's helo, it arced forward and upward to meet the oncoming attackers. The bandit helo's pilot, perhaps a bit faster on the uptake, was also in motion, buzzing past above Flanders's head and coming up behind the Harrier as it rose back to altitude, crowding in as close as he could without getting caught in the turbulence.

And as the two aircraft blurred over and under Flanders, clearing the area in front of him, he saw something he hadn't noticed until that moment.

The ship below was on the move.

"The ship's rabbiting," he reported, swinging his helo into pursuit. "Heading northwest at high speed."

"Northwest?" Belford asked. "Out to sea?"

"Yes, sir," Flanders confirmed, frowning. The ship was still picking up speed. A *lot* of speed. "It's pulling fifty knots and still accelerating. What kind of ship *is* this, anyway?"

"A disguised racing cat," Vaughn said. "Can you stay with it?"

"I can try," Flanders said, swinging in behind it and gunning his engine.

"Backup's on the way," Vaughn said. "Maintain visual as long as you can, but try to stay out of attack range."

"Yes, sir," Flanders said, putting the helo's nose down and giving it full throttle. There was no way they were going to get away from him. Not now. No way in hell.

~

The plan had been for Three to parachute from his Harrier as close to U.S. 101 as possible; and as Nine sped north along the highway he could see through his windshield that Three was following that plan to the letter.

So much so, in fact, that traffic was starting to snarl as the southbound line of morning commuters became aware of the parachute dropping from the sky and slowed to watch. Keeping one eye on his comrade and the other on the erratic traffic flow, Nine headed for the extrapolated drop point, wondering which of them would get there first.

Three won, but not by much. He was in the process of collapsing his chute when Nine did a quick and slightly reckless U-turn and pulled off the highway beside him. "You all right?" he asked, hitting the emergency flashers and hopping out to help.

"No problems," Three said, looking warily at the traffic driving slowly past them, the drivers rubbernecking for all they were worth. "You look a mess."

Nine looked down at the mud coating his coat and trousers. "I had to backstop the general from under the van," he explained. "I'll dump the coat before we get moving."

"Did everything work?"

"Our end did," Nine said as he started folding the far end of the chute. "So did yours, apparently."

"So far," Three said, looking warily at the passing traffic. "You realize that half these people are probably calling the authorities. We'll need to grab a new car."

"Don't worry," Nine assured him as he carried the folded chute toward the rear of his car. "The general has that covered. Come and see."

Three did so; and as he rounded the rear of the car his lip twitched in a wry smile. "Ah," he said. "Clever."

"Isn't it?" Nine agreed, gazing at the boldly hand-lettered SKYDIVER CHASE TEAM sign fastened to the back of the car as he fished out the trunk key. "You'll notice how it's accidentally slipped down just enough to obscure part of the license plate. We'll have plenty of time to get that new car."

They stuffed the chute into the trunk. Nine unfastened the sign and tossed it in on top of the mass of nylon, then pulled off his muddy coat and added it to the pile. They closed the trunk and got into the car, and as Nine waited for an opening in the traffic flow, Three ducked down and slipped on the bright red coat and blond woman's wig that had been waiting for him. A minute later, looking for all the world like a respectable couple heading in to work, they were driving sedately back toward town.

They were nearly to the bridge when they had to pull off onto the shoulder as four police cars blew past heading north, lights and sirens bellowing their determination.

Irreverently, Nine wondered how loudly they would bellow when they found their quarry gone.

~

The bandit Harrier dropped close to the ocean as if planning a suicide ditch; then, roaring back to power and altitude, it charged fangs-out toward the kill.

"That's right," Hamilton murmured. "Come to papa, you son of a bitch."

As if in reply, the plane opened up with its 25mm cannon, tracing a line toward its opponents. Hamilton twisted hard right as the cannon shells tore through the air past him, aware that Hofstetter was peeling left at the same time. "Bandit has opened fire," he reported, swinging around in a tight turn. "Authorization to return fire?"

"Does the bandit have missiles?" Vaughn asked.

"I didn't see any," Hamilton said. "He's opened fire with cannon only."

"He has no missiles," Hofstetter confirmed. "I got a clear look as he turned. Watch it, Boxcar; he's on your tail."

"Got it," Hamilton said, twisting his plane aside and checking his six. Another burst of cannon shells tore past his canopy, and he dropped toward the ground, waggling as he arced back up.

The maneuver was a waste of effort. The bandit had already abandoned the chase and returned to helo escort duty, both aircraft climbing into the clouds. Hamilton swung back into pursuit, Hofstetter coming back to formation beside him. They drove up through the clouds together into the sunlight. "Back on target," he announced, drifting a little to the side so that the bandits wouldn't be directly between him and the rising sun. "Understand cleared to engage?"

"Any chance you can lure them over uninhabited territory?" Vaughn asked.

"No need," Hofstetter reported. "They're on a heading of one-sixty, paralleling Highway 42. If they keep that course, they'll be over empty ground soon enough."

"If they keep that course, they'll wind up back at Roseburg," Hamilton pointed out. "Maybe they're trying to put the Harrier back where they found it."

"More likely drawing us into an ambush," Hofstetter countered. "You could put fifty guys with Stingers on those hills, and even without the clouds we'd never see them."

Hamilton glared at the fighter and helo ahead. Hofstetter was right. A sucker's ambush was definitely Kalil's style.

And having already lost one Harrier to thieves, he was damned if he'd lose another to a battery of surface-to-air missiles. "Then we'd better splash them first," he said. "General, I don't think we can wait for the territory to get any more uninhabited."

"Very well," Vaughn said reluctantly. "You're cleared to engage the Harrier. Repeat, you are cleared to engage the Harrier only."

"Take him down, Marines."

31

THE BANDIT WAS fast. But F-15s on afterburners were faster.

Even so, it was a hard chase, and the rogue Harrier was halfway to Portland before Galway's group caught up with it.

"Hostile Harrier in range," Galway reported, settling into position behind the runaway, fighting the buffeting of the other's slipstream. "Request permission to fire."

"Position?" Belford asked.

"Just west of Corvallis," Galway said, glancing out at the landscape below. "If we don't splash him soon, we'll be raining debris on downtown Salem."

"Understood," Belford growled. "You are cleared to engage; repeat, you are cleared to engage."

"Acknowledged," Galway said, flipping the master arm switch and arming one of his Sidewinders. "Good tone; Fox-2."

He pulled the trigger. The F-15 lurched slightly as the Sidewinder accelerated off the rail; and then the missile was sizzling through the air toward the Harrier. Galway glanced at his tracker, confirmed the missile was locked, and looked up again. The Sidewinder disappeared into the glare from the Harrier's engine—

With a brilliant flash, the Harrier's aft end blew up.

"Send that one back to the taxpayers," Galway muttered. "All right, gentlemen. Let's get back to the coast and see if that party's still on."

~

Six minutes later, precisely on Belford's six-minutes-and-counting timetable, the backup arrived at Flanders's side.

There were three of them, F-14s, flying in close formation. "Major Diefenback," a voice crackled in his ear. "I'm tally on the ship."

"Good," Belford said. "Flanders, stand down and return to base."

"With the colonel's permission, I'd like to stay," Flanders said. "You might need a helo on the scene."

"We have four helos on the way," Diefenback told him. "Sea Stallions, with twenty Marines on each, in case we need to board her. If the bandits decide they want to shoot it out, you'll be a sitting duck *and* in our way."

Flanders set his jaw firmly. "Colonel Belford?"

It was General Vaughn who answered. "Diefenback, what's ETA on those Sea Stallions?"

"Seventeen minutes, sir," Diefenback said.

"Flanders, what's your fuel status? Can you hold another seventeen minutes?"

"Yes, sir." Flanders glanced at the fuel gauge and did a quick calculation. "I can probably cover another hour."

"You can stay until the Sea Stallions arrive," Vaughn said. "But keep well back. If the ship starts shooting, you get clear. Diefenback's right about you being a sitting duck, and with this group you never know what to expect."

"Yes, sir," Flanders said.

Three seconds later, the ship blew up.

Instinctively, Flanders twisted the HH-65 away, wincing as debris rained past him. In his ears Diefenback and the other pilots gasped or snapped orders or swore. "Diefenback!" Vaughn's voice shouted over the confusion. "What the *hell*—?"

"Ship's self-destructed, General," Diefenback said, sounding stunned. "Scattered itself all over the Pacific."

"Engine or fuel tank explosion?" Belford asked.

"No idea," Diefenback said.

"I don't think it was either, sir," Flanders said. "I've seen both scenarios, and the blasts are always more localized than this. The whole ship must have been rigged."

"What about debris?" Vaughn asked. "Any bodies?"

"I don't know," Flanders said. "Permission to move in closer?"

"Go ahead," Vaughn said. "Diefenback, pull back and give him room."

The F-14s veered off, and Flanders eased his helo over the explosion site. Most of the ship seemed to have gone straight to the bottom, but there were enough bits and pieces of floating flammables to keep some smoke going, which dispersed wildly under the blast from his blades. "I can see a few pieces of the hull," he reported. "Some interior equipment, a chair and what looks like part of a fold-up table. Boxes, including a bunch of food cartons. Probably empty, the way they're floating."

He frowned. "Lots of Styrofoam, too, and some big rubbery pieces that look like they came from a weather balloon. Parts of the mast, but the way it's been splintered it was either wired with its own set of explosives or else wasn't very strong to begin with."

"Probably the latter," Vaughn said.

"No sign of a sail," Flanders went on. "Life vests . . . one, two, three of them. All empty." He gave the scene another careful look. "No bodies."

"There have to be bodies," Diefenback protested. "Somebody was driving the damn thing."

"Or it was running on its own like the first Harrier," Belford growled.

"It does look that way, sir, yes," Flanders agreed.

"So where the hell are they?" Belford demanded. "There *were* people on that ship, weren't there?"

"Should have been at least three of them," Vaughn said. "Not to mention the two who stole the Coast Guard helo from North Bend."

"They must all be with the helo, then," Flanders said.

"So it would seem," Vaughn agreed grimly. "All units with or converging on the southbound bandits: be advised that we want that helo intact."

~

"Roger that, General," Hamilton growled an acknowledgment, twisting his plane around as the rogue Harrier shot overhead again, sending yet another blast of cannon fire raking across his fuselage. Damn the pilot, anyway.

And while he was at it, damn Vaughn and Belford and all the rest of the gas burners discussing their plans out in the open where any enemy with half a working ear could listen in. He and Hofstetter had hoped to take out the bandit's engine, with an eye toward bringing it down more or less in one piece and minimizing collateral damage to the landscape below.

But every time they'd tried to get into position to do so, the rogue had perversely broken from escort duty and swung back for a flailing pass at his pursuers. It was like a dog snapping at a pair of bobcats on his tail: not doing any real damage, but still managing to keep them back and off-balance.

Every time he did that he left the helo totally unprotected. That alone made it clear that he knew they were under orders not to splash it.

The helo's pilot knew it, too. He hadn't altered his heading or altitude since they left sight of the Pacific. Just tootling blissfully along like he was on vacation.

Well, that was about to change, Hamilton decided as he recovered from the bandit's latest lunge and swung back into position behind him. The Air Force backup coming up from San Francisco would be here in five more minutes. But this was Corps business, and it should be Corps planes and pilots that settled it. The landscape below would just have to take care of itself.

Besides, that was his plane out there. A man should be allowed to shoot his own dog.

Flipping the master arm switch, he armed one of his Sidewinders. The seeker growled confirmation of positive lock, and with a squeeze of the trigger the missile fired.

As it sputtered toward the bandit, the Harrier's canopy shattered and the pilot seat blasted upward.

"He's ejected," Hofstetter barked, the second word almost lost in the thunderclap as the Harrier flashed spectacularly into scrap and metallic dust. "Heading—where the hell's he heading? I've lost him in the sun."

"I've got him," Hamilton said, cutting into a sharp turn. "Going in for a closer look."

"Back away!" Belford ordered sharply. "We want him alive."

"I'm not crowding him," Hamilton assured them, changing his turn into a wide, lazy circle and dropping through the clouds. A moment later the pilot appeared as well, his chute deployed, heading for the curving thread of pavement below. "We're still over Highway 42," he reported. "Looks like he's aiming for the road."

"Ten to one he's got a ride waiting," Vaughn said.

"Probably," Belford agreed. "Boxcar, you see any likely candidates?"

"I don't see anyone sitting by the side of the road," Hamilton said, studying the area below. "If they're coming for him, they must not be here yet."

"No one could be waiting for him, anyway," Hofstetter pointed out. "They couldn't have known when Boxcar would fire and he'd have to eject."

"Don't underestimate these people," Vaughn warned. "They're smart and devious, and so far seem to know exactly what they're doing."

"Maybe this time they've outsmarted themselves," Hamilton said. "There isn't a lot of traffic down there. Even if he hops a car, there's no way they can lose themselves in a crowd." He studied the parachute a moment, gauging its trajectory. "Besides, he's not even going to make it to the road," he amended. "He'll hit about a hundred meters west and downhill to boot. Riptide and I should be able to put down and introduce him to the grass."

"It can't be that easy," Vaughn rumbled. "There's a catch here somewhere."

"What's the terrain like?" Belford asked. "Is there anywhere besides the road where he can run or hide?"

"There's a cluster of buildings on that side of the highway," Hamilton told them. "A junkyard or machine shop with storage sheds. He's coming down in the middle of open grassland to the west of it— shrubs and a few trees. There's some forest surrounding the area, with a river hemming him in on the west."

"Maybe he's hoping to take hostages from the junkyard," Belford suggested uneasily.

"So we don't let him get near it," Hamilton said impatiently. Sitting in a comfy chair out in Fort Fumble, you could speculate on all sorts of possible complications. But he was here, he was looking at the actual situation, and it really *was* that easy. "Riptide can chase the helo while I put down between him and the road. Unless he's got a Stinger in his boot, he's in the bag."

"You'd better be right about that," Belford said, a hint of menace in his voice.

"I am, sir," Hamilton said. "As I said, he's landing in the middle of—"

"Holy sh—" Hofstetter bit the word in half with an audible click of his teeth. "Boxcar, you'd better take a look at this."

"What is it?" Hamilton demanded, tightening down the back half of his circle and giving the sky a quick search for his wingman. But he and the helo were still on the wrong side of the clouds.

"There's no one in it," Hofstetter said, sounding completely floored. "The damn helo's flying by wire."

Hamilton blinked. "You're joking."

"Do I *sound* like I'm joking?" Hofstetter retorted. "There's a black box sitting where the pilot ought to be."

"Passengers?" Belford asked.

"There aren't any," Hofstetter insisted. "That's what I'm saying. It's a ghost ship."

"It can't be empty," Belford insisted, sounding as bewildered as Hofstetter. "The ship was empty. How can the helo be empty too? Where did they all go?"

"You still have eyes on yours, Boxcar?" Vaughn asked.

"Affirmative," Hamilton said. "Coming to ground now, about a hundred meters from the road."

"Watch him," Vaughn warned. "Riptide, stay on the helo."

Below him, Hamilton saw the parachute give the slight bounce that indicated the pilot had hit ground, followed by the unmistakable ripple as the fabric was released from the strain. "Pigeon is down."

And without warning, the collapsing chute abruptly disappeared into a roiling burst of smoke. "Smoke bomb!" he snapped, turning his Harrier around in a tight curve and angling toward the ground.

"Can you see him?" Belford snapped back.

"Negative," Hamilton said, biting back a more pungent retort. The smoke screen was a mass of whipped-cream color and nearly whipped-cream consistency, hugging the ground for all it was worth. It was already a good twenty meters across from north to south and still expanding, especially along its eastward edge as the westerly breeze pushed it toward the highway.

"Expansion mainly toward the highway," he reported, pointing the Harrier toward the open ground between the cloud and the strip of pavement. "I'm moving to cut him off."

"Riptide, get back and assist," Belford ordered. "Stay in high cover—we don't want him backtracking while Boxcar is watching the road. Boxcar, can you keep the smoke clear of the highway?"

"I'll try, sir," Hamilton said. Adjusting his nozzles, he eased into a hover over the edge of the cloud.

For a few seconds he thought it was going to work. The blast from his jets blew the smoke back and sideways, opening a hole straight through to the ground.

But the cloud was too big, and the Harrier's engine hadn't been designed with this maneuver in mind. He could clear out a given spot, but the rest of the smoke simply flowed both ways around the turbulence and continued its drift toward the highway. "Negative, sir, negative," he called. "Cloud's too big."

And then, just inside the leading edge of the drifting smoke directly ahead of him, a second cloud burst into existence.

"Second grenade!" Hamilton snapped, dropping his nose and trying to get to the rapidly expanding cloud.

But he was too late. The second cloud had already flowed out in all directions, and even as the Harrier headed toward it the smoke rolled across the highway.

And the rogue pilot had a completely enclosed corridor to the road.

"Blow it away," Belford ordered. "You hear me? Get it clear."

"Impossible, sir," Hamilton said between clenched teeth as he glided across the expanding cloud. Just as with the first one, he could clear out only a small portion at a time. "If he's headed this way, I can't stop him."

"Then block the traffic," Vaughn ordered. "Put down across the road to the south. Riptide, ditto to the north. If he's getting out, he's doing it on foot."

"Acknowledged," Hamilton said, shifting direction toward the road.

Though the traffic itself was already closing that escape route. On the northbound pair of lanes a log truck hit his brakes too quickly and jackknifed across that half of the road. Southbound, an eighteen-wheeler avoided a similar fate by not stopping at all, following an equally reckless panel truck through the smoke. The cars and pickups still outside the cloud squealed to a chaotic halt, creating an instant traffic jam in both directions.

Twenty seconds later, Hamilton preempted any further decisions by putting his Harrier down across the southbound lanes.

He popped his canopy and drew his Beretta, staring into the roiling smoke. No sign of anyone yet. "I'm down," he reported.

"Any sign of our pilot?"

"Not yet," Hamilton said, raising his voice over the noise as Hofstetter's Harrier settled into its own blocking position a hundred meters north. "Unless he was flat-out running, I doubt he could have made it this far by now. He's probably still inside the smoke."

"Or inside one of the buildings," Belford said. "What about the river? How far away is it?"

"Quarter to half a mile," Hamilton said. "The traffic seems to be stopped for now. Should I go back to blowing away his cover?"

"Stay put," Vaughn ordered. "I don't know what his plan is, but I already don't like it. Two of the Sea Stallions have been diverted your direction—they'll be there in three minutes, and they can do a quicker job of clearing the smoke. You two stand guard until they arrive, and make sure he doesn't get to a car."

"And stay *in* your planes," Belford added. "We sure as hell don't want him grabbing another Harrier."

Hamilton winced. "Yes, sir."

The minutes ticked by. Hamilton watched the area around him, occasionally revving his engine to blow the smoke away from his immediate vicinity, and listened to the various reports as they came filtering in. The first Harrier—what was left of it—had come down on farmland north of Corvallis, pre-plowing someone's field but otherwise not doing significant damage. Two Sea Stallions had joined the Coast Guard helo at the site of the ship explosion and were starting to collect debris. Still no bodies. Some Air Force whiz kid was walking the San Francisco squad through various high-tech contortions involving resonances and override codes, trying to find a way to take control of the runaway HH-65's autopilot and land it before it smashed itself into the next mountain in line. The search for the pilot who had ejected north of the Coos River was still coming up dry.

After what seemed more like three hours than three minutes, the two Sea Stallions that Vaughn had promised arrived.

They did a wide circle around the area first, confirming that no one in a flight suit was tearing across the wet grass making for the river or the woods. They landed long enough to discharge their complement of Marines, who spread out to completely encircle the cloud. With the Marines in place, and one of the helos hovering overhead with machine guns at the ready, the other flew back and forth across the smoke screen, methodically driving it away. A few minutes later, the pilot's hiding place had vanished into the damp air.

So had the pilot.

"What do you mean, he's not there?" Vaughn rumbled disbelievingly.

"I don't know what to say, General," Hamilton said, feeling sick as he watched two of the Marines gather up the vanished pilot's parachute and harness. His last forlorn hope, that the pilot had been hunkered down under his parachute like a four-year-old hiding from monsters, was now gone. "They've searched the buildings and every other place he could be hiding. He's not there, and no one saw him. He must have gotten out with the traffic before it stopped."

"How?" Vaughn demanded. "I thought you said nobody stopped inside the smoke screen."

"Nobody did, sir," Hamilton said. "He had to have jumped aboard something as it slowed down."

"You have any idea what kind of split-second timing you're talking about with a stunt like that?" Belford growled. "Who was flying that plane, anyway, Superman?"

Hamilton took a deep breath. "I'm sorry, sir," he said stiffly. "I take full responsibility for his escape."

Someone sighed, a long, snake-like hiss. "Are the police there yet?" Vaughn asked. To Hamilton's ears he no longer sounded furious, merely tired.

"Yes, sir," Hamilton said, shifting his attention to the police cars lined up along the shoulder beside the growing tangle of stalled cars and trucks, and the cadre of cops moving purposefully among the vehicles. "Some of them are heading in to search the buildings again, the rest are checking driver and passenger IDs. Why, I don't know."

"Because that's what they've been ordered to do," Belford snapped. He, on the other hand, *did* still sound furious. "Because maybe while you hotshots were busy staring at the smoke or your own navels the son of a bitch sneaked past you and strolled over to one of the waiting cars. Or did that possibility ever occur to you?"

Hamilton clamped his teeth together. "I don't believe it could have happened that way, sir."

"Well, we'll find out soon enough, won't we?" Belford growled. "There'll be an investigation team from Washington there this afternoon." His voice dropped ominously. "And if it turns out he sneaked around behind you, your heads are going to be decorating the Pentagon's flagpoles."

"The Marines will be putting up a cordon line to warn people away from the area," Vaughn said. "Make sure they enclose the whole region the smoke screen covered, including the relevant parts of the highway. The police will be closing off that section and detouring traffic around it."

"You two wait there until that's finished," Belford said. "Then go back to Roseburg and start working up your reports. And they'd better be good."

"Yes, sir," Hamilton murmured.

The radio went silent. With a sigh, Hamilton shifted his gaze from the cops to the other Harrier and the back of Hofstetter's head and then out into the field again. A field of open grassland from which a single man—a single man on foot, yet—had effortlessly evaded two highly trained Marine pilots and their super-powered AV-8B+ Harriers. It took an exceptional man, he decided glumly, to be able to feel like a complete ass twice in the same week.

Clearly, he was just such an exceptional man.

~

The Marines along Highway 42 had nearly finished laying out their poles and yellow tape, and the runaway Coast Guard HH-65 was less than five minutes away from a mountain looming in its path, when the Air Force whiz kid finally came up with the right combination of frequencies and internal codes to bypass the black box sitting in the helo's pilot seat. Triumphantly, he sent the lock-breaker code into the system via satellite, and took control of the helo.

The HH-65 showed its gratitude by blowing up.

~

The Marines set up their little yellow-taped picket fence around the landing site, then climbed back into their helos and flew off into the leaden sky. Disappearing toward the east, Four noted with interest, the direction where the borrowed Coast Guard helo should by now have either exploded or crashed. The two Harriers followed shortly thereafter, also heading east.

Behind them, the military left a small mob of local police with the task of clearing out the stalled traffic, posting the detour signs that would send future vehicles around the area, and explaining matters as best they could to the frightened or outraged populace. Eventually, they sorted everything out, and then they too pulled out, leaving a single squad car to stand guard over the crime scene.

Leaving Four with nothing to do but gaze out at the fluttering yellow tape that encircled him like a fool's paddock and wait for his ride.

He hoped it wouldn't be too long. True, others had had worse privations on this mission. There were Ten and Eleven, who'd ridden that Pakistani freighter inside oversized packing crates. There was Six, sitting motionless for two days in the Lees' living room. But most of the rest of the group were commandos, accustomed to such hardships. Reveling in it, even. Hotshot pilots like Four preferred a little more in the way of creature comforts.

At the moment he was about as creature uncomfortable as he cared to be. The ground was cold and wet, his flight suit had long since given up and let the chill through, and the hand-held launcher that had sent the second grenade shooting far away toward the highway, giving the illusion that he was moving that direction himself, was digging into his lower rib cage.

And while the Cloak stretched over him might be a miracle in its own right, it nevertheless had all the thermal properties of cheap newspaper. The only heat source besides his own body was the plastic-wrapped laptop lying on the ground beside his head, and it wasn't putting out very much.

Mentally, he shook his head. He'd watched with the others as the General tested the Cloaks; watched too as the Harriers he and Three had stolen from Captain Hamilton had vanished beneath the large Cloak in the middle of an empty beach. But it wasn't until this past hour that the true possibilities of this device had fully and finally hit home. Some of those Marines had passed within two meters of him as he lay quietly here in the open, a handful of paces from the spot where he'd parachuted to the ground. Yet not a single one of them had had the slightest notion that he was there. At times, in fact, as he'd listened in on bits and pieces of their frustrated speculations, it was all he could do to keep from laughing out loud.

For the first time, in a way he'd never really believed before, Four knew now that their mission could succeed. *Would* succeed.

He shivered. And not just from the cold.

~

The sky was clear of aircraft, and the ocean clear of ships, when the general and the rest of the group from the catamaran and helo waded ashore through the final set of breakers and arrived at the secluded beach where the stolen Harriers had sat for two days concealed from all those prying eyes.

Two, Six, and Seven were waiting for them. "That was quite a show," Two commented as he poured the general a steaming cup of tea from a vacuum bottle. "A shame you weren't in position to see it."

"That's all right," the general said, taking a careful sip of the tea. The trip had been longer and colder than he'd expected, and he was chilled to the bone. "All the really exciting parts happened a long ways away. Any news?"

"Everything seems to have gone according to plan," Two said, nodding back over his shoulder toward an otherwise unremarkable section of empty beach. By inference, that was where their two trucks and military monitoring gear were sitting, hidden beneath the large Cloak. "Three successfully ejected on target, and Nine got to him before the police did. They're in Coos Bay now, getting a new vehicle. Four also successfully ejected, into an ideal area as it turned out, and reported that he successfully evaded discovery. Nine and Three will be picking him up as soon as it's clear to move in."

"And the aircraft?"

"All shot down or self-destructed, according to the reports," Two said. "The Coast Guard helo spectacularly so, as did the ship."

"Excellent," the general said. "Particularly the news about Three. His was the part I was most concerned about."

"Changed plans always carry risks," Two agreed. "But things worked out despite the loss of the small Cloak."

The general looked across at Six. But if the other had heard he gave no sign. "Any other problems?"

"No problems, but one unexpected wrinkle," Two said. "Two Harriers were somewhere nearby when the scramble order was given. They were the planes that chased and ultimately shot down Four."

His eyebrows lifted slightly. "One of them was piloted by the same Captain Hamilton whose plane Four was flying."

"Odd," the general said, frowning.

"I thought so, too," Two said soberly. "I'm wondering if they might have been hidden just over the hills waiting for us to make our move. That might imply our opponents have anticipated us more accurately than they should have."

For a moment the general sipped his tea in silence, gazing out at the rolling gray waves as he turned that thought over in his mind. "If there was any anticipation it was minor or coincidental," he said. "The current lack of eyes on us shows they don't truly know what we're doing."

"I suppose," Two said. He didn't sound entirely convinced.

"But those eyes will return soon enough," the general said briskly. "We'd best pack the equipment and be on our way."

"Yes, sir," Two said. "Though I doubt anyone will be coming here any time soon."

"Sooner than you think," the general warned. "You didn't know, but Ten mentioned to a passing ship that they had diving gear aboard the catamaran. Eventually, our opponents will remember that and send people to all the beaches within swimming distance of our transfer point."

"I didn't know that." Two looked over at Ten, dragging a heavy scuba tank through the sand toward the hidden trucks. "That may not have been wise."

The general shrugged. "Perhaps," he agreed. "But it shouldn't cause any serious problems."

"Yes, sir," Two said, clearly not convinced on that point, either. "We can shut down the large Cloak and fold it as soon as everything else is inside. There should be enough room in the panel truck for it and your equipment both. That will free up the entire back of the pickup for the weapon."

"You made sure the shell is weatherproof?" the general asked, thinking back to his doubts about the shell-equipped truck the others had procured.

"Yes, sir," Two said. "It looks terrible, but it's perfectly watertight. We won't need to take any special precautions."

"Let's get to it, then," the general said. "There's still a long road ahead."

"But with a light waiting at the end of the tunnel," Two suggested.

The general looked across at Twelve and Thirteen as they carefully carried the nuclear weapon toward the cloaked trucks. All the deceptions and distractions were past, and only the future would tell whether they had accomplished their purpose. Now, all that lay before them was the mission itself. "Yes," he agreed quietly. "A very bright light indeed."

32

THE LOUNGE DOWN the hall from the satellite room had done a brisk business throughout most of the evening as the analysts and their supervisors dropped in for a cup of coffee, to compare notes or talk shop, or simply to give their eyes a chance to focus on something farther than two feet away. On the three occasions he'd stopped by, McPherson had noted that the men and women from the rival agencies had tended to clump together, the CIA people and their borrowed Bureau counterparts each sitting with their own kind.

Now, an hour past midnight, the analysts were all gone, either snatching a few hours of sleep or else simply too tired to leave their keyboards. Sitting alone in the dark, watching the snow falling outside the windows, McPherson found himself reflecting on that earlier observation. A good deal had been written and discussed over the years about the rivalries between the various branches of the military, but relatively little about the similar situation in the intelligence community. Possibly it was because the different agencies' spheres of responsibility didn't overlap as much, with less need for the daily cooperation required by the military, and consequently less official angst over the squabbling.

Or perhaps the angst was simply not being expressed, at least not at the top of the chain of command. Verbal breast-beating wasn't President Whitcomb's style. Perhaps that was the reason he'd instituted his Wednesday breakfast meetings, hoping that the informal atmosphere and truncated personnel list would limit the political jockeying that always seemed to lurk below the surface at full Security Council meetings.

Maybe it was working. True, the rank and file might choose to eat donuts at different tables, but back in the analysis room they were working together as efficiently as he'd ever seen. Certainly he and Cohn and

Vaughn were coordinating their activities and keeping the lines of communication open. Even Logan, for all his seeming inability to grasp the big picture sometimes, wasn't being nearly as contrary as DHS often seemed. It was, in short, a triumph of statesmanship over history, of logic over pride, of necessity over inertia.

It was too bad that none of this enlightenment and efficiency had done them a damn bit of good.

Across the room, the door opened. "Hello?" a voice called tentatively.

"Over here, Swenson," McPherson called to her. "Leave the lights off, please."

"There you are," she said, sounding almost accusing as she started across the room, the door swinging shut behind her. "Sorry. I would have been here sooner, but with the lights off I thought you'd gone."

"Just watching the snow," he told her, waving toward the window.

"Ah," she said, coming up to his conversation cluster, a collection of four chairs and two couches grouped around a low coffee table. McPherson had taken one of the couches; Swenson selected the chair to his right. "You know, I haven't been outside once since I got here Sunday."

"You're not missing anything," he assured her. "Any news?"

"Nothing you'll want to hear," she said. "Banderlaine and I have been over every scrap of data since the cat got to within fifty miles of the coast. If it stopped anywhere along the way to let off passengers, we can't find the spot."

McPherson grimaced. That had been his last hopeful guess as to how the cat's crew had pulled their vanishing act. "Could they have done it without stopping? Dropped a dinghy off the back, say, which then rowed or motored in?"

In the backwash of light coming through the windows he saw her shake her head. "Not a chance," she said. "For starters, there were no extra hot spots peeling off from the cat, which means either a very small motor or else oars the whole way in."

"It could happen," McPherson said stubbornly.

"No," she said. "For one thing, at fifty miles offshore it would have taken them forever to get here. For another, there isn't any dinghy I've ever heard of that could take to the water at a hundred knots without instantly capsizing or breaking up. Even with the relatively smooth surface conditions at the time."

"Maybe they slowed down," McPherson suggested. "Not a full stop, but slow enough to put the dinghy in the water, doing it between satellite passes so we wouldn't notice. They could then have bumped their speed up a few extra knots until the next pass so that the average speed between photos would stay the same."

"Doesn't work," Swenson said. "They presumably don't have a schedule for the retasked satellites, so they wouldn't know how to avoid them. More importantly, they were already doing their top speed on that last surge. They didn't have any extra knots left."

McPherson frowned. "That was a rather significant-sounding comment. Have you found out who they are?"

"Not who, but maybe what," she said. "I dug up some references to a big-time drug lord out in Southeast Asia who had a customized ocean-going gas turbine/water jet racing catamaran built a couple of years ago that could be gimmicked to look like an ordinary monohull yacht. It had some inflatable camouflage bladders around the hull edges, and could even raise and lower various sections of its superstructure and deck to give it a range of topside silhouettes. Sound familiar?"

"Very," McPherson said. "I don't suppose it also had a telescoping sailboat mast?"

"As a matter of fact, it did," Swenson confirmed. "Not strong enough to be functional, but it apparently looked like the real thing. The whole package was obscenely expensive, of course, but it must have come in handy when he was hauling contraband and the patrol boats pulled alongside."

"So now we've got drug involvement," McPherson growled. "Terrific."

"Actually, no," she said. "The full history's not clear—nothing from that part of the world is—but it looks like the patrol boats pulled alongside one time too many, and even with the quick-change super-structure the authorities got wise to the masquerade. The cat hasn't been seen in Asian waters for six months, and informed opinion is that the owner probably sold it off."

"To . . . ?"

"To person or persons unknown," Swenson said. "Apparently at a fire-sale price, too, considering what it cost to build. Still, it *is* a money trail, and that means we should eventually be able to run it down."

"Though probably not soon enough."

"Probably not," she conceded.

McPherson shook his head. "Hanna, make all of this make sense for me, will you? These people have an ocean-going cat. They have access to fuel bladders and can get them into the middle of the ocean, so they presumably can sail the cat straight across the Pacific all by itself. Right?"

"Sounds reasonable," she agreed.

"So why bother with that Pakistani freighter?"

Swenson shrugged. "Probably so they could scatter all those red herrings," she said. "The North Korean agent thing, the Chinese CitationJet—"

"Yes, I know the list," McPherson interrupted. "The question is *why*. Was it all a massive feint to keep our attention away from the Middle East, like Whitcomb believes? Or was it to keep us in the dark about who's behind it so that when the nuke goes off we won't know who to pound back to the Stone Age?"

"I'd guess the latter," Swenson said. "Though if it goes off in Jerusalem, we'll know who to blame."

"Will we?" McPherson countered. "How will we know if it was Rabbi Salomon or someone trying to discredit him?"

"Point," Swenson admitted. "There are plenty of people out there afraid of his popularity."

"Or at least afraid of his movement," McPherson agreed. "Chop off the head and the whole movement collapses, or so says the conventional wisdom. But that's beside the point. Fine; let's say the nuke goes off under the Temple Mount. We've then got two possibilities: Salomon's bunch or someone out to destroy Salomon's bunch. You see where I'm going?"

"I think so," Swenson said, gazing out at the snow. "No one would believe anymore that North Korea was involved. What reason would they have to mess with Israel?"

"Exactly," McPherson said. "Same goes for China and India. Iran and Pakistan might still be question marks, given they probably consider Salomon an enemy of Islam. But, yes, that's precisely my point. As soon as the nuke goes off, the suspect list instantly gets cut in half, or even smaller. So why bother with the red herrings?"

"Maybe because if we knew who was involved we'd know which targets needed protection," Swenson suggested slowly. "Or even what dates to watch out for. If we figured out it was a local fringe group, say, we might be on special alert on the anniversaries of Waco and Oklahoma City."

"Could be," McPherson murmured, an odd thought suddenly striking him. "Has it occurred to you that in all this flurry of planted clues not a single one of them has pointed to any group here in the U.S.?"

"No, it hadn't," Swenson said thoughtfully. "Interesting. You'd think they'd want to pin the tail on at least one of our home-grown donkeys. Especially if the nuke is here."

McPherson grimaced. "Oh, it's here, all right," he told her darkly. "Apparently gone to ground, too—we've had southwest Oregon hemmed in with checkpoints since ten o'clock this morning, with every radiation detector we could scrounge from Seattle to San Diego to Denver pressed into service. So far no one's tried to get it through."

"Could they be planning to use it right there?" Swenson suggested. "Some place inside the cordon?"

"I can't see anything that would make even a halfway reasonable target," McPherson said. "No government labs, no major military bases, no nothing."

"Then maybe it was all just a feint after all."

McPherson grunted. "You can believe that if you want," he said. "Whitcomb believes it, Vaughn wants to believe it, and even Cohn goes back and forth. But I know it's here. You can't convince me that this morning was just a diversion."

"What exactly did happen?" Swenson asked. "I've been too busy working on ship photos to get the whole story."

"They ran circles around us, that's what," McPherson said sourly. "Two of them stole a Coast Guard chopper and rendezvoused with the cat a mile off the coast. When we scrambled fighters, out popped the two Harriers they stole Monday and have been hiding God only knows where. Within half an hour both Harriers had been shot down, the chopper and cat had self-destructed, and the whole bunch of them had vanished into the woodwork."

"What about the Harrier pilots?" Swenson asked. "Did we recover the bodies?"

"There weren't any," McPherson told her. "Both pilots ejected, the second one into an open field with a pair of Marine pilots following him the whole way down."

"And?"

"And he set off a couple of smoke bombs and disappeared," McPherson said with a sigh. "Best guess is he hopped a slow-moving car while it was going through the smoke."

"*That's* somebody's best guess?" Swenson asked scornfully. "He found a car, opened the door, hopped in, and closed the door again, all without the Marines noticing?"

"It doesn't make sense to me, either," McPherson agreed. "But everyone on the scene swore up and down that they'd searched every possible hiding place."

He snorted. "They were wrong, of course. Half an hour after the Marines and police left, someone came by and maced the two cops who'd been left behind to watch the scene. Either he *was* hiding there, some place he couldn't come out of without the cops spotting him, or else his own buddies didn't know he'd gotten away. Maybe in the river with scuba gear like our friend off the *Rabah Jamila*—they hadn't had a chance to drag the area yet."

"But he didn't just float down the river instead of coming up in the same place?"

"I'm just telling you what happened," McPherson said. "They did get a barricade set up downstream a ways—Vaughn suggested that—so maybe he tried that direction and had to go back."

"He could have gone upstream," Swenson pointed out. "Maybe the police didn't think of—"

She broke off. "What?" McPherson asked.

"Oh, no," she murmured, her voice suddenly stricken. "An open field. *The Cloaks.*"

"The what?" McPherson frowned, an unpleasant sensation stirring inside him.

"The Cloaks," she said. "High-tech fiberoptic cloaks of invisibility. You remember—that was what Talbot and I were working on when you called me back here."

"Lyman said you were working on something important," McPherson said, frowning at her. Cloaks of *invisibility*? What the hell kind of joke was this? "But we had a nuke to find and I wasn't interested in the details."

"Wait a minute, let me think," she said, her voice abruptly full of rekindled dread. "There were three Cloaks. No, four: two small, one mid-sized, one large. The small one ought to cover a pilot hiding in the middle of an open field. Question: would the large one be big enough to cover two Harriers?"

The unpleasant sensation in McPherson's gut was growing stronger. "You're serious, aren't you?" he said. "Look, I'll buy a really good camouflage system for the Harriers. But an open field, with Marines stomping all over it?"

"I don't know," Swenson said. "I haven't seen them work. All I know is that Talbot told me an assassin used one to slip through a fifty-cop trap in San Jose yesterday morning."

"But an *open field*?"

"And he said the people he was up against were clever and inventive," she went on, ignoring his objection. "That they liked finesse better than brute force. In all the explosions and dogfights this morning, did anyone die?"

"We lost one Marine during the chopper hijacking," McPherson said darkly. "But he pulled a gun on the hijackers when he'd been warned not to. As far as I know, no one else even got a scratch. Why didn't you say something about all this sooner?"

"It never even occurred to me that the two cases might be related," Swenson said quietly. "I'm sorry."

"Forget it," McPherson said, feeling a flicker of guilt at having jumped on her. "I should have listened when Lyman was trying to tell me what you were working on." He got to his feet and headed for the door. "Is there any way to get hold of Talbot's data on these things?"

"Yes, I can access his files," Swenson said, hurrying to catch up with him. "We'd do better to talk to him directly. They recovered one of the Cloaks, so you could even see how it works."

"Just pull up the files," he told her. "We don't have time to haul him out here."

"It wouldn't take that long," Swenson said hesitantly. "Actually, he's already here."

McPherson skidded to a halt. "He's *what*?"

"He's in D.C.," Swenson said. With her back to the windows McPherson couldn't see her face, but her voice sounded defensive. "He called me late last night and said the thieves had added some kind of password lock to the software of the recovered Cloak. The Sand/Star techs hadn't been able to break it, and he wanted to know if I could point him to someone at the Bureau who was good at that sort of thing. Since they were also looking for a secure place for the techs to work on a countermeasure, I offered them space in the FBI Lab. They were supposed to get in early this morning."

"And *did* they find a countermeasure?"

"I don't know," she said. "I haven't talked to him today."

"Call and find out," McPherson told her. "Then tell him to get his butt over here. I'm fresh out of ideas, and so is everyone else I know who's been banging his forehead against this wall. Maybe fresh eyes will do some good."

"Yes, sir," she said, sounding a little uncertain. Apparently she'd been expecting a different reaction. "Uh . . . "

"You don't agree?"

"Yes, sir, of course," she said. "I just thought . . . "

"Then get on the phone," he interrupted her verbal floundering. "I need to make some calls of my own, then I'll clear him a pass to get in. Once he's on his way, get back to your workstation and pull together everything we've got on the nuke hunt, in chronological order—we'll want him up to speed as quickly as possible. I'll meet you both back here."

Swenson squared her shoulders. "Yes, sir," she said. Slipping past him, she hurried out into the hallway.

Taking a deep breath, fatigue tugging at his eyes and lungs, McPherson followed. If the terrorists' target was on the West Coast, and if they'd managed to slip through the cordon, the nuke could already be in position. If it was on the East Coast, they still had only two or three days at the most before it arrived.

He hoped to hell Talbot was a fast reader.

~

"Sir?"

The general opened his eyes to find a young woman standing over him. "Yes?" he asked, slipping the headphones off his ears.

"I asked if you'd like something to drink," the flight attendant repeated.

"Ah," he said. "No. Thank you."

She nodded and moved on, pushing her cart past his seat down the aisle. The general glanced at his watch, already set to Eastern Time. A few minutes after one in the morning. By now the two trucks carrying the Cloaks and the weapon should have reached Idaho, with the chase vehicle running backup ten kilometers behind it.

They might even be a bit farther along. The three vehicles had gotten an early jump on his advance team, successfully passing through the military cordon via smaller back roads while the general's group was still stuck in the long line of traffic behind the Highway 101 roadblock.

He'd been mildly surprised that the pickup, at least, hadn't had to shoot its way through the cordon. Apparently, the soldiers on duty had decided that waving their radiation detector into the back of a clearly empty pickup truck would be a waste of valuable time.

And now the path was clear, with the last leg of the mission before them. Resettling his headphones, he leaned back in his seat and again closed his eyes. It would be several hours before they landed, and he ought to get some sleep.

But sleep refused to come. The last leg of the mission was ahead . . . and for the first time he truly had to deal with what that meant. For the first time since Nagasaki, a nuclear weapon was about to be detonated in a populated area.

And he was the man who was going to do it.

He squirmed uncomfortably against the soft cloth of the airline seat. It had been easy to talk about numbers back in that small, dark, dusty room. Easy to blithely speak about killing a thousand people, or even ten thousand, for the good of the people and the survival of the nation. Particularly easy when standing far removed from the event, both in time and in distance, with all of it neat numbers and figures on paper.

Perhaps neither of them had wanted to think about the numbers at the time. Perhaps neither of them had seriously believed the mission would ever get this far.

But it had. The road ahead was open . . . and in approximately forty-three hours, those numbers would become real people.

Is there no other way? The general had heard that question a hundred times in the past few months, the last of those times there at the end, in that small, dark, dusty room. And the general had assured him that, no, there was no other way.

At the time, he'd believed it, too. But now, with the reading light of the seat beside him forcing its way beneath his eyelids, he found himself wondering if perhaps he'd been wrong.

But no. Tactics and strategy were his business, and it was a business he knew well. This was no sudden spur-of-the-moment impulse, but something he'd carefully thought out over months, always with the hope and indeed the expectation that something better would occur to him along the way.

But nothing had, at least nothing that would eliminate the threat without making a martyr of the man's memory. It had to be done, and there was no other way to do it.

So he would push the button, and he would send several thousand innocent people to their deaths.

For the good of the people. For the survival of the nation.

33

THE CALLS TOOK longer than McPherson had expected, and it was nearly an hour before he was able to get back to the lounge. Swenson was already there, seated in the same chair, her laptop on the coffee table in the center of the conversation cluster. Talbot had arrived, too, and was sitting in McPherson's former seat on the couch, reading through the material on the laptop's display.

And to McPherson's annoyed surprise, he'd brought a couple of friends.

"Talbot," he grunted as he strode across the lounge. "I assumed you'd realize this was a private party."

"Hello, Director," Talbot said politely, standing up and offering his hand. "It's good to see you again, sir."

"Private party means *private*," McPherson said, ignoring the proffered hand and glaring at the two interlopers. "Bureau business. Governmental security. You understand the concepts?"

"Certainly, sir," Talbot said, shifting his outstretched hand smoothly into a gesture toward the woman sitting quietly opposite Swenson. "May I present Mrs. Angie Chandler, widow of Dr. James Chandler, one of the Cloak's inventors? I thought she might have some useful insights."

"Mrs. Chandler," McPherson said, nodding to her. An Asian, probably Chinese, with all of the stereotypical inscrutability of that people. "I'm sorry for your loss."

"Thank you, Director," she said, nodding back.

"And," Talbot continued, "I'm sure you remember former agent Adam Ross."

McPherson's annoyance tightened another couple of turns. "Oh, yes," he said softly. "I remember Mr. Ross quite well. Including the fact that he's supposed to be in witness protection."

Ross shrugged slightly. "I was needed."

"Actually, you're not," McPherson said shortly. "I'll have someone escort you out."

"Sir, I respectfully request you reconsider," Talbot said quietly. "Ross has been on the Cloak case for some time now. He's tangled with the thieves, and at one point actually had a conversation with one of them. His insights and experience could be invaluable."

"I just said we don't need him," McPherson repeated.

"With all due respect, Director," Talbot said, putting a little steel into his unassuming tone. "We have a rogue nuclear weapon in the country and a cloak of invisibility to wrap it in. It seems to me that right now we need everyone we can get."

McPherson took a deep breath. *And you know it,* Talbot might as well have added.

And he would have been right. Right now they needed everyone, even wild cards. Maybe even especially wild cards.

What had he just been thinking, he reminded himself sourly, about interagency cooperation?

"Fine," he growled. "But you, Talbot, are responsible for him. For both of them." He gestured at the laptop. "How up to speed are you?"

"Not very," Talbot said, his voice all brisk business now that he'd won. "I've hit the high points, but there are plenty of details I still need to sort through. But I think I can at least fill in some of the blanks from this morning." He nodded toward Swenson. "Hanna's guess is almost certainly right, that that second Harrier pilot just stayed quietly inside his smoke screen with the Baby Bear Cloak over him. My guess is that the first Harrier pilot was supposed to pull a similar stunt after he delayed those National Guard fighters."

"Or else was supposed to help escort the chopper," Ross added. "Either way, having a Cloak with him would let him go wherever he needed to, knowing he could eject whenever it got too hot and vanish."

"Makes sense," McPherson agreed reluctantly. "So why did they change plans?"

"Because they lost the second Baby Bear," Talbot said. "So they had to improvise, having him eject before engaging and parachute into a carefully defined area where a car could pick him up."

"Mm." McPherson stroked his lip thoughtfully. "Which in effect wasted one of their Harriers. The move forced the Guard planes to circle back and destroy it, but that didn't delay them as much as a full-fledged dogfight would have."

"Right," Talbot said. "The farther away from the landing point they could get the cat and the chopper before we realized they were both empty, the longer the group handling the nuke would have to bring it ashore and disappear."

McPherson looked sideways at Mrs. Chandler. Her lips were pressed tightly together, but she seemed to be holding herself together well enough. "Speaking of which, the mystery of how they pulled that off has also been solved," he said. "A group checking out the beach found a mess of footprints and tire tracks about five miles north of where the chopper and cat parted ways. Among other things, they found the impressions and heat marks where a pair of Harriers put down and took off, plus the mark of a scuba tank being dragged across the sand."

"You're joking," Talbot said. "They *swam* to shore?"

"Why not?" McPherson said. "I don't mean they did a Sea Hunt with snorkel and flippers, lugging the nuke behind them. They probably had a motorized underwater carrier and rode the thing to shore. The team said the footprints indicated people carrying something heavy that was too wide to be the nuke itself."

"At least that solves the question of how they got off the cat early," Swenson murmured. "They didn't."

"Why didn't the Navy get something with anti-sub capabilities to the area right away?" Ross asked.

"Everyone was too busy with the cat and chopper," McPherson said. "First chasing them and then looking at the wreckage. It was a good hour before they got anything back to the coast."

"Even if they'd gotten there sooner, it might not have helped," Talbot pointed out. "The cat's engines would have drowned out any underwater noise for quite a distance."

"They even told the *Shimizu Nakama* they had diving gear aboard," Swenson said suddenly. "Remember, sir?"

"I'd forgotten that," McPherson admitted. "Damn, but these people are brazen."

"That's our Cloak thieves, all right," Ross said sourly. "The one who captured me in Monterey even had the chutzpah to tell me the rest of the gang had gone north. That must have been just before they took off with those Harriers."

"Chutzpah may indeed be the word," McPherson said. "There's a possibility that there might be an Israeli connection."

"Hanna mentioned that," Talbot said. "And I agree with both of you that this morning's activities are way out of line for a feint or diversion. The bomb's definitely here, which begs the question of why any group of Israelis might want to nuke U.S. territory."

"Or some group of North Koreans or Iranians," Swenson added.

"Maybe we're looking at this wrong," Ross said thoughtfully. "We're calling it a nuclear weapon. But as nukes go, it's really pretty puny."

"Two hundred tons of TNT is nothing to be sneered at," McPherson said.

"My point is that we're thinking forty megatons, twenty-mile blast radius, a major city leveled in a few milliseconds," Ross said. "Serious mass destruction."

"So how *should* we think about it?" Talbot asked.

"Like what they've got is the world's biggest pipe bomb," Ross said. "Question: what does somebody do with a pipe bomb?"

"Interesting point," McPherson said, intrigued in spite of himself. The world's biggest pipe bomb . . . "They're usually terrorist weapons or booby traps," he said slowly. "You use them against a specific locale, like a courthouse or police station, or more randomly against crowds at a shopping mall or on the street."

Swenson stirred. "Or for an assassination."

For a long, dark moment the five of them looked around the table at each other. "A nuke as an assassination weapon," McPherson said at last. "My God. They're after President Whitcomb."

"The *President*?" Mrs. Chandler asked, sounding stunned.

"Who else?" McPherson said heavily. "He's the one-man driving force behind our foreign policy these days, the one most likely to be irritating or threatening the kind of people who could pull off this theft in the first place. Who else in the country would be worth hitting with the world's biggest pipe bomb?"

"What about Congress?" Mrs. Chandler suggested. "Or some military installation?"

"The military's too decentralized for a single nuke to be worth the effort," Talbot told her. "Not even if you hit the Pentagon. The chain of command's too well defined."

"And taking out Congress doesn't gain them anything," Ross added. "Maybe make a political statement, but it would hardly throw the country into mass chaos."

"Or throw some unpopular foreign policy off the rails," McPherson said. "The more I think about this, the more sense it makes. There's no way you could get a normal bomb within half a mile of the President. But with a nuke, half a mile would do just fine. Even a mile or more if he's out in the open."

"Though there's no reason they couldn't go for both Whitcomb and Congress," Swenson pointed out. "The State of the Union address is coming up pretty soon. They'll all be together in a single room."

"Along with most of the Cabinet," Talbot agreed. "They'd get to make a political statement *and* eliminate Whitcomb's foreign policy at the same time."

"But why would Israel want to kill the President?" Mrs. Chandler asked. "I thought he was mostly on their side."

"I doubt the Israeli government has anything to do with this," Ross told her. "If it's Israelis, we're talking fringe group"

"Possibly the Third Temple controversy," Talbot said grimly. "One side of it or the other."

"Or the Israeli connection could be just a red herring," Ross offered. "Trouble is, one of the supposed red herrings in this fish stew might not be a diversion at all. I can certainly see North Korea wanting Whitcomb out of the way and planting evidence against themselves just to throw everyone off. Ditto for the Iranians, or the Russian mob."

"Or Colombian drug lords looking for revenge over Operation Calling Birds," Talbot added. "You'll note that none of our playmate's pointers has gotten anywhere near South America."

"At this point you could almost throw a dart into a map," Swenson murmured. "You should see the Goose List."

McPherson felt his eyes narrow. "The Goose List?" he echoed, giving her a long, hard stare.

She at least had the grace to blush. "I'm sorry, sir," she said. "But you said to pull together everything Madison might need."

"I didn't mean for you to raid my private files," he bit out. "Or was it someone *else's* private files?"

She seemed to shrink into her chair. "No, sir. Yours."

"Just as well," Ross murmured. "We don't want the CIA mad at us."

McPherson shifted his glare that direction. Ross wasn't quite looking at him, his eyes focused on the coffee table somewhere between the laptop and McPherson's knees. "I'd be very careful about adopting Talbot's attitude shortcomings if I were you," he warned. "That short leash you're on has a choke collar at your end."

"No," Talbot said thoughtfully. He was staring at the coffee table, too, his forehead wrinkled in thought. "No, it doesn't fit. Red herrings. Cloaks . . ."

"If you're talking to yourself, talk softer," McPherson growled. "If you're talking to us, make more sense."

Talbot looked up again, almost as if noticing the others for the first time. "Okay," he said slowly. "Logic time. Taking out the White House or the Capitol would be trivial with a nuke in hand. You get a room at one of the nearby hotels, you park your car in their lot with the bomb in the trunk, and you walk away. So why do you need a Cloak?"

"To get the nuke into the country," Ross said. "I thought that was the whole point of this morning's exercise."

"No, Madison's right," Swenson said slowly. "They could have gotten the nuke ashore without any of those fireworks if they hadn't been so busy scattering red herrings around the Pacific. They could have just brought it straight in on that cat and we'd never have known the difference."

"Which brings us back to the red herrings," Talbot said. "Question: why?"

"So we wouldn't know who did it?" Mrs. Chandler suggested.

"That's the obvious answer," Talbot agreed. "But it seems to me that automatically eliminates any drug cartels from the suspect list. When you carry out a reprisal you *want* your victim to know who did it, as a warning against future action. Ditto anyone who wants to wave us off something specific. "

"So it's not a reprisal," McPherson said. "A preemptive strike, then?"

"Which takes us back to your unpopular foreign policy theory," Talbot agreed. "But let's troll beneath the headlines a bit. Has Whitcomb made any private threats against anyone in, say, the past month? Specific threats, I mean, against specific countries or groups?"

"You'd have to go back at least two months," Swenson warned. "That's when work started on the decoy *Eureka* yacht."

"Okay, let's be generous and call it six months," Talbot said. "Director?"

McPherson shook his head. "Nothing I know about."

"It doesn't have to be a real threat," Ross pointed out. "The *perception* of threat would be enough."

"So now you want to delve into international and multicultural psyches?" McPherson said, scowling. "Terrific."

"Lucky for us, we're in the right place for that," Ross pointed out. "If anyone knows who might think we're a threat, it's the CIA."

"Speaking of which, where *is* Director Cohn?" Talbot asked. "He really should be in on this."

"I tried to get him," McPherson said. "He's asleep, with strict instructions not to be awakened until six-thirty." He made a face. "My fault, really. I suggested he needed more rest."

"Six-thirty could be too late," Ross warned.

"I know, I know," McPherson said. "Give him a break. He's an old man."

"He'll age a lot faster if that nuke goes off while he's napping," Ross said bluntly.

"I don't think there's any need to wake him," Talbot said, an odd gleam in his eye. "A man like Cohn should have transcripts of all his phone calls, incoming and outgoing both."

"No," McPherson said firmly. "Don't even think it."

"You're right, I'll bet he does," Ross agreed. "I'd also bet Hanna could access them."

"Don't you start, either," McPherson warned. "You want that war with the CIA you just mentioned?"

"Not particularly," Ross said. "But I'm even less crazy about having a nuke go off in downtown Washington."

"Or downtown San Francisco," Talbot pointed out soberly. "Whitcomb still has a breakfast meeting there tomorrow before he flies back."

"Today, you mean," Ross corrected, glancing at his watch. "The bomb could already be in place, just waiting for someone to light the fuse."

McPherson grimaced. So much for all the agencies working and playing well together. "I can't believe I'm even listening to this," he growled. "Swenson? Can you do it?"

"You really want to know?"

"No," he said. "Just get whatever Talbot thinks he needs. I'll leave the details up to you."

He looked at Talbot. "Up to the both of you," he amended. "If Swenson gets busted, you're going down with her, so be damn careful what you copy and read. *And* what you remember of it."

Talbot nodded. "Understood."

Ross tapped Mrs. Chandler on the arm. "This looks like a good time for us to go, Angie," he said. "Official Bureau business and governmental security, you know."

"Yes," she said, closing her eyes briefly. Earlier, McPherson had thought she looked inscrutable. Now, he realized the lack of emotion in her face was merely fatigue. "You said you had hotel rooms reserved, Mr. Talbot?"

"I've got all the details," Ross said before Talbot could answer. "Come on, I'll drive you. Hopefully, we won't have to shoot our way out this time."

Mrs. Chandler's only response was a wan smile as she stood up. "Thank you for your time, Director McPherson," she said. "And for allowing me to sit in on this discussion. I appreciate the chance to know why James was murdered."

"We'll get his killers, Mrs. Chandler," McPherson said quietly. "I wish we could do more."

"Just stop them," she said. "I don't want anyone else to die because of my husband's work."

She looked at Ross and nodded. He took her arm, and together they left the room.

"What are you going to need to get into the files?" McPherson asked, gazing after them.

"Just a workstation," Swenson said. "I could go back to the satellite room, only someone might notice what I was doing. I'll see if I can hunt up some other place."

"Come on," McPherson grunted, heaving himself to his feet. "Cohn lent me an office. There's a terminal there you can use."

"You sure you want to do that?" Swenson asked, frowning as she also stood up. "If I get caught doing this from your office, you'll be in as much trouble as Madison and I are."

"Don't kid yourself," McPherson said sourly. "My neck's already on the line. You'd just better get something useful out of it." He jerked his head toward the door. "You come with me. Talbot, you sit there and read."

"Yes, sir," Talbot said, his eyes already back on the laptop screen.

They left the room. "I appreciate your confidence in me, sir," Swenson said as McPherson led the way down the corridor. "And in Madison, too."

McPherson shrugged. "He's one of the best we've got at this sort of thing," he said. "I'm glad we've got him on board."

"So am I," she said, sounding puzzled. "I just thought . . . "

"That I didn't like him?" McPherson gestured ahead as he fished out his key card. "Over there."

Out of the corner of his eye, he saw her gazing at him as he unlocked the door. "You kicked him out of D.C.," she reminded him. "If it wasn't for incompetence, and it wasn't because you didn't like him, what exactly did he *do*?"

McPherson ushered her into the office and flipped on the light. "You really want to know?"

"Of course."

"All right," he said, watching her face closely as he closed the door behind them. "He blackmailed me."

The parade of emotions across her face was the most entertaining thing he'd seen in days. "He *blackmailed* you?" she gasped. "Madison *Talbot*?"

"Madison Talbot," he nodded. "You sure you want to know more?"

She clamped her jaws back together. "Yes," she said stubbornly.

"It was right after you and he broke the Clarkston kidnapping case last summer," McPherson said, waving her to the desk. "There was a scheduled appropriations hearing, and I thought it would be nice to trot Talbot out in front of the committee. Square-jawed hero, glowing example of Bureau prowess—you know the song and dance."

"Sounds perfect for him," Swenson said, locating the desk chair with her hands and sinking down into it, her eyes never leaving McPherson's face.

"Oh, it was," McPherson agreed. "Only not the way I expected. Instead of turning his reflected glory onto the Bureau, he completely downplayed our role while singing the praises of the local cops you'd been working with. Especially the one who picked up on the car with the fake wooden tag as it went by."

"He did a good job," Swenson murmured. "All the cops did."

"Of course," McPherson said. "It was a team effort. We all know that. But that's not the point. The point is that you don't share credit in front of the people writing the checks. Unless they ask you point-blank about it, and even then you wiggle as much as you can. Frankly, I was more than a little put out, and as soon as I got him alone I let him know that."

She smiled faintly. "I can imagine."

"You wouldn't have had to," McPherson said bluntly. "The S.O.B. recorded it."

Her jaw dropped open again. "He *recorded* it?"

"From soup to nuts," McPherson said, grimacing at the memory. "He'd obviously anticipated the rant—in fact, he probably deliberately set me up—and had himself wired. He got the whole thing, including my highly professional treatise on how exactly you go about conning Congressmen out of more money than they intended to give you."

"Oh, boy," Swenson murmured.

"I'm sure you could find more appropriate words than that," McPherson said. "Anyway, after I cooled down, he played me back part of it and offered a trade."

"I'm surprised you didn't arrest him on the spot," Swenson said.

McPherson shrugged. "The essence of blackmail is that the victim doesn't want the information getting out. That tape would have wrecked my career and certainly made me a lot of powerful enemies. Worse, it would have made me look exactly as childish and petty as I'd been behaving. Besides, what he wanted was really quite modest." He raised his eyebrows slightly. "Want to take a guess?"

Swenson's forehead was wrinkled with concentration. "Are you saying . . . all he wanted was a transfer to San Francisco?"

"Bingo," McPherson said. "Only he didn't want it for himself. He wanted it for you."

He hadn't thought her eyes could get any wider. He was wrong. "For *me*?" she gasped.

"He told me you were miserable in D.C.," McPherson said. "You were either roasting or freezing, you were getting sick about once a month from some bug or other, you hated the petty political maneuvering all around you from people trying to claw their way up the ladder, and all your family and friends were in the Bay Area."

For the first time since McPherson had known her, Swenson was genuinely at a loss for words. "I . . . no," she managed at last. "No, it wasn't that bad."

"Come on, Swenson," McPherson admonished. "It's a sin to lie to your director."

She reddened. "Okay, I guess I really didn't like it here," she admitted. "But I don't remember ever complaining about it. At least, not that strongly."

"Well, whatever you said, he picked up on it," McPherson told her. "So that was the deal: you went back to San Francisco, with the same pay and benefits you had here, and I got the recording."

She pondered that a minute. "And once you had it," she said, "that's when you kicked him out of D.C.?"

"That's what he thinks," McPherson said. "That's what I *want* him to think. The fact of the matter—and you are to keep this an absolute secret, especially from Talbot—is that I just didn't want to break up a winning team."

She blinked. "Excuse me?"

McPherson sighed. It was so obvious . . . but perhaps not to Swenson. Someone who focused so tightly on her work that she didn't even notice she was eating lunch could easily miss something like this. "Didn't it ever occur to you that you and Talbot had been assigned to an awful lot of cases together?" he asked. "Well, you were. And it wasn't because I liked the snappy repartee the two of you could get going."

"Well . . ."

"No *well* about it," McPherson said. "It just so happens that you two are a perfect investigative team. You dig out all the pieces, even the ones you have to snag from way out in left field, and assemble them into a coherent form. Talbot then takes that jigsaw puzzle and reads past the pieces to the underlying pattern. The way you do your job exactly meshes with the way he does his."

Swenson had been staring at him like he'd just sprouted flowers. But now she nodded. A slow, hesitant, not quite believing nod, but a nod nevertheless. "I hadn't noticed," she said. "You really think so?"

"I've seen it before with other teams," McPherson assured her. "Trust me; I know what it looks like."

He jabbed a finger at the workstation. "But you have to do your part before he can do his. So get busy and pull up whatever you think he'll need."

"Yes, sir," Swenson said. She still sounded a little dazed, but the briskness was starting to creep back into her voice. "Yes, sir."

"Good." He glanced at his watch. It was after two already. "I'm going to go home and crash for a few hours. Tell Talbot to call me immediately if he finds anything."

~

It was after four o'clock when Swenson returned to the lounge. Talbot was sitting where she'd left him, still reading through her assembled files. "It isn't all of Cohn's conversations, not by a long shot," she said as she handed him a flash drive. "But it covers the whole period since New Delhi informed us the weapon was missing, plus about two weeks before that. That's the best I could do."

"Thanks," he said, taking the flash drive absently, his eyes still on the screen. "Anything juicy in there?"

"If you think I read through all of it, you're nuts," she told him. "But I did notice a couple of conversations with the President where they discuss who might be behind this. Could make for interesting reading."

"I'll bet," he said, yawning. "Come on, you can read over my shoulder."

"I'm going to read the inside of my eyelids, thank you," she countered, yawning herself. "Good night."

"Good night," he said, waving vaguely toward her. "Wait a second," he added. "You said earlier that you and McPherson had discussed the reason for all the red herrings. But you never told me what you came up with."

"That's because we didn't," she told him ruefully. "Director McPherson pointed out that a lot of the false leads would evaporate as soon as the nuke went off and we found out what the target was. That raised the question of why bother with them in the first place. I thought maybe they were there to keep us from figuring out what the target was ahead of time and protecting it."

"Like knowing it was aimed at Whitcomb would have us sweeping everything ahead of his speaking tour."

"Right," Swenson said. "But that was as far as we got. And of course, it's all moot now. If they're after Whitcomb, none of the false leads evaporates anyway. Speaking of the Director, he said to call him at home if you find anything."

"Okay, thanks. Where are you going to be?"

"I'm in room 387 if you absolutely need me," she said, vaguely aware that giving him her room number was probably not the smartest thing she'd done that day. "But don't need me until at least ten."

"Got it," he said, already engrossed again in his reading. "Pleasant dreams."

"Six hours' worth, anyway," she said, heading for the door. "Good luck."

She didn't get six hours' worth of dreams. She had exactly two hours and forty minutes before she was jolted awake by an insistent knocking on her door. "Wait a second," she called, groping for her robe and prying her eyes open just far enough to see the clock. Six fifty-six. "Madison, that had better not be you."

"Open up, Hanna," Talbot's voice called with muffled insistence through the door. "I need you."

A minute later she fumbled the door open. "This had better be good," she warned, standing pointedly in the middle of the doorway as she tugged her robe sash tighter around her.

"It is," he assured her, pointing toward the chair where she'd laid out the next day's clothing. "Get dressed and meet me in McPherson's office. I know who's behind it; and I think I know where the nuke's headed."

She came fully awake in an instant. "You *know*? Who?"

"Get dressed and I'll tell you," he said, starting back down the hall. "Come on, I need you to pull up more information for me."

"At least tell me where it's going," she said, stepping part way out into the hall. "D.C.? 'Frisco?"

"Neither," he said. "New York.

"They're going to hit the United Nations."

THE
NINTH
DAY

34

HE WAS IN that same small dusty room, the room where the final decision had been made, when the phone rang.

He'd spent a great deal of time in that room in the past few days. The story he'd told his staff and family was that it was a place for him to get away from the pressures of everyday life, to do some reading or a little work, or to simply relax. They'd all accepted that, and had respected his wish for solitude.

He had indeed gotten a little work done, at least at first. But lately, most of his time had been spent gazing out the window, thinking about what was about to happen. The horror he was about to unleash upon unsuspecting men and women.

All in the name of saving the nation.

He was gazing out that window now when the sudden ringing of the phone jarred him out of his dark thoughts. He hurried to the desk, his first thought that it was the general with news. Bad news, perhaps; news that the weapon had been lost or captured, or that the mission for some other reason had to be canceled. He almost hoped that was it, for while it might well ultimately spell doom for the nation it would at least lift the terrible weight pressing down on his shoulders. Perhaps he was not the man who should have made this decision in the first place.

He scooped up the phone on the third ring. "Hello?"

It was not the general. It was, in fact, the last voice he'd expected to hear. "Hello, Father," his son said. "Greetings from the snow fields of New York. How are you?"

It was a frozen second before he could get his mouth working again. "Well, hello," he said lamely. "I'm sorry, I thought it would be someone else."

"Ah," his son said. "I'm sorry, too—I didn't intend to intrude. Shall I call back later?"

"No, no, not at all," he hastened to assure him. This was exactly what he needed, he realized now: the voice of his son, a young man who loved and respected him. The voice of the future, for whose sake he had set all of this in motion in the first place. "How are you? Don't tell me: you need tuition money again?"

The boy laughed. "Hardly," he said. "No, I just wanted to say hello and see how you were doing. And also to share some exciting news and possibly some gratitude."

The man frowned. What could he be talking about? "You're engaged?" he hazarded.

The boy snorted. "You know I didn't come here looking for women."

"I certainly hope not," the man said, smiling at the memory of the boy's firm resolve to focus exclusively on his studies while he was at college. "You've made the Dean's List, then?"

"Not yet, but I'm sure I will," the boy said with casual confidence. "No, this is something more immediate. You know that big human rights conference at the UN this weekend?"

A cold hand wrapped itself around his heart. "Yes?" he said cautiously.

"I'm going to be attending the opening ceremonies tomorrow night," the boy said, his voice bubbling with the pleasure of someone delivering good news. "Isn't that marvelous?"

The cold hand squeezed hard, freezing his heart within him. His own hand reciprocated, squeezing the phone as if trying to break it. "Yes, indeed," he said through lips suddenly as stiff as elephant hide. "How did this happen?"

"That was my question, actually," the youth said cheerfully. Clearly, he hadn't noticed the sudden chill in his father's voice. "I got a call this morning, just a few minutes ago, in fact, from my political science professor. Someone has donated passes for the entire class to attend the ceremonies."

"Ah," was all the man could think to say. "Who?"

"The call was from some UN official. I don't remember the name— it wasn't one I recognized." He paused, and the man could imagine him smiling that sly smile he always used when they were sharing a private secret. "Professor Sloane thought maybe you'd pulled a few strings with them. Did you?"

He squeezed the phone even harder. No. This couldn't be happening. "No," he managed. "No, I had nothing to do with it."

"Ah," his son said. "I thought that since you'd once planned to attend and had then canceled—never mind. Perhaps someone else in the class has the right kind of connections. At any rate, Professor Sloane asked me to thank you if you were the one responsible. I suppose I'll have to save his thanks for some other time."

The one responsible. The cold hand around his heart had developed knives, their hardened points digging into the tissue. "No, it wasn't me," he said. "But—but look, perhaps I can do something now," he hurried on, trying desperately to unfreeze his mind from the awful image of his son flashing to fiery nothingness as the UN Building disintegrated around him. "The opening ceremonies really won't be that interesting, certainly not for a political science class. You'd do better to attend one of the speeches or workshops on Saturday or Sunday. Perhaps I can arrange that."

"That would be wonderful," the boy said, his excitement bubbling all the more. "I knew you'd come through. With enough people pulling strings, we may be able to attend the entire conference. I think John Seymour's father is a Congresswoman's aide—"

"No, no, I was thinking of you doing the workshops instead of opening ceremonies," he interrupted quickly. "You surely can't afford to take an entire weekend away from your studies."

"Trust me, Father, this is well worth whatever late nights it will cost to make up my other work," his son assured him. "Besides, Professor Sloane is going to give us class credit for this. I have to go now—my next class is about to start. How are *you* doing, anyway?"

It took two tries for him to get any words out. "I'm fine," he said. "Just fine. Look, I'll talk to you later. All right?"

"Of course," the boy said. "Take care of yourself, Father. I'll let you know how the conference goes."

"Yes. Good-bye."

"Good-bye."

The phone went dead in his hand. He sat there, motionless, staring at the empty wall in front of him, until clicks on the line reminded him to hang up.

It was a nightmare come to earth. His son was going to the UN. Friday night.

To die.

The cold hand was still wrapped around his heart, but abruptly the paralysis freezing his mind vanished a in blaze of sudden heat. His son would not die. He would *not*. The general would call, and he would cancel the operation, and that would be that.

Only the general might not call. Probably wouldn't, in fact. He'd only called once since the mission started, and that was early on, just after he'd obtained the Cloaks. Since then there'd been only silence.

Was there anyone else he might call? Someone in New York itself, perhaps, who could lure his son to safety at the critical hour?

But again, no. He couldn't involve anyone else in this. Not only for their sake, but for his as well. An urgent request to effectively kidnap his son away from the UN Building would surely be remembered afterward, a memory as damning as fingerprints left at the scene of a crime. Saving his son from death would be of little value if he couldn't also protect him from the eternal shame of a disgraced father.

No. If he was to save his son, he would have to do it himself.

He flipped open his appointment book, mind racing as he turned to the proper pages. He couldn't simply cancel everything in sight and rush off guiltily on the very next plane. He had to do it quietly, and subtly, and invisibly. It had to look natural, not impulsive. It would have to look natural to those who would later scrutinize all such movements with hard and bitter eyes.

Yes, it could be done. It would be tricky, and he would have to be clever if he was to make it work. But it could be done. He still had time to fulfill his most important obligations, shift away the minor ones that fell within the necessary timeframe, and arrive in New York well ahead of zero hour. To the future investigators with the bitter eyes, it would look like nothing more than a mildly impulsive decision to use some spare time to visit his son at school, and a change of heart regarding the conference itself. To his son, it would appear the same way. Surely it would not be beyond the stretch of reasonable men to accept that a man might change his mind on such a matter.

And if he took his son to dinner beforehand, and they were delayed by traffic or slow restaurant service, no one could possibly find fault or suspicion in that. Surely not.

But in any event he would have to risk it. His son would not die.

Picking up the phone again, he punched in a number.

~

Another day, another cemetery. Or maybe another dozen cemeteries.

Shana Donahue was thinking evil thoughts as she pulled her squad car up to yet another modest, tastefully designed cemetery office building. It had been two days since she'd come to the twin conclusions that somebody up there didn't like her, and that this was that somebody's idea of police officer purgatory. She was tired of the driving, not to mention the odd looks and no doubt ghoulish thoughts from cemetery officials.

She was even tired of springing this on her fellow cops when they started comparing the dumbness levels of their current duties. Most of her friends had already heard the whole story, and they were nearly as tired of it as she was.

The man inside this particular office was younger than most she'd encountered, definitely on the short side of twenty-five. Also unlike most of the others, he greeted the sudden appearance of a uniformed cop with the kind of jolted wariness most people reserved for unexpected snakes in the garden. "Uh . . . hello, officer," he said. "Can I—what can I do for you?"

"I'm investigating a possible irregularity in a burial sometime since last Friday," she said, launching into her well-worn speech.

She never made it to the second line. "Look, I don't know what anyone told you," he insisted. "But that Bodinacce grave *was* dug the full eight feet down."

"Really," Donahue said, studying the young man's face as she took a moment to shut off her mental tape player and jumpstart her brain back into gear. "Tell me about it."

"I measured it myself," he said firmly, or as firmly as someone could who was so clearly on the defensive. "The evening before the service. If it wasn't deep enough, then it must have been kids getting over the fence and kicking dirt back in. That happens sometimes, and there's nothing we can do about it. I mean, we offered to redo it, but all the family wanted was to yell and accuse us of not doing our jobs—"

"Just a minute," Donahue cut in. "How much too shallow was it?"

"I don't know," the young man admitted. "I was working on another grave at the time, and it was already filled in by the time they came to complain. Look, if someone kicks in dirt—"

"How much too shallow did they say it was?" Donahue persisted.

"I don't *know*. They said two feet, but Jack said it couldn't have been more than a foot at the most. Jack was the one who filled it in."

"How soon was Jack there after the service ended?" Donahue asked. A purely routine question; at this point she was pretty sure she already knew the answer.

"He was there when the last people left," the young man said. "He usually gets there a little early, though he stays out of sight. People don't like to see us hanging around."

"Thank you," Donahue said. "I need to make a call, and then I'll want you to show me the grave."

"Yeah, sure," he said, ducking his head like a pigeon.

"And I'll want you to get your digging equipment out there, too," she added.

His face was suddenly stricken. "You mean—? But I can't let you—"

"Relax," she said. "I'll have all the legalities in place before you start digging. And no, this has nothing to do with the complaints," she added as his face began a fast drift toward panic. "I just want to get the coffin out of there."

His eyes bugged. "You want to look in the coffin?"

"Not *in*," she corrected. "*Under.*"

~

Cohn shook his head. "I don't believe it," he declared tiredly, turning his empty coffee cup around in his fingers.

"It's all right there," McPherson reminded him from his equally tired slouch in a chair near the window. "It was there practically from the start."

"I know that," Cohn rumbled, sending a sudden look at Talbot, seated quietly back in one corner of the room. Talbot braced himself; but there was no reproach or anger in the older man's eyes that he could see. "Trust me—I can see perfectly well when something is written in thirty-point type and hung on the wall in front of me. What I'm mostly not believing is that I didn't spot it myself. I must be getting old."

"If you are, then so are the rest of us," McPherson said. "I think it's more the old forest-for-the-trees problem. We were just too close."

"Bull," Cohn said succinctly, still eying Talbot. "Nice try, but bull nonetheless. Special Agent Talbot's simply got more of what I wish I had. If I weren't so damn tired, I'd probably be jealous."

"You give me too much credit, Director Cohn," Talbot said. "You and Director McPherson and the rest of your people put most of the puzzle together. I just noticed a piece that had fallen on the floor, that's all."

"And he's modest along with it," Cohn said sourly.

"Oh, he's an expert at sharing credit," McPherson said, giving Talbot a look of his own. "Trust me."

"And don't forget we aren't entirely sure yet that I even put that one piece in correctly," Talbot added quickly. Letting McPherson get started down that particular memory lane would be begging for trouble. "The theory won't be confirmed until he takes the bait."

"The bait is set, then?" McPherson asked.

Talbot nodded. "I got through to your friend at the UN and had him call the boy's poli sci professor."

"No names, I hope," Cohn said. "We don't want it to be too obvious."

"No names," Talbot assured him, "but a few broad hints that a VIP had pulled some strings to get them the passes. We'll just have to wait and see how it plays out."

"I still want to know how you tagged the UN Building," Cohn said. "The rest certainly follows, but what got you pointed that direction?"

"Actually, it was Director McPherson and Ms. Swenson who laid all the groundwork," Talbot told him. "Plus a big boost from a comment suggesting that we think of the weapon as the world's biggest pipe bomb. That's what led us to wonder if the plan might be simply a straightforward assassination."

Cohn snorted gently. "Talk about your TNT-based insecticide."

"Definitely," Talbot nodded. "But the very outrageousness of the idea made it worth exploring. What reasonable person would even think of such a thing?"

"The Pentagon has thought about it, actually," Cohn commented. "But in the context of a war footing, not as an isolated act."

"He said a reasonable person," McPherson reminded him. "Go on, Talbot."

"Last night Hanna told me she and Director McPherson had been speculating on the reason for all the red herrings," Talbot said. "The Director had noted that once the bomb went off it would likely be obvious who had been responsible. Hanna's take was that perhaps they simply didn't want us guessing the target beforehand."

McPherson nodded. "So you just put the two of them together."

"The three of them, yes," Talbot said. "The thieves had gone to a great deal of time and effort, not to mention risk, to create an international collection of false leads. If assassination was the goal, why not look for an equally international group of plausible targets? Not only would it leave all those expensive red herrings still in place, but it would also nicely mask our string-puller's true motivation. At that point, the UN was the only logical answer."

He shrugged slightly. "After that . . . well, as you said, the rest mostly followed."

"Like a murderer who pretends to be a serial killer," McPherson ruminated. "Taking out three random victims, then the one he really wants to kill, then maybe one more at random so that the real motive gets buried in the crowd."

"Exactly," Talbot agreed. "The only difference here is that all the random killings would happen at the same time."

McPherson shook his head. "The politics of desperation."

"Not if we can help it," Cohn said firmly. "Frank, what did you find out about tomorrow evening's schedule?"

"Officially, it starts with opening ceremonies and five-minute speeches at seven o'clock," McPherson said. "Unofficially, both the regular delegates and invited speakers will be drifting in as early as noon for news conferences, interviews, and informal get-togethers. There's also a dinner scheduled for five, which most of the speakers will be attending."

"And which many of the regular delegates will be boycotting, I imagine," Cohn said, grimacing. "You know, it occurs to me that half the governments in the world will be secretly relieved if that nuke does go off, taking their loudest dissident gadflies with it."

"Another reason to have staged it this way," Talbot agreed. "Even if we were able to sift the actual motive out of all the possibilities, the attack team would have quite a few grateful governments they could go to for quiet sanctuary."

Across the room, the door opened. Swenson came in, her face set into hard lines. "News?" McPherson asked, straightening in his chair.

"Good and bad," she said, closing the door behind her. "The bad news is that the first sweep of satellite photos has drawn a negative on anything that looks like our proposed convoy. Some of the techs are trying to program a recognition pattern into the computers, but so far they haven't been able to give it the breadth it needs while still keeping it manageable."

"They're still looking for two trucks?" Talbot asked.

"That was what the first sweep covered," Swenson nodded. "Some of them are trying the truck/RV or truck/SUV combination now. Burke and Esteban both agree that even folded down completely the Papa Bear Cloak will require at least a panel truck or gutted RV to transport it. Unfortunately, the weapon itself is much smaller, and might even fit inside a big enough car trunk."

"I wish to God we could put up some roadblocks," Cohn muttered. "At least keep it away from New York."

"And have it go off next week in Miami?" McPherson countered. "If we tip them off more than five minutes before we're ready to pounce, they'll slip away and we'll never find them. At least this way we know where they're going."

"What about the password lock on the Cloak computer?" Talbot asked. "Have they had any luck breaking it?"

"That's the good news," Swenson said. "They've gotten through the lock and have the Cloak up and running. Last I heard they had it draped over a big waste basket in their lab and were going to try a modified police laser gun on it."

"Standard speed trap variety?" McPherson asked, frowning.

"Right, except they're adapting it to use visible light," Swenson said. "Burke tells me there's a very short time delay as the light goes through the Cloak, reflects from whatever surface is behind it, and comes back through again. We're hoping the laser gun's computer will interpret that delay as a speed differential."

"So that a stationary waste basket will read like it's going ninety miles an hour?" Cohn asked.

"Right," Swenson said. "They said they should have the preliminary tests done in an hour or so and will keep me informed. They're also experimenting with a sonar rangefinder setup, though there are distance restrictions that may keep that from being of much use."

Her lips compressed briefly. "The other news," she continued quietly, "is that the airline computer is now showing the flight reservation we expected. He'll be arriving at JFK tomorrow afternoon at one-thirty."

For a long minute the office was silent. "I would say, Special Agent Talbot," Cohn said at last, "that your theory has now been confirmed."

"Yes," Talbot agreed soberly. "I believe it has."

~

The chubby little man seated at the security desk by the elevators shook his head in disbelief as he peered at the work order. "You gotta be kidding," he said, his New York accent as thick as a movie caricature's. "Air conditioning upgrades in *January*?"

"Hey, buddy, that's the best time," Eleven assured him, shifting his feet in feigned tiredness and impatience as he leaned against the side of the big box strapped to its dolly. "You try getting this stuff installed in August. June, even—folks are starting to wake up then and remembering what August was like. But January? Who thinks about August in January?"

"Besides, you get bargains this way," Ten pointed out, leaning on his own box.

"Yeah, that too," Eleven agreed. "Last year's models, right out of the crate. Only we gotta get 'em out of the warehouse for when the new models start coming in around May." He gestured toward the guard. "You know, if you're in the market for a new unit . . . ?"

"Yeah, don't I wish," the guard said with a sniff, handing back the order and pulling open the center drawer of his desk. "Super in my building doesn't believe in air conditioning. Here you go."

He pulled out a swipe card and handed it to Eleven. "Freight elevator's around the corner over there," he continued, hooking a thumb past the main elevator bank. "This'll get you to the roof."

"Whoa," Eleven said, sounding impressed as he turned the card over in his hand. "Buttons not good enough for you people?"

"Security," the guard said succinctly. "That card'll take you exactly two places: the roof and the lobby. Nowhere else."

"Cute," Ten put in.

"Yeah, we like it," the guard said dryly. "Saves one of us having to tag along on every service call. 'Specially up on the roof. Move it—it's getting late, and I don't want to be here all night."

"Don't worry," Eleven assured him, stepping behind his box and swinging the dolly up on its wheels. Ten already had his box and dolly moving the indicated direction. "We're just delivering it and doing some preliminary setup. Most of the work's gonna be done tomorrow."

"And don't lose that card," the guard called after them. "You need to turn it back in when you check out."

"Right," Eleven called back.

The freight elevator was roomy and plain, and as they headed up Eleven couldn't help but think back to the oversized packing crates he and Ten had ridden in across the South China sea. From the amused smile playing across Ten's lips, he guessed his partner was reliving the same memories.

They reached the roof and maneuvered their crates outside. The bright sunshine earlier in the day had warmed the rooftop enough to partially melt the layer of snow, but as the afternoon had cooled, it had refrozen into textured ice that crunched underfoot as they manhandled their cargoes north. Ten lugged his box to the very edge; Eleven, with the heavier load, was thankfully able to stop five meters short.

It was three minutes' work to unfasten and remove the sides of the two crates, revealing the heavy-duty winch and steel cables packed inside Eleven's and the equally heavy-duty pulley-and-boom system inside Ten's. Anchoring both pieces of machinery to the roof took longer but was equally straightforward; a simple matter of using spike drivers to shoot connectors through the snow and roofing material into the underlying layer of reinforced concrete. A few similarly anchored guy lines on the winch, just to make sure, and they were done.

"I trust you tested this," Eleven commented, carrying the connector end of the heavy steel cable toward the edge of the tripod as Ten used the remote to uncoil it from its reel.

"Of course," Ten said, sounding surprised that Eleven would even have to ask. "I *did* arrive here five days ago, you know. What else did I have to do but check the equipment?"

"You might have taken in a Broadway show," Eleven suggested, feeding the cable carefully into the pulley system. "You know, while Broadway's still there. Five more meters."

Ten fed out the cable. "Broadway should come out of this all right."

"So the theory goes," Eleven said. "Still, it *is* all theory, isn't it? Untested for half a century and more."

Ten shook his head. "Sometimes I can't believe we're actually doing this," he said. "I just hope it's worth what it's going to cost."

"So do I," Eleven said. "But the general says it will. He hasn't been wrong yet."

"Yet," Ten echoed ominously. "You finished there?"

Eleven checked the end of the cable, making sure enough of its weight hung down the side of the building. "All set," he confirmed. "Let's get back down. The general wants to bring up the first two loads no later than five tomorrow morning, and the trucks could be here as early as eleven. We'd better get some rest while we can."

"And meanwhile get ourselves out of this cold."

Eleven gazed across the roof at the sun settling behind the New York skyline, feeling a sudden tightness in his chest. In a little over twenty-four hours, for a few minutes anyway, the cold he could feel settling around them would be banished from this part of the city. "Yes," he murmured. "Let's go get warm."

~

The legal paperwork had slid through the system as only officially-greased paperwork can slide, and by late afternoon the coffin of the late Mr. Raymond Bodinacce had been dug up and carefully lifted out of the too-shallow grave.

There, buried underneath it, protected from crushing by a surrounding ring of similarly buried cement blocks, was the missing body.

"So that's Talbot's body, eh?" Chief Garcia commented, watching with folded arms as Barry and two of his assistants knelt precariously on the cement blocks, carefully cutting away the thick plastic wrapping the bundle.

"Ross's, actually," Delgado corrected, taking a cautious sniff of the air. After nearly a week underground, the body would be well into decomposition phase. Just as well he and Garcia were standing upwind of the hole. "The one he shot at Greenleaf Center."

"I meant the one Talbot was so hot that we look for," Garcia rumbled. "Buried with another body, too, just like he said. Must be a real pain to be right all the time."

"Well, he *did* guess wrong about which side of the coffin it would be buried on," Delgado pointed out. "But don't worry. He'll give Officer Donahue and us the full credit for finding it."

Garcia grunted. "Right. FBI types always share the glory with the peons."

Delgado smiled to himself. "It could happen," he said.

Barry looked up. "Looks like Ross's body, all right," he announced, his voice muffled by his protective mask. "Single 9mm gunshot wound to the chest, with trauma evidence of a face-forward fall onto pavement or concrete. I'll be able to tell you more after we get him home."

Garcia nodded. "Let's do it, then."

"Sure thing," Barry said. Turning, he waved to the men waiting a short distance away with the lifting equipment.

"I'm heading back," Garcia added to Delgado. "You coming?"

"I think I'll stay on top of this," Delgado told him. "Talbot *did* say to rush it."

Garcia grunted. "Suit yourself," he said. "Have fun."

"Yes, sir."

He headed back toward the line of cars on the access road. For a minute Delgado watched as he picked his way almost gingerly between the graves. Garcia didn't know the full truth about this. No one outside D.C. did. Or at least no one was supposed to.

But Delgado was Talbot's friend, and Talbot had needed someone to make sure this final piece of the puzzle didn't get shunted off into a corner somewhere until it was too late.

He swallowed hard, visions of nuclear holocaust over New York dancing before his eyes like a foretaste of hell. No, Garcia didn't have the inside track on this one, and if he knew he'd been cut out he would undoubtedly be furious. But at least he would sleep well tonight.

Sometimes friendship was a blessing. Other times, it could be a curse.

With a sigh, Delgado turned back to watch them lift the body from its grave.

THE
LAST
DAY

35

It HAD BEEN cold on the rooftop the previous afternoon. It was even colder at four-thirty Friday morning when the panel truck pulled to a stop along the north side of the building. Eleven wiggled his toes inside his boots, trying not to be obvious about the fact they were freezing, wondering uneasily if the winch mechanism would refuse to work in such temperatures.

He needn't have worried. The winch worked perfectly, lowering the cable to street level, and a few minutes later the group had the first and largest crate out of the truck and securely fastened to the end. Ten touched the remote again, and the box slid silently up into the street-lit night.

"You can swing it all the way onto the roof?" the general asked, watching the crate's progress.

"Yes, sir," Ten confirmed. "The boom's fully operable from here, too."

"Good," the general said. "Swing this one as far to the right as you can before you set it down. That will leave all the room on the left for the other crates."

"Yes, sir."

"Is there any late word on the trucks?" Eleven asked.

"They're making good time," the general said. "They may be to the outskirts as early as nine-thirty, though maneuvering through the city will take extra time."

He looked at Eleven. "When you see the security man later this morning, makes sure he knows we're bringing another package up along here around midday. We don't want him being surprised by that."

Eleven nodded. "I know how to handle it."

"Good," the general said again. "Then we're set."

"And nothing can stop us now," Eight murmured under his breath.

"On the contrary," the general said. "Any number of things could still stop us."

He looked back at the ascending crate. "But," he added quietly, "none of them will."

~

One thirty-nine. JFK Airport.

His plane had just arrived at the gate.

Talbot loitered back beside the windows, the bright sunshine coming in over his shoulder as the gate personnel opened the door. It was an uncommonly clear day for New York in January, though the forecast was promising more snow before midnight.

"Here he comes," McPherson's voice came through the earphone tucked unobtrusively in Talbot's left ear.

"Our other guest has also arrived," General Vaughn's voice came back. "Bring him in."

"Acknowledged," McPherson said. "Talbot?"

"Ready," Talbot confirmed, moving casually toward the gate and the line of passengers starting to emerge through the door.

He was third in line, a small overnight bag over his shoulder, clearly impatient to get past the business-suited woman walking in front of him. His dark face was sheened with a thin layer of perspiration, his eyes darting about with anxiety and restlessness and probably the fatigue of a sleepless night.

He was past the rows of waiting area chairs, and was just ducking around the woman, when McPherson rose quietly from his seat in the back row and stepped in behind him. "Home Minister Naveen Rao?" he said.

Rao jumped as if he'd stepped on an electrically charged nail. "Yes?" he said cautiously.

"Director Frank McPherson, FBI," McPherson introduced himself, showing the other his badge wallet. "We've spoken on the phone quite a bit over the past few days."

Some of Rao's tightness faded into cautious relief. "Yes, of course," he said. "I wish we could have met under more pleasant circumstances."

"So do I," McPherson said solemnly as Talbot came up to them. "This is Special Agent Talbot. Would you come with us, please?"

The eyes went tight again. "I understand that we have a great deal to discuss," Rao said, speaking toward McPherson as he looked at Talbot. "That was why I came personally. But at the moment—"

"I'm afraid I have to insist," McPherson said firmly, gesturing him forward. "This way, please."

"Yes," Rao murmured. "Of course."

They walked in silence down the corridor, bypassing the normal customs lines in favor of a back route manned by silent FBI and Homeland Security agents. A minute later they arrived at the secure Port Authority conference room McPherson had requisitioned. Still without speaking, the director opened the door and ushered Rao inside.

There had been four people in the office when Talbot had left to go to the gate: Cohn, Hanna Swenson, General Vaughn, and Vijay Prasad, the Indian ambassador to the United States. Those four were still there, but now four more had been added. Three of them were Secret Service agents, spread watchfully around the edges of the room.

The fourth, seated behind the desk, was President Whitcomb.

"Good morning, Minister Rao," Whitcomb said evenly, gesturing him to the single chair that had been placed in front of the desk. "Please sit down."

"Mr. President," Rao said, moving to the chair but standing beside it instead of sitting. "It's an honor to meet you. Regretfully, I must ask that this meeting be postponed until a later time. I have important governmental business to attend to."

"You're not here on governmental business, Minister," Whitcomb said. "At least, I hope not. Otherwise, I'll have no choice but to conclude that all of New Delhi is part of this plot."

The dark eyes went suddenly flat. "I have no idea what you're talking about."

"I'm talking about a tactical nuclear weapon you arranged to have stolen from an Indian research facility," Whitcomb said, his eyes and words boring into Rao like drop-forged steel drill bits. "I'm talking about your co-conspirator, General Raksha Bakht, who smuggled that weapon into the United States and in so doing caused the death of a United States Marine. I'm talking about four other civilian deaths caused or ordered by General Bakht during and following the theft of three advanced technological devices known as Cloaks, which he subsequently used to bring the weapon into this country."

His gaze hardened even more. "And I'm talking about your intention to detonate the weapon against us. Have you anything to say?"

There had, Talbot thought, been a brief flicker of reaction in Rao's eyes at the name of General Bakht. But by the time Whitcomb finished, the minister's face had closed over again. "With all due respect, Mr. President," he said, his voice under rigid control, "this makes no sense at all. Why on Earth would I do such a thing?"

"That's what we're here to find out," Whitcomb said.

"But it makes no sense," Rao insisted. "Or do you seek in me a scapegoat for your own failures?"

Whitcomb gestured to McPherson. "Director?" he invited.

"You were good at your job, Minister," McPherson said, his voice cold as he gazed at Rao. "Both jobs, I should say. Your first task, of course, was to use hand-wringing and moaning about world censure to deflect our attention away from India, despite the obviously suspicious fact that the weapon had originated there. But even more important was your second task, that of making sure we stayed on track for all the false leads Bakht was scattering behind him."

"This is absurd," Rao protested.

"Unfortunately for you, you were a little too good at it," McPherson continued as if Rao hadn't spoken. "Or perhaps I should say, a little too quick. The CitationJet incident, for instance. Bakht was expecting us to catch the feint he'd worked up between a totally innocent Chinese plane and his own copycat version, with an eye toward implicating both China and Iran in the theft. Both countries were marked for additional suspicion later on, but he wanted us to start thinking in those directions. He couldn't have anticipated that the cloud cover would roll in at just the wrong moment, blanking out satellite surveillance, and that for a couple of days we would miss the trick completely.

"It would have been a major triumph, of course, if the plan had been to actually throw us off track. Unfortunately, it wasn't. Bakht's hijackers aboard the *Rabah Jamila* were poised to send their mayday and coded Chinese signal, and then pull a vanishing act that would ultimately throw suspicion on Captain Syed. All that cleverness would go to waste if we didn't already have some idea that the freighter was important and therefore move in immediately once we picked up the mayday.

"What you didn't know, Minister, was that a pirate incident off Taiwan had already brought the ship to our attention. So, not knowing that, you had to conveniently discover that a particular Pakistani freighter had been in a particular Indian harbor at the same time as an alleged security disturbance a few days before the weapon disappeared."

McPherson threw a slightly grudging glance at Talbot. "The point, though we didn't notice it at the time, was that there was absolutely no reason for you to have picked on that particular freighter."

"This is your proof of conspiracy?" Rao demanded scathingly. "That my people did their job better than yours? I told you at the time that the *Rabah Jamila* was scheduled to load eight containers, yet only loaded six."

"Which sounded reasonable enough at the time," McPherson agreed, throwing a far less grudging look at Swenson. "Unfortunately for you, we've since run the analysis ourselves. It turns out that the *Rabah Jamila* was one of seven freighters during that same time period that ended up with changed manifests. Why pick on one and ignore the others?"

"You were also a little too startled when we mentioned the pirate attack," Cohn pointed out. "That alone should have suggested you might have more than a passing interest in the freighter's welfare."

"Still, once might have been a lucky guess or even the expertise you claim," McPherson continued. "The freighter in question was Pakistani, after all, which would make it stand out on any Indian list of suspects. The problem was that you turned right around and did it again. As the ship carrying the weapon approached the U.S., Bakht wanted our attention drawn elsewhere so that they could ease into position without being spotted and challenged too far from shore."

Vaughn snorted. "Into position for this *quiet* landing of theirs," he muttered.

"You're missing the true subtlety of the situation, General," McPherson told him. "Bakht's idea was never for the cat to just slink ashore without anyone noticing, though it probably could have, any more than that CitationJet was supposed to permanently throw us off the trail. Again, he wanted to muddy the waters as much as possible, and he'd gone to too much trouble and planted too many false clues not to do something spectacular at that end."

"But as Director McPherson said, he didn't need or want us on the scene too early," Cohn added. "The open theft of the Coast Guard helo was what was supposed to stir up the anthill."

"As it happened, we'd already penetrated the incoming cat's shifting disguise system and sent out an alert," McPherson said. "But Director Cohn is right. Even if we hadn't, the Coast Guard incident would have brought us back onto Bakht's script at the right time.

"But back to your part," he went on, his gaze hardening. "As I said, Bakht wanted our eyes turned away from our own shores, to which end he'd planted evidence pointing to Israel in the containers the *Rabah Jamila* hijackers had used. We caught on as soon as the containers were flown to the FBI labs, so there too we were right where Bakht wanted us.

"But again, you didn't know that, and you assumed we'd missed yet another clue. Granted, it was a far more subtle one this time. So you called with yet another out-of-the-blue discovery, this one concerning an alleged secret Iranian meeting between Captain Syed and one of Rabbi Salomon's top people."

"Joshua Barez *was* in Bandar-e 'Abbas," Rao said stubbornly. But to Talbot's ear he was starting to weaken. "You can confirm that yourself."

"Oh, I don't doubt he was," McPherson said. "I imagine Bakht engineered the whole visit, possibly even calling Barez personally to invite him to Iran. The issue isn't whether Barez and Syed were in the same port together, but rather why you'd gone looking for such a connection in the first place. Why suspect Israeli involvement at all?"

"Again, you condemn me for my thoroughness," Rao protested.

"Perhaps," McPherson said. "And I'll grant you that even two such lucky guesses could still be coincidence."

"Or simple competence."

"Which was why Special Agent Talbot decided to arrange a little test," McPherson concluded quietly. "A test in the form of complementary passes for your son Sanjay and his political science class to attend tonight's opening UN ceremonies.

"So tell me, Minister Rao: why exactly *are* you here in New York?"

The question hung in the silence like a dew-heavy spider web. Rao looked desperately at Prasad; but there was no help or comfort there. The ambassador's face had grown steadily harder throughout McPherson's recitation, to the point where it was now as grim and unyielding as Whitcomb's. Only in Prasad's case the darkness was edged with a deep shame. "Is President Whitcomb correct, Minister?" Prasad asked. "Is it indeed your intention to detonate a nuclear weapon against the United States?"

Rao's eyes slipped away from that implacable gaze. "You Americans," he murmured, a hint of contempt all that remained of his earlier attempts at righteous indignation. "You think everything in the world must somehow revolve around you. This has nothing to do with you. Nothing at all."

"What does it have to do with, then?" Prasad demanded. "The murder of Dr. Tahir Kazi, perhaps?"

"Don't you understand?" Rao bit out, shifting his gaze again to Prasad. His voice was angry and demanding, yet at the same time almost pleading. "He's a threat to our nation. A terrible, deadly threat. And not only to us, but to the entire world. Surely you can see that."

"And that is your excuse?" Prasad countered. "That you do not wish to be the Home Affairs Minister who must preside over the departure of Jammu and Kashmir from the union?"

"You are a fool," Rao snarled. The pleading had disappeared, replaced by bitterness. "You understand nothing. If Kazi succeeds in persuading the world community to wrench Jammu and Kashmir from its place in the Indian state, that precedent will become a rolling Juggernaut against which no nation will be able to stand for long.

"Within a year, which other Indian states and ethnic minorities will decide they no longer wish to be ruled from New Delhi? For there *will* be others. Many others. Bit by bit, piece by piece, state by state, India will disintegrate, until there is nothing left but a thousand different peoples living behind their self-imposed walls, squabbling endlessly among themselves. Nothing will be left but the memory of what once was and the fading vision of what might have been."

He jabbed an accusing finger at Whitcomb. "And don't think it would stop with India, Mr. President. Within five years, the world will have disintegrated into a chaos of tiny ethnic groups, each too small to sustain itself, each forever embroiled in wars of hatred or greed or desperation with its neighbors. Neither would your country be spared—even now some of your Hispanic minorities clamor for their own land."

"All of this chaos from a single man?" McPherson asked.

"A spark can ignite a forest," Rao countered. "Kazi has the eyes and ears of the world, and a skill for manipulating emotions and inciting action rarely seen on the world stage. Perhaps he won't succeed. But we cannot afford to take that risk."

"You may view Dr. Kazi as an enemy of your nation if you choose," Whitcomb's deep voice broke in. "You may even take steps to eliminate him if circumstances and your own conscience permit. We aren't the world's policeman, and wouldn't have the authority to stop you even if we could."

His face darkened like a thundercloud, and even seated behind the desk he suddenly seemed to tower above Rao. "But do *not* try to tell me this has nothing to do with us. If it happens on U.S. soil, it most definitely concerns us."

Rao's mouth worked. "What I meant—"

"And you will therefore now explain to me," Whitcomb continued softly, "why I should not declare a state of war between our two nations."

Behind the film of sweat, Rao's dark face went pale. "Surely you don't intend to hold an entire nation accountable for the actions of a few," he managed. "General Bakht and I take full responsibility for this plot."

"That will be of no comfort to the thousands of people your bomb will burn to their deaths," Whitcomb shot back. "Their ghosts will demand justice, and your life and General Bakht's together won't even begin to balance the scales. We've been through this before, Minister, with 9/11 and its aftermath. You really should have learned what it means to attack the United States."

Whitcomb turned to Prasad. "We've spoken long with your government about the dangers of nuclear proliferation, Mr. Ambassador," he said. "We've spoken relatively little about the inevitable consequences. You're about to see one of those consequences first-hand. Within a few days at the most, New Delhi will see the other."

"I will contact my government immediately, Mr. President," Prasad said, his voice trembling. "But Minister Rao is right. Apologies we can give. Restitution, so far as it is possible, for lives unjustly snuffed out. But how can you suggest taking indiscriminate vengeance on an innocent people?"

"We have only the minister's word that the rest of the government is innocent," Vaughn pointed out. "Besides, the American people won't be interested in the fine distinctions between mass murderers and those who will be quietly relieved that the threat of Kashmiri independence is gone."

"The people will demand vengeance," Whitcomb agreed. "You saw that on 9/11, too. And vengeance *will* be theirs."

"I beg of you, Mr. President," Prasad pleaded, his face now nearly as pale as Rao's. "I cannot go to my government with such a message. You must offer us an alternative."

"There is none," Whitcomb said, his voice the quiet of a grave. "If the weapon is detonated, the United States and the Republic of India will be at war."

He turned back to Rao. "Your only alternative is to make it not happen."

Prasad took a step toward Rao. "He means it, Minister," he said urgently. "Do you understand? You must call off the operation."

Rao closed his eyes, fatigue and tension seeming to melt him into something small and pathetic as he stood leaning on the empty chair. "Don't you think I want to?" he whispered. "My own son is going to be in the weapon's path. But I can't. General Bakht has not contacted me in nearly a week, and I have no way of contacting him."

"Then tell us the plan," McPherson said. "We'll stop him ourselves."

Rao covered his face with his hands. "I don't *know* the plan," he all but wailed. "Not the details. All I know is that the explosion is scheduled for seven o'clock tonight."

For a long moment the only sound in the room was Rao's stifled sobbing. Then Whitcomb turned to Swenson. "What do you need?"

"We can start with his computer access codes and passwords, sir," she said, her voice tight but controlled. "After that, the numbers of any government accounts he controls that General Bakht might have had access to. Ditto for his personal accounts."

"You heard the lady, Minister," Whitcomb said. "Give her the numbers."

With an effort, Rao pulled himself together and finally sat down in the chair he'd been leaning on for so long. Swenson set her notebook on the corner of the desk beside him, and under Whitcomb's unblinking gaze Rao began haltingly giving her the information.

McPherson caught Talbot's eye, nodded minutely toward the corner Cohn and Vaughn had already drifted toward. "Five hours," Vaughn muttered when the four men were gathered in a tight group. "Hell's bells."

"And we only get that much if Bakht doesn't find out we're onto him," McPherson pointed out grimly. "Dr. Kazi is already at the UN— Bakht could jump the timetable and blow it any time."

"And anywhere within a quarter mile of the UN will guarantee its destruction," Vaughn added. "Within half a mile, possibly, if he assumes debris and the shockwave will do most of the job for him."

"I don't think he will," Talbot said thoughtfully. "I'd be willing to bet it'll be as close to the UN as he can get it. *And* that he'll wait until seven if at all possible, or at least until after rush hour winds down."

"Why?" Vaughn asked. "So their getaway will be easier?"

Talbot shook his head. "Look at their pattern, not only with the *Rabah Jamila* and the coastal operation, but also the Cloak theft. All along the way, they've tried very hard to keep the killing to an absolute minimum."

"Of course." Vaughn snorted. "That's why they're only using a *little* nuclear weapon."

"I'm serious," Talbot insisted. "Look at their pattern, then look at the landscape. The UN Building is about as isolated a structure as you can get in Manhattan—the East River on one side, lots of open space on the other three. The closer in they can get the bomb, the less collateral damage there'll be to everything else."

"What about the hotels in the area?" McPherson asked. "Lot of people in those."

"I don't know," Talbot said. "But I'm betting he has something in mind. Maybe a series of bomb threats around six o'clock to get them emptied."

"You may be right," Cohn grunted. "But if push comes to shove, I vote with Frank and General Vaughn. He'll set it off wherever he can get it, and whenever he can get it there, and to hell with collateral damage. The last thing he wants now is to get caught with it in his possession."

"So we search quietly," McPherson said. "We don't let them know we're on to them."

"Easier said than done," Vaughn warned. "Check Bakht's record— he doesn't take anything for granted. He'll have spotters in place, probably before he even tries to move the weapon."

Cohn, facing the desk, lifted a finger. "They're finished."

The others turned to look. Swenson was closing her notebook as Rao pulled himself up from his chair, looking like a man preparing for his own execution. The man had broken, all right, and it had been as quick a collapse as Talbot had ever seen.

It made him wonder how firmly Rao had been on board with this plot in the first place, and how much Bakht had bullied him into it. Yet another reason for the general to have kept his distance since the operation began.

Which meant that any tenuous hope they might have had that Bakht would call for a final confirmation before detonating the bomb could be put to rest. This was a political strike, but it was the general, not the politician, who was the driving force behind it.

Talbot caught Swenson's eye, lifted his eyebrows questioningly. Her lip twitched, her shoulders shrugged microscopically. Whatever information Rao had given her apparently wasn't very much.

"Thank you for your cooperation, Minister," Whitcomb said. He didn't stand up, nor did he offer to shake hands. "If you think of anything else that might help, I trust you'll inform one of your guards immediately."

"Of course," Rao murmured. "What will happen to me now?"

"You came here to visit the United Nations," Whitcomb said. "So that's where you're going. You'll be kept in a room near our command center."

Prasad stirred, but didn't speak. "And my son?" Rao asked.

Whitcomb's expression didn't change. "He'll be attending the ceremonies along with his class."

Rao stiffened. "Sir, I beg of you. Keep me there—I no longer care. But please let the boy live."

"He lives or dies with the rest of us, Minister," Whitcomb said. "Perhaps that thought will help sharpen your memory. The men outside will escort you out."

For a moment Talbot thought Rao was actually going to drop to his knees and plead. But the last shreds of pride won out, or else the realization that it would do no good. Silently, he turned and walked to the door. Talbot caught a glimpse of the two FBI agents waiting there as the minister stepped outside and closed the door behind him.

Ambassador Prasad took a deep breath. "This is a nightmare come to Earth," he murmured.

"It is indeed," Whitcomb agreed heavily. "But given the global political climate I suppose it was inevitable that something like this would eventually happen."

"You will of course evacuate the UN immediately?"

Whitcomb shook his head. "No."

Prasad's mouth dropped open. "*No*? But—"

"It's too late for that, Mr. Ambassador," Whitcomb said. "Dr. Kazi is already in range, along with most of the other delegates. If we try to sneak him out, they'll simply detonate the weapon earlier."

"Even if we somehow catch them napping, we'd still have the problem of the weapon itself," Vaughn rumbled. "If they can't get to it, they'll blow it just to be rid of the thing. If they *can* get to it, they might cart it off to Boston or LA or God only knows where and set it off there. Our best chance of recovering the weapon is right here and right now."

Prasad shook his head. "I can't believe General Bakht would allow himself to be drawn into such madness," he said, as if talking to himself. "He's a dedicated and highly decorated officer, the hero of our most recent border confrontation with the Chinese. Are you certain he is involved?"

"Minister Rao himself confirmed it," Whitcomb reminded him.

"After you had named him," Prasad pointed out. "Could he merely have been trying to shift some of the responsibility?"

"Director McPherson?" Whitcomb invited.

"I'm afraid there's no doubt, Mr. Ambassador," McPherson said. "Last night we recovered the body of one of his men and made a positive fingerprint identification. He was one of fifteen men Bakht handpicked six months ago from the various units under his command. Three of them were arrested in India this morning, charged with the actual theft of the weapon. Bakht and the other eleven have disappeared."

"And are presumably already in New York," Whitcomb added. "I suggest, Mr. Ambassador, that you return to Washington immediately and consult with your government."

Prasad drew himself up. "Thank you, Mr. President," he said. "But I can consult with them as easily from our UN mission as I can from Washington."

Whitcomb frowned. "You're going to the UN?"

"Yes, sir," Prasad said. His face was still pale, but his jaw was set. "If an Indian weapon is to be used against innocent people, the least an Indian diplomat can do is not run while others die. With your permission?"

Whitcomb nodded. "Very well, Mr. Ambassador. I'll see you there."

Prasad nodded back, and like Rao before him left without another word. "You didn't actually mean that last, did you, sir?" Talbot asked, frowning. "Surely you're not going to the UN yourself."

"I'm scheduled to speak at the opening ceremonies, Special Agent Talbot," Whitcomb said gravely. "If we can't risk a complete evacuation of the building—and we can't—then I can hardly sneak off and hide in the White House basement, can I?"

Talbot looked at McPherson. "Director?"

McPherson shook his head. "Sorry, Talbot," he said. "We've been to the mat with him already on this. He's made up his mind."

"Besides, if Bakht's spotters notice he's not there, they may smell a rat," Cohn added. "We can't risk that."

"Not to mention the international repercussions if I stay away and let others die," Whitcomb said, standing up. "I will compromise this far, though. Since I'm not scheduled to arrive until six-thirty, I'll stay away until then. What progress have we made?"

"We started searching the building itself around midnight," Vaughn said. "So far we haven't found anything, but there are all sorts of back corridors and cubbyholes yet to check." He grimaced. "Complicating things, of course, is the need to keep anyone from noticing what we're doing and realizing there's more than just a routine bomb check underway. A panic is the last thing we need."

"Complicating things even more are these Cloaks," McPherson added grimly. "The bomb could be sitting right out in the open somewhere, and unless someone tripped over it they'd never even know it was there."

"There's no way to detect them?" Whitcomb asked.

"We've got some speed trap guns that seem to work pretty well," McPherson said. "Unfortunately, the things are pulsed, so you can't just sweep the laser around a storeroom and see if you hit something. We've got people playing with the electronics, but I don't know if they'll be retooled in time to be of any use."

"We're also trying radar guns and long-scan metal detectors," Vaughn said. "They're of no use inside, but they might pick up the bomb casing if Bakht has it stashed out in the middle of the grounds somewhere."

"A shame the snow isn't supposed to show up until later tonight," Whitcomb commented. "A fresh blanket of snow on top of even a cloaked bomb would probably show something."

"And if it had snowed last night, we might have footprints to work with," McPherson said. "But we have to make do with what we have."

"We've also begun a search of the buildings nearest to the UN itself, including the various hotels," Vaughn went on. "That one's a bit trickier, since we don't know where Bakht might have his observers located. New Delhi sent us photos of all of them, but we know from the Harrier and Coast Guard thefts that Bakht has an amateur makeup artist in the group who likes playing with theatrical putty and colored contact lenses."

"Plus there's a hell of a lot of real estate to be covered," McPherson said. "I don't know how strong the UN building is, but we have to assume that a point two kiloton weapon going off anywhere within a quarter mile will pretty well demolish it."

"Yes," Whitcomb murmured. "Well, at least we don't have to worry about buildings in the East River."

"No, just boats and the chance they buried it underwater," Vaughn said. "We've got divers down there now, with a mini-submarine on the way. There's also the Midtown Tunnel, which we're also checking."

"What about the weapon itself?" Whitcomb asked. "Once we find it, how hard will it be to disarm?"

"There, at least, we have some good news," Vaughn said. "There's a single electronics box that slides into a slot in one end. Pull out the box, and it's disarmed. Simplicity itself."

Whitcomb frowned. "Seems almost *too* simple."

"It would be useless in a combat situation," Vaughn agreed. "But remember, the bomb came from a research lab, not an armory. It was an experimental model, without all the usual safeties and locks."

"Let's hope New Delhi knows what they're talking about," Whitcomb said. "Is there anything else you need from me? More people, more resources—anything?"

"We've got about as many people as we can safely field right now," McPherson said. "Unless the Executive Branch has a secret stockpile of luck somewhere, I think we're on our own."

"I'll check with Cynthia," Whitcomb said soberly. "If we can't locate any luck, maybe some prayers will do."

McPherson nodded. "Even better."

Whitcomb looked at his watch. "We have five hours. Let's make them count."

~

By three-thirty, the unofficial but de facto start of Friday afternoon rush hour, the final rooftop preparations were finished.

"All set, sir," Thirteen reported, crawling out from under the section of empty air that was the Cloak. "The lines are secure."

"Very good," General Bakht said, checking his watch. They were nearly an hour ahead of schedule. Excellent. "The final stage will begin in two hours."

"And until then?" Six asked, shivering once. Bakht could sympathize—even the light wind drifting steadily in from the west was enough to make the roof feel much colder than it actually was.

"Until then?" The general smiled. "Why, the fleshpots of Manhattan lie at our feet. Let us go down, make our way through the police lines and military searchers, and find something warm to drink."

36

THERE WAS SOME long and involved explanation going on over the tac radio system, a conversation which for some reason Talbot needed to be involved in. Swenson leaned back in her chair, rubbed her tired fingertips, and cultivated her patience.

At five minutes to four, with three hours left, she didn't have a lot of patience left to cultivate.

Talbot finished his conversation and pulled his headset off. "Go," he said, dropping into the chair beside her.

"Okay," Swenson said, pulling up the first spreadsheet. "Near as I can figure, this is the total list of funds Bakht was able to sneak out of Rao's various sources."

"A tidy sum," Talbot commented. "Next?"

Swenson pulled up her second window. "Here, mixed in with a lot of guesswork, is a probable list of disbursements."

"Why so much guesswork?"

"There are some big question marks," Swenson explained. "The chameleon racing cat they bought from that drug lord, for one. I've got a number that seems likely, but Bakht's bookkeeping hasn't exactly been CPA quality. A lot of the numbers simply aren't identified."

"There's the *Eureka*," he muttered, half to himself. "The sailing yacht they wound up sinking. That was an expensive fifteen minutes. What's that?—oh, yes, the other decoy, their sailboat-shaped balloon. Compressed air to fill it with . . . the fuel bladder, and the stuff to fill *it* with. No ammo listed. I guess they stole those Israeli armaments instead of buying them."

He leaned closer. "Surface-to-air missiles?" he asked, tapping a number on the screen.

"Five of them, looks like," she said. "Purchased four months ago from Iran, if the Pentagon's black-market tracking system is right."

"Iran," Talbot growled. "Still throwing out red herrings. I wonder what those are for."

"Maybe they were part of the cat's defense system," Swenson suggested. "In case we tumbled too early and they had to make a run for the coast with half the Navy on their tail."

"I don't know," Talbot said, tugging thoughtfully at his lower lip. "More likely they're for defense here. Something to shoot back with if we find them."

"Which might suggest they're setting the bomb in a place where they have to worry about an air attack," Swenson pointed out. "Like a boat or rooftop."

"Or the SAMs could be part of a diversion, fired off to make us *think* they're on a boat or rooftop," Talbot said. "Either way, we need to warn the choppers and air spotters."

"Right." Swenson tapped a number on the screen with her pencil. "But here's what I mostly wanted you to see. I've covered all the equipment we know they have or can reasonably guess that they have. I've even figured in food and lodging allowances. But I still come up with this one disbursement I can't account for."

Talbot whistled softly. "A hundred and fifty thousand dollars. That's one hell of a petty cash fund."

"I can't think what that could be for," Swenson went on. "My best guess is that it's the vehicles they used to bring the nuke and Cloaks across country."

"Way too high for that," Talbot said. "Besides, up to now they've done just fine hot-wiring whatever they needed."

"You suppose they might have changed the pattern this once?" Swenson asked. "Hoped they could make us waste time looking for stolen vehicles that weren't stolen?"

"Seems sort of petty," Talbot said doubtfully. "And again, it's way too much money. Maybe it has to do with their escape route."

Behind them, the door opened. "Talbot?" the FBI man on liaison duty called. "Visitors."

Swenson turned, to see Ross step into the room, carrying what looked like an oversized version of an old-style Geiger counter on a strap over his shoulder. "Ross!" she exclaimed.

Talbot swiveled around, too. "What are you doing here?" he demanded.

"Brought you a present," Ross said. "Hi, Hanna."

"Thoughtful of you," Talbot growled. "Only you're supposed to be in D.C. watching over Angie and the techs."

Ross's lips puckered. "Well, you're half right," he conceded, stepping aside out of the doorway.

"Hello, Hanna," Angie Chandler said quietly as she walked in behind him. "Special Agent Talbot."

Talbot threw Swenson a startled look. "Mrs. Chandler," he managed, sounding like he was talking through chapped lips. "Ross, pardon the question, but what the hell is she doing here?"

"I asked him to bring me," Angie said before Ross could answer. "I want to help."

"I appreciate your willingness," Talbot said. "But you're one of exactly three sources of information and expertise we have on the Cloaks. We can't afford to risk you."

She shook her head. "Burke and Esteban have the expertise," she said. "I'm just the widow."

"Fine," Talbot bit out. "Let me put it more bluntly. If we don't find and defuse the bomb in the next three hours, this is going to be a very unhealthy place to be. I appreciate your bravery. Ross, kindly get her out of here."

Neither of them moved. "There's nothing for me in Washington, Special Agent Talbot," Angie said. Her face was smooth and emotionless, but Swenson could hear the depth of sadness in her voice. "Or anywhere else. I'd rather die here, today, than live with the knowledge of what my husband's work has done."

"It isn't your husband's fault that his invention was twisted to this use," Talbot countered. "But we don't have time to discuss it, and I can't spare anyone to physically toss you off the island. If you want to stay, I can't stop you."

"That's Madison's way of saying welcome," Swenson added dryly.

Talbot threw her a patient look. "So what's this present?" he asked.

"Something the lab boys whipped up," Ross said, sliding the box off his shoulder onto the table beside Swenson's computer. The resemblance she'd already noted to a Geiger counter was still there, except that where the usual dial indicator should have been was a small LCD screen. "It's a thermal-gradient imaging something or other," Ross continued, flipping the on switch and pulling the microphone-shaped probe from its clamp. "Unlike standard infrared detectors, this does a gradient mapping of local ambient heat changes, looking for objects with different heating or cooling rates."

"Like, for instance, a nuclear bomb casing sitting in the middle of a field?" Talbot asked.

"Exactly," Ross confirmed. "As a nice bonus, since the basic Cloak material is black, which absorbs and radiates faster than other colors, we even get a slight enhancement of the effect. Particularly when the temperature is changing rapidly."

"Like at sunset," Swenson said, feeling a cautious new hope.

"Exactly," Ross said. "Even now, with building shadows starting to cut across the grounds, it should have a fair chance of working."

"That should take a bite out of the search time," Talbot agreed. "Better get this to the troops scouring the lawn out there."

"They already have theirs," Ross assured him. "I ran into General Vaughn on my way in and he's passing them out. This one's mine."

"How many do we have?"

"Only five, I'm afraid, including this one," Ross said. "The other downside is that the detection angle is narrow, though that can be adjusted a little. Unfortunately, the wider the angle, the shorter the distance it'll work over. The sampling rate also kind of stinks."

"How badly?" Swenson asked.

"You basically have to point the thing at your target zone for seven to ten seconds before you get enough data for it to paint you a picture," Ross told her. "They're trying to throw together some faster ones that you can sweep across the landscape like a video camera, but I don't know if they'll be done in time."

"Why don't they send the schematics here?" Swenson suggested. "Build them in Manhattan instead of D.C. That would at least save delivery time."

"Already thought of that," Ross said. "McPherson's got a dozen techs in one of those semis by the river working on the Mark II models, plus another dozen turning out more of these Mark I's. We also brought the Cloak up so that they'll be able to give the Mark II's a field test if and when they get them running."

"At least we have these five," Talbot said. "What are you planning to do with yours?"

"I thought I'd go wander the streets out there," Ross said. "Poke my head into some alleys near the quarter-mile perimeter. The main search teams are working their way outward from the UN Building itself, but I don't see Bakht being quite that obvious."

"Neither do I," Talbot said. "But McPherson and Vaughn decided we need to start from the presumed blast point."

"I suppose they have to," Ross conceded. "We'd all look pretty silly if the bomb went off under the General Assembly podium while everyone was searching Broadway dressing rooms."

"I'll be going with Mr. Ross," Angie said. "There's still the question of why they were trying to kill me. Maybe there's still time to figure it out."

Talbot cleared his throat. "I presume it's occurred to you that they may not take kindly to seeing you alive and well."

"I know," she said quietly. "As I said, I'm not afraid to die."

"We've still got those turtle vests, and I've told Angie she has to wear hers," Ross said. "But frankly, I can't see them blowing their cover just for another crack at us. For all they know, we might be deliberate bait trying to draw them out."

"I suppose," Talbot said reluctantly.

"Besides, you already admitted you have no authority over Angie's movements," Ross added. "Or mine, for that matter."

"I wouldn't push McPherson on that one if I were you," Talbot warned.

"Wouldn't dream of it," Ross assured him. "Speaking of whom, I need to check in with him on something. He's down the hall, right?"

"Three doors on the left," Talbot confirmed.

Ross nodded. "Can I leave Angie here for a minute?"

"Sure," Talbot said. "Make it fast."

"I will." He slipped out the door, closing it behind him.

"You're sure you're okay with this?" Talbot asked Angie. "There really isn't any need for you to be here."

"I want to be." Angie hesitated. "May I ask you a question?"

"Sure," Talbot said. "I hope it's one I can answer for a change."

"Who exactly is Mr. Ross?" she asked. "Back in Monterey he said you used to be partners. But then Director McPherson said something about him being in witness protection?"

Swenson looked at Talbot, found him looking back at her. "You want to take this one?" he invited.

"Don't look at me," Swenson countered. "He's *your* colleague."

"I suppose," Talbot said. "Okay. Yes, he was my partner for three years. A good partner, and a good agent. We tackled a lot of cases together, and solved a pretty fair number of them. Not enough for Ross, though, who is something of a workaholic. In his spare time he went off and dabbled around the edges of other people's cases, mostly just for the fun of it, usually finding stuff the assigned investigators had missed."

"That probably made him very popular," Angie murmured.

"Oh, you have no idea," Talbot agreed sourly. "Especially in the high-pressure competition that's the true heart and soul of D.C. Anyway, during one of these private excavations he more or less accidentally dug up some major dirt on a high-level Justice Department official."

"Who?" Angie asked.

"Sorry, that one's classified," Talbot said. "Ross's evidence was genuine, but unfortunately unprovable. The official caught some heat and returned the favor by getting Ross kicked out of the Bureau."

Angie looked at Swenson, her eyes wide. "They can do that?"

"This one could," Talbot said grimly. "Anyway, Ross didn't take it well and disappeared for a couple of years. There were rumors he hooked up with the CIA during that time and did some undercover work for them, but I've never had that confirmed. Then, he suddenly popped up in D.C. again, this time with a brand-new connection between the same DOJ official and the mob. And he made sure this one *was* provable."

"Only no one wanted the awkward publicity of a trial," Swenson put in. "So he was allowed to resign and flip on the crime bosses he'd been taking payoffs from."

"All of which resulted in both him and Ross going into WitSec," Talbot said.

"All right," Angie said, frowning. "So why doesn't Director McPherson like him?"

"Because Ross won't put his feet up and enjoy his early retirement," Talbot told her. "Remember I said he liked dabbling in other people's cases? Well, he still does. Only now he does it without a badge or any official backing. *And* usually without the knowledge of the investigators. Certainly without their permission."

"Though usually with good results," Swenson pointed out.

"Almost always with good results," Talbot agreed. "He can shake out clues and smoke out bad guys like nobody's business. Of course, every time he does that he puts his WitSec status at risk and drives the Marshals crazy."

"The biggest problem is that since he's not official, most of the evidence he turns up is tainted and can't be used in court," Swenson said.

"But it usually points the investigators to answers and evidence that *can* be used," Talbot added. "In my mind, it's a pretty fair trade."

"But not in everyone's," Swenson said.

"And they just let him do this?" Angie asked, clearly still puzzled.

"Oddly enough, they do," Talbot said. "Personally, I think he's got a quiet protector somewhere, someone who likes having this kind of wild card running around poking sticks into anthills. In fact, I wouldn't be surprised if McPherson himself was secretly running the guy."

"He's not," Swenson murmured.

"So he says," Talbot countered. "I still wouldn't be surprised." He hesitated. "In fact, Angie, Ross's lack of official status was the main reason I asked him to investigate you. Your husband thought there might be something irregular with your family's immigration status that the Chinese were using as leverage against you."

"There's a problem?" Angie breathed, her eyes going wide. "But I thought—"

"No, no, everything's fine," Talbot said hastily. "But your husband didn't want you getting in trouble if there was some problem. Ross's lack of official status meant he could ignore anything he found instead of being legally obligated to turn it over to ICE."

The door opened and Ross poked his head in. "All set," he said. "You still want to do this, Angie?"

"Yes," she said, standing up. "Thank you."

"Take care of her," Talbot warned. "Better take one of the tac radios in case you spot something."

"Already got one," Ross said, tapping his pocket. "See you later."

"Before you go," Swenson spoke up, "can either of you think what you might do with a spare hundred and fifty thousand dollars if you were trying to nuke the UN?"

Angie exchanged looks with Ross. "No idea," she said.

"I'd probably turn it into singles and pile them on top of the bomb," Ross offered. "Who'd notice an extra wheelbarrow full of money vanishing into the UN?"

"Funny," Talbot said with a grunt. "Go on, get out."

"And watch your backs," Swenson added.

"Yeah," Talbot said quietly. "Watch them very carefully."

~

General Bakht had found a place that served good tea and even had a distant view of one corner of the UN Building. The group had finished their drinks, warming life back into fingers and toes, and he was sorting out money to pay the bill when Six suddenly stiffened across the table. "Sir," he hissed urgently. "Five o'clock—coming this way. Man in navy-blue pea jacket, woman in dark brown mid-calf coat."

Taking a last sip from his mug, Bakht turned casually to look out the window beside him. He spotted them at once amid the throng of people hurrying along the sidewalks toward the subways and busses.

And felt his breath catch in his throat.

It was Ross and Angie Chandler.

"I thought you got them," Seven said.

"So did I," Six ground out. "I'll have to remedy that."

"Steady, Six," the general warned. "We're not going to jeopardize matters at this late hour for the sake of injured pride."

"I disagree, sir," Six said stiffly. "Even now, she's still a threat."

"No," Bakht said. "Hooker's assessment was wrong. She knows nothing. If she did, we'd never have made it this far. Forget her."

"I'm not sure I agree, sir," Seven put in. "We should at least find out what they're doing here."

"They've joined with those looking for us, of course," Bakht said. "Notice the device Ross is carrying?"

"It looks like an old Geiger counter," Six suggested.

"It does indeed," Bakht agreed. "And if it is, I see no reason why we shouldn't let them waste their time with it."

There was a movement beside him, and Thirteen slid back into his seat. "Sir, I took the liberty of calling Three while I was in the rest room," he said quietly. "He says several of the men searching the fields have a new piece of equipment, a small box with a detector wand connected by a coaxial cable—"

"Like that one?" Six interrupted, pointing out the window.

Thirteen craned his neck. "I think so," he confirmed. "It matches the description." He inhaled sharply as he seemed to focus for the first time on the man carrying it. "Is that—?"

"Yes, it is," Six growled. "Sir, I submit that this isn't a matter of injured pride. Geiger counters like that are at least thirty years out of date, and the military isn't likely to press archaic equipment into service. I think that's something entirely new."

"I agree, sir," Seven said. "We should at least try to get a closer look at it."

"Or see how it's used," Six added. "That may provide a clue to its capabilities."

The general watched as the couple passed the restaurant window and continued west down the sidewalk, mentally weighing the odds. To reveal themselves now would spell disaster, particularly if they were tracked back to their base.

But Six was right. If this was a new weapon their opponents had devised, they really should check it out. "Very well," he said, picking up the bill and adding it to the top of the stack of dollars he'd counted out. "Six, you and I will follow them."

He glanced at his watch. Just after four-fifteen. "Thirteen, Seven; go relieve Three and Four. You know where their posts are?"

"Yes, sir."

"Tell them they have one hour to warm up and get whatever food or drink they wish before returning to their posts," he continued. "Six and I will do the same for Two and the others after we've had a look at our opponents' new toy."

They left the restaurant in silence, splitting into pairs as they headed off on their assigned tasks. Bakht and Six wove quickly through the crowds until they were within sight of their quarry. Keeping a safe distance, they followed.

It was unrewarding duty. At each side street Ross and the woman would stop, and Ross would stand for several seconds pointing the wand down the alley as if spraying invisible roach killer. They would then peer at the box itself, sometimes exchanging a few words before continuing to the next street and repeating the process.

"Doesn't work like any radiation detector I'm familiar with," Six murmured after the fourth such performance. "Even those that run a long sampling time or weigh against a background work faster than that."

"Agreed," Bakht said. "There also appears to be a display on the box."

"I could try to get a closer look," Six offered. "I doubt either of them would recognize me, and the labels on the controls might give a clue as to its function."

For a moment Bakht was tempted. One of the requirements for staying ahead of an opponent was to know what he knew, or at least be able to form an educated guess. New equipment, by its very nature, put severe limitations on such foreknowledge.

But no. They'd spent more time on this than they had to spare and had already moved closer to known enemies than was prudent. "Let them be," he told Six, taking the other's arm and steering him toward a crosswalk. "As long as they stay here, whatever they're doing is none of our concern."

"Perhaps," Six said, clearly not convinced. "Sir, I request permission to trade assignments with Three."

"That would put Three in a probable combat situation," Bakht reminded the other. "He's primarily a pilot, not a soldier."

"Which is precisely why I should take his place," Six said. "We may need a spotter with more ground combat experience than either Three or Four."

Bakht sent him a long, cool look. "Are you genuinely expecting trouble near the UN?" he asked pointedly. "Or are you hoping for another try at Ross and the woman?"

"I've already said this isn't a matter of injured pride," Six reminded him. "Ross has demonstrated time and again his ability to make trouble. He bears watching."

Bakht pondered the question the rest of the way across the street. "All right," he said when they reached the other side. "I'll call Three and tell him to join us at the base after his break."

"Thank you, sir."

"Just see that you keep your mind and attention on the mission," Bakht warned. "Nothing more."

"That's all I've ever had my mind on," Six assured him. "You can count on me."

~

McPherson had joined Talbot in the ops center and was skimming through Swenson's financial report when the final word came in. "The search team coordinator reports all UN buildings and grounds are secure," Talbot announced. "They're going to security maintenance mode now, shifting the bulk of their personnel to city search."

"Make sure it's a damn good maintenance mode," McPherson warned. "There's nothing that says Bakht can't bring the bomb in at the last minute. Did they check the parking areas, including all the cars?"

"Parking areas, yes," Talbot said, half his attention on his tac radio as the coordinator and team leaders conversed back and forth. "All cars with trunks or interiors big enough to contain the bomb have also been looked into."

"What if they removed the outer casing?" McPherson asked. "That would make the package smaller."

"It would also mean higher radiation readings," Talbot pointed out. "All the cars were also checked with detectors."

McPherson grunted. "So I guess he isn't worried about limiting collateral damage after all," he said, his tone implying that that was somehow Talbot's personal fault. "He's got it stashed somewhere in the city."

"I still think it's close by," Talbot insisted.

McPherson grunted again and turned to Swenson, slapping at the papers in his hand. "What is this hundred and fifty grand discrepancy?"

"We don't know," Swenson said, her tone making it clear that this was certainly not *her* fault. "Possibly more weaponry, possibly a vehicle."

"About the right range for a nice expensive yacht," Talbot suggested, the idea just occurring to him. "Something you might ignore as it putters up the East River."

"Not even if my own grandmother was sailing it," McPherson assured him. "Besides, all boat traffic's been stopped a mile away in both directions.

"A small plane, then?" Swenson suggested. "They've already shown a fondness for remote-controlled vehicles. Could they pull a 9/11 and crash a plane on the building with the nuke inside?"

McPherson shook his head. "All general aviation traffic has been grounded for the next four hours. Air traffic control has been instructed to divert anything coming into the city from outside, and under no circumstances are they to let *anything* except our own helos fly into or over this area for that same period. That includes medical choppers or anything else claiming an emergency."

"And if those orders are ignored?" Talbot asked.

"The F-16s circling the city aren't there just for show," McPherson said grimly. "The air attack thing worked once. It's not going to work again. Ever. Swenson, is there any way to dig deeper on this missing money? Bakht isn't the sort to collect souvenir postcards."

"I'm still trying," Swenson said, her forehead tight with thought. "Madison, they *did* check the UN building rooftops, didn't they?"

Talbot and McPherson exchanged looks. "I suppose they did," Talbot said slowly. "I'm sure they did. They must have."

"Maybe you'd better check," McPherson said.

"Maybe I'd better," Talbot agreed, keying his tac radio as he peered out the window toward the Manhattan cityscape and the stream of headlights moving up and down First Avenue. Somewhere beyond all those buildings, the sun was beginning to set.

~

The pudgy guard at the security desk looked up in obvious annoyance as the six men appeared around the corner from the freight elevator. "There you are," he said accusingly. "Where have you been? I was about to send Jerry up to throw your butts out of here."

"It's only a few minutes after five," Bakht reminded him mildly.

The guard sniffed. "Here in the business world, pal, the Friday ghost-town impression starts at four-thirty. How long you been in New York, anyway?"

"So everyone else in the building is gone?" Bakht asked, handing over the elevator access card.

"Long gone," the guard assured them, taking the card.

"Except for you and Jerry," Seven put in. "Where *is* Jerry, by the way?"

"He's on the cameras," the guard said, pulling open his desk drawer and dropping the card into its proper slot.

"And where would that be?"

"Why, you want to say good-bye personally?" the guard retorted, looking up as he started to close the drawer.

And came to a jerking halt as he saw the guns leveled at his face. "Not exactly," Bakht said. "Where is he?"

The guard opened his mouth. Closed it again. "What the hell?" he demanded weakly.

"You have three seconds," Bakht said mildly. "After that we kill you and find him ourselves."

"Down there," the guard said hurriedly, pointing along one of the cross corridors. "Third door on the right."

Without a word, Seven, Twelve, and Thirteen headed that direction. "Push back from your desk a bit, if you would," Bakht instructed the guard. "Just leave the drawer open."

The guard did as ordered. Handing his gun to Bakht, making sure to stay out of Eight's line of fire, Three stepped around behind the prisoner and pulled a roll of duct tape from his jacket pocket. By the time the others returned with their catch, the guard was securely trussed.

"Hello, Jerry," Bakht said courteously to the second guard as the four of them came up. Jerry's face was ashen, his knees trembling noticeably, and he probably would have collapsed in a heap if Twelve and Thirteen hadn't had a grip on his arms. "Our apologies for this brief postponement of your weekend. Any trouble?"

"He was trying to call for help when we got there," Seven said. "Oddly enough, all the phone lines were dead."

"Imagine that," Bakht said. "Lock them up."

Eight hoisted the first guard to his feet, and the group headed down another cross corridor to the electrical closet Twelve had checked out earlier. Bakht sat down at the desk, methodically opening the other drawers. One of them yielded a complete listing of the elevator coding system, as he'd known it would, and he spent a moment studying it. By the time the others returned—minus the two guards—he'd collected the key cards they needed.

"Ninth floor cards," he said, passing them out. "Seven, start checking out positions. Eight, Twelve: take the rest of the heavy weapons from the roof and get them over to Nine, Ten, and Eleven—they should be in position by now. When everything there is in order, Twelve, you and Ten will come back and help Seven with his defense setup. Three, Thirteen: relieve Two on the roof and send him down to me on the tenth floor. Then wait until everything is finished—I'll let you know when you can join the others. Here are your roof keys, and here's a tenth floor key for Two. And remember: cell phones only. The radios are certain to be compromised by now. Questions?"

"No, sir," Seven said for all of them.

Bakht nodded curtly. "Then get to it."

37

THEY HAD INDEED checked all the rooftops, Talbot was testily informed. McPherson, equally testy, insisted they do it again.

It was ten after five, and the city lights had become a blaze of fluorescent and neon and halogen against the blackness of winter's night by the time they once again confirmed that the rooftops were clear.

"Sometimes the hunches work," McPherson rumbled, sitting in a corner of the ops room gazing out the window toward the city, a twisting ache growing in his gut. Less than an hour and a half to go.

Less than an hour before President Whitcomb entered the death zone.

Behind him the room was filled with the tense buzz of low voices and the shuffling of chairs and papers, all against the soft background hum of a hundred tiny computer cooling fans. It was a massive operation, with units drawn from the Bureau, Homeland Security, the Pentagon's best search and strike teams, and the New York City police. All of them thrown together with the kind of speed and efficiency McPherson could most of the time only dream about.

All of them furiously and efficiently running in place. "And sometimes they don't," he added.

"I'm sorry," Swenson said. She was gazing, not at the city, but at her computer screen, her fingers sitting in tense idleness on the keyboard, looking as miserable as he'd ever seen her. For once, it seemed, the Jigsaw Girl had run out of pieces to put together. "It seemed like a perfect place to hide a bomb, right out in the open that way."

"It *was* a perfect place," McPherson agreed. "Don't worry about it."

"You mean don't worry about wasting half an hour of everyone's time?"

"I said don't worry about it," he said, making it an order. "I've explained about the Cloaks to these people until I'm blue down to my socks, and I'm still not convinced they understand what we're dealing with. No, hiding the nuke in the open is exactly the sort of thing Bakht would do."

"And don't forget, he wanted the Cloaks for *something*," Talbot put in. He was leaning against the side of the window McPherson was staring out of, his arms folded across his chest as he too gazed at the cityscape.

"We'll nail him," McPherson promised, trying to put some conviction into his words. No point in the troops being as demoralized as their leader was feeling at the moment. "Talbot, what's the latest from the NSA?"

"They've got full-blanket surveillance up and running on all communications inside Manhattan," Talbot said. "Line and cell phones, the whole radio spectrum, and as much of the Internet as they can get into. They're running all their usual flag words, plus about fifty more they've added for the occasion. Everyone in Fort Meade has been put on instant analysis duty. General Vaughn has people doubled up on the radio surveillance, too."

"What about that voiceprint thing we came up with?"

"They all loved it," Talbot said. "It's already been implemented."

"What voiceprint thing?" Swenson asked.

"The NSA created a general profile from the *Rabah Jamila* Mayday transmission," Talbot explained. "They're running it in parallel with their monitors. If Bakht brought that particular hijacker with him, and if he talks to anyone, they may be able to tag him."

Swenson made a face. "Which means that if he *is* here, he probably has tape over his mouth," she said. "Bakht is still two steps ahead of us."

"Maybe not," Talbot said thoughtfully. "Maybe you had the right idea, just not the right place."

"You mean about the rooftop?" McPherson asked.

"Exactly," Talbot said. "If not the UN rooftop, why not one of the buildings over on First Avenue?"

McPherson shrugged. "We've got three helos already checking out rooftops, and I've reminded the search team leaders to do more than just visually clear open areas like that. The second batch of thermal gradient imagers should be here any time. That should help." He grimaced. "Assuming everyone's taking the Cloaks seriously."

"It's just past sundown," Swenson murmured. "That should be the best time for the imagers to work."

"If they can get the continual-scan versions operational," McPherson agreed. "Last I heard, they were still having trouble with the electronics."

"I keep coming back to that missing hundred and fifty thousand," Talbot murmured. "What can you buy with that kind of money?" He gestured out the window. "One of those, maybe?"

"One of what?" McPherson asked, standing up and crossing to his side. Parked halfway between them and First Avenue was a pair of military helos and a big New York City S.W.A.T. van. "You mean the van or the chopper?"

"Either," Talbot said. "Did anyone bother to search all the official equipment we drove, flew, or lugged in?"

"I don't know," McPherson said thoughtfully, reaching for a tac radio. "Let's find out."

~

The tenth-floor office window wasn't one of the unbreakable, high-security types routinely used in more modern office structures. It was, however, jammed closed, and after working at it for a few minutes, Bakht gave up and simply cut out the necessary panes.

"Going to get chilly in here," Two commented as he maneuvered the last box of equipment into the office on one of their collapsible dollies.

"It'll get warmer soon enough," Bakht reminded him, easing his head out through the opening and looking up. Two floors above him on the roof one of the others was looking down, the face unrecognizable in the darkness. The general waved, the figure waved back, and a moment later the first of the slender cables came snaking down the side of the building toward him. He caught it as it came by the window and ducked back in, pulling the end inside with him. "How long will it take you to set up?" he asked Two.

"Not long," the other said. He already had the top off the larger of the packing crates; with a brief moan of distressed nails, he pried off the front. "Twenty minutes, perhaps twenty-five."

Well within schedule. "Good," Bakht said. "Unless you need help, I'm going to check the guard posts."

"Go ahead," Two said, grunting as he pried off another side of the crate. "I can manage."

Bakht made his way down the elevator and out into the cold night air. Manhattan was hardly the ghost town the pudgy guard had implied, with a considerable amount of vehicular and pedestrian traffic still plying the streets. But having earlier made his way through the rush hour crowds, he had to agree that the contrast was a respectable one.

He couldn't help but wonder which of the people hurrying by would soon be dead.

The first guard post was on top of the building due south of their base. He made his way through the unlocked outer door and up the elevator, alert the whole way for a challenge or other unexpected confrontation.

But there was none. Ten, who'd arrived several days ahead of the others after lying submerged for a day in the *Rabah Jamila*'s wake, had spent part of that time scouting possible locations and checking for potential security problems. So far, he'd done his job admirably.

The general reached the roof to find Eight and Nine setting the second of their heavy weapons in place. "Situation?" he asked.

"No problems," Nine said. "Everything's intact. We'll be ready in half an hour."

"I wish we had a few more of those Cloaks, though," Eight added as he surveyed their work. "I know this camouflage is supposed to make them look like normal building protrusions, but I'd rather they weren't visible at all."

"You're welcome to use the Cloak here instead of on yourselves if you'd rather," Bakht offered.

Eight smiled. "Yes, sir. Point taken."

Bakht nodded. "What about the laptop?"

"Battery's fully charged," Eight said. "The power should last as long as we need."

"Certainly longer than the UN," Nine put in with a smirk.

Bakht managed a small smile in return. Nine was an excellent soldier, but he could never see past the primary focus of the mission itself. It would probably come as a complete surprise to him when he learned how many more people had died than just those in the UN Building itself.

But there was no point clouding his enthusiasm with such issues. "Good," Bakht said instead. "Remember that after your first shot they'll be hunting for you, so make sure you're wearing your suits and gas masks."

"Yes, sir."

The second flanking position was on the building northwest of the base. Eleven was on that roof alone, already partially suited up, checking out his Galil sniper rifle and laying out ammunition magazines. Bakht confirmed that he, too, would be ready on schedule, then headed back to street level. A block further north, he reached the deserted garage Ten had scouted out and let himself in.

The panel truck they'd brought cross country was where they'd left it, apparently undisturbed, ready for a quick escape if all went well, or an even quicker retreat if it didn't. The box of magnetic decals and other equipment was in the back, and a few minutes later he'd transformed it into a more impressive-looking vehicle complete with rotating red lights on top and the word "POLICE" boldly printed on both sides.

And all was now ready. Locking the garage behind him, he headed back toward the base.

Trying not to see all of the pedestrians and vehicles as they passed.

~

It was five twenty-five when the word finally came that all official vehicles had been checked and cleared.

"For a minute there, I thought we had him," McPherson commented.

Swenson stole a quick glance at him, then turned guiltily back to her computer. McPherson looked like a coiled spring, and down deep she knew that it was partly her fault. If she hadn't pushed for a second check of the UN rooftops, that particular search team would have had an extra half hour to search somewhere else. With only ninety minutes to go, the loss of those thirty could mean all the difference in the world.

There was nothing she could do to help make up that time. Nothing except maybe solve the problem of Bakht's missing money and figure out what it meant.

The problem was that she was stuck. Every avenue she tried, every clever, underhanded, or flat-out illegal approach she could come up with had failed. Whatever Bakht had spent that hundred and fifty thousand on, she simply couldn't find it.

McPherson and Talbot were discussing the searches in low voices. Taking a deep breath, Swenson blanked them out and started down her listing again. Maybe the missing money had nothing to do with the nuke per se, as Talbot had suggested, but was part of their escape plan. Maybe it was all sitting somewhere in hundred-dollar bills, a nest egg for thirteen men who would have to go underground for quite a while. She scrolled down the list, looking again at each item, trying to see past the names. Bakht, she reminded herself firmly, liked to think sideways, too.

Her eyes and fingers paused. Five surface-to-air missiles.

Surface-to-air missiles . . .

"Madison?" she called.

She had their instant attention. "Something?" McPherson asked hopefully.

"I was just wondering," she said hesitantly, painfully aware that this was nothing more than a wild guess. "What would happen if they strapped five surface-to-air missiles to the bomb and fired them all together? How far would it travel? Or would it even get off the ground?"

"I have no idea," Talbot said, looking at McPherson. "Director?"

"It couldn't get very far," McPherson said slowly. "SAMs aren't designed to carry loads."

"But maybe they've got something else that will," Talbot suggested. "Could that missing money have gone toward an actual short-range missile?"

"What, a hundred fifty Gs?" McPherson scoffed. "That's not even a down payment."

"Besides, a transaction like that should show up on the Pentagon's tracking system," Swenson reminded herself. "Unless they stole a missile when they stole the bomb," she added as that thought suddenly occurred to her.

"How in the world could they have gotten it cross-country?" Talbot asked. "Forget a panel truck—you'd need a semi at least. Not to mention a crane at both ends of the trip."

"They don't have a missile," McPherson said, shaking his head. "As soon as Rao's plane left New Delhi we had the Indians do a complete military inventory. There's nothing significant missing but the nuke."

Swenson felt her face warm. "So another washout."

"Well, let's hold on a second," McPherson cautioned, staring out the window again. "Maybe not. A cluster of SAM's wouldn't get the bomb very far; but then, how far do they have to send it? A mile? Half a mile?"

"Maybe even less," Talbot agreed. "Just far enough to get it from somewhere outside the primary blast radius to somewhere *inside* the primary blast radius."

"Or to put it another way, from somewhere outside our search perimeter to somewhere inside it," McPherson added grimly. "This is starting to make sense."

"It also instantly doubles the area we have to search," Talbot warned.

"Not quite," McPherson said, his voice starting to sound alive again. "They aren't going to try a stunt like that from the ground. Except maybe from across the river—we'll have to check that out. And firing through a window is too ludicrous to even think about."

"Which means a rooftop," Talbot said, some cautious excitement starting to creep into his voice as well. "Which means chopper searches using thermal imagers."

"Or plain old-fashioned IR detectors," McPherson said. "A nuke sitting alone in its casing might not radiate much heat, but a launch team getting a rocket ready to fly sure as hell will. All we need to do is shift the helos' search pattern around."

"We can even leave the building teams alone," Talbot said, nodding.

"In case we're wrong," Swenson murmured.

"We're not wrong," McPherson said. "Not this time. I've got a feeling."

He turned toward the main part of the ops center and raised his voice. "Crenna? Has that new batch of thermal imagers arrived yet?"

"No, sir," one of the coordinators called back. "We're expecting them any time."

McPherson swore under his breath. "Fine," he called back, getting to his feet and heading that direction. "Get Colonel Zebrinski on the line. Tell him I want a reconfiguration of his helo search pattern."

~

With Bakht's full concentration on the last stages of the equipment check, his first warning was the sudden realization that the distant throbbing of helicopter blades was growing louder. Crossing to the window, careful not to trip over the half dozen cables snaking their way across the floor, he looked out.

They were coming, all right: six of them, by the lights. As he watched, they broke formation, two each peeling away to north and south, the last two continuing west.

Directly toward them.

"Alert the men on the roof," he called to Two, stepping to the side out of sight and pulling out his phone. "The helos seem to have suddenly expanded their search range."

Two already had his phone out. "Orders?" he asked as he jabbed at the keys.

"Tell them to get out of sight," Bakht said, punching in Nine's number. "In fact, have them get back into the stairway. The helos may have IR detectors, and the Cloak won't protect against those."

There was a click in Bakht's ear. "Yes?" Nine's voice came.

"Company," the general said. "Are you both dressed?"

"Yes," Nine said. "So is Eleven—I just spoke to him."

The general nodded satisfaction. Sealed inside their insulated suits, the men on the two flanking rooftops would be as secure from infrared scans as it was possible to be. And lying beneath their Cloaks, they were safe from prying eyes, as well. "The potted plants?"

"They've all been watered," Nine said. "We're ready for company."

"Good. We may soon be having visitors at the front and side doors."

"We're on it," Nine promised.

"Call me if anyone rings the bell."

He punched the off button. "Report?" he asked Two.

"They were already in the stairway," the other said. "They saw the helos and thought it would be prudent. Orders?"

Bakht scratched his chin, running the checklist through his mind. Everything should be ready to go. "Was there anything left for them to do up there?"

Two shrugged. "Watch over the weapon."

"The weapon can watch over itself," Bakht decided. "They may as well join Seven and the others on the ninth floor."

"I don't like this," Two said darkly. "They must surely still have a large area to search within the blast zone. What are they doing this far out? Unless Ross and the woman were bait," he added, throwing a sharp look at the window. "If you and Six were spotted—" He swore suddenly and headed toward the control panel on the desk in the center of the room.

Bakht got there first. "What are you doing?" he asked mildly, stepping between Two and the controls.

"Don't you see?" Two demanded. "If you were tracked here, then those helos will be merely the final phase of the assault. The commandos will already be inside the building."

"Calm down," Bakht ordered, putting steel into his voice. "You're jumping at shadows."

"If they're on to us—"

"They're not on to us," Bakht said firmly.

"—and we don't launch the weapon—"

"The weapon is in no danger," Bakht said, hardening his voice. "We have a schedule, Colonel, and we're going to stay on that schedule."

For a moment the two men stood facing each other. Then, with visible effort, Two pulled himself back together. "Yes, sir," he said between stiff lips.

"We have to be sure the target is in the building," Bakht reminded him quietly. "Just as importantly, all the other possible targets have to be in there with him. That's the only way to ensure that no one traces this back to us, and that situation isn't guaranteed until seven o'clock."

"Are you sure you aren't just stalling, General?" Two asked pointedly. "The targets are there. You know that as well as I do—Four has been counting them as they go in. Are you sure you aren't having second thoughts?"

"We'll carry out the mission," Bakht said quietly. "And we'll launch when the time is right. Not before."

Two swallowed. "Yes, sir."

"Now," Bakht said, pointing to the phone still clutched in Two's hand. "Order Three and Thirteen to the ninth floor."

He turned and looked out the window behind him. The two helos had passed overhead, and from the subtle change in the sound he guessed they were veering apart, angling north and south. Whatever they were looking for, they apparently hadn't spotted it on this pass.

Maybe on the next pass they would. "And then call Seven," he added. "Tell him company may soon be arriving."

~

Standing a few feet back from the lieutenant at the helo command station, gazing at the semicircle of TV monitors showing the views from the various aircraft nose cameras, Colonel Zebrinski shook his head. "Nothing," he said, throwing a dark look at Talbot. "Which is about what I expected."

"Give it another couple of passes," Talbot told him, turning away from the other's annoyed glare to study the city map tacked to the side wall. "Let's try south this time, the 37th and 38th Street areas."

"It's a waste of time," Zebrinski insisted. "I talked to General Vaughn again, and he confirms there's no way they can have a missile out there big enough to carry the nuke."

"No one's suggesting they do," Talbot said.

"Right," Zebrinski rumbled. "*Your* idea is that they've strapped a bunch of SAMs to it." He snorted. "Do us a favor, Talbot. Stick to your wiretaps and let us handle the military thinking."

There was a brush of air from beside Talbot. "Anything?" McPherson asked.

"Not yet," Talbot said. "Yours?"

"False alarm," the director said. "Some Wall Street headcheese who decided the interdiction on East River traffic didn't apply to yachts in his price category."

Talbot shook his head in disgust. "You should have let him stay in the blast zone."

"I was tempted," McPherson admitted. "Oh, and I'm sure you'll be amused by this one. As you predicted, the four closest hotels have just had bomb threats phoned in. The police are evacuating them now."

"It gets those people out, and also ties up a large chunk of our resources," Talbot commented. "I wonder which part Bakht's more interested in."

"We were going to evacuate and search anyway," McPherson pointed out. "This way we kill two birds with one stone."

"The hell with this," Zebrinski said abruptly, turning back to Talbot. "There's nothing out there. I'm pulling the helos back to support the ground teams."

McPherson looked at Talbot, then back at Zebrinski. "All right," he said. "Pull all of them back except one."

Zebrinski drew himself up to his full six-three. "Director McPherson—"

"Because I'll need that one myself," McPherson continued. "I want to go up and look around."

The colonel blinked in surprise. "You?"

"Yes, me," McPherson said impatiently. "I was a field agent once, you know. I still remember how to do this. Whatever coordination is needed I can do from up there as well as from down here." He raised his eyebrows, as if daring Zebrinski to argue the point.

With anyone else, Talbot decided, he probably would have. But even full colonels knew when they were outranked. Zebrinski scowled, but gave a reluctant nod. "Get Hastings back here," he ordered the lieutenant. "Tell him FBI Director McPherson wants a lift. The rest are to return to their original assignments."

The lieutenant nodded and relayed the orders. "The fine art of getting what you want," Talbot murmured to McPherson. "I bow to the master."

"Knock it off," McPherson growled. "You keep an eye on things in here. Let Zebrinski and his people handle the straightforward stuff. That's what they're best at. Your job is to keep thinking sideways."

"Yes, sir. I'll try."

"And keep Swenson at her computer," McPherson added. "I've seen her pull last-minute rabbits out of the hat before."

"So have I," Talbot agreed. "Watch yourself up there."

McPherson grunted and started to walk away. "Wait a second," he said, turning back. "Did you say Ross had one of the thermal imagers?"

"Yes, sir," Talbot said. "He wanted to do some checking ahead of the search teams."

"Get him back here," McPherson ordered. "I've just commandeered it."

~

It was ten minutes after six.

And it was time.

"Arming release mechanism," Bakht announced, opening the safety cover. "Is the wind still holding steady?"

"Steady enough," Two confirmed, peering at the display tied into the compact meteorological station they'd set up on the roof. "Running mostly between thirty to forty kilometers per hour, directly out of the west."

Bakht nodded. That was what the weather report had predicted, and what he'd banked on when setting all this up. It was gratifying to see they'd gotten it right.

"The helos have gone, too," Two added, stepping over to the window and looking outside.

"I told you they didn't have anything," Bakht reminded him, gazing at the switch. It was the end of the road, and the mission was about to be completed.

And thousands of people were about to die.

He was suddenly aware of the sounds of traffic below, tires hissing across wet pavement, the seemingly never-ending honking of taxi horns, the occasional sudden squeal of brakes. At ten floors up, they were far too high to hear individual pedestrian voices, but as the eddy currents from the westerly wind flowed past and into the room he could almost imagine he could hear them as well.

Thousands of people were going to die. Maybe tens of thousands. Maybe even hundreds of thousands.

"Sir?" Two prompted.

Bakht took a deep breath. *For the good of the people,* he reminded himself silently. *For the survival of the nation.* "Yes," he said. "We're ready. On my command, stand by to launch."

38

ANGIE AND ROSS had been sifting through the darkened doorways on Third Avenue when Ross received the call to return to the UN grounds. They had obediently turned north, and they'd just reached 44th when Talbot called again to cancel the order. The new batch of imagers had arrived, and McPherson would be taking one of those instead.

As they stood at the corner of 44th and Third, waiting for the light to change and pondering their next move, Angie gazed out at the city around her and shivered. "Cold?" Ross asked, instantly solicitous, putting his arm around her shoulders.

She shook her head. "No," she said quietly, a painful tightness in her throat. "I was just looking at all the cars and people. What kind of man would do this to us, Adam?"

"They're not doing it to us, Angie," he told her. "At least, not technically. They're doing it to someone they consider a dangerous enemy. This just happens to be the place they've chosen to have it out with him."

"I'm sure the distinction will be of great comfort to the dead," she murmured bitterly.

His arm tightened around her. "That's why we have to stop him."

Angie shivered again, this time not just from the horror of the situation. The air temperature itself was probably no lower than the upper twenties, but the wind sweeping out of the west made it feel far colder. It had been steadily increasing over the two and a half hours they'd been walking the streets, to the point where it was now uncomfortable to look straight into it. A portent of serious weather coming into the city, and she could imagine that the biggest worry of the people hurrying along was how heavy the snowfall would be.

If they only knew. "Why don't they get them out of here?" she asked. "Director McPherson and the others. Are they just going to let them die? Why can't they block off the streets and blow sirens and get them away?"

"For the same reason they can't evacuate the UN," Ross told her quietly. "Bakht will have people watching everything. If he sees us trying to clear the area, he'll almost certainly blow the bomb early rather than let his pigeon get away."

"So we're just going to let them all die?"

Ross shrugged. "My guess is that they're planning to search until, say, six forty-five, then give up and shift to a massive push to get the civilians out of the blast area. Gamble that at that point it'll be too late for Bakht to change his timer."

"That won't help the people in the UN, though."

Ross shook his head. "Nothing is going to help them except finding the bomb."

"Maybe we ought to tell him," Angie said. "The man they want to kill. I know it's terrible, but couldn't we see if he would offer his life to save everyone else? He's going to die anyway."

"Now we get into questions of ethics and civilization and lifeboat scenarios," Ross said ruefully. "I don't know. If I was in his place, I suppose I'd want to know . . . or maybe not. I don't know. But in this case it's a moot point. I presume the reason they haven't simply shot him down in the streets somewhere is that they don't want to make a martyr out of him. Once this bomb goes off, who's going to know who the target really was? He'll be lost in the shuffle, his memory will fade away, and that'll be that. Or so goes the theory."

Angie felt her stomach trying to be sick, and she closed her eyes until she could force back the feeling. "They must be insane."

"Desperation often looks that way."

The light changed, and they started across 44th. Angie turned her face away from the wind whistling through the man-made canyons, and found herself gazing east toward the brightly lit UN Building two and a half long New York blocks away. Thirty-five minutes from now, at seven o'clock precisely, Secretary-General Muluzi would be banging his gavel and bringing the Human Rights Conference to order. Between now and then the delegates and speakers would be gathering in the big assembly room, if they weren't there already.

President Whitcomb, she remembered someone saying, would be arriving precisely at six-thirty. Distantly, she wondered if he would smile and wave at the cameras as he always did. Knowing he had thirty minutes to live.

A car horn blared practically in her ear. She jumped, twisting her head back around, as a taxi swerved through the slush around a slow-moving panel truck. The cabby expressed his annoyance with another blare and was gone, speeding his way north on Third. "Of course," Ross added as they made it to the relative safety of the sidewalk, "there are some who would say New York needs something like this every few years just to remind them to stay civil to each other."

"That's not funny," Angie growled.

Ross sighed. "I know. Sorry. Look, let's go one more block north. If we don't find anything, we'll head west toward Lexington. Unless you want to go inside somewhere for a couple of minutes and warm up."

"We don't have time for that," Angie said, still staring at the lumbering panel truck that had so annoyed the impatient cabby. Why should a panel truck be grabbing her attention right now?

"Angie?"

Angie blinked, the train of thought whispering away into the cold. Ross was staring at her, an odd expression on his face. "I don't know," she said. "I thought I had something. But it's gone now. It must not have been anything."

"Maybe not," he said. His eyes, she saw, were also on the truck disappearing into the general flow of taillights. "You said you were in the room when your husband told Kingsley to go get the semi, right?"

"Yes," she said, her heart suddenly pounding. He was on to something, all right. Maybe the very thing they'd tried to kill her for. "Scott was the one who could drive an eighteen-wheeler."

"But why a semi?" Ross countered. "Why something that big?"

"To take the Cloaks and other equipment to the reservoir," she said. "There was supposed to be a demo for the Army the next morning."

"Except that we know now that the Cloaks and all their gear will fit inside a panel truck," Ross persisted. "So why a semi?"

And suddenly, she had it. "Oh, no," she breathed. "Are you saying—?"

"Yeah," Ross bit out, grabbing the mike switch for his tac radio. "Talbot? Talbot, you copy?"

Angie leaned close to him, straining to hear. Ross responded by pulling out the ear bud and turning it sideways, leaning his head close to hers with the ear bud between them. "Talbot," she heard Talbot's voice faintly above the traffic noise.

"We've been had," Ross snarled. "The damn Cloaks can move."

"They what?"

"You heard me," Ross said. "That semi Dr. Chandler ordered the night before the murders? It wasn't for transport to the demonstration. It *was* the demonstration."

"That's impossible," Talbot insisted. "All three techs told us the Cloaks couldn't work while moving."

"They also all said it was a software problem," Ross reminded him. "I guess the problem got fixed."

"James and Barbara came out of his office together that evening," Angie said. The memory of that scene, and her childish overreaction to it, bit into her like a serrated icicle. "James looked so happy. And it was right after that he told Scott to get the semi."

"Kingsley must have known from his pillow talk with Underwood that they were on the verge of a breakthrough," Ross said. "The minute Chandler told him to get the semi he would have known they'd done it. Think about it—why make a hundred-foot Quonset hut vanish when you can do it to a rolling semi instead? The Army would have fallen all over themselves signing up the project."

"But why didn't Chandler tell the other techs?" Talbot objected.

"James loved to pull that sort of surprise on people," Angie said, her eyes filling with tears despite the urgency of the situation. "He would have stood there and watched their faces as an invisible truck drove past and loved every minute."

"That was why they had to kill Angie," Ross said, his voice suddenly grim. "Kingsley would have assumed Dr. Chandler had told her about their breakthrough during their few minutes alone."

Talbot swore suddenly. "*That's* how they got off the cat in Oregon," he said. "Nothing as complicated as a mass scuba dive. The Coast Guard helo delivered them a Cloak and they just rode a dinghy in."

"This is McPherson," the Director's voice cut in. "Never mind the history. What does this translate into right now?"

"It means we're not necessarily looking for a stationary bomb anymore," Talbot said. "In fact, I'd say we're not looking for something stationary at all. They wouldn't have been so worried about what Angie knew if they were just going to park it somewhere."

"And with all due respect, sir, the history *is* important," Ross added. "If the Cloak's sampling rate was the limitation before, then even with a software breakthrough that limitation is probably still there in one form or another."

"Right," Talbot said. "That means a limit to how fast they can move the things and still keep them invisible."

"The fact that they didn't Cloak the whole catamaran to bring it in to the coast tells me the top speed is probably pretty slow," Ross offered.

"And the larger the Cloak, the slower it probably has to move," Angie said. "There's always more sampling data needed with a larger one."

"Makes sense," McPherson agreed. "Unfortunately, the smallest Cloak is already big enough to cover the nuke. Ross, you said you brought our small one with you?"

"It's in the electronics assembly semi down by the river," Ross said.

"Maybe they'll have time to do some tests," McPherson grunted.

"I've got someone on it," Colonel Zebrinski's voice cut in. "Personally, I'd guess Manhattan traffic speeds may be enough of a limitation all by themselves."

"Maybe," McPherson said. "So what, we're now looking for a convertible cruising past the UN with its top down?"

"Or an open pickup," Talbot said. "Or an SUV, or maybe a Prius with an empty luggage carrier on its roof. Something we normally wouldn't waste a second glance on because we know the Cloaks have to be stationary."

"Sir, I recommend we block off the streets right now," Zebrinski said tightly. "This situation is suddenly a hell of a lot more unmanageable."

"We've been through this, Colonel," McPherson said firmly. "If they can't get the weapon to the UN, they sure as hell aren't going to smuggle it back into India. They'll blow it somewhere else, maybe Wall Street or Broadway, and try to make it look like a second 9/11."

"Our job is to protect the UN," Zebrinski said.

"Our job is to protect United States citizens," McPherson shot back. "If it comes to choosing between them, we'll go ahead and put up the roadblocks. But not while we still have half an hour to find them."

"Find them *where*?" Zebrinski retorted. "They could be sitting in Queens right now for all we know."

"Which is another point," Talbot put in. "They're hardly going to drive up to the UN in the next two minutes and park. Blocking the streets now will just warn them off."

"So we wait?"

"We keep searching the buildings," McPherson told him. "I like the logic here, but that doesn't mean it's right. And we get ourselves set for a complete stop-and-search along the perimeter starting at ten minutes to seven."

"Which according to you will just warn them off," Zebrinski argued.

"Not if we're careful," McPherson said. "We'll only pick on vehicles that to all appearances can't possibly be carrying anything the size of our nuke. If we limit it that way, we won't have long checkpoint lines and snarled traffic to alert them."

Zebrinski muttered something under his breath. "I still don't like it," he said. "But I don't have anything better."

"Just keep looking," McPherson said. "Until you or someone else comes up with a better plan, we're stuck with this one. Talbot, start getting the Bureau people organized."

"Yes, sir," Talbot said. "Ross, what about you and Angie?"

"I thought we'd do a little more searching," Ross said. "As long as we're this far out anyway."

There was just the barest pause. "Fine," Talbot said. "All team leaders, check in."

~

McPherson clicked off his mike. "So let me get this straight," his pilot, Hastings, said. "These friggin' Cloak things can move."

"That's what the man said," McPherson told him, peering out the open helo window at the rooftops not all that far below.

"But these detectors of yours, these thermal-gradient imagers, have to be pointed somewhere for a few seconds to work?"

McPherson grimaced, seeing where the other was going. "Yes."

"So in other words," Hastings concluded, "if the target's moving at anything better than rush-hour speeds, it'll be to hell and gone before you even get a reading on it."

"Pretty much," McPherson growled. "That's why we're using them up here and not down there. Let's head north—I want to look at the next block up."

~

Ross stepped away from Angie, suddenly aware that he was standing closer to her than she was probably comfortable with, and slid the ear bud back in place.

"So we're going to search some more?" she asked.

Ross frowned. There'd been something odd in her voice just then. "We might as well," he said, forcing a briskness he didn't particularly feel. "We'll go another block up Third and then cut over to Lexington. Come on."

She didn't move. "We're not going back, are we?" she asked quietly. "You and Special Agent Talbot have already set this up. When the bomb goes off, you plan to have me as far away as you can. Tell me I'm wrong."

Damn. "Angie—"

"I told you I wanted to help," she said, and he could see that she was trying hard to be angry or outraged, or at least indignant. But the cold, the waiting, and the dread had drained all such emotions out of her. "Instead, you're treating me like a child."

"You *are* helping," he told her. "In the past five minutes you've done more to help the situation than the rest of us have done in the past two hours. Thanks to you, we've now got a real shot at stopping this."

"Then why are you sneaking me away?" she asked. "Because I'm a woman?"

Ross felt his stomach tighten. "Hanna Swenson's also a woman," he reminded her quietly. "She's sitting right in the center of the blast zone."

Angie lowered her eyes. "I'm sorry," she murmured. "I didn't mean it that way."

"The point is that you're a civilian," he went on. "You never signed up for this kind of risk."

"Neither did any of these people," she countered, waving at the traffic still flowing past them. "Neither did the people there," she added, pointing back along 44th toward the distant lights of the UN Building.

"They're diplomats," he pointed out. "Politicians. These days, that automatically means accepting risks. I wish that weren't true, but it is."

She gazed at the UN in silence a moment, then resolutely turned her back on it, bowing her head against the stiff westerly wind now blowing squarely in her face. "So why even bother with the pretense?" she said. "If we're going to go, let's just go. Or why don't I just go, and let you get back to work? I'm sure you still have something useful to contribute."

"Come on, Angie," he said, stepping behind her and putting his hands on her shoulders. Even through her heavy coat he could feel the stiffness of her muscles. "Look, you want to help? Then start thinking. Think about what kind of vehicle they might use to sneak the bomb in."

"What do you mean?" Angie asked. Her muffled voice still sounded dejected, but there was a faint spark of interest to it now.

"Well, it won't be a convertible, for instance," he said, trying to muster his own thoughts. There had to be a logical way to attack this. "A convertible with its top down in this weather would be as obvious as Lady Godiva."

"Yes, I see," she said, raising her head again. "It has to look natural."

"Right," Ross said, blinking against the wind as he peered at the traffic. "It also has to look empty.

"What about if it doesn't look at all?" she suggested. "Why couldn't they just roll a cloaked golf cart down the sidewalk or something?"

Ross blinked. But even as the excitement rose inside him, common sense throttled it down again. "Too risky," he said. "Too many people to dodge on the sidewalks. Someone would be bound to bump into it sooner or later. It'd be even worse when they hit the UN grounds, with all the people we've got running around there."

"I suppose it would leave tracks in any snow it ran across, too, wouldn't it?" she conceded with a sigh.

"Snow and puddles both," he agreed. "Though I have to say that watching a cloaked golf cart trying to dodge New York traffic—"

And then, abruptly, it hit him. "Hell," he said, very quietly.

Angie spun around, her eyes wide. "What is it?"

He looked down into her eyes, and then lifted his gaze into the wind, to the lights of Grand Central Station a block away.

Angie turned again to see what he was looking at. "A train?" she asked, catching her breath. "A subway train under the UN?"

"Not a train," he said softly. "And not under." Almost unwillingly, he lifted his gaze to the empty sky overhead. "Over."

She said something startled sounding, but he wasn't really listening. Letting go of her shoulders, he got his thermal imager in hand, twisted the knob to its longest distance setting, and pointed it directly upward.

Nothing. He reset it, angled it slightly east of vertical, and tried again. Still nothing. Resetting again, vaguely aware that pedestrians were slowing down and staring as they passed him, he tried a little further east.

"There's still half an hour to go," Angie's voice broke into his concentration. "And the UN's only two blocks away."

"You're right," he agreed, turning around and aiming up and to the west instead of east. Ten seconds later, the imager's display cleared and came back on.

And there it was. A huge cigar-shaped image with a baggy underside where the Papa Bear Cloak wrapped around it, perhaps eighty feet long, floating like a ghost a hundred feet above the street.

A dirigible.

He took a careful breath and keyed on his mike. "Talbot, this is Ross," he said, fighting to keep his voice steady. "Tell Hanna I've found her missing hundred fifty thousand dollars."

39

McPHERSON STARED OUT the helo window at the city lights below. "You've got to be kidding," he said. "A *dirigible*?"

"Bakht's own little Goodyear blimp," Ross's voice confirmed in his ear. "Heading straight down 44th toward the UN."

"I'm not getting anything on the IR," Hastings spoke up. "What kind of power is it under?"

"The oldest kind in the book," Ross said. "Wind power. It's being blown east."

"Probably unmanned, too," Talbot put in. "I should have thought of that when we first came up with this moving-Cloak idea. If General Bakht doesn't like killing civilians unnecessarily, he's not likely to be big on suicide missions, either."

"But they wouldn't have just let the thing go on a wing and a prayer," McPherson pointed out. "They must have some kind of control over it."

"I'd guess a tether line," Ross said. "But if it's there, it's too thin and too high for me to see."

"If it has to play out a half mile or more, it'll have to be light," Talbot pointed out. "Kevlar, maybe. Even so, it'll bow down toward the street somewhat."

"Whatever it is, we ought to be able to track it back to its source," McPherson said. "Colonel, are any of your spotters close enough to zoom in on a Kevlar tether line?"

"We may not have to," Zebrinski said as a faint rustle of papers came over McPherson's headphones. "The NSA just sent the transcript of a tagged cell conversation from fifty-two minutes ago. Smudgy, they say, like two people talking near an open phone that one of them was covering with his hand . . . bingo. Listen to this. Quote:

"'Unless Ross and the woman were bait. If you and Six were spotted.'

"'What are you doing?'

"'Don't you see? If you were tracked here, then those helos will be merely the final phase of the assault. The commandos will already be inside the building.'

"'Calm down. You're jumping at shadows.'

"'If they're on to us.'

"'They're not on to us.'

"'And we don't launch the weapon.'

"'The weapon is in no danger. We have a schedule, Colonel, and we're going to stay on that schedule.'

"'Yes, sir.' End quote."

"That's them," McPherson confirmed grimly. "Could they get a location on that call?"

"Got the address right here." Zebrinski read it off. "They couldn't pull the floor number, but there's another line in the transcript that talks about sending Three and Thirteen to someone on the ninth floor, so there are at least that many stories. Wait a second."

There was another rustle of paper. "Got the schematics. Twelve floors."

"Then we've got them," McPherson said. "Question is whether we can nail them before they get the bomb in position."

"More to the point, can we get to them before they blow it?" Ross put in.

"The assault teams are already on the way," Zebrinski said. "As to the second . . . we'll just have to see."

~

The assault was three-pronged, quiet and stealthy. The first two prongs were obvious and unimaginative: three darkened and engine-muffled helos, one attack and two troop carriers, all doing their best to sneak up on the base's roof, while far below squads of combat-garbed commandos with shoulder-slung submachine guns stole through the suddenly deserted streets and took up positions at doors and windows.

The third prong was slightly more interesting, Eleven thought, peering through his binoculars as best he could through the lenses of his gas mask. Six of the men in the street below, more or less evenly spaced around the two sides of the building that he could see, lifted slender, meter-long cylinders to their shoulders and simultaneously fired upward. There was a muffled group *chummpf*; and suddenly six grappling hooks were snaking upward, trailing rapidly uncoiling ropes behind them. The hooks arched over the edge of the roof and were dragged back to the parapet, catching solidly there. Blinking the sweat from his eyes, Eleven watched as the commandos hooked their powered harnesses to the ropes and started smoothly up the sides of the building.

He wondered what kind of motor was small enough yet powerful enough to pull the commandos upward so quickly, but was unable to get a clear view of the mechanism. Pity.

"Company at the side doors," he reported into the mike of the headset connected to the cell phone lying beneath his chin on his mechanic's creeper. "Company also at the front and back doors . . . correction, company has come in the front door," he amended as one of the street-level commando squads got the main door open and slipped inside the building. "Orders?"

"Discourage side-door visitors on my signal," the general said.

"Acknowledged." Eleven punched off the phone and got his Galil in hand, the same kind of gun that had served Ten so well on the *Rabah Jamila*. Their earlier Israeli deception was probably no longer needed, but stirring a little more mud into the murky water couldn't hurt.

The five reverse-rappelling commandos were passing the seventh floor now, coming into optimal kill range. Remembering the body armor that had defeated Six's attempts to eliminate Ross and Mrs. Chandler in San Jose, Eleven set his crosshairs on the back of the head of the commando most distant from his position and waited.

And with a suddenness that even startled him, every second-story window exploded outward as the entire floor erupted into flame.

Someone shouted something, but the words were lost in the roar of flames and the muffled crack of Eleven's rifle. The target commando jerked once and went limp, his ascent stopping as his dead hand dropped from the control. Shifting aim, Eleven fired again, and a second commando joined his comrade in death.

He was lining his sights on the third when the sky above the building lit up with a brilliance that momentarily rivaled the glow from the blaze below. Across on the other flanking roof, Nine had apparently introduced a surface-to-air missile to one of the stealthy helos, which would never be stealthy again. The flaming aircraft veered sharply away, the commandos who'd been preparing to drop onto the rooftop holding on for their lives as they careened toward the streets below.

Dismissing them from his mind and attention, Eleven returned to his own private duck shoot.

Twenty seconds later he had finished, leaving six corpses dangling like broken marionettes along the side of the building. He took a quick look below and tucked the rifle back under him. "Side-door company has been discouraged," he reported.

"Acknowledged," the general said. "Relocate."

"Yes, sir," Eleven said, sliding his legs a little ways off the sides of his creeper, making sure they stayed hidden beneath the protection of the small Cloak lying across his back. Getting a grip on the rough roof surface with his toes, he started pushing himself forward.

He'd moved perhaps four meters when a sudden staccato of machine gun fire came from behind him, and the sound of slugs tearing into the spot he'd just vacated. Setting his teeth, he kept going, mindful of the danger of ricochets or erratic marksmanship on the one hand and the speed limitations of his Cloak on the other.

The gunnery practice continued for a few more seconds, then stopped. The down-blast of a helo passed somewhere close overhead and then was gone.

He made it to his secondary position and stopped, sweat dripping off his nose as he eased one eye beneath the edge of the Cloak. The enemy's first, mostly subtle approach had failed. The next assault would be less subtle and considerably noisier.

Hefting his rifle, he settled in to wait.

~

Hovering well away from the fiasco, McPherson clenched his teeth and tried not to swear out loud on an open mike. "I thought you said there were no flankers," he snarled.

"Every rooftop for six blocks showed clear," the Delta Force commander snarled back. From the tone of his voice, he was choking back a few choice words, too. "Visual and IR both. I thought these damn Cloaks of yours don't block IR."

"They don't," McPherson said. "The flankers must be wearing insulated suits."

"We had a visual on the sniper's muzzle flashes," another voice cut in. "But there's no body or blood, so he must have moved before we got there."

"Or else he's dead under the Cloak," McPherson muttered.

"Okay, fine," Delta Leader growled. "They want to play games? We can play games, too. We'll just saturate those two rooftops and *then* see what good these Cloaks do them."

"Wait a second," McPherson said. "The primary goal isn't to take out the snipers, or even get to Bakht. It's to keep the weapon from blowing."

"And how do you propose we do that?" Delta Leader asked. "I hope you're not going to suggest we just shoot the dirigible out of the sky. With the nuke already armed, you'd have a better than even chance of blowing it right there and then."

"I wasn't," McPherson told him, glaring at the burning wreckage of the downed helo and trying to force his nebulous idea into something workable. "Have you got more of those tube-launched grapples?"

"Yes, plenty."

"All right," McPherson said. "That dirigible is moving slowly down 44th Street, no faster than a couple of miles per hour. We should be able to get on top of a building somewhere ahead of it, something the same height or a little lower than it is. We wait for it to come by, snag it with the grapples, use the winch from one of your helos to haul it sideways to the roof, get into the gondola, and disarm the damn thing. That sound like a plan to you?"

Delta Leader grunted. "Doesn't sound any crazier than the rest of it," he conceded. "Problem: how do we tag the dirigible when we can't see it?"

"We use the imagers," McPherson told him. "Better yet, we get another helo above it and use one of our modified speed-trap laser guns. Those don't need nearly as much sampling time, but they have to have something behind the cloaked object to bounce the beam off of."

"Worth a try," Delta Leader said. "Delta Four, head back to base and grab one of those lasers. Once you've got it, we'll find ourselves a likely rooftop. I suppose you'll want the rest of us to sit on our hands until then?"

McPherson pursed his lips. "Yes, hang back for a minute," he said. "You can't get your ground-level people in through that second-floor fire anyway, and sending in more helos will just be asking for them to be shot down. We know they've got four SAMs left."

"They're going to find it damn suspicious if we don't do something," Zebrinski warned.

"Oh, we'll do something," McPherson assured him. "Colonel, when the NSA gave you the location of that cell call, did they also happen to give you the phone's number?"

~

"They're still hanging back," Two reported, peering cautiously out the window. "I'd say our response was something of a surprise."

"They're discussing options," Bakht said, checking on the slender cable being unwound from the portable winch they'd anchored to the room's floor. The next length marker on the cable came into view, and Bakht did a quick mental calculation. Yes—at the current pace the dirigible would reach its position above the UN Building at precisely seven o'clock.

And though his opponents didn't realize it, they'd already lost. The dirigible had moved within the magic quarter-mile of its target, the distance at which the building's devastation was guaranteed. If they were pressed too hard and he was forced to detonate the weapon early, the UN would still be demolished, and the renegade Dr. Kazi would still die.

Two's cell phone chirped, and he punched it on. "Yes?"

Bakht glanced at him; paused for a second look. Two's eyes had gone wide, his mouth falling slightly open as he let the phone drop from his ear and pressed his palm against the microphone. "It's FBI Director McPherson," he hissed. "He wants to speak with you."

Bakht nodded. A not unexpected development, though he was mildly surprised they'd made his phone connection this quickly. "It's all right," he told Two, beckoning him forward. "Let me have it."

Silently, Two handed him the phone. "Yes?" Bakht said.

"This is FBI Director McPherson," a voice said. A hard, cool, professional voice, Bakht decided. The voice of a worthy opponent. "Is this General Raksha Bakht?"

Bakht felt something tight close around his throat. No wonder Two had looked so stunned. He hadn't realized that McPherson had asked for him by name.

And in that sliced moment of time, everything was suddenly poised on the edge of disaster. Because if they knew about him, they knew everything.

Everything?

Involuntarily, he glanced out the window down 44th Street, logic forcing down the sudden surge of panic. No, they couldn't know everything. Only those few loyal men who were with him now knew the entire plan, and none of them would have talked or betrayed him. That was a certainty as solid as the sun's rising in the east. It had to be something else that had given him away. Something else, or someone else.

Minister Rao.

He smiled bitterly. Of course. Rao had broken, or been caught in a lie, or trapped some other way. He'd never been strong enough—Bakht had known that from the beginning. Rao had broken, and in guilt or fear or cowardice he had told them everything he knew.

Which meant there was still hope. Rao knew nothing about this part of the plan, which meant McPherson didn't, either. Certainly he couldn't know about the invisible dirigible slowly wending its way toward destiny. Even if by some miracle he suspected, the large Cloak wrapped snugly around the dirigible made it impossible to locate, certainly in any stealthy manner. Without any engines the vehicle gave off no heat; with relatively little metal aside from the weapon itself, it would be virtually transparent to radar, especially against the ground clutter surrounding it.

And Hooker had personally assured him that IR and radar were the only two ways of penetrating the Cloak. The Americans' only other hope would be if someone ran a helo into the dirigible or its tether line, and either of those would show up instantly on the winch's stress indicator.

No, the weapon was safe enough. And McPherson's knowledge of his name would not make that much of a difference in the conversation he'd been planning to have here anyway. It was time to present his final red herring. "Ah," he said. "So that was his name. Bakht."

There was just the barest hesitation. "We know about your mission, General," McPherson said. "Everything, including Minister Rao's involvement. I'm here to tell you that your plan to bury Dr. Kazi's murder in the middle of mass slaughter has failed. All you'll accomplish will be to make him a martyr, which we both know will be as bad as having him still alive and well."

"This is most interesting," Bakht said, putting a menacing casualness into his voice. "So that was what Bakht was planning, was it? Well, he may yet get his wish."

There was another pause, a slightly longer one this time. "Did you hear me, General?" McPherson said. "Did you hear what I said?"

"General Bakht and his followers are dead," Bakht said flatly. Two was looking slightly sandbagged; Bakht sent him a reassuring wink. "You would have learned of this afterwards through our communiqué," he continued. "But since you went to the effort of tracking down my phone number, I do you the courtesy of telling you now."

"All right," McPherson said. He didn't believe it for a minute, of course. But Bakht could nevertheless hear a grain of doubt in his voice. "I'll play. If you're not General Bakht, who are you?"

"You may call me Simon," Bakht told him, "after that greatest of heroes, Simon Bolivar, who remains our inspiration."

"So you're a terrorist?"

"We are soldiers," Bakht corrected sternly. "Warriors for causes the world has chosen to forget or ignore."

"And what is your cause today?"

"One that would be near to your own heart if you were an honest man and not merely a political beast of burden," Bakht said. "The freedom to choose one's own way in life, using whatever pleasures and assists and crutches one wishes."

"I don't understand."

"Last month your President made a despicable and cowardly attack on an innocent and unarmed populace in Colombia," Bakht said, letting his voice harden. "Many innocents were killed, their homes and livelihoods destroyed, all in the name of denying your people their own rightful freedoms."

"The targets of that operation were murderous drug lords," McPherson countered calmly. "Men who made themselves rich from enslaved people and shattered lives, who think nothing of killing anyone who gets in their way. They're the ones who put the people you mention in harm's way, deliberately hiding behind them. If your concern is for the downtrodden, you should be on our side here."

"Ah, the traditional American noble cause," Bakht said sarcastically. "And the other deaths merely regrettable collateral damage? Very well. In that case, our noble cause is the elimination of a single murderous man, President Whitcomb alone. All the rest will merely be regrettable collateral damage."

"And how much collateral damage are we talking about?" McPherson asked carefully.

"Please," Bakht reproved him. "If you know about General Bakht, you surely know what he brought into the country."

"And you just borrowed it from him?"

"My people were to meet him at a rendezvous point in Montana with munitions obtained from another repressive regime," Bakht said. "We decided we had a better use for his device than he did." He snorted into the phone. "I see now we could simply have let him continue and achieve our goal for us. Still, if we had, our message would have been lost on you and the world. So perhaps it is better this way."

"All right," McPherson said. "You've made your point. Let's talk."

"We have nothing to talk about," Bakht said stiffly. "Whitcomb will die tonight. There is nothing you or anyone else can do to stop us."

"I understand," McPherson said. "But you don't need to kill every-one in the UN just to get to him. How about permitting us to evacuate the rest of the building if Whitcomb promises to stay behind?"

Bakht smiled. McPherson still wasn't buying the Simon masquer-ade. But there was still enough uncertainty for him to try this probe. "I make you a counteroffer," he said. "You may quietly—*quietly*, I say—evacuate the diplomats of the following nations: Colombia, Mexico, Argentina, Ecuador, Ukraine, and Iran. Those were the only nations to publicly denounce Whitcomb for his so-named Calling Birds operation."

"There were many other nations who also didn't support the President's action," McPherson pointed out. "How about letting them off the hook, too?"

"Those who do not defend the people's lives are the people's ene-mies," Bakht retorted. "I have given you the list. Evacuate them or not—your choice. But I warn you, there is little time left. The weapon is planted and ready, and the timer is set to detonate as Whitcomb reaches the podium."

"Which will be, when, an hour from now?"

"It will be in precisely thirty-nine minutes, at seven-fifteen," Bakht said. "Do you think I do not know their schedule?"

"Sorry," McPherson apologized. "It wasn't a trick, just a question—I don't have the schedule in front of me. But look, Simon. If it's the people of Colombia you really care about, they don't need revenge. What they need is the means to rebuild their lives. Destroying the United Nations won't get that for them."

"So it comes to this," Bakht said contemptuously. "You think all you have to do is offer American money and I will forget the faces of the dead?"

"I'm not asking you to forget the dead," McPherson said. "I'm sug-gesting a way for you to help the living."

"The only ones living will be the diplomats from the six coun-tries I listed," Bakht said coldly. "Your time is running swiftly, Director McPherson. And this conversation is over."

He punched the off button. "Interesting," he commented, offering the phone back to Two.

Automatically, the other took it. "How did they find us?" he asked.

"Probably the phone," Bakht said, gesturing to it. "The conversa-tion you and I had earlier—I didn't think about it at the time, but even though you had the microphone covered they must have gleaned enough key words to flag it. Impressive, really, considering the amount of traffic they must have had to sift through. We won't use that particular phone again, of course."

"Not that it matters," Two said tautly, studying his commander's face as he put the phone away. "They know, don't they?"

"They know," Bakht confirmed soberly. "I may have planted a few doubts. But, yes, they know."

"Then it's over," Two said, his cheeks sagging, his face suddenly old. "We've failed."

"We haven't failed," Bakht said firmly. "They don't know where the weapon is, and in any event they cannot stop it now. We *will* detonate on schedule."

"And accomplish what?" Two murmured. "Mass murder?"

"The silencing of a great threat," Bakht corrected.

"And the destruction of our nation."

"Our nation will survive," Bakht assured him. "Certainly there will be great anger over what we've done. There will be resignations and trials and perhaps even convictions of innocent men and women in our government. We ourselves, should they track us down, will be held as criminals of the highest order."

"And in the midst of it all Jammu and Kashmir will still be lost to us," Two shot back. "Kazi will be raised to martyrdom, and world outrage will demand the partition of our land. So tell me again: what will we have accomplished?"

"We can hold out against world outrage," Bakht said. "As for Kazi, he will be remembered for a day, or a week, or a month. But the sheer number of prominent deaths this night will bury that memory, and for everyone outside India itself he'll be relegated to the back page of history. Less effective men will rise to take his place, and the world will forget him. And with him will be forgotten the cause he stood for."

Two snorted. "The world does not forget their martyrs, General."

Bakht shook his head. "The world has no martyrs anymore, Colonel," he said quietly, a twinge of unexpected sadness in his heart. "Small groups may remember for a time, but the larger world outside will not. The media have become the world's memory, and they live solely to suck the life-blood from the living. The dry bones of the dead are of no interest to them."

He took a deep breath, forcing from his mind all thoughts of the shallowness the world had become. "So we'll continue," he said. "We'll do what has to be done. For the good of the people, and the survival of the nation."

40

THE NEGOTIATIONS, SUCH as they were, were over. "Comments?" McPherson's voice came in Talbot's ear.

"Worst try at a snow job I've ever heard," Zebrinski said contemptuously. "He must think we're morons."

"He thinks the public are morons," someone else said acidly. "He knows the recording will come out eventually, and he's playing to the conspiracy nuts."

"Forget the political fallout," McPherson growled. "I'm more interested in that comment about a timer. Does anyone think that's really how it's set?"

"Not a chance," Zebrinski said firmly. "It'll be a radio control that he can trigger whenever he wants. Either broadcast or on a wire piggybacking the tether line."

"If it's the former, could we blanket the radio frequencies?" McPherson asked. "Keep him from transmitting whatever the go signal is?"

"Sure," Zebrinski said. "Unless what he's got is a dead-man setup where cutting off a hold signal is what blows it. In that case, jamming the radio just sets it off right then and there."

"I was afraid of that," McPherson muttered.

Standing at the ops room window, Talbot gazed through his binoculars at the bright lights where 44th Street intersected First Avenue, trying to tune out the running commentary in his ear. There was something about this whole plan that was sending danger signals through the base of his brain. But in ten minutes of trying he hadn't been able to force the vague disquiet to coalesce into anything concrete.

And he was rapidly running out of time to do so. On the lawn below, the Delta Force helo had landed, and someone was running out to it with one of their modified speed-trap lasers in hand. Another minute and they would be off to try and lasso the dirigible.

He turned away from the window and went over to Swenson's desk. She was tapping away at her keyboard, oblivious as always, an oasis of silence amid the noise and tension swirling through the room. "Anything?" he asked, laying a hand on her shoulder.

She blinked up at him, taking a few seconds to replay and process his question. "I'm closing in on it," she said. "There aren't a lot of places that even make seventy-foot dirigibles, and the sales aren't what you'd call brisk."

She gestured to her screen. "I've got a tentative match with a Canadian company. Right size, right cost, and enough room in the gondola for the nuke."

Talbot leaned over for a look at the schematic she'd pulled up. It was a typical fat cigar shape, with a pair of small prop-equipped wings on the sides of the envelope and a small gondola riding beneath it. "Anything there for a grappling hook to grab onto?"

"Precious little," she said, tapping spots on the schematic. "You've got these stub wings and engines, but since they're not using them they may have just taken them off."

"Which means the guy wires or stabilizers anchoring the wings to the envelope would likely be gone, too," Talbot said.

"Right," Swenson agreed. "That just leaves the tricycle landing gear and the gondola itself."

"And in order to hit any of those spots, you first have to go through the Cloak," Talbot murmured. "Do we have any idea what happens if you cut the Cloak material?"

"I assume that at some point you cut something vital and the thing becomes visible again," she said. "You want me to call Burke and Esteban for details?"

Talbot straightened up and looked back out the window. The helo was taking off, its nose turning back toward 44th Street as it lifted from the ground.

And abruptly, he had it. Grabbing for his mike switch, he flicked it on. "This is Talbot," he said hurriedly. "Delta Four, Delta Leader: do not move to intercept the dirigible. Repeat, do *not* move to intercept."

"What?" Delta Leader growled. "Who do you think—?"

"Explain," McPherson cut him off.

"The dirigible is cloaked, and it's not radiating heat," Talbot said. "That means that as far as Bakht is concerned *we don't know it's there.*"

"Oh, God, he's right," McPherson breathed. "Delta Four, confirm that order. Head straight back to the target group. Don't stop, don't pause along the way, and make damn sure you don't bump into the dirigible."

"Wait a minute," Delta Leader objected. "If Bakht doesn't know, then we've got the drop on him. Isn't that what we want?"

"The problem is we won't have the drop on him for long if he sees us gathering helos together right where his pet dirigible is located," McPherson gritted. "Because I'll guarantee *he* sure as hell knows exactly where it is."

"And even if he can't see it himself, he'll have spotters along the way," Talbot added. "We can't let them notice anything unusual."

"So what, we're back to assaulting his base?"

"Not until we confirm whether or not he's on a deadman configuration," McPherson said.

Someone was tugging at his sleeve. Talbot looked down, annoyed, to see Swenson holding out her cell phone to him. "You'd better take this," she said, an odd note to her voice.

Frowning, he pulled the tac radio out of his ear and handed it to her as he took the phone. "Talbot."

"Ross," Ross's voice came back. "Listen, I've got an idea. The old fighting fire with fire thing."

"Great," Talbot said. "Hang on; I'll put you on tac."

"No, don't," Ross said quickly. "If I wanted the world to listen, I'd have put it on my own tac. This is just between you and me."

Talbot ground his teeth. "Ross, this isn't a game."

"No kidding," Ross countered. "The point is that if we mention this scheme to the military people, they're going to insist on doing it themselves."

"Isn't that their job?"

"Sure," Ross agreed. "Only they don't have time. The Delta Force grunts are dug in half a mile away around Bakht's building, the police and SEAL search teams are who knows where inside these other buildings. One of the S.W.A.T. trucks is parked fifty yards ahead of me, but I've yet to see a single cop anywhere. By the time we got any of them back here it would be too late."

"Too late for what?" Talbot demanded.

"Besides, like you said, Bakht will have spotters," Ross went on. "If they reported a helo discharging Marines on First Avenue, he'd realize the balloon had gone up and blow the thing. It's already within range of the UN—if he's waiting until it gets directly overhead it's purely from professional pride and not mission necessity."

"Okay, okay, you've sold me," Talbot said. "So who *do* we get?"

"Who do you think?" Ross retorted. "I'm already in place. How fast can you get that spare Cloak to First and 44th?"

"About three minutes, assuming I can snag one of those police bikes down there," Talbot told him, frowning. Whatever Ross had in mind, he was pretty sure he wasn't going to like it. "The Cloak's three doors down the hall—the techs brought it in to run tests."

"Perfect," Ross said. "Grab it and meet me on the north side of 44th, at the first building you hit past the hotel. Don't forget the laptop."

"Right," Talbot said. "You want to tell me what this is all about?"

"Hold on," Ross said as a faint voice came in the background. There was a brief, unintelligible conversation, and then Ross was back on the line. "Hell and biscuits," he said grimly. "We've run out of time, Madison. The temperatures have equalized, and the thermal imagers have gone useless."

Talbot felt his throat tighten. "It's invisible again?"

"Completely," Ross confirmed. "All we've got left are the laser guns, and we can't use those without a background. Just get over here."

"I'm on my way."

He turned off the phone and handed it back to Swenson. "You'd better call McPherson," he told her, taking the tac radio back. "Tell him what's going on."

"*I* don't even know what's going on," she protested.

"That makes two of us," Talbot said, heading for the door. "Just tell him Ross and I are playing a hunch."

~

The S.W.A.T. truck had been backed into a narrow driveway out of the traffic flow on the north side of 44th Street, half a block west of First Avenue. It was unoccupied, as Ross had already noted, with the cops belonging to it scattered throughout the surrounding buildings.

It was also locked, with the kind of security that came of big-city cops who knew the kind of PR hell that would come of having one of their own vehicles stolen by the bad guys.

Ross had the back door open in forty seconds.

"What are we looking for?" Angie asked as Ross shone his pocket flash around the back of the truck. It was as well-equipped a police vehicle as he'd ever seen, with equipment ranging from the mundane to the exotic.

In this case, he was going to need something from each end of that spectrum.

"This, for starters," he told her, pulling a slender, yard-long cylinder from a rack on one wall and handing it through the door to her. "Careful—it's heavier than it looks."

"Got it," she said, taking the weight and pulling it outside.

"And this," he added, selecting one of the bulky harnesses racked alongside the cylinders and also passing it back. "This might be handy," he said, pulling a long combat knife from its sheath and looking it over. It had an eight-inch ceramic blade, one edge wickedly serrated, both edges painfully sharp. Resheathing it, he slid it into his belt beneath his coat. "And this," he finished, sliding a tranquilizer dart kit from one of the shelves and popping it open for a quick inspection. Inside was a long-barreled air gun and four darts with bright red pom-pom ends. Probably designed for taking down dangerous animals, but the particular chemical mixture inside wouldn't matter. Closing the kit, he tucked it under one arm and stepped back to the door.

He paused there, glancing around toward the front of the truck as a sudden thought struck him. If he took another minute to hot-wire the vehicle and sat Angie down in the driver's seat, she could be on the street in a matter of seconds. In the fifteen minutes left before the presumed seven o'clock detonation she should have no trouble getting out of the blast zone . . .

"I'm coming with you," she said into his thoughts. "You might need an extra pair of hands."

"Yeah, okay," Ross sighed, hopping out of the truck and slamming the doors behind him. Loosening his belt, he took the cylinder from Angie and slid it part way down his left pant leg, concealing the rest beneath his coat. The harness he stuffed beneath the right side of his coat; the trank kit he handed to her to carry. "Let's go."

~

"It looks like he's trying to get it open," Six murmured into his phone, trying to look inconspicuous as he huddled in a doorway out of the wind and watched Ross work on the lock of the building across the street. Mrs. Chandler stood at his side, looking nervous and twitchy.

"Either of them carrying anything?" the general asked.

"The woman's got a small box," Six reported. "He doesn't have anything obvious. But his left leg seemed stiff when he was walking. He could be carrying something there. Shall I follow them inside?"

There was a pause, and Six took advantage of the opportunity to check his watch. Fourteen minutes until seven. Fourteen minutes, if all went according to schedule, until the blast.

The general was apparently thinking along the same lines. "Better not," he said. "Time is getting short. I don't want to close the party early, but I don't think we can afford to close it late, either. You and Four had best pull out now."

Six hesitated. His motorcycle was parked around the corner on First Avenue, and he most definitely didn't want to be anywhere in the vicinity when the bomb went off. But he also didn't like the idea of leaving Ross running around this close to the bomb, even if he didn't know how close he actually was. "With your permission, sir, I'd like to stay a bit longer," he said. "I don't trust this man."

"I don't want you pressing your luck, Six," Bakht warned. "We're expecting new visitors any minute now. If they're too noisy, the party will have to be closed right at seven."

"Understood," Six said. "Can you give me the reading?"

The general read off the distance marker on the tether line. Six did the calculation in his head, watching as Ross straightened up and pushed open the now unlocked door. The dirigible was just a little ways west at the moment, he concluded. Another five to eight minutes, and the weapon would have passed the last of these buildings and be crossing First Avenue onto UN grounds. "Let me have eight minutes," he said.

"Five minutes," the general said. "No more. Let me know when you're on your way."

"Yes, sir."

Six closed down his phone and folded his arms across his chest, shivering once with the sudden redistribution of heat through his torso. The primary blast radius, he knew, was about a quarter mile, but the blast damage and resulting firestorm would extend far beyond that. Pushing his time limit would make his escape considerably more problematic.

But it was worth the risk to find out what Ross was up to. Besides, once the weapon was safely hovering over the UN the general might decide he could afford to hold the detonation another few minutes.

He frowned. A police motorcycle had just appeared through the traffic flow on First Avenue, its lights blazing but its siren silent. It headed down the sidewalk on the far side of the street and skidded to a halt directly in front of the door Ross and the woman had just disappeared through. The rider wasn't an officer, or at least wasn't in uniform, and had a bulky backpack on over his light jacket. He dismounted, hunched his shoulders once as if to resettle the backpack's weight, and then followed the other two inside.

And as the door closed behind him, Six saw him pull out a cell phone.

He pulled his out, too, but then hesitated. The general had cautioned them against using the phones more than necessary, especially now that the enemy had demonstrated his ability to monitor all communication systems and, even more impressive, to pluck specific conversations from the mass.

He dropped the phone back in his pocket. The follow-up report could wait until he had some actual information to offer. Whatever Ross and the others were up to, they had to come out into the open to do it.

When they did, he would be waiting.

~

"You had better be joking," McPherson said. His voice was flat and colorless, the kind of voice Swenson always had difficulty reading on phones or radios.

For once, though, she had no trouble visualizing the expression that went with that voice. "No, sir," she said, wincing as she visualized the Director's face going purple. "Ross seemed to think this was the only way to stop the nuke."

"Of all the damn fool stunts—" McPherson broke off. "Are they on tac? Talbot? Ross?"

Swenson listened carefully to the clipped comments and replies coming in on the tac. But there was no reply from either of the two men. "They may be getting Ross ready," she suggested.

"God save us from self-appointed Lone Rangers," McPherson snarled. "I swear, Swenson, that if we get out of this alive I'm transferring him to the Aleutians. What's their timetable?"

Swenson checked her watch. "Talbot joined them about two minutes ago, while Ross was giving me the plan. He guessed it would take five minutes to get ready, so call it another three."

"Another three minutes," McPherson said. "Delta Leader, you get all that?"

"Yes, sir," Delta Leader said. "I agree it's a damn-fool stunt. But it might actually work."

"If Bakht doesn't tumble to it," McPherson said. "In about a minute and a half we're going to want one hell of a diversion."

"We're on it," Delta Leader promised grimly. "All right, gentlemen, we tried it the quiet way. Time to try it the loud way."

"Just don't hit Bakht directly," McPherson warned. "We still don't know if he's running a dead-man setup."

Swenson could almost see Delta Leader's cold smile. "Leave it to us."

There was more, but Swenson wasn't listening. There was a flaw in Ross's scheme, she suddenly realized. A potentially disastrous flaw.

But if she was fast, maybe she could fix it. Maybe.

~

Eleven's first warning that the helos were back was the sudden brilliant flash from the flanking rooftop where Eight and Nine lay hidden under their Cloak, a flash that was dazzling even at his distance. His second warning, even as he reflexively squeezed his eyes shut, was the near-simultaneous flash from somewhere behind him, bright enough to see even through closed eyelids, and the violent concussion that seemed to lift him straight up into the air. Even as he grabbed for the edges of the creeper another set of flashes drilled through his eyelids, with an accompanying set of explosions that hammered into his skull even with full hearing protection in place.

It was several seconds before he could pull himself together and get his brain functioning again. Shaking his head, he blinked a few times and peered cautiously over the edge of the roof.

There was only one reason he could think of why they would bother using flash-bangs on him. And as he got his eyes focused on the base of the building across the street he saw that his guess had been right. The fire on the second and now third floors was still burning fiercely, the flames forming a highly effective barrier to anyone attempting to enter the building from street level.

But now, where there had been six grappler-equipped ropes hanging from the rooftop, each with its own dead commando, there were now a dozen such ropes.

And the new ones were swaying empty in the wind, each hanging beside a fifth-floor window from which the glass had mysteriously disappeared.

With the fire blocking the lower floors, and with Eleven's marksmanship blocking the upper ones, the commandos had made themselves a new door in the middle.

Fingers still trembling with reaction, Eleven punched Bakht's number on his phone. "Company in front door," he said, his voice sounding slurred in his ringing ears. "In through fifth."

"We're ready," the general's voice answered, infinitely reassuring in its calmness and stability. "Are you hurt?"

"No," Eleven said. His voice sounded better this time. "Just flash-bangs."

"Pull back and watch the back door," the general ordered. "The company may try that way again."

"Yes, sir," Eleven said, feeling an easing of his tension as he sidled his creeper carefully backward. Keeping an eye on street-level activities meant staying near the edge of his roof, which gave the enemy an uncomfortably narrow zone in which to hunt for him. Now, with the whole rooftop available to hide in, they could blast away forever without ever hitting him.

Especially since they didn't have forever. They had exactly twelve minutes, if the general was on schedule. At that point the eastern sky would light up, and the shock wave would sweep across the rooftops, swatting the helos down like large insects.

That would be a sight to see.

He came to a halt at a spot near a vent, well away from the edge. Hefting his rifle, he peered across at the other roof and waited for the enemy's next move.

~

"That should have gotten their attention," Delta Leader said. "IR reading shows two warm bodies on ten and five more backstopping them on nine. We'll let our people get a little closer, then hit nine with a few flash-bangs, too."

"Just keep it off ten," McPherson reminded him, peering out the helo window at the burning building. "Swenson?"

"Angie says he's going now," Swenson reported.

McPherson nodded. "Stay on it."

"Well, well," Hastings commented, swinging the helo around in a gentle curve and pointing downward. "Guess what doesn't like flash-bangs."

Frowning, McPherson looked that direction. There, amid the lingering wisps of residue smoke from the stun grenades, was what looked like a human figure lying on the rooftop with a black cloth draped over him. "I'll be damned," he murmured. "You're right. The Cloaks don't like flash-bangs at all."

"The one over here's gone visible, too," Delta Leader said. "You want us to take them?"

"Not yet," McPherson told him. "We don't want to upset General Bakht."

He smiled tightly. "Let's let the emperor think he still has clothes."

~

There was a muffled *chummpf* from behind him at the eighth-story window. Ross started to turn his head— "Hold still," Angie ordered, grabbing his arm with her left hand as she finished the stitch with her right. "I'm almost done."

"Hurry it up," Ross said. In his mind's eye he could see the invisible dirigible out there slipping past the window while they delayed, ending their last hope of preventing this insanity. "Madison?"

"The line seems secure," Talbot told him. "We won't really know until we try it, though."

"Yeah," Ross growled. "Come *on*, Angie."

"Finished," she declared, pulling the needle though the heavy Cloak material one final time. She did something complicated below his chin that he couldn't see from his angle, probably tying a knot, then leaned in to bite off the thread.

"Good," he said, taking a step back and cautiously raising his arms a little. The Cloak now wrapped cocoon-style around him shrugged with his shoulders but stayed fastened at his neck and knees where Angie had tacked the edges together with needlepoint thread. "I hope this looks better than it feels."

"How *does* it feel?" Angie asked as Talbot stepped up to Ross with the laptop.

"Somewhere between a monk's robe and a burial shroud," he said, taking the computer.

"*I* just hope it works," Talbot countered, plugging the cable hanging from the edge of the cloak at Ross's left cheek into the back of the computer. He tapped a key, glanced at Ross, and shook his head. "This still takes getting used to," he said. "Okay, you're on—nothing showing but your face. Got a place to put that thing?"

"Same place everything else goes," Ross grunted, closing the laptop's screen and sliding it beneath the Cloak and behind the harness beneath that and finally into his open jacket, making sure it wasn't blocking access to his borrowed knife. "Okay," he said, walking as quickly as he could toward the window, making sure to keep his stride short enough that his knees didn't tear out the stitching in front of them.

The rope from the grappling hook gun was lying across the sill of the open window, disappearing out and up toward the rooftop of the building across 44th Street where Talbot had fired it. "Can someone help me connect this harness?"

"Angie?" Talbot said as he worked to belay the end of the rope around a heavy oak desk.

"Got it." She eased the clamp from the motorized harness up past her stitching and fastened it around the grappling line. Reaching under the connection, she freed up the remote on its slender wire and pressed it into Ross's left hand. "Be careful," she murmured.

"Right," he said, easing into a seated position on the sill with his back to the window, running the motor on his harness to take up the slack. Angie knelt at his feet with her needle and thread, pulling the flap of the Cloak up over his feet and tacking it together like a diaper hanging too low. "Can you hand me the gun?"

From the distance came a multiple flash of reflected light, and the multiple booms of Fourth of July fireworks. "McPherson's diversion, right on schedule," Talbot commented, rounding the corner of the desk with his end of the belayed rope in hand and handing Ross the tranquilizer gun. "I squeezed most of the drug out of the darts," he added as he pinned the three spare darts into the front of Ross's harness where they would be accessible. "Try not to stick yourself anyway."

"I'll do that," Ross promised, sliding the gun into his waistband beside the knife and pulling out his pocket flash. Flicking it on, he put the end in his mouth like a cigarette, swiveling it around with his lips to shine past his right ear inside the cowl of his Cloak.

"And don't forget this," Talbot said, handing him the tac radio. "Damn, I wish you'd grabbed two harnesses."

"And what, had Angie belay the rope?" Ross countered around the flashlight as he set the ear bud and mike in place. "Besides, there's only room out there for one."

"Finished," Angie declared, standing up and picking up the cell phone from the desk. "Hanna? He's ready."

"Okay." Ross took a deep breath. "Here goes." With a touch on the control button, he slid out the window and up along the rope.

The first two seconds were the worst, as his sheathed legs came clear of the window and he swung back and forth on the gimbaled harness connector, looking down past the folds of the Cloak at 44th Street eighty feet beneath his feet. Then the pendulum movement dampened out, and with it the sensation that he was about to come loose and plummet to the pavement below. Pressing the button again, he continued sliding across and up.

With his free hand he turned on his tac radio. "Talbot?" he called.

"Ross?" McPherson's voice answered sharply.

"Yes, sir," Ross said as he pulled out the tranquilizer gun and pointed it forward at waist level, making sure the barrel wasn't blocked but at the same time didn't stick out past the protection of the Cloak. "I'm at the middle of the street. Time to play pin the tail on the donkey." Mentally crossing his fingers, he fired.

He'd known the dirigible would be close, but it was even closer than he'd expected. The red pom-pom stopped abruptly in apparent midair no more than fifty yards ahead and immediately started creeping back toward him. "Fifty yards and closing," he reported, quickly loading another dart.

He fired again, lower and to the left. This dart didn't get quite as far before its flight was arrested by the unseen bulk in front of it. Ross reloaded and fired again, this time still lower and to the right. Again, the dart stopped short of the other two.

"Okay, I can see two of them," Talbot reported in his ear. "Looks like you're right in front of it."

"I'm also a few yards too high," Ross said, looking at the three darts and trying to fit the dirigible shape to their positions. The Cloak hung like a loose shirtsleeve beneath the dirigible, he knew from the imager picture, which meant the curved area he'd been shooting his darts into had to be the top surface of the dirigible envelope. "Give me about ten feet of slack."

The rope sagged as Talbot let it out, carrying Ross down and to the side. He hit the backup button on the remote, moving still further down and back toward the window, recentering himself on the incoming darts. "More?" Talbot asked.

"No, this is good," Ross said, loading his last dart. He fired straight ahead, and it stuck into the air about as far back as the last one had. "Okay, I should be beneath it," he reported, stuffing the gun back into his waistband and drawing his borrowed knife. "Get ready to give me slack, and lots of it. Here we go . . . "

~

Time was growing short, Six knew as he gazed upward toward the building Ross and the others had entered a few minutes ago. Dangerously short, in fact.

So what was Ross waiting for?

Because he was definitely up to *something*. A couple of minutes ago Six had caught a flicker of movement from behind one of the eighth-floor windows, and despite the height and lack of good illumination he'd had the impression that the window had been opened. A minute later there'd been a brief and subdued flash of light, and an even more subtle sense of movement, though he hadn't yet been able to figure out what that one had entailed. He thought he'd seen more movement behind the darkened window, but aside from those glimpses there had been nothing.

What was Ross planning? Had he somehow guessed the plan, deducing the dirigible's existence either via some sophisticated radar system or direct observation of the tether line? If so, had that stiff-legged walk been because Ross had had a short-range rocket launcher down his trouser leg?

If so, both he and Six had looked upon their last sunrise. Trying to blow up the weapon with the arming box in place would succeed beyond Ross's wildest dreams.

Or was Six overestimating the enemy? Were Ross and the others merely following up on some hunch and searching the building again?

He shifted his gaze to the sky above, trying to estimate where the dirigible would be. Almost directly opposite the building, he guessed.

And the five minutes the general had granted him were nearly up. Taking one last look at Ross's building, he pushed away from his doorway and headed down the street toward the corner where his motorcycle was parked. As soon as the dirigible was over First Avenue, he promised himself, he would be out of here.

~

Even at three miles an hour, the dirigible was coming at him fast. Much too fast.

Ross bit down on the hardened aluminum of his flashlight as he watched the red pom-poms sweeping through the air toward him. This plan had sounded a lot more feasible when he was raiding the S.W.A.T. truck, he realized belatedly, than it was now that he was hanging over Manhattan like an amateur spider with half a ton of dirigible bearing down on him.

But it was too late to back out now. Gripping his knife in his left hand, holding it horizontally out in front of him with the serrated edge gleaming forward, he braced himself for the impact. And hoped like hell that the NYPD's knife-sharpener took exceptional pride in his work.

The lowest of the dart pom-poms slid past over his head; and abruptly something solid slapped into the tip of his knife, the impact nearly wrenching it out of his hand. Instantly he jabbed sideways, and half the blade abruptly vanished as it slid through the Cloak material.

The blade's vanishing act didn't last long. As the dirigible's motion carried it forward against Ross's rigid grip, the knife edge sliced smoothly through the Cloak, opening up a slit in the material. Grabbing the lower edge of the cut with his right hand as it lengthened past his head, he pulled it open and flipped the flashlight around in his mouth to point inside.

There it was. A dirigible, all right, and from that first quick glance it looked to be the exact model Swenson had described to him over the phone.

But he didn't have time for more than that one quick glance. Suddenly the bulk of the Cloak was squeezing hard against his chest as the dirigible pushed against the rope holding him suspended over the street. Another second or two and the pressure would either snap the line or, more likely, yank the other end from Talbot's grip, sending Ross swinging helplessly into the side of the building across the street.

There was no time to get to the harness release. Spitting the flashlight out of his mouth through the opening, he flipped his legs up around his more or less braced right hand like a gymnast on a vaulting horse, trying to swing his lower body in through the gap. "Let go the rope!" he barked into the tac, slashing backward with his knife against the rope above his head.

The knife bit through the rope like it was cheap string. His legs bounced off the edge of the cut and slid through; and suddenly Ross was completely inside the Cloak enclosure, holding onto the edge with one hand.

But contrary to his shouted instructions the other end of the rope was still holding fast; and even as his feet slapped against the inside of the Cloak he realized to his horror that he was starting to be pulled back out through the opening again. He slashed at the lower part of the rope with his knife, but it was already buried within a crease of the material and he succeeded only in making another slice in the Cloak.

And then there was no time to try again as he was forced to drop the knife and grab for the top edge of the cut with his left hand as his torso was pulled irresistibly back out through the opening. "Talbot!" he shouted frantically.

Almost too late, the tension on the rope vanished; and suddenly the pressure he'd been applying was again shoving him inward.

The sudden change in direction proved too much for his tentative grip. With a startled curse, he found himself sliding helplessly down the inside of the Cloak.

41

FROM THE FLOOR below came the thunder-cracks of more flash-bang grenades, the noise only slightly muffled by the flooring material between them, and Bakht winced with each burst. The commandos were knocking at the door.

Still, there was time. His men on the floor below might not leave the city alive—none of them might, for that matter—but that had always been a possibility. What was important was that Kazi was about to be burned down to his component atoms, and with him would die the threat to the nation.

This particular threat, at least. There would be others in the future. There always were. Bakht could only hope that those who came after him would prove as equal to those challenges as he had proved himself with this one.

"Sir!" Two said sharply. He was over by the winch, his gun in hand, his face obscured by his gas mask. "Reading a sudden loss of tension."

Bakht was at his side in an instant. "Where?" he asked, his eyes flicking over the gauges. They looked normal to him.

"It's gone now," Two said, his voice sounding odd. "But it was there. For a moment the tension in the tether line dipped. I swear it."

"I'm not doubting you," Bakht said, lifting his binoculars to the goggles of his own gas mask.

Everything seemed all right. The dirigible was still cloaked, and there was no sign of anything or anyone near it.

Squatting down, he sighted along the tether line. Aside from the inevitable dip it was running straight down the street, exactly as it was supposed to. No one had winched the dirigible to a rooftop or down to street level, as they surely would have if they'd somehow discovered its

presence. "What are the readings now?" he asked, lowering the binoculars and pulling out his phone.

"Normal," Two said, sounding uncomfortable. "Perhaps it was just
a momentary pause in the wind."

"Perhaps," Bakht said darkly, punching in Six's number. "Let's find
out."

~

"Ross!" Talbot snapped. "Are you all right?"

"I'm fine," Ross grunted, easing himself around and up into a sitting position at the bottom of the Cloak enclosure and taking quick
stock of the situation. His flashlight was laying a couple of feet away,
its beam buried in a fold of the black material. Pressed tightly across his
chest and shoulder, the section of rope still hooked to his harness angled
up to the cut he'd made in the Cloak and disappeared outside.

"Where are you?" Talbot asked.

"Where do you think?" Ross retorted. "I'm sitting on the bottom
of the Cloak."

"I thought you were going for the gondola," McPherson's voice cut
in.

"I took a detour."

"So what now?" McPherson demanded.

"Hang on," Ross said. Gingerly, he picked up his flashlight and
aimed it downward.

It was as good as he'd hoped and as bad as he'd figured. The seam
where the two ends of the Cloak had been fastened together, as he had
feared, ran straight along the bottom of the enclosure in keel-line position. Precisely, in fact, where he was currently sitting.

The good news was that Bakht's men had clearly had more time and
resources than Angie had. Unlike the small Cloak still tangled around
his shoulders, this one had been more than simply tacked together with
needlepoint thread. From the slickness of the seam, he guessed it had
been sealed with a hot glue gun or something similar.

Still, it was unlikely they'd designed the connection with passengers in mind. He needed to get off it before it ripped through and
dropped him onto the pavement below.

He aimed the light upward. There, too, the situation was decidedly
mixed. "The good news is that I'm directly beneath the gondola," he
reported. "The bad news is that I'm ten feet beneath it."

"Can you climb up the Cloak material?" Talbot asked.

"I don't even know how much longer I can sit on it," Ross countered. "This stuff's carrying enough weight already without my pounds added in."

"What are you going to do?" McPherson asked.

"Hope that the glorious spirit of the Lone Ranger hasn't completely faded away," Ross told him. Somewhere in the past minute, he saw, his flailing legs had broken the stitches holding his own Cloak together at feet and knees. Reaching to his chest, he ripped out the last remaining threads, freeing himself from the confinement of his cocoon. Removing the laptop from inside his coat, he set it aside, making sure the cable connecting it to his Cloak wasn't tangled in either the rope or the harness.

"What in hell's name are you talking about?" McPherson demanded.

"The Old West, of course," Ross said. Sticking the flashlight back in his mouth, he started pulling in the rope. "I'm going to try to lasso the gondola."

~

Six had reached the corner and started around it when some premonition or subtle sound made him turn halfway around and look back.

For a second he saw nothing. Then his eyes focused, and he jerked to an abrupt halt.

Angling up from the street and disappearing into the air like a fakir's magic trick was a thin rope. Even as he felt his jaw drop in amazement, he saw that the rope was in motion, being dragged down the middle of the street as if pulled by an unseen hand.

Moving eastward. Toward the UN.

He looked up. Against the hazy darkness of the New York night sky was a rectangular piece of still darker blackness where the cloaked dirigible should have been. In the center of that patch, looking like a tear in the fabric of space, was a narrow horizontal slit. A faint light shone through the gap, and as Six stared at it the light shifted subtly, revealing just a hint of the dirigible's shiny gas bag surface and the stub-wing protruding from its side.

The Cloak had been breached. Somehow, despite Six's vigilance, Ross had gotten inside.

And he was about to disarm the bomb.

Cursing violently, Six snatched out his cell phone. He'd been mistaken earlier. Ross would indeed see one more sunrise.

The one about to go off directly in his face.

~

"Uh-oh," the controller warned as he gazed through his binoculars out the ops room window. "The front starboard section of the Cloak has gone visible. And—*damn*—the rope hanging down is dragging along the street."

"How obvious is it?" Swenson asked, her fingers skating across the computer keys. Almost there.

"Well, *I* can see it," the controller shot back. "If Bakht still has spotters hanging around, they sure as hell can, too."

Swenson nodded. "I'm on it," she said. A half dozen more keystrokes—

Done. "Hang on," she muttered, mentally crossing her fingers as she keyed in the final command.

And to her immense relief and satisfaction, the entire Manhattan cell phone network quietly crashed.

~

Slowly, Bakht lowered the phone. "What is it?" Two asked.

"The phone system has gone down," the general told him.

Two hissed behind his mask. "You think they're making a move against the bomb?"

His answer was the sudden staccato of gunfire from the near distance. "I would say they're making their move against the flankers," Bakht told him grimly.

But that was all right. The flankers were still protected by their Cloaks; and he didn't need phones to give them their evacuation signal. "Fire the rooftop flares," he ordered Two, stepping to the winch and the control box on the desk beside it. A quick confirmation via binoculars that the dirigible was still cloaked, and he lifted the safety cover on the switch. It was four minutes to seven, and four minutes should be enough time for the flankers to spot the signal and make it off their rooftops to relative safety.

Kazi and his treason had four more minutes to live.

~

With a vicious curse, Six hurled his phone against the ice-edged pavement. So the enemy had been a step ahead this time. They'd shut down the cell phone system, cutting off any chance he might have to warn the general and leaving him completely isolated.

Fine. He would deal with this on his own.

His motorcycle was twenty meters away. By the time he kicked it to life, the trailing rope was making its way across First Avenue, much to the consternation of the Friday night traffic. Only a handful of drivers had actually noticed the rope, but their startled panic stops had snarled everything for a block in both directions. Taking advantage of the frozen traffic flow, Six roared across the lanes, weaving around the halted cars as he chased after the rope.

He caught up with it at the far side of the street. Skidding to a halt, he grabbed the end and wrapped a quick bowline around his handlebars. Then, gunning his engine, he roared off toward the north, at right angles to the dirigible's motion. Whatever the rope was for, it wasn't going to be there for long. Moreover, if the general was paying attention to the tether line readings, yanking the rope loose might also jolt the dirigible enough to get his attention.

Or maybe the rope was still attached to Ross. In that case, he might even be able to pull him bodily through the cut he'd made and into a hundred-foot freefall.

He rather hoped that would be the case.

~

It was the last thing Ross had expected, and it nearly killed him before he could even react to it. One minute he was hauling in the rope, trying to decide how much he would need; the next, the rope had been snatched out of his hands and he was being yanked up along the side of the Cloak again. "Watch out!" someone shouted belatedly as he scrabbled uselessly for a grip on the smooth sides of the enclosure. "Someone's trying to pull you out."

"He's on a motorcycle," Swenson's voice cut in. "Ross?"

"Yeah, thanks," Ross grunted. Abruptly, the tension vanished, and he went sliding again to the bottom of the enclosure. "What's happening?"

"He's swinging around," the first voice said. "Turning south—probably going to get up a head of steam and try again."

Ross hissed between his teeth, looking for inspiration. Something to grab onto, or to belay the rope around. Anything.

But there wasn't anything. And as the rope abruptly snapped taut and again yanked him upward he knew with the acrid taste of defeat that there was only one thing he could do. Groping at his chest, he found the harness's quick release and popped it.

The rope snaked up and through the opening and vanished into the night. "Ross?" Swenson called.

"I'm okay," Ross told her as he once again slid to the bottom.

But this time the landing was different. As his feet hit bottom there was a faint sound of tearing cloth. A two-foot gap appeared in the black material along the edge of the center seam, revealing the network of thin wires and tiny fibers inside.

With nothing beyond it but the distant ground.

Instantly, Ross twisted around to get his feet away from the tear, rolling onto his back to spread his weight as evenly across the material as he could. He slid to a halt, and for a moment lay motionless, listening for the sound of more tearing. Directly above him, the belly of the gondola hung mockingly, as inaccessible as the far side of the moon now that his rope was gone.

He took a deep breath. "Ladies and gentlemen," he said quietly. "I think we're in trouble."

~

The tension in the rope abruptly vanished, overbalancing the motorcycle and nearly throwing Six over the handlebars. He caught his balance and hit the brake, spinning around to a halt as the rope snaked to the ground around him. Neither Ross nor anyone else was tied to it.

He looked up. The crack in the side of the Cloak had gone mostly dark, but there was still a hint of light there. Ross, he guessed, had lost his flashlight during the turbulence he'd just been through. It was too much to hope he'd been incapacitated; on the other hand, it was likely he was at least temporarily dazed.

Dismounting from the motorcycle, Six crouched down on the side away from the UN building and drew his gun. He'd always liked dazed targets. They tended to hold still.

Flicking off the safety, he braced his arm on the handlebars, aimed toward where the bottom of the dirigible's Cloak enclosure ought to be, and opened fire.

~

"He's shooting at him now," Swenson's frantic voice reported in Talbot's ear as the elevator indicator flicked from five to four.

Talbot squeezed the grip of his gun. "Get some people out there," he ordered.

"Already on their way."

The elevator light flicked from four to three, and Talbot glanced at his watch. Three minutes to seven. Damn, and damn, and damn again.

~

The first bullet slapped through the Cloak less than a yard from Ross's head. The second, before he could even react to this new threat, whistled past no more than six inches from his ear. "Madison!" he yelped.

"Hang in there," Talbot's voice came back. "We're on our way."

Ross braced himself. But the third shot tore through the Cloak a good two feet past his shoes, with the fourth farther along still. The methodical sort, Ross thought as he consciously relaxed his muscles and tried to get his brain back into gear. The shots continued on for another few seconds, then stopped. Probably changing magazines, he decided, wondering distantly how heavily armed the attacker was.

And now, in the ringing silence, he heard a new sound: a soft hissing noise coming from somewhere above him.

The bullets, having missed their intended target, had instead punched a set of holes in the gasbag.

He shook his head in disgust-edged amazement. Whoever this guy was, he had a truly amazing sense of overkill. Two minutes from nuclear detonation, and he was doing his damnedest to sink the dirigible.

Or maybe all he was trying to do was sink Ross. Carefully, mindful of the increasingly fragile material between him and a long first step, he rolled up onto his side.

His hip banged into something solid as he did so. The laptop, lying uselessly where he'd set it down earlier.

The irony of it struck him oddly. Even if he'd still had his Cloak on, invisibility didn't do a bit of good when your opponent was firing blind anyway. He pushed the laptop out of his way, his hand brushing against the cable as he did so.

The cable . . .

Suddenly, the mental fumbling and uncertainty were gone. The Papa Bear Cloak covering the dirigible had a cable and a computer, too. But Bakht would surely not have simply left the laptop lying loose on the bottom of the enclosure, no matter how good with a glue gun his people were.

It had to be somewhere else. And the only possible somewhere else available was the gondola.

He sat up sharply, fears about ripping through the material abruptly forgotten. Somewhere along the way he'd lost his flashlight, but all that motorcycle-assisted yanking on the rope had carved a new rip in the Cloak, perpendicular to the one he'd made with his knife, and the resulting pair of loose flaps was letting enough street light in for him to see.

There it was, a taut dark line angling up from the bottom of the Cloak about two yards back from the gondola, with the other end disappearing through a channel that had been drilled around the edge of the door.

Putting a hand against the side of the Cloak for balance, Ross headed back toward the cable. The upward rain of bullets resumed as he hurried along, one of the shots tearing through the Cloak just ahead of him, another smashing through the laptop that had started him on this chain of thought in the first place.

And then he was at the cable. Hoping the connector had been fastened solidly into the back of the computer, he got a grip and started to climb.

~

The men were coming from the UN toward him across the frozen field, Six saw as he shook the empty magazine from his gun: two jeeps worth, plus three motorcycles. Some of the soldiers, he noted with mild astonishment, were shouting at him to stop. As if he might actually obey.

He smiled grimly as he slapped another magazine home and crouched a bit lower beside the motorcycle. Let them come. The body of the motorcycle would protect him from any distance shots they might try, and in one more minute they'd all be part of the same cloud of superheated plasma anyway.

But before that happened, he would at least have the personal satisfaction of finishing off Ross. Releasing the slide, keeping half an eye on the incoming soldiers, he braced his arm again and commenced firing.

He'd sent five shots into the sky and was deciding where to put the next pattern, when something from the opposite edge of his peripheral vision caught his attention. He spun his head around—

The man riding the motorcycle toward him skidded to a halt just past First Avenue, dropping the machine to the ground beneath him and lifting his gun in a two-handed marksman's stance. "FBI!" he shouted over the noise of the traffic and the echoes of Six's own shots. "Drop it!"

Reflexively, Six spun his gun around toward this new threat. The FBI man's first shot was wide, careening off the metal of the bike beside him. Smiling tightly, Six fired back, his shot twitching the shoulder of the other's coat.

And then, before he could adjust his aim, there was a flash of light and fire above his right shoulder, and a wave of sudden heat washed over him.

The nuke! was his first reflexive thought. But even as he flung himself away from the heat, and the fire fell with him, he realized his attacker's first shot hadn't simply ricocheted away as he'd thought. It had instead punctured the gas tank, and the flash or ejected casing from Six's own shot had ignited it.

His arm and shoulder were on fire.

He was writhing on the ground, trying to roll out the fire as he centered his gun on the approaching enemy, when the FBI man fired one last time.

~

The connection cable was a lot thinner than it looked, at least as far as climbing purposes were concerned, and there was no place for Ross to brace his feet or even get a purchase on the cable with them. But at least the shooting from below seemed to have stopped.

He grunted his way up, hand over hand, painfully aware that there was probably nothing anchoring the other end of the cable but a couple of tiny screws and whatever support the gondola door was providing. He had the vague sense that someone was calling his name, but his headset had gotten knocked off in that last mad scramble and was banging against his hip with each surge upward.

It seemed to take forever, hanging and twisting in midair, but it was probably no more than half a minute before he reached the gondola. Swinging his left foot up and over, he got it braced on the nearest rear wheel of the tricycle landing gear; and with a half kick, half surging pull upward, he lunged up and got a grip on the door handle with his right hand.

For a moment he hung there, gathering his strength. Then, with another lunge, he tripped the latch. The door swung open—

And his left hand, still gripping the cable, suddenly lost all support as the laptop sitting on the seat inside the door flew out and disappeared beneath his feet.

With a curse, Ross let go of the cable and grabbed for the edge of the door. He got half a handhold, squeezing hard as his right hand scrabbled for something more solid to hang onto. But the door was too smooth. He could feel his foot starting to slip off the wheel; and with one final all-or-nothing surge, he kicked upward off the wheel with all his strength, his right hand stretching toward the top of the door.

For a single terrifying heartbeat he thought he wasn't going to make it. Then his fingertips got a grip, just enough, and he swung his legs up, twisting his body around, and got his left foot on the door sill. The door swung farther open in response, but with the bulk of his weight now supported he was able to dart his left hand up and get a firm grip on the top of the door. The right hand followed, freeing up his left to grab the gondola frame above the door opening and pull the door he was straddling partially closed.

And for the first time he had a chance to pause and assess the situation inside the gondola.

The nuke was there, all right, lying across the seat, the chunky rectangular shape of its arming box jutting out near Ross's end. A pair of cables connected to the box ran to a small junction cube resting on top of the bomb casing, then slithered across the seat and out through a hole drilled in the gondola's far side. Easing his body around the edge of the door he was still clinging to, he pulled himself all the way inside the gondola and settled with a thud onto his knees on the floor. Making sure not to touch the bomb, he swiveled carefully around to face it.

~

The second hand on Bakht's watch swept past the six. Thirty seconds to go. Gazing one last time out the window at the distant lights of the UN, he turned around and put his back to the view. He hadn't come all this way, after all, to be blinded by his own weapon.

~

"Okay," Ross said, pulling his headset up by its cord and pressing it to his ear as he gave the mechanism a quick once-over. "I'm here. What do I do?"

"Pull out the arming box," McPherson's taut voice came. "Quickly."

Ross nodded, dropping the headset again as he got both hands on the arming box's handles. He braced himself—

And paused, a sudden ugly thought slicing through him. General Raksha Bakht, arguably the greatest tactical genius India had produced in the past century. More to the point, a tactical genius who had managed to stay ahead of them every single step of the way.

Ross's flashlight was still buried in the folds of the Cloak below. Twisting his left wrist around toward the shadowy arming box, he pressed the light button on his watch.

In the soft blue-green glow, he saw the subtle glints from a pair of hair-thin wires angling loosely across the upper right and lower left corners of the box.

Someone was shouting again on the dangling headset, but Ross didn't have time to respond. Holding down the watch button to keep the light going, he traced the wires with his eyes, following them back around the corners of the box to tiny junction cubes at each end. From there, insulated cables circled around back to the main junction cube.

Gingerly, he touched one of the thin wires. It was loose, with what appeared to be enough slack for him to pull it over the corner it was lying across. There was no sign of the spring-loading that would indicate that any movement of the wires, either in or out, would trigger something unpleasant. With no insulation on the wires there couldn't be any heavy current involved. Apparently, they were simple trip wires: a booby trap designed to let Bakht's people get the box out quickly if they needed to but last-minute insurance against careless handling by anyone else.

At least, that was how he was going to have to gamble. There was no time for anything more sophisticated. Easing the wires gingerly over the corners, he held them out of the way against the casing with the backs of his little fingers and again got a grip on the handles. Mentally crossing his fingers, he started to pull.

~

The second hand swept past the twelve, and the four minutes Bakht had allotted the flankers were up. It was seven o'clock, and the weapon was as near to optimal position as it needed to be. Rotating the switch a half turn, saying a brief prayer for the innocents who were about to die, he pressed it.

~

For a long moment Ross knelt there, breathing hard as he cradled the arming box in one arm. There had been a loud buzz from the electronics in the main junction cube just as he'd gotten the box free of its long-pronged connectors, accompanied by an answering thud from somewhere inside the box itself, and for a brief but terrible fraction of a second he thought he'd failed.

But the nuke was still there. More to the point, so was he.

He took a deep breath and again retrieved his headset. "Director McPherson?" he said into his mike, trying to sound calm and cool and collected, and not entirely succeeding. "I've got the arming box."

And still gripping the box, he closed his eyes and let the roar of spontaneous cheers from the tac radio wash over him.

~

General Bakht stood motionless, looking down at the switch. He reset and tried it again. And again. And again.

Slowly, he turned around and looked out the window. The sky to the east was still dark, the lights of the UN still burning bravely against them.

"General?" Two asked tentatively from behind him.

"Did the flankers make it off their roofs?" Bakht asked.

"Their reply flares went up three minutes ago," Two said. "There were a few random shots from the helos after that, but none of the saturation pattern that would be necessary to destroy them. They're surely clear and on their way to the rendezvous."

"Any casualties below?"

"No, sir."

Bakht took a deep breath. "Order Seven to lay down the gas and thermite cover and evacuate his force. You'll go with them. Four and Six should also be on their way to the outer rendezvous; meet with them there and leave the country via the planned escape route."

"Yes, sir. And you?"

The general didn't turn. "I have one last duty to perform," he said quietly. "Carry out your orders, Colonel."

There was a moment of silence, broken only by the gunfire from below. "Yes, sir," the other said at last. "Good-bye, General."

Bakht nodded silently.

He stood there until the multiple pop of the gas grenades had passed and reflected glow outside from the thermite burn on the roof had faded away. Then, still gazing out at the UN building in the distance, he removed his gas mask and protective hood, and pulled a grenade from the pouch at his belt. *The media have become the world's memory,* his own words from earlier that evening echoed through his mind, *and they live solely to suck the life-blood from the living. The dry bones of the dead are of no interest to them.* For the sake of his nation, he hoped he'd been right about that.

Lifting the grenade to his chin, he pulled the pin and settled down to wait.

~

Slowly, wearily, Talbot placed his foot on the gun lying beside the still-smoldering figure sprawled on the lawn and kicked the weapon away across the frozen grass. Only then did he lower his own gun and look up.

The patch of visible Cloak with the multiple tears in it, still drifting along on the westward wind, was already starting to sink toward the ground as the dirigible's helium leaked out. Even if the Delta Force assault team didn't get to the tether line and tie it off, he decided, the dirigible ought to run into the UN Building and stop before it reached the East River. Ross would be glad to hear that.

He looked at his watch. It was two minutes past seven.

~

Standing at the podium, the lights shining in his eyes obscuring the faces of those in the packed assembly hall before him, Secretary General Muluzi banged his gavel. "The United Nations Special Conference on Human Rights is hereby brought to order," he intoned solemnly. "In the name of peace and justice, I welcome you all."

EPILOGUE

"**WILL YOU BE** going back to the Bay Area?" Ross asked.

Angie took a sip of her tea. It was her second cup since they'd brought her into the UN and planted her here in this otherwise unoccupied lounge, and only now was the chill of the night air finally starting to recede.

The chill in her soul would take longer to heal. Maybe it never would. "I don't think so," she said. "I may go stay with my parents for a while. I haven't really thought about it."

"Well, you *have* been kind of busy," Ross agreed, setting his coffee cup down on the low table between them. He lifted his left leg up onto the couch, wincing at the effort. "But there's time," he added. "It's all over now."

"Is it?" she asked. "What about the ones who got away?"

"They'll be running for the border and far too busy to bother with you," Ross assured her. "Still, Director McPherson would probably be willing to assign you some protection if it would make you feel safer. At least send you back with Special Agent Talbot."

"Not unless she's going to Alaska," Talbot's voice came from the doorway. "I'm being transferred to the Aleutians, remember?"

Angie turned to see Talbot and Swenson come into the lounge. "Any news?" she asked.

"A little," Talbot said, pulling up a chair for Swenson and then snagging one for himself. "It looks like most of the gang in the main building got out by rappelling down the elevator shafts, getting around the locked-down cars somehow, and getting into the subbasement. From there they used a section of the sewer system to get to a garage a block away. They must have had a vehicle parked there; from the tire marks, probably a panel truck. We're on the lookout for it."

"You said most of them went that way," Ross said. "Which ones didn't?"

Talbot's eyes flicked to Angie. "I'll tell you later."

"Please," Angie said. "I want to know."

"It's not very pleasant," he warned.

"I've already been through more unpleasantness than I ever thought I could endure," she reminded him quietly. "Uncertainties are more frightening than anything you could say."

"All right," Talbot said reluctantly. "General Bakht was waiting for the attack team when it burst in on him. At least, we assume it was General Bakht. The image we got from the Delta Force helmet cams didn't look a thing like his photos."

"Wait a minute," Ross cut in, frowning. "The image from the helmet cams?"

"Afraid that's all we've got," Talbot said. "He shouted something about vengeance for the people of Colombia, pressed the nuke detonation button, which of course didn't do anything—" His mouth tightened. "And then set off a grenade under his chin."

"My God," Angie breathed. "Why would he do something like that?"

"One last attempt to muddy the water, I guess," Talbot said. "His makeup artist had evidently given him a new face for the occasion, and he must have figured the grenade would take that, his real face, and his fingerprints when it went off. He'd told McPherson earlier that he was someone named Simon who'd rendezvoused with Bakht in Montana, killed him and his men, and taken the nuke for himself. He had a proclamation to that effect in his pocket, too."

"And he seriously expected us to buy that?" Ross asked incredulously.

Talbot shrugged. "Like I said, muddying the water. His last-ditch effort to shift as much of the blame away from India as he could. Whatever else the man was, he clearly considered himself a patriot."

"Also an idiot," Ross growled. "Or hasn't DNA testing made it to India yet?"

"Years ago," Talbot confirmed. "Which is probably why he erased the DNA data on himself and his team from all the official records."

"When did he do *that*?" Angie asked.

"About a month before all this started," Swenson said. "The man was three steps ahead of us the whole way."

"Except at the end," Ross reminded her. "The only place that matters."

"It was wasted effort anyway," Talbot said. "He didn't know that even before the main group set off their smoke and thermite we'd already gotten the three on the other rooftops. They were shot as they shuffled toward the stairway in their no longer invisible Cloaks."

"There's the one on the motorcycle, too," Swenson added.

"Right," Talbot nodded. "And those four bodies alone are in good enough shape to prove it was Bakht's operation, DNA or no DNA."

"If anyone's interested in assigning blame, anyway," Ross said. "My guess is that the whole thing will be swept as far under the rug as possible." He smiled ruefully. "I have a certain amount of experience in such things."

"From a slightly less cynical point of view," Talbot added, "we'll also want to keep it quiet to keep from panicking the public and also to avoid giving ideas to the rest of the world's lunatic fringe. Don't worry, though—we'll either grab the rest of the team here or India will nab them when they come home. And that'll be that."

"Aside from lessons learned," Swenson murmured.

Talbot made a face. "We can hope."

Angie looked down at the cup of tea gripped in her hands. "So it really is mostly over?"

"It's completely over as far as you're concerned," Talbot assured her. "You can go back home anytime you want. Director McPherson's already said he'll have a private jet for you whenever you're ready."

Angie smiled wanly. "Is this the same Director McPherson who's sending you to the Aleutians?"

"I'll talk to him," Talbot assured her. "Maybe he'll settle for giving me two weeks' leave in Nome." He gestured toward Swenson. "Besides, if he sends me, he'll have to send Hanna, too."

It seemed to Angie that Swenson twitched oddly at that. "What's that supposed to mean?" Swenson asked, her eyes narrowing.

"You were the one who dropped the whole Manhattan cell phone system," Talbot reminded her. "If I get kicked out of the lower forty-eight for not keeping him in the loop, it's only reasonable that you get kicked out, too."

"And McPherson would never do that to me?" Swenson asked, still sounding suspicious.

"Not a chance," Talbot said. "If only because it would take too long to get you back to D.C. when he needs you to fix the next problem for him."

Ross cleared his throat. "I can see you two have some private game to play," he said, easing his leg off the couch and standing up. "Personally, I hear dinner and a bed somewhere calling me."

"There's a car waiting downstairs whenever you want it," Swenson told him. "And McPherson already has a whole block of hotel rooms set up for those of us who are staying."

"Sounds good," Ross said. "Angie? Want to see what kind of spaghetti Manhattan has to offer? My treat this time."

"Yes, why not?" Angie said, taking one last sip from her tea and standing up. The delayed shock of all this would hit her soon enough, she knew: James's murder, the unrelenting threat to her own life, the deeper and far darker danger they'd barely managed to avert. When it did, if past experience was a guide, she would retreat within herself for days or weeks until she'd worked through it and was ready to face the world again.

But at the moment, all was simply fatigue and numbness and, paradoxically perhaps, a remnant of sociability. Best to make use of it while she could. "There's one thing I'd still like to know."

"Sure," Ross said as they walked together toward the door. "What is it?"

Angie hesitated. Should she ask him about his past, his time with the FBI or CIA? Should she ask about his life in WitSec, and why he continually risked that to come out and dabble in cases that weren't his concern? Should she even be so bold as to ask about Talbot's suspicion that he was working quietly for McPherson or someone else?

No. Not now. Maybe not ever, but certainly not now. "How exactly," she asked, "did you hurt your leg?"

THE END

KICKSTARTER BACKERS

A Fan of Books; Adam Alexander; Adam G. Pugh; Adam Wynn;
Adriane Ruzak; Adrianne Middleton; Alex Caligiuri;
Alex, Johanna, Hal and Jack Newbold; Amelia Smith;
Anakin and Scout Young; Andreas Welch; Andrew Barnes;
Andrew Bednara; Andrew Clody; Andy Santoro; Anna Marie Stern;
Anna Mitchell; Anonymous Supporter; Anthony Capuano Jr;
Antonio Gutiérrez Peña; Antony Gusscott; Arne Radtke;
Ashli T.; Barbara Silcox; Becky Bergmann; Becky Smith;
Ben Seeley; Benjamin Abbott; Big Al; Bill Tng; BJ Bjornson;
Bjørge Vevik; Bo Aakersoe; Bob Michiels; Bob Quinlan;
Breeanna Sveum; Brendan Lonehawk; Bria LaVorgna;
Brian Barrett; Brian Hartman; Brian Mahoney; Brian T. Hall;
C. M. Boyer; Calvin G. Dodge; Camdon Wright; Carly Schneider;
Casey Harris; Cato; Charles Moorhead; Charlie Tibbert;
Chris Quinn; Chris Regan; Christa D. Brolley; Christian Steudtner;
Christopher S. Sanders; Cole Peel; Corie Weaver; CyndiGaw;
D-Rock; Damin Toell; Dani Hall; Daniel Flucke;
Daniel H. MacMillan; Danielle Mathieson Pederson;
Darrell Grizzle; David Gunter; David Hernly; David I. Oxley;
David J Rios; Deanna Stanley; Derek "Pineapple Steak" Swoyer;
Derry Salewski; Devin R. Streur; Diana Castillo;
Diana Peterfreund; Dom Robinson; Dorothy Spackman;
Doug Grimes; Doug Hibbard; Elaine Tindill-Rohr;
Elizabeth Bridges; Emilio Desalvo; Emily Haberstroh;
Emily Scherping and Raphael Ahad; Eric Allen; Eric Buetikofer;
Eric Christensen; Erik Mulloon; Erin M. Klitzke; Erin Nagelkirk;

Eva Thompson; Evaristo Ramos, Jr.; Fen Eatough; Gail Z. Martin;
Gareth Turner; Gavin H Norris; Gawin Grimm; Greg L Tucker;
Greg Plonowski; Greg Resnik; Gregory A. Wilson; Greta Humphrey;
Gunnar Högberg; Guy McLimore; Halsted M. Larsson;
Heather Wilke; Helen Savore; Henning Hönicke; Hrvoje Bukša;
Ian Harvey; Ian Hopkins; Ian Miller; Ira Tabankin; Jackie Werner;
Jacob BoomShadow Tirey; Jada Hope Diaz; James;
James & Tera Fulbright; James, Mostly Harmless;
James H. Murphy Jr.; Janine Martinez; Janito Vaqueiro Ferreira Filho;
Jared Zimmer; Jason Chen; Jason Hunt; Jason L Martin;
Jason Trosen; Jeff; Jeff Prichard; Jeffrey Kromer;
Jeffrey M Nichols; Jen Maccioli; Jennifer Brozek;
Jennifer Simmons; Jeremy Crist; Jeremy Reppy; Jessica Schulze;
Jill Bradley; Jill Maddox; Jim Cebulka; Joelle Paxton;
Johannes Borgström; John A; John Cantrell Jr; John Collicott;
John Green; John Idlor; Jon Furniss; Jonathan Woolums;
Jordan Zipkin; Joseph Petrides; Joshua Lannik; Justin Nelson;
Karl F Maurer; Kat Feete; Katherine Malloy; Keith Hall;
Kelli Neier; Kelly Lloyd; Kelly Swails; Ken Mencher;
Kevin G. Fisher; Kevin Harp; Kirstin Faughn; Kit Wetzler;
Kotova Marika Igorevna; Kristen; Kristin Evenson Hirst; Kristina;
Leah Webber; Leslie Barkley; Liang Gao; Linda Silverman;
Lisa Kruse; Lisa Richelle Jensen; Lissa Capo; Logan Bruce Poole;
Louise Löwenspets; Luke Dore; M. Crowe; Maarten Leo daalder;
Marcelo Germano; Margaret M. St. John; Mario J Lara;
Mark coley; Mark Jones; Mark Sergeant; Mark Sidden; Marmæl;
Martin F Kramer; Matt Grierson; Matt Lowe; Matt Schmitt;
Matthew Edward Speed; Matthias Wallner-Géhri; Michael Crill;
Michael Jarett; Michael McAfee; Michael Newbold;
Michael Steinbach; Mike Bavister; Mike Davidson and Gloria Sheu;
Mike Inguagiato; Mike Maurer; Mike Rockwell; Mike Van Ee;
monkeygrudge; Moorkh; Nadine Sehnert; Nate L.; Nate Rethorn;
Nathan Aaron Jones; Nathan Marchand; Nathan Turner;
Nicholas Ahlhelm; Nicholas Watson; NovaPrime; Pat O'Hara;
Paul Bulmer; Paul Leone; Paul Swaine; Paula Rosenberg;
Peggy Rae Sapienza; Pepita Hogg-Sonnenberg; Phillip H.;
Raymond Danbakli; Revan Kane; Revek; Rhel ná DecVandé;
Rhetta Akamatsu; Rhiannon L Crothers; Richard Blackburn;
Rick Ashford; Rick House; Rob Holland; Robert "R2" Robertson;
Robert Early; Robert Martincic; Roman Pauer; Ron & Janine;
Russell Martens; Ruth Ellison; Ryan Davis; Ryan Headlee;
Sally Novak Janin; Samuel Murphy; Sarah Cornell; Sarah Edwards;

Sarah Faith Gaspar; Sarah Faith Morris; Sarah M Stewart;
Scott A Johnson; Scott and Cindy Kuntzelman; Scott Schaper;
Shaowen Wu & Rodney Romasanta; Sharlene Glennie;
Sharona Ginsberg; Shervyn; Sheryl R. Hayes; Sit-a-Spell Used
Books, Games & More; Stephen Cheng; Stephen Howard;
Stephen Lornie; Stephen May; Steve Gayler; Steve Grigson;
Steve Lord; Steve Weiner; Steven "Sparkles" Collins;
Steven Howie; Steven Mentzel; Stijn Vanderstraeten;
Stuart Walters; Svend Andersen; SwordFire; T.Rob;
The Amazing Amber Bessire; The Tandy Family;
Thomas McManus; Thomas Zilling; Timothy Brown;
Timothy Murphy; Timothy Paulson; Tina & John Tipton;
Tish Pahl; Tony Hansen; Tory Shade; Travis Skinner; Trevor Arat;
Trip Space-Parasite; Tyler Owen; Vincent Morrone; Vita A.;
Wade Hull; Walt Bryan; Wesley Bevens; wraith808;
Zach Whittaker; zSpidet

ABOUT THE AUTHOR

Timothy Zahn was born in Chicago in 1951. In 1975, while working on a doctorate in physics, he began a new hobby: writing science fiction. In December 1978, he sold his first story, and in 1980 left grad school and began writing full time.

Since then he has published forty-five novels, over a hundred short stories and novelettes, and four collections of short fiction. Best known for his ten *Star Wars* novels, he is also the author of the Quadrail series, the Cobra series, the Conquerors Trilogy, and the young-adult Dragonback series. His latest books are *Cobra Slave*, the first of the Cobra Rebellion Trilogy, and *Star Wars: Scoundrels*.

Upcoming books include *Cobra Outlaw*, the second Cobra Rebellion novel, and *A Call to Duty*, the first of a three-book collaboration with David Weber set in the Honor Harrington universe. You can contact him at Facebook.com/TimothyZahn.

ABOUT SILENCE IN THE LIBRARY

Founded in 2011 by a group of authors, Silence in the Library, LLC was established with the goal of creating an environment that allows authors, artists, editors, and other publishing professionals to work collaboratively to showcase their work. Our model keeps the creative decisions, throughout the publishing process, as close to the actual *creators* (i.e. authors and artists) as possible. Authors are deeply involved in their projects from start to finish. By closely controlling the quality of inputs to the process, we ensure a high level of quality in the final product while allowing space for imagination to flourish.

One of our goals is to prove that there is no "standard" face to a protagonist or an author of speculative fiction. Talent and strength know no race, sex, or other artificial boundary. Our projects, in particular our anthologies, strive to reflect this.

The *Athena's Daughters* anthology (and its sister volumes) were conceived, developed, and driven by women. The books have one unifying theme: all of the protagonists are women, and they exhibit a wide range of physical attributes, ages, abilities, ethnicities, and orientations.

For *HEROES!*, a collection of stories about superheroes, we focused on diversity with respect to gender, ethnicity, age, body type, and life experience.

We consider representation a priority—all readers should be able to find someone like themselves in the books they read. We hope to contribute towards this goal by continuing to offer our customers a diverse selection of authors and characters.

WWW.SILENCEINTHELIBRARYPUBLISHING.COM

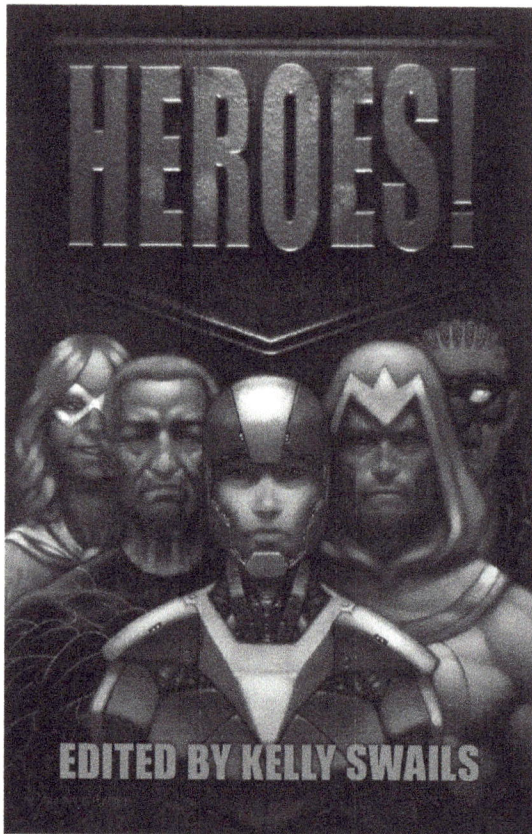

HEROES!

Includes stories by Timothy Zahn as well as Aaron Allston, John Kovalic, Gail Z. Martin, Michael A. Stackpole, Sarah Hans, Jean Rabe, Alan Dean Foster, and many more.

This anthology includes a wide range of works that capture the entire spectrum of heroism in speculative fiction. Some of the protagonists have superpowers, others survive purely on their wits and sometimes dumb luck. Some of the stories focus on the battles between costumed crusaders and their enemies, and others focus on battles against the demons within.

Each of the stories in this anthology is beautifully illustrated by renowned artist Mark Dos Santos.

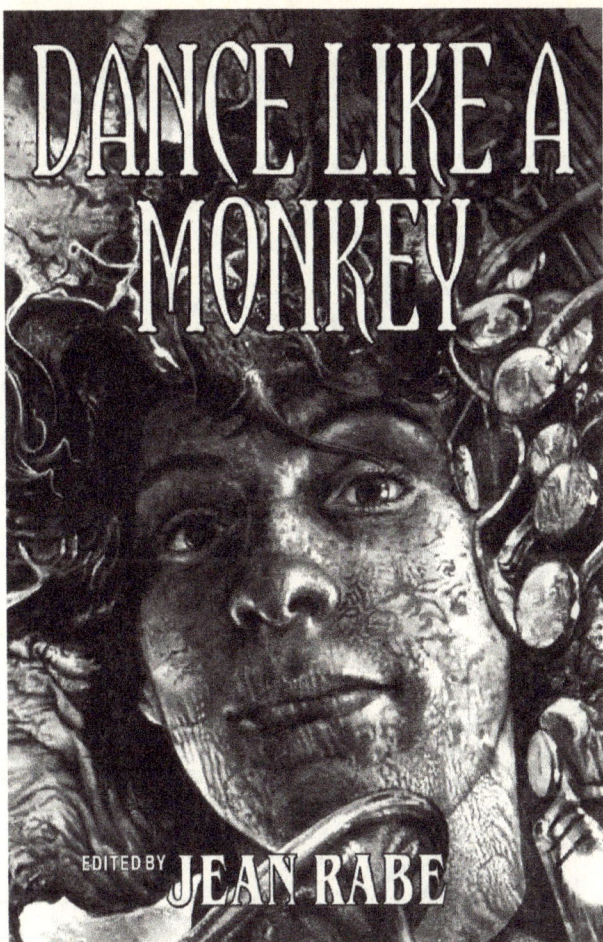

DANCE LIKE A MONKEY

This anthology of nearly 700 pages is a tribute to author C.J. Henderson. It contains short speculative fiction from some of the most popular authors in the industry. Proceeds from the sale of this book benefit C.J.'s family.

Two of C.J. Henderson's own stories are included, along with stories by Alan M. Clark, Tera Fulbright, John G. Hartness, Stuart Jaffe, Gail Z. Martin, Mike Resnick, Kelly Swails, Robert E. Vardeman, Gene Wolfe, Timothy Zahn, and over a dozen others.

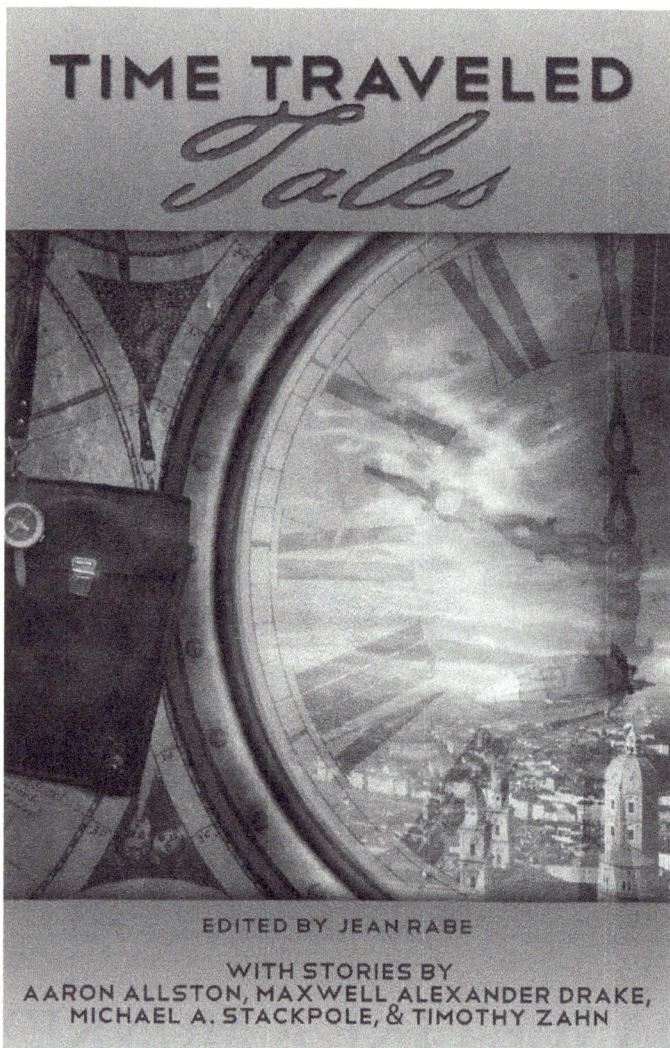

TIME TRAVELED TALES

Time Traveled Tales is an exciting journey through stories of time travel, possible futures, and supernatural and alien beings from authors like Aaron Allston, Maxwell Alexander Drake, R.T. Kaelin, Janine Spendlove, Michael A. Stackpole, Bryan Young, Timothy Zahn, and many others. Each story is beautifully illustrated by artist Matt Slay.

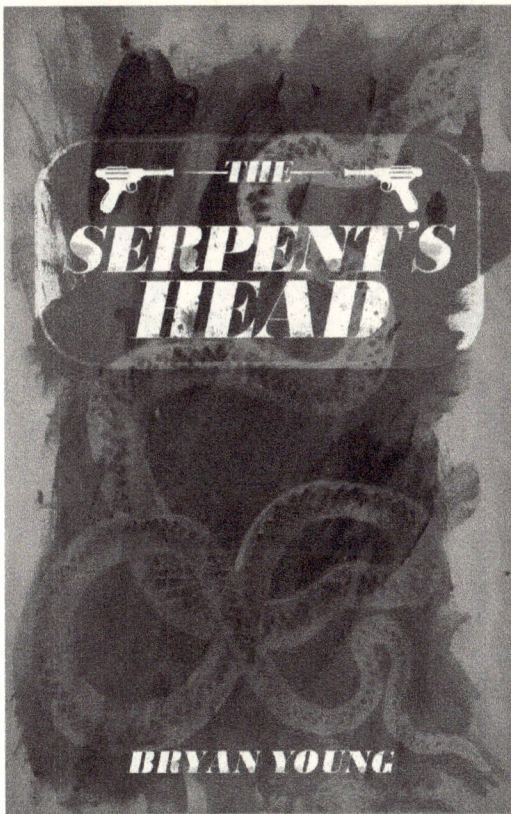

THE SERPENT'S HEAD

BRYAN YOUNG

The man called Twelve is a hired gun, taking his laser pistol from planet to planet, hiring his services out to the highest bidder. He finds himself on Glycon-Prime, a new colony at the edge of space. On the hunt for work, Twelve blows into a small, frontier town only to find a massacre. The only survivors? A trio of young children, devastated by the murder of their families and hellbent on hiring the gunslinger to help them get revenge on the leader of the vicious mutants responsible, the man known only as "The Serpent's Head."

SOOTHE THE SAVAGE BEAST

What happens when you come back from the dead?
Or when a girl falls for the monster under her bed?
What is it that makes a monster terrifying?

In Soothe the Savage Beast you'll learn the answer to these questions and many others, in stories by some of today's best known genre authors: Carrie Ryan, Maxwell Alexander Drake, Beth Revis, and Aaron Rosenberg. This collection of monster stories features werewolves, zombies, vampires, and every other sort of creature that goes bump in the night, sure to thrill and terrify.

Every story in this collection is illustrated by Erin Kubinek.